The Editor

WERNER SOLLORS is Henry B. and Anne M. Cabot Professor of English Literature and Afro-American Studies and Chair of History of American Civilization at Harvard University. He previously taught at Columbia University, the Free University of Berlin, and the Università degli Studi di Venezia. He is the author of *Neither Black Nor White Yet Both: Thematic Explorations of Interracial Literature; Beyond Ethnicity: Consent and Descent in American Culture;* and *Amiri Baraka/ LeRoi Jones: The Quest for a "Populist Modernism."* His edited works include *The Multilingual Anthology of American Literature: A Reader of Original Texts with English Translations; Multilingual America: Transnationalism, Ethnicity, and the Languages of America; The Return of Thematic Criticism; Theories of Ethnicity: A Classical Reader;* and *The Invention of Ethnicity.*

W. W. NORTON & COMPANY, INC.
Also Publishes

ENGLISH RENAISSANCE DRAMA: A NORTON ANTHOLOGY
edited by David Bevington et al.

THE NORTON ANTHOLOGY OF AFRICAN AMERICAN LITERATURE
edited by Henry Louis Gates Jr. and Nellie Y. McKay et al.

THE NORTON ANTHOLOGY OF AMERICAN LITERATURE
edited by Nina Baym et al.

THE NORTON ANTHOLOGY OF CHILDREN'S LITERATURE
edited by Jack Zipes et al.

THE NORTON ANTHOLOGY OF DRAMA
edited by J. Ellen Gainor, Stanton B. Garner Jr., and Martin Puchner

THE NORTON ANTHOLOGY OF ENGLISH LITERATURE
edited by M. H. Abrams and Stephen Greenblatt et al.

THE NORTON ANTHOLOGY OF LITERATURE BY WOMEN
edited by Sandra M. Gilbert and Susan Gubar

THE NORTON ANTHOLOGY OF MODERN AND CONTEMPORARY POETRY
edited by Jahan Ramazani, Richard Ellmann, and Robert O'Clair

THE NORTON ANTHOLOGY OF POETRY
edited by Margaret Ferguson, Mary Jo Salter, and Jon Stallworthy

THE NORTON ANTHOLOGY OF SHORT FICTION
edited by R. V. Cassill and Richard Bausch

THE NORTON ANTHOLOGY OF THEORY AND CRITICISM
edited by Vincent B. Leitch et al.

THE NORTON ANTHOLOGY OF WORLD LITERATURE
edited by Sarah Lawall et al.

THE NORTON FACSIMILE OF THE FIRST FOLIO OF SHAKESPEARE
prepared by Charlton Hinman

THE NORTON INTRODUCTION TO LITERATURE
edited by Alison Booth and Kelly J. Mays

THE NORTON READER
edited by Linda H. Peterson and John C. Brereton

THE NORTON SAMPLER
edited by Thomas Cooley

THE NORTON SHAKESPEARE, BASED ON THE OXFORD EDITION
edited by Stephen Greenblatt et al.

For a complete list of Norton Critical Editions, visit
www.wwnorton.com/college/English/nce_home.htm

Olaudah Equiano

THE INTERESTING NARRATIVE OF THE LIFE OF OLAUDAH EQUIANO, OR GUSTAVUS VASSA, THE AFRICAN, WRITTEN BY HIMSELF

AUTHORITATIVE TEXT

CONTEXTS

CRITICISM

Edited by
WERNER SOLLORS

HARVARD UNIVERSITY

W • W • NORTON & COMPANY • *New York* • *London*

Copyright © 2001 by W. W. Norton & Company, Inc.

All rights reserved.
Printed in the United States of America.
First Edition.

The text of this book is composed in Electra
with the display set in Bernhard Modern.
Composition by Binghamton Valley Composition
Manufacturing by Maple-Vail Book Group
Book design by Antonina Krass.

Library of Congress Cataloging-in-Publication Data

Equiano, Olaudah, b. 1745.
    The interesting narrative of the life of Olaudah Equiano, or Gustavus Vassa,
the African : an authoritative text/written by himself; contexts, criticism, edited
by Werner Sollors.
        p. cm. — (A Norton critical edition)
    Includes bibliographical references.

    ISBN 0-393-97494-4 (pbk.)

    1. Equiano, Olaudah, b. 1745. 2. Slaves—Great Britain—Biography.
3. Slaves—United States—Biography. I. Sollors, Werner. II. Title.
HT869.E6 A3 2000
305.5'67'092—dc21
[B]
                                                            00-058386

W. W. Norton & Company Inc., 500 Fifth Avenue, New York, N.Y. 10110
www.wwnorton.com

W. W. Norton & Company Ltd., Castle House, 75/76 Wells Street, London W1T 3QT

0

Contents

Criticism

Introduction

Approximately fifty-three thousand Africans were transported as slaves to the Americas each year in the 1750s; and many, many of them died in the process. The total number of Africans who were forced into New World slavery from the sixteenth to the nineteenth century has been estimated at between eleven and twelve million.[1] How did these Africans experience their enslavement and the forced Atlantic crossing of the Middle Passage, "the rupture and the ordeal," as Nathan Huggins described the second leg of the triangular voyage among Europe, Africa, and the Americas?[2] One early answer was given by this book, *The Interesting Narrative of the Life of Olaudah Equiano, or Gustavus Vassa, The African, Written by Himself*, first published in the memorable revolutionary year, 1789. The memoir, written before the word "autobiography" had been coined, describes the author's life before, during, and after his enslavement. Equiano's haunting account of his experience aboard a slave ship in the 1750s is unforgettable:

> The stench of the hold while we were on the coast was so intolerably loathsome, that it was dangerous to remain there for any time, and some of us had been permitted to stay on the deck for the fresh air; but now that the whole ship's cargo were confined together, it became absolutely pestilential. The closeness of the place, and the heat of the climate, added to the number in the ship, which was so crowded that each had scarcely room to turn himself, almost suffocated us. This produced copious perspirations, so that the air soon became unfit for respiration, from a variety of loathsome smells, and brought on a sickness among the slaves, of which many died, thus falling victims to the improvident avarice, as I may call it, of their purchasers. This wretched situation was again aggravated by the galling of the chains, now become insupportable; and the filth of the necessary tubs, into which the children often fell, and were almost suffocated. The shrieks of the

1. According to the database of Stephen Behrendt, David Richardson, and David Eltis at the W. E. B. Du Bois Institute, Harvard University, the total number of Africans transported to the Americas was 11,569,000; the figure is based on records for 27,233 voyages by slavers. Estimates vary; the "probably very conservative" figure of 14,650,000 is the one reported by Charles Nichols. See his essay below, pp. 217–21.
2. See Huggins, *Black Odyssey: The Afro-American Ordeal in Slavery*, a part of which is excerpted below, pp. 222–28.

women, and the groans of the dying, rendered the whole a scene
of horror almost inconceivable. (40–41)[3]

The author offers his life as a "history of neither a saint, a hero, nor
a tyrant" (19). He casts himself as a representative African who, though
his sufferings were extraordinary by European standards, was still more
fortunate than many of his fellow Africans.

The stages of Equiano's life also represent a model of history. The
development starts with an ideal state in West Africa, which is interrupted by kidnapping, enslavement, and the brutal Middle Passage,
and culminates in freedom of economic enterprise, scientific exploration, and devout Christianity. This representative life story would help
end the slave trade and convince readers that the African slave trade
was not only contrary to Enlightenment principles and incompatible
with Christian religion but also ultimately an impediment to English
economic growth. But this book goes far beyond these two themes as
it tells the story of a generally interesting life.

According to the *Narrative*, Olaudah Equiano (o-lah-*oo*-day ek-wee-
ah-no) was born in West Africa in 1745. He explains that his first name
means "vicissitude or fortune also, one favoured, and having a loud
voice and well spoken" (27). Paul Edwards and Catherine Obianju
Acholonu have tried to identify in present-day Nigeria the precise
birthplace Equiano mentions, the vale of Essaka, province of Eboe,
kingdom of Benin, Guinea.[4] When Olaudah was about eleven years
old, he and his sister were kidnapped; after a brief, chance meeting
subsequent to their initial parting, the siblings were separated from
each other forever. Equiano was taken on board a slave ship to Barbados, and sent to a plantation in Virginia. He was soon purchased by
the British naval officer Michael Henry Pascal, who took him to
England and who, inspired by a popular English play about the sixteenth-century hero of Swedish independence, renamed him Gustavus
Vassa. Previously, Equiano had also been called Michael and Jacob,
and he at first resisted the new name Vassa but ultimately came to use
it more frequently than his Ibo name. With the exception of the *Narrative* itself, a single letter from 1789, and one use of the signature
"Aethiopianus," Equiano appears to have signed publications, letters,
and legal documents with the name Gustavus Vassa.

Equiano served with Pascal in the Seven Years' War (the American
part of it is known as the French and Indian War) and was present at
the siege of Louisbourg in Nova Scotia, was then resold into slavery
and worked on ships for a Philadelphia Quaker merchant, Robert King,
trading between the West Indies and the mainland American colonies,

---

3. In the Introduction, citations to pages in this Norton Critical Edition will appear in paren-
theses.
4. See essays below by Edwards, pp. 302–38, and Acholonu, pp. 351–61.

ultimately earning enough money to buy his own freedom. He lived through shipwrecks, sailed the Mediterranean, and participated in an expedition to the Arctic. He converted to Anglicanism and was admitted to communion in Westminster Church (though he also expressed Methodist leanings). He took part in an English settlement among the Miskito Indians in Central America, sailed to North America again, and was appointed commissary for a Sierra Leone settlement by the Committee for the Relief of the Black Poor in 1787, though he lost the appointment for political reasons. He published letters in London newspapers and often expressed his support of the movement to abolish the slave trade. In 1787 he sent a brief to Lord Hawkesbury that was virtually identical to the penultimate paragraphs of the *Narrative*, in which he argued that the slave trade was an impediment to British manufacturing interests. In 1788 he presented an antislavery petition to Queen Charlotte, the Royal Consort of King George III, that is incorporated into Chapter XII of the *Narrative*.

After the publication of his book—which went through nine English editions, was reprinted in America, and translated into Dutch, German, and Russian—he continued to live in England, and remained connected with opponents of the slave trade; in 1791, for example, he spoke in Ireland, where nearly two thousand copies of his book were sold. In 1792, as he proudly added to later editions of the *Narrative*, he married Susan Cullen of Ely, Cambridgeshire, with whom he had two daughters, Ann Maria Vassa (who died in infancy) and Joanna Vassa. Susan Cullen Vassa was buried on February 21, 1796, and Gustavus Vassa died on March 31, 1797. Upon her father's death, Joanna Vassa inherited a fair amount of money.

The Slave Trade Opposed and Africa Remembered

The author of the *Narrative* lived in the intellectual ambience of English anti–slave-trade activists. As Charles Nichols pointed out, it was Equiano who called the British abolitionist Granville Sharp's attention to the so-called *Zong* massacre, the case of a captain who in November 1781 had ordered 132 ailing African slaves drowned alive during the Middle Passage and who then collected the insurance on them. (In 1789 Sharp was among the subscribers whose support made possible the publication of the *Narrative*.) Gustavus Vassa knew British public figures of African origin, with whom he formed the "Sons of Africa," and he cosigned public appeals with Quobna Ottobah Cugoano (a subscriber), Yahne Aelane, Jasper Goree, and others. Equiano knew, quoted, and defended celebrated abolitionists such as Thomas Clarkson and James Ramsey against pro–slave-trade attacks.[5] (Both Clarkson and Ramsay subscribed to the *Narrative*.) In 1789

5. See essay below by Robert J. Allison, pp. 393–95.

Equiano wrote a letter to the Committee for the Abolition of the Slave Trade in which he commented on the famous illustration of the cross section of the slave ship *Brookes* that had accompanied Clarkson's essays and that was frequently reproduced.[6] The Committee attempted to move British parliament to curb and ultimately abolish the lucrative slave trade, a campaign that began in 1788 and did not come to a successful end until 1807.[7] Equiano's book also strengthened John Wesley, the founder of Methodism, in his opposition to slavery.[8]

Equiano's contemporaries were, with varying degrees of enthusiasm, drawn to the *Narrative*. Here was a first-person singular account by a man who had himself been captured and taken away on a slave ship and who was an eyewitness to the enormous and the more subtle cruelties that accompanied the slave trade. This was not just a book written against the slave trade; it was a book written by an African who had firsthand memories of his childhood in West Africa.

In his vivid account of customs and staples, Equiano provided all readers interested in West African origins with rich details such as the following:

> We compute the year from the day on which the sun crosses the line, and on its setting that evening there is a general shout throughout the land; at least I can speak from my own knowledge throughout our vicinity. The people at the same time make a great noise with rattles, not unlike the basket rattles used by children here, though much larger, and hold up their hands to heaven for a blessing. (27)

> The natives are extremely cautious about poison. When they buy any eatable the seller kisses it all round before the buyer, to shew him it is not poisoned; and the same is done when any meat or drink is presented, particularly to a stranger. We have serpents of different kinds, some of which are esteemed ominous when they appear in our houses, and these we never molest. I remember two of those ominous snakes, each of which was as thick as the calf of a man's leg, and in colour resembling a dolphin in the water, crept at different times into my mother's night-house, where I always lay with her, and coiled themselves into folds, and each time they crowed like a cock. (29)

The fact that Equiano could remember so much and that he recorded his observations makes the *Interesting Narrative*, as Charles Nichols stressed, one of the "rarest historical documents, for millions of the

---

6. See illustration below, p. 204, and Equiano's letter, also below, p. 205.
7. An extract below, pp. 282–83, from the famous address by William Wilberforce, and the minutes of the representative 1791 parliamentary debate, also below, pp. 283–87, give readers a sense of the nature of the debate.
8. See documents below by Wesley, pp. 281–82, and the excerpt from Eva Dykes, also below, pp. 210–16.

men, women, and children who crossed the Atlantic during two or three centuries of the slave trade have left no word of their experiences."[9] Edwards and Acholonu have traced and identified features such as scarification, cam wood, and salt made of wood ash, all mentioned in the *Narrative*. Equiano's memories symbolically bridge the rupture of the Middle Passage.

The parts of the *Narrative* that seem to have affected its audience most were the descriptions of African life and of the Middle Passage in the first three chapters, the account of the atrocities of slave life in the West Indies in Chapter V, and the episode in which the author buys his freedom in Chapter VII. Contemporary reviewers, later American abolitionists like Lydia Maria Child, and twentieth-century critics all tended to focus on these passages.

Readers who shared Equiano's faith or who were interested in religious autobiography were also moved by the account of his conversion in Chapter X; but those who, like Mary Wollstonecraft, were Enlightenment freethinkers wished that Equiano had stopped before getting religion and had ended the book at the moment he purchased his freedom on July 11, 1766.[1] For Equiano, however, these themes were intimately connected.

Literacy and Religion

Since the slave trade was a great *moral* evil (though very profitable for those who were engaged or invested in it), Equiano firmly believed in Christian education for Africans as well as in the need to convert those who were Christians in name only into true believers. Part of this process included his acquisition and use of literacy. Equiano draws on the comic potential of the old topos of the book that is encountered by someone who does not know how to read.

> I had often seen my master and Dick employed in reading; and I had a great curiosity to talk to the books, as I thought they did; and so to learn how all things had a beginning: for that purpose I have often taken up a book, and have talked to it, and then put my ears to it, when alone, in hopes it would answer me; and I have been very much concerned when I found it remained silent. (48)

This scene, pioneeringly highlighted in its context by Paul Edwards and brilliantly examined by Henry Louis Gates, Jr., as part of the encounter of orally communicating with lettered cultures, echoed many others in colonial and postcolonial texts—for example, ("El

9. Nichols, *Many Thousand Gone: The Ex-Slaves' Account of Their Bondage and Freedom* (1963), p. xi; see also the excerpt below, pp. 217–21, from Nichols's book.
1. Early reviews and assessments are included below, pp. 293–301.

Inca") Garcilaso de la Vega's *Royal Commentaries of the Incas and General History of Peru* (1609)[2] and the memoirs by contemporary Afro-British and African American authors like James Albert Ukawsaw Gronniosaw (1770), John Marrant (1785), and Quobna Ottobah Cugoano (1787).[3]

The initiation into the magic of the lettered world interests Equiano most especially in connection with his meditations on the Bible. In fact, he tells us when the book finally speaks to him that the one remaining "silent" at first was God. Equiano's conversion occurred at that very moment. He is reading Acts 4.12, the page to which the Bible in his hand in the frontispiece is opened—"And there is salvation in no one else, for there is no other name under heaven given among men by which we must be saved"—when he finds that "the scriptures became an unsealed book. * * * The word of God was sweet to my taste, yea sweeter than honey and the honeycomb" (144). This experience makes the Bible his "only companion and comfort" (145):

> I prized it much, with many thanks to God that I could read it for myself. * * * Whenever I looked in the bible I saw things new, and many texts were immediately applied to me with great comfort, for I knew that to me was the word of salvation sent. (145)

In faith, the book has really spoken to Equiano, and resting on this revelation, he can dare to write his own book. It is after his conversion, too, that Equiano—who interlaced his *Narrative* with snippets from poets, including Milton and Thomas Day, and who wrote an appreciative letter to the poet Samuel Jackson Pratt—presents a long poem of his own, a religious meditation that culminates in the phrase "Salvation is by Christ alone!" freely adapted from Acts 4. For any religious reader, this section must constitute the center of Equiano's book. Incidentally, Equiano also contemplated Islam and Judaism as possible religions and rejected a Spanish offer to study for the Catholic priesthood on the grounds that Catholics do not read the Bible enough. And as a reader-believer he was shocked to see Portuguese Catholics banning Protestant Bible translations.

The *Interesting Narrative* devotes much space to registering surprising deliverances and providential reversals as well as to describing the wonders of seafaring and of the whole natural world; and it is telling

---

2. For Garcilaso, see *Royal Commentaries of the Incas and General History of Peru, Part One. 1609*, transl. Harold V. Livermore (Austin: University of Texas Press, 1966), pp. 604–05. Also see essays below by Edwards, pp. 302–38, and Gates, pp. 361–67; see also Adam Potkay's essay below, pp. 382–92.

3. As Ernst Robert Curtius's work on "The Book as Symbol" suggests, this topos is also derived from the long legacy of book metaphors going back at least to Isidore of Sevilla (560–632), who had observed in his *Etymologiae* that letters are "signs" that have the "power [to] bring the speech of one absent to our ears." *European Literature and the Latin Middle Ages* (1949), transl. Willard Trask (Bollingen Series 36; New York: Pantheon Books, 1953), pp. 302–47, esp. p. 313.

that of the two illustrations accompanying the first edition, one showed Equiano holding the Bible, the other the wreck of the slave ship *Nancy* in a storm at Bahama Banks in 1767, subtitled with a text from Job 33.14–30. Equiano's tale is undoubtedly a spiritual autobiography; and the turning point of his life is his conversion and religious rebirth on October 6, 1775.

Equiano's Transatlantic World

Although spiritual autobiography can be quite otherworldly, Equiano takes a deep, naturalistic, and scientific interest in the secular world; it was not only God's book that spoke to him but others as well. He was obviously someone who enjoyed books more generally. The *Interesting Narrative* is also a memoir by a seaman who, during his travels around the globe, observes flying fishes (amazingly, right from the slave ship that brings him to Barbados), whales, and flamingoes; the customs of Central American Indians; the volcano Mount Vesuvius; the wonders of the Arctic; and the mysteries of human skin color. If Vassa marshals the power of literacy and writing against the slave trade, he also writes in heterogeneous literary traditions. He is well-versed in the Old and New Testaments and is clearly inspired by St. Paul in the Acts of the Apostles and by St. Augustine's *Confessions*; but he also writes in the novelistic manner of Daniel Defoe;[4] he freely quotes the classics, from Homer to Shakespeare, Milton, and contemporary English poets; and he draws on travel literature as well as religious, political, and scientific tracts, following the scholarly procedure of indicating several sources in footnotes.

Equiano's literary language made his book much more than a generic abolitionist tract or conversion narrative; for at a peak period of the culture of the printed book, here was one written by an African writer and reader whose image, holding the Bible, must have appealed to an audience that he impressed by his self-conscious employment of literary devices and allusions. Equiano's particular command of literacy helped to strengthen his case against the slave trade by establishing him not only as a representative African but also as a well-rounded cosmopolitan and well-read Christian or, in short, a "bourgeois subject" whose views deserved serious attention and whose very abilities were a refutation of racist justifications of the African slave trade.[5] In this

---

4. Henri Grégoire was the first to note this; see his assessment below, pp. 298–300.
5. On the "bourgeois subject," see Geraldine Murphy's essay below, pp. 368–82.
   One only has to remember David Hume's racist footnote on Negro inferiority in his essay "Of National Characters" (1753–54) to understand what notions Equiano and other early African writers in England were up against. The passage is reprinted in Wylie Sypher, *Guinea's Captive Kings: British Anti-Slavery Literature of the XVIIIth Century* (Chapel Hill: University of North Carolina Press, 1942), pp. 52–53; Sypher points out, however, that Hume also argued against domestic slavery. Many Enlightenment thinkers were extremely contradictory on the subject of African slavery.

sense, his many asides on topics such as bullfighting or George Whitefield's style of preaching, his amazing interest in a Shropshire coal-pit
or in the Portuguese carnival are not distractions from his central
political and religious subjects—the need to end the slave trade and
to find universal salvation in Christ. His random observations, such as
his reaction to seeing snow for the first time, and his spontaneous, and
at times quite humorous, comments help to get the central, serious
points across.

Equiano is remarkably comparative in his contribution to interpre-
tations of the Atlantic World in which he lived. For example, African
dances remind him of oppressed Greeks whom he later observed in
Turkish Smyrna, the Ibo robes are reminiscent of Scottish highland
plaid (which he saw in the Seven Years' War), and even the snake's
color in land-locked Essaka is described to the reader in terms of a
dolphin. Equiano was impressively broad in his global framework of
perception.

Rousseau, Montesquieu, Woolman, and Benezet

Among the many strains of philosophical, political, and religious
thought that permeated Equiano's intellectual world, three reached
him through a source he cites in the *Narrative* (*Some Historical Account
of Guinea*; see below).

First, Equiano's representation of Africa was in part a response to
the theme of the "noble savage," as well as a close fit to the Rousseau-
inspired European predilection for a natural simplicity that was not
yet contaminated by the depradations of urban luxury and education.[6]
Jean-Jacques Rousseau made the argument in *A Discourse upon the
Origin and Foundation of the Inequality among Mankind* (1753, English
transl. 1755) that "savage Man" or "Man in a State of Nature" had
strength, courage, and good health; however, "as he becomes sociable
* * * he becomes weak, fearful, mean-spirited, and his soft and effeminate Way of Living at once completes the Enervation of his Strength
and of his Courage."[7] With property comes selfishness, destroying
man's original goodness and unlimited ability to empathize. This
belief—which would have held an obvious appeal to Equiano—pervaded European intellectual life in the last decades of the eighteenth
century and particularly inspired authors of travel writing who were
fond of finding Rousseau's natural men in Africa and the Americas.
Though Rousseau had said little on the subject of slavery, the Rous-

6. Eva Dykes and Wylie Sypher were the first to stress this aspect; Paul Edwards was skeptical
   and viewed Equiano as distinct from the "noble savage" tradition. See Rousseau excerpt
   below, pp. 206–09.
7. Rousseau, *A Discourse upon the Origin and Foundation of the Inequality among Mankind*
   (London: Dodsley, 1761), p. 30; see below, p. 206.

seauvian view of Africa was an argument against the pro–slave-trade faction that tended to disparage Africa as backward.

Second, Montesquieu offered a rationalist critique of slavery as incompatible with any form of government except despotism. Charles-Louis de Secondat Montesquieu made the important argument in *The Spirit of the Laws* (1748, English transl. 1750) that slavery must not exist under a monarchy, in which it is decisively important not to sub-ject human nature to oppression and indignity; or in a democracy where all humans are equal; or even in an aristocracy, in which laws attempt to equalize men as much as that form of government permits. Montesquieu made his case as a matter of principle—an important one, for it permitted intellectuals to view slavery as incompatible with democracy or monarchy and to describe a slaveholding society as a tyranny. But Montesquieu also wrote what some readers have seen as a strong, ironic passage directed at supporters of slavery on racial grounds: "It is impossible to imagine that those people"—Montes-quieu appears to be parodying the pro-slavery position on Africans—"could be human beings, for if we considered them humans we would have to start doubting whether we ourselves are Christian men." Other readers believed this passage was serious and an "instance of the prej-udice under which even a liberal mind can labor."[8] Montesquieu's posi-tion on African slavery and on the climate theory of human character was full of contradictions. Yet no matter how Montesquieu is read, in the eyes of his antislavery readers he offered strong support for their cause: African slavery was antithetical to political principles, served only the undeserved luxury of Europeans, and stemmed from a hypo-critical violation of that same human empathy that Christians pro-fessed to believe in.

Third, the Pennsylvania Society of Friends felt that the contradic-tion between Christian faith and African slavery was simply unsustain-able.[9] The Philadelphia Quaker John Woolman began to articulate this tension in his diary in 1742, and in 1754 he published the tract *Some Consideration on the Keeping of Negroes; Recommended to the Professors of Christianity, of Every Denomination*. Motivated by a "real Sadness" he felt about the fate of the "poor *African*," Woolman cited the shared human origin in Adam and Eve as evidence that all humans are of "one

8. *De l 'Esprit des lois*, ed. Victor Goldschmidt (Paris: Garnier-Flammarion, 1979), livre 15, vol. I, pp. 389–407; here p. 393. The English translation is adapted from *The Spirit of the Laws*, ed. Franz Neumann (New York, 1949), I: 238–40. Whereas Bitterli (see Selected Bibliogra-phy, p. 399) sees Montesquieu as ironist, Neumann reads him as making a straight comment.
9. Francis Daniel Pastorius, the German-American founder of Germantown, articulated the first protest against slavery in British North America as early as 1688. As Alfred Brophy has shown, Pastorius addressed the Quaker Monthly Meeting, calling attention to the inappropriateness of holding humans in bondage and reminding immigrant Quakers that they, too, might have been enslaved by Turkish pirates. And he exhorted Quakers to follow the golden rule. See Brophy's introduction to Pastorius's *Bee-Hive* in *The Multilingual Anthology of American Literature*, ed. Marc Shell et al. (New York: New York University Press, 2000), p. 14.

Blood." He emphasized the golden rule as the core of Christian doctrine: "*Whatsoever ye would that Men should do unto you, do ye even so to them*" (Matthew 7.12). He invited Christian readers to imagine themselves in the Africans' place, to "make their case ours." He proceeded with a novel consideration that proved persuasive to many readers in the second half of the eighteenth century. Woolman examined the effects of slaveholding on *whites* and focused perceptively on the danger of a rise of racial prejudice. In contemplating the effects of slavery on a Christian commonwealth, Woolman feared for the loss of "that Humility and Meekness in which alone lasting Happiness can be enjoyed." Beginning in 1761, Quakers were increasingly exhorted to release their slaves and to cease all participation in the slave trade. It is no coincidence that Equiano's master, who permitted him, however reluctantly, to buy his freedom in 1766, was a Philadelphia Quaker.[1] Even though Equiano did not wish to become a Quaker himself (he preferred Bible-reading to silent meetings), he held Quakers in highest esteem.

These different strands of mid-eighteenth-century thought coalesced perfectly in the once extremely popular (though now less-well-known) work by the Pennsylvania Quaker abolitionist quotation-gatherer Anthony Benezet, *Some Historical Account of Guinea* (published in 1771 and reprinted many times).[2] Benezet, who also founded a Philadelphia Free School for colored children that Equiano visited in 1785 (see Chapter XII of the *Narrative*), absorbed from his sources many positive and admiring descriptions of Africa; he devoted a section to a praise of Montesquieu's critique of slavery; and, following the Quaker concern about the effects of slavery on Christianity, he vehemently opposed slavery from a Christian universalist position. The long title of his book included the programmatic phrase, *An Inquiry into the Rise and Progress of the Slave-Trade, Its Nature and Lamentable Effects*, and his opening epigraph on the title page is taken from Acts 17: "God that made the World—hath made of one Blood all Nations of Men." He also included long descriptions of the extraordinary cruelties toward African slaves on the West Indian islands and extracts from Granville Sharp's attack on slavery.

Benezet was a strong presence in the writings of English opponents to the slave trade who were rallying to their cause in the 1780s. This is certainly true for Thomas Clarkson's important work, *An Essay on the Slavery and Commerce of the Human Species, Particularly the African* (1786), in which the author traced "the situation of man from unbounded liberty to subordination" in order to attack African slavery as contrary to "*reason, justice, nature, the principles of law and government, the whole doctrine, in short, of natural religion, and the revealed*

1. See Edwards's annotation to this passage in his edition of the *Narrative*, Chapter VII.
2. Some extracts from Benezet's compendium are included below, pp. 250–53.

voice of God."³ Clarkson named Benezet's *Account* as one of his central sources: "In this precious book I found almost all I wanted," he stated.⁴ Appeals to original goodness, a natural right to liberty, human oneness ("one blood"), the golden rule, and the incompatibility of slavery with Christianity pervaded antislavery writing; and Benezet also influenced Tom Paine and John Wesley. It was impossible for Equiano not to encounter and appreciate Benezet's glowing account of Africa. With his footnotes to Benezet and Clarkson, Equiano signals his participation in this tradition of anti–slave-trade and antislavery writing.⁵

Equiano's Voice

Equiano's voice is both that of "the African" (as the title page of his book promises) and that of a European.⁶ He is the African who cherishes his past and the culture within which he was raised and who, when he sees Europeans for the first time, can describe his fear of being "eaten by those white men with horrible looks, red faces, and loose hair" (39). And he is the English intellectual who can speak with the voice of Ajax in Pope's translation of the *Iliad*, or describe the hell of slavery in Montserrat in the words of *Paradise Lost*. In fact, his English erudition appears well before he describes his first encounter with Englishmen. It is manifest from the rhetorical opening—in which Equiano expresses feigned concern that a writer of memoirs might be considered vain—to the sources through which he represents Africa. It reaches extreme moments, as when he describes his fear of perishing in the African woods while escaping his capture by a neighboring nation. "Thus was I like the hunted deer," he writes.

—Ev'ry leaf and ev'ry whisp'ring breath,
Convey'd a foe, and ev'ry foe a death. (34)

To have a repertoire of even minor literary quotations available—this one adapted from John Denham's *Cooper's Hill* (1642)—and to

3. Clarkson, p. 256; see also excerpt below, pp. 277–81.
4. Sypher, p. 17. Clarkson's printer, who was a Quaker, advertised, on a page facing the essay's "Preface," Benezet's works and James Ramsay's *Essay on the Treatment and Conversion of African Slaves* (1784), an essay that Clarkson (and Equiano) defended on rationalist principles against James Tobin's pro-slavery attacks. See excerpt included in this edition, pp. 250–53. See also brief excerpt from Tobin and Equiano's public letter below, pp. 195–99.
5. In the descriptive details of his place of birth, Equiano follows closely the idyllic accounts collected in Benezet, even to the extent of incorporating whole sentences. Through Benezet's writings, Equiano drew on eighteenth-century works such as the French traveler Michel Adanson's *Voyage to Senegal* (translated in 1759); and Benezet, in turn, in his *Account of Guinea*, drew on Adanson. Adanson's *Voyage* was also cited in authenticating footnotes to Thomas Day and John Bicknell's immensely popular poem *The Dying Negro* (1773), which Equiano quotes in his *Narrative*, apparently from memory. See the excerpt below, pp. 288–91, from the first edition of *The Dying Negro*. Edwards has disentangled the different editions from which Equiano adapted and conflated his rendition.
6. As Stefania Piccinato observed, Equiano embodied biculturalism or bipolarism. See her "Olaudah Equiano Gustavus Vassa: Un Uomo del '700 fra due culture," in Lynn Salkin Sbiroli, ed., *Il senso del nonsenso* (Roma: Edizioni Scientifiche Italiane, 1994), pp. 237–45.

employ them even in situations charged with emotions (for example, great anxiety) reveals not merely literacy but a close approximation of a contemporary literary ideal. Equiano's literary sophistication and rhetorical skills do not constitute a contradictory interference with his "Africanness": they rather help to define the terms in which he came to present and view African life.

Yet Equiano could not assume a readily available collective identification ("Afro-Briton"? "Anglo-African"?). This causes a certain instability of the first-person-singular observer and of the pronouns he uses to describe collective belonging. Both "they" and "we" may refer to Equiano's Africans as well as to Europeans. The following sentences from Chapter I is representative:

> As to religion, the natives believe that there is one Creator of all things, and that he lives in the sun, and is girted round with a belt that he may never eat or drink; but, according to some, he smokes a pipe, which is our own favourite luxury. They believe he governs events. . . . (26)

There is a subtle distinction between "our own" luxury and what "they" believe.[7] The Ibo sun-God referred to may be *Chukwu*, as Edwards suggested. However, the presence of a pipe-smoking God also makes for a certain humor here, as it points to a post-Columbian origin of this "original" custom (in a part of the world in which Indian corn had also become a staple). The appeal to Rousseauvian ideas of simplicity is explicitly articulated: "Our manner of living is entirely plain; for as yet the natives are unacquainted with those refinements in cookery which debauch the taste" (22).

If "Africa" meant for Equiano the presence of natural man, simple, unrefined, and still capable of empathy unmediated by selfishness, his land of birth was also associated with biblical origins. Equiano explicitly casts the Ibos as typologically related to the biblical Israelites. "We practised circumcision like the Jews, and made offerings and feasts on that occasion in the same manner as they did. Like them also, our children were named from some event, some circumstance, or fancied foreboding at the time of their birth" (27). Equiano repeatedly mentions examples of African-Jewish parallels and even offers a general observation concerning, as he puts it, "the strong analogy * * * in the manners and customs of my countrymen and those of the Jews, before they reached the Land of Promise" (29).[8] Equiano here followed contemporary efforts to connect all human history to the biblical story.

---

7. Geraldine Murphy also examines the pronoun shift and sees in it a technique by which Equiano distances himself from African religious beliefs. See Murphy's essay below, pp. 378–79.

8. See Adam Potkay on this issue, pp. 384–88 below.

This reinforced the perception that Africans were living in an earlier, more original, positively conceived "primitive" state: "Like the Israelites in their primitive state, our government was conducted by our chiefs or judges, our wise men and elders; and the head of a family with us enjoyed a similar authority over his household with that which is ascribed to Abraham and the other patriarchs" (30). This simile casts Africans as the symbolic ancestors of the British, what the Hebrew patriarchs were for Christianity. This analogy also created an expectation of a possible return, on a higher, Christian level, to the state of nature he describes, and to a realm of full, unselfish empathy, of which Christian Africans could be the harbingers.

Equiano ends both Chapters I and II with strong exhortations to European readers that are augmented by the familiar biblical quotations ("one blood" from Acts 17.26 and the "golden rule" of Matthew 7.12):

> Let the polished and haughty European recollect that his ancestors were once, like the Africans, uncivilized, and even barbarous. Did Nature make *them* inferior to their sons? and should *they too* have been made slaves? Every rational mind answers, No. * * * If, when they [the Europeans] look round the world, they feel exultation, let it be tempered with benevolence to others, and gratitude to God, "who hath made of one blood all nations of men for to dwell on all the face of the earth. . . ." (31)

And:

> O, ye nominal Christians! might not an African ask you, learned you this from your God, who says unto you, Do unto all men as you would men should do unto you? (43)

Free Trade

Whether or not African aborigines lived in an original state of nature (as the English aborigines once did), that state was brought to an abrupt and brutal end by the slave trade. One thinks that this experience might generate a nostalgic wish in Equiano for a return to origins or the development of a position from which *all* British trade would be attacked as destructive of original goodness. Yet far from yearning for a return to an original state of respose,[9] Equiano actually cherishes the hustle-bustle of the world of modern free trade, in which *only* the slave trade is an obstacle to an otherwise thoroughly appreciated and endorsed free exchange of goods and the opening of untapped markets. As Houston A. Baker, Jr., stressed, the very fact that Equiano *purchased*

---

9. Even the unfulfilled plans Equiano made to return to West Africa defined his role as commissary of a British resettlement scheme.

himself was a sign of his recognition "that only the acquisition of property will enable him to alter his designated status *as property*."[1] It was thus Equiano's ability to trade that freed him from his slave status. "As the inhuman traffic of slavery is to be taken into the consideration of the British legislature," he states in his *Narrative* and, adapting passages from a letter he had written to the president of the English Board of Trade, Lord Hawkesbury, he continues:

> I doubt not, if a system of commerce was established in Africa, the demand for manufactures would most rapidly augment, as the native inhabitants will insensibly adopt the British fashions, manners, customs, &c. In proportion to the civilization, so will be the consumption of British manufactures. (177)

He believes that the "manufacturing interest and the general interests are synonymous" (177), and it is in the area of consumption growth that African history will repeat English history:

> It cost the Aborigines of Britain little or nothing in clothing, &c. The difference between their forefathers and the present generation, in point of consumption, is literally infinite. The supposition is most obvious. It will be equally immense in Africa—The same cause, viz. civilization, will ever have the same effect. (177)

Civilization and property spelled the end of Rousseau's state of nature, but Equiano deemed such progress beneficial.[2] Hence the slave trade appears to be not only morally wrong but also bad for all commerce—except the trade in shackles and chains, as Equiano sarcastically adds.

Cultural Relativism

Equiano's autobiographical self had multiple perspectives: the eyewitness of Ibo life and of the slave ship; the extoller of primitive man; the writer, reader, and Protestant convert; the political abolitionist and economic free-trade advocate. These various aspects do not easily merge into a single point of view. Speaking with different voices, Equiano is also remarkably curious about many of the details of the worlds he encounters in his largely episodic book.[3] He is, as Geraldine Murphy writes, an "accidental tourist" who finds something to marvel at wherever he goes—from the predictable to the unexpected.

In his observations, Equiano provides some evidence of cultural relativism, most pronounced in his explicit and implicit comparisons

1. Baker, *Blues, Ideology, and Afro-American Literature: A Vernacular Theory*, p. 35. See excerpt below, pp. 339–47.
2. In this respect, Equiano was close to Benezet's position. See David Dabydeen's treatment of commerce and slavery below pp. 228–49.
3. Angelo Costanzo assigned Equiano's *Narrative* to the picaresque tradition. See excerpt below, pp. 348–50.

between black and white, African and English. He writes that "in regard to complexion, ideas of beauty are wholly relative" (25), an idea to which some English intellectuals gave currency, going back at least to Thomas Browne's study *Pseudodoxia* (1646). Browne had stressed that Africans take so much content in blackness "that they esteem deformity by other colours, describing the Devil, and terrible objects, white," and concluded that "Beauty is determined by opinion, and seems to have no essence that holds one notion with all."[4] Equiano supports a similar observation by his life: "I remember while in Africa to have seen three negro children, who were tawny, and another quite white, who were universally regarded by myself, and the natives in general, as far as related to their complexions, as deformed" (25).

Equiano's relativism is less clear-cut when he observes other cultures. He is often inclined to see the world through British eyes. His anti-Catholicism is pronounced; his double-edged reference to the "morality and common sense of a Samaide or a Hottentot" (81) does not betray an African point of view; and in such decisive cultural markers as monogamy, Equiano can come out on different sides of the issue. He described the Ibo men understandingly as not preserving "the same constancy to their wives, which they expect from them; for they indulge in a plurality, though seldom in more than two" (21). Yet when he is offered two wives by a Turkish officer in Smyrna, he comments with irony, but now also from a firmly Western point of view: "I refused the temptation" (128). (He added in a later edition that he thought "one was as much as some could manage, and more than others would venture on.")

Language, Free Black Life, and Interracialism

Equiano, who views himself as an open-minded observer, renders many other interesting aspects of eighteenth-century Atlantic life that a modern reader may enjoy. His observations on language, free black life, and on interracialism are examples. He is, from childhood, accustomed to language difference, and he continually comments on languages. Scholars have endeavored to offer additional explanations of Equiano's Ibo terms such as "Embrenche" or "Ah-affoe-way-cah." Yet his memory of his mother tongue also serves to support the theory of natural goodness: "I remember we never polluted the name of the object of our adoration; on the contrary, it was always mentioned with the greatest reverence; and we were totally unacquainted with swearing, and all those terms of abuse and reproach which find their way so readily and copiously into the languages of more civilized people" (27). Still, switching from one natural language to another was not

---

4. "Of the Blackness of Negroes," *Pseudodoxia* (1646), in *The Works of Sir Thomas Browne*, ed. Charles Sayle (London: Grant Richards, 1904), vol. II, p. 385.

difficult. "From the time I left my own nation I always found somebody that understood me till I came to the sea coast. The languages of different nations did not totally differ, nor were they so copious as those of the Europeans, particularly the English. They were therefore easily learned; and, while I was journeying thus through Africa, I acquired two or three different tongues" (35).

This (idealized) family resemblance of various African languages ("we understood each other perfectly" (37)) changes radically when he has his first encounter with Europeans who are absolutely different in "manners, customs, and language" (37). More than that, "the language they spoke, (which was very different from any I had ever heard)" (38) strengthens his belief that they must be bad spirits, not human beings at all. Yet as his fear of Europeans disappears, he can also master English: "I could now speak English tolerably well, and I perfectly understood every thing that was said. I now not only felt myself quite easy with these new countrymen, but relished their society and manners" (56).

One could probably add that Equiano particularly relished the language of the sea and that modern readers could assemble a whole phrase book from his *Narrative*, including, for example, vessels such as wherry, punt, drogger, hoy, sloop, frigate, snow, privateer, schooner, man of war, or fire ship; abbreviations from the compass such as S.W. and E.N.E.; and nautical terms such as quadrant, ensign, sounding, battery, press-gang, half-musket shot, quarter-deck, jib, gunwale, leebeam, mizzenmast, and maintop gallant mast-head. He even liked to spin sailors' yarns, like the story of his sea-horses "which neighed exactly like any other horses" (132).

How cosmopolitan this multilingual African becomes in the course of the book is driven home by another Rousseauvian encounter he has when he takes part in an English expedition to Central America. In the same manner in which he described his own West Africans, he views the Miskito Indians as original men: "Upon the whole, I never met any nation that were so simple in their manners as these people, or had so little ornament in their houses. Neither had they, as I ever could learn, one word expressive of an oath" (156). Yet in Indian eyes Equiano seems to be an Englishman, even if somewhat better than the others. He reports the double-edged comment by a Miskito who is struck by the many curse words that were used by the English Christians: "How comes it that all the white men on board who can read and write, and observe the sun, and know all things, yet swear, lie, and get drunk, only excepting yourself?" (154)

Natural people speak natural languages that are proto-Protestant and pure. "The worst word I ever heard amongst them when they were quarreling, was one that they had got from the English, which was 'you rascal' " (156). Adopting English can thus be a mixed blessing. But from there Equiano proceeds to make pronouncements about the negative effect of culture contacts on pure languages, and his reading of aspects of Creole language is not admiring: "The Musquito people within our vicinity * * * made entertainments of the grand kind, called in their tongue *tourrie* or *dryckbot*. The English of this expression is, a feast of drinking about, of which it seems a corruption of language" (158). This may not be good etymology, but it does raise questions about Equiano's view of multilingual encounters. Does culture contact bring about better understanding, or does it merely corrupt? Are natural people purer and more truly Christian than they become after mingling with nominally Christian Englishmen?

Equiano's answer to this question is different when he considers race rather than language. Again, his answer, informed by free black life, does not easily fit into a predictable mold. Equiano was aware that the issue of race had a dynamic of its own that could unfold outside and after slavery, too. He was perceptive in describing the difficulties and legal oppression of free blacks such as the Georgia carpenter who was imprisoned when he asked for his pay, or the free Mulatto sailor Joseph Clipson from the Bermudas who was wrongfully reenslaved. Equiano's legal efforts to regain the liberty of his friend, the cook John Annis, were thwarted: Annis was kidnapped on the river Thames and taken to St. Kitts where he was, "according to custom, staked to the ground with four pins through a cord, two on his wrists, and two on his ancles, was cut and flogged most unmercifully, and afterwards loaded cruelly with irons about his neck" (137).

Equiano states forcefully that the liberty of free blacks is "nominal, for they are universally insulted and plundered without the possibility of redress" (90). John Wesley (whose antislavery position was aroused earlier when he read Benezet's *Account of Guinea*) reacted with particular empathy when he learned in Equiano's *Narrative* of the curtailment of the rights of free blacks: they were not permitted to bear witness against whites in court.[5] Like John Woolman, Equiano understood the dangers of racial prejudice; but unlike Woolman, Equiano was repeatedly exposed to racial injustices in the colonies after his manumission. When a Mr. Hughes ties and hoists him up, intending to sell him as a slave in Cartagena, Equiano comments: "Thus I hung, without any crime committed, and without judge or jury; merely because I was a free man, and could not by the law get any redress from a white person in those parts of the world" (160). It is significant that in Chapter V Equiano explicitly expresses his sympathy for Moses, who found redress only by slaying an Egyptian (as in Exodus 2.11–12). In this discerning allusion to Moses, Equiano supported militant, violent retaliation to racial injustice as one of the expectable and under-

5. See extracts below from Wesley, pp. 281–82, and Dykes, pp. 210–16.

standable responses. It is as if Equiano had said, by any means necessary. The year was, after all, 1789, and bourgeois and colonial subjects were rallying to the cause of Revolution.

Equiano also examined the meaning of reciprocity implied by the golden rule in order to advocate a course of action that would seem to make him a prophet of the modern interracial movement. His theoretical starting point is the premise from the abolitionists' favorite passage in Acts 17 that all human beings are "of one blood" and that racial differences are of secondary significance and are due to different climates. He invokes John Mitchell's "Essay on the Causes of the Different Colours of People in Different Climates" (1744), which had argued that both blacks and whites "were descended from people of an intermediate tawny colour; whose posterity became more and more tawny, i.e., black, in the southern regions and less so, or white, in the northern climes."[6] From Clarkson, Equiano adopts Mitchell's example of the Spaniards in America who had become "as dark coloured as our native Indians of Virginia" (30). Given the original "tawny colour" of Adam, Eve, and Noah, there was really no "black" or "white" in the world—there was only more or less "tawny." Hence Equiano saw interracial marriage, on which he commented in the *Narrative* and in one of his public letters, as a desirable expression of human nature.[7]

Of course, Equiano was aware of the opposition to interracial unions that was particularly strong in the colonies and that was articulated by pro-slavery authors.[8] He describes, for example, the "curious imposition on human nature" in an episode in St. Kitts, when a "white man wanted to marry in the church a free black woman":

> [T]he clergyman told him it was against the law of the place to marry a white and a black in the church. The man then asked to be married on the water, to which the parson consented, and the two lovers went in one boat, and the parson and clerk in another, and thus the ceremony was performed. (88)

As this episode suggests, Equiano did not favor the "curious imposition" of intermarriage restrictions. He not only lived an interracial life, he also advocated a general program of intermarriage. In an open letter to *The Public Advertiser* (January 28, 1788), Equiano wrote that

6. "Essay on the Causes of the Different Colours of People in Different Climates," Royal Society, *Philosophical Transactions* 1744 (London: C. R. Baldwin, 1809), vol. 9, p. 65. See p. 256 below.

7. In the manner of many of his contemporaries who were interested in African color variation, Equiano mentions the red-skinned Oye-Eboe, whose existence complicates notions of color, and he describes an interracial family scene that would seem to appeal to his sense of wonder as well as express his belief that complexion is merely an accidental human quality: "Soon after my arrival in London, I saw a remarkable circumstance relative to African complexion, which I thought so extraordinary, that I beg leave just to mention it: A white negro woman, that I had formerly seen in London and other parts, had married a white man, by whom she had three boys, and they were every one mulattoes, and yet they had fine light hair (166)."

8. See, for example, the extract below, pp. 195–96, from James Tobin's *Cursory Remarks*, which provoked Equiano's response.

the "mutual commerce of the sexes of both Blacks and Whites" would help the situation of black women who are sexually exploited because of the legal restraints on intermarriage. He asks the London reader: "[W]hy not establish intermarriages at home, and in our Colonies? and encourage open, free, and generous love upon Nature's own wide and extensive plan, subservient only to moral rectitude, without distinction of the colour of a skin?" (199). In Equiano's eyes, interracial "mutual commerce" was part of the free flow of commercial activity that he generally favored.

Here he again adopts his favorite typological role model of Moses, this time as the loving husband of an Ethiopian woman (Numbers 12) rather than as the militant slayer of an Egyptian.

> That ancient, most wise, and inspired politician, Moses, encouraged strangers to unite with the Israelites, upon this maxim, that every addition to their number was an addition to their strength, and as an inducement, admitted them to most of the immunities of his own people. He established marriage with strangers by his own example—The Lord confirmed them—and punished Aaron and Miriam for vexing their brother for marrying the Ethiopian— Away then with your narrow impolitic notion of preventing by law what will be a national honour, national strength, and productive of national virtue—Intermarriages! (199)

Gustavus Vassa's work may not have been the ideal prototype of the American slave narrative; as Charles T. Davis put it so memorably, the *Interesting Narrative* was "neither an Afro-American work nor a slave narrative."[9] But Olaudah Equiano did participate in the eighteenth-century project of self-representation in autobiographic writing, of which Rousseau's *Confessions* and Benjamin Franklin's memoirs also were a part.[1] Proud of Africa, tireless in his opposition to the slave trade, and serious about spiritual matters, he led an active life and wrote an autobiography of true political significance. In Equiano's openness in encountering the whole world of the eighteenth century and in representing it in the different voices he developed in his *Narrative*, he has left posterity a remarkable legacy that is as intriguing for today's readers as it was for his contemporaries.

Reception

While there were many editions of the *Interesting Narrative* between 1789 and 1819, and the next English edition appeared only in 1964,

9. See Davis's essay below, pp. 338–39.
1. For interesting comparisons between Franklin and Equiano, see Rafia Zafar, *We Wear the Mask: African Americans Write American Literature, 1760–1870* (New York: Columbia University Press, 1997), and Martin Christadler, "Selbstkonstitution und Lebensgeschichte in der Autobiographie der Aufklärung: Benjamin Franklin und Olaudah Equiano." In Carola Hilmes et al., ed,. *Skepsis oder das Spiel mit dem Zweifel. Festschrift für Ralph-Rainer Wuthenow zum 65. Geburtstag* (Würzburg: Königshausen & Neumann, 1994), pp. 191–211.

Equiano was not forgotten in the intervening years. His memory was kept alive by American abolitionists; the last two editions published in the nineteenth century appeared in the United States, in 1829 and 1837, respectively; Lydia Maria Child drew on Equiano's sympathetic depiction of African manners in her short story "Jumbo and Zairee" (1831) and included a one-page sketch of Equiano, "better known by the name of Gustavus Vassa," in *An Appeal in Favor of that Class of Americans Called Africans* (1833); and Wilson Armistead's *A Tribute for the Negro* (1848) gave a forty-page summary of Equiano's *Narrative* and cited documents such as Equiano's appeal to Queen Charlotte. Though surprisingly I have not been able to find any reference to Equiano in Frederick Douglass's writing, efforts at stock-taking of the African American tradition have continued to remember Equiano. Gertrude Mossell's "Sketch of Afro-American Literature" (1894) mentions him; Arthur Schomburg's bibliography in Alain Locke's *The New Negro* (1925) lists the American 1791 edition "with portrait by Tiebout"; Vernon Loggins offers a positive appraisal in *The Negro Author* (1931); in *The Negro Genius* (1937), Benjamin Brawley sketches Gustavus Vassa's life and quotes a page from Chapter II of the *Narrative*; Benjamin E. Mays, *The Negro's God as Reflected in His Literature* (1938), gives a one-page account of the *Narrative*; and Sterling Brown's *Negro Caravan* (1941) lists the book in the chronology. Dorothy Porter, who had assisted in the production of Brown's path-breaking anthology, pioneered in sorting out more than a dozen different Equiano editions in her "Early American Negro Writings: A Bibliographical Study" (1945). In 1942 no fewer than three books devoted some space to Vassa: Eva Beatrice Dykes's *The Negro in English Romantic Thought* and Wylie Sypher's *Guinea's Captive Kings: British Anti-Slavery Literature of the XVIIIth Century* discuss Equiano, and Joel Rogers's *Sex and Race* includes Equiano's image with a few accompanying words. The dissertations by Marion W. Starling (1946) and Charles H. Nichols (1948) opened up the field of African American autobiography in the slavery period. Despite this continued recognition, Vassa remained a minor figure in historical and literary scholarship until his text was republished in the 1960s, reexamined in the 1980s, and widely anthologized in the 1990s.

The turning point in the Equiano reception is easily marked by the definitive facsimile of the first edition that was prepared and magisterially introduced by Paul Edwards in 1969. Starting with the Edwards edition, it has also been more common to discuss the author under his African name Equiano than under the name the author himself used far more frequently, Gustavus Vassa. American readers and students began to pay more attention to Equiano after Arna Bontemps included the full *Narrative* in his collection, *Great Slave Narratives* (1969).

Since the autobiography itself remains the most important source of Equiano's life story, much of the critical literature has offered summaries of the author's account, interlaced with excerpts from the *Narrative*. However, this state of affairs has inspired readers from Edwards to Acholonu to locate related historical documents, and the question of the book's reliability has been raised more than once. Equiano's authenticity was disputed repeatedly from 1792 (when rumors circulated that he had been born in St. Croix rather than in West Africa) to the present. Thus Edwards (see below, p. 302) noticed a problem in the text concerning Equiano's age. Most recently, Vincent Carretta, working with British Admiralty records (see sample, p. xxx), has found that Equiano was truthful in many of the details of his life. However, Carretta also reopened the question of the place and date of Equiano's nativity. Carretta did so, not in the Equiano edition he prepared but in separate essays, in which he pondered

> the tantalizing possibility that Equiano's African identity may have been a rhetorical invention. * * * In 1792 he vigorously disputed an assertion in a London newspaper that charged he was not born in Africa but rather in the Danish West Indies. In the documentary evidence of his baptism and naval records while serving with Pascal, Equiano had no control over the name recorded or the baptismal location of his nativity "in Carolina." But on the voyage to the North Pole, he was a free man and presumably the only source of the information in the muster book of the *Racehorse* identifying him as "Gustavus Weston" (non-English names were often misspelled), an able seaman, aged 28, who had been born in South Carolina.[2]

This raised the question "why, if he had indeed been born Olaudah Equiano in Africa, he chose to suppress these facts." Carretta surmised that "Pascal must have bought Equiano from Campbell, and renamed him Gustavus Vassa in early September 1754"—"two years earlier than the date Vassa offers in the *Narrative*."[3] Carretta added that these disparities were particularly odd in the case of an autobiographer who

2. "Three West Indian Writers of the 1780s Revisited and Revised," *Research in African Literatures* 29.4 (Winter 1998): 73–86. The corresponding information in Carretta's edition appears in footnote 485, in which the editor argues that "Gustavus Weston was almost certainly Gustavus Vassa" but without drawing any conclusions concerning Equiano's African identity, even though he mentions in footnote 197 that the baptismal record of St. Margaret's Church in Westminster reads, "Gustavus Vassa a Black born in Carolina 12 years old" (February 9, 1759).

3. Carretta, "Olaudah Equiano or Gustavus Vassa? New Light on an Eighteenth-Century Question of Identity," *Slavery and Abolition* 20.3 (December 1999): 96–105, here, pp. 102, 100, and 101. Carretta suggests as possible carriers the snow *Ogden* for the Middle Passage from the Bight of Biafra to Barbados and the sloop *Nancy* for the voyage from Barbados to the York River, on June 13, 1754. Interestingly, another ship named *Nancy* appears as the frontispiece to the second volume of the first edition.

   Robert Allison examined the arrival of slave ships in Virginia in 1756 and found only two, one of which, the *Kingston*, did sell two or three slaves; up the York River there also was a plantation owned by a man named Campbell or Kammel. See Allison, ed., p. 25, n. 24.

Bounty paid.	Nº Entry.	Year	Appearance.	Whence and whether Prest or not.	Place and County where Born.	Age at Time of Entry in this Ship.	Nº and Letter of Tickets	MENS NAMES.	Qualities	D.D. or R.	Time of Discharge.
	3	May 17 1773	May 17 Deptford		Derry Ireland	21		Davd Lovell to A Janc pd Corporal	Att		
					Exeter	20		Jos.h Godfrey	Att	R	26 May
					S.o Carolina	28		Gus.o Weston	Att		
	5				London	29		Cotr.d Stakions	Att		
					Philadelphia	24		Will.m McPaul	Att		
					Dagnam Essex	25		Henry Teton to A June 73 Lut.t M.r Mas.	Att		
					S.t Andrews Esq 30			Sr.d Moore	Att		

May 17, 1773, entry in the Racehorse muster book for the Arctic expedition under Captain Constantine Phipps (PUBLIC RECORD OFFICE, ADMIRALTY ARCHIVES: PRO/ADM 36/7490). Courtesy of The National Archives, Public Record

was so verifiably accurate about the later stages of his career. If Carretta's hypothesis of Equiano's Carolina birth were ever to be fully substantiated, Equiano might just turn out to be one of the very first black American expatriates in Europe. This would, of course, also require a new interpretation of the *Narrative*.

The present edition is the first to include all known contemporary reviews the *Narrative* received, selected public letters in the contexts in which they emerged, and a representative sampling of Equiano criticism from all periods as well as related historical documents and sources.

WERNER SOLLORS
Cambridge, Massachusetts

Acknowledgments

This edition was made possible by the energetic and resourceful research and editorial assistance of Erica Michelstein, who traced even the most elusive sources, helped select the materials that accompany this edition, and proofread. The Introduction was written during a research period supported by the National Endowment for the Humanities.

The librarians at Widener Library, Houghton Library, and the Bayerische Staatsbibliothek München, and Paul Johnson at the British Public Record Office were all extraordinarily helpful at the research stage of this edition. I am grateful to Robert Allison for comments and leads, to Gert Buelens for locating the Dutch translation, to Heike Paul for procuring and examining a copy of the German translation, to Karen C. F. Dalton and Image of the Black in Western Art Research Project and Photo Archive, Harvard University, for assistance in searching for images, to Keren McGinity at Brown University for helping locate a difficult source, and to Vincent Carretta for alerting me to his recent publications on Equiano. I benefited from a seminar at the Université de Paris (Charles V) and wish to express my gratitude to Geneviève Fabre, Marc Mve Bekale, Françoise Charras, and Helena Woodard for their helpful comments. At W. W. Norton, Carol Bemis supervised this edition from the planning stage to the proofs, and I wish to thank her as well as Kathy Talalay, Brian Baker, and David Hawkins for many helpful suggestions, queries, and corrections.

I am deeply indebted to the pathbreaking and wide-ranging work undertaken by Paul Edwards as well as to the editions and annotations by Robert Allison, Vincent Carretta, Henry Louis Gates, Jr., and Adam Potkay.

The Text of
THE INTERESTING NARRATIVE OF THE LIFE OF OLAUDAH EQUIANO, OR GUSTAVUS VASSA, THE AFRICAN, WRITTEN BY HIMSELF

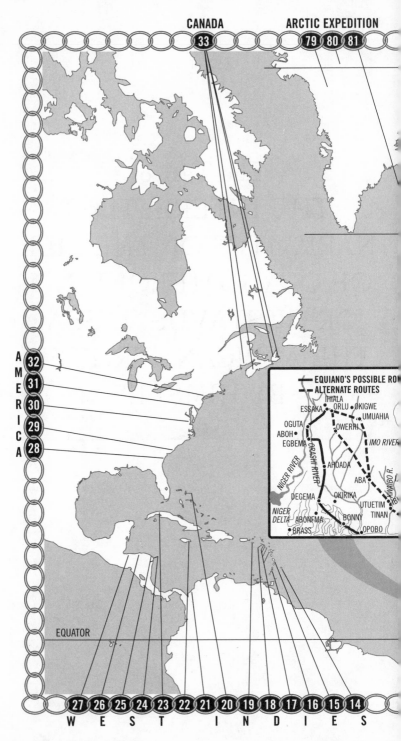

A
M
E
R
I
C
A

32
31
30
29
28

EQUIANO'S POSSIBLE RO
ALTERNATE ROUTES

IHIALA
ESSAKA   ORLU • OKIGWE
                    • UMUAHIA
OGUTA   OWERRI
ABOH •
EGBEMA •   IMO RIVER

NIGER RIVER   ORASHI RIVER   AHOADA

DEGEMA   OKIRIKA   ABA   KWAIBO R.

NIGER   BONNY   UTUETIM
DELTA   ABONEMA   TINAN
   • BRASS   OPOBO

EQUATOR

27 26 25 24 23 22 21 20 19 18 17 16 15 14

W E S T   I N D I E S

Equiano's World

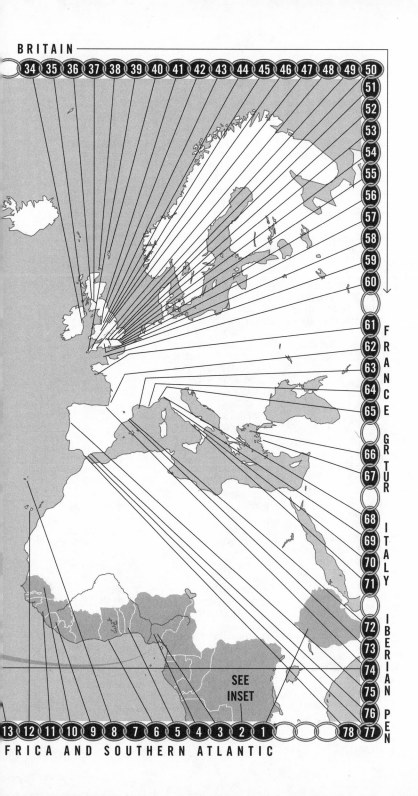

BRITAIN

34 35 36 37 38 39 40 41 42 43 44 45 46 47 48 49 50

51
52
53
54
55
56
57
58
59
60

61
62
63
64
65

66
67

68
69
70
71

72
73
74
75
76
77

F R A N C E

GR TUR

ITALY

IBERIAN PEN

SEE
INSET

13 12 11 10 9 8 7 6 5 4 3 2 1 78 77

FRICA AND SOUTHERN ATLANTIC

LEGEND FOR MAP ON PAGES 2 AND 3

AFRICA AND THE SOUTHERN ATLANTIC

1 ABYSSINIA (ETHIOPIA)
2 POSSIBLE ROUTE FROM ESSAKA TO THE COAST
3 ESSAKA?
4 EBOE? (unidentified)
5 BENIN
6 COAST FRON SENEGAL TO ANGOLA
7 TINMAH (unidentified, perhaps Tinan in inset)
8 MADEIRA
9 SIERRA LEONE
10 SENEGAMBIA (REGION IN WEST AFRICA BETWEEN THE SENEGAL & GAMBIA RIVERS, IN PRESENT-DAY SENEGAL, MALI, & GAMBIA)
11 GUINEA
12 TENERIFE AND CANARY ISLANDS
13 "THE LINE" (THE EQUATOR)

WEST INDIES

14 BRIDGE TOWN (BRIDGETOWN), BARBADOS
15 MARTINICO (MARTINIQUE)
16 GRENADES (GRENADINES)
17 LEEWARD ISLANDS:
   GAURDELOUPE (GUADELOUPE), MONTSERRAT, ANTIGUA, NEVIS, ST. KITTS
18 ST. EUSTATIA (SINT EUSTATIUS)
19 SANTA CRUZ (ST. CROIX)
20 BAHAMA ISLANDS:
   NEW PROVIDENCE AND OBBICO (GREAT ABACO)
21 CARTHAGENA (CARTAGENA, COLOMBIA)
22 KINGSTON, JAMAICA
23 THE HAVANNAH (HAVANA, CUBA)
24 CAPE GRACIAS Á DIOS (CABO GRACIAS Á DIOS, NICARAGUA)
25 MOSQUITO COAST, (COSTA DE MOSQUITOS, NICARAGUA)
26 BLACK RIVER (RIO NEGRO, HONDURAS)
27 DUPEUPY (HONDURAS) (unidentified)

AMERICA AND CANADIAN EAST COAST

28 SAVANNAH, GEORGIA
29 CHARLES TOWN (CHARLESTON, S.C.)
30 VIRGINIA
31 PHILADELPHIA
32 NEW YORK
33 NOVA SCOTIA:
   ST. GEORGE, LOUISBOURG, CAPE BRETON

EUROPE

a. BRITAIN
34 DUBLIN
35 BELFAST
36 GREENOCK (SCOTLAND)
37 CLYDE RIVER
38 ORKNEYS
39 LAND'S END
40 SHETLANDS
41 LIVERPOOL
42 NEWCASTLE (-ON-TYNE)
43 ST. HELEN'S
44 SHROPSHIRE
45 MANCHESTER
46 FALMOUTH
47 PEAK OF DERBYSHIRE
48 PLYMOUTH
49 PORTSMOUTH
50 LONDON
52 CAMBRIDGE
52 THAMES RIVER
53 ORFORDNESS (ORFORD NESS)
54 GRAVESEND
55 NORE
56 SHEERNESS
57 DEAL
58 SPITHEAD
59 DEPTFORD
60 GUERNSEY

EUROPE

b. FRANCE
61 BELLE-ÎLE
62 BAYONNE
63 GULF OF LYONS
64 TOULON
65 NICE

c. GREECE AND TURKEY
66 ARCHIPELAGO ISLANDS (GREEK ISLANDS, AEGEAN SEA)
67 SYMRNA (IZMIR), TURKEY

d. ITALY
68 GENOA
69 LEGHORN (LIVORNO)
70 NAPLES
71 MT. VESUVIUS

EUROPE

e. IBERIAN PENINSULA
72 BARCELONA
73 VILLA FRANCA (VILLA-FRANCA DE PENEDÉS, NEAR BARCELONA)
74 ST. SEBASTIAN (SAN SEBASTIÁN)
75 OPORTO
76 MALAGA
77 GIBRALTAR
78 CADIZ

f. ARCTIC EXPEDITION
79 GREENLAND
80 LATITUDE 73
81 LATITUDE 58-59

THE
INTERESTING NARRATIVE
OF
THE LIFE
OF
OLAUDAH EQUIANO,
OR
GUSTAVUS VASSA,
THE AFRICAN.

WRITTEN BY HIMSELF.

---

*Behold, God is my salvation; I will trust, and not be
afraid, for the Lord Jehovah is my strength and my
song; he also is become my salvation.*

*And in that day shall ye say, Praise the Lord, call upon his
name, declare his doings among the people.* Isa. xii. 2. 4.

NINTH EDITION ENLARGED.

LONDON:
PRINTED FOR, AND SOLD BY THE AUTHOR.

1794.

PRICE FIVE SHILLINGS,
Formerly sold for 7s.

Olaudah Equiano,
or
GUSTAVUS VASSA,
the African.

Publish'd March 1 1789 by G. Vassa

To the Lords Spiritual and Temporal, and the Commons of the Parliament of Great Britain.

My Lords and Gentlemen,

Permit me, with the greatest deference and respect, to lay at your feet the following genuine Narrative; the chief design of which is to excite in your august assemblies a sense of compassion for the miseries which the Slave-Trade has entailed on my unfortunate countrymen. By the horrors of that trade was I first torn away from all the tender connexions that were naturally dear to my heart; but these, through the mysterious ways of Providence, I ought to regard as infinitely more than compensated by the introduction I have thence obtained to the knowledge of the Christian religion, and of a nation which, by its liberal sentiments, its humanity, the glorious freedom of its government, and its proficiency in arts and sciences, has exalted the dignity of human nature.

I am sensible I ought to entreat your pardon for addressing to you a work so wholly devoid of literary merit; but, as the production of an unlettered African, who is actuated by the hope of becoming an instrument towards the relief of his suffering countrymen, I trust that *such a man*, pleading in *such a cause*, will be acquitted of boldness and presumption.

May the God of heaven inspire your hearts with peculiar benevolence on that important day when the question of Abolition is to be discussed, when thousands, in consequence of your Determination, are to look for Happiness or Misery!

I am,

MY LORDS AND GENTLEMEN,

Your most obedient,

And devoted humble Servant,

OLAUDAH EQUIANO,

or

GUSTAVUS VASSA.

Union-Street, Mary-le-bone,
March 24, 1789.

LIST OF SUBSCRIBERS.

His Royal Highness the Prince of Wales.
His Royal Highness the Duke of York.

A
The Right Hon. the Earl of Ailesbury
Admiral Affleck
Mr. William Abington, 2 copies
Mr. John Abraham
James Adair, Esq.
Reverend Mr. Aldridge
Mr. John Almon
Mrs. Arnot
Mr. Joseph Armitage
Mr. Joseph Ashpinshaw
Mr. Samuel Atkins
Mr. John Atwood
Mr. Thomas Atwood
Mr. Ashwell
J. C. Ashworth, Esq.

B
His Grace the Duke of Bedford
Her Grace the Duchess of Buccleugh
The Right Rev. the Lord Bishop of Bangor
The Right Hon. Lord Belgrave
The Rev. Doctor Baker
Mrs. Baker
Matthew Baillie, M.D.
Mrs. Baillie
Miss Baillie
Miss J. Baillie
David Barclay, Esq.
Mr. Robert Barrett
Mr. William Barrett
Mr. John Barnes
Mr. John Basnett
Mr. Bateman
Mrs. Baynes, 2 copies
Mr. Thomas Bellamy
Mr. J. Benjafield
Mr. William Bennett
Mr. Bensey
Mr. Samuel Benson
Mrs. Benton
Reverend Mr. Bentley
Mr. Thomas Bently

Sir John Berney, Bart.
Alexander Blair, Esq.
James Bocock, Esq.
Mrs. Bond
Miss Bond
Mrs. Borckhardt
Mrs. E. Bouverie
————Brand, Esq.
Mr. Martin Brander
F. J. Brown, Esq. M. P. 2 copies
W. Buttall, Esq.
Mr. Buxton
Mr. R. L. B.
Mr. Thomas Burton, 6 copies
Mr. W. Button

C
The Right Hon. Lord Cathcart
The Right Hon. H. S. Conway
Lady Almiria Carpenter
James Carr, Esq.
Charles Carter, Esq.
Mr. James Chalmers
Captain John Clarkson, of the Royal Navy
The Rev. Mr. Thomas Clarkson, 2 copies
Mr. R. Clay
Mr. William Clout
Mr. George Club
Mr. John Cobb
Miss Calwell
Mr. Thomas Cooper
Richard Cosway, Esq.
Mr. James Coxe
Mr. J. C.
Mr. Croucher
Mr. Cruickshanks
Ottobah Cugoano, or John Stewart

D
The Right Hon. the Earl of Dartmouth
The Right Hon. the Earl of Derby
Sir William Dolben, Bart.
The Reverend C. E. De Coetlogon
John Delamain, Esq.
Mrs. Delamain
Mr. Davis
Mr. William Denton
Mr. T. Dickie
Mr. William Dickson

Mr. Charles Dilly, 2 copies
Andrew Drummond, Esq.
Mr. George Durant

E

The Right Hon. the Earl of Essex
The Right Hon. the Countess of Essex
Sir Gilbert Elliot, Bart. 2 copies
Lady Ann Erskine
G. Noel Edwards, Esq. M. P. 2 copies
Mr. Durs Egg
Mr. Ebenezer Evans
The Reverend Mr. John Eyre
Mr. William Eyre

F

Mr. George Fallowdown
Mr. John Fell
F. W. Foster, Esq.
The Reverend Mr. Foster
Mr. J. Frith
W. Fuller, Esq.

G

The Right Hon. the Earl of Gainsborough
The Right Hon. the Earl of Grosvenor
The Right Hon. Viscount Gallway
The Right Hon. Viscountess Gallway
————Gardner, Esq.
Mrs. Garrick
Mr. John Gates
Mr. Samuel Gear
Sir Philip Gibbes, Bart 6 copies
Miss Gibbes
Mr. Edward Gilbert
Mr. Jonathan Gillett
W. P. Gilliess, Esq.
Mrs. Gordon
Mr. Grange
Mr. William Grant
Mr. John Grant
Mr. R. Greening
S. Griffiths
John Grove, Esq.
Mrs. Guerin
Reverend Mr. Gwinep

H

The Right Hon. the Earl of Hopetoun
The Right Hon. Lord Hawke

Right Hon. Dowager Countess of Huntingdon
Thomas Hall, Esq.
Mr. Haley
Hugh Josiah Hansard, Esq.
Mr. Moses Hart
Mrs. Hawkins
Mr. Haysom
Mr. Hearne
Mr. William Hepburn
Mr. J. Hibbert
Mr. Jacob Higman
Sir Richard Hill, Bart.
Reverend Rowland Hill
Miss Hill
Captain John Hills, Royal Navy
Edmund Hill, Esq.
The Reverend Mr. Edward Hoare
William Hodges, Esq.
Reverend Mr. John Holmes, 3 copies
Mr. Martin Hopkins
Mr. Thomas Howell
Mr. R. Huntley
Mr. J. Hunt
Mr. Philip Hurlock, jun.
Mr. Hutson

J
Mr. T. W. J. Esq.
Mr. James Jackson
Mr. John Jackson
Reverend Mr. James
Mrs. Anne Jennings
Mr. Johnson
Mrs. Johnson
Mr. William Jones
Thomas Irving, Esq. 2 copies
Mr. William Justins

K
The Right Hon. Lord Kinnaird
William Kendall, Esq.
Mr. William Ketland
Mr. Edward King
Mr. Thomas Kingston
Reverend Dr. Kippis
Mr. William Kitchener
Mr. John Knight

L
The Right Reverend the Lord Bishop of London
Mr. John Laisne

Mr. Lackington, 6 copies
Mr. John Lamb
Bennet Langton, Esq.
Mr. S. Lee
Mr. Walter Lewis
Mr. J. Lewis
Mr. J. Lindsey
Mr. T. Litchfield
Edward Loveden Loveden, Esq. M.P
Charles Lloyd, Esq.
Mr. William Lloyd
Mr. J. B. Lucas
Mr. James Luken
Henry Lyte, Esq.
Mrs. Lyon

M

His Grace the Duke of Marlborough
His Grace the Dake [Duke] of Montague
The Right Hon. Lord Mulgrave
Sir Herbert Mackworth, Bart.
Sir Charles Middleton, Bart.
Lady Middleton
Mr. Thomas Macklane
Mr. George Markett
James Martin, Esq. M P.
Master Martin, Hayes-Grove, Kent
Mr. William Massey
Mr. Joseph Massingham
John M'Intosh, Esq.
Paul Le Mesurier, Esq. M. P.
Mr. James Mewburn
Mr. N. Middleton,
T. Mitchell, Esq.
Mrs. Montague, 2 copies
Miss Hannah More
Mr. George Morrison
Thomas Morris, Esq.
Miss Morris
Morris Morgann, Esq.

N

His Grace the Duke of Northumberland
Captain Nurse

O

Edward Ogle, Esq.
James Ogle, Esq.
Robert Oliver, Esq.

P

Mr. D. Parker,
Mr. W. Parker,
Mr. Richard Packer, jun.
Mr. Parsons, 6 copies
Mr. James Pearse
Mr. J. Pearson
J. Penn, Esq.
George Peters, Esq.
Mr. W. Phillips,
J. Philips, Esq.
Mrs. Pickard
Mr. Charles Pilgrim
The Hon. George Pitt, M. P.
Mr. Thomas Pooley
Patrick Power, Esq.
Mr. Michael Power
Joseph Pratt, Esq.

Q

Robert Quarme, Esq.

R

The Right Hon. Lord Rawdon
The Right Hon. Lord Rivers, 2 copies
Lieutenant General Rainsford
Reverend James Ramsay, 3 copies
Mr. S. Remnant, jun.
Mr. William Richards, 2 copies
Mr. J. C. Robarts
Mr. James Roberts
Dr. Robinson
Mr. Robinson
Mr. C. Robinson
George Rose, Esq. M. P.
Mr. W. Ross
Mr. William Rouse
Mr. Walter Row

S

His Grace the Duke of St. Albans
Her Grace the Duchess of St. Albans
The Right Reverend the Lord Bishop of St. Davi'ds [David's]
The Right Hon. Earl Stanhope, 3 copies
The Right Hon. the Earl of Scarbrough
William, the Son of Ignatius Sancho
Mrs. Mary Ann Sandiford
Mr. William Sawyer
Mr. Thomas Seddon

W. Seward, Esq.
Reverend Mr. Thomas Scott
Granville Sharp, Esq. 2 copies
Captain Sidney Smith, of the Royal Navy
Colonel Simcoe
Mr. John Simco
General Smith
John Smith, Esq.
Mt. George Smith
Mr. William Smith
Reverend Mr. Southgate
Mr. William Starkey
Thomas Steel, Esq. M. P.
Mr. Staples Steare,
Mr. Joseph Stewardson
Mr. Henry Stone, jun. 2 copies
John Symmons, Esq.

T
Henry Thornton, Esq. M. P.
Mr. Alexander Thomson, M. D.
Reverend John Till
Mr. Samuel Townly
Mr. Daniel Trinder
Reverend Mr. C. La Trobe
Clement Tudway, Esq.
Mrs. Twisden

U
Mr. M. Underwood

V
Mr. John Vaughan
Mrs. Vendt

W
The Right Hon. Earl of Warnick
The Right Reverend the Lord Bishop of Worcester
The Hon. William Windham, Esq. M. P.
Mr. C. B. Wadstrom
Mr. George Walne
Reverend Mr. Ward
Mr. S. Warren
Mr. J. Waugh
Josiah Wedgwood, Esq.
Reverend Mr. John Wesley
Mr. J. Wheble
Samuel Whitbread, Esq. M. P.
Reverend Thomas Wigzell

Mr. W. Wilson
Reverend Mr. Wills
Mr. Thomas Wimsett
Mr. William Winchester
John Wollaston, Esq.
Mr. Charles Wood
Mr. Joseph Woods
Mr. John Wood
J. Wright, Esq.

Y
Mr. Thomas Young
Mr. Samuel Yockney

CONTENTS
of
VOLUME I.

CHAP. I.

VOLUME II.

CHAP. VII.

16

CHAP. X.

CHAP. XI.

CHAP. XII.

Volume I

THE LIFE, &c.

Chapter I.] skim

The authors account of his country, and their manners and customs—Administration of justice—Embrenche—Marriage ceremony, and public entertainments—Mode of living—Dress—Manufactures Buildings—Commerce—Agriculture—War and religion—Superstition of the natives—Funeral ceremonies of the priests or magicians—Curious mode of discovering poison—Some hints concerning the origin of the author's countrymen, with the opinions of different writers on that subject.

I believe it is difficult for those who publish their own memoirs to escape the imputation of vanity; nor is this the only disadvantage under which they labour: it is also their misfortune, that what is uncommon is rarely, if ever, believed, and what is obvious we are apt to turn from with disgust, and to charge the writer with impertinence. People generally think those memoirs only worthy to be read or remembered which abound in great or striking events, those, in short, which in a high degree excite either admiration or pity: all others they consign to contempt and oblivion. It is therefore, I confess, not a little hazardous in a private and obscure individual, and a stranger too, thus to solicit the indulgent attention of the public; especially when I own[1] offer here the history of neither a saint, a hero, nor a tyrant. I believe there are few events in my life, which have not happened to many: it is true the incidents of it are numerous; and, did I consider myself an European, I might say my sufferings were great: but when I compare my lot with that of most of my countrymen, I regard myself as a *particular favourite of Heaven*, and acknowledge the mercies of Providence in every occurrence of my life. If then the following narrative does not appear sufficiently interesting to engage general attention, let my motive be some excuse for its publication. I am not so foolishly vain as to expect from

---

1. Acknowledge.

19

it either immortality or literary reputation. If it affords any satisfaction to my numerous friends, at whose request it has been written, or in the smallest degree promotes the interests of humanity, the ends for which it was undertaken will be fully attained, and every wish of my heart gratified. Let it therefore be remembered, that, in wishing to avoid censure, I do not aspire to praise.

That part of Africa, known by the name of Guinea, to which the trade along for slaves is carried on, extends along the coast above 3400 miles, from the Senegal to Angola, and includes a variety of kingdoms. Of these the most considerable is the kingdom of Benen,[2] both as to extent and wealth, the richness and cultivation of the soil, the power of its king, and the number and warlike disposition of the inhabitants. It is situated nearly under the line, and extends along the coast about 170 miles, but runs back into the interior part of Africa to a distance hitherto I believe unexplored by any traveller; and seems only terminated at length by the empire of Abyssinia,[3] near 1500 miles from its beginning. This kingdom is divided into many provinces or districts: in one of the most remote and fertile of which, called Eboe,[4] I was born, in the year 1745, in a charming fruitful vale, named Essaka.[5] The distance of this province from the capital of Benin and the sea coast must be very considerable; for I had never heard of white men or Europeans, nor of the sea: and our subjection to the king of Benin was little more than nominal; for every transaction of the government, as far as my slender observation extended, was conducted by the chiefs or elders of the place. The manners and government of a people who have little commerce with other countries are generally very simple; and the history of what passes in one family or village may serve as a specimen of a nation. My father was one of those elders or chiefs I have spoken of, and was styled Embrenche;[6] a term, as I remember, importing the highest distinction, and signifying in our language a *mark* of grandeur. This mark is conferred on the person entitled to it, by cutting the skin across at the top of the forehead, and drawing it down to the eye-brows; and while it is in this situation applying a warm hand, and rubbing it until it shrinks up into a thick *weal*[7] across the lower part of the forehead. Most of the judges and senators were thus marked; my father had long born it: I had seen it conferred on one of my brothers, and I was also *destined* to receive it by my parents. Those Embrence, or chief men, decided disputes and punished crimes; for

2. Or Benin. The kingdom of Benin reached from the Niger delta to the present-day city of Lagos, Nigeria, West Africa.
3. Ancient name for Ethiopia; it included present-day Ethiopia and parts of the Sudan. *Under the line*: the equator.
4. Ibo, or Igbo people, live in what is now southern Nigeria.
5. See essays below by Paul Edwards, pp. 308–14, and Catherine Acholonu, pp. 351–61.
6. "A mark of grandeur." According to Edwards and Acholonu, the modern equivalent is *mgbur-ichi*, the name given to those who either receive or make the *ichi* facial scars.
7. A mark, line, or ridge raised on the skin, as by a blow; a welt.

which purpose they always assembled together. The proceedings were generally short; and in most cases the law of retaliation prevailed. I remember a man was brought before my father, and the other judges, for kidnapping a boy; and, although he was the son of a chief or senator, he was condemned to make recompense by a man or woman slave. Adultery, however, was sometimes punished with slavery or death; a punishment which I believe is inflicted on it throughout most of the nations of Africa:[8] so sacred among them is the honour of the marriage bed, and so jealous are they of the fidelity of their wives. Of this I recollect an instance:—a woman was convicted before the judges of adultery, and delivered over, as the custom was, to her husband to be punished. Accordingly he determined to put her to death: but it being found, just before her execution, that she had an infant at her breast; and no woman being prevailed on to perform the part of a nurse, she was spared on account of the child. The men, however, do not preserve the same constancy to their wives, which they expect from them; for they indulge in a plurality, though seldom in more than two. Their mode of marriage is thus:—both parties are usually betrothed when young by their parents, (though I have known the males to betroth themselves). On this occasion a feast is prepared, and the bride and bridegroom stand up in the midst of all their friends, who are assembled for the purpose, while he declares she is thenceforth to be looked upon as his wife, and that no other person is to pay any addresses to her. This is also immediately proclaimed in the vicinity, on which the bride retires from the assembly. Some time after she is brought home to her husband, and then another feast is made, to which the relations of both parties are invited: her parents then deliver her to the bridegroom, accompanied with a number of blessings, and at the same time they tie round her waist a cotton string[9] of the thickness of a goose-quill, which none but married women are permitted to wear: she is now considered as completely his wife; and at this time the dowry is given to the new married pair, which generally consists of portions of land, slaves, and cattle, household goods, and implements of husbandry. These are offered by the friends of both parties; besides which the parents of the bridegroom present gifts to those of the bride, whose property she is looked upon before marriage; but after it she is esteemed the sole property of her husband. The ceremony being now ended the festival begins, which is celebrated with bonefires, and loud acclamations of joy, accompanied with music and dancing.

We are almost a nation of dancers, musicians, and poets. Thus every great event, such as a triumphant return from battle, or other cause of

---

8. See Benezet's "Account of Guinea." throughout [Equiano's note]. See excerpt below, from Anthony Benezet 1713–1784), *Some Historical Account of Guinea*, pp. 250–53.
9. This might be the *eme*, a cotton string tied round a girl's waist, but on her reaching puberty, not on her marriage.

public rejoicing is celebrated in public dances, which are accompanied with songs and music suited to the occasion. The assembly is separated into four divisions, which dance either apart or in succession, and each with a character peculiar to itself. The first division contains the married men, who in their dances frequently exhibit feats of arms, and the representation of a battle. To these succeed the married women, who dance in the second division. The young men occupy the third; and the maidens the fourth. Each represents some interesting scene of real life, such as a great achievement, domestic employment, a pathetic story or some rural sport; and as the subject is generally founded on some recent event, it is therefore ever new. This gives our dances a spirit and variety which I have scarcely seen elsewhere.[1] We have many musical instruments, particularly drums of different kinds, a piece of music which resembles a guitar, and another much like a stickado.[2] These last are chiefly used by betrothed virgins, who play on them on all grand festivals.

As our manners are simple, our luxuries are few. The dress of both sexes is nearly the same. It generally consists of a long piece of callico, or muslin, wrapped loosely round the body, somewhat in the form of a highland plaid. This is usually dyed blue, which is our favourite colour. It is extracted from a berry, and is brighter and richer than any I have seen in Europe. Besides this, our women of distinction wear golden ornaments; which they dispose with some profusion on their arms and legs. When our women are not employed with the men in tillage, their usual occupation is spinning and weaving cotton, which they afterwards dye, and make it into garments. They also manufacture earthen vessels, of which we have many kinds. Among the rest tobacco pipes, made after the same fashion, and used in the same manner, as those in Turkey.[3]

Our manner of living is entirely plain; for as yet the natives are unacquainted with those refinements in cookery which debauch the taste: bullocks, goats, and poultry, supply the greatest part of their food. These constitute likewise the principal wealth of the country, and the chief articles of its commerce. The flesh is usually stewed in a pan; to make it savoury we sometimes use also pepper, and other spices, and we have salt made of wood ashes.[4] Our vegetables are mostly plantains, eadas,[5] yams, beans, and Indian corn. The head of the family usually

---

1. When I was in Smyrna I have frequently seen the Greeks dance after this manner [Equiano's note]. The Greek city of Smyrna in Asia Minor is now Izmir, Turkey.
2. Or *ngelenge*, a musical instrument resembling a xylophone; the guitarlike instrument is known as *obe* and is considered a precursor of the banjo.
3. The bowl is earthen, curiously figured, to which a long reed is fixed as a tube. This tube is sometimes so long as to be born by one, and frequently out of grandeur by two boys. [Equiano's note].
4. A principal item of trade at this time, salt was commonly extracted from wood or leaves.
5. Eddoes, or coco-yams, commonly spelled "eddas" in the eighteenth century. *Plantains*: banana-like fruit, usually eaten cooked before ripe.

eats alone; his wives and slaves have also their separate tables. Before we taste the food we always wash our hands: indeed our cleanliness on all occasions is extreme; but on this it is an indispensable ceremony. After washing, libation is made, by pouring out a small portion of the food, in a certain place, for the spirits of departed relations, which the natives suppose to preside over their conduct, and guard them from evil. They are totally unacquainted with strong or spirituous liquours; and their principal beverage is palm wine. This is gotten from a tree of that name by tapping it at the top, and fastening a large gourd to it; and sometimes one tree will yield three or four gallons in a night. When just drawn it is of a most delicious sweetness; but in a few days it acquires a tartish and more spirituous flavour: though I never saw any one intoxicated by it. The same tree also produces nuts and oil. Our principal luxury is in perfumes; one sort of these is an odoriferous wood of delicious fragrance: the other a kind of earth; a small portion of which thrown into the fire diffuses a most powerful odour.[6] We beat this wood into powder, and mix it with palm oil; with which both men and women perfume themselves.

In our buildings we study convenience rather than ornament. Each master of a family has a large square piece of ground, surrounded with a moat or fence, or enclosed with a wall made of red earth tempered; which, when dry, is as hard as brick. Within this are his houses to accommodate his family and slaves; which, if numerous, frequently present the appearance of a village. In the middle stands the principal building, appropriated to the sole use of the matter, and consisting of two apartments; in one of which he sits in the day with his family, the other is left apart for the reception of his friends. He has besides these a distinct apartment in which he sleeps, together with his male children. On each side are the apartments of his wives, who have also their separate day and night houses. The habitations of the slaves and their families are distributed throughout the rest of the enclosure. These houses never exceed one story in height: they are always built of wood, or stakes driven into the ground, crossed with wattles,[7] and neatly plastered within, and without. The roof is thatched with reeds. Our day-houses are left open at the sides; but those in which we sleep are always covered, and plastered in the inside, with a composition mixed with cow-dung, to keep off the different insects, which annoy us during the night. The walls and floors also of these are generally covered with mats. Our beds consist of a platform, raised three or four feet from the ground, on which are laid skins, and different parts of a spungy tree called plaintain. Our covering is calico or muslin, the same as our dress.

6. When I was in Smyrna I saw the same kind of earth, and brought some of it with me to England; it resembles musk in strength, but is more delicious in scent, and is not unlike the smell of a rose [Equiano's note]. This is probably cam wood, or *uhie*.
7. A woven work made of sticks intertwined with twigs or branches.

The usual seats are a few logs of wood; but we have benches, which are generally perfumed, to accommodate strangers: these compose the greater part of our household furniture. Houses so constructed and furnished require but little skill to erect them. Every man is a sufficient architect for the purpose. The whole neighbourhood afford their unanimous assistance in building them and in return receive, and expect no other recompense than a feast.

As we live in a country where nature is prodigal of her favours, our wants are few and easily supplied; of course we have few manufactures. They consist for the most part of calicoes, earthern ware, ornaments, and instruments of war and husbandry. But these make no part of our commerce, the principal articles of which, as I have observed, are provisions. In such a state money is of little use; however we have some small pieces of coin, if I may call them such. They are made something like an anchor; but I do not remember either their value or denomination. We have also markets, at which I have been frequently with my mother. These are sometimes visited by stout mahogany-coloured men from the south west of us: we call them Oye-Eboe,[8] which term signifies red men living at a distance. They generally rally bring us fire-arms, gunpowder, hats, beads, and dried fish. The last we esteemed a great rarity, as our waters were only brooks and springs. These articles they barter with us for odoriferous woods and earth, and our salt of wood ashes. They always carry slaves through our land; but the strictest account is exacted of their manner of procuring them, before they are suffered to pass. Sometimes indeed we sold slaves to them, but they were only prisoners of war, or such among us as had been convicted of kidnapping, or adultery, and some other crimes, which we esteemed heinous. This practice of kidnapping induces me to think, that, notwithstanding all our strictness, their principal business among us was to trepan[9] our people. I remember too they carried great sacks along with them, which not long after I had an opportunity of fatally seeing applied to that infamous purpose.

Our land is uncommonly rich and fruitful, and produces all kinds of vegetables in great abundance. We have plenty of Indian corn, and vast quantities of cotton and tobacco. Our pine apples grow without culture; they are about the size of the largest sugar-loaf,[1] and finely flavoured. We have also spices of different kinds, particularly pepper; and a variety of delicious fruits which I have never seen in Europe; together with gums of various kinds, and honey in abundance. All our industry is exerted to improve those blessings of nature. Agriculture is our chief employment; and every one, even the children and women, are engaged in it. Thus we are all habituated to labour from our earliest

8. Or *onye Aboh*, people from Aboh; the term may also refer to *Oyibo*, or light-skinned person.
9. To trick, trap, or ensnare.
1. A conical mass of crystallized sugar; or refined sugar molded into a cone.

years. Every one contributes something to the common stock; and as
we are unacquainted with idleness, we have no beggars. The benefits
of such a mode of living are obvious. The West India planters prefer
the slaves of Benin or Eboe to those of any other part of Guinea, for
their hardiness, intelligence, integrity, and zeal. Those benefits are felt
by us in the general healthiness of the people, and in their vigour and
activity; I might have added too in their comeliness. Deformity is
indeed unknown amongst us, I mean that of shape. Numbers of the
natives of Eboe now in London might be brought in support of this
assertion: for, in regard to complexion, ideas of beauty are wholly relative. I remember while in Africa to have seen three negro children,
who were tawny, and another quite white, who were universally
regarded by myself, and the natives in general, as far as related to their
complexions, as deformed. Our women too were in my eyes at least
uncommonly graceful, alert, and modest to a degree of bashfulness;
nor do I remember to have ever heard of an instance of incontinence
amongst them before marriage. They are also remarkably cheerful.
Indeed cheerfulness and affability are two of the leading characteristics
of our nation.

Our tillage is exercised in a large plain or common, some hours walk
from our dwellings, and all the neighbours resort thither in a body.
They use no beasts of husbandry; and their only instruments are hoes,
axes, shovels, and beaks, or pointed iron to dig with. Sometimes we
are visited by locusts, which come in large clouds, so as to darken the
air, and destroy our harvest. This however happens rarely, but when it
does, a famine is produced by it. I remember an instance or two
wherein this happened. This common is often the theatre of war; and
therefore when our people go out to till their land, they not only go in
a body, but generally take their arms with them for fear of a surprise;
and when they apprehend an invasion they guard the avenues to their
dwellings, by driving sticks into the ground, which are so sharp at one
end as to pierce the foot, and are generally dipt in poison. From what
I can recollect of these battles, they appear to have been irruptions of
one little state or district on the other, to obtain prisoners or booty.
Perhaps they were incited to this by those traders who brought the
European goods I mentioned amongst us. Such a mode of obtaining
slaves in Africa is common; and I believe more are procured this way,
and by kidnaping, than any other.[2] When a trader wants slaves, he
applies to a chief for them, and tempts him with his wares. It is not
extraordinary, if on this occasion he yields to the temptation with as
little firmness, and accepts the price of his fellow creatures liberty with
as little reluctance as the enlightened merchant. Accordingly he falls
on his neighbours, and a desperate battle ensues. If he prevails and

2. See Benezet's Account of Africa throughout [Equiano's note]. See excerpt below, pp. 250–
    53.

takes prisoners, he gratifies his avarice by selling them; but, if his party be vanquished, and he falls into the hands of the enemy, he is put to death: for, as he has been known to foment their quarrels, it is thought dangerous to let him survive, and no ransom can save him, though all other prisoners may be redeemed. We have fire-arms, bows and arrows, broad two-edged swords and javelins: we have shields also which cover a man from head to foot. All are taught the use of these weapons; even our women are warriors, and march boldly out to fight along with the men. Our whole district is a kind of militia: on a certain signal given, such as the firing of a gun at night, they all rise in arms and rush upon their enemy. It is perhaps something remarkable, that when our people march to the field a red flag or banner is borne before them. I was once a witness to a battle in our common. We had been all at work in it one day as usual, when our people were suddenly attacked. I climbed a tree at some distance, from which I beheld the fight. There were many women as well as men on both sides; among others my mother was there, and armed with a broad sword. After fighting for a considerable time with great fury, and after many had been killed our people obtained the victory, and took their enemy's Chief prisoner. He was carried off in great triumph, and, though he offered a large ransom for his life, he was put to death. A virgin of note among our enemies had been slain in the battle, and her arm was exposed in our market-place, where our trophies were always exhibited. The spoils were divided according to the merit of the warriors. Those prisoners which were not sold or redeemed we kept as slaves: but how different was their condition from that of the slaves in the West Indies! With us they do more work than other members of the community, even their masters; their food, clothing and lodging were nearly the same as theirs, (except that they were not permitted to eat with those who were free-born); and there was scarce any other difference between them, than a superior degree of importance which the head of a family possesses in our state, and that authority which, as such, he exercises over every part of his household. Some of these slaves have even slaves under them as their own property, and for their own use.

As to religion, the natives believe that there is one Creator of all things, and that he lives in the sun, and is girted round with a belt that he may never eat or drink; but, according to some, he smokes a pipe, which is our own favourite luxury. They believe he governs events, especially our deaths or captivity; but, as for the doctrine of eternity, I do not remember to have ever heard of it: some however believe in the transmigration of souls[3] in a certain degree. Those spirits, which are not transmigrated, such as our dear friends or relations, they believe always attend them, and guard them from the bad spirits or their foes.

---

3. The passing of the soul into a new life-form after death; reincarnation.

For this reason they always before eating, as I have observed, put some small portion of the meat, and pour some of their drink, on the ground for them; and they often make oblations[4] of the blood of beasts or fowls at their graves. I was very fond of my mother, and almost constantly with her. When she went to make these oblations at her mother's tomb, which was a kind of small solitary thatched house, I sometimes attended her. There she made her libations, and spent most of the night in cries and lamentations. I have been often extremely terrified on these occasions. The loneliness of the place, the darkness of the night, and the ceremony of libation, naturally awful and gloomy, were heightened by my mother's lamentations; and these, concuring with the cries of doleful birds, by which these places were frequented, gave an inexpressible terror to the scene.

We compute the year from the day on which the sun crosses the line, and on its setting that evening there is a general shout throughout the land; at least I can speak from my own knowledge throughout our vicinity. The people at the same time make a great noise with rattles, not unlike the basket rattles used by children here, though much larger, and hold up their hands to heaven for a blessing. It is then the greatest offerings are made; and those children whom our wise men foretel will be fortunate are then presented to different people. I remember many used to come to see me, and I was carried about to others for that purpose. They have many offerings, particularly at full moons; generally two at harvest before the fruits are taken out of the ground: and when any young animals are killed, sometimes they offer up part of them as a sacrifice. These offerings, when made by one of the heads of a family, serve for the whole. I remember we often had them at my father's and my uncle's, and their families have been present. Some of our offerings are eaten with bitter herbs. We had a saying among us to any one of a cross temper, "That if they were to be eaten, they should be eaten with bitter herbs."

We practised circumcision like the Jews, and made offerings and feasts on that occasion in the same manner as they did. Like them also, our children were named from some event, some circumstance, or fancied foreboding at the time of their birth. I was named *Olaudah*,[5] which, in our language, signifies vicissitude or fortune also, one favoured, and having a loud voice and well spoken. I remember we never polluted the name of the object of our adoration; on the contrary, it was always mentioned with the greatest reverence; and we were totally unacquainted with swearing, and all those terms of abuse and reproach which find their way so readily and copiously into the languages of more civilized people. The only expressions of that kind I

4. Offerings.
5. *Ola*, or ring, signals good fortune. The second element of the name may be either *ude*, "fame," or *øda*, "resonant, resounding."

remember were "May you rot, or may you swell, or may a beast take you."

I have before remarked that the natives of this part of Africa are extremely cleanly. This necessary habit of decency was with us a part of religion, and therefore we had many purifications and washings; indeed almost as many, and used on the same occasions, if my recollection does not fail me, as the Jews. Those that touched the dead at any time were obliged to wash and purify themselves before they could enter a dwelling-house. Every woman too, at certain times, was forbidden to come into a dwelling-house, or touch any person, or any thing we ate. I was so fond of my mother I could not keep from her, or avoid touching her at some of those periods, in consequence of which I was obliged to be kept out with her, in a little house made for that purpose, till offering was made, and then we were purified.

Though we had no places of public worship, we had priests and magicians, or wise men. I do not remember whether they had different offices, or whether they were united in the same persons, but they were held in great reverence by the people. They calculated our time, and foretold events, as their name imported, for we called them Ah-affoe-way-cah,[6] which signifies calculators or yearly men, our year being called Ah-affoe. They wore their beards, and when they died they were succeeded by their sons. Most of their implements and things of value were interred along with them. Pipes and tobacco were also put into the grave with the corpse, which was always perfumed and ornamented, and animals were offered in sacrifice to them. None accompanied their funerals but those of the same profession or tribe. These buried them after sunset, and always returned from the grave by a different way from that which they went.

These magicians were also our doctors or physicians. They practised bleeding by cupping;[7] and were very successful in healing wounds and expelling poisons. They had likewise some extraordinary method of discovering jealousy, theft, and poisoning; the success of which no doubt they derived from their unbounded influence over the credulity and superstition of the people. I do not remember what those methods were, except that as to poisoning: I recollect an instance or two, which I hope it will not be deemed impertinent here to insert, as it may serve as a kind of specimen of the rest, and is still used by the negroes in the West Indies. A virgin had been poisoned, but it was not known by whom: the doctors ordered the corpse to be taken up by some persons, and carried to the grave. As soon as the bearers had raised it on their shoulders, they seemed seized with some[8] sudden impulse, and ran to

---

6. Or *ofo-nwanchi*, traveling men who calculated time. They were sometimes called *afo-nwa-ika* or "funny monkeys."
7. Drawing blood by means of a vacuum created by a heated glass cup.
8. See also Leut. Matthew's Voyage, p. 123 [Equiano's note]. See excerpt below, from John Matthews, A *Voyage to the River Sierra-Leone*, pp. 253–55.

and fro unable to stop themselves. At last, after having passed through a number of thorns and prickly bushes unhurt, the corpse fell from them close to a house, and defaced it in the fall; and, the owner being taken up, he immediately confessed the poisoning.[9]

The natives are extremely cautious about poison. When they buy any eatable the seller kisses it all round before the buyer, to shew him it is not poisoned; and the same is done when any meat or drink is presented, particularly to a stranger. We have serpents of different kinds, some of which are esteemed ominous when they appear in our houses, and these we never molest. I remember two of those ominous snakes, each of which was as thick as the calf of a man's leg, and in colour resembling a dolphin in the water, crept at different times into my mother's night-house, where I always lay with her, and coiled themselves into folds, and each time they crowed like a cock. I was desired by some of our wise men to touch these, that I might be interested in the good omens, which I did, for they were quite harmless, and would tamely suffer themselves to be handled; and then they were put into a large open earthen pan, and set on one side of the highway. Some of our snakes, however, were poisonous: one of them crossed the road one day when I was standing on it, and passed between my feet without offering to touch me, to the great surprise of many who saw it; and these incidents were accounted by the wise men, and therefore by my mother and the rest of the people, as remarkable omens in my favour.

Such is the imperfect sketch my memory has furnished me with of the manners and customs of a people among whom I first drew my breath. And here I cannot forbear suggesting what has long struck me very forcibly, namely, the strong analogy which even by this sketch, imperfect as it is, appears to prevail in the manners and customs of my countrymen and those of the Jews,[1] before they reached the Land of Promise, and particularly the patriarchs[2] while they were yet in that pastoral state which is described in Genesis—an analogy, which alone

---

9. An instance of this kind happened at Montserrat in the West Indies in the year 1763. I then belonged to the Charming Sally, Capt. Doran.—The chief mate, Mr. Mansfield, and some of the crew being one day on shore, were present at the burying of a poisoned negro girl. Though they had often heard of the circumstance of the running in such cases, and had even seen it, they imagined it to be a trick of the corpse-bearers. The mate therefore desired two of the sailors to take up the coffin, and carry it to the grave. The sailors, who were all of the same opinion, readily obeyed; but they had scarcely raised it to their shoulders, before they began to run furiously about, quite unable to direct themselves, till, at last, without intention, they came to the hut of him who had poisoned the girl. The coffin then immediately fell from their shoulders against the hut, and damaged part of the wall. The owner of the hut was taken into custody on this, and confessed the poisoning.—I give this story as it was related by the mate and crew on their return to the ship. The credit which is due to it I leave with the reader [Equiano's note].
1. The biblical descent of Africans was a common topic at this time, for example in essays by Anthony Benezet (1713–1784), Thomas Clarkson (1760–1846), and Quobna Ottobah Cugoano (1757–?).
2. Founders of the ancient Hebrew families: Abraham, Isaac, Jacob, and Jacob's twelve sons. *The Land of Promise*: the biblical Canaan, promised by God to Abraham and his descendants; see Genesis 15.18 and 17.8.

would induce me to think that the one people had sprung from the other. Indeed this is the opinion of Dr. Gill,[3] who, in his commentary on Genesis, very ably deduces the pedigree of the Africans from Afer and Afra, the descendants of Abraham by Keturah his wife and concubine (for both these titles are applied to her). It is also conformable to the sentiments of Dr. John Clarke, formerly Dean of Sarum,[4] in his Truth of the Christian Religion: both these authors concur in ascribing to us this original. The reasonings of these gentlemen are still further confirmed by the scripture chronology; and if any further corroboration were required, this resemblance in so many respects is a strong evidence in support of the opinion. Like the Israelites in their primitive state, our government was conducted by our chiefs or judges, our wise men and elders; and the head of a family with us enjoyed a similar authority over his household with that which is ascribed to Abraham and the other patriarchs. The law of retaliation obtained almost universally with us as with them: and even their religion appeared to have shed upon us a ray of its glory, though broken and spent in its passage, or eclipsed by the cloud with which time, tradition, and ignorance might have enveloped it; for we had our circumcision (a rule I believe peculiar to that people:) we had also our sacrifices and burnt-offerings, our washings and purifications, on the same occasions as they had.

As to the difference of colour between the Eboan Africans and the modern Jews, I shall not presume to account for it. It is a subject which has engaged the pens of men of both genius and learning, and is far above my strength. The most able and Reverend Mr. T. Clarkson, however, in his much admired Essay on the Slavery and Commerce of the Human Species,[5] has ascertained the cause, in a manner that at once solves every objection on that account, and, on my mind at least, has produced the fullest conviction. I shall therefore refer to that performance for the theory,[6] contenting myself with extracting a fact as related by Dr. Mitchel.[7] "The Spaniards, who have inhabited America, under the torrid zone, for any time, are become as dark coloured as our native Indians of Virginia; of which I myself have been a witness." There is also another instance[8] of a Portuguese settlement at Mitomba, a river in Sierra Leona;[9] where the inhabitants are bred from a mixture of the first Portuguese discoverers with the natives, and are now become in

3. John Gill (1697–1771), English Baptist theologian and author of An Exposition of the Old Testament, 4 vols. (1763–66).
4. Ecclesiastical name for Salisbury, England. John Clarke (1682–1757), English translator of Hugo Grotius, whose The Truth of the Christian Religion (1711) was popular.
5. See excerpt below, pp. 277–81.
6. Page 178 to 216 [Equiano's note]. See excerpt below, from Thomas Clarkson, pp. 277–81.
7. Philos. Trans. No 476, Sect, 4, cited by Mr. Clarkson, p. 205. [Equiano's note]. See excerpt below, from John Mitchell, pp. 256–58.
8. Same page [Equiano's note].
9. A West African port for the Portuguese trade, later a resettlement colony for ex-slaves established by British abolitionists, for whose Committee for the Relief of the Black Poor Equiano later became commissary.

their complexion, and in the woolly quality of their hair, *perfect negroes*, retaining however a smattering of the Portuguese language.

These instances, and a great many more which might be adduced, while they shew how the complexions of the same persons vary in different climates, it is hoped may tend also to remove the prejudice that some conceive against the natives of Africa on account of their colour. Surely the minds of the Spaniards did not change with their complexions! Are there not causes enough to which the apparent inferiority of an African may be ascribed, without limiting the goodness of God, and supposing he forbore to stamp understanding on certainly his own image, because "carved in ebony."[1] Might it not naturally be ascribed to their situation? When they come among Europeans, they are ignorant of their language, religion, manners, and customs. Are any pains taken to teach them these? Are they treated as men? Does not slavery itself depress the mind, and extinguish all its fire and every noble sentiment? But, above all, what advantages do not a refined people possess over those who are rude and uncultivated. Let the polished and haughty European recollect that his ancestors were once, like the Africans, uncivilized, and even barbarous. Did Nature make *them* inferior to their sons? and should *they too* have been made slaves? Every rational mind answers, No. Let such reflections as these melt the pride of their superiority into sympathy for the wants and miseries of their sable[2] brethren, and compel them to acknowledge, that understanding is not confined to feature or colour. If, when they look round the world, they feel exultation, let it be tempered with benevolence to others, and gratitude to God, "who hath made of one blood all nations of men for to dwell on all the face of the earth;[3] and whose wisdom is not our wisdom, neither are our ways his ways."

Chap. II.

The author's birth and parentage—His being kidnapped with his sister—Their separation—Surprise at meeting again—Are finally separated—Account of the different places and incidents the author met with till his arrival on the coast—The effect the sight of a slave ship had on him—He sails for the West Indies— Horrors of a slave ship—Arrives at Barbadoes, where the cargo is sold and dispersed.

I hope the reader will not think I have trespassed on his patience in introducing myself to him with some account of the manners and

1. An allusion to Thomas Fuller (1608–1661), *The Holy State* (1642), in which a captain sees God's image cut in ebony.
2. Black.
3. Acts, c. xvii. v. 26 [Equiano's note]. The last line is adapted from Isaiah 55.8.

customs of my country. They had been implanted in me with great care, and made an impression on my mind, which time could not erase, and which all the adversity and variety of fortune I have since experienced served only to rivet[1] and record; for, whether the love of one's country be real or imaginary, or a lesson of reason, or an instinct of nature, I still look back with pleasure on the first scenes of my life, though that pleasure has been for the most part mingled with sorrow.

I have already acquainted the reader with the time and place of my birth. My father, besides many slaves, had a numerous family, of which seven lived to grow up, including myself and a sister, who was the only daughter. As I was the youngest of the sons, I became, of course, the greatest favourite with my mother, and was always with her; and she used to take particular pains to form my mind. I was trained up from my earliest years in the art of war; my daily exercise was shooting and throwing javelins; and my mother adorned me with emblems, after the manner of our greatest warriors. In this way I grew up till I was turned the age of eleven, when an end was put to my happiness in the following manner:—Generally when the grown people in the neighborhood were gone far in the fields to labour, the children assembled together in some of the neighbours' premises to play; and commonly some of us used to get up a tree to look out for any assailant, or kidnapper, that might come upon us; for they sometimes took those opportunities of our parents' absence to attack and carry off as many as they could seize. One day, as I was watching at the top of a tree in our yard, I saw one of those people come into the yard of our next neighbour but one, to kidnap, there being many stout young people in it. Immediately on this I gave the alarm of the rogue, and he was surrounded by the stoutest of them, who entangled him with cords, so that he could not escape till some of the grown people came and secured him. But alas! ere long it was my fate to be thus attacked, and to be carried off, when none of the grown people were nigh. One day, when all our people were gone out to their works as usual, and only I and my dear sister were left to mind the house, two men and a woman got over our walls, and in a moment seized us both, and, without giving us time to cry out, or make resistance, they stopped our mouths, and ran off with us into the nearest wood. Here they tied our hands, and continued to carry us as far as they could, till night came on, when we reached a small house, where the robbers halted for refreshment, and spent the night. We were then unbound, but were unable to take any food; and, being quite overpowered by fatigue and grief, our only relief was some sleep, which allayed our misfortune for a short time. The next morning we left the house, and continued travelling all the day. For a long time we had kept the woods, but at last we came into a road which I believed

1. To fix or hold (the eyes, attention, etc.) firmly.

I knew. I had now some hopes of being delivered; for we had advanced but a little way before I discovered some people at a distance, on which I began to cry out for their assistance: but my cries had no other effect than to make them tie me faster and stop my mouth, and then they put me into a large sack. They also stopped my sister's mouth, and tied her hands; and in this manner we proceeded till we were out of the sight of these people. When we went to rest the following night they offered us some victuals;[2] but we refused it; and the only comfort we had was in being in one another's arms all that night, and bathing each other with our tears. But alas! we were soon deprived of even the small comfort of weeping together. The next day proved a day of greater sorrow than I had yet experienced; for my sister and I were then separated, while we lay clasped in each other's arms. It was in vain that we besought them not to part us; she was torn from me, and immediately carried away, while I was left in a state of distraction not to be described. I cried and grieved continually; and for several days I did not eat any thing but what they forced into my mouth. At length, after many days travelling, during which I had often changed masters, I got into the hands of a chieftain, in a very pleasant country. This man had two wives and some children, and they all used me extremely well, and did all they could to comfort me; particularly the first wife, who was something like my mother. Although I was a great many days journey from my father's house, yet these people spoke exactly the same language with us. This first master of mine, as I may call him, was a smith, and my principal employment was working his bellows, which were the same kind as I had seen in my vicinity. They were in some respects not unlike the stoves here in gentlemen's kitchens; and were covered over with leather, and in the middle of that leather a stick was fixed, and a person stood up, and worked it, in the same manner as is done to pump water out of a cask with a hand pump. I believe it was gold he worked, for it was of a lovely bright yellow colour, and was worn by the women in their wrists and ancles. I was there I suppose about a month, and they at last used to trust me some little distance from the house. This was liberty I used in embracing every opportunity to inquire the way to my own home: and I also sometimes, for the same purpose, went with the maidens, in the cool of the evenings, to bring pitchers of water from the springs for the use of the house. I had also remarked where the sun rose in the morning, and set in the evening, as I had travelled along; and I had observed that my father's house was towards the rising of the sun. I therefore determined to seize the first opportunity of making my escape, and to shape my course for that quarter; for I was quite oppressed and weighed down by grief after my mother and friends; and my love of liberty, ever great, was strengthened by the mortifying

2. Food.

circumference of not daring to eat with the free-born children, although I was mostly their companion. While I was projecting my escape, one day an unlucky event happened, which quite disconcerted my plan, and put an end to my hopes. I used to be sometimes employed in assisting an elderly woman slave to cook and take care of the poultry; and one morning, while I was feeding some chickens, I happened to toss a small pebble at one of them, which hit it on the middle and directly killed it. The old slave, having soon after missed the chicken, inquired after it; and on my relating the accident (for I told her the truth, because my mother would never suffer me to tell a lie) she flew into a violent passion, threatened that I should suffer for it; and, my master being out, she immediately went and told her mistress what I had done. This alarmed me very much, and I expected an instant flogging, which to me was uncommonly dreadful; for I had seldom been beaten at home. I therefore resolved to fly; and accordingly I ran into a thicket that was hard by, and hid myself in the bushes. Soon afterwards my mistress and the slave returned, and, not seeing me, they searched all the house, but not finding me, and I not making answer when they called to me, they thought I had run away, and the whole neighborhood was raised in the pursuit of me. In that part of the country (as in ours) the houses and villages were skirted with woods, or shrubberies, and the bushes were so thick that a man could readily conceal himself in them, so as to elude the strictest search. The neighbors continued the whole day looking for me, and several times many of them came within a few yards of the place where I lay hid. I then gave myself up for lost entirely, and expected every moment, when I heard a rustling among the trees, to be found out, and punished by my master: but they never discovered me, though they were often so near that I even heard their conjectures as they were looking about for me; and I now learned from them, that any attempt to return home would be hopeless. Most of them supposed I had fled towards home; but the distance was so great, and the way so intricate, that they thought I could never reach it, and that I should be in lost in the woods. When I heard this I was seized with a violent panic, and abandoned myself to despair. Night too began to approach, and aggravated all my fears. I had before entertained hopes of getting home, and I had determined when it should be dark to make the attempt; but I was now convinced it was fruitless, and I began to consider that, if possibly I could escape all other animals, I could not those of the human kind; and that, not knowing the way, I must perish in the woods. Thus was I like the hunted deer:

> ——"Ev'ry leaf and ev'ry whisp'ring breath
> Convey'd a foe, and ev'ry foe a death.[3]

---

3. Adapted from John Denham (1615–1669), *Cooper's Hill* (1642), lines 287–88. Vassa usually quotes from memory, and many of his quotations follow the originals only loosely.

I heard frequent rustling among the leaves; and being pretty sure they were snakes I expected every instant to be stung by them. This increased my anguish, and the horror of my situa- [situation] became now quite insupportable. I at length quitted the thicket, very faint and hungry, for I had not eaten or drank any thing all the day; and crept to my master's kitchen, from whence I set out at first, and which was an open shed, and laid myself down in the ashes with an anxious wish for death to relieve me from all my pains. I was scarcely awake in the morning when the old woman slave, who was the first up, came to light the fire, and saw me in the fire place. She was very much surprised to see me, and could scarcely believe her own eyes. She now promised to intercede for me, and went for her master, who soon after came, and, having slightly reprimanded me, ordered me to be taken care of, and not to be ill-treated.

Soon after this my master's only daughter, and child by his first wife, sickened and died, which affected him so much that for some time he was almost frantic, and really would have killed himself, had he not been watched and prevented. However, in a small time afterwards he recovered, and I was again sold. I was now carried to the left of the sun's rising, through many different countries, and a number of large woods. The people I was sold to used to carry me very often, when I was tired, either on their shoulders or on their backs. I saw many convenient well-built sheds along the roads, at proper distances, to accommodate the merchants and travellers, who lay in those buildings along with their wives, who often accompany them; and they always go well armed.

From the time I left my own nation I always found somebody that understood me till I came to the sea coast. The languages of different nations did not totally differ, nor were they so copious as those of the Europeans, particularly the English. They were therefore easily learned; and, while I was journeying thus through Africa, I acquired two or three different tongues. In this manner I had been travelling for a considerable time, when one evening, to my great surprise, whom should I see brought to the house where I was but my dear sister! As soon as she saw me she gave a loud shriek, and ran into my arms—I was quite overpowered: neither of us could speak; but, for a considerable time, clung to each other in mutual embraces unable to do any thing but weep. Our meeting affected all who saw us; and indeed I must acknowledge, in honour of those sable destroyers of human rights, that I never met with any ill treatment, or saw any offered to their slaves, except tying them, when necessary, to keep them from running away. When these people knew we were brother and sister they indulged us together; and the man, to whom I supposed we belonged, lay with us, he in the middle, while she and I held one another by the hands across his breast all night; and thus for a while we forgot our misfortunes in the joy of being together: but even this small comfort was soon to have an end; for scarcely had the fatal morning appeared, when she was again torn from me for ever! I was now more miserable, if possible, than before. The small relief which her presence gave me from pain was gone, and the wretchedness of the situation was redoubled by my anxiety after her fate, and my apprehensions lest her sufferings should be greater than mine, when I could not be with her to alleviate them. Yes, thou dear partner of all my childish sports! thou sharer of my joys and sorrows! happy should I have ever esteemed myself to encounter every misery for you, and to procure your freedom by the sacrifice of my own. Though you were early forced from my arms, your image has been always rivetted in my heart, from which neither *time nor fortune* have been able to remove it; so that, while the thoughts of your sufferings have damped my prosperity, they have mingled with adversity and increased its bitterness. To that Heaven which protects the weak from the strong, I commit the care of your innocence and virtues, if they have not already received their full reward, and if your youth and delicacy have not long since fallen victims to the violence of the African trader, the pestilential stench of a Guinea ship, the seasoning[4] in the European colonies, or the lash and lust of a brutal and unrelenting overseer.

I did not long remain after my sister. I was again sold, and carried through a number of places, till, after travelling a considerable time, I came to a town called Tinmah, in the most beautiful country I had yet seen in Africa. It was extremely rich, and there were many rivulets which flowed through it, and supplied a large pond in the centre of the town, where the people washed. Here I first saw and tasted cocoa-nuts, which I thought superior to any nuts I had ever tasted before; and the trees, which were loaded, were also interspersed amongst the houses, which had commodious shades adjoining, and were in the same manner as ours, the insides being neatly plastered and whitewashed. Here I also saw and tasted for the first time sugar-cane. Their money consisted of little white shells, the size of the finger nail. I was sold here for one hundred and seventy-two of them by a merchant who lived and brought me there. I had been about two or three days at his house, when a wealthy widow, a neighbour of his, came there one evening, and brought with her an only son, a young gentleman about my own age and size. Here they saw me; and, having taken a fancy to me, I was bought of the merchant, and went home with them. Her house and premises were situated close to one of those rivulets I have mentioned, and were the finest I ever saw in Africa: they were very extensive, and she had a number of slaves to attend her. The next day

---

4. Rigorous preparation for use; for African slaves, the preparation for rigors of work on plantations. Equiano here reviews the stages of the African slave trade: capture, Middle Passage, "seasoning," and ultimate enslavement.

I was washed and perfumed, and when meal-time came I was led into the presence of my mistress, and ate and drank before her with her son. This filled me with astonishment; and I could scarce help expressing my surprise that the young gentleman should suffer[5] me, who was bound, to eat with him who was free; and not only so, but that he would not at any time either eat or drink till I had taken first, because I was the eldest, which was agreeable to our custom. Indeed every thing here, and all their treatment of me, made me forget that I was a slave. The language of these people resembled ours so nearly, that we understood each other perfectly. They had also the very same customs as we. There were likewise slaves daily to attend us, while my young master and I with other boys sported with our darts and bows and arrows, as I had been used to do at home. In this resemblance to my former happy state I passed about two months; and I now began to think I was to be adopted into the family, and was beginning to be re-reconciled [reconciled] to my situation, and to forget by degrees my misfortunes, when all at once the delusion vanished; for, without the least previous knowledge, one morning early, while my dear master and companion was still asleep, I was wakened out of my reverie to fresh sorrow, and hurried away even amongst the uncircumcised.

Thus, at the very moment I dreamed of the greatest happiness, I found myself most miserable; and it seemed as if fortune wished to give me this taste of joy, only to render the reverse more poignant. The change I now experienced was as painful as it was a sudden and unexpected. It was a change indeed from a state of bliss to a scene which is inexpressible by me, as it discovered[6] to me an element I had never before beheld, and till then had no idea of, and wherein such instances of hardship and cruelty continually occurred as I can never reflect on but with horror.

All the nations and people I had hitherto passed through resembled our own in their manners, customs, and language: but I came at length to a country, the inhabitants of which differed from us in all those particulars. I was very much struck with this difference, especially when I came among a people who did not circumcise, and ate without washing their hands. They cooked also in iron pots, and had European cutlasses[7] and cross bows, which were unknown to us, and fought with their fists amongst themselves. Their women were not so modest as ours, for they ate, and drank, and slept, with their men. But, above all, I was amazed to see no sacrifices or offerings among them. In some of those places the people ornamented themselves with scars, and likewise filed their teeth very sharp. They wanted sometimes to ornament me in the same manner, but I would not suffer them; hoping that I might

5. Allow.
6. Revealed.
7. Short, broad, curved sword with a single cutting edge.

some time be among a people who did not thus disfigure themselves, as I thought they did. At last I came to the banks of a large river, which was covered with canoes, in which the people appeared to live with their household utensils and provisions of all kinds. I was beyond measure astonished at this, as I had never before seen any water larger than a pond or a rivulet: and my surprise was mingled with no small fear when I was put into one of these canoes, and we began to paddle and move along the river. We continued going on thus till night; and when we came to land, and made fires on the banks, each family by themselves, some dragged their canoes on shore, others stayed and cooked in theirs, and laid in them all night. Those on the land had mats, of which they made tents, some in the shape of little houses: in these we slept; and after the morning meal we embarked again and proceeded as before. I was often very much astonished to see some of the women, as well as the men, jump into the water, dive to the bottom, come up again, and swim about. Thus I continued to travel, sometimes by land, sometimes by water, through different countries and various nations, till, at the end of six or seven months after I had been kidnapped, I arrived at the sea coast. It would be tedious and uninteresting to relate all the incidents which befell me during this journey, and which I have not yet forgotten; of the various hands I passed through, and the manners and customs of all the different people among whom I lived: I shall therefore only observe, that in all the places where I was the soil was exceedingly rich; the pomkins,[8] eadas, plantains, yams, &c. &c. were in great abundance, and of incredible size. There were also vast quantities of different gums, though not used for any purpose; and every where a great deal of tobacco. The cotton even grew quite wild; and there was plenty of red-wood. I saw no mechanics[9] whatever in all the way, except such as I have mentioned. The chief employment in all these countries was agriculture, and both the males and females, as with us, were brought up to it, and trained in the arts of war.

The first object which saluted my eyes when I arrived on the coast was the sea, and a slave ship, which was then riding at anchor, and waiting for its cargo. These filled me with astonishment, which was soon converted into terror when I was carried on board. I was immediately handled and tossed up to see if I were sound by some of the crew; and I was now persuaded that I had gotten into a world of bad spirits, and that they were going to kill me. Their complexions too differing so much from ours, their long hair, and the language they spoke, (which was very different from any I had ever heard) united to confirm me in this belief. Indeed such were the horrors of my views and fears at the moment, that, if ten thousand worlds had been my own, I would have freely parted with them all to have exchanged my condition with that

8. Pumpkins
9. Artisans, craftsmen.

of the meanest slave in my own country. When I looked round the ship too and saw a large furnace or copper boiling, and a multitude of black people of every description chained together, every one of their countenances expressing dejection and sorrow, I no longer doubted of my fate; and, quite overpowered with horror and anguish, I fell motionless on the deck and fainted. When I recovered a little I found some black people about me, who I believed were some of those who brought me on board, and had been receiving their pay; they talked to me in order to cheer me, but all in vain. I asked them if we were not to be eaten by those white men with horrible looks, red faces, and loose hair. They told me I was not; and one of the crew brought me a small portion of spirituous liquor in a wine glass; but, being afraid of him, I would not take it out of his hand. One of the blacks therefore took it from him and gave it to me, and I took a little down my palate, which, instead of reviving me, as they thought it would, threw me into the greatest consternation at the strange feeling it produced, having never tasted any such liquor before. Soon after this the blacks who brought me on board went off, and left me abandoned to despair. I now saw myself deprived of all chance of returning to my native country, or even the least glimpse of hope of gaining the shore, which I now considered as friendly; and I even wished for my former slavery in preference to my present situation, which was filled with horrors of every kind, still heightened by my ignorance of what I was to undergo. I was not long suffered to indulge my grief; I was soon put down under the decks, and there I received such a salutation in my nostrils as I had never experienced in my life: so that, with the loathsomeness of the stench, and crying together, I became so sick and low that I was not able to eat, nor had I the least desire to taste any thing. I now wished for the last friend, death, to relieve me; but soon, to my grief, two of the white men offered me eatables; and, on my refusing to eat, one of them held me fast by the hands, and laid me across I think the windlass,[1] and tied my feet, while the other flogged me severely. I had never experienced any thing of this kind before; and although, not being used to the water, I naturally feared that element the first time I saw it, yet nevertheless, could I have got over the nettings, I would have jumped over the side, but I could not; and, besides, the crew used to watch us very closely who were not chained down to the decks, lest we should leap into the water: and I have seen some of these poor African prisoners most severely cut for attempting to do so, and hourly whipped for not eating. This indeed was often the case with myself. In a little time after, amongst the poor chained men, I found some of my own nation, which in a small degree gave ease to my mind. I inquired of these what was to be done with us; they gave me to understand we were to be carried to

---

1. An apparatus for winding rope.

these white people's country to work for them. I then was a little revived, and thought, if it were no worse than working, my situation was not so desperate: but still I feared I should be put to death, the white people looked and acted, as I thought, in so savage a manner; for I had never seen among any people such instances of brutal cruelty; and this not only shewn towards us blacks, but also to some of the whites themselves. One white man in particular I saw, when we were permitted to be on deck, flogged so unmercifully with a large rope near the foremast, that he died in consequence of it; and they tossed him over the side as they would have done a brute. This made me fear these people the more; and I expected nothing less than to be treated in the same manner. I could not help expressing my fears and apprehensions to some of my countrymen: I asked them if these people had no country, but lived in this hollow place (the ship): they told me they did not, but came from a distant one. "Then," said I, "how comes it in all our country we never heard of them?" They told me because they lived so very far off. I then asked where were their women? had they any like themselves? I was told they had: "and why," said I, "do we not see them?" they answered, because they were left behind. I asked how the vessel could go? they told me they could not tell; but that there were cloths put upon the masts by the help of the ropes I saw, and then the vessel went on; and the white men had some spell or magic they put in the water when they liked in order to stop the vessel. I was exceedingly amazed at this account, and really thought they were spirits. I therefore wished much to be from amongst them, for I expected they would sacrifice me: but my wishes were vain; for we were so quartered that it was impossible for any of us to make our escape. While we stayed on the coast I was mostly on deck; and one day, to my great astonishment, I saw one of these vessels coming in with the sails up. As soon as the whites saw it, they gave a great shout, at which we were amazed; and the more so as the vessel appeared larger by approaching nearer. At last she came to an anchor in my sight, and when the anchor was let go I and my countrymen who saw it were lost in astonishment to observe the vessel stop; and were now convinced it was done by magic. Soon after this the other ship got her boats out, and they came on board of us, and the people of both ships seemed very glad to see each other. Several of the strangers also shook hands with us black people, and made motions with their hands, signifying I suppose we were to go to their country; but we did not understand them. At last, when the ship we were in had got in all her cargo, they made ready with many fearful noises, and we were all put under deck, so that we could not see how they managed the vessel. But this disappointment was the least of my sorrow. The stench of the hold while we were on the coast was so intolerably loathsome, that it was dangerous to remain there for any time, and some of us had been permitted to stay on the deck for the fresh air; but now that the whole ship's cargo were confined together, it became absolutely pestilential. The closeness of the place, and the heat of the climate, added to the number in the ship, which was so crowded that each had scarcely room to turn himself, almost suffocated us. This produced copious perspirations, so that the air soon became unfit for respiration, from a variety of loathsome smells, and brought on a sickness among the slaves, of which many died, thus falling victims to the improvident avarice, as I may call it, of their purchasers. This wretched situation was again aggravated by the galling of the chains, now become insupportable; and the filth of the necessary tubs,[2] into which the children often fell, and were almost suffocated. The shrieks of the women, and the groans of the dying, rendered the whole a scene of horror almost inconceivable. Happily perhaps for myself I was soon reduced so low here that it was thought necessary to keep me almost always on deck; and from my extreme youth I was not put in fetters. In this situation I expected every hour to share the fate of my companions, some of whom were almost daily brought upon deck at the point of death, which I began to hope would soon put an end to my miseries. Often did I think many of the inhabitants of the deep much more happy than myself. I envied them the freedom they enjoyed, and as often wished I could change my condition for theirs. Every circumstance I met with served only to render my state more painful, and heighten my apprehensions, and my opinion of the cruelty of the whites. One day they had taken a number of fishes; and when they had killed and satisfied themselves with as many as they thought fit, to our astonishment who were on the deck, rather than give any of them to us to eat as we expected, they tossed the remaining fish into the sea again, although we begged and prayed for some as well as we could, but in vain; and some of my countrymen, being pressed by hunger, took an opportunity, when they thought no one saw them, of trying to get a little privately; but they were discovered, and the attempt procured them some very severe floggings. One day, when we had a smooth sea and moderate wind, two of my wearied countrymen who were chained together (I was near them at the time), preferring death to such a life of misery, somehow made through the nettings and jumped into the sea: immediately another quite dejected fellow, who, on one account of his illness, was suffered to be out of irons, also followed their example; and I believe many more would very soon have done the same if they had not been prevented by the ship's crew, who were instantly alarmed. Those of us that were the most active were in a moment put down under the deck, and here was such a noise and confusion amongst the people of the ship as I never heard before, to stop her, and get the boat out to go after the slaves. However two of the wretches were drowned, but they got

2. Latrines.

the other, and afterwards flogged him unmercifully for thus attempting to prefer death to slavery. In this manner we continued to undergo more hardships than I can now relate, hardships which are inseparable from this accursed trade. Many a time we were near suffocation from the want of fresh air, which we were often without for whole days together. This, and the stench of the necessary tubs, carried off many. During our passage I first saw flying fishes, which surprised me very much: they used frequently to fly across the ship, and many of them fell on the deck. I also now first saw the use of the quadrant;[3] I had often with astonishment seen the mariners make observations with it, and I could not think what it meant. They at last took notice of my surprise; and one of them, willing to increase it, as well as to gratify my curiosity, made me one day look through it. The clouds appeared to me to be land, which disappeared as they passed along. This heightened my wonder; and I was now more persuaded than ever that I was in another world, and that every thing about me was magic. At last we came in sight of the island of Barbadoes,[4] at which the whites on board gave a great shout, and made many signs of joy to us. We did not know what to think of this; but as the vessel drew nearer we plainly saw the harbour, and other ships of different kinds and sizes; and we soon anchored amongst them off Bridge Town.[5] Many merchants and planters now came on board, though it was in the evening. They put us in separate parcels, and examined us attentively. They also made us jump, and pointed to the land, signifying we were to go there. We thought by this we should be eaten by these ugly men, as they appeared to us; and, when soon after we were all put down under the deck again, there was much dread and trembling among us, and nothing but bitter cries to be heard all the night from these apprehensions, insomuch that at last the white people got some old slaves from the land to pacify us. They told us we were not to be eaten, but to work, and were soon to go on land, where we should see many of our country people. This report eased us much; and sure enough, soon after we were landed, there came to us Africans of all languages. We were conducted immediately to the merchant's yard, where we were all pent up together like so many sheep in a fold, without regard to sex or age. As every object was new to me every thing I saw filled me with surprise. What struck me first was that the houses were built with stories, and in every other respect different from those in Africa: but I was still more astonished on seeing people on horseback. I did not know what this could mean; and indeed I thought these people were full of nothing but magical arts. While I was in this astonishment one of my fellow prisoners spoke to a country-man of his about the horses, who said they were the same kind they

3. Instrument used to determine geographical latitude.
4. Or Barbados, the most easterly of the Caribbean islands.
5. Capital of Barbados.

had in their country. I understood them, though they were from a distant part of Africa, and I thought it odd I had not seen any horses there; but afterwards, when I came to converse with different Africans, I found they had many horses amongst them, and much larger than those I then saw. We were not many days in the merchant's custody before we were sold after their usual manner, which is this:—On a signal given, (as the beat of a drum) the buyers rush at once into the yard where the slaves are confined, and make choice of that parcel they like best. The noise and clamour with which this is attended, and the eagerness visible in the countenances of the buyers, serve not a little to increase the apprehensions of the terrified Africans, who may well be supposed to consider them as the ministers of that destruction to which they think themselves devoted. In this manner, without scruple, are relations and friends separated, most of them never to see each other again. I remember in the vessel in which I was brought over, in the men's apartment, there were several brothers, who, in the sale, were sold in different lots; and it was very moving on this occasion to see and hear their cries at parting. O, ye nominal Christians! might not an African ask you, learned you this from your God, who says unto you, Do unto all men as you would men should do unto you?[6] Is it not enough that we are torn from our country and friends to toil for your luxury and lust of gain? Must every tender feeling be likewise sacrificed to your avarice? Are the dearest friends and relations, now rendered more dear by their separation from their kindred, still to be parted from each other, and thus prevented from cheering the gloom of slavery with the small comfort of being together and mingling their sufferings and sorrows? Why are parents to lose their children, brothers their sisters, or husbands their wives? Surely this is a new refinement in cruelty, which, while it has no advantage to atone for it, thus aggravates distress, and adds fresh horrors even to the wretchedness of slavery.

Chap. III. ~~skim the Boscawen part~~

The author is carried to Virginia—His distress—Surprise at seeing a picture and a watch—Is brought by Captain Pascal, and sets out for England—His terror during the voyage—Arrives in England—His wonder at a fall of snow—Is sent to Guernsey, and in some time goes on board a ship of war with his master—Some account of the expedition against Louisbourg under the command of Admiral Boscawen, in 1758.

I now totally lost the small remains of comfort I had enjoyed in conversing with my countrymen; the women too, who used to wash

6. Adapted from the "golden rule" of Matthew 7.12: "Therefore all things whatsoever ye would that men should do to you, do ye even so to them." *Nominal*: in name only.

and take care of me, were all gone different ways, and I never saw one of them afterwards.

I stayed in this island for a few days; I believe it could not be above a fortnight;[1] when I and some few more slaves, that were not saleable amongst the rest, from very much fretting, were shipped off in a sloop for North America. On the passage we were better treated than when we were coming from Africa, and we had plenty of rice and fat pork. We were landed up a river a good way from the sea, about Virginia county, where we saw few or none of our native Africans, and not one soul who could talk to me. I was a few weeks weeding grass, and gathering stones in a plantation; and at last all my companions were distributed different ways, and only myself was left. I was now exceedingly miserable, and thought myself worse off than any of the rest of my companions; for they could talk to each other, but I had no person to speak to that I could understand. In this state I was constantly grieving and pining, and wishing for death rather than any thing else. While I was in this plantation the gentleman, to whom I suppose the estate belonged, being unwell, I was one day sent for to his dwelling house to fan him; when I came into the room where he was I was very much affrighted at some things I saw, and the more so as I had seen a black woman slave as I came through the house, who was cooking the dinner, and the poor creature was cruelly loaded with various kinds of iron machines; she had one particularly on her head, which locked her mouth so fast that she could scarcely speak; and could not eat nor drink. I was much astonished and shocked at this contrivance, which I afterwards learned was called the iron muzzle. Soon after I had a fan put into my hand, to fan the gentleman while he slept; and so I did indeed with great fear. While he was fast asleep I indulged myself a great deal in looking about the room, which to me appeared very fine and curious. The first object that engaged my attention was a watch which hung on the chimney, and was going. I was quite surprised at the noise it made, and was afraid it would tell the gentleman any thing I might do amiss: and when I immediately after observed a picture hanging in the room, which appeared constantly to look at me, I was still more affrighted, having never seen such things as these before. At one time I thought it was something relative to magic; and not seeing it move I thought it might be some way the whites had to keep their great men when they died, and offer them libation as we used to do to our friendly spirits. In this state of anxiety I remained till my master awoke, when I was dismissed out of the room, to my no small satisfaction and relief; for I thought that these people were all made up of wonders. In this place I was called Jacob; but on board the African

1. Two weeks.

snow[2] I was called Michael. I had been some time in this miserable, forlorn, and much dejected state, without having any one to talk to, which made my life a burden, when the kind and unknown hand of the Creator (who in very deed leads the blind in a way they know not) now began to appear, to my comfort; for one day the captain of a merchant ship, called the Industrious Bee, came on some business to my master's house. This gentleman, whose name was Michael Henry Pascal, was a lieutenant in the royal navy, but now commanded this trading ship, which was somewhere in the confines of the country many miles off. While he was at my master's house it happened that he saw me, and liked me so well that he made a purchase of me. I think I have often heard him say he gave thirty or forty pounds sterling for me; but I do not now remember which. However, he meant me for a present to some of his friends in England: and I was sent accordingly from the house of my then master, one Mr. Campbell, to the place where the ship lay; I was conducted on horseback by an elderly black man, (a mode of travelling which appeared very odd to me). When I arrived I was carried on board a fine large ship, loaded with tobacco, &c. and just ready to sail for England. I now thought my condition much mended; I had sails to lie on, and plenty of good victuals to eat; and every body on board used me very kindly, quite contrary to what I had seen of any white people before; I therefore began to think that they were not all of the same disposition. A few days after I was on board we sailed for England. I was still at a loss to conjecture my destiny. By this time, however, I could smatter a little imperfect English; and I wanted to know as well as I could where we were going. Some of the people of the ship used to tell me they were going to carry me back to my own country, and this made me very happy. I was quite rejoiced at the sound of going back; and thought if I should get home what wonders I should have to tell. But I was reserved for another fate, and was soon undeceived when we came within sight of the English coast. While I was on board this ship, my captain and master named me *Gustavus Vasa*.[3] I at that time began to understand him a little, and refused to be called so, and told him as well as I could that I would be called Jacob; but he said I should not, and still called me Gustavus; and when I refused to answer to my new name, which at first I did, it gained me many a cuff; so at length I submitted, and was obliged to bear the present name, by which I have been known ever since. The ship had a very long passage; and on that account we had very short

2. A ship equipped with two masts. Equiano uses a great variety of names for vessels, among them wherry, punt, drogger, hoy, sloop, frigate, snow, privateer, schooner, man of war, and fire ship.
3. Swedish nobleman (1496–1560) who fought for independence from Denmark and ruled Sweden (1523–60) as Gustavus I; he was the subject of a popular historical play by Henry Brooke, *Gustavus Vasa, the Deliverer of His Country* (1738).

allowance of provisions. Towards the last we had only one pound and a half of bread per week, and about the same quantity of meat, and one quart of water a-day. We spoke with only one vessel the whole time we were at sea, and but once we caught a few fishes. In our extremities the captain and people told me in jest they would kill and eat me; but I thought them in earnest, and was depressed beyond measure, expecting every moment to be my last. While I was in this situation one evening they caught, with a good deal of trouble, a large shark, and got it on board. This gladdened my poor heart exceedingly, as I thought it would serve the people to eat instead of their eating me; but very soon, to my astonishment, they cut off a small part of the tail, and tossed the rest over the side. This renewed my consternation; and I did not know what to think of these white people, though I very much feared they would kill and eat me. There was on board the ship a young lad who had never been at sea before, about four or five years older than myself: his name was Richard Baker. He was a native of America, had received an excellent education, and was of a most amiable temper. Soon after I went on board he shewed me a great deal of partiality and attention, and in return I grew extremely fond of him. We at length became inseparable; and, for the space of two years, he was of very great use to me, and was my constant companion and instructor. Although this dear youth had many slaves of his own, yet he and I have gone through many sufferings together on shipboard; and we have many nights lain in each other's bosoms when we were in great distress. Thus such a friendship was cemented between us as we cherished till his death, which, to my very great sorrow, happened in the year 1759, when he was up the Archipelago,[4] on board his majesty's ship the Preston: an event which I have never ceased to regret, as I lost at once a kind interpreter, an agreeable companion, and a faithful friend; who, at the age of fifteen, discovered a mind superior to prejudice; and who was not ashamed to notice, to associate with, and to be the friend and instructor of one who was ignorant, a stranger, of a different complexion, and a slave! My master had lodged in his mother's house in America: he respected him very much, and made him always eat with him in the cabin. He used often to tell him jocularly that he would kill me to eat. Sometimes he would say to me—the black people were not good to eat, and would ask me if we did not eat people in my country. I said, No: then he said he would kill Dick (as he always called him) first, and afterwards me. Though this hearing relieved my mind a little as to myself, I was alarmed for Dick and whenever he was called I used to be very much afraid he was to be killed; and I would peep and watch to see if they were going to kill him: nor was I free from this consternation till we

4. A group of islands; here, the Greek islands.

made the land. One night we lost a man overboard; and the cries and noise were so great and confused, in stopping the ship, that I, who did not know what was the matter, began, as usual, to be very much afraid, and to think they were going to make an offering with me, and perform some magic; which I still believed they dealt in. As the waves were very high I thought the Ruler of the seas was angry, and I expected to be offered up to appease him. This filled my mind with agony, and I could not any more that night close my eyes again to rest. However, when daylight appeared I was a little eased in my mind; but still every time I was called I used to think it was to be killed. Some time after this we saw some very large fish, which I afterwards found were called grampusses.[5] They looked to me extremely terrible, and made their appearance just at dusk; and were so near as to blow the water on the ship's deck. I believed them to be the rulers of the sea; and, as the white people did not make any offerings at any time, I thought they were angry with them: and, at last, what confirmed my belief was, the wind just then died away, and a calm ensued, and in consequence of it the ship stopped going. I supposed that the fish had performed this, and I hid myself in the fore part of the ship, through fear of being offered up to appease them, every minute peeping and quaking: but my good friend Dick came shortly towards me, and I took an opportunity to ask him, as well as I could, what these fish were. Not being able to talk much English, I could but just make him understand my question; and not at all, when I asked him if any offerings were to be made to them: however, he told me these fish would swallow any body; which sufficiently alarmed me. Here he was called away by the captain, who was leaning over the quarter-deck railing and looking at the fish; and most of the people were busied in getting a barrel of pitch[6] to light, for them to play with. The captain now called me to him, having learned some of my apprehensions from Dick; and having diverted himself and others for some time with my fears, which appeared ludicrous enough in my crying and trembling, he dismissed me. The barrel of pitch was now lighted and put over the side into the water: by this time it was just dark, and the fish went after it; and, to my great joy, I saw them no more.

However, all my alarms began to subside when we got sight of land; and at last the ship arrived at Falmouth,[7] after a passage of thirteen weeks. Every heart on board seemed gladdened on our reaching the shore, and none more than mine. The captain immediately went on shore, and sent on board some fresh provisions, which we wanted very much: we made good use of them, and our famine was soon turned into feasting, almost without ending. It was about the beginning of

5. Small, black, toothed whales ("killer whales"), related to dolphins.
6. Black sticky substance used hot for waterproofing.
7. Port city in Cornwall, England.

the spring 1757 when I arrived in England, and I was near twelve years of age at that time. I was very much struck with the buildings and the pavement of the streets in Falmouth; and, indeed, any object I saw filled me with new surprise. One morning, when I got upon deck, I saw it covered all over with the snow that fell over-night: as I had never seen any thing of the kind before, I thought it was salt; so I immediately ran down to the mate and desired him, as well as I could, to come and see how somebody in the night had thrown salt all over the deck. He, knowing what it was, desired me to bring some of it down to him: accordingly I took up a handful of it, which I found very cold indeed; and when I brought it to him he desired me to taste it. I did so, and I was surprised beyond measure. I then asked him what it was; he told me it was snow: but I could not in anywise understand him. He asked me if we had no such thing in my country; and I told him, No. I then asked him the use of it, and who made it; he told me a great man in the heavens, called God: but here again I was to all intents and purposes at a loss to understand him; and the more so, when a little after I saw the air filled with it, in a heavy shower, which fell down on the same day. After this I went to church; and having never been at such a place before, I was again amazed at seeing and hearing the service. I asked all I could about it; and they gave me to understand it was worshipping God, who made us and all things. I was still at a great loss, and soon got into an endless field of inquiries, as well as I was able to speak and ask about things. However, my little friend Dick used to be my best interpreter; for I could make free with him, and he always instructed me with pleasure: and from what I could understand by him of this God, and in seeing these white people did not sell one another, as we did, I was much pleased; and in this I thought they were much happier than we Africans. I was astonished at the wisdom of the white people in all things I saw; but was amazed at their not sacrificing, or making any offerings, and eating with unwashed hands, and touching the dead. I likewise could not help remarking the particular slenderness of their women, which I did not at first like; and I thought they were not so modest and shamefaced as the African women.

I had often seen my master and Dick employed in reading; and I had a great curiosity to talk to the books, as I thought they did; and so to learn how all things had a beginning: for that purpose I have often taken up a book, and have talked to it, and then put my ears to it, when alone, in hopes it would answer me; and I have been very much concerned when I found it remained silent.

My master lodged at the house of a gentleman in Falmouth, who had a fine little daughter about six or seven years of age, and she grew prodigiously fond of me; insomuch that we used to eat together, and had servants to wait on us. I was so much caressed by this family that it often reminded me of the treatment I had received from my little

noble African master. After I had been here a few days, I was sent on
board of the ship; but the child cried so much after me that nothing
could pacify her till I was sent for again.

It is ludicrous enough, that I began to fear I should be betrothed to
this young lady; and when my master asked me if I would stay there
with her behind him, as he was going away with the ship, which had
taken in the tobacco again, I cried immediately, and said I would not
leave her. At last, by stealth, one night I was sent on board the ship
again; and in a little time we sailed for Guernsey,[8] where she was in
part owned by a merchant, one Nicholas Doberry. As I was now
amongst a people who had not their faces scarred, like some of the
African nations where I had been, I was very glad I did not let them
ornament me in that manner when I was with them. When we arrived
at Guernsey, my master placed me to board and lodge with one of his
mates, who had a wife and family there; and some months afterwards
he went to England, and left me in care of this mate, together with
my friend Dick: This mate had a little daughter, aged about five or six
years, with whom I used to be much delighted. I had often observed
that when her mother washed her face it looked very rosy; but when
she washed mine it did not look so: I therefore tried oftentimes myself
if I could not by washing make my face of the same colour as my little
play-mate (Mary), but it was all in vain; and I now began to be mortified at the difference in our complexions. This woman behaved to
me with great kindness and attention; and taught me every thing in
the same manner as she did her own child, and indeed in every respect
treated me as such. I remained here till the summer of the year 1757;
when my master, being appointed first lieutenant of his majesty's ship
the Roebuck, sent for Dick and me, and his old mate: on this we all
left Guernsey, and set out for England in a sloop bound for London.
As we were coming up towards the Nore, where the Roebuck lay, a
man of war's boat came alongside to press[9] our people; on which each
man ran to hide himself. I was very much frightened at this, though I
did not know what it meant, or what to think or do. However I went
and hid myself also under a hencoop.[1] Immediately afterwards the
press-gang came on board with their swords drawn, and searched all
about, pulled the people out by force, and put them into the boat. At
last I was found out also: the man that found me held me up by the
heels while they all made their sport of me, I roaring and crying out
all the time most lustily: but at last the mate, who was my conductor,
seeing this, came to my assistance, and did all he could to pacify me;
but all to very little purpose, till I had seen the boat go off. Soon

8. Island in the English Channel.
9. To force into service. *Nore*: area near the mouth of the Thames where naval military fleets
   assembled. *Man of war's boat*: warship equipped with artillery. See n. 2, p. 45.
1. A coop or pen for poultry.

afterwards we came to the Nore, where the Roebuck lay; and, to our great joy, my master came on board to us, and brought us to the ship. When I went on board this large ship, I was amazed indeed to see the quantity of men and the guns. However my surprise began to diminish as my knowledge increased; and I ceased to feel those apprehensions and alarms which had taken such strong possession of me when I first came among the Europeans, and for some time after. I began now to pass to an opposite extreme; I was so far from being afraid of any thing new which I saw, that, after I had been some time in this ship, I even began to long for a battle.

My griefs too, which in young minds are not perpetual, were now wearing away; and I soon enjoyed myself pretty well, and felt tolerably easy in my present situation. There was a number of boys on board, which still made it more agreeable; for we were always together, and a great part of our time was spent in play. I remained in this ship a considerable time, during which we made several cruises, and visited a variety of places: among others we were twice in Holland, and brought over several persons of distinction from it, whose names I do not now remember. On the passage, one day, for the diversion of those gentle-men, all the boys were called on the quarter-deck, and were paired proportionably, and then made to fight; after which the gentleman gave the combatants from five to nine shillings each.[2] This was the first time I ever fought with a white boy; and I never knew what it was to have a bloody nose before. This made me fight most desperately; I suppose considerably more than an hour: and at last, both of us being weary, we were parted. I had a great deal of this kind of sport afterwards, in which the captain and the ship's company used very much to encourage me. Sometime afterwards the ship went to Leith in Scot-

2. Equiano makes many references to British and colonial money. The major unit was the pound sterling (£), which consisted of 20 shillings (s.); and each shilling in turn was worth 12 pence (d.). A guinea was 21 shillings, a crown 5 shillings, and a farthing one quarter of a penny. A pisterine in the West Indies had the value of an English shilling, as did two bits; and equiv-alent amounts in local pound currency were often much higher than British pound sterling (which was worth more).

Vincent Carretta estimates that multiplying by 80 yields an approximate modern equivalent; James Heldman suggests that £1 around 1800 would be worth about $33 in today's money.

Equiano's Narrative sold for 5s. in 1794, just a little less than a four-pound loaf of bread. Equiano remembers that he was bought by Michael Henry Pascal for £30 or £40, which may have been higher than average for a young slave. Working for Robert King, Equiano received 10 to 15 pence per day; other slaves were paid only 6 to 9 pence daily while they earned their masters three or four shillings. Equiano made £47 sterling by trading, and he bought his freedom for £70 Montserrat currency, or £40. As an able-bodied sailor, he was paid 36s per month. Upon his death he left his daughter an estate worth £950.

Charles Nichols (see p. 220) cites sources showing that a slave-carrying sea captain could make £360 and a slave trader £465 on a single trip; and a ship with 250 slaves aboard could net as much as £7,000. The slavery advocate James Tobin cited sources indicating that in 1785 West Indian slave labor brought England and annual income of £2,000,000, one sixth of the total national revenue. In the parliamentary debate of 1791, British exports to Africa were estimated to be worth £800,000, and imports of the West India trade £6,000,000 (see p. 195 and p. 286 below).

land, and from thence to the Orkneys,[3] where I was surprised in seeing scarcely any night: and from thence we sailed with a great fleet, full of soldiers, for England. All this time we had never come to an engagement, though we were frequently cruising off the coast of France: during which we chased many vessels, and took in all seventeen prizes.[4] I had been learning many of the manœuvres of the ship during our cruise; and I was several times made to fire the guns. One evening, off Havre de Grace, just as it was growing dark, we were standing off shore, and met with a fine large French-built frigate. We got all things immediately ready for fighting; and I now expected I should be gratified in seeing an engagement, which I had so long wished for in vain. But the very moment the word of command was given to fire we heard those on board the other ship cry "Haul down the jib"; and in that instant she hoisted English colours. There was instantly with us an amazing cry of—Avast! or stop firing; and I think one or two guns had been let off, but happily they did no mischief. We had hailed them several times; but they not hearing, we received no answer, which was the cause of our firing. The boat was then sent on board of her, and she proved to be the Ambuscade man of war, to my no small disappointment. We returned to Portsmouth, without having been in any action, just at the trial of Admiral Byng[5] (whom I saw several times during it): and my master having left the ship, and gone to London for promotion, Dick and I were put on board the Savage sloop of war, and we went in her to assist in bringing off the St. George man of war, that had ran ashore somewhere on the coast. After staying a few weeks on board the Savage, Dick and I were sent on shore at Deal, where we remained some short time, till my master sent for us to London, the place I had long desired exceedingly to see. We therefore both with great pleasure got into a waggon, and came to London, where we were received by a Mr. Guerin, a relation of my master. This gentleman had two sisters, very amiable ladies, who took much notice and great care of me. Though I had desired so much to see London, when I arrived in it I was unfortunately unable to gratify my curiosity; for I had at this time the chilblains[6] to such a degree that I could not stand for several months, and I was obliged to be sent to St. George's Hospital. There I grew so ill, that the doctors wanted to cut my left leg off at different times, apprehending a mortification;[7] but I always said I would rather die than suffer it; and happily (I thank God) I recovered without the operation. After being there several weeks, and just as I had recovered,

3. Islands north of Scotland.
4. Captured warship or its cargo.
5. Admiral John Byng (1704–1757) was executed for cowardice in the Seven Years' War. *Portsmouth*: port city in England.
6. Inflammation of hands and feet due to exposure to cold.
7. Gangrene.

the small-pox broke out on me, so that I was again confined; and I thought myself now particularly unfortunate. However I soon recovered again; and by this time my master having been promoted to be first lieutenant of the Preston man of war of fifty guns, then new at Deptford, Dick and I were sent on board her, and soon after we went to Holland to bring over the late Duke of ——— to England.—While I was in this ship an incident happened, which, though trifling, I beg leave to relate, as I could not help taking particular notice of it, and considering it then as a judgment of God. One morning a young man was looking up to the fore-top,[8] and in a wicked tone, common on shipboard, d——d his eyes about something. Just at the moment some small particles of dirt fell into his left eye, and by the evening it was very much inflamed. The next day it grew worse; and within six or seven days he lost it. From this ship my master was appointed a lieutenant on board the Royal George.

When he was going he wished me to stay on board the Preston, to learn the French horn; but the ship being ordered for Turkey I could not think of leaving my master, to whom I was very warmly attached; and I told him if he left me behind it would break my heart. This prevailed on him to take me with him; but he left Dick on board the Preston, whom I embraced at parting for the last time. The Royal George was the largest ship I had ever seen; so that when I came on board of her I was surprised at the number of people, men, women, and children, of every denomination; and the largest of the guns, many of them also of brass, which I had never seen before. Here were also shops or stalls of every kind of goods, and people crying their different commodities about the ship as in a town. To me it appeared a little world, into which I was again cast without a friend, for I had no longer my dear companion Dick. We did not stay long here. My master was not many weeks on board before he got an appointment to be sixth lieutenant of the Namur, which was then at Spithead, fitting up for Vice-admiral Boscawen, who was going with a large fleet on an expedition against Louisburgh.[9] The crew of the Royal George were turned over to her, and the flag of that gallant admiral was hoisted on board, the blue at the maintop-gallant mast head.[1] There was a very great fleet of men of war of every description assembled together for this expedition, and I was in hopes soon to have an opportunity of being gratified with a sea-fight. All things being now in readiness, this mighty fleet (for there was also Admiral Cornish's fleet in company, destined

8. Platform at the head of a ship's foremast. For an illustration of nautical terms, see p. 193.
9. Or Louisbourg. Equiano also spells it Louisbourgh. Located at the entrance of the St. Lawrence River on Cape Breton Island in Nova Scotia, Louisbourg had been under British attack from June to September, 1757. Louisbourg surrendered July 26, 1758. *Spithead:* name of an anchorage and a strait that lie off Portsmouth. *Fitting up:* being prepared. *Edward Boscawen* (1711–1761), or "Old Dreadnought," commanded navel fleet at Louisbourgh.
1. Top of the ship's middle, or main, mast.

for the East Indies) at last weighed anchor, and sailed. The two fleets continued in company for several days, and then parted; Admiral Cornish, in the Lenox, having first saluted our admiral in the Namur, which he returned. We then steered for America; but, by contrary winds, we were driven to Teneriffe,[2] where I was struck with its noted peak. Its prodigious height, and its form, resembling a sugar-loaf, filled me with wonder. We remained in sight of this island some days, and then proceeded for America, which we soon made, and got into a very commodious harbour called St. George, in Halifax,[3] where we had fish in great plenty, and all other fresh provisions. We were here joined by different men of war and transport ships with soldiers; after which, our fleet being increased to a prodigious number of ships of all kinds, we sailed for Cape Breton in Nova Scotia. We had the good and gallant General Wolfe[4] on board our ship, whose affability made him highly esteemed and beloved by all the men. He often honoured me, as well as other boys, with marks of his notice; and saved me once a flogging for fighting with a young gentleman. We arrived at Cape Breton in the summer of 1758: and here the soldiers were to be landed, in order to make an attack upon Louisbourgh. My master had some part in superintending the landing; and here I was in a small measure gratified in seeing an encounter between our men and the enemy. The French were posted on the shore to receive us, and disputed our landing for a long time; but at last they were driven from their trenches, and a complete landing was effected. Our troops pursued them as far as the town of Louisbourgh. In this action many were killed on both sides. One thing remarkable I saw this day:—A lieutenant of the Princess Amelia, who, as well as my master, superintended the landing, was giving the word of command, and while his mouth was open a musquet ball went through it, and passed out at his cheek. I had that day in my hand the scalp of an indian king, who was killed in the engagement: the scalp had been taken off by an Highlander. I saw this king's ornaments too, which were very curious, and made of feathers.

Our land forces laid siege to the town of Louisbourgh, while the French men of war were blocked up in the harbour by the fleet, the batteries[5] at the same time playing upon them from the land. This they did with such effect, that one day I saw some of the ships set on fire by the shells from the batteries, and I believe two or three of them were quite burnt. At another time, about fifty boats belonging to the English men of war, commanded by Captain George Balfour of the Ætna fire-ship, and another junior captain, Laforey, attacked and boarded the only two remaining French men of war in the harbour.

2. Or Tenerifa. The largest of the Canary Islands.
3. Nova Scotia.
4. General James Wolfe (1727–1759) defeated French power in Quebec in 1759, but was killed during the last assault on the city.
5. Array of guns.

They also set fire to a seventy-gun ship, but a sixty-four, called the Bienfaisant, they brought off. During my stay here I had often an opportunity of being near Captain Balfour, who was pleased to notice me, and liked me so much that he often asked my master to let him have me, but he would not part with me; and no consideration could have induced me to leave him. At last Louïsbourgh was taken,[6] and the English men of war came into the harbour before it, to my very great joy; for I had now more liberty of indulging myself, and I went often on shore. When the ships were in the harbour we had the most beautiful procession on the water I ever saw. All the admirals and captains of the men of war, full dressed, and in their barges, well ornamented with pendants, came alongside of the Namur. The vice-admiral then went on shore in his barge, followed by the other officers in order of seniority, to take possession, as I suppose, of the town and fort. Some time after this the French governor and his lady, and other persons of note, came on board our ship to dine. On this occasion our ships were dressed with colours of all kinds, from the topgallant-mast head to the deck; and this, with the firing of guns, formed a most grand and magnificent spectacle.

As soon as every thing here was settled Admiral Boscawen sailed with part of the fleet for England, leaving some ships behind with Rear-admirals Sir Charles Hardy and Durell. It was now winter; and one evening, during our passage home, about dusk, when we were in the channel, or near soundings, and were beginning to look for land, we descried[7] seven sail of large men of war, which stood off shore. Several people on board of our ship said, as the two fleets were (in forty minutes from the first sight) within hail of each other, that they were English men of war; and some of our people even began to name some of the ships. By this time both fleets began to mingle, and our admiral ordered his flag to be hoisted. At that instant the other fleet, which were French, hoisted their ensigns, and gave us a broadside as they passed by. Nothing could create greater surprise and confusion among us than this: the wind was high, the sea rough, and we had our lower and middle deck guns housed in, so that not a single gun on board was ready to be fired at any of the French ships. However, the Royal William and the Somerset being our sternmost ships, became a little prepared, and each gave the French ships a broadside as they passed by. I afterwards heard this was a French squadron, commanded by Mons. Conflans; and certainly had the Frenchmen known our condition, and had a mind to fight us, they might have done us great mischief. But we were not long before we were prepared for an engagement. Immediately many things were tossed overboard; the ships were made ready for fighting as soon as possible; and about ten at night we had bent a

6. On July 26, 1758.
7. Caught sight of.

new main sail, the old one being split. Being now in readiness for fighting, we wore ship, and stood after[8] the French fleet, who were one or two ships in number more than we. However we gave them chase, and continued pursuing them all night: and at day-light we saw six of them, all large ships of the line, and an English East Indiaman, a prize they had taken. We chased them all day till between three and four o'clock in the evening, when we came up with, and passed within a musquet shot of, one seventy-four gun ship, and the Indiaman also, who now hoisted her colours, but immediately hauled them down again. On this we made a signal for the other ships to take possession of her; and, supposing the man of war would likewise strike, we cheered, but she did not; though if we had fired into her, from being so near, we must have taken her. To my utter surprise the Somerset, who was the next ship a-stern of the Namur, made way likewise; and, thinking they were sure of this French ship, they cheered in the same manner, but still continued to follow us. The French Commodore was about a gun-shot ahead of all, running from us with all speed; and about four o'clock he carried his foretop-mast overboard. This caused another loud cheer with us; and a little after the topmast came close by us; but, to our great surprise, instead of coming up with her, we found she went as fast as ever, if not faster. The sea grew now much smoother; and the wind lulling, the seventy-four gun ship we had passed came again by us in the very same direction, and so near, that we heard her people talk as she went by; yet not a shot was fired on either side; and about five or six o'clock, just as it grew dark, she joined her commodore. We chased all night; but the next day they were out of sight, so that we saw no more of them; and we only had the old Indiaman (called Carnarvon I think) for our trouble. After this we stood in for[9] the channel, and soon made the land; and, about the close of the year 1758–9, we got safe to St. Helen's. Here the Namur ran aground; and also another large ship astern of us; but, starting our water, and tossing many things overboard to lighten her, we got the ships off without any damage. We stayed for a short time at Spithead, and then went into Portsmouth harbour to refit; from whence the admiral went to London; and my master and I soon followed, with a press-gang, as we wanted some hands to complete our complement.

Chap. IV. *skim the mediterranean part*

The author is baptized—Narrowly escapes drowning—Goes on an expedition to the Mediterranean—Incidents he met with there—Is witness to an engagement between some English and French ships—

8. Changed course, and chased.
9. Held course for.

A particular account of the celebrated engagement between Admiral Boscawen and Mons. Le Clue, off Cape Logas, in August 1759—Dreadful explosion of a French ship—The author sails for England—His master appointed to the command of a fire-ship—Meets a negro boy, from whom he experiences much benevolence—Prepares for an expedition against Belle-Isle—A remarkable story of a disaster which befel his ship—Arrives at Belle-Isle—Operations of the landing and siege—The author's danger and distress, with his manner of extricating himself—Surrender of Belle-Isle—Transactions afterwards on the coast of France—Remarkable instance of kidnapping—The author returns to England—Hears a talk of peace, and expects his freedom—His ship sails for Deptford to be paid off, and when he arrives there he is suddenly seized by his master and carried forcibly on board a West India ship and sold.

It was now between two and three years since I first came to England, a great part of which I had spent at sea; so that I became inured to that service, and began to consider myself as happily situated; for my master treated me always extremely well; and my attachment and gratitude to him were very great. From the various scenes I had beheld on ship-board, I soon grew a stranger to terror of every kind, and was, in that respect at least, almost an Englishman. I have often reflected with surprise that I never felt half the alarm at any of the numerous dangers I have been in, that I was filled with at the first sight of the Europeans, and at every act of theirs, even the most trifling, when I first came among them, and for some time afterwards. That fear, however, which was the effect of my ignorance, wore away as I began to know them. I could now speak English tolerably well, and I perfectly understood every thing that was said. I now not only felt myself quite easy with these new countrymen, but relished their society and manners. I no longer looked upon them as spirits, but as men superior to us; and therefore I had the stronger desire to resemble them; to imbibe their spirit, and imitate their manners; I therefore embraced every occasion of improvement; and every new thing that I observed I treasured up in my memory. I had long wished to be able to read and write; and for this purpose I took every opportunity to gain instruction, but had made as yet very little progress. However, when I went to London with my master, I had soon an opportunity of improving myself, which I gladly embraced. Shortly after my arrival, he sent me to wait upon the Miss Guerins, who had treated me with much kindness when I was there before; and they sent me to school.

While I was attending these ladies their servants told me I could not go to Heaven unless I was baptized. This made me very uneasy; for I had now some faint idea of a future state: accordingly I communicated my anxiety to the eldest Miss Guerin, with whom I was become a favourite, and pressed her to have me baptized; when to my great joy she told me I should. She had formerly asked my master to let me be baptized, but he had refused; however, she now insisted on it; and he being under some obligation to her brother complied with her requests; so I was baptized in St. Margaret's church, Westminster, in February 1759, by my present name. The clergyman, at the same time, gave me a book, called a Guide to the Indians, written by the Bishop of Sodor and Man.[1] On this occasion Miss Guerin did me the honour to stand as godmother, and afterwards gave me a treat. I used to attend these ladies about the town, in which service I was extremely happy; as I had thus many opportunities of seeing London, which I desired of all things. I was sometimes, however, with my master at his rendezvous-house[2] which was at the foot of Westminster-bridge. Here I used to enjoy myself in playing about the bridge stairs, and often in the watermen's wherries,[3] with other boys. On one of these occasions there was another boy with me in a wherry, and we went out into the current of the river: while we were there two more stout boys came to us in another wherry, and abusing us for taking the boat, desired me to get into the other wherry-boat. Accordingly I went to get out of the wherry I was in; but just as I had got one of my feet into the other boat the boys shoved it off, so that I fell into the Thames; and, not being able to swim, I should unavoidably have been drowned, but for the assistance of some watermen who providentially came to my relief.

The Namur being again got ready for sea, my master, with his gang,[4] was ordered on board; and, to my no small grief, I was obliged to leave my schoolmaster, whom I liked very much, and always attended while I stayed in London, to repair on board with my master. Nor did I leave my kind patronesses, the Miss Guerins, without uneasiness and regret. They often used to teach me to read, and took great pains to instruct me in the principles of religion and the knowledge of God. I therefore parted from those amiable ladies with reluctance; after receiving from them many friendly cautions how to conduct myself, and some valuable presents.

When I came to Spithead, I found we were destined for the Mediterranean, with a large fleet, which was now ready to put to sea. We only waited for the arrival of the admiral, who soon came on board; and about the beginning of the spring 1759, having weighed anchor, and got under way, sailed for the Mediterranean; and in eleven days,

1. Sodor and Man are the Hebrides and the Isle of Man respectively, both islands off the coast of Scotland. Bishop Thomas Wilson (1697–1755) wrote *The Knowledge and Practice of Christianity Made Easy for the Meanest Mental Capacities; or, an Essay towards an Instruction for the Indians* (1740, 1781).
2. A place for enlisting seamen into naval service.
3. Light rowboats.
4. Crew.

from the Land's End,[5] we got to Gibraltar. While we were here I used to be often on shore, and got various fruits in great plenty, and very cheap.

I had frequently told several people, in my excursions on shore, the story of my being kidnapped with my sister, and of our being separated, as I have related before; and I had as often expressed my anxiety for her fate, and my sorrow at having never met her again. One day, when I was on shore, and mentioning these circumstances to some persons, one of them told me he knew where my sister was, and, if I would accompany him, he would bring me to her. Improbable as this story was I believed it immediately, and agreed to go with him, while my heart leaped for joy: and, indeed, he conducted me to a black young woman, who was so like my sister, that, at first sight, I really thought it was her: but I was quickly undeceived; and, on talking to her, I found her to be one of another nation.

While we lay there the Preston came in from the Levant.[6] As soon as she arrived, my master told me I should now see my old companion, Dick, who had gone with her when she sailed for Turkey. I was much rejoiced at this news, and expected every minute to embrace him; and when the captain came on board of our ship, which he did immediately after, I ran to inquire after my friend; but, with inexpressible sorrow, I learned from the boat's crew that the dear youth was dead! and that they had brought his chest, and all his other things, to my master: these he afterwards gave to me, and I regarded them as a memorial of my friend, whom I loved, and grieved for, as a brother.

While we were at Gibraltar, I saw a soldier hanging by his heels, at one of the moles:[7] I thought this a strange sight, as I had seen a man hanged in London by his neck. At another time I saw the master of a frigate towed to shore on a grating,[8] by several of the men of war's boats, and discharged the fleet, which I understood was a mark of disgrace for cowardice. On board the same ship there was also a sailor hung up at the yard-arm.[9]

After lying at Gibraltar for some time, we sailed up the Mediterranean a considerable way above the Gulf of Lyons;[1] where we were one night overtaken with a terrible gale of wind, much greater than any I had ever yet experienced. The sea ran so high that, though all the guns were well housed, there was a great reason to fear their getting loose, the ship rolled so much; and if they had it must have proved our destruction. After we had cruised here for a short time, we came to Barcelona, a Spanish sea-port, remarkable for its silk manufactures.

---

5. Westernmost point of England, in Cornwall.
6. Region in eastern Mediterranean, from Greece to Egypt.
7. He had drowned himself in endeavouring to desert [Equiano's note]. A mole is a pier.
8. Moveable floor of a boat, resembling latticework.
9. Either end of a ship's yard (or spar) supporting a square sail.
1. Near southern France.

Here the ships were all to be watered;[2] and my master, who spoke different languages, and used often to interpret for the admiral, superintended the watering of ours. For that purpose he and the officers of the other ships, who were on the same service, had tents pitched in the bay; and the Spanish soldiers were stationed along the shore, I suppose to see that no depredations[3] were committed by our men.

I used constantly to attend my master; and I was charmed with this place. All the time we stayed it was like a fair with the natives, who brought us fruits of all kinds, and sold them to us much cheaper than I got them in England. They used also to bring wine down to us in hog and sheep skins, which diverted me very much. The Spanish officers here treated our officers with great politeness and attention; and some of them, in particular, used to come often to my master's tent to visit him; where they would sometimes divert themselves by mounting me on the horses or mules, so that I could not fall, and setting them off at full gallop; my imperfect skill in horsemanship all the while affording them no small entertainment. After the ships were watered, we returned to our old station of cruizing off Toulon, for the purpose of intercepting a fleet of French men of war that lay there. One Sunday, in our cruise, we came off a place where there were two small French frigates lying in shore; and our admiral, thinking to take or destroy them, sent two ships in after them—the Culloden and the Conqueror. They soon came up to the Frenchmen; and I saw a smart fight here, both by sea and land: for the frigates were covered by batteries,[4] and they played upon our ships most furiously, which they as furiously returned, and for a long time a constant firing was kept up on all sides at an amazing rate. At last one frigate sunk; but the people escaped, though not without much difficulty: and a little after some of the people left the other frigate also, which was a mere wreck. However, our ships did not venture to bring her away, they were so much annoyed from the batteries, which raked them both in going and coming: their topmasts were shot away, and they were otherwise so much shattered, that the admiral was obliged to send in many boats to tow them back to the fleet. I afterwards sailed with a man who fought in one of the French batteries during the engagement, and he told me our ships had done considerable mischief that day on shore and in the batteries.

After this we sailed for Gibraltar, and arrived there about August 1759. Here we remained with all our sails unbent, while the fleet was watering and doing other necessary things. While we were in this situation, one day the admiral, with most of the principal officers, and many people of all stations, being on shore, about seven o'clock in the evening we were alarmed by signals from the frigates stationed for that

2. Supplied with fresh drinking water.
3. Acts of stealing or looting.
4. I.e., guns.

purpose; and in an instant there was a general cry that the French fleet was out, and just passing through the streights. The admiral immediately came on board with some other officers; and it is impossible to describe the noise, hurry and confusion throughout the whole fleet, in bending their sails and slipping their cables;[5] many people and ships' boats were left on shore in the bustle. We had two captains on board of our ship who came away in the hurry and left their ships to follow. We shewed lights from the gun-whale to the main topmast-head;[6] and all our lieutenants were employed amongst the fleet to tell the ships not to wait for their captains, but to put the sails to the yards, slip their cables and follow us; and in this confusion of making ready for fighting we set out for sea in the dark after the French fleet. Here I could have exclaimed with Ajax,

> Oh Jove! O father! if it be thy will
> That we must perish, we thy will obey,
> But let us perish by the light of day.[7]

They had got the start of us so far that we were not able to come up with them during the night; but at day-light we saw seven sail of the line of battle some miles ahead. We immediately chased them till about four o'clock in the evening, when our ships came up with them; and, though we were about fifteen large ships, our gallant admiral only fought them with his own division, which consisted of seven; so that we were just ship for ship. We passed by the whole of the enemy's fleet in order to come at their commander, Mons. La Clue, who was in the Ocean, an eighty-four gun ship: as we passed they all fired on us; and at one time three of them fired together, continuing to do so for some time. Notwithstanding which our admiral would not suffer a gun to be fired at any of them, to my astonishment; but made us lie on our bellies on the deck till we came quite close to the Ocean, who was ahead of them all; when we had orders to pour the whole three tiers into her at once.

The engagement now commenced with great fury on both sides: the Ocean immediately returned our fire, and we continued engaged with each other for some time; during which I was frequently stunned with the thundering of the great guns, whose dreadful contents hurried many of my companions into awful eternity. At last the French line was entirely broken, and we obtained the victory, which was immediately proclaimed with loud huzzas and acclamations. We took three prizes, La Modess, of sixty-four guns, and Le Temeraire and Centaur, of seventy-four guns each. The rest of the French ships took to flight

---

5. Raising their sails and taking their ropes aboard.
6. I.e., from top to bottom. *Gun-whale*: gunwale or gunnel, the upper edge of a ship's side (see p. 193 below.)
7. Adapted from Alexander Pope's (1680–1744) translation of the *Iliad* 17.728–32.

with all the sail they could crowd. Our ship being very much damaged, and quite disabled from pursuing the enemy, the admiral immediately quitted her, and went in the broken and only boat we had left on board the Newark, with which, and some other ships, he went after the French. The Ocean, and another large French ship, called the Redoubtable, endeavouring to escape, ran ashore at Cape Logas, on the coast of Portugal; and the French admiral and some of the crew got ashore; but we, finding it impossible to get the ships off, set fire to them both. About midnight I saw the Ocean blow up, with a most dreadful explosion. I never beheld a more awful scene. In less than a minute the midnight for a certain space seemed turned into day by the blaze, which was attended with a noise louder and more terrible than thunder, that seemed to rend every element around us.

My station during the engagement was on the middle-deck, where I was quartered with another boy, to bring powder to the aftermost gun; and here I was a witness of the dreadful fate of many of my companions, who, in the twinkling of an eye, were dashed in pieces, and launched into eternity. Happily I escaped unhurt, though the shot and splinters flew thick about me during the whole fight. Towards the latter part of it my master was wounded, and I saw him carried down to the surgeon; but though I was much alarmed for him and wished to assist him I dared not leave my post. At this station my gun-mate (a partner in bringing powder for the same gun) and I ran a very great risk for more than half an hour of blowing up the ship. For, when we had taken the cartridges out of the boxes, the bottoms of many of them proving rotten, the powder ran all about the deck, near the match tub:[8] we scarcely had water enough at the last to throw on it. We were also, from our employment, very much exposed to the enemy's shots; for we had to go through nearly the whole length of the ship to bring the power. I expected therefore every minute to be my last; especially when I saw our men fall so thick about me; but, wishing to guard as much against the dangers as possible, at first I thought it would be safest not to go for the powder till the Frenchmen had fired their broadside; and then, while they were charging, I could go and come with my powder: but immediately afterwards I thought this caution was fruitless; and, cheering myself with the reflection that there was a time allotted for me to die as well as to be born,[9] I instantly cast off all fear or thought whatever of death, and went through the whole of my duty with alacrity; pleasing myself with the hope, if I survived the battle, of relating it and the dangers I had escaped to the dear Miss Guerin, and others, when I should return to London.

Our ship suffered very much in this engagement; for, besides the

8. Tub for keeping matches, fuses, and wicks for firing guns.
9. See Ecclesiastes 3.2.

number of our killed and wounded, she was almost torn to pieces, and our rigging so much shattered, that our mizen-mast and main-yard,[1] &c. hung over the side of the ship; so that we were obliged to get many carpenters, and others from some of the ships of the fleet, to assist in setting us in some tolerable order; and, notwithstanding, it took us some time before we were completely refitted; after which we left Admiral Broderick to command, and we, with the prizes, steered for England. On the passage, and as soon as my master was something recovered of his wounds, the admiral appointed him captain of the Ætna fire-ship, on which he and I left the Namur, and went on board of her at sea. I liked this little ship very much. I now became the captain's steward, in which situation I was very happy: for I was extremely well treated by all on board; and I had leisure to improve myself in reading and writing. The latter I had learned a little of before I left the Namur, as there was a school on board. When we arrived at Spithead the Ætna went into Portsmouth harbour to refit, which being done, we returned to Spithead and joined a large fleet that was thought to be intended against the Havannah; but about that time the king died: whether that prevented the expedition I know not; but it caused our ship to be stationed at Cowes, in the isle of Wight,[2] till the beginning of the year sixty-one. Here I spent my time very pleasantly; I was much on shore all about this delightful island, and found the inhabitants very civil.

While I was here, I met with a trifling incident, which surprised me agreeably. I was one day in a field belonging to a gentleman who had a black boy about my own size; this boy having observed me from his master's house, was transported at the sight of one of his own countrymen, and ran to meet me with the utmost haste. I not knowing what he was about turned a little out of his way at first, but to no purpose: he soon came close to me and caught hold of me in his arms as if I had been his brother, though we had never seen each other before. After we had talked together for some time he took me to see his master's houses, where I was treated very kindly. This benevolent boy and I were very happy in frequently seeing each other till about the month of March 1761, when our ship had orders to fit out again for another expedition. When we got ready, we joined a very large fleet at Spithead, commanded by Commodore Keppel, which was destined against Belle-Isle,[3] and with a number of transport ships with troops on board to make a descent on the place. We sailed once more in quest of fame. I longed to engage in new adventures and see fresh wonders.

1. The main yard is the spar on which the mainsail is extended, supported by the mainmast. The mizzenmast supports the middle; it is the mast closest to the stern of a ship with two or three masts (see p. 193 below).
2. Island in the English Channel.
3. Belle-Île is in the Bay of Biscay, off the French coast. The siege took place from April to June 1761.

I had a mind on which every thing uncommon made its full impression, and every event which I considered as marvellous. Every extraordinary escape, or signal deliverance, either of myself or others, I looked upon to be effected by the interposition of Providence. We had not been above ten days at sea before an incident of this kind happened; which, whatever credit it may obtain from the reader, made no small impression on my mind.

We had on board a gunner, whose name was John Mondle; a man of very indifferent morals. This man's cabin was between the decks, exactly over where I lay, abreast of the quarter-deck ladder. One night, the 20th of April, being terrified with a dream, he awoke in so great a fright that he could not rest in his bed any longer, nor even remain in his cabin; and he went upon deck about four o'clock in the morning extremely agitated. He immediately told those on the deck of the agonies of his mind, and the dream which occasioned it; in which he said he had seen many things very awful, and had been warned by St. Peter to repent, who told him time was short. This he said had greatly alarmed him, and he was determined to alter his life. People generally mock the fears of others when they are themselves in safety; and some of his shipmates who heard him only laughed at him. However, he made a vow that he never would drink strong liquors again; and he immediately got a light, and gave away his sea-stores of liquor. After which, his agitation still continuing, he began to read the Scriptures, hoping to find some relief; and soon afterwards he laid himself down again on his bed, and endeavoured to compose himself to sleep, but to no purpose; his mind still continuing in a state of agony. By this time it was exactly half after seven in the morning : I was then under the half-deck at the great cabin door; and all at once I heard the people in the waist[4] cry out, mostly fearfully—'The Lord have mercy upon us! We are all lost! The Lord have mercy upon us!' Mr. Mondle hearing the cries, immediately ran out of his cabin; and we were instantly struck by the Lynne, a forty-gun ship, Captain Clark, which nearly ran us down. This ship had just put about, and was by the wind, but had not got full headway, or we must all have perished; for the wind was brisk. However, before Mr. Mondle had got four steps from his cabin-door, she struck our ship with her cutwater right in the middle of his bed and cabin, and ran it up to the combings[5] of the quarter-deck hatchway, and above three feet below water, and in a minute there was not a bit of wood to be seen where Mr. Mondle's cabin stood; and he was so near being killed that some of the splinters tore his face. As Mr. Mondle must inevitably have perished from this accident had he not been alarmed in the very extraordinary way I have related, I could not

4. Area between the ship's quarterdeck and forecastle, both parts of the upper deck.
5. The raised sides of the hatch, an opening in the ship's deck. *Cutwater*: foremost part of a ship's prow, which cuts the water.

help regarding this as an awful interposition of Providence for his preservation. The two ships for some time swinged alongside of each other;
for ours being a fireship, our grappling-irons[6] caught the Lynne every
way, and the yards and rigging went at an astonishing rate. Our ship
was in such a shocking condition that we all thought she would
instantly go down, and every one ran for their lives, and got as well as
they could on board the Lynne; but our lieutenant being the aggressor,
he never quitted the ship. However, when we found she did not sink
immediately, the captain came on board again, and encouraged our
people to return and try to save her. Many on this came back, but some
would not venture. Some of the ships in the fleet, seeing our situation,
immediately sent their boats to our assistance; but it took us the whole
day to save the ship with all their help. And by using every possible
means, particularly frapping her together with many hawsers,[7] and putting a great quantity of tallow below water where she was damaged,
she was kept together: but it was well we did not meet with any gales
of wind, or we must have gone to pieces; for we were in such a crazy
condition that we had ships to attend us till we arrived at Belle-Isle,
the place of our destination; and then we had all things taken out of
the ship, and she was properly repaired. This escape of Mr. Mondle,
which he, as well as myself, always considered as a singular act of Providence, I believe had a great influence on his life and conduct ever
afterwards.

Now that I am on this subject I beg leave to relate another instance
or two which strongly raised my belief of the particular interposition
of Heaven, and which might not otherwise have found a place here,
from their insignificance. I belonged for a few days in the year 1758 to
the Jason, of fifty-four guns, at Plymouth; and one night, when I was
on board, a woman, with a child at her breast, fell from the upper-deck
down into the hold, near the keel. Every one thought that the mother
and child must be both dashed to pieces; but, to our great surprise,
neither of them was hurt. I myself one day fell headlong from the
upper-deck of the Etna[Ætna] down the after-hold, when the ballast
was out; and all who saw me fall cried out I was killed: but I received
not the least injury. And in the same ship a man fell from the mast-
head on the deck without being hurt. In these, and in many more
instances, I thought I could plainly trace the hand of God, without
whose permission a sparrow cannot fall. I began to raise my fear from
man to him alone, and to call daily on his holy name with fear and
reverence: and I trust he heard my supplications, and graciously condescended to answer me according to his holy word, and to implant

---

6. Or grapplings, instrument consisting of an iron bar with several iron claws at one end for
   grappling and holding things. Used in naval warfare to grip and hold enemy ship for boarding.
7. Large ropes used for towing and mooring ships. *Frapping*: binding together by cables or ropes;
   tightening.

the seeds of piety in me, even one of the meanest[8] of his creatures.

When we had refitted our ship, and all things were in readiness for attacking the place, the troops on board the transports were ordered to disembark; and my master, as a junior captain, had a share in the command of the landing. This was on the 8th of April. The French were drawn up on the shore, and had made every disposition to oppose the landing of our men, only a small part of them this day being able to effect it; most of them, after fighting with great bravery, were cut off; and General Crawford, with a number of others, were taken prisoners. In this day's engagement we had also our lieutenant killed.

On the 21st of April we renewed our efforts to land the men, while all the men of war were stationed along the shore to cover it, and fired at the French batteries and breastworks[9] from early in the morning till about four o'clock in the evening, when our soldiers effected a safe landing. They immediately attacked the Fench [French]; and, after a sharp encounter, forced them from the batteries. Before the enemy retreated they blew up several of them, lest they should fall into our hands. Our men now proceeded to besiege the citadel, and my master was ordered on shore to superintend the landing of all the materials necessary for carrying on the siege; in which service I mostly attended him. While I was there I went about to different parts of the island; and one day, particularly, my curiosity almost cost me my life. I wanted very much to see the mode of charging the mortars[1] and letting off the shells, and for that purpose I went to an English battery that was but a very few yards from the walls of the citadel. There, indeed, I had an opportunity of completely gratifying myself in seeing the whole operation, and that not without running a very great risk, both from the English shells that burst while I was there, but likewise from those of the French. One of the largest of their shells bursted within nine or ten yards of me: there was a single rock close by, about the size of a butt;[2] and I got instant shelter under it in time to avoid the fury of the shell. Where it burst the earth was torn in such a manner that two or three butts might easily have gone into the hole it made, and it threw great quantities of stones and dirt to a considerable distance. Three shot [shots] were also fired at me and another boy who was along with me, one of them in particular seemed

Wing'd with red lightning and impetuous rage;[3]

for with a most dreadful sound it hissed close by me, and struck a rock at a little distance, which it shattered to pieces. When I saw what perilous circumstances I was in, I attempted to return the nearest way

8. Humblest.
9. A low, quickly constructed barrier to protect gunners.
1. Firing the cannons.
2. A measure of 126 liquid gallons; a large cask.
3. From John Milton (1608–1674), *Paradise Lost* 1.175.

I could find, and thereby I got between the English and the French centinels. An English serjeant, who commanded the outposts, seeing me, and surprised how I came there, (which was by stealth along the seashore), reprimanded me very severely for it, and instantly took the centinel off his post into custody, for his negligence in suffering me to pass the lines. While I was in this situation I observed at a little distance a French horse, belonging to some islanders, which I thought I would now mount, for the greater expedition of getting off. Accordingly I took some cord which I had about me, and making a kind of bridle of it, I put it round the horse's head, and the tame beast very quietly suffered me to tie him thus and mount him. As soon as I was on the horse's back I began to kick and beat him, and try every means to make him go quick, but all to very little purpose: I could not drive him out of a slow pace. While I was creeping along, still within reach of the enemy's shot, I met with a servant well mounted on an English horse. I immediately stopped; and, crying, told him my case; and begged of him to help me, and this he effectually did; for, having a fine large whip, he began to lash my horse with it so severely, that he set off full speed with me towards the sea, while I was quite unable to hold or manage him. In this manner I went along till I came to a craggy precipice. I now could not stop my horse; and my mind was filled with apprehensions of my deplorable fate should he go down the precipice, which he appeared fully disposed to do: I therefore thought I had better throw myself off him at once, which I did immediately with a great deal of dexterity, and fortunately escaped unhurt. As soon as I found myself at liberty I made the best of my way for the ship, determined I would not be so fool-hardy again in a hurry.

We continued to besiege the citadel till June, when it surrendered. During the siege I have counted above sixty shells and carcases in the air at once. When this place was taken I went through the citadel, and in the bomb-proofs under it, which were cut in the solid rock; and I thought it a surprising place, both for strength and building: notwithstanding which our shots and shells had made amazing devastation, and ruinous heaps all around it.

After the taking of this island our ships, with some others commanded by Commodore Stanhope in the Swiftsure, went to Basse-road, where we blocked up a French fleet. Our ships were there from June till February following; and in that time I saw a great many scenes of war, and stratagems on both sides to destroy each others fleet. Sometimes we would attack the French with some ships of the line; at other times with boats; and frequently we made prizes. Once or twice the French attacked us by throwing shells with their bomb-vessels: and one day as a French vessel was throwing shells at our ships she broke from her springs, behind the isle of I de Re: the tide being complicated, she came within a gun shot of the Nassau; but the Nassau could not bring a gun to bear upon her, and thereby the Frenchman got off. We were twice attacked by their fire-floats,[4] which they chained together, and then let them float down with the tide; but each time we sent boats with graplings, and towed them safe out of the fleet.

We had different commanders while we were at this place, Commodores Stanhope, Dennis, Lord Howe, &c. From hence, before the Spanish war began, our ship and the Wasp sloop were sent to St. Sebastian in Spain, by Commodore Stanhope; and Commodore Dennis afterwards sent our ship as a cartel to Bayonne in France,[5] after which[6] we went in February in 1762 to Belle-Isle, and there stayed till the summer, when we left it, and returned to Portsmouth.

After our ship was fitted out again for service, in September she went to Guernsey, where I was very glad to see my old hostess, who was now a widow, and my former little charming companion, her daughter. I spent some time here very happily with them, till October, when we had orders to repair to Portsmouth. We parted from each other with a great deal of affection; and I promised to return soon, and see them again, not knowing what all-powerful fate had determined for me. Our ship having arrived at Portsmouth, we went into the harbour, and remained there till the latter end of November, when we heard great talk about peace; and, to our very great joy, in the beginning of December we had orders to go up to London with our ship to be paid off. We received this news with loud huzzas, and every other demonstration of gladness; and nothing but mirth was to be seen throughout every part of the ship. I too was not without my share of the general joy on this occasion. I thought now of nothing but being freed, and working for myself, and thereby getting money to enable me to get a good education; for I always had a great desire to be able at least to read and write; and while I was on ship-board I had endeavoured to improve myself in both. While I was in the Ætna particularly, the captain's clerk taught me to write, and gave me a smattering of arithmetic as far as the rule of three.[7] There was also one Daniel Queen, about forty years of age, a man very well educated, who messed[8] with me on board

---

4. Low flat vessels filled with combustibles to be exploded among enemy ships in battle.
5. Among others whom we brought from Bayonne, two gentleman, who had been in the West Indies, where they sold slaves; and they confessed they had made at one time a false bill of sale, and sold two Portuguese white men among a lot of slaves [Equiano's note].
6. Some people have it, that sometimes shortly before persons die their ward has been seen; that is, some spirit exactly in their likeness, though they are themselves at other places at the same time. One day while we were at Bayonne Mr. Mondle saw one of our men, as he thought, in the gun-room; and a little after, coming on the quarter-deck, he spoke of some circumstances of this man to some of the officers. They told him that the man was then out of the ship, in one of the boats with the Lieutenant: but Mr. Mondle would not believe it, and we searched the ship, when he found the man was actually out of her; and when the boat returned some time afterwards, we found the man had been drowned at the very time Mr. Mondle thought he saw him [Equiano's note].
7. In mathematics, the method of finding the fourth term of a proportion when three are given. The fourth number is to the third as the second is to the first.
8. Had meals together.

this ship, and he likewise dressed and attended the captain. Fortunately this man soon became very much attached to me, and took very great pains to instruct me in many things. He taught me to shave and dress hair a little, and also to read in the Bible, explaining many passages to me, which I did not comprehend. I was wonderfully surprised to see the laws and rules of my country written almost exactly here; a circumstance which I believe tended to impress our manners and customs more deeply on my memory. I used to tell him of this resemblance; and many a time we have sat up the whole night together at this employment. In short, he was like a father to me; and some even used to call me after his name; they also styled me the black Christian. Indeed I almost loved him with the affection of a son. Many things I have denied myself that he might have them; and when I used to play at marbles or any other game, and won a few halfpence, or got any little money, which I sometimes did, for shaving any one, I used to buy him a little sugar or tobacco, as far as my stock of money would go. He used to say, that he and I never should part; and that when our ship was paid off, as I was as free as himself or any other man on board, he would instruct me in his business, by which I might gain a good livelihood. This gave me new life and spirits; and my heart burned within me, while I thought the time long till I obtained my freedom. For though my master had not promised it to me, yet, besides the assurances I had received that he had no right to detain me, he always treated me with the greatest kindness, and reposed[9] in me an unbounded confidence; he even paid attention to my morals; and would never suffer me to deceive him, or tell lies, of which he used to tell me the consequences; and that if I did so God would not love me; so that, from all this tenderness, I had never once supposed, in all my dreams of freedom, that he would think of detaining me any longer than I wished.

In pursuance of our orders we sailed from Portsmouth for the Thames, and arrived at Deptford the 10th of December, where we cast anchor just as it was high water. The ship was up about half an hour, when my master ordered the barge to be manned; and all in an instant, without having before given me the least reason to suspect any thing of the matter, he forced me into the barge; saying, I was going to leave him, but he would take care I should not. I was so struck with the unexpectedness of this proceeding, that for some time I did not make a reply, only I made an offer to go for my books and chest of clothes, but he swore I should not move out of his sight; and if I did he would cut my throat, at the same time taking his hanger.[1] I began, however, to collect myself; and, plucking up courage, I told him I was free, and

---

9. Placed.
1. A short sword hanging from the belt.

he could not by law serve me so. But this only enraged him the more; and he continued to swear, and said he would soon let me know whether he would or not, and at that instant sprung himself into the barge from the ship, to the astonishment and sorrow of all on board. The tide, rather unluckily for me, had just turned downward, so that we quickly fell down the river along with it, till we came among some outward-bound West Indiamen; for he was resolved to put me on board the first vessel he could get to receive me. The boat's crew, who pulled against their will, became quite faint different times, and would have gone ashore; but he would not let them. Some of them strove then to cheer me, and told me he could not sell me, and that they would stand by me, which revived me a little; and I still entertained hopes; for as they pulled along he asked some vessels to receive me, but they could not. But, just as we had got a little below Gravesend, we came alongside of a ship which was going away the next tide for the West Indies; her name was the Charming Sally, Captain James Doran; and my master went on board and agreed with him for me; and in a little time I was sent for into the cabin. When I came there Captain Doran asked me if I knew him; I answered that I did not; 'Then,' said he 'you are now my slave.' I told him my master could not sell me to him, nor to any one else. 'Why,' said he, 'did not your master buy you?' I confessed he did. 'But I have served him,' said I, 'many years, and he has taken all my wages and prize-money,[2] for I only got one sixpence during the war; besides this I have been baptized; and by the laws of the land no man has a right to sell me:' And I added, that I had heard a lawyer and others at different times tell my master so. They both then said that those people who told me so were not my friends; but I replied—it was very extraordinary that other people did not know the law as well as they. Upon this Captain Doran said I talked too much English; and if I did not behave myself well, and be quiet, he had a method on board to make me. I was too well convinced of his power over me to doubt what he said; and my former sufferings in the slaveship presenting themselves to my mind, the recollection of them made me shudder. However, before I retired I told them that as I could not get any right among men here I hoped I should hereafter in Heaven; and I immediately left the cabin, filled with resentment and sorrow. The only coat I had with me my master took away with him, and said if my prize-money had been 10,000£[3] he had a right to it all, and would have taken it. I had about nine guineas, which, during my long sea-faring life, I had scraped together from trifling perquisites[4] and little ventures; and I hid it that instant, lest my master should take

---

2. A prize is a captured warship or its cargo.
3. See n. 2, p. 50. Equiano's use of the lower-case l. for pound has been regularized by substituting the sign £ throughout.
4. Wages or tips.

that from me likewise, still hoping that by some means or other I should make my escape to the shore; and indeed some of my old shipmates told me not to despair, for they would get me back again; and that, as soon as they could get their pay, they would immediately come to Portsmouth to me, where this ship was going: but, alas! all my hopes were baffled,[5] and the hour of my deliverance was yet far off. My master, having soon concluded his bargain with the captain, came out of the cabin, and he and his people got into the boat and put off; I followed them with aching eyes as long as I could, and when they were out of sight I threw myself on the deck, while my heart was ready to burst with sorrow and anguish.

Chap. V.

The author's reflections on his situation—Is deceived by a promise of being delivered—His despair at sailing for the West Indies— Arrives at Montserrat, where he is sold to Mr. King—Various interesting instances of oppression, cruelty, and extortion, which the author saw practised upon the slaves in the West Indies during his captivity from the year 1763 to 1766—Address on it to the planters.

Thus, at the moment I expected all my toils to end, was I plunged, as I supposed, in a new slavery; in comparison of which all my service hitherto had been 'perfect freedom;' and whose horrors, always present to my mind, now rushed on it with tenfold aggravation. I wept very bitterly for some time: and began to think that I must have done something to displease the Lord, that he thus punished me so severely. This filled me with painful reflections on my past conduct; I recollected that on the morning of our arrival at Deptford I had rashly sworn that as soon as we reached London I would spend the day in rambling and sport. My conscience smote me for this unguarded expression: I felt that the Lord was able to disappoint me in all things, and immediately considered my present situation as a judgment of Heaven on account of my presumption in swearing: I therefore, with contrition of heart, acknowledged my transgression to God, and poured out my soul before him with unfeigned repentance, and with earnest supplications I besought him not to abandon me in my distress, nor cast me from his mercy for ever. In a little time my grief, spent with its own violence, began to subside; and after the first confusion of my thoughts was over I reflected with more calmness on my present condition: I considered that trials and disappointments are sometimes for our good, and I

5. Thwarted or dashed.

thought God might perhaps have permitted this in order to teach me wisdom and resignation; for he had hitherto shadowed me with the wings of his mercy, and by his invisible but powerful hand brought me the way I knew not. These reflections gave me a little comfort, and I rose at last from the deck with dejection and sorrow in my countenance, yet mixed with some faint hope that the Lord would appear for my deliverance.

Soon afterwards, as my new master was going ashore, he called me to him, and told me to behave myself well, and do the business of the ship the same as any of the rest of the boys, and that I should fare the better for it; but I made him no answer. I was then asked if I could swim, and I said, No. However I was made to go under the deck, and was well watched. The next tide the ship got under way, and soon after arrived at the Mother Bank, Portsmouth; where she waited a few days for some of the West India convoy. While I was here I tried every means I could devise amongst the people of the ship to get me a boat from the shore, as there was none suffered to come alongside of the ship; and their own, whenever it was used, was hoisted in again immediately. A sailor on board took a guinea from me on pretence of getting me a boat; and promised me, time after time, that it was hourly to come off. When he had the watch upon deck I watched also; and looked long enough, but all in vain; I could never see either the boat or my guinea again. And what I thought was still the worst of all, the fellow gave information, as I afterwards found, all the while to the mates, of my intention to go off, if I could in any way do it; but, rogue like, he never told them he had got a guinea from me to procure my escape. However, after we had sailed, and his trick was made known to the ship's crew, I had some satisfaction in seeing him detested and despised by them all for his behaviour to me. I was still in hopes that my old shipmates would not forget their promise to come for me to Portsmouth: and, indeed, at last, but not till the day before we sailed, some of them did come there, and sent me off some oranges, and other tokens of their regard. They also sent me word they would come off to me themselves the next day or the day after; and a lady also, who lived in Gosport, wrote to me that she would come and take me out of the ship at the same time. This lady had been once very intimate with my former master: I used to sell and take care of a great deal of property for her, in different ships; and in return she always shewed great friendship for me, and used to tell my master that she would take me away to live with her: but, unfortunately for me, a disagreement soon afterwards took place between them; and she was succeeded in my master's good graces by another lady, who appeared sole mistress of the Ætna, and mostly lodged on board. I was not so great a favourite with this lady as with the former; she had conceived a pique against me on some occasion when she was on board, and she did not fail to instigate my master to treat me in the manner he did.[1]

However, the next morning, the 30th of December, the wind being brisk and easterly, the Œolus frigate, which was to escort the convoy, made a signal for sailing. All the ships then got up their anchors; and, before any of my friends had an opportunity to come off to my relief, to my inexpressible anguish our ship had got under way. What tumultuous emotions agitated my soul when the convoy got under sail, and I a prisoner on board, now without hope! I kept my swimming eyes upon the land in a state of unutterable grief; not knowing what to do, and despairing how to help myself. While my mind was in this situation the fleet sailed on, and in one day's time I lost sight of the wished-for land. In the first expressions of my grief I reproached my fate, and wished I had never been born. I was ready to curse the tide that bore us, the gale that wafted my prison, and even the ship that conducted us; and I called on death to relieve me from the horrors I felt and dreaded, that I might be in that place

> Where slaves are free, and men oppress no more.
> Fool that I was, inur'd so long to pain,
> To trust to hope, or dream of joy again.
> . . . .
> Now dragg'd once more beyond the western main,
> To groan beneath some dastard planter's chain;
> Where my poor countrymen in bondage wait
> The long enfranchisement of ling'ring fate:
> Hard ling'ring fate! while, ere the dawn of day,
> Rous'd by the lash they go their cheerless way;
> And as their souls with shame and anguish burn,
> Salute with groans unwelcome morn's return,
> And, chiding ev'ry hour the slow-pac'd sun,
> Pursue their toils till all his race is run.
> No eye to mark their suff'rings with a tear;
> No friend to comfort, and no hope to cheer:
> Then, like the dull unpity'd brutes, repair
> To stalls as wretched, and as coarse a fare;
> Thank heaven one day of mis'ry was o'er,
> Then sink to sleep, and wish to wake no more.[2]

1. Thus was I sacrificed to the envy and resentment of this woman for knowing that the lady whom she had succeeded in my master's good graces designed to take me into her service; which, had I once got on shore, she would not have been able to prevent. She felt her pride alarmed at the superiority of her rival in being attended by a black servant: it was not less to prevent this than to be revenged on me, that she caused the captain to treat me thus cruelly [Equiano's note].
2. "The Dying Negro," a poem originally published in 1773. Perhaps it may not be deemed impertinent here to had [add], that this elegant and pathetic little poem was occasioned, as appears by the advertisement prefixed to it, by the following incident. "A black, who, a few days before add [had] ran away from his master, and got himself christened, with intent to marry a white woman his fellow-servant, being taken and sent on board a ship in the Thames,

The turbulence of my emotions however naturally gave way to calmer thoughts, and I soon perceived what fate had decreed no mortal on earth could prevent. The convoy sailed on without any accident, with a pleasant gale and smooth sea, for six weeks, till February, when one morning the Œolus ran down a brig, one of the convoy, and she instantly went down and was ingulfed in the dark recesses of the ocean. The convoy was immediately thrown into great confusion till it was day-light; and the Œolus was illumined with lights to prevent any farther mischief. On the 13th of February 1763, from the mast-head, we descried our destined island Montserrat;[3] and soon after I beheld those

> Regions of sorrow, doleful shades, where peace
> And rest can rarely dwell. Hope never comes
> That comes to all, but torture without end
> Still urges.[4]

At the sight of this land of bondage, a fresh horror ran through all my frame, and chilled me to the heart. My former slavery now rose in dreadful review to my mind, and displayed nothing but misery, stripes,[5] and chains; and, in the first paroxysm of my grief, I called upon God's thunder, and his avenging power, to direct the stroke of death to me, rather than permit me to become a slave, and be sold from lord to lord.

In this state of my mind our ship came to an anchor, and soon after discharged her cargo. I now knew what it was to work hard; I was made to help to unload and load the ship. And, to comfort me in my distress in that time, two of the sailors robbed me of all my money, and ran away from the ship. I had been so long used to an European climate that at first I felt the scorching West India sun very painful, while the dashing surf would toss the boat and the people in it frequently above high water mark. Sometimes our limbs were broken with this, or even attended with instant death, and I was day by day mangled and torn.

About the middle of May, when the ship was got ready to sail for England, I all the time believing that Fate's blackest clouds were gathering over my head, and expecting their bursting would mix me with the dead, Captain Doran sent for me ashore one morning, and I was told by the messenger that my fate was then determined. With fluttering steps and trembling heart I came to the captain, and found with him one Mr. Robert King, a quaker, and the first merchant in the place. The captain then told me my former master had sent me there to be sold; but that he had desired him to get me the best master

---

took an opportunity of shooting himself through the head" [Equiano's note]. See excerpt below (pp. 288–91) of Thomas Day and John Bicknell's poem, as well as Edwards's discussion on the different versions Equiano conflated, p. 327.
3. One of the Leeward Islands in the Lesser Antilles, West Indies.
4. From Milton, *Paradise Lost* 1:65–68.
5. Flogging.

he could, as he told him I was a very deserving boy, which Captain Doran said he found to be true: and if he were to stay in the West Indies he would be glad to keep me himself; but he could not venture to take me to London, for he was very sure that when I came there I would leave him. I at that instant burst out a crying, and begged much of him to take me to England with him, but all to no purpose. He told me he had got me the very best master in the whole island, with whom I should be as happy as if I were in England, and for that reason he chose to let him have me, though he could sell me to his own brother-in-law for a great deal more money than what he got from this gentleman. Mr. King, my new master, then made a reply, and said the reason he had bought me was on account of my good character; and, as he had not the least doubt of my good behaviour, I should be very well off with him. He also told me he did not live in the West Indies, but at Philadelphia, where he was going soon; and, as I understood something of the rules of arithmetic, when we got there he would put me to school, and fit me for a clerk. This conversation relieved my mind a little, and I left those gentlemen considerably more at ease in myself than when I came to them; and I was very grateful to Captain Doran, and even to my old master, for the character they had given me; a character which I afterwards found of infinite service to me. I went on board again, and took leave of all my shipmates; and the next day the ship sailed. When she weighed anchor I went to the waterside and looked at her with a very wishful and aching heart, and followed her with my eyes and tears until she was totally out of sight. I was so bowed down with grief that I could not hold up my head for many months; and if my new master had not been kind to me I believe I should have died under it at last. And indeed I soon found that he fully deserved the good character which Captain Doran had given me of him; for he possessed a most amiable disposition and temper, and was very charitable and humane. If any of his slaves behaved amiss he did not beat or use them ill, but parted with them. This made them afraid of disobliging him; and as he treated his slaves better than any other man on the island, so he was better and more faithfully served by them in return. By his kind treatment I did at last endeavour to compose myself; and with fortitude, though moneyless, determined to face whatever fate had decreed for me. Mr. King soon asked me what I could do; and at the same time said he did not mean to treat me as a common salve. I told him I knew something of seamanship, and could shave and dress hair pretty well; and I could refine wines, which I had learned on shipboard, where I had often done it; and that I could write, and understood arithmetic tolerably well as far as the Rule of Three.[6] He then asked me if I knew

6. See n. 7, p. 67.

any thing of gauging;[7] and, on my answering that I did not, he said one of his clerks should teach me to gauge.

Mr. King dealt in all manner of merchandize, and kept from one to six clerks. He loaded many vessels in a year; particularly to Philadelphia, where he was born, and was connected with a great mercantile house in that city. He had besides many vessels and droggers,[8] of different sizes, which used to go about the island; and others to collect rum, sugar, and other goods. I understood pulling and managing those boats very well; and this hard work, which was the first that he set me to, in the sugar seasons used to be my constant employment. I have rowed the boat, and slaved at the oars, from one hour to sixteen in the twenty-four; during which I had fifteen pence sterling[9] per day to live on, though sometimes only ten pence. However this was considerably more than was allowed to other slaves that used to work with me, and belonged to other gentlemen on the island: those poor souls had never more than nine pence per day, and seldom more than six pence, from their masters or owners, though they earned them three or four pisterines:[1] for it is a common practice in the West Indies for men to purchase slaves though they have not plantations themselves, in order to let them out to planters and merchants at so much a piece by the day, and they give what allowance they chuse out of this produce of their daily work to their slaves for subsistence; this allowance is often very scanty. My master often gave the owners of these slaves two and a half of these pieces per day, and found the poor fellows in victuals himself, because be thought their owners did not feed them well enough according to the work they did. The slaves used to like this very well; and, as they knew my master to be a man of feeling, they were always glad to work for him in preference to any other gentleman: some of whom, after they had been paid for these poor people's labours, would not give them their allowance out of it. Many times have I even seen these unfortunate wretches beaten for asking for their pay; and often severely flogged by their owners if they did not bring them their daily or weekly money exactly to the time; though the poor creatures were obliged to wait on the gentlemen they had worked for sometimes for more than half the day before they could get their pay; and this generally on Sundays, when they wanted the time for themselves. In particular, I knew a countryman of mine who once did not bring the weekly money directly that it was earned; and though he brought it the same day to his master, yet he was staked to the ground for this pretended negligence, and was just going to receive a hundred lashes, but for a gentleman who begged him off fifty. This poor man was very

7. Measuring.
8. Slow boats.
9. See n. 2, p. 50.
1. These pisterines are of the value of a shilling [Equiano's note].

industrious; and, by his frugality, had saved so much money by working on shipboard, that he had got a white man to buy him a boat, unknown to his master. Some time after he had this little estate the governor wanted a boat to bring his sugar from different parts of the island; and, knowing this to be a negro-man's boat, he seized upon it for himself, and would not pay the owner a farthing. The man on this went to his master, and complained to him of this act of the governor; but the only satisfaction he received was to be damned very heartily by his master, who asked him how dared any of his negroes to have a boat. If the justly-merited ruin of the governor's fortune could be any gratification to the poor man he had thus robbed, he was not without consolation. Extortion and rapine are poor providers; and some time after this the governor died in the King's Bench[2] in England, as I was told, in great poverty. The last war favoured this poor negro-man, and he found some means to escape from his Christian master: he came to England; where I saw him afterwards several times. Such treatment as this often drives these miserable wretches to despair, and they run away from their masters at the hazard of their lives. Many of them, in this place, unable to get their pay when they have earned it, and fearing to be flogged, as usual, if they return home without it, run away where they can for shelter, and a reward is often offered to bring them in dead or alive. My master used sometimes, in these cases, to agree with their owners, and to settle with them himself; and thereby he saved many of them a flogging.

Once, for a few days, I was let out to fit a vessel, and I had no victuals allowed me by either party; at last I told my master of this treatment, and he took me away from it. In many of the estates, on the different islands where I used to be sent for rum or sugar, they would not deliver it to me, or any other negro; he was therefore obliged to send a white man along with me to those places; and then he used to pay him from six to ten pisterines a day. From being thus employed, during the time I served Mr. King, in going about the different estates on the island, I had all the opportunity I could wish for to see the dreadful usage of the poor men; usage that reconciled me to my situation, and made me bless God for the hands into which I had fallen.

I had the good fortune to please my master in every department in which he employed me; and there was scarcely any part of his business, or household affairs, in which I was not occasionally engaged. I often supplied the place of a clerk, in receiving and delivering cargoes to the ships, in tending stores, and delivering goods: and, besides this, I used to shave and dress my master when convenient, and take care of his horse; and when it was necessary, which was very often, I worked likewise on board of different vessels of his. By these means I became very

2. Prison for debtors in London's Southwark.

useful to my master; and saved him, as he used to acknowledge, above a hundred pounds a year. Nor did he scruple to say I was of more advantage to him than any of his clerks; though their usual wages in the West Indies are from sixty to a hundred pounds current a year.[3]

I have sometimes heard it asserted that a negro cannot earn his master the first cost; but nothing can be further from the truth. I suppose nine tenths of the mechanics throughout the West Indies are negro slaves; and I well know the coopers[4] among them earn two dollars a day; the carpenters the same, and oftentimes more; as also the masons, smiths, and fishermen, &c. and I have known many slaves whose masters would not take a thousand pounds current for them. But surely this assertion refutes itself; for, if it be true, why do the planters and merchants pay such a price for slaves? And, above all, why do those who make this assertion exclaim the most loudly against the abolition of the slave trade? So much are men blinded, and to such inconsistent arguments are they driven by mistaken interest! I grant, indeed, that slaves are some times, by half-feeding, half-clothing, over-working and stripes, reduced so low, that they are turned out as unfit for service, and left to perish in the woods, or expire on a dunghill.

My master was several times offered by different gentlemen one hundred guineas for me; but he always told them he would not sell me, to my great joy: and I used to double my diligence and care for fear of getting into the hands of those men who did not allow a valuable slave the common support of life. Many of them even used to find fault with my master for feeding his slaves so well as he did; although I often went hungry, and an Englishman might think my fare very indifferent; but he used to tell them he always would do it, because the slaves thereby looked better and did more work.

While I was thus employed by my master I was often a witness to cruelties of every kind, which were exercised on my unhappy fellow slaves. I used frequently to have different cargoes of new negroes in my care for sale; and it was almost a constant practice with our clerks, and other whites, to commit violent depredations on the chastity of the female slaves; and these I was, though with reluctance, obliged to submit to at all times, being unable to help them. When we have had some of these slaves on board my master's vessels to carry them to other islands, or to America, I have known our mates to commit these acts most shamefully, to the disgrace, not of Christians only, but of men. I have even known them gratify their brutal passion with females not ten years old; and these abominations some of them practised to such scandalous excess, that one of our captains discharged the mate and others on that account. And yet in Montserrat I have seen a negro man staked to the ground, and cut most shockingly, and then his ears

3. See n. 2, p. 50.
4. Barrel makers.

cut off bit by bit, because he had been connected with a white woman who was a common prostitute: as if it were no crime in the whites to rob an innocent African girl of her virtue; but most heinous in a black man only to gratify a passion of nature, where the temptation was offered by one of a different colour, though the most abandoned woman of her species. Another negro man was half hanged, and then burnt, for attempting to poison a cruel overseer. Thus by repeated cruelties are the wretched first urged to despair, and then murdered, because they still retain so much of human nature about them as to wish to put an end to their misery, and retaliate on their tyrants! These overseers are indeed for the most part persons of the worst character of any denomination of men in the West Indies. Unfortunately, many humane gentlemen, by not residing on their estates, are obliged to leave the management of them in the hands of these human butchers, who cut and mangle the slaves in a shocking manner on the most trifling occasions, and altogether treat them in every respect like brutes: They pay no regard to the situation of pregnant women, nor the least attention to the lodging of the field negroes. Their huts, which ought to be well covered, and the place dry where they take their little repose, are often open sheds, built in damp places; so that, when the poor creatures return tired from the toils of the field, they contract many disorders, from being exposed to the damp air in this uncomfortable state, while they are heated, and their pores are open. This neglect certainly conspires with many others to cause a decrease in the births as well as in the lives of the grown negroes. I can quote many instances of gentlemen who reside on their estates in the West Indies, and then the scene is quite changed; the negroes are treated with lenity[5] and proper care, by which their lives are prolonged, and their masters are profited. To the honour of humanity, I knew several gentlemen who managed their estates in this manner; and they found that benevolence was their true interest. And, among many I could mention in several of the islands, I knew one in Montserrat[6] whose slaves looked remarkably well, and never needed any fresh supplies of negroes; and there are many other estates, especially in Barbadoes, which, from such judicious treatment, need no fresh stock of negroes at any time. I have the honour of knowing a most worthy and humane gentleman, who is a native of Barbadoes, and has estates there.[7] This gentleman has written a treatise on the usage of his own slaves. He allows them two hours for refreshment at mid-day; and many other indulgencies and comforts, particularly in their lying;[8] and besides this, he raises more

5. Leniency.
6. Mr. Dubury, and many others, Montserrat [Equiano's note].
7. Sir. Philip Gibbes, Baronet, Barbadoes [Equiano's note].
8. Confinement after childbirth.

provisions on his estate than they can destroy; so that by these attentions he saves the lives of his negroes, and keeps them healthy, and
as happy as the condition of slavery can admit. I myself, as shall appear
in the sequel, managed an estate, where, by those attentions, the
negroes were uncommonly cheerful and healthy, and did more work
by half than by the common mode of treatment they usually do. For
want, therefore, of such care and attention to the poor negroes, and
otherwise oppressed as they are, it is no wonder that the decrease
should require 20,000 new negroes annually to fill up the vacant places
of the dead.

Even in Barbadoes, notwithstanding those humane exceptions
which I have mentioned, and others I am acquainted with, which justly
make it quoted as a place where slaves meet with the best treatment,
and need fewest recruits of any in the West Indies, yet this island
requires 1000 negroes annually to keep up the original stock, which is
only 80,000. So that the whole term of a negro's life may be said to be
there but sixteen years![9] And yet the climate here is in every respect
the same as that from which they are taken, except in being more
wholesome. Do the British colonies decrease in this manner? And yet
what a prodigious difference is there between an English and West
India climate?

While I was in Montserrat I knew a negro man, named Emanuel
Sankey, who endeavoured to escape from his miserable bondage, by
concealing himself on board of a London ship: but fate did not favour
the poor oppressed man; for, being discovered when the vessel was
under sail, he was delivered up again to his master. This *Christian
master* immediately pinned the wretch down to the ground at each
wrist and ancle, and then took some sticks of sealing wax, and lighted
them, and droped it all over his back. There was another master who
was noted for cruelty; and I believe he had not a slave but what had
been cut, and had pieces fairly taken out of the flesh: and, after they
had been punished thus, he used to make them get into a long wooden
box or case he had for that purpose, in which he shut them up during
pleasure.[1] It was just about the height and breadth of a man; and the
poor wretches had no room, when in the case, to move.

It was very common in several of the islands, particularly in St.
Kitt's,[2] for the slaves to be branded with the initial letters of their
master's name; and a load of heavy iron hooks hung about their necks.
Indeed on the most trifling occasions they were loaded with chains;
and often instruments of torture were added. The iron muzzle, thumbscrews, &c. are so well known, as not to need a description, and were

9. Benezet's Account of Guinea, p. 16 [Equiano's note]. See excerpt below, pp. 250–53.
1. As long as he pleased.
2. One of the Leeward Islands.

sometimes applied for the slightest faults. I have seen a negro beaten till some of his bones were broken, for even letting a pot boil over.[3] Is it surprising that usage like this should drive the poor creatures to despair, and make them seek a refuge in death from those evils which render their lives intolerable—while,

> With shudd'ring horror pale, and eyes aghast,
> They view their lamentable lot, and find
> No rest![4]

This they frequently do. A negro-man on board a vessel of my master, while I belonged to her, having been put in irons for some trifling misdemeanor, and kept in that state for some days, being weary of life, took an opportunity of jumping overboard into the sea; however, he was picked up without being drowned. Another, whose life was also a burden to him, resolved to starve himself to death, and refused to eat any victuals; this procured him a severe flogging: and he also, on the first occasion which offered, jumped overboard at Charles Town, but was saved.

Nor is there any greater regard shewn to the little property than there is to the persons and lives of the negroes. I have already related an instance or two of particular oppression out of many which I have witnessed; but the following is frequent in all the islands. The wretched field-slaves, after toiling all the day for an unfeeling owner, who gives them but little victuals, steal sometimes a few moments from rest or refreshment to gather some small portion of grass, according as their time will admit. This they commonly tie up in a parcel; (either a bit, worth six pence; or half a bit's-worth) and bring it to town, or to the market, to sell. Nothing is more common than for the white people on this occasion to take the grass from them without paying for it; and not only so, but too often also, to my knowledge, our clerks, and many others, at the same time have committed acts of violence on the poor, wretched, and helpless females; whom I have seen for hours stand crying to no purpose, and get no redress or pay of any kind. Is not this one common and crying sin enough to bring down God's judgment on the islands? He tells us the oppressor and the oppressed are both in his hands; and if these are not the poor, the broken-hearted, the blind, the captive, the bruised, which our Saviour speaks of, who are they?[5]

---

3. pot boil over.] Beginning in the fifth edition (1792), this was followed by: "It is not uncommon, after a flogging, to make slaves go on their knees, and thank their owners, and pray, or rather say, God bless them. I have often asked many of the men slaves (who used to go several miles to their wives, and late in the night, after having been wearied with a hard day's labour) why they went so far for wives, and why they did not take them of their own master's negro women, and particularly those who lived together as household slaves? Their answers have ever been—'Because when the master or mistress choose to punish the women, they make the husbands flog their own wives, and that they could not bear to do.' "
4. From Milton, *Paradise Lost* 2.661–18.
5. Luke 4.8.

One of these depredators once, in St. Eustatia,[6] came on board of our vessel, and bought some fowls and pigs of me; and a whole day after his departure with the things he returned again and wanted his money back: I refused to give it; and, not seeing my captain on board, he began the common pranks with me; and swore he would even break open my chest and take my money. I therefore expected, as my captain was absent, that he would be as good as his word: and he was just proceeding to strike me, when fortunately a British seaman on board, whose heart had not been debauched by a West India climate, interposed and prevented him. But had the cruel man struck me I certainly should have defended myself at the hazard of my life; for what is life to a man thus oppressed? He went away, however, swearing; and threatened that whenever he caught me on shore he would shoot me, and pay for me afterwards.

The small account in which the life of a negro is held in the West Indies is so universally known, that it might seem impertinent to quote the following extract, if some people had not been hardy enough of late to assert that negroes are on the same footing in that respect as Europeans. By the 329th Act, page 125, of the Assembly of Barbadoes, it is enacted 'That if any negro, or other slave, under punishment by his master, or his order, for running away, or any other crime or misdemeanor towards his said master, unfortunately shall suffer in life or member, no person whatsoever shall be liable to a fine; but if any man shall out of *wantonness, or only of bloody-mindedness, or cruel intention, wilfully kill a negro, or other slave, of his own, he shall pay into the public treasury fifteen pounds sterling.*' And it is the same in most, if not all, of the West India islands. Is not this one of the many acts of the islands which call loudly for redress? And do not the assembly which enacted it deserve the appellation of savages and brutes rather than of Christians and men? It is an act at once unmerciful, unjust, and unwise; which for cruelty would disgrace an assembly of those who are called barbarians; and for its injustice and *insanity* would shock the morality and common sense of a Samaide or a Hottentot.[7]

Shocking as this and many more acts of the bloody West India code at first view appear, how is the iniquity of it heightened when we consider to whom it may be extended! Mr. James Tobin, a zealous labourer in the vineyard of slavery, gives an account of a French planter of his acquaintance, in the island of Martinico,[8] who shewed him many mulattoes working in the fields like beasts of burden; and he told Mr. Tobin these were all the produce of his own loins! And I myself have known similar instances. Pray, reader, are these sons and daughters of

6. Or Sint Eustatius. One of the Leeward Islands in the Lesser Antilles, West Indies.
7. Hottentots come from South Africa; Samoyeds are Mongolians.
8. Present-day Martinique. *James Tobin:* an English defender of slavery who attacked abolitionist James Ramsay (1733–1789). See excerpts below, from Tobin's *Cursory Remarks* (pp. 195–96) and Equiano's letter to Tobin in defense of his friend Ramsay (pp. 196–99).

the French planter less his children by being begotten on a black woman? And what must be the virtue of those legislators, and the feelings of those fathers, who estimate the lives of their sons, however begotten, at no more than fifteen pounds; though they should be murdered, as the act says, *out of wantonness and bloody-mindedness!* But is not the slave trade entirely a war with the heart of man? And surely that which is begun by breaking down the barriers of virtue involves in its continuance destruction to every principle, and buries all sentiments in ruin!

I have often seen slaves, particularly those who were meagre, in different islands, put into scales and weighed; and then sold from three pence to six pence or nine pence a pound. My master, however, whose humanity was shocked at this mode, used to sell such by the lump. And at or after a sale it was not uncommon to see negroes taken from their wives, wives taken from their husbands, and children from their parents, and sent off to other islands, and wherever else their merciless lords chose; and probably never more during life to see each other! Oftentimes my heart has bled at these partings; when the friends of the departed have been at the water side, and, with sighs and tears, have kept their eyes fixed on the vessel till it went out of sight.

A poor Creole negro I knew well, who, after having been often thus transported from island to island, at last resided in Montserrat. This man used to tell me many melancholy tales of himself. Generally, after he had done working for his master, he used to employ his few leisure moments to go a fishing. When he had caught any fish, his master would frequently take them from him without paying him; and at other times some other white people would serve him in the same manner. One day he said to me, very movingly, 'Sometimes when a white man take away my fish I go to my maser, and he get me my right; and when my maser by strength take away my fishes, what me must do? I can't go to any body to be righted: then' said the poor man, looking up above 'I must look up to God Mighty in the top for right.' This artless tale moved me much, and I could not help feeling the just cause Moses had in redressing his brother against the Egyptian.[9] I exhorted the man to look up still to the God on the top, since there was no redress below. Though I little thought then that I myself should more than once experience such imposition, and read the same exhortation hereafter, in my own transactions in the islands; and that even this poor man and I should some time after suffer together in the same manner, as shall be related hereafter.

Nor was such usage as this confined to particular places or individ-

9. See Exodus 2.11–12: "And it came to pass in those days, when Moses was grown, that he went out unto his brethren, and looked on their burdens: and he spied an Egyptian smiting an Hebrew, one of his brethren. And he looked this way and that way, and when he saw that there was no man, he slew the Egyptian, and hid him in the sand."

uals; for, in all the different islands in which I have been (and I have visited no less than fifteen) the treatment of the slaves was nearly the same; so nearly indeed, that the history of an island, or even a plantation, with a few such exceptions as I have mentioned, might serve for a history of the whole. Such a tendency has the slave-trade to debauch men's minds, and harden them to every feeling of humanity! For I will not suppose that the dealers in slaves are born worse than other men—No; it is the fatality of this mistaken avarice, that it corrupts the milk of human kindness and turns it into gall.[1] And, had the pursuits of those men been different, they might have been as generous, as tender-hearted and just, as they are unfeeling, rapacious and cruel. Surely this traffic cannot be good, which spreads like a pestilence, and taints what it touches! which violates that first natural right of mankind, equality and independency, and gives one man a dominion over his fellows which God could never intend! For it raises the owner to a state as far above man as it depresses the slave below it; and, with all the presumption of human pride, sets a distinction between them, immeasurable in extent, and endless in duration! Yet how mistaken is the avarice even of the planters? Are slaves more useful by being thus humbled to the condition of brutes, than they would be if suffered to enjoy the privileges of men? The freedom which diffuses health and prosperity throughout Britain answers you—No. When you make men slaves you deprive them of half their virtue, you set them in your own conduct an example of fraud, rapine, and cruelty, and compel them to live with you in a state of war; and yet you complain that they are not honest or faithful! Your stupify them with stripes, and think it necessary to keep them in a state of ignorance; and yet you assert that they are incapable of learning; that their minds are such a barren soil or moor, that culture would be lost on them; and that they come from a climate, where nature, though prodigal of her bounties in a degree unknown to yourselves, has left man alone scant and unfinished, and incapable of enjoying the treasures she has poured out for him!—An assertion at once impious and absurd. Why do you use those instruments of torture? Are they fit to be applied by one rational being to another? And are ye not struck with shame and mortification, to see the partakers of your nature reduced so low? But, above all, are there no dangers attending this mode of treatment? Are you not hourly in dread of an insurrection? Nor would it be surprising: for when

> ————No peace is given
> To us enslav'd, but custody severe;
> And stripes and arbitrary punishment
> Inflicted—What peace can we return?
> But to our power, hostility and hate;

1. See Shakespeare, *Macbeth* I.v.48.

Untam'd reluctance, and revenge, though slow.
Yet ever plotting how the conqueror least
May reap his conquest, and may least rejoice
In doing what we most in suffering feel.[2]

But by changing your conduct, and treating your slaves as men, every
cause of fear would be banished. They would be faithful, honest, intelligent and vigorous; and peace, prosperity, and happiness, would attend
you.

Chap. VI

*Some account of Brimstone-Hill in Montserrat—Favourable
change in the author's situation—He commences merchant with
three pence—His various success in dealing in the different
islands, and America, and the impositions he meets with in his
transactions with Europeans—A curious imposition on human
nature—Danger of the surfs in the West Indies—Remarkable
instance of kidnapping a free mulatto—The author is nearly
murdered by Doctor Perkins in Savannah.*

In the preceding chapter I have set before the reader a few of those
many instances of oppression, extortion, and cruelty, which I have been
a witness to in the West Indies: but, were I to enumerate them all,
the catalogue would be tedious and disgusting. The punishments of
the slaves on every trifling occasion are so frequent, and so well known,
together with the different instruments with which they are tortured,
that it cannot any longer afford novelty to recite them; and they are
too shocking to yield delight either to the writer or the reader. I shall
therefore hereafter only mention such as incidentally befel myself in
the course of my adventures.

In the variety of departments in which I was employed by my master,
I had an opportunity of seeing many curious scenes in different islands;
but, above all, I was struck with a celebrated curiosity called Brimstone-
Hill, which is a high and steep mountain, some few miles from the
town of Plymouth in Montserrat. I had often heard of some wonders
that were to be seen on this hill, and I went once with some white and
black people to visit it. When we arrived at the top, I saw under different cliffs great flakes of brimstone, occasioned by the steams of
various little ponds, which were then boiling naturally in the earth.
Some of these ponds were as white as milk, some quite blue, and many
others of different colours. I had taken some potatoes with me, and I
put them into different ponds, and in a few minutes they were well
boiled. I tasted some of them, but they were very sulphurous; and the

2. From Milton, *Paradise Lost* 2.232–40.

silver shoe buckles, and all the other things of that metal we had among us, were, in a little time, turned as black as lead.

Some time in the year 1763 kind Providence seemed to appear rather more favourable to me. One of my master's vessels, a Bermudas sloop, about sixty tons, was commanded by one Captain Thomas Farmer, an Englishman, a very alert and active man, who gained my master a great deal of money by his good management in carrying passengers from one island to another; but very often his sailors used to get drunk and run away from the vessel, which hindered him in his business very much. This man had taken a liking to me; and many different times begged of my master to let me go a trip with him as a sailor; but he would tell him he could not spare me, though the vessel sometimes could not go for want of hands, for sailors were generally very scarce in the island. However, at last, from necessity or force, my master was prevailed on, though very reluctantly, to let me go with this captain; but he gave great charge to him to take care that I did not run away, for if I did he would make him pay for me. This being the case, the captain had for some time a sharp eye upon me whenever the vessel anchored; and as soon as she returned I was sent for on shore again. Thus was I slaving as it were for life, sometimes at one thing, and sometimes at another; so that the captain and I were nearly the most useful men in my master's employment. I also became so useful to the captain on shipboard, that many times, when he used to ask for me to go with him, though it should be but for twenty-four hours, to some of the islands near us, my master would answer he could not spare me, at which the captain would swear, and would not go the trip; and tell my master I was better to him on board than any three white men he had; for they used to behave ill in many respects, particularly in getting drunk; and then they frequently got the boat stove,[1] so as to hinder the vessel from coming back as soon as she might have done. This my master knew very well; and at last, by the captain's constant entreaties, after I had been several times with him, one day, to my great joy, my master told me the captain would not let him rest, and asked me whether I would go aboard as a sailor, or stay on shore and mind the stores, for he could not bear any longer to be plagued in this manner. I was very happy at this proposal, for I immediately thought I might in time stand some chance by being on board to get a little money, or possibly make my escape if I should be used ill: I also expected to get better food, and in greater abundance; for I had felt much hunger oftentimes, though my master treated his slaves, as I have observed, uncommonly well. I therefore, without hesitation, answered him, that I would go and be a sailor if he pleased. Accordingly I was ordered on board directly. Nevertheless, between the vessel and the shore, when

---

1. Broke a hole in the boat; got the boat crushed inward.

she was in port, I had little or no rest, as my master always wished to have me along with him. Indeed he was a very pleasant gentleman, and but for my expectations on shipboard I should not have thought of leaving him. But the captain liked me also very much, and I was entirely his right-hand man. I did all I could to deserve his favour, and in return I received better treatment from him than any other I believe ever met with in the West Indies in my situation.

After I had been sailing for some time with this captain, at length I endeavoured to try my luck and commence merchant. I had but a very small capital to begin with; for one single half bit,[2] which is equal to three pence in England, made up my whole stock. However I trusted to the Lord to be with me; and at one of our trips to St. Eustatia, a Dutch island, I bought a glass tumbler with my half bit, and when I came to Montserrat I sold it for a bit, or sixpence. Luckily we made several successive trips to St. Eustatia (which was a general mart for the West Indies, about twenty leagues from Montserrat); and in our next, finding my tumbler so profitable, with this one bit I bought two tumblers more; and when I came back I sold them for two bits, equal to a shilling sterling. When we went again I bought with these two bits four more of these glasses, which I sold for four bits on our return to Montserrat: and in our next voyage to St. Eustatia I bought two glasses with one bit, and with the other three I bought a jug of Geneva,[3] nearly about three pints in measure. When we came to Montserrat I sold the gin for eight bits, and the tumblers for two, so that my capital now amounted in all to a dollar, well husbanded[4] and acquired in the space of a month or six weeks, when I blessed the Lord that I was so rich. As we sailed to different islands, I laid this money out in various things occasionally, and it used to turn out to very good account, especially when we went to Guadaloupe, Grenada, and the rest of the French islands. Thus was I going all about the islands upwards of four years, and ever trading as I went, during which I experienced many instances of ill usage, and have seen many injuries done to other negroes in our dealings with Europeans: and, amidst our recreations, when we have been dancing and merry-making, they, without cause, have molested and insulted us. Indeed I was more than once obliged to look up to God on high, as I had advised the poor fisherman some time before. And I had not been long trading for myself in the manner I have related above, when I experienced the like trial in company with him as follows: This man being used to the water, was upon an emergency put on board of us by his master to work as another hand, on a voyage to Santa Cruz;[5] and at our sailing he had brought his little all for a ven-

2. Small West Indian silver coin.
3. Gin.
4. Managed.
5. Or St. Croix, then Danish Antilles, now U.S. Virgin Islands.

ture, which consisted of six bits' worth of limes and oranges in a bag; I had also my whole stock, which was about twelve bits' worth of the same kind of goods, separate in two bags; for we had heard these fruits sold well in that island. When we came there, in some little convenient time he and I went ashore with our fruits to sell them; but we had scarcely landed when we were met by two white men, who presently took our three bags from us. We could not at first guess what they meant to do; and for some time we thought they were jesting with us; but they too soon let us know otherwise, for they took our ventures immediately to a house hard by, and adjoining the fort, while we followed all the way begging of them to give us our fruits, but in vain. They not only refused to return them, but swore at us, and threatened if we did not immediately depart they would flog us well. We told them these three bags were all we were worth in the world, and that we brought them with us to sell when we came from Montserrat, and shewed them the vessel. But this was rather against us, as they now saw we were strangers as well as slaves. They still therefore swore, and desired us to be gone, and even took sticks to beat us; while we, seeing they meant what they said, went off in the greatest confusion and despair. Thus, in the very minute of gaining more by three times than I ever did by any venture in my life before, was I deprived of every farthing I was worth. An insupportable misfortune! but how to help ourselves we knew not. In our consternation we went to the commanding officer of the fort and told him how we had been served by some of his people; but we obtained not the least redress: he answered our complaints only by a volley of imprecations against us, and immediately took a horse-whip, in order to chastise us, so that we were obliged to turn out much faster than we came in. I now, in the agony of distress and indignation, wished that the ire of God in his forked lightning might transfix these cruel oppressors among the dead. Still however we persevered; went back again to the house, and begged and besought them again and again for our fruits, till at last some other people that were in the house asked if we would be contented if they kept one bag and gave us the other two. We, seeing no remedy whatever, consented to this; and they, observing one bag to have both kinds of fruit in it, which belonged to my companion, kept that; and the other two, which were mine, they gave us back. As soon as I got them, I ran as fast as I could, and got the first negro man I could to help me off; my companion, however, stayed a little longer to plead; he told them the bag they had was his, and likewise all that he was worth in the world; but this was of no avail, and he was obliged to return without it. The poor old man, wringing his hands, cried bitterly for his loss; and, indeed, he then did look up to God on high, which so moved me with pity for him, that I gave him nearly one third of my fruits. We then proceeded to the markets to sell them; and Providence was more favourable to us than we could have expected, for we sold our fruits uncommonly well; I got for mine about thirty-seven bits. Such a surprising reverse of fortune in so short a space of time seemed like a dream to me, and proved no small encouragement for me to trust the Lord in any situation. My captain afterwards frequently used to take my part, and get me my right, when I have been plundered or used ill by these tender Christian depredators; among whom I have shuddered to observe the unceasing blasphemous execrations which are wantonly thrown out by persons of all ages and conditions, not only without occasion, but even as if they were indulgences and pleasure.

At one of our trips to St. Kitt's I had eleven bits of my own; and my friendly captain lent me five bits more, with which I bought a Bible. I was very glad to get this book, which I scarcely could meet with any where. I think there was none sold in Montserrat; and, much to my grief, from being forced out of the Ætna in the manner I have related, my Bible, and the Guide to the Indians,[6] the two books I loved above all others, were left behind.

While I was in this place, St. Kitt's, a very curious imposition on human nature took place:—A white man wanted to marry in the church a free black woman that had land and slaves in Montserrat: but the clergyman told him it was against the law of the place to marry a white and a black in the church. The man then asked to be married on the water, to which the parson consented, and the two lovers went in one boat, and the parson and clerk in another, and thus the ceremony was performed. After this the loving pair came on board our vessel, and my captain treated them extremely well, and brought them safe to Montserrat.

The reader cannot but judge of the irksomeness of this situation to a mind like mine, in being daily exposed to new hardships and impositions, after having seen many better days, and having been as it were in a state of freedom and plenty; added to which, every part of the world I had hitherto been in seemed to me a paradise in comparison of the West Indies. My mind was therefore hourly replete with inventions and thoughts of being freed, and, if possible, by honest and honourable means; for I always remembered the old adage; and I trust it has ever been my ruling principle, that honesty is the best policy; and likewise that other golden precept—to do unto all men as I would they should do unto me. However, as I was from early years a predestinarian, I thought whatever fate had determined must ever come to pass; and therefore, if ever it were my lot to be freed nothing could prevent me, although I should at present see no means or hope to obtain my freedom; on the other hand, if it were my fate not to be freed I never should be so, and all my endeavours for that purpose would be fruitless.

6. See n. 1, p. 57.

In the midst of these thoughts I therefore looked up with prayers anxiously to God for my liberty; and at the same time I used every honest means, and endeavoured all that was possible on my part to obtain it. In process of time I became master of a few pounds, and in a fair way of making more, which my friendly captain knew very well; this occasioned him sometimes to take liberties with me: but whenever he treated me waspishly I used plainly to tell him my mind, and that I would die before I would be imposed on as other negroes were, and that to me life had lost its relish when liberty was gone. This I said although I foresaw my then well-being or future hopes of freedom (humanly speaking) depended on this man. However, as he could not bear the thoughts of my not sailing with him, he always became mild on my threats. I therefore continued with him; and, from my great attention to his orders and his business, I gained him credit, and through his kindness to me I at last procured my liberty. While I thus went on, filled with the thoughts of freedom, and resisting oppression as well as I was able, my life hung daily in suspense, particularly in the surfs I have formerly mentioned, as I could not swim. These are extremely violent throughout the West Indies, and I was ever exposed to their howling rage and devouring fury in all the islands. I have seen them strike and toss a boat right up an [on] end, and maim several on board. Once in the Grenada islands, when I and about eight others were pulling a large boat with two puncheons[7] of water in it, a surf struck us, and drove the boat and all in it about half a stone's throw, among some trees, and above the high water mark. We were obliged to get all the assistance we could from the nearest estate to mend the boat, and launch it into the water again. At Montserrat one night, in pressing hard to get off the shore on board, the punt[8] was overset with us four times; the first time I was very near being drowned; however the jacket I had on kept me up above water a little space of time, while I called on a man near me who was a good swimmer, and told him I could not swim; he then made haste to me, and, just as I was sinking, he caught hold of me, and brought me to sounding,[9] and then he went and brought the punt also. As soon as we had turned the water out of her, lest we should be used ill for being absent, we attempted again three times more, and as often the horrid surfs served us as at first; but at last, the fifth time we attempted, we gained our point, at the imminent hazard of our lives. One day also, at Old Road in Montserrat, our captain, and three men besides myself, were going in a large canoe in quest of rum and sugar, when a single surf tossed the canoe an amazing distance from the water, and some of us even a stone's throw from each other: most of us were very much bruised; so that I and many

7. Large casks.
8. Flat-bottomed pontoon boat.
9. I.e., Where one could stand.

more often said, and really thought, that there was not such another place under the heavens as this. I longed therefore much to leave it, and daily wished to see my master's promise performed of going to Philadelphia. While we lay in this place a very cruel thing happened on board of our sloop which filled me with horror; though I found afterwards such practices were frequent. There was a very clever and decent free young mulatto-man who sailed a long time with us: he had a free woman for his wife, by whom he had a child; and she was then living on shore, and all very happy. Our captain and mate, and other people on board, and several elsewhere, even the natives of Bermudas, all knew this young man from a child that he was always free, and no one had ever claimed him as their property: however, as might too often overcomes right in these parts, it happened that a Bermudas captain, whose vessel lay there for a few days in the road, came on board of us, and seeing the mulatto-man, whose name was Joseph Clipson, he told him he was not free, and that he had orders from his master to bring him to Bermudas. The poor man could not believe the captain to be in earnest; but he was very soon undeceived, his men laying violent hands on him: and although he shewed a certificate of his being born free in St. Kitt's, and most people on board knew that he served his time[1] to boat-building, and always passed for a free man, yet he was taken forcibly out of our vessel. He then asked to be carried ashore before the secretary or magistrates, and these infernal invaders of human rights promised him he should; but, instead of that, they carried him on board of the other vessel: and the next day, without giving the poor man any hearing on shore, or suffering him even to see his wife or child, he was carried away, and probably doomed never more in this world to see them again. Nor was this the only instance of this kind of barbarity I was a witness to. I have since often seen in Jamaica and other islands free men, whom I have known in America, thus villainously trepanned and held in bondage. I have heard of two similar practices even in Philadelphia: and were it not for the benevolence of the quakers in that city many of the sable race, who now breathe the air of liberty, would, I believe, be groaning indeed under some planter's chains. These things opened my mind to a new scene of horror to which I had been before a stranger. Hitherto I had thought only slavery dreadful; but the state of a free negro appeared to me now equally so at least, and in some respects even worse, for they live in constant alarm for their liberty; and even this is but nominal, for they are universally insulted and plundered without the possibility of redress; for such is the equity of of the West Indian laws, that no free negro's evidence will be admitted in their courts of justice. In this situation is it surprising that slaves, when mildly treated, should prefer even the misery

---

1. Was apprenticed.

of slavery to such a mockery of freedom? I was now completely disgusted with the West Indies, and thought I never should be entirely free until I had left them.

> With thoughts like these my anxious boding mind
> Recall'd those pleasing scenes I left behind;
> Scenes where fair Liberty in bright array
> Makes darkness bright, and e'en illumines day;
> Where nor complexion, wealth, or station, can
> Protect the wretch who makes a slave of man.[2]

I determined to make every exertion to obtain my freedom, and to return to Old England. For this purpose I thought a knowledge of navigation might be of use to me; for, though I did not intend to run away unless I should be ill used, yet, in such a case, if I understood navigation, I might attempt my escape in our sloop, which was one of the swiftest sailing vessels in the West Indies, and I could be at no loss for hands to join me: and if I should make this attempt, I had intended to have gone for England; but this, as I said, was only to be in the event of my meeting with any ill usage. I therefore employed the mate of our vessels to teach me navigation, for which I agreed to give him twenty-four dollars, and actually paid him part of the money down; though when the captain, some time after, came to know that the mate was to have such a sum for teaching me, he rebuked him, and said it was a shame for him to take any money from me. However, my progress in this useful art was much retarded by the constancy of our work. Had I wished to run away I did not want opportunities, which frequently presented themselves; and particularly at one time, soon after this. When we were at the island of Gaurdeloupe[3] there was a large fleet of merchantmen bound for Old France; and, seamen then being very scarce, they gave from fifteen to twenty pounds a man for the run. Our mate, and all the white sailors, left our vessels on this account, and went on board of the French ships. They would have had me also to go with them, for they regarded me; and they swore to protect me, if I would go: and, as the fleet was to sail the next day, I really believe I could have got safe to Europe at that time. However, as my master was kind, I would not attempt to leave him; and, remembering the old maxim, that 'honesty is the best policy,' I suffered them to go without me. Indeed my captain was much afraid of my leaving him and the vessel at that time, as I had so fair an opportunity: but, I thank God, this fidelity of mine turned out much to my advantage hereafter, when I did not in the least think of it; and made me so much in favour with the captain, that he used now and then to teach me some parts of navigation himself: but some of our passengers, and others, seeing this,

2. Unidentified verse.
3. Or Guadeloupe. One of the Leeward Islands.

found much fault with him for it, saying it was a very dangerous thing to let a negro know navigation; thus I was hindered again in my pursuits. About the latter end of the year 1764 my master bought a larger sloop, called the Providence, about seventy or eighty tons, of which my captain had the command. I went with him into this vessel, and we took a load of new slaves for Georgia and Charles Town. My master now left me entirely to the captain, though he still wished for me to be with him; but I, who always much wished to lose sight of the West Indies, was not a little rejoiced at the thoughts of seeing any other country. Therefore, relying on the goodness of my captain, I got ready all the little venture I could; and, when the vessel was ready, we sailed, to my great joy. When we got to our destined places, Georgia and Charles Town, I expected I should have an opportunity of selling my little property to advantage: but here, particularly in Charles Town, I met with buyers, white men, who imposed on me as in other places. Notwithstanding, I was resolved to have fortitude; thinking no lot or trial is too hard when kind Heaven is the rewarder. We soon got loaded again, and returned to Montserrat; and there, amongst the rest of the islands, I sold my goods well; and in this manner I continued trading during the year 1764; meeting with various scenes of imposition, as usual. After this, my master fitted out his vessel for Philadelphia, in the year 1765; and during the time we were loading her, and getting ready for the voyage, I worked with redoubled alacrity, from the hope of getting money enough by these voyages to buy my freedom in time, if it should please God; and also to see the town of Philadelphia, which I had heard a great deal about for some years past; besides which, I had always longed to prove[4] my master's promise the first day I came to him. In the midst of these elevated ideas, and while I was about getting my little merchandize in readiness, one Sunday my master sent for me to his house. When I came there I found him and the captain together; and, on my going in, I was struck with astonishment at his telling me he heard that I meant to run away from him when I got to Philadelphia: 'And therefore,' said he, 'I must sell you again: you cost me a great deal of money, no less than forty pounds sterling; and it will not do to lose so much. You are a valuable fellow,' continued he; 'and I can get any day for you one hundred guineas, from many gentlemen in this island.' And then he told me of Captain Doran's brother-in-law, a severe master, who ever wanted to buy me to make me his overseer. My captain also said he could get much more than a hundred guineas for me in Carolina. This I knew to be a fact; for the gentleman that wanted to buy me came off several times on board of us, and spoke to me to live with him, and said he would use me well.

4. Test.

When I asked what work he would put me to he said, as I was a sailor, he would make me a captain of one of his rice vessels. But I refused: and fearing, at the same time, by a sudden turn I saw in the captain's temper, he might mean to sell me, I told the gentleman I would not live with him on any condition, and that I certainly would run away with his vessel: but he said he did not fear that, as he would catch me again; and then he told me how cruelly he would serve me if I should do so. My captain, however, gave him to understand that I knew something of navigation: so he thought better of it; and, to my great joy, he went away. I now told my master I did not say I would run away in Philadelphia; neither did I mean it, as he did not use me ill, nor yet the captain: for if they did I certainly would have made some attempts before now; but as I thought that if it were God's will I ever should be freed it would be so, and, on the contrary, if it was not his will it would not happen; so I hoped, if ever I were freed, whilst I was used well, it should be by honest means; but, as I could not help myself, he must do as he pleased; I could only hope and trust to the God of Heaven; and at that instant my mind was big with inventions and full of schemes to escape. I then appealed to the captain whether he ever saw any sign of my making the least attempt to run away; and asked him if I did not always come on board according to the time for which he gave me liberty; and, more particularly, when all our men left us at Gaurdeloupe and went on board of the French fleet, and advised me to go with them, whether I might not, and that he could not have got me again. To my no small surprise, and very great joy, the captain confirmed every syllable that I had said: and even more; for he said he had tried different times to see if I would make any attempt of this kind, both at St. Eustatia and in America, and he never found that I made the smallest; but, on the contrary, I always came on board according to his orders; and he did really believe, if I ever meant to run away, that, as I could never have had a better opportunity, I would have done it the night the mate and all the people left our vessel at Gaurdeloupe. The captain then informed my master, who had been thus imposed on by our mate, though I did not know who was my enemy, the reason the mate had for imposing this lie upon him; which was, because I had acquainted the captain of the provisions the mate had given away or taken out of the vessel. This speech of the captain was like life to the dead to me, and instantly my soul glorified God; and still more so on hearing my master immediately say that I was a sensible fellow, and he never did intend to use me as a common slave; and that but for the entreaties of the captain, and his character of me, he would not have let me go from the stores about as I had done; that also, in so doing, he thought by carrying one little thing or other to different places to sell I might make money. That he also intended to encourage me in this by crediting me with half a puncheon of rum and half a hogshead[5] of sugar at a time; so that, from being careful, I might have money enough, in some time, to purchase my freedom; and, when that was the case, I might depend upon it he would let me have it for forty pounds sterling money, which was only the same price he gave for me. This sound gladdened my poor heart beyond measure; though indeed it was no more than the very idea I had formed in my mind of my master long before, and I immediately made him this reply: 'Sir, I always had that very thought of you, indeed I had, and that made me so diligent in serving you.' He then gave me a large piece of silver coin, such as I never had seen or had before, and told me to get ready for the voyage, and he would credit me with a tierce[6] of sugar, and another of rum; he also said that he had two amiable sisters in Philadelphia, from whom I might get some necessary things. Upon this my noble captain desired me to go aboard; and, knowing the African metal,[7] he charged me not to say any thing of this matter to any body; and he promised that the lying mate should not go with him any more. This was a change indeed; in the same hour to feel the most exquisite pain, and in the turn of a moment the fullest joy. It caused in me such sensations as I was only able to express in my looks; my heart was so overpowered with gratitude that I could have kissed both of their feet. When I left the room I immediately went, or rather flew, to the vessel, which being loaded, my master, as good as his word, trusted me with a tierce of rum, and another of sugar, when we sailed, and arrived safe at the elegant town of Philadelphia. I soon sold my goods here pretty well; and in this charming place I found every thing plentiful and cheap.

While I was in this place a very extraordinary occurrence befell me. I had been told one evening of a *wise* woman, a Mrs. Davis, who revealed secrets, foretold events, &c. I put little faith in this story at first, as I could not conceive that any mortal could foresee the future disposals of Providence, nor did I believe in any other revelation than that of the Holy Scriptures; however, I was greatly astonished at seeing this woman in a dream that night, though a person I never before beheld in my life; this made such an impression on me, that I could not get the idea the next day out of my mind, and I then became as anxious to see her as I was before indifferent; accordingly in the evening, after we left off working, I inquired where she lived, and being directed to her, to my inexpressible surprise, beheld the very woman in the very same dress she appeared to me to wear in the vision. She immediately told me I had dreamed of her the preceding night; related to me many things that had happened with a correctness that aston-

5. Large barrel or cask.
6. Liquid measure; a cask between a barrel and a hogshead in size; originally "a third."
7. Mettle; character.

ished me; and finally told me I should not be long a slave: this was the more agreeable news, as I believed it the more readily from her having so faithfully related the past incidents of my life. She said I should be twice in very great danger of my life within eighteen months, which, if I escaped, I should afterwards go on well, so, giving me her blessing, we parted. After staying here some time till our vessel was loaded, and I had bought in my little traffic, we sailed from this agreeable spot for Montserrat, once more to encounter the raging surfs.

We arrived safe at Montserrat, where we discharged our cargo; and soon after that we took slaves on board for St. Eustatia, and from thence to Georgia. I had always exerted myself and did double work, in order to make our voyages as short as possible; and from thus over-working myself while we were at Georgia I caught a fever and ague.[8] I was very ill for eleven days and near dying; eternity was now exceedingly impressed on my mind, and I feared very much that awful event. I prayed the Lord therefore to spare me; and I made a promise in my mind to God, that I would be good if ever I should recover. At length, from having an eminent doctor to attend me, I was restored again to health; and soon after we got the vessel loaded, and set off for Mont-serrat. During the passage, as I was perfectly restored, and had much business of the vessel to mind, all my endeavours to keep up my integ-rity, and perform my promise to God, began to fail; and, in spite of all I could do, as we drew nearer and nearer to the islands, my resolutions more and more declined, as if the very air of that country or climate seemed fatal to piety. When we were safe arrived at Montserrat, and I had got ashore, I forgot my former resolutions.—Alas! how prone is the heart to leave that God it wishes to love! and how strongly do the things of this world strike the senses and captivate the soul!—After our vessel was discharged, we soon got her ready, and took in, as usual, some of the poor oppressed natives of Africa, and other negroes, we then set off again for Georgia and Charlestown. We arrived at Georgia, and, having landed part of our cargo, proceeded to Charlestown with the remainder. While we were there I saw the town illuminated; the guns were fired, and bonfires an [and] other demonstrations of joy shewn, on account of the repeal of the stamp act.[9] Here I disposed of some goods on my own account; the white men buying them with smooth promises and fair words, giving me however but very indifferent payment. There was one gentleman particularly who bought a pun-cheon of rum of me, which gave me a great deal of trouble; and, although I used the interest of my friendly captain, I could not obtain any thing for it; for, being a negro man, I could not oblige him to pay

---

8. Paroxysms of cold, or shivering; chilliness.
9. Duty imposed in 1765 by British Parliament on all paper and parchment used in American colonies. Writing on unstamped paper was declared null and void. This unpopular measure, enacted in order to pay for the French and Indian Wars, was repealed on March 18, 1766.

me. This vexed me much, not knowing how to act; and I lost some time in seeking after this Christian; and though, when the Sabbath came (which the negroes usually make their holiday) I was much inclined to go to public worship, I was obliged to hire some black men to help to pull a boat across the water to go in quest of this gentleman. When I found him, after much entreaty, both from myself and my worthy captain, he at last paid me in dollars; some of them, however, were copper, and of consequence of no value; but he took advantage of my being a negro man, and obliged me to put up with those or none, although I objected to them. Immediately after, as I was trying to pass them in the market, amongst other white men, I was abused for offering to pass bad coin; and, though I shewed them the man I got them from, I was within one minute of being tied up and flogged without either judge or jury; however, by the help of a good pair of heels, I ran off, and so escaped the bastinadoes[1] I should have received. I got on board as fast as I could, but still continued in fear of them until we sailed, which I thanked God we did not long after; and I have never been amongst them since.

We soon came to Georgia, where we were to complete our lading;[2] and here worse fate than ever attended me: for one Sunday night, as I was with some negroes in their master's yard in the town of Savannah, it happened that their master, one Doctor Perkins, who was a very severe and cruel man, came in drunk; and, not liking to see any strange negroes in his yard, he and a ruffian of a white man he had in his service beset me in an instant, and both of them struck me with the first weapons they could get hold of. I cried out as long as I could for help and mercy; but, though I gave a good account of myself, and he knew my captain, who lodged hard by him,[3] it was to no purpose. They beat and mangled me in a shameful manner, leaving me near dead. I lost so much blood from the wounds I received, that I lay quite motionless, and was so benumbed that I could not feel any thing for many hours. Early in the morning they took me away to the jail. As I did not return to the ship all night, my captain, not knowing where I was, and being uneasy that I did not then make my appearance, he made inquiry after me; and, having found where I was, immediately came to me. As soon as the good man saw me so cut and mangled, he could not forbear weeping; he soon got me out of jail to his lodgings, and immediately sent for the best doctors in the place, who at first declared it as their opinion that I could not recover. My captain on this went to all the lawyers in the town for their advice, but they told him they could do nothing for me as I was a negro. He then went to Doctor Perkins, the hero who had vanquished me, and menaced him, swearing he would

1. Beatings with stick or cudgel, especially on soles of feet.
2. Loading.
3. Close by him.

be revenged of him, and challenged him to fight.—But cowardice is ever the companion of cruelty—and the Doctor refused. However, by the skilfulness of one Doctor Brady of that place, I began at last to amend; but, although I was so sore and bad with the wounds I had all over me that I could not rest in any posture, yet I was in more pain on account of the captain's uneasiness about me than I otherwise should have been. The worthy man nursed and watched me all the hours of the night; and I was, through his attention and that of the doctor, able to get out of bed in about sixteen or eighteen days. All this time I was very much wanted on board, as I used frequently to go up and down the river for rafts, and other parts of our cargo, and stow them when the mate was sick or absent. In about four weeks I was able to go on duty; and in a fortnight after, having got in all our lading, our vessel set sail for Montserrat; and in less than three weeks we arrived there safe towards the end of the year. This ended my adventures in 1764; for I did not leave Montserrat again till the beginning of the following year.

END OF THE FIRST VOLUME.

BAHAMA BANKS. 1767.

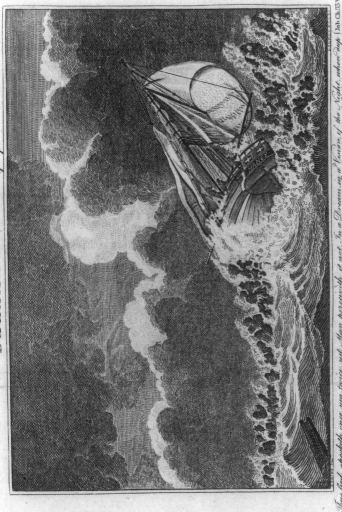

For God speaketh once, yea twice, yet Man perceiveth it not. In a Dream, in a Vision of the Night, when deep (Job Ch.33.Ver.14
sleep falleth upon Men in slumbrings upon the Bed. Then he openeth the Ears of Men & sealeth their instruction) 15.16.&29.&30

Frontispiece for Volume II

They ran the ship aground: and the fore part stuck fast, and remained unmoveable, but the hinder part was broken with the violence of the waves. ACTS XXXVI. 41.

Howbeit, we must be cast upon a certain island;
Wherefore, sirs, be of good cheer: for I believe God, that it shall be even as it was told me. ACTS XXVII. 26, 25.

Now a thing was secretly brought to me, and mine ear received a little thereof.
In thoughts from the visions of the night, when deep sleep falleth on men. JOB IV. 12, 13.

Lo, all these *things* worketh God oftentimes with man,
To bring back his soul from the pit, to be enlightened with the light of the living. JOB XXXIII. 29, 30.

Volume II

THE LIFE, &C.

Chap. VII.

The author's disgust at the West Indies—Forms schemes to obtain his freedom—Ludicrous disappointment he and his Captain meet with in Georgia—At last, by several successful voyages, he acquires a sum of money sufficient to purchase it—Applies to his master, who accepts it, and grants his manumission,[1] to his great joy—He afterwards enters as a freeman on board one of Mr. King's ships, and sails for Georgia—Impositions on free negroes as usual—His venture of turkies—Sails for Montserrat, and on his passage his friend, the Captain, falls ill and dies.

Every day now brought me nearer my freedom, and I was impatient till we proceeded again to sea, that I might have an opportunity of getting a sum large enough to purchase it. I was not long ungratified; for, in the beginning of the year 1766, my master bought another sloop, named the Nancy, the largest I had ever seen. She was partly laden, and was to proceed to Philadelphia; our Captain had his choice of three, and I was well pleased he chose this, which was the largest; for, from his having a large vessel, I had more room, and could carry a larger quantity of goods with me. Accordingly, when we had delivered our old vessel, the Prudence, and completed the lading of the Nancy, having made near three hundred per cent. by four barrels of pork I brought from Charlestown, I laid in as large a cargo as I could, trusting to God's providence to prosper my undertaking. With these views I sailed for Philadelphia. On our passage, when we drew near the land, I was for the first time surprised at the sight of some whales, having never seen any such large sea monsters before; and as we sailed by the land one morning I saw a puppy whale close by the vessel; it was about the length of a wherry boat,[2] and it followed us all the day till we got within the Capes. We arrived safe and in good time at Philadelphia,

1. Document declaring formal emancipation from slavery.
2. Long, light rowboat.

and I sold my goods there chiefly to the quakers. They always appeared to be a very honest discreet sort of people, and never attempted to impose on me; I therefore liked them, and ever after chose to deal with them in preference to any others. One Sunday morning while I was here, as I was going to church, I chanced to pass a meeting-house. The doors being open, and the house full of people, it excited my curiosity to go in. When I entered the house, to my great surprise, I saw a very tall woman standing in the midst of them, speaking in an audible voice something which I could not understand. Having never seen any thing of this kind before, I stood and stared about me for some time, wondering at this odd scene. As soon as it was over I took an opportunity to make inquiry about the place and people, when I was informed they were called Quakers. I particularly asked what that woman I saw in the midst of them had said, but none of them were pleased to satisfy me; so I quitted them, and soon after, as I was returning, I came to a church crowded with people; the church-yard was full likewise, and a number of people were even mounted on ladders, looking in at the windows. I thought this a strange sight, as I had never seen churches, either in England or the West Indies, crowded in this manner before. I therefore made bold to ask some people the meaning of all this, and they told me the Rev. Mr. George Whitfield[3] was preaching. I had often heard of this gentleman, and had wished to see and hear him; but I had never before had an opportunity. I now therefore resolved to gratify myself with the sight, and I pressed in amidst the multitude. When I got into the church I saw this pious man exhorting the people with the greatest fervour and earnestness, and sweating as much as I ever did while in slavery on Montserrat beach. I was very much struck and impressed with this; I thought it strange I had never seen divines exert themselves in this manner before, and I was no longer at a loss to account for the thin congregations they preached to. When we had discharged our cargo here, and were loaded again, we left this fruitful land once more, and set sail for Montserrat. My traffic[4] had hitherto succeeded so well with me, that I thought, by selling my goods when we arrived at Montserrat, I should have enough to purchase my freedom. But, as soon as our vessel arrived there, my master came on board, and gave orders for us to go to St. Eustatia, and discharge our cargo there, and from thence proceed for Georgia. I was much disappointed at this; but thinking, as usual, it was of no use to encounter with[5] the decrees of fate, I submitted without repinning,[6] and we went to St. Eustatia. After we had discharged our cargo there we took in a live cargo, as we call a cargo of slaves. Here I

3. English Methodist clergyman 1714–1770. Though they were not in Philadelphia at the same time, there is the possibility that Equiano heard Whitefield in Savannah.
4. Trade.
5. To go against.
6. Feeling dejected.

sold my goods tolerably well; but, not being able to lay out[7] all my money in this small island to as much advantage as in many other places, I laid out only part, and the remainder I brought away with me neat.[8] We sailed from hence for Georgia, and I was glad when we got there, though I had not much reason to like the place from my last adventure in Savannah; but I longed to get back to Montserrat and procure my freedom, which I expected to be able to purchase when I returned. As soon as we arrived here I waited on my careful doctor, Mr. Brady, to whom I made the most grateful acknowledgments in my power for his former kindness and attention during my illness. While we were here an odd circumstance happened to the Captain and me, which disappointed us both a good deal. A silversmith, whom we had brought to this place some voyages before, agreed with the Captain to return with us to the West Indies, and promised at the same time to give the Captain a great deal of money, having pretended to take a liking to him, and being, as we thought, very rich. But while we stayed to load our vessel this man was taken ill in a house where he worked, and in a week's time became very bad. The worse he grew the more he used to speak of giving the Captain what he had promised him, so that he expected something considerable from the death of this man, who had no wife or child, and he attended him day and night. I used also to go with the Captain, at his own desire, to attend him; especially when we saw there was no appearance of his recovery: and, in order to recompense me for my trouble, the Captain promised me ten pounds, when he should get the man's property. I thought this would be of great service to me, although I had nearly money enough to purchase my freedom, if I should get safe this voyage to Montserrat. In this expectation I laid out above eight pounds of my money for a suit of superfine clothes to dance with at my freedom, which I hoped was then at hand. We still continued to attend this man, and were with him even on the last day he lived, till very late at night, when we went on board. After we were got to bed, about one or two o'clock in the morning, the Captain was sent for, and informed the man was dead. On this he came to my bed, and, waking me, informed me of it, and desired me to get up and procure a light, and immediately go to him. I told him I was very sleepy, and wished he would take somebody else with him; or else, as the man was dead, and could want no farther attendance, to let all things remain as they were till the next morning. 'No, no,' said he, 'we will have the money to-night, I cannot wait till to-morrow; so let us go.' Accordingly I got up and struck a light, and away we both went and saw the man as dead as we could wish. The Captain said he would give him a grand burial, in gratitude for the promised treasure; and desired that all the things belonging to the

7. Spend.
8. Completely, or cleverly.

deceased might be brought forth. Among others, there was a nest of trunks of which he had kept the keys whilst the man was ill, and when they were produced we opened them with no small eagerness and expectation; and as there were a great number within one another, with much impatience we took them one out of the other. At last, when we came to the smallest, and had opened it, we saw it was full of papers, which we supposed to be notes; at the sight of which our hearts leapt for joy; and that instant the Captain, clapping his hands, cried out, 'Thank God, here it is.' But when we took up the trunk, and began to examine the supposed treasure and long-looked-for bounty, (alas! alas! how uncertain and deceitful are all human affairs!) what had we found! While we thought we were embracing a substance we grasped an empty nothing. The whole amount that was in the nest of trunks was only one dollar and a half; and all that the man possessed would not pay for his coffin. Our sudden and exquisite joy was now succeeded by as sudden and exquisite pain; and my Captain and I exhibited, for some time, most ridiculous figures—pictures of chagrin and disappointment! We went away greatly mortified, and left the deceased to do as well as he could for himself, as we had taken so good care of him when alive for nothing. We set sail once more for Montserrat, and arrived there safe; but much out of humor with our friend the silversmith. When we had unladen the vessel, and I had sold my venture, finding myself master of about forty-seven pounds,[9] I consulted my true friend, the Captain, how I should proceed in offering my master the money for my freedom. He told me to come on a certain morning, when he and my master would be at breakfast together. Accordingly, on that morning I went, and met the Captain there, as he had appointed. When I went in I made my obeisance to my master, and with my money in my hand, and many fears in my heart, I prayed him to be as good as his offer to me, when he was pleased to promise me my freedom as soon as I could purchase it. This speech seemed to confound him; he began to recoil; and my heart that instant sunk within me. 'What,' said he, 'give you your freedom? Why, where did you get the money? Have you got forty pounds sterling?' 'Yes, sir,' I answered. 'How did you get it?' replied he. I told him, very honestly. The Captain then said he knew I got the money very honestly and with much industry, and that I was particularly careful. On which my master replied, I got money much faster than he did; and said he would not have made me the promise he did if he had thought I should have got money so soon. 'Come, come,' said my worthy Captain, clapping my master on the back, 'Come, Robert, (which was his name) I think you must let him have his freedom; you have laid your money out very well; you have received good interest for it all this time, and here is now the

9. See n. 2, p. 50.

principal at last. I know Gustavus has earned you more than an hundred a-year, and he will still save you money, as he will not leave you:—
Come, Robert, take the money.' My master then said, he would not
be worse than his promise; and, taking the money, told me to go to
the Secretary at the Register Office, and get my manumission drawn
up. These words of my master were like a voice from heaven to me: in
an instant all my trepidation was turned into unutterable bliss; and I
most reverently bowed myself with gratitude, unable to express my
feelings, but by the overflowing of my eyes, while my true and worthy
friend, the Captain, congratulated us both with a peculiar degree of
heart-felt pleasure. As soon as the first transports of my joy were over,
and that I had expressed my thanks to these my worthy friends in the
best manner I was able, I rose with a heart full of affection and reverence, and left the room, in order to obey my master's joyful mandate
of going to the Register Office. As I was leaving the house I called to
mind the words of the Psalmist, in the 126th Psalm,[1] and like him, 'I
glorified God in my heart, in whom I trusted.' These words had been
impressed on my mind from the very day I was forced from Deptford
to the present hour, and I now saw them, as I thought, fulfilled and
verified. My imagination was all raptures as I flew to the Register
Office, and, in this respect, like the apostle Peter,[2] (whose deliverance
from prison was so sudden and extraordinary, that he thought he was
in a vision) I could scarcely believe I was awake. Heavens! who could
do justice to my feelings at this moment! Not conquering heroes themselves, in the midst of a triumph—Not the tender mother who has just
regained her long-lost infant, and presses it to her heart—Not the
weary hungry mariner, at the sight of the desired friendly port—Not
the lover, when he once more embraces his beloved mistress, after she
had been ravished from his arms!—All within my breast was tumult,
wildness, and delirium! My feet scarcely touched the ground, for they
were winged with joy, and, like Elijah, as he rose to Heaven,[3] they 'were
with lightning sped as I went on.' Every one I met I told of my happiness, and blazed about the virtue of my amiable master and captain.

When I got to the office and acquainted the Register with my errand
he congratulated me on the occasion, and told me he would draw up
my manumission for half price, which was a guinea. I thanked him for
his kindness; and, having received it and paid him, I hastened to my
master to get him to sign it, that I might be fully released. Accordingly
he signed the manumission that day, so that, before night, I who had
been a slave in the morning, trembling at the will of another, was
become my own master, and completely free. I thought this was the

---

1. Psalm 126 is known as "Thanksgiving for Return from Captivity." The words Equiano cites
   come from Psalms 28.7, 33.21, and 86.12.
2. Acts, chap. xii. ver. 9 [Equiano's note].
3. 2 Kings 2.11.

happiest day I had ever experienced; and my joy was still heightened by the blessings and prayers of the sable race, particularly the aged, to whom my heart had ever been attached with reverence.

As the form of my manumission has something peculiar in it, and expresses the absolute power and dominion one man claims over his fellow, I shall beg leave to present it before my readers at full length:

> *Montserrat.*—To all men unto whom these presents[4] shall come: I Robert King, of the parish of St. Anthony in the said island, merchant, send greeting: Know ye, that I the aforesaid Robert King, for and in consideration of the sum of seventy pounds current money of the said island, to me in hand paid, and to the intent that a negro man-slave, named Gustavus Vassa, shall and may become free, have manumitted, emancipated, enfranchised, and set free, and by these presents do manumit, emancipate, enfranchise, and set free, the aforesaid negro man-slave, named Gustavus Vassa, for ever, hereby giving, granting, and releasing unto him, the said Gustavus Vassa, all right, title, dominion, sovereignty, and property, which, as lord and master over the aforesaid Gustavus Vassa, I had, or now I have, or by any means whatsoever I may or can hereafter possibly have over him the aforesaid negro, for ever. In witness whereof I the abovesaid Robert King have unto these presents set my hand and seal, this tenth day of July, in the year of our Lord one thousand seven hundred and fixty-six.
>
> ROBERT KING.
>
> Signed, sealed, and delivered in the presence of Terrylegay, Montserrat.
> Registered the within manumission at full length, this eleventh day of July, 1766, in liber D.[5]
>
> TERRYLEGAY, Register.

In short, the fair as well as black people immediately styled me by a new appellation, to me the most desirable in the world, which was Freeman, and at the dances I gave my Georgia superfine blue clothes made no indifferent appearance, as I thought. Some of the sable females, who formerly stood aloof, now began to relax and appear less coy; but my heart was still fixed on London, where I hoped to be ere long. So that my worthy captain and his owner, my late master, finding that the bent of my mind was towards London, said to me, 'We hope

4. The present words; this document.
5. Book D.

you won't leave us, but that you will still be with the vessels.' Here
gratitude bowed me down; and none but the generous mind can judge
of my feelings, struggling between inclination and duty. However, notwithstanding my wish to be in London, I obediently answered my benefactors that I would go in the vessel, and not leave them; and from
that day I was entered on board as an able-bodied sailor, at thirty-six
shillings per month, besides what perquisites[6] I could make. My intention was to make a voyage or two, entirely to please these my honoured
patrons; but I determined that the year following, if it pleased God, I
would see Old England once more, and surprise my old master, Capt.
Pascal, who was hourly in my mind; for I still loved him, notwithstanding his usage of me, and I pleased myself with thinking of what he
would say when he saw what the Lord had done for me in so short a
time, instead of being, as he might perhaps suppose, under the cruel
yoke of some planter. With these kind of reveries I used often to entertain myself, and shorten the time till my return; and now, being as in
my original free African state, I embarked on board the Nancy, after
having got all things ready for our voyage. In this state of serenity we
sailed for St. Eustatia; and, having smooth seas and calm weather, we
soon arrived there: after taking our cargo on board, we proceeded to
Savannah in Georgia, in August, 1766. While we were there, as usual,
I used to go for the cargo up the rivers in boats; and on this business
I have been frequently beset by alligators, which were very numerous
on that coast, and I have shot many of them when they have been near
getting into our boats; which we have with great difficulty sometimes
prevented, and have been very much frightened at them. I have seen
a young one sold in Georgia alive for six pence. During our stay at this
place, one evening a slave belonging to Mr. Read, a merchant of Savannah, came near our vessel, and began to use me very ill. I entreated
him, with all the patience I was master of, to desist, as I knew there
was little or no law for a free negro here; but the fellow, instead of
taking my advice, persevered in his insults, and even struck me. At this
I lost all temper, and I fell on him and beat him soundly. The next
morning his master came to our vessel as we lay alongside the wharf,
and desired me to come ashore that he might have me flogged all round
the town, for beating his negro slave. I told him he had insulted me,
and have given the provocation, by first striking me. I had told my
captain also the whole affair that morning, and wished him to have
gone along with me to Mr. Read, to prevent bad consequences; but he
said that it did not signify,[7] and if Mr. Read said any thing he would
make matters up, and had desired me to go to work, which I accordingly
did. The Captain being on board when Mr. Read came, he told him I
was a free man; and when Mr. Read applied to him to deliver me up,

6. Wages or tips.
7. Did not matter.

he said he knew nothing of the matter. I was astonished and frightened at this, and thought I had better keep where I was than go ashore and be flogged round the town, without judge or jury. I therefore refused to stir; and Mr. Read went away, swearing he would bring all the constables in the town, for he would have me out of the vessel. When he was gone, I thought his threat might prove too true to my sorrow; and I was confirmed in this belief, as well by the many instances I had seen of the treatment of free negroes, as from a fact that had happened within my own knowledge here a short time before. There was a free black man, a carpenter, that I knew, who, for asking a gentleman that he worked for for the money he had earned, was put into gaol; and afterwards this oppressed man was sent from Georgia, with false accusations, of an intention to set the gentleman's house on fire, and run away with his slaves. I was therefore much embarrassed, and very apprehensive of a flogging at least. I dreaded, of all things, the thoughts of being striped, as I never in my life had the marks of any violence of that kind. At that instant a rage seized my soul, and for a little I determined to resist the first man that should offer to lay violent hands on me, or basely use me without a trial; for I would sooner die like a free man, than suffer myself to be scourged by the hands of ruffians, and my blood drawn like a slave. The captain and others, more cautious, advised me to make haste and conceal myself; for they said Mr. Read was a very spiteful man, and he would soon come on board with constables and take me. At first I refused this counsel, being determined to stand my ground; but at length, by the prevailing entreaties of the captain and Mr. Dixon, with whom he lodged, I went to Mr. Dixon's house, which was a little out of town, at a place called Yea-ma-chra.[8] I was but just gone when Mr. Read, with the constables, came for me, and searched the vessel; but, not finding me there, he swore he would have me dead or alive. I was secreted about five days; however, the good character which my captain always gave me as well as some other gentlemen who also knew me, procured me some friends. At last some of them told my captain that he did not use me well, in suffering me thus to be imposed upon, and said they would see me redressed, and get me on board some other vessel. My captain, on this, immediately went to Mr. Read, and told him, that ever since I eloped from the vessel his work had been neglected, and he could not go on with her loading, himself and mate not being well; and, as I had managed things on board for them, my absence must retard his voyage, and consequently hurt the owner; he therefore begged of him to forgive me, as he said he never had any complaint of me before, for the many years that I had been with him. After repeated entreaties, Mr. Read said I might go to hell, and that he would not meddle with me; on which my

8. Yammacraw Indian name for area near Savannah.

captain came immediately to me at his lodging, and, telling me how pleasantly matters had gone on, he desired me to go on board. Some of my other friends then asked him if he had got the constable's warrant from them; the captain said, No. On this I was desired by them to stay in the house; and they said they would get me on board of some other vessel before the evening. When the captain heard this he became almost distracted. He went immediately for the warrant, and, after using every exertion in his power, he at last got it from my hunters; but I had all the expenses to pay. After I had thanked all my friends for their attention, I went on board again to my work, of which I had always plenty. We were in haste to complete our lading, and were to carry twenty head of cattle with us to the West Indies, where they are a very profitable article. In order to encourage me in working, and to make up for the time I had lost, my captain promised me the privilege of carrying two bullocks of my own with me; and this made me work with redoubled ardour. As soon as I had got the vessel loaded, in doing which I was obliged to perform the duty of the mate as well as my own work, and that the bullocks were near coming on board, I asked the captain leave to bring my two, according to his promise; but, to my great surprise, he told me there was no room for them. I then asked him to permit me to take one; but he said he could not. I was a good deal mortified at this usage, and told him I had no notion that he intended thus to impose on me; nor could I think well of any man that was so much worse than his word. On this we had some disagreement, and I gave him to understand, that I intended to leave the vessel. At this he appeared to be very much dejected; and our mate, who had been very sickly, and whose duty had long devolved upon me, advised him to persuade me to stay: in consequence of which he spoke very kindly to me, making many fair promises, telling me that, as the mate was so sickly, he could not do without me, and that, as the safety of the vessel and cargo depended greatly upon me, he therefore hoped that I would not be offended at what had passed between us, and swore he would make up all matters when we arrived in the West Indies; so I consented to slave on as before. Soon after this, as the bullocks were coming on board, one of them ran at the captain, and butted him so furiously in the breast, that he never recovered of the blow. In order to make me some amends for his treatment about the bullocks, the captain now pressed me very much to take some turkeys, and other fowls, with me, and gave me liberty to take as many as I could find room for; but I told him he knew very well I had never carried any turkeys before, as I always thought they were such tender birds that they were not fit to cross the seas. However, he continued to press me to buy them for once; and, what was very surprising to me, the more I was against it, the more he urged my taking them, insomuch that he ensured me from all losses that might happen by them, and I was prevailed on to take them; but I though this very strange, as he had never acted so with me before. This, and not being able to dispose of my paper-money in any other way, induced me at length to take four dozen. The turkeys, however, I was so dissatisfied about that I determined to make no more voyages to this quarter, nor with this captain; and was very apprehensive that my free voyage would be the worst I had ever made. We set sail for Montserrat. The captain and mate had been both complaining of sickness when we sailed, and as we proceeded on our voyage they grew worse. This was about November, and we had not been long at sea before we began to meet with strong northerly gales and rough seas; and in about seven or eight days all the bullocks were near being drowned, and four or five of them died. Our vessel, which had not been tight at first, was much less so now; and, though we were but nine in the whole, including five sailors and myself, yet we were obliged to attend to the pumps every half or three quarters of an hour. The captain and mate came on deck as often as they were able, which was now but seldom; for they declined so fast, that they were not well enough to make observations above four or five times the whole voyage. The whole care of the vessel rested, therefore, upon me, and I was obliged to direct her by my former experience, not being able to work a traverse.[9] The captain was now very sorry he had not taught me navigation, and protested, if ever he should get well again, he would not fail to do so; but in about seventeen days his illness increased so much, that he was obliged to keep his bed, continuing sensible, however, till the last, constantly having the owner's interest at heart; for this just and benevolent man ever appeared much concerned about the welfare of what he was intrusted with. When this dear friend found the symptoms of death approaching, he called me by my name; and, when I came to him, he asked (with almost his last breath) if he had ever done me any harm? 'God forbid I should think so,' I replied, 'I should then be the most ungrateful of wretches to the best of benefactors.' While I was thus expressing my affection and sorrow by his bedside, he expired without saying another word; and the day following we committed his body to the deep. Every man on board loved this man, and regretted his death; but I was exceedingly affected at it, and I found that I did not know, till he was gone, the strength of my regard for him. Indeed I had every reason in the world to be attached to him; for, besides that he was in general mild, affable, generous, faithful, benevolent, and just, he was to me a friend and a father; and, had it pleased Providence that he had died but five months before, I verily believed I should not have obtained my freedom when I did; and it is not improbable that I might not have been able to get it at any rate afterwards. The captain being dead, the mate came on

9. To zigzag a course against contrary winds.

the deck, and made such observations as he was able, but to no purpose. In the course of a few days more, the few bullocks that remained were found dead; but the turkies I had, though on the deck, and exposed to so much wet and bad weather, did well, and I afterwards gained near three hundred per cent. on the sale of them; so that in the event it proved a happy circumstance for me that I had not bought the bullocks I intended, for they must have perished with the rest; and I could not help looking on this, otherwise trifling circumstance, as a particular providence of God, and I was thankful accordingly. The care of the vessel took up all my time, and engaged my attention entirely. As we were now out of the variable winds, I thought I should not be much puzzled to hit upon the islands. I was persuaded I steered right for Antigua, which I wished to reach, as the nearest to us; and in the course of nine or ten days we made this island, to our great joy; and the next day after we came safe to Montserrat. Many were surprised when they heard of my conducting the sloop into the port, and I now obtained a new appelation, and was called Captain. This elated me not a little, and it was quite flattering to my vanity to be thus styled by as high a title as any free man in this place possessed. When the death of the captain became known, he was much regretted by all who knew him; for he was a man universally respected. At the same time the sable captain lost no fame; for the success I had met with increased the affection of my friends in no small measure.

Chap. VIII.

The author, to oblige Mr. King, once more embarks for Georgia in one of his vessels—A new captain is appointed—They sail, and steer a new course—Three remarkable dreams—The vessel is shipwrecked on the Bahama bank, but the crew are preserved, principally by means of the author—He sets out from the island with the captain, in a small boat, in quest of a ship—Their distress—Meet with a wrecker—Sail for Providence—Are overtaken again by a terrible storm, and are all near perishing— Arrive at New Providence—The author, after some time, sails from thence to Georgia—Meets with another storm, and is obliged to put back and refit—Arrives at Georgia—Meets new impositions— Two white men attempt to kidnap him—Officiates as a parson at a funeral ceremony—Bids adieu to Georgia, and sails for Martinico.

As I had now, by the death of my captain, lost my great benefactor and friend, I had little inducement to remain longer in the West Indies, except my gratitude to Mr. King, which I thought I had pretty well discharged in bringing back his vessel safe, and delivering his cargo to his satisfaction. I began to think of leaving this part of the world, of which I had been long tired, and returning to England, where my heart had always been; but Mr. King still pressed me very much to stay with his vessel; and he had done so much for me that I found myself unable to refuse his requests, and consented to go another voyage to Georgia, as the mate, from his ill state of health, was quite useless in the vessel. Accordingly a new captain was appointed, whose name was William Phillips, an old acquaintance of mine; and, having refitted our vessel, and taken several slaves on board, we set sail for St. Eustatia, where we stayed but a few days; and on the 30th of January 1767 we steered for Georgia. Our new captain boasted strangely of his skill in navigating and conducting a vessel; and in consequence of this he steered a new course, several points more to the westward than we ever did before; this appeared to me very extraordinary.

On the fourth of February, which was soon after we had got into our new course, I dreamt the ship was wrecked amidst the surfs and rocks, and that I was the means of saving every one on board; and on the night following I dreamed the very same dream. These dreams however made no impression on my mind; and the next evening, it being my watch below, I was pumping the vessel a little after eight o'clock, just before I went off the deck, as is the custom; and being weary with the duty of the day, and tired at the pump, (for we made a good deal of water) I began to express my impatience, and I uttered with an oath, 'Damn the vessel's bottom out.' But my conscience instantly smote me for the expression. When I left the deck I went to bed, and had scarcely fallen asleep when I dreamed the same dream again about the ship that I had dreamt the two preceeding nights. At twelve o'clock the watch was changed; and, as I had always the charge of the captain's watch, I then went upon deck. At half after one in the morning the man at the helm saw something under the lee-beam that the sea washed against, and he immediately called to me that there was a grampus,[1] and desired me to look at it. Accordingly I stood up and observed it for some time; but, when I saw the sea wash up against it again and again. I said it was not a fish but a rock. Being soon certain of this, I went down to the captain, and with some confusion, told him the danger we were in, and desired him to come upon deck immediately. He said it was very well, and I went up again. As soon as I was upon deck the wind, which had been pretty high, having abated a little, the vessel began to be carried sideways towards the rock, by means of the current. Still the captain did not appear. I therefore went to him again, and told him the vessel was then near a large rock, and desired he would come up with speed. He said he would, and I returned to the deck. When I was upon the deck again I saw we were not above a

---

1. See n. 5, p. 47. *Lee-beam*: the side of the ship away from the wind.

pistol shot from the rock, and I heard the noise of the breakers all around us. I was exceedingly alarmed at this; and the captain having not yet come on the deck I lost all patience; and, growing quite enraged, I ran down to him again, and asked him why he did not come up, and what he could mean by all this? 'The breakers,' said I, 'are round us, and the vessel is almost on the rock.' With that he came on the deck with me, and we tried to put the vessel about, and get her out of the current, but all to no purpose, the wind being very small. We then called all hands up immediately; and after a little we got up one end of a cable, and fastened it to the anchor. By this time the surf was foaming round us, and made a dreadful noise on the breakers, and the very moment we let the anchor go the vessel struck against the rocks. One swell now succeeded another, as it were one wave calling on its fellow: the roaring of the billows increased, and, with one single heave of the swells, the sloop was pierced and transfixed among the rocks! In a moment a scene of horror presented itself to my mind, such as I never had conceived or experienced before. All my sins stared me in the face; and especially, I thought that God had hurled his direful vengeance on my guilty head for cursing the vessel on which my life depended. My spirits at this forsook me, and I expected every moment to go to the bottom: I determined if I should still be saved that I would never swear again. And in the midst of my distress, while the dreadful surfs were dashing with unremitting fury among the rocks, I remembered the Lord, though fearful that I was undeserving of forgiveness, and I thought that as he had often delivered he might yet deliver; and, calling to mind the many mercies he had shewn me in times past, they gave me some small hope that he might still help me. I then began to think how we might be saved; and I believe no mind was ever like mine so replete with inventions and confused with schemes, though how to escape death I knew not. The captain immediately ordered the hatches to be nailed down on the slaves in the hold, where there were above twenty, all of whom must unavoidably have perished if he had been obeyed. When he desired the man to nail down the hatches I thought that my sins was the cause of this, and that God would charge me with these people's blood. This thought rushed upon my mind that instant with such violence, that it quite overpowered me, and I fainted. I recovered just as the people were about to nail down the hatches; perceiving which, I desired them to stop. The captain then said it must be done: I asked him why? He said that every one would endeavour to get into the boat, which was but small, and thereby we should be drowned; for it would not have carried above ten at the most. I could no longer restrain my emotion, and I told him he deserved drowning for not knowing how to navigate the vessel; and I believe the people would have tossed him overboard if I had given them the least hint of it. However the hatches were not nailed down; and, as none of us could leave the vessel then on account of the darkness, and as we knew not where to go, and were convinced besides that the boat could not survive the surfs, we all said we would remain on the dry part of the vessel, and trust to God till day-light appeared, when we should know better what to do.

I then advised to get the boat prepared against morning, and some of us began to set about it; but some abandoned all care of the ship and themselves, and fell to drinking. Our boat had a piece out of her bottom near two feet long, and we had no materials to mend her; however, necessity being the mother of invention, I took some pump leather and nailed it to the broken part, and plastered it over with tallow-grease. And, thus prepared, with the utmost anxiety of mind we watched for day-light, and thought every minute an hour till it appeared. At last it saluted our longing eyes, and kind Providence accompanied its approach with what was no small comfort to us; for the dreadful swell began to subside; and the next thing that we discovered to raise our drooping spirits, was a small key or island, about five or six miles off; but a barrier soon presented itself; for there was not water enough for our boat to go over the reefs, and this threw us again into a sad consternation; but there was no alternative, we were therefore obliged to put but a few in the boat at once; and, what is still worse, all of us were frequently under the necessity of getting out to drag and lift it over the reefs. This cost us much labour and fatigue; and, what was yet more distressing, we could not avoid having our legs cut and torn very much with the rocks. There were only four people that would work with me at the oars; and they consisted of three black men and a Dutch creole sailor; and, though we went with the boat five times that day, we had no others to assist us. But, had we not worked in this manner, I really believe the people could not have been saved; for not one of the white men did any thing to preserve their lives; and indeed they soon got so drunk that they were not able, but lay about the deck like swine, so that we were at last obliged to lift them into the boat and carry them on shore by force. This want of assistance made our labour intolerably severe; insomuch, that, by putting on shore so often that day, the skin was entirely stript off my hands.

However, we continued all the day to toil and strain our exertions, till we had brought all on board safe to the shore; so that out of thirty-two people we lost not one. My dream now returned upon my mind with all its force; it was fulfilled in every part; for our danger was the same I had dreamt of: and I could not help looking on myself as the principal instrument in effecting our deliverence; for, owing to some of our people getting drunk, the rest of us were obliged to double our exertions; and it was fortunate we did, for in a very little time longer the patch of leather on the boat would have been worn out, and she would have been no longer fit for service. Situated as we were, who could think that men should be so careless of the danger they were in? for, if the wind had but raised the swell as it was when the vessel struck, we must have bid a final farewell to all hopes of deliverance; and though, I warned the people who were drinking and entreated them to embrace the moment of deliverance, nevertheless they persisted, as if not possessed of the least spark of reason. I could not help thinking, that, if any of these people had been lost, God would charge me with their lives, which, perhaps, was one cause of my labouring so hard for their preservation, and indeed every one of them afterwards seemed so sensible of the service I had rendered them; and while we were on the key[2] I was a kind of chieftain amongst them. I bought some limes, oranges, and lemons ashore; and, finding it to be a good soil where we were, I planted several of them as a token to any one that might be cast away hereafter. This key, as we afterwards found, was one of the Bahama islands, which consist of a cluster of large islands, with smaller ones or keys, as they are called, interspersed among them. It was about a mile in circumference, with a white sandy beach running in a regular order along it. On that part of it where we first attempted to land there stood some very large birds, called flamingoes: these, from the reflection of the sun, appeared to us at a little distance as large as men; and, when they walked backwards and forwards, we could not conceive what they were: our captain swore they were cannibals. This created a great panic among us; and we held a consultation how to act. The captain wanted to go to a key that was within sight, but a great way off; but I was against it, as in so doing we should not be able to save all the people; 'And therefore,' said I, 'let us go on shore here, and perhaps these cannibals may take to the water.' Accordingly we steered towards them; and when we approached them, to our very great joy and no less wonder, they walked off one after the other very deliberately; and at last they took flight and relieved us entirely from our fears. About the key there were turtles and several sorts of fish in such abundance that we caught them without bait, which was a great relief to us after the salt provisions on board. There was also a large rock on the beach, about ten feet high, which was in the form of a punch-bowl at the top; this we could not help thinking Providence had ordained to supply us with rainwater; and it was something singular that, if we did not take the water when it rained, in some little time after it would turn as salt as sea-water.

Our first care, after refreshment, was to make ourselves tents to lodge in, which we did as well as we could with some sails we had brought from the ship. We then began to think how we might get from this place, which was quite uninhabited; and we determined to repair our boat, which was very much shattered, and to put to sea in quest of a

2. A low island or reef.

ship or some inhabited island. It took us up however eleven days before we could get the boat ready for sea in the manner we wanted it, with a sail and other necessaries. When we had got all things prepared the captain wanted me to stay on shore while he went to sea in quest of a vessel to take all the people off the key; but this I refused; and the captain and myself, with five more, set off in the boat towards New Providence.[3] We had no more than two musket load of gun-powder with us if any thing should happen; and our stock of provisions consisted of three gallons of rum, four of water, some salt beef, some biscuit; and in this manner we proceeded to sea.

On the second day of our voyage we came to an island called Obbico,[4] the largest of the Bahama islands. We were much in want of water; for by this time our water was expended, and we were exceedingly fatigued in pulling two days in the heat of the sun; and it being late in the evening, we hauled the boat ashore to try for water and remain during the night: when we came ashore we searched for water, but could find none. When it was dark, we made a fire around us for fear of the wild beasts, as the place was an entire thick wood, and we took it by turns to watch. In this situation we found very little rest, and waited with impatience for the morning. As soon as the light appeared we set off again with our boat, in hopes of finding assistance during the day. We, were now much dejected and weakened, by pulling the boat; for our sail was of no use, and we were almost famished for want of fresh water to drink. We had nothing left to eat but salt beef, and that we could not use without water. In this situation we toiled all day in sight of the island, which was very long; in the evening, seeing no relief, we made ashore again, and fastened our boat. We then went to look for fresh water, being quite faint for the want of it; and we dug and searched about for some all the remainder of the evening, but could not find one drop, so that our dejection at this period became excessive, and our terror so great, that we expected nothing but death to deliver us. We could not touch our beef, which was as salt as brine, without fresh water; and we were in the greatest terror from the apprehension of wild beasts. When unwelcome night came we acted as on the night before; and the next morning we set off again from the island in hopes of seeing some vessel. In this manner we toiled as well as we were able till four o'clock, during which we passed several keys, but could not meet with a ship; and, still famishing with thirst, went ashore on one of those keys again in hopes of finding some water. Here we found some leaves with a few drops of water in them, which we lapped with much eagerness; we then dug in several places, but without success. As we were digging holes in search of water there came forth some very thick and black stuff; but none of us could touch it, except the

3. Island of the Bahamas on which Nassau is located.
4. Or Abbico. Present-day Great Abaco, Bahamas.

poor Dutch Creole, who drank above a quart of it as eagerly as if it had been wine. We tried to catch fish, but could not; and we now began to repine at our fate, and abandon ourselves to despair; when, in the midst of our murmuring, the captain all at once cried out 'A sail! a sail! a sail!' This gladdening sound was like a reprieve to a convict, and we all instantly turned to look at it; but in a little time some of us began to be afraid it was not a sail. However, at a venture, we embarked and steered after it; and, in half an hour, to our unspeakable joy, we plainly saw that it was a vessel. At this our drooping spirits revived, and we made towards her with all the speed imaginable. When we came near to her, we found she was a little sloop, about the size of a Gravesend hoy,[5] and quite full of people; a circumstance which we could not make out the meaning of. Our captain, who was a Welchman, swore that they were pirates, and would kill us. I said, be that as it might, we must board her if we were to die for it; and, if they should not receive us kindly, we must oppose them as well as we could; for there was no alternative between their perishing and ours. This counsel was immediately taken; and I really believe that the captain, myself, and the Dutchman, would then have faced twenty men. We had two cutlasses[6] and a musquet, that I brought in the boat; and, in this situation, we rowed alongside, and immediately boarded her. I believe there were about forty hands on board; but how great was our surprises, as soon as we got on board, to find that the major part of them were in the same predicament as ourselves!

They belonged to a whaling schooner that was wrecked two days before us about nine miles to the north of our vessel. When she was wrecked some of them had taken to their boats and had left some of their people and property on a key, in the same manner as we had done; and were going, like us, to New Providence in quest of a ship, when they met with this little sloop, called a wrecker; their employment in those seas being to look after wrecks. They were then going to take the remainder of the people belonging to the schooner; for which the wrecker was to have all things belonging to the vessel, and likewise their people's help to get what they could out of her, and were then to carry the crew to New Providence.

We told the people of the wrecker the condition of our vessel, and we made the same agreement with them as the schooner's people; and, on their complying, we begged of them to go to our key directly, because our people were in want of water. They agreed, therefore, to go along with us first; and in two days we arrived at the key, to the inexpressible joy of the people that we had left behind, as they had been reduced to great extremities for want of water in our absence. Luckily for us, the wrecker had now more people on board than she

5. *Gravesend*: on the Thames River, east of London. A hoy is a small vessel used as ferry.
6. See n. 7, p. 37.

could carry or victual for any moderate length of time; they therefore hired the schooner's people to work on our wreck, and we left them our boat, and embarked for New Providence.

Nothing could have been more fortunate than our meeting with this wrecker, for New Providence was at such a distance that we never could have reached it in our boat. The island of Abbico was much longer than we expected; and it was not till after sailing for three or four days that we got safe to the farther end of it, towards New Providence. When we arrived there we watered, and got a good many lobsters and other shellfish; which proved a great relief to us, as our provisions and water were almost exhausted. We then proceeded on our voyage; but the day after we left the island, late in the evening, and whilst we were yet amongst the Bahama keys, we were overtaken by a violent gale of wind, so that we were obliged to cut away the mast. The vessel was very near foundering; for she parted from her anchors, and struck several times on the shoals. Here we expected every minute that she would have gone to pieces, and each moment to be our last; so much so that my old captain and sickly useless mate, and several others, fainted; and death stared us in the face on every side. All the swearers on board now began to call on the God of Heaven to assist them: and, sure enough, beyond our comprehension he did assist us, and in a miraculous manner delivered us! In the very height of our extremity the wind lulled for a few minutes; and, although the swell was high beyond expression, two men, who were expert swimmers, attempted to go to the buoy of the anchor, which we still saw on the water, at some distance, in a little punt that belonged to the wrecker, which was not large enough to carry more than two. She filled different times in their endeavours to get into her alongside of our vessel; and they saw nothing but death before them, as well as we; but they said they might as well die that way as any other. A coil of very small rope, with a little buoy, was put in along with them; and, at last, with great hazard, they got the punt clear from the vessel; and these two intrepid water heroes paddled away for life towards the buoy of the anchor. The eyes of us all were fixed on them all the time, expecting every minute to be their last: and the prayers of all those that remained in their senses were offered up to God, on their behalf, for a speedy deliverance; and for our own, which depended on them; and he heard and answered us! These two men at last reached the buoy; and, having fastened the punt to it, they tied one end of their rope to the small buoy that they had in the punt, and sent it adrift towards the vessel. We on board observing this threw out boat-hooks and leads fastened to lines, in order to catch the buoy: at last we caught it, and fastened a hawser[7] to the end of the small rope; we then gave them a sign to pull, and they pulled

7. See n. 7, p. 64.

the hawser to them, and fastened it to the buoy: which being done we hauled for our lives; and, through the mercy of God, we got again from the shoals into deep water, and the punt got safe to the vessel. It is impossible for any to conceive our heart-felt joy at this second deliverance from ruin, but those who have suffered the same hardships. Those whose strength and senses were gone came to themselves, and were now as elated as they were before depressed. Two days after this the wind ceased, and the water became smooth. The punt then went on shore, and we cut down some trees; and having found our mast and mended it we brought it on board, and fixed it up. As soon as we had done this we got up the anchor, and away we went once more for New Providence, which in three days more we reached safe, after having been above three weeks in a situation in which we did not expect to escape with life. The inhabitants here were very kind to us; and, when they learned our situation, shewed us a great deal of hospitality and friendship. Soon after this every one of my old fellow-sufferers that were free parted from us, and shaped their course where their inclination led them. One merchant, who had a large sloop, seeing our condition, and knowing we wanted to go to Georgia, told four of us that his vessel was going there; and, if we would work on board and load her, he would give us our passage free. As we could not get any wages whatever, and found it very hard to get off the place, we were obliged to consent to his proposal; and we went on board and helped to load the sloop, though we had only our victuals allowed us. When she was entirely loaded he told us she was going to Jamaica first, where we must go if we went in her. This, however, I refused; but my fellow-sufferers not having any money to help themselves with, necessity obliged them to accept of the offer, and to steer that course, though they did not like it.

We stayed in New Providence about seventeen or eighteen days; during which time I met with many friends, who gave me encouragement to stay there with them: but I declined it; though, had not my heart been fixed on England, I should have stayed, as I liked the place extremely, and there were some free black people here who were very happy, and we passed our time pleasantly together, with the melodious sound of the catguts,[8] under the lime and lemon trees. At length Captain Phillips hired a sloop to carry him and some of the slaves that he could not sell to Georgia; and I agreed to go with him in this vessel, meaning now to take my farewell of that place. When the vessel was ready we all embarked; and I took my leave of New Providence, not without regret. We sailed about four o'clock in the morning, with a fair wind, for Georgia; and about eleven o'clock the same morning a short and sudden gale sprung up and blew away most of our sails; and,

---

8. Dried and twisted animal intestines used for strings of musical instruments.

as we were still amongst the keys, in a very few minutes it dashed the
sloop against the rocks. Luckily for us the water was deep; and the sea
was not so angry but that, after having for some time laboured hard,
and being many in number, we were saved through God's mercy; and,
by using our greatest exertions, we got the vessel off. The next day we
returned to Providence, where we soon got her again refitted. Some of
the people swore that we had spells set upon us by somebody in Montserrat; and others that we had witches and wizzards amongst the poor
helpless slaves; and that we never should arrive safe at Georgia. But
these things did not deter me; I said, 'Let us again face the winds and
seas, and swear not, but trust to God, and he will deliver us.' We
therefore once more set sail; and, with hard labour, in seven day's time
arrived safe at Georgia.

After our arrival we went up to the town of Savannah; and the same
evening I went to a friend's house to lodge, whose name was Mosa, a
black man. We were very happy at meeting each other; and after supper
we had a light till it was between nine and ten o'clock at night. About
that time the watch or patrol came by; and, discerning a light in the
house, they knocked at the door: we opened it; and they came in and
sat down, and drank some punch with us: they also begged some limes
of me, as they understood I had some, which I readily gave them. A
little after this they told me I must go to the watch-house with them:
this surprised me a good deal, after our kindness to them; and I asked
them, Why so? They said that all negroes who had light in their houses
after nine o'clock were to be taken into custody, and either pay some
dollars or be flogged. Some of those people knew that I was a free man;
but, as the man of the house was not free, and had his master to protect
him, they did not take the same liberty with him they did with me. I
told them that I was a free man, and just arrived from Providence; that
we were not making any noise, and that I was not a stranger in that
place, but was very well known there: 'Besides,' said I, 'what will you
do with me?'—'That you shall see,' replied they, 'but you must go to
the watch-house with us.' Now whether they meant to get money from
me or not I was at a loss to know; but I thought immediately of the
oranges and limes at Santa Cruz: and seeing that nothing would pacify
them I went with them to the watch-house, where I remained during
the night. Early the the next morning these imposing ruffians flogged
a negro-man and woman that they had in the watch-house, and then
they told me that I must be flogged too. I asked why? and if there was
no law for free men? And told them if there was I would have it put
in force against them. But this only exasperated them the more; and
instantly they swore they would serve me as Doctor Perkins had done;
and they were going to lay violent hands on me; when one of them,
more humane than the rest, said that as I was a free man they could

not justify stripping me by law. I then immediately sent for Doctor Brady, who was known to be an honest and worthy man; and on his coming to my assistance they let me go.

This was not the only disagreeable incident I met with while I was in this place; for, one day, while I was a little way out of the town of Savannah, I was beset by two white men, who meant to play their usual tricks with me in the way of kidnapping. As soon as these men accosted me, one of them said to the other, 'This is the very fellow we are looking for that you lost:' and the other swore immediately that I was the identical person. On this they made up to me, and were about to handle me; but I told them to be still and keep off; for I had seen those kind of tricks played upon other free blacks, and they must not think to serve me so. At this they paused a little, and one said to the other—it will not do; and the other answered that I talked too good English. I replied, I believed I did; and I had also with me a revengeful stick equal to the occasion; and my mind was likewise good. Happily however it was not used; and, after we had talked together a little in this manner, the rogues left me. I stayed in Savannah some time, anxiously trying to get to Montserrat once more to see Mr. King, my old master, and then to take a final farewell of the American quarter of the globe. At last I met with a sloop called the Speedwell, Captain John Bunton, which belonged to Grenada, and was bound to Martinico, a French island, with a cargo of rice, and I shipped myself on board of her. Before I left Georgia a black woman, who had a child lying dead, being very tenacious of the church burial service, and not able to get any white person to perform it, applied to me for that purpose. I told her I was no parson; and besides, that the service over the dead did not affect the soul. This however did not satisfy her; she still urged me very hard: I therefore complied with her earnest entreaties, and at last consented to act the parson for the first time in my life. As she was much respected, there was a great company both of white and black people at the grave. I then accordingly assumed my new vocation, and performed the funeral ceremony to the satisfaction of all present; after which I bade adieu to Georgia, and sailed for Martinico.

Chap. IX.

The author arrives at Martinico—Meets with new difficulties—
Gets to Montserrat, where he takes leave of his old master, and
sails for England—Meets Capt. Pascal—Learns the French horn—
Hires himself with Doctor Irving, where he learns to freshen sea
water—Leaves the doctor, and goes a voyage to Turkey and
Portugal; and afterwards goes a voyage to Grenada, and another

to Jamaica—Returns to the Doctor, and they embark together on
a voyage to the North Pole, with the Hon. Capt. Phipps—Some
account of that voyage, and the dangers the author was in—He
returns to England.

I thus took a final leave of Georgia; for the treatment I had received
in it disgusted me very much against the place; and when I left it and
sailed for Martinico I determined never more to revisit it. My new captain conducted his vessel safer than my former one; and, after an agreeable voyage, we got safe to our intended port. While I was on this island
I went about a good deal, and found it very pleasant: in particular I
admired the town of St. Pierre, which is the principal one in the island,
and built more like an European town than any I had seen in the West
Indies. In general also, slaves were better treated, had more holidays,
and looked better than those in the English islands. After we had done
our business here, I wanted my discharge, which was necessary; for it
was then the month of May, and I wished much to be at Montserrat to
bid farewell to Mr. King, and all my other friends there, in time to sail
for Old England in the July fleet. But, alas! I had put a great stumbling
block in my own way, by which I was near losing my passage that season
to England. I had lent my captain some money, which I now wanted to
enable me to prosecute my intentions. This I told him; but when I
applied for it, though I urged the necessity of my occasion, I met with
so much shuffling from him, that I began at last to be afraid of losing
my money, as I could not recover it by law: for I have already mentioned, that throughout the West Indies no black man's testimony is
admitted, on any occasion, against any white person whatever, and
therefore my own oath would have been of no use. I was obliged,
therefore, to remain with him till he might be disposed to return it to
me. Thus we sailed from Martinico for the Grenades.[1] I frequently
pressing the captain for my money to no purpose; and, to render my
condition worse, when we got there, the captain and his owners quarrelled; so that my situation became daily more irksome: for besides that
we on board had little or no victuals allowed us, and I could not get my
money nor wages, I could then have gotten my passage free to Montserrat had I been able to accept it. The worst of all was, that it was growing late in July, and the ships in the islands must sail by the 26th of that
month. At last, however, with a great many entreaties, I got my money
from the captain, and took the first vessel I could meet with for St. Eustatia. From thence I went in another to Basseterre in St. Kitts, where I
arrived on the 19th of July. On the 22d, having met with a vessel bound
to Montserrat, I wanted to go in her; but the captain and others would
not take me on board until I should advertise myself, and give notice of
my going off the island. I told them of my haste to be in Montserrat,

1. The Grenadines, or Lesser Antilles.

and that the time then would not admit of advertising, it being late in the evening, and the captain about to sail; but he insisted it was necessary, and otherwise he said he would not take me. This reduced me to great perplexity; for if I should be compelled to submit to this degrading necessity, which every black freeman is under, of advertising himself like a slave, when he leaves an island, and which I thought a gross imposition upon any freeman, I feared I should miss that opportunity of going to Montserrat, and then I could not get to England that year. The vessel was just going off, and no time could be lost; I immediately therefore set about, with a heavy heart, to try who I could get to befriend me in complying with the demands of the captain. Luckily I found, in a few minutes, some gentlemen of Montserrat whom I knew; and, having told them my situation, I requested their friendly assistance in helping me off the island. Some of them, on this, went with me to the captain, and satisfied him of my freedom; and, to my very great joy, he desired me to go on board. We then set sail, and the next day, the 23d, I arrived at the wished-for place, after an absence of six months, in which I had more than once experienced the delivering hand of Providence, when all human means of escaping destruction seemed hopeless. I saw my friends with a gladness of heart which was increased by my absence and the dangers I had escaped, and I was received with great friendship by them all, but particularly by Mr. King, to whom I related the fate of his sloop, the Nancy, and the causes of her being wrecked. I now learned with extreme sorrow, that his house was washed away during my absence, by the bursting of a pond at the top of a mountain that was opposite the town of Plymouth. It swept great part of the town away, and Mr. King lost a great deal of property from the inundation, and nearly his life. When I told him I intended to go to London that season, and that I had come to visit him before my departure, the good man expressed a great deal of affection for me, and sorrow that I should leave him, and warmly advised me to stay there; insisting, as I was much respected by all the gentlemen in the place, that I might do very well, and in a short time have land and slaves of my own. I thanked him for this instance of his friendship; but, as I wished very much to be in London, I declined remaining any longer there, and begged he would excuse me. I then requested he would be kind enough to give me a certificate of my behaviour while in his service, which he very readily compiled with, and gave me the following:

Montserrat, January 26, 1767.
The bearer hereof, Gustavus Vassa, was my slave for upwards of three years, during which he has always behaved himself well, and discharged his duty with honesty and assiduity.

ROBERT KING.

To all whom this may concern.

Having obtained this, I parted from my kind master, after many sincere professions of gratitude and regard, and prepared for my departure for London. I immediately agreed to go with one Capt. John Hamer, for seven guineas, the passage to London, on board a ship called the Andromache; and on the 24th and 25th I had free dances, as they are called, with some of my countrymen, previous to my setting off; after which I took leave of all my friends, and on the 26th I embarked for London, exceeding glad to see myself once more on board of a ship; and still more so, in seeing the course I had long wished for. With a light heart I bade Montserrat farewell, and never had my feet on it since; and with it I bade adieu to the sound of the cruel whip, and all other dreadful instruments of torture; adieu to the offensive sight of the violated chastity of the sable females, which has too often accosted my eyes; adieu to oppressions (although to me less severe than most of my countrymen); and adieu to the angry howling, dashing surfs. I wished for a grateful and thankful heart to praise the Lord God on high for all his mercies!

We had a most prosperous voyage, and, at the end of seven weeks, arrived at Cherry-Garden stairs.[2] Thus were my longing eyes once more gratified with a sight of London, after having been absent from it above four years. I immediately received my wages, and I never had earned seven guineas so quick in my life before; I had thirty-seven guineas in all, when I got cleared of the ship. I now entered upon a scene, quite new to me, but full of hope. In this situation my first thoughts were to look out for some of my former friends, and amongst the first of those were the Miss Guerins. As soon, therefore, as I had regaled myself I went in quest of those kind ladies, whom I was very impatient to see; and with some difficulty and perseverance, I found them at May's-hill, Greenwich. They were most agreeably surprised to see me, and I quite overjoyed at meeting with them. I told them my history, at which they expressed great wonder, and freely acknowledged it did their cousin, Capt. Pascal, no honour. He then visited there frequently; and I met him four or five days after in Greenwich park. When he saw me he appeared a good deal surprised, and asked me how I came back? I answered, 'In a ship.' To which he replied dryly, 'I suppose you did not walk back to London on the water.' As I saw, by his manner, that he did not seem to be sorry for his behavior to me, and that I had not much reason to expect any favour from him, I told him that he had used me very ill, after I had been such a faithful servant to him for so many years; on which, without saying any more, he turned about and went away. A few days after this I met Capt. Pascal at Miss Guerin's

2. Landing place on the river Thames.

house, and asked him for my prize-money.[3] He said there was none due to me; for, if my prize money had been 10,000£[4] he had a right to it all. I told him I was informed otherwise; on which he bade me defiance; and, in a bantering tone, desired me to commence a lawsuit against him for it: 'There are lawyers enough,' said he, 'that will take the cause in hand, and you had better try it.' I told him then that I would try it, which enraged him very much; however, out of regard to the ladies, I remained still, and never made any farther demand of my right. Some time afterwards these friendly ladies asked me what I meant to do with myself, and how they could assist me. I thanked them, and said, if they pleased, I would be their servant; but if not, as I had thirty-seven guineas, which would support me for some time, I would be much obliged to them to recommend me to some person who would teach me a business whereby I might earn my living. They answered me very politely, that they were sorry it did not suit them to take me as their servant, and asked me what business I should like to learn? I said, hair-dressing. They then promised to assist me in this; and soon after they recommended me to a gentleman whom I had known before, one Capt. O'Hara, who treated me with much kindness, and procured me a master, a hair-dresser, in Coventry-court, Haymarket, with whom he placed me. I was with this man from September till the February following. In that time we had a neighbour in the same court who taught the French horn. He used to blow it so well that I was charmed with it, and agreed with him to teach me to blow it. Accordingly he took me in hand, and began to instruct me, and I soon learned all the three parts. I took great delight in blowing on this instrument, the evenings being long; and besides that I was fond of it, I did not like to be idle, and it filled up my vacant hours innocently. At this time also I agreed with the Rev. Mr. Gregory, who lived in the same court, where he kept an academy and an evening-school, to improve me in arithmetic. This he did as far as barter and alligation;[5] so that all the time I was there I was entirely employed. In February 1758 I hired myself to Dr. Charles Irving,[6] in Pall-mall, so celebrated for his successful experiments in making sea water fresh; and here I had plenty of hair-dressing to improve my hand. This gentleman was an excellent master; he was exceedingly kind and good tempered; and allowed me in the evenings to attend my schools, which I esteemed a

---

3. See n. 2, p. 69.
4. See n. 2, p. 50.
5. Barter is an arithmetical method for computing value or quantity of one commodity in return for another. Alligation is a rule of arithmetic for finding the price or value of compounds of ingredients of different values and varying proportions.
6. Irving's method was used on the Arctic expedition in which Equiano participated (p. 131, below). See Constantine John Phipps, A *Voyage towards the North Pole Undertaken by His Majesty's Command, 1773* (1774).

great blessing; therefore I thanked God and him for it, and used all my diligence to improve the opportunity. This diligence and attention recommended me to the notice and care of my three preceptors, who on their parts bestowed a great deal of pains in my instruction, and besides were all very kind to me. My wages, however, which were by two thirds less than I ever had in my life (for I had only 12£ per annum) I soon found would not be sufficient to defray this extraordinary expense of masters, and my own necessary expenses; my old thirty-seven guineas had by this time worn all away to one. I thought it best, therefore, to try the sea again in quest of more money, as I had been bred to it, and had hitherto found the profession of it successful. I had also a very great desire to see Turkey, and I now determined to gratify it. Accordingly, in the month of May, 1768, I told the doctor my wish to go to sea again, to which he made no opposition; and we parted on friendly terms. The same day I went into the city in quest of a master. I was extremely fortunate in my inquiry; for I soon heard of a gentleman who had a ship going to Italy and Turkey, and he wanted a man who could dress hair well. I was overjoyed at this, and went immediately on board of his ship, as I had been directed, which I found to be fitted up with great taste, and I already foreboded no small pleasure in sailing in her. Not finding the gentleman on board, I was directed to his lodgings, where I met with him the next day, and gave him a specimen of my dressing. He liked it so well that he hired me immediately, so that I was perfectly happy; for the ship, master, and voyage, were entirely to my mind. The ship was called the Delawar, and my master's name was John Jolly, a neat smart good humoured man, just such an one as I wished to serve. We sailed from England in July following, and our voyage was extremely pleasant.

We went to Villa Franca, Nice, and Leghorn;[7] and in all these places I was charmed with the richness and beauty of the countries, and struck with the elegant buildings with which they abound. We had always in them plenty of extraordinary good wines and rich fruits, which I was very fond of; and I had frequent occasions of gratifying both my taste and curiosity; for my captain always lodged on shore in those places, which afforded me opportunities to see the country around. I also learned navigation of[8] the mate, which I was very fond of. When we left Italy we had delightful sailing among the Archipelago[9] islands, and from thence to Smyrna in Turkey. This is a very ancient city; the houses are built of stone, and most of them have graves adjoining to them; so that they sometimes present the appearance of church-yards. Provisions are very plentiful in this city, and good wine less than a penny a

7. Or Livorno, Italian port on the Ligurian coast; *Villafranca de Penedés*: near Barcelona; *Nice*: in present-day southern France.
8. From.
9. See n. 4, p. 46.

pint. The grapes, pomegranates, and many other fruits, were also the richest and largest I ever tasted. The natives are well looking and strong made, and treated me always with great civility. In general I believe they are fond of black people; and several of them gave me pressing invitations to stay amongst them, although they keep the franks, or Christians, separate, and do not suffer them to dwell immediately amongst them. I was astonished in not seeing women in any of their shops, and very rarely any in the streets; and whenever I did they were covered with a veil from head to foot, so that I could not see their faces, except when any of them out of curiosity uncovered them to look at me, which they sometimes did. I was surprised to see how the Greeks are, in some measure, kept under by the Turks, as the Negroes are in the West Indies by the white people. The less refined Greeks, as I have already hinted, dance here in the same manner as we do in my nation. On the whole, during our stay here, which was about five months, I liked the place and the Turks extremely well. I could not help observing one very remarkable circumstance there: the tails of the sheep are flat, and so very large, that I have known the tail even of a lamb to weigh from eleven to thirteen pounds. The fat of them is very white and rich, and is excellent in puddings, for which it is much used. Our ship being at length richly loaded with silk, and other articles, we sailed for England.

In May 1769, soon after our return from Turkey, our ship made a delightful voyage to Oporto in Portugal, where we arrived at the time of the carnival. On our arrival, there were sent on board to us thirty-six articles to observe, with very heavy penalties if we should break any of them; and none of us even dared to go on board any other vessel or on shore till the Inquisition[1] had sent on board and searched for every thing illegal, especially bibles. Such as were produced, and certain other things, were sent on shore till the ships were going away; and any person in whose custody a bible was found concealed was to be imprisoned and flogged, and sent into slavery for ten years. I saw here many very magnificent sights, particularly the garden of Eden, where many of the clergy and laity went in procession in their several orders with the host, and sung Te Deum.[2] I had a great curiosity to go into some of their churches, but could not gain admittance without using the necessary sprinkling of holy water at my entrance. From curiosity, and a wish to be holy, I therefore complied with this ceremony, but its virtues were lost on me, for I found myself nothing the better for it. This place abounds with plenty of all kinds of provisions. The town is well built

1. General tribunal of the Roman Catholic Church established for the discovery and suppression of heresy and the punishment of heretics. Protestant translations of the Bible were considered heretical.
2. Beginning of Latin chant in praise of God. *Host:* the bread of the Eucharist; wafer symbolizing Christ's body in Catholic Mass.

and pretty, and commands a fine prospect.[3] Our ship having taken in a load of wine, and other commodities, we sailed for London, and arrived in July following. Our next voyage was to the Mediterranean. The ship was again got ready, and we sailed in September for Genoa. This is one of the finest cities I ever saw; some of the edifices were of beautiful marble, and made a most noble appearance; and many had very curious fountains before them. The churches were rich and magnificent, and curiously adorned both in the inside and out. But all this grandeur was in my eyes disgraced by the galley slaves, whose condition both there and in other parts of Italy is truly piteous and wretched. After we had stayed there some weeks, during which we bought many different things which we wanted, and got them very cheap, we sailed to Naples, a charming city, and remarkably clean. The bay is the most beautiful I ever saw; the moles[4] for shiping are excellent. I thought it extraordinary to see grand operas acted here on Sunday nights, and even attended by their majesties. I too, like these great ones, went to those sights, and vainly served God in the day while I thus served mammon[5] effectually at night. While we remained here there happened an eruption of mount Vesuvius, of which I had a perfect view. It was extremely awful; and we were so near that the ashes from it used to be thick on our deck. After we had transacted our business at Naples we sailed with a fair wind once more for Smyrna, where we arrived in December. A seraskier or officer took a liking to me here, and wanted me to stay, and offered me two wives; however I refused the temptation. The merchants here travel in caravans or large companies. I have seen many caravans from India, with some hundreds of camels, laden with different goods. The people of these caravans are quite brown. Among other articles, they brought with them a great quantity of locusts, which are a kind of pulse,[6] sweet and pleasant to the palate, and in shape resembling French beans, but longer. Each kind of goods is sold in a street by itself, and I always found the Turks very honest in their dealings. They let no Christians into their mosques or churches, for which I was very sorry; as I was always fond of going to see the different modes of worship of the people wherever I went. The plague broke out while we were in Smyrna, and we stopped taking goods into the ship till it was over. She was then richly laden, and we sailed in about March 1770 for England. One day in our passage we met with an accident which was near burning the ship. A black cook, in melting some fat, overset the pan into the fire under the deck, which immediately began to blaze, and the flame went up very high under the foretop. With the fright the poor cook became almost white, and

---

3. Offers a fine view.
4. See n. 7, p. 58.
5. The false god of riches and avarice. See Matthew 6.24
6. Edible seeds of plants having pods. *Locusts*: beans of locust trees.

altogether speechless. Happily however we got the fire out without doing much mischief. After various delays in this passage, which was tedious, we arrived in Standgate creek in July; and, at the latter end of the year, some new event occurred, so that my noble captain, the ship, and I all separated.

In April 1771 I shipped myself as a steward with Capt. Wm. Robertson of the ship Grenada Planter, once more to try my fortune in the West Indies; and we sailed from London for Madeira,[7] Barbadoes, and the Grenades. When we were at this last place, having some goods to sell, I met once more with my former kind of West India customers. A white man, an islander, bought some goods of me to the amount of some pounds, and made me many fair promises as usual, but without any intention of paying me. He had likewise bought goods from some more of our people, whom he intended to serve in the same manner; but he still amused us with promises. However, when our ship was loaded, and near sailing, this honest buyer discovered no intention or sign of paying for any thing he had bought of us; but on the contrary, when I asked him for my money he threatened me and another black man he had bought goods of, so that we found we were like to get more blows than payment. On this we went to complain to one Mr. M'Intosh, a justice of the peace; we told his worship of the man's villainous tricks, and begged that he would be kind enough to see us redressed: but being negroes, although free, we could not get any remedy; and our ship being then just upon the point of sailing, we knew not how to help ourselves, though we thought it hard to lose our property in this manner. Luckily for us however, this man was also indebted to three white sailors, who could not get a farthing from him; they therefore readily joined us, and we all went together in search of him. When we found where he was, I took him out of a house and threatened him with vengeance; on which, finding he was likely to be handled roughly, the rogue offered each of us some small allowance, but nothing near our demands. This exasperated us much more; and some were for cutting his ears off; but he begged hard for mercy, which was at last granted him, after we had entirely stripped him. We then let him go, for which he thanked us, glad to get off so easily, and ran into the bushes, after having wished us a good voyage. We then repaired on board, and shortly after set sail for England. I cannot help remarking here a very narrow escape we had from being blown up, owing to a piece of negligence of mine. Just as our ship was under sail, I went down into the cabin to do some business, and had a lighted candle in my hand, which, in my hurry, without thinking, I held in a barrel of gunpowder. It remained in the powder until it was near catching fire, when fortunately I observed it and snatched it out in time, and prov-

7. Portuguese island in the Atlantic.

identially no harm happened; but I was so overcome with terror that I immediately fainted at this deliverance.

In twenty-eight days time we arrived in England, and I got clear of this ship. But, being still of a roving disposition, and desirous of seeing as many different parts of the world as I could, I shipped myself soon after, in the same year, as steward on board of a fine large ship, called the Jamaica, Captain David Watt; and we sailed from England in December 1771 for Nevis and Jamaica. I found Jamaica to be a very fine large island, well peopled, and the most considerable of the West India islands. There was a vast number of negroes here, whom I found as usual exceedingly imposed upon by the white people, and the slaves punished as in the other islands. There are negroes whose business it is to flog slaves; they go about to different people for employment, and the usual pay is from one to four bits. I saw many cruel punishments inflicted on the slaves in the short time I stayed here. In particular I was present when a poor fellow was tied up and kept hanging by the wrists at some distance from the ground, and then some half hundred weights were fixed to his ancles, in which posture he was flogged most unmercifully. There were also, as I heard, two different masters noted for cruelty on the island, who had staked up two negroes naked, and in two hours the vermin stung them to death. I heard a gentleman I well knew tell my captain that he passed sentence on a negro man to be burnt alive for attempting to poison an overseer. I pass over numerous other instances, in order to relieve the reader by a milder scene of roguery. Before I had been long on the island, one Mr. Smith at Port Morant bought goods of me to the amount of twenty-five pounds sterling; but when I demanded payment from him, he was going each time to beat me, and threatened that he would put me in goal. One time he would say I was going to set his house on fire, at another he would swear I was going to run away with his slaves. I was astonished at this usage from a person who was in the situation of a gentleman, but I had no alternative; I was therefore obliged to submit. When I came to Kingston, I was surprised to see the number of Africans who were assembled together on Sundays; particularly at a large commodious place, called Spring Path. Here each different nation of Africa meet and dance after the manner of their own country. They still retain most of their native customs: they bury their dead, and put victuals, pipes and tobacco, and other things, in the grave with the corps, in the same manner as in Africa. Our ship having got her loading we sailed for London, where we arrived in the August following. On my return to London, I waited on my old and good master, Dr. Irving, who made me an offer of his service again. Being now tired of the sea I gladly accepted it. I was very happy in living with this gentleman once more; during which time we were daily employed in reducing old Neptune's dominions[8] by purifying the briny element and making it fresh. Thus I went on till May 1773, when I was roused by the sound of fame, to seek new adventures, and to find, towards the north pole, what our Creator never intended we should, a passage to India.[9] An expedition was now fitting out to explore a north-east passage, conducted by the Honourable John Constantine Phipps, since Lord Mulgrave, in his Majesty's sloop of war the Race Horse. My master being anxious for the reputation of this adventure, we therefore prepared every thing for our voyage, and I attended him on board the Race Horse, the 24th day of May 1773. We proceeded to Sheerness,[1] where we were joined by his Majesty's sloop the Carcass, commanded by Captain Lutwidge. On the 4th of June we sailed towards our destined place, the pole; and on the 15th of the same month we were off Shetland.[2] On this day I had a great and unexpected deliverance from an accident which was near blowing up the ship and destroying the crew, which made me ever after during the voyage uncommonly cautious. The ship was so filled that there was very little room on board for any one, which placed me in a very aukward situation. I had resolved to keep a journal of this singular and interesting voyage; and I had no other place for this purpose but a little cabin, or the doctor's store-room, where I slept. This little place was stuffed with all manner of combustibles, particularly with tow and aquafortis,[3] and many other dangerous things. Unfortunately it happened in the evening as I was writing my journal, that I had occasion to take the candle out of the lanthorn,[4] and a spark having touched a single thread of the tow, all the rest caught the flame, and immediately the whole was in a blaze. I saw nothing but present death before me, and expected to be the first to perish in the flames. In a moment the alarm was spread, and many people who were near ran to assist in putting out the fire. All this time I was in the very midst of the flames; my shirt, and the handkerchief on my neck, were burnt, and I was almost smothered with the smoke. However, through God's mercy, as I was nearly giving up all hopes, some people brought blankets and mattresses and threw them on the flames, by which means in a short time the fire was put out. I was severely reprimanded and menaced by such of the officers who knew it, and strictly charged never more to go there with a light: and, indeed, even my own fears made me give heed to this command for a little time; but at last, not being able to write my journal in any other part of the ship, I was tempted again to venture

8. The sea. Neptune was the Roman name for Poseidon, the God of the sea.
9. The contemporary hope that it might be possible to reach India by way of the Arctic Sea. The Phipps expedition sailed to Spitsbergen and went further north than had any precursors.
1. Port at the mouth of the Thames.
2. Scottish islands, directly north of the Orkneys.
3. Nitric acid. Tow: flax or hemp fibers used for spinning or making ropes.
4. Lantern.

by stealth with a light in the same cabin, though not without considerable fear and dread on my mind. On the 20th of June we began to use Dr. Irving's apparatus for making salt water fresh; I used to attend the distillery: I frequently purified from twenty-six to forty gallons a day. The water thus distilled was perfectly pure, well tasted, and free from salt; and was used on various occasions on board the ship. On the 28th of June, being in lat. 78, we made Greenland, where I was surprised to see the sun did not set. The weather now became extremely cold; and as we sailed between north and east, which was our course, we saw many very high and curious mountains of ice; and also a great number of very large whales, which used to come close to our ship, and blow the water up to a very great height in the air. One morning we had vast quantities of sea-horses[5] about the ship, which neighed exactly like any other horses. We fired some harpoon guns amongst them, in order to take some, but we could not get any. The 30th, the captain of a Greenland ship came on board, and told us of three ships that were lost in the ice; however we still held on our course till July the 11th, when we were stopt by one compact impenetrable body of ice. We ran along it from east to west above ten degrees; and on the 27th we got as far north as 80, 37; and in 19 or 20 degrees east longitude from London. On the 29th and 30th of July we saw one continued plain of smooth unbroken ice, bounded only by the horizon; and we fastened to a piece of ice that was eight yards eleven inches thick. We had generally sunshine, and constant daylight; which gave cheerfulness and novelty to the whole of this striking, grand, and uncommon scene; and, to heighten it still more, the reflection of the sun from the ice gave the clouds a most beautiful appearance. We killed many different animals at this time, and among the rest nine bears. Though they had nothing in their paunches but water yet they were all very fat. We used to decoy them to the ship sometimes by burning feathers or skins. I thought them coarse eating, but some of the ship's company relished them very much. Some of our people once, in the boat, fired at and wounded a sea-horse, which dived immediately; and, in a little time after, brought up with it a number of others. They all joined in an attack upon the boat, and were with difficulty prevented from staving or oversetting her; but a boat from the Carcass having come to assist ours, and joined it, they dispersed, after having wrested an oar from one of the men. One of the ship's boats had before been attacked in the same manner, but happily no harm was done. Though we wounded several of these animals we never got but one. We remained hereabouts until the 1st of August; when the two ships got completely fastened in the ice, occasioned by the loose ice that set in from the sea. This made our situation very dreadful and alarming;

5. Arctic walruses

so that on the 7th day we were in very great apprehension of having the ships squeezed to pieces. The officers now held a council to know what was best for us to do in order to save our lives; and it was determined that we should endeavour to escape by dragging our boats along the ice towards the sea; which, however, was farther off than any of us thought. This determination filled us with extreme dejection, and confounded us with despair; for we had very little prospect of escaping with life. However, we sawed some of the ice about the ships to keep it from hurting them; and thus kept them in a kind of pond. We then began to drag the boats as well as we could towards the sea; but, after two or three days labour, we made very little progress; so that some of our hearts totally failed us, and I really began to give up myself for lost, when I saw our surrounding calamities. While we were at this hard labour I once fell into a pond we had made amongst some loose ice, and was very near being drowned; but providentially some people were near who gave me immediate assistance, and thereby I escaped drowning. Our deplorable condition, which kept up the constant apprehension of our perishing in the ice, brought me gradually to think of eternity in such a manner as I never had done before. I had the fears of death hourly upon me, and shuddered at the thoughts of meeting the grim king of terrors in the *natural* state I then was in, and was exceedingly doubtful of a happy eternity if I should die in it. I had no hopes of my life being prolonged for any time; for we saw that our existence could not be long on the ice after leaving the ships, which were now out of sight, and some miles from the boats. Our appearance now became truly lamentable; pale dejection seized every countenance; many, who had been before blasphemers, in this our distress began to call on the good God of heaven for his help; and in the time of our utter need he heard us, and against hope or human probability delivered us! It was the eleventh day of the ships being thus fastened, and the fourth of our drawing the boats in this manner, that the wind changed to the E.N.E. The weather immediately became mild, and the ice broke towards the sea, which was to the S.W. of us. Many of us on this got on board again, and with all our might we hove[6] the ships into every open water we could find, and made all the sail on them in our power; and now, having a prospect of success, we made signals for the boats and the remainder of the people. This seemed to us like a reprieve from death; and happy was the man who could first get on board of any ship, or the first boat he could meet. We then proceeded in this manner till we got into the open water again, which we accomplished in about thirty hours, to our infinite joy and gladness of heart. As soon as we were out of danger we came to anchor and refitted; and on the 19th of August we sailed from this uninhabited extremity of the world,

6. Heaved.

where the inhospitable climate affords neither food nor shelter, and not a tree or shrub of any kind grows amongst its barren rocks; but all is one desolate and expanded waste of ice, which even the constant beams of the sun for six months in the year cannot penetrate or dissolve. The sun now being on the decline the days shortened as we sailed to the southward; and, on the 28th, in latitude 73,[7] it was dark by ten o'clock at night. September the 10th, in latitude 58–59, we met a very severe gale of wind and high seas, and shipped a great deal of water in the space of ten hours. This made us work exceedingly hard at all our pumps a whole day; and one sea, which struck the ship with more force than any thing I ever met with of the kind before, laid her under water for some time, so that we thought she would have gone down. Two boats were washed from the booms, and the long-boat from the chucks: all other moveable things on the deck were also washed away, among which were many curious things of different kinds which we had brought from Greenland; and we were obliged, in order to lighten the ship, to toss some of our guns overboard. We saw a ship, at the same time, in very great distress, and her masts were gone; but we were unable to assist her. We now lost sight of the Carcass till the 26th, when we saw land about Orfordness,[8] off which place she joined us. From thence we sailed for London, and on the 30th came up to Deptford. And thus ended our Arctic voyage, to the no small joy of all on board, after having been absent four months; in which time, at the imminent hazard of our lives, we explored nearly as far towards the Pole as 81 degrees north, and 20 degrees east longitude;[9] being much farther, by all accounts, than any navigator had ever ventured before; in which we fully proved the impracticability of finding a passage that way to India.

Chap. X.

The author leaves Doctor Irving and engages on board a Turkey ship—Account of a black man's being kidnapped on board and sent to the West Indies, and the author's fruitless endeavours to procure his freedom—Some account of the manner of the author's conversion to the faith of Jesus Christ.

Our voyage to the North Pole being ended, I returned to London with Doctor Irving, with whom I continued for some time, during which I began seriously to reflect on the dangers I had escaped, par-

---

7. In the Arctic Ocean, latitude 73 is to the north of Iceland and Scandinavia and traverses Greenland in the west and Novaya Zemlya in the east.
8. Or Orford Ness, on the Suffolk coast, approximately 60 miles northeast of the mouth of the Thames.
9. Near the east coast of northern Greenland.

ticularly those of my last voyage, which made a lasting impression on my mind, and, by the grace of God, proved afterwards a mercy to me; it caused me to reflect deeply on my eternal state, and to seek the Lord with full purpose of heart ere it was too late. I rejoiced greatly; and heartily thanked the Lord for directing me to London, where I was determined to work out my own salvation, and in so doing procure a title to heaven, being the result of a mind blended by ignorance and sin.

In process of time I left my master, Doctor Irving, the purifier of waters, and lodged in Coventry-court, Haymarket, where I was continually oppressed and much concerned about the salvation of my soul, and was determined (in my own strength) to be a first-rate Christian. I used every means for this purpose; and, not being able to find any person amongst my acquaintance that agreed with me in point of religion, or, in scripture language, 'that would shew me any good;' I was much dejected, and knew not where to seek relief; however, I first frequented the neighbouring churches, St. James's, and others, two or three times a day, for many weeks: still I came away dissatisfied; something was wanting that I could not obtain, and I really found more heartfelt relief in reading my bible at home than in attending the church; and, being resolved to be saved, I pursued other methods still. First I went among the quakers, where the word of God was neither read or preached, so that I remained as much in the dark as ever. I then searched into the Roman catholic principles, but was not in the least satisfied. At length I had recourses to the Jews, which availed me nothing, for the fear of eternity daily harassed my mind, and I knew not where to seek shelter from the wrath to come. However this was my conclusion, at all events, to read the four evangelists,[1] and whatever sect or party I found adhering thereto such I would join. Thus I went on heavily without any guide to direct me the way that leadeth to eternal life. I asked different people questions about the manner of going to heaven, and was told different ways. Here I was much staggered, and could not find any at that time more righteous than myself, or indeed so much inclined to devotion. I thought we should not all be saved (this is agreeable to the holy scriptures), nor would all be damned. I found none among the circle of my acquaintance that kept wholly the ten commandments. So righteous was I in my own eyes, that I was convinced I excelled many of them in that point, by keeping eight out of ten; and finding those who in general termed themselves Christians not so honest or so good in their morals as the Turks, I really thought the Turks were in a safer way of salvation than my neighbours: so that between hopes and fears I went on, and the chief comforts I enjoyed were in the musical French horn, which I then practised, and

1. The four writers of the gospels, Matthew, Mark, Luke, and John, whose texts comprise the first four books of the New Testament.

also dressing of hair. Such was my situation some months, experiencing the dishonesty of many people here. I determined at last to set out for Turkey, and there to end my days. It was now early in the spring 1774. I sought for a master, and found a captain John Hughes, commander of a ship called Anglicania, fitting out in the river Thames, and bound to Smyrna in Turkey. I shipped myself with him as a steward; at the same time I recommended to him a very clever black man, John Annis, as a cook. This man was on board the ship near two months doing his duty: he had formerly lived many years with Mr. William Kirkpatrick, a gentleman of the island of St. Kitts, from whom he parted by consent, though he afterwards tried many schemes to inveigle the poor man. He had applied to many captains who traded to St. Kitts to trepan[2] him; and when all their attempts and schemes of kidnapping proved abortive, Mr. Kirkpatrick came to our ship at Union Stairs on Easter Monday, April the fourth, with two wherry boats and six men, having learned that the man was on board; and tied, and forcibly took him away from the ship, in the presence of the crew and the chief mate, who had detained him after he had notice to come away. I believe that this was a combined piece of business: but, at any rate, it certainly reflected great disgrace on the mate and captain also, who, although they had desired the oppressed man to stay on board, yet he did not in the least assist to recover him, or pay me a farthing of his wages, which was about five pounds. I proved the only friend he had, who attempted to regain him his liberty if possible, having known the want of liberty myself. I sent as soon as I could to Gravesend, and got knowledge of the ship in which he was; but unluckily she had sailed the first tide after he was put on board. My intention was then immediately to apprehend Mr. Kirkpatrick, who was about setting off for Scotland; and, having obtained a *habeas corpus* for him, and got a tipstaff[3] to go with me to St. Paul's church-yard, where he lived, he, suspecting something of this kind, set a watch to look out. My being known to them occasioned me to use the following deception: I whitened my face, that they might not know me, and this had its desired effect. He did not go out of his house that night, and next morning I contrived a well plotted stratagem notwithstanding he had a gentleman in his house to personate him. My direction to the tipstaff, who got admittance into the house, was to conduct him to a judge, according to the writ. When he came there, his plea was, that he had not the body in custody, on which he was admitted to bail. I proceeded immediately to that philanthropist, Granville Sharp, Esq.[4] who received me with the utmost kindness, and gave me every instruction that was needful on the occa-

2. Snare or entrap.
3. Officer; constable. *Habeas corpus*: A legal order requiring that a restrained person be brought before a judge to decide the legality of the detention; safeguard against illegal imprisonment.
4. Abolitionist (1735–1813) who chaired the Society for the Abolition of Slavery and rescued blacks from being shipped to the West Indies, arguing that they were free in England.

sion. I left him in full hope that I should gain the unhappy man his liberty, with the warmest sense of gratitude towards Mr. Sharp for his kindness; but, alas! my attorney proved unfaithful; he took my money, lost me many months employ, and did not do the least good in the cause: and when the poor man arrived at St. Kitts, he was, according to custom, staked to the ground with four pins through a cord, two on his wrists, and two on his ancles, was cut and flogged most unmercifully, and afterwards loaded cruelly with irons about his neck. I had two very moving letters from him, while he was in this situation; and also was told of it by some very respectable families now in London, who saw him in St. Kitts, in the same state in which he remained till kind death released him out of the hands of his tyrants. During this disagreeable business I was under strong convictions of sin, and thought that my state was worse than any man's; my mind was unaccountably disturbed; I often wished for death, though at the same time convinced I was altogether unprepared for that awful summons. Suffering much by villains in the late cause, and being much concerned about the state of my soul, these things (but particularly the latter) brought me very low; so that I became a burden to myself, and viewed all things around me as emptiness and vanity, which could give no satisfaction to a troubled conscience. I was again determined to go to Turkey, and resolved, at that time, never more to return to England. I engaged as steward on board a Turkeyman (the Wester Hall, Capt. Linna); but was prevented by means of my late captain, Mr. Hughes, and others. All this appeared to be against me, and the only comfort I then experienced was, in reading the holy scriptures, where I saw that 'there is no new thing under the sun,' Eccles. i. 9; and what was appointed for me I must submit to. Thus I continued to travel in much heaviness, and frequently murmured against the Almighty, particularly in his providential dealings; and, awful to think! I began to blaspheme, and wished often to be any thing but a human being. In these severe conflicts the Lord answered me by awful 'visions of the night, when deep sleep falleth upon men, in slumberings upon the bed,' Job xxxiii. 15. He was pleased, in much mercy, to give me to see, and in some measure to understand, the great and awful scene of the judgment-day, that 'no unclean person, no unholy thing, can enter into the kingdom of God,' Eph. v. 5. I would then, if it had been possible, have changed my nature with the meanest worm on the earth; and was ready to say to the mountains and rocks 'fall on me,' Rev. vi. 16; but all in vain. I then requested the divine Creator that he would grant me a small space of time to repent of my follies and vile iniquities, which I felt were grievous. The Lord, in his manifold mercies, was pleased to grant my request, and being yet in a state of time, the sense of God's mercies was so great on my mind when I awoke, that my strength entirely failed me for many minutes, and I was exceedingly weak. This was the first spiritual mercy I ever was sensible of, and being on praying ground, as soon as I recovered a little strength, and got out of bed and dressed myself, I invoked Heaven from my inmost soul, and fervently begged that God would never again permit me to blaspheme his most holy name. The Lord, who is long-suffering, and full of compassion to such poor rebels as we are, condescended to hear and answer. I felt that I was altogether unholy, and saw clearly what a bad use I had made of the faculties I was endowed with; they were given me to glorify God with; I thought, therefore, I had better want them here, and enter into life eternal, than abuse them and be cast into hell fire. I prayed to be directed, if there were any holier than those with whom I was acquainted, that the Lord would point them out to me. I appealed to the Searcher of hearts, whether I did not wish to love him more, and serve him better. Notwithstanding all this, the reader may easily discern, if he is a believer, that I was still in nature's darkness. At length I hated the house in which I lodged, because God's most holy name was blasphemed in it; then I saw the word of God verified, viz. 'Before they call, I will answer; and while they are yet speaking, I will hear.'[5]

I had a great desire to read the bible the whole day at home; but not having a convenient place for retirement, I left the house in the day, rather than stay amongst the wicked ones; and that day as I was walking, it pleased God to direct me to a house where there was an old sea-faring man, who experienced much of the love of God shed abroad in his heart. He began to discourse with me; and, as I desired to love the Lord, his conversation rejoiced me greatly; and indeed I had never heard before the love of Christ to believers set forth in such a manner, and in so clear a point of view. Here I had more questions to put to the man than his time would permit him to answer; and in that memorable hour there came in a dissenting[6] minister; he joined our discourse, and asked me some few questions; among others, where I heard the gospel preached. I knew not what he meant by hearing the gospel; I told him I had read the gospel: and he asked where I went to church, or whether I went at all or not. To which I replied, 'I attended St. James's, St. Martin's, and 'St. Ann's, Soho;'—'So,' said he, 'you are a churchman.' I answered, I was. He then invited me to a lovefeast[7] at his chapel that evening. I accepted the offer, and thanked him; and soon after he went away, I had some further discourse with the old Christian, added to some profitable reading, which made me exceedingly happy. When I left him he reminded me of coming to the feast; I assured him I would be there. Thus we parted, and I weighed over the heavenly conversation that had passed between these two men, which cheered my then heavy and drooping spirit more than any thing

5. Isaiah 65.24.
6. Non-Anglican; Methodist.
7. Evangelical commemoration of Christ's Last Supper, with singing and praying.

I had met with for many months. However, I thought the time long in going to my supposed banquet. I also wished much for the company of these friendly men; their company pleased me much; and I thought the gentlemen very kind, in asking me, a stranger, to a feast; but how singular did it appear to me, to have it in a chapel! When the wished-for hour came I went, and happily the old man was there, who kindly seated me, as he belonged to the place. I was much astonished to see the place filled with people, and no signs of eating and drinking. There were many ministers in the company. At last they began by giving out hymns, and between the singing the minister engaged in prayer; in short, I knew not what to make of this sight, having never seen any thing of the kind in my life before now. Some of the guests began to speak their experience, agreeable to what I read in the Scriptures; much was said by every speaker of the providence of God, and his unspeakable mercies, to each of them. This I knew in a great measure, and could most heartily join them. But when they spoke of a future state, they seemed to be altogether certain of their calling and election of God; and that no one could ever separate them from the love of Christ, or pluck them out of his hands. This filled me with utter consternation, intermingled with admiration. I was so amazed as not to know what to think of the company; my heart was attracted and my affections were enlarged. I wished to be as happy as them, and was persuaded in my mind that they were different from the world 'that lieth in wickedness,' I John v. 19. Their language and singing, &c. did well harmonize; I was entirely overcome, and wished to live and die thus. Lastly, some persons in the place produced some neat baskets full of buns, which they distributed about; and each person communicated with his neighbour, and sipped water out of different mugs, which they handed about to all who were present. This kind of Christian fellowship I had never seen, nor ever thought of seeing on earth; it fully reminded me of what I had read in the holy scriptures, of the primitive Christians,[8] who loved each other and broke bread. In partaking of it, even from house to house, this entertainment (which lasted about four hours) ended in singing and prayer. It was the first soul feast I ever was present at. This last twenty-four hours produced me things, spiritual and temporal, sleeping and waking, judgment and mercy, that I could not but admire the goodness of God, in directing the blind, blasphemous sinner in the path that he knew not of, even among the just; and instead of judgment he has shewed mercy, and will hear and answer the prayers and supplications of every returning prodigal:

> O! to grace how great a debtor
> Daily I'm constrain'd to be![9]

---

8. Followers of Jesus before the establishment of the Christian church.
9. From hymn by Robert Robinson (1735–1790), "Come, Thou Fountain of Every Blessing."

After this I was resolved to win Heaven if possible; and if I perished I thought it should be at the feet of Jesus, in praying to him for salvation. After having been an eye-witness to some of the happiness which attended those who feared God, I knew not how, with any propriety, to return to my lodgings, where the name of God was continually profaned, at which I felt the greatest horror. I paused in my mind for some time, not knowing what to do; whether to hire a bed elsewhere, or go home again. At last, fearing an evil report might arise, I went home, with a farewell to card-playing and vain jesting, &c. I saw that time was very short, eternity long, and very near, and I viewed those persons alone blessed who were found ready at midnight call, or when the Judge of all, both quick[1] and dead, cometh.

The next day I took courage, and went to Holborn, to see my new and worthy acquaintance, the old man, Mr. C——; he, with his wife, a gracious woman, were at work at silk weaving; they seemed mutually happy, and both quite glad to see me, and I more so to see them. I sat down, and we conversed much about soul matters, &c. Their discourse was amazingly delightful, edifying, and pleasant. I knew not at last how to leave this agreeable pair, till time summoned me away. As I was going they lent me a little book, entitled "The Conversion of an Indian."[2] It was in questions and answers. The poor man came over the sea to London, to inquire after the Christian's God, who, (through rich mercy) he found, and had not his journey in vain. The above book was of great use to me, and at that time was a means of strengthening my faith; however, in parting, they both invited me to call on them when I pleased. This delighted me, and I took care to make all the improvement from it I could; and so far I thanked God for such company and desires. I prayed that the many evils I felt within might be done away, and that I might be weaned from my former carnal acquaintances. This was quickly heard and answered, and I was soon connected with those whom the scripture calls the excellent of the earth. I heard the gospel preached, and the thoughts of my heart and actions were laid open by the preachers, and the way of salvation by Christ alone was evidently set forth. Thus I went on happily for near two months; and I once heard, during this period, a reverend gentleman speak of a man who had departed this life in full assurance of his going to glory. I was much astonished at the assertion; and did very deliberately inquire how he could get at this knowledge. I was answered fully, agreeable to what I read in the oracles of truth; and was told also, that if I did not experience the new birth, and the pardon of my sins, through the blood of Christ, before I died, I could not enter the kingdom of heaven. I knew not what to think of this report, as I thought I kept eight commandments out of ten; then my worthy interpreter told me

1. Alive.
2. Lawrence Harlow's *The Conversion of the Indian, in a Letter to a Friend* (1774).

I did not do it, nor could I; and he added, that no man ever did
or could keep the commandments, without offending in one point.
I thought this sounded very strange, and puzzled me much for
many weeks; for I thought it a hard saying. I then asked my friend, Mr.
L——d, who was a clerk in a chapel, why the commandments of God
were given, if we could not be saved by them? To which he replied,
'The law is a schoolmaster to bring us to Christ,' who alone could and
did keep the commandments, and fulfilled all their requirements for
his elect people, even those to whom he had given a living faith, and
the sins of those chosen vessels *were already* atoned for and forgiven
them whilst living; and if I did not experience the same before my exit,
the Lord would say at that great day to me 'Go ye cursed,' &c. &c. for
God would appear faithful in his judgments to the wicked, as he would
be faithful in shewing mercy to those who were ordained to it before
the world was; therefore Christ Jesus seemed to be all in all to that
man's soul. I was much wounded at this discourse, and brought into
such a dilemma as I never expected. I asked him, if *he* was to die that
moment, whether he was sure to enter the kingdom of God? and
added, 'Do you *know* that your sins are forgiven you?' He answered in
the affirmative. Then confusion, anger, and discontent seized me, and
I staggered much at this sort of doctrine; it brought me to a stand, not
knowing which to believe, whether salvation by works or by faith only
in Christ. I requested him to tell me how I might know when my sins
were forgiven me. He assured me he could not, and that none but God
alone could do this. I told him it was very mysterious; but he said it
was really matter of fact, and quoted many portions of scripture immediately to the point, to which I could make no reply. He then desired
me to pray to God to shew me these things. I answered, that I prayed
to God every day? He said, 'I perceive you are a church-man.' I
answered I was. He then entreated me to beg of God to shew me what
I was, and the true state of my soul. I thought the prayer very short
and odd; so we parted for that time. I weighed all these things well
over, and could not help thinking how it was possible for a man to
know that his sins were forgiven him in this life. I wished that God
would reveal this self same thing unto me. In a short time after this I
went to Westminster chapel; the Rev. Mr. P—— preached, from Lam.
iii. 39.[3] It was a wonderful sermon; he clearly shewed that a living man
had no cause to complain for the punishment of his sins; he evidently
justified the Lord in all his dealings with the sons of men; he also
shewed the justice of God in the eternal punishment of the wicked
and impenitent. The discourse seemed to me like a two-edged sword
cutting all ways; it afforded me much joy, intermingled with many
fears, about my soul; and when it was ended, he gave it out that he

---

3. "Wherefore doth a living man complain, a man for the punishment of his sins?"

intended, the ensuing week, to examine all those who meant to attend the Lord's table. Now I thought much of my good works, and at the same time was doubtful of my being a proper object to receive the sacrament; I was full of meditation till the day of examining. However, I went to the chapel, and, though much distressed, I addressed the reverend gentleman, thinking, if I was not right, he would endeavour to convince me of it. When I conversed with him, the first thing he asked me was, what I knew of Christ? I told him I believed in him, and had been baptized in his name. 'Then,' said he, 'when were you brought to the knowledge of God? and how were you convinced of sin?' I knew not what he meant by these questions; I told him I kept eight commandments out of ten; but that I sometimes swore on board ship, and sometimes when on shore, and broke the sabbath. He then asked me if I could read? I answered, 'Yes.'—'Then,' said he, 'do you not read in the bible, he that offends in one point is guilty of all?'[4] I said, 'Yes.' Then he assured me, that one sin unatoned for was as sufficient to damn a soul as one leak was to sink a ship. Here I was struck with awe; for the minister exhorted me much, and reminded me of the shortness of time, and the length of eternity, and that no unregenerate soul, or any thing unclean, could enter the kingdom of Heaven. He did not admit me as a communicant; but recommended me to read the scriptures, and hear the word preached, not to neglect fervent prayer to God, who has promised to hear the supplications of those who seek him in godly sincerity; so I took my leave of him, with many thanks, and resolved to follow his advice, so far as the Lord would condescend to enable me. During this time I was out of employ, nor was I likely to get a situation suitable for me, which obliged me to go once more to sea. I engaged as steward of a ship called the Hope, Capt. Richard Strange, bound from London to Cadiz in Spain. In a short time after I was on board I heard the name of God much blasphemed, and I feared greatly, lest I should catch the horrible infection. I thought if I sinned again, after having life and death set evidently before me, I should certainly go to hell. My mind was uncommonly chagrined, and I murmured much at God's providential dealings with me, and was discontented with the commandments, that I could not be saved by what I had done; I hated all things, and wished I had never been born; confusion seized me, and I wished to be annihilated. One day I was standing on the very edge of the stern of the ship, thinking to drown myself; but this scripture was instantly impressed on my mind—'that no murderer hath eternal life abiding in him,' 1 John iii. 15. Then I paused, and thought myself the unhappiest man living. Again I was convinced that the Lord was better to me than I deserved, and I was better off in the world than many. After this I began to fear death; I

4. See James 2.10.

fretted, mourned, and prayed, till I became a burden to others, but more so to myself. At length I concluded to beg my bread on shore rather than go again to sea amongst a people who feared not God, and I entreated the captain three different times to discharge me; he would not, but each time gave me greater and greater encouragement to continue with him, and all on board shewed me very great civility: notwithstanding all this I was unwilling to embark again. At last some of my religious friends advised me, by saying it was my lawful calling, consequently it was my duty to obey, and that God was not confined to place, &c. &c. particularly Mr. G. S.[5] the governor of Tothil-fields Bridewell, who pitied my case, and read the eleventh chapter of the Hebrews to me, with exhortations. He prayed for me, and I believed that he prevailed on my behalf, as my burden was then greatly removed, and I found a heartfelt resignation to the will of God. The good man gave me a pocket Bible and Allen's Alarm to the unconverted.[6] We parted, and the next day I went on board again. We sailed for Spain, and I found favour with the captain. It was the fourth of the month of September when we sailed from London; we had a delightful voyage to Cadiz, where we arrived the twenty-third of the same month. The place is strong, commands a fine prospect, and is very rich. The Spanish galloons[7] frequent that port, and some arrived whilst we were there. I had many opportunities of reading the scriptures. I wrestled hard with God in fervent prayer, who had declared in his word that he would hear the groanings and deep sighs of the poor in spirit. I found this verified to my utter astonishment and comfort in the following manner:

On the morning of the 6th of October, (I pray you to attend) or all that day, I thought I should either see or hear something supernatural. I had a secret impulse on my mind of something that was to take place, which drove me continually for that time to a throne of grace. It pleased God to enable me to wrestle with him, as Jacob did:[8] I prayed that if sudden death were to happen, and I perished, it might be at Christ's feet.

In the evening of the same day, as I was reading and meditating on the fourth chapter of the Acts, twelfth verse[9] under the solemn apprehensions of eternity, and reflecting on my past actions, I began to think I had lived a moral life, and that I had a proper ground to believe I had an interest in the divine favour; but still meditating on the subject, not knowing whether salvation was to be had partly for our own good deeds, or solely as the sovereign gift of God; in this deep consternation the Lord was pleased to break in upon my soul with his bright beams

5. George Smith (d.1784), a frequently praised prison-keeper.
6. Joseph Alleine's *An Alarme to Unconverted Sinners* (1674) was a popular conversion treatise.
7. Or galleons, large Spanish warships with three or four decks.
8. In Genesis 32.24–30, Jacob wrestles with God.
9. Quoted by Equiano below (see p. 145), with the added phrase "but only Christ Jesus."

of heavenly light; and in an instant as it were, removing the veil, and letting light into a dark place,[1] I saw clearly with the eye of faith the crucified Saviour bleeding on the cross on mount Calvary: the scriptures became an unsealed book, I saw myself a condemned criminal under the law, which came with its full force to my conscience, and when 'the commandment came sin revived, and I died.'[2] I saw the Lord Jesus Christ in his humiliation, loaded and bearing my reproach, sin, and shame. I then clearly perceived that by the deeds of the law no flesh living could be justified. I was then convinced that by the first Adam sin came, and by the second Adam (the Lord Jesus Christ) all that are saved must be made alive. It was given me at that time to know what it was to be born again, John iii. 5. I saw the eighth chapter to the Romans, and the doctrines of God's decrees, verified agreeable to his eternal, everlasting, and unchangeable purposes. The word of God was sweet to my taste, yea sweeter than honey and the honeycomb. Christ was revealed to my soul as the chiefest among ten thousand. These heavenly moments were really as life to the dead, and what John calls an earnest of the Spirit.[3] This was indeed unspeakable, and I firmly believe undeniable by many. Now every leading providential circumstance that happened to me, from the day I was taken from my parents to that hour, was then in my view, as if it had but just then occurred. I was sensible of the invisible hand of God, which guided and protected me when in truth I knew it not: still the Lord pursued me although I slighted and disregarded it; this mercy melted me down. When I considered my poor wretched state I wept, seeing what a great debtor I was to sovereign free grace. Now the Ethiopian[4] was willing to be saved by Jesus Christ, the sinner's only surety, and also to rely on none other person or thing for salvation. Self was obnoxious, and good works he had none, for it is God that worketh in us both to will and to do. The amazing things of that hour can never be told—it was joy in the Holy Ghost! I felt an astonishing change; the burden of sin, the gaping jaws of hell, and the fears of death, that weighed me down before, now lost their horror; indeed I thought death would now be the best earthly friend I ever had. Such were my grief and joy as I believe are seldom experienced. I was bathed in tears, and said, What am I that God should thus look on me the vilest of sinners? I felt a deep concern for my mother and friends, which occasioned me to pray with fresh ardour; and, in the abyss of thought, I viewed the unconverted people of the world in a very awful state, being without God and without hope.

It pleased God to pour out on me the Spirit of prayer and the grace

1. Isaiah 25.7.
2. Romans 7.9
3. John xvi. 13, 14. &c [Equiano's note].
4. See Psalms 68.31, Jeremiah 13.23, and Acts 8.27–39.

of supplication, so that in loud acclamations I was enabled to praise and glorify his most holy name. When I got out of the cabin, and told some of the people what the Lord had done for me, alas, who could understand me or believe my report!—None but to whom the arm of the Lord was revealed. I became a barbarian to them in talking of the love of Christ: his name was to me as ointment poured forth; indeed it was sweet to my soul, but to them a rock of offence. I thought my case singular, and every hour a day until I came to London, for I much longed to be with some to whom I could tell of the wonders of God's love towards me, and join in prayer to him whom my soul loved and thirsted after. I had uncommon commotions within, such as few can tell aught about. Now the bible was my only companion and comfort; I prized it much, with many thanks to God that I could read it for myself, and was not left to be tossed about or led by man's devices and notions. The worth of a soul cannot be told.—May the Lord give the reader an understanding in this. Whenever I looked in the bible I saw things new, and many texts were immediately applied to me with great comfort, for I knew that to me was the word of salvation sent. Sure I was that the Spirit which indited the word opened my heart to receive the truth of it as it is in Jesus—that the same Spirit enabled me to act faith upon the promises that were so precious to me, and enabled me to believe to the salvation of my soul. By free grace I was persuaded that I had a part in the first resurrection, and was 'enlightened with the light of the living,' Job xxxiii. 30. I wished for a man of God with whom I might converse: my soul was like the chariots of Aminidab,[5] Canticles vi. 12. These, among others, were the precious promises that were so powerfully applied to me: 'All things whatsoever ye shall ask in prayer, believing, ye shall receive,' Mat. xxi. 22. 'Peace I leave with you, my peace I give unto you,' John xiv. 27. I saw the blessed Redeemer to be the fountain of life, and the well of salvation. I experienced him all in all; he had brought me by a way that I knew not, and he had made crooked paths straight. Then in his name I set up my Ebenezer,[6] saying, Hitherto he hath helped me: and could say to the sinners about me, Behold what a Saviour I have! Thus I was, by the teaching of that all-glorious Deity, the great One in Three, and Three in One, confirmed in the truths of the bible, those oracles of everlasting truth, on which every soul living must stand or fall eternally, agreeable to Acts iv. 12. 'Neither is there salvation in any other, for there is none other name under heaven given among men whereby we must be saved, but only Christ Jesus.' May God give the reader a right understanding in these facts! To him that believeth all things are pos-

5. Or Amminadib; minor biblical figure mentioned only in genealogies and in the passage from Canticles that Equiano cites.
6. Literally, "stone of help." Samuel set up the Ebenezer to commemorate God's help in defeating the Philistines (1 Samuel 7.12); hence, any memorial of divine aid; among English dissenters, a place of worship.

sible, but to them that are unbelieving nothing is pure, Titus i. 15. During this period we remained at Cadiz until our ship got laden. We sailed about the fourth of November; and, having a good passage, we arrived in London the month following, to my comfort, with heartfelt gratitude to God for his rich and unspeakable mercies. On my return I had but one text which puzzled me, or that the devil endeavoured to buffet me with, viz. Rom. xi. 6.[7] and, as I had heard of the Reverend Mr. Romaine,[8] and his great knowledge in the scriptures, I wished much to hear him preach. One day I went to Blackfriars church, and, to my great satisfaction and surprise, he preached from that very text. He very clearly shewed the difference between human works and free election, which is according to God's sovereign will and pleasure. These glad tidings set me entirely at liberty, and I went out of the church rejoicing, seeing my spots[9] were those of God's children. I went to Westminster Chapel, and saw some of my old friends, who were glad when they perceived the wonderful change that the Lord had wrought in me, particularly Mr. G—S—, my worthy acquaintance, who was a man of a choice spirit, and had great zeal for the Lord's service. I enjoyed his correspondence till he died in the year 1784. I was again examined at the same chapel, and was received into church fellowship amongst them: I rejoiced in spirit, making melody in my heart to the God of all my mercies. Now my whole wish was to be dissolved, and to be with Christ—but, alas! I must wait mine appointed time.

Micellaneous Verses,

or
Reflections on the State of my mind during my first Convictions; of the Necessity of believing the Truth, and experiencing the inestimable Benefits of Christianity.

Well may I say my life has been
One scene of sorrow and of pain;
From early days I griefs have known,
And as I grew my griefs have grown:

Dangers were always in my path;
And fear of wrath, and sometimes death;

7. "And if by grace, then is it no more of works: otherwise grace is no more grace. But if it be of works, then is it no more grace; otherwise work is no more work."
8. William Romaine (1714–1795) preached salvation through faith alone.
9. Sins. Perhaps also an allusion to the question in Jeremiah 13: 23: "Can the Ethiopian change his skin, or the leopard his spots?"

While pale dejection in me reign'd
I often wept, by grief constrain'd.

When taken from my native land,
By an unjust and cruel band,
How did uncommon dread prevail!
My sighs no more I could conceal.

'To ease my mind I often strove,
And tried my trouble to remove:
I sung, and utter'd sighs between—
Assay'd to stifle guilt with sin.

'But O! not all that I could do
Would stop the current of my woe;
Conviction still my vileness shew'd;
How great my guilt—how lost from God!

'Prevented, that I could not die,
Nor might to one kind refuge fly;
An orphan state I had to mourn,—
Forsook by all, and left forlorn.'

'Those who beheld my downcast mien
Could not guess at my woes unseen:
They by appearance could not know
The troubles that I waded through.

'Lust, anger, blasphemy, and pride,
With legions of such ills beside,
Troubled my thoughts,' while doubts and fears
Clouded and darken'd most my years.

'Sighs now no more would be confin'd—
They breath'd the trouble of my mind:
I wish'd for death, but check'd the word,
And often pray'd unto the Lord.'

Unhappy, more than some on earth,
I thought the place that gave me birth—
Strange thoughts oppress'd—while I replied
"Why not in Ethiopia died?"

And why thus spared, nigh to hell?—
God only knew—I could not tell!
'A tott'ring fence, a bowing wall,
I thought myself ere since the fall.'

'Oft times I mused, nigh despair,
While birds melodious fill'd the air:
Thrice happy songsters, ever free,
How bless'd were they compar'd to me!'

Thus all things added to my pain,
While grief compell'd me to complain;
When sable clouds began to rise
My mind grew darker than the skies.

The English nation call'd to leave,
How did my breast with sorrows heave!
I long'd for rest—cried "Help me, Lord!
"Some mitigation, Lord, afford!"

Yet on, dejected, still I went—
Heart-throbbing woes within were pent;
Nor land, nor sea, could comfort give,
Nothing my anxious mind relieve.

Weary with travail, yet unknown
To all but God and self alone,
Numerous months for peace I strove,
And numerous foes I had to prove.

Inur'd to dangers, griefs, and woes,
Train'd up 'midst perils, deaths, and foes,
I said "Must it thus ever be?—
"No quiet is permitted me."

Hard hap, and more than heavy lot!
I pray'd to God, "Forget me not—
"What thou ordain'st willing I'll bear;
But O! deliver from despair!"

Strivings and wrestlings seem'd in vain;
Nothing I did could ease my pain:
Then gave I up my works and will,
Confess'd and own'd my doom was hell!

Like some poor pris'ner at the bar,
Conscious of guilt, of sin and fear,
Arraign'd, and self-condemned, I stood—
'Lost in the world, and in my blood!'

Yet here, 'midst blackest clouds confin'd,
A beam from Christ, the day-star, shin'd;
Surely, thought I, if Jesus please,
He can at once sign my release.

I, ignorant of his righteousness,
Set up my labours in its place;
'Forgot for why his blood was shed,
And pray'd and fasted in its stead.'

He dy'd for sinners—I am one!
Might not his blood for me atone?
Tho' I am nothing else but sin,
Yet surely he can make me clean!

Thus light came in, and I believ'd;
Myself forgot, and help receiv'd!
My Saviour then I know I found,
For, eas'd from guilt, no more I groan'd.

O, happy hour, in which I ceas'd
To mourn, for then I found a rest!
My soul and Christ were now as one—
Thy light, O Jesus, in me shone!

Bless'd be thy name, for now I know
I and my works can nothing do;
"The Lord alone can ransom man—
For this the spotless Lamb was slain!"

When sacrifices, works, and pray'r,
Prov'd vain, and ineffectual were,
"Lo, then I come!" the Saviour cry'd,
And, bleeding, bow'd his head and dy'd!

He dy'd for all who ever saw
No help in them, nor by the law:—
I this have seen; and gladly own
"Salvation is by Christ alone!"[1]

---

1. Acts iv. 12 [Equiano's note]. A freely expanded rendition of Acts.

Chap. XI.

The author embarks on board a ship bound for Cadiz—Is near
being shipwrecked—Goes to Malaga—Remarkable fine cathedral
there—The author disputes with a pepish priest—Picking up
eleven miserable men at sea in returning to England—Engages
again with Doctor Irving to accompany him to Jamaica and the
Mosquito Shore—Meets with an Indian prince on board—The
author attempts to instruct him in the truths of the Gospel—
Frustrated by the bad example of some in the ship—They arrive
on the Mosquito Shore with some slaves they purchased at
Jamaica, and begin to cultivate a plantation—Some account of
the manners and customs of the Mosquito Indians—Successful
device of the author's to quell a riot among them—Curious
entertainment given by them to Doctor Irving and the author, who
leaves the shore and goes for Jamaica—Is barbarously treated by a
man with whom he engaged for his passage—Escapes and goes to
the Mosquito admiral, who treats him kindly—He gets another
vessel and goes on board—Instances of bad treatment—Meets
Doctor Irving—Gets to Jamaica—Is cheated by his captain—
Leaves the Doctor and goes for England.

When our ship was got ready for sea again, I was entreated by the
captain to go in her once more; but, as I felt myself now as happy as I
could wish to be in this life, I for some time refused; however, the
advice of my friends at last prevailed; and, in full resignation to the
will of God, I again embarked for Cadiz in March 1775.

We had a very good passage, without any material accident, until
we arrived off the Bay of Cadiz; when one Sunday, just as we were
going into the harbour, the ship struck against a rock and knocked off
a garboard plank, which is the next to the keel. In an instant all hands
were in the greatest confusion, and began with loud cries to call on
God to have mercy on them. Although I could not swim, and saw no
way of escaping death, I felt no dread in my then situation, having no
desire to live. I even rejoiced in spirit, thinking this death would be
sudden glory. But the fulness of time was not yet come. The people
near to me were much astonished in seeing me thus calm and resigned;
but I told them of the peace of God, which through sovereign grace I
enjoyed, and these words were that instant in my mind:

> Christ is my pilot wise, my compass is his word;
> My soul each storm defies, while I have such a Lord.
> I trust his faithfulness and power,
> To save me in the trying hour.
> Though rocks and quicksands deep through all my passage lie,
> Yet Christ shall safely keep and guide me with his eye.

How can I sink with such a prop,
That bears the world and all things up?[1]

At this time there were many large Spanish flukers or passage-vessels full of people crossing the channel; who seeing our condition, a number of them came alongside of us. As many hands as could be employed began to work; some at our three pumps, and the rest unloading the ship as fast as possible. There being only a single rock called the Porpus on which we struck, we soon got off it, and providentially it was then high water, we therefore run the ship ashore at the nearest place to keep her from sinking. After many tides, with a great deal of care and industry, we got her repaired again. When we had dispatched our business at Cadiz, we went to Gibraltar, and from thence to Malaga,[2] a very pleasant and rich city, where there is one of the finest cathedrals I had ever seen. It had been above fifty years in building, as I heard, though it was not then quite finished; great part of the inside, however, was completed and highly decorated with the richest marble columns and many superb paintings; it was lighted occasionally by an amazing number of wax tapers of different sizes, some of which were as thick as a man's thigh; these, however, were only used on some of their grand festivals.

I was very much shocked at the custom of bull-baiting, and other diversions which prevailed here on Sunday evenings, to the great scandal of Christianity and morals. I used to express my abhorrence of it to a priest whom I met with. I had frequent contests about religion with the reverend father, in which he took great pains to make a proselyte of me to his church; and I no less to convert him to mine. On these occasions I used to produce my Bible, and shew him in what points his church erred. He then said he had been in England, and that every person there read the Bible, which was very wrong; but I answered him that Christ desired us to search the Scriptures. In his zeal for my conversion, he solicited me to go to one of the universities in Spain, and declared that I should have my education free; and told me, if I got myself made a priest, I might in time become even pope; and that Pope Benedict was a black man.[3] As I was ever desirous of learning, I paused for some time upon this temptation; and thought by being crafty I might catch some with guile; but I began to think that it would be only hypocrisy in me to embrace his offer, as I could not in conscience conform to the opinions of his church. I was therefore enabled to regard the word of God, which says, 'Come out

1. Adapted from the Methodist hymn "Jesus at Thy Command."
2. City in southern Spain.
3. Though not a pope, St. Benedict the Black (San Benedetto il Moro, 1526–1589), a Sicilian whose parents had been African slaves, entered a Franciscan convent and became well known for his humility, devotion, fasting, and self-chastisement. Miracles were attributed to him, and he was made the patron saint of Palermo in 1713. Pope Benedict XIV (and this may have caused the confusion) beatified Benedict the Black in 1743; sainthood followed in 1807.

from amongst them,'[4] and refused Father Vincent's offer. So we parted without conviction on either side.

Having taken at this place some fine wines, fruits, and money, we proceeded to Cadiz, where we took about two tons more of money, &c. and then sailed for England in the month of June. When we were about the north latitude 42, we had contrary wind for several days, and the ship did not make in that time above six or seven miles straight course. This made the captain exceeding fretful and peevish: and I was very sorry to hear God's most holy name often blasphemed by him. One day, as he was in that impious mood, a young gentleman on board, who was a passenger, reproached him, and said he acted wrong; for we ought to be thankful to God for all things, as we were not in want of any thing on board; and though the wind was contrary for us, yet it was fair for some others, who, perhaps, stood in more need of it than we. I immediately seconded this young gentleman with some boldness, and said we had not the least cause to murmur, for that the Lord was better to us than we deserved, and that he had done all things well. I expected that the captain would be very angry with me for speaking, but he replied not a word. However, before that time on the following day, being the 21st of June, much to our great joy and astonishment, we saw the providential hand of our benign Creator, whose ways with his blind creatures are past finding out. The preceding night I dreamed that I saw a boat immediately off the starboard main shrouds;[5] and exactly at half past one o'clock, the following day at noon, while I was below, just as we had dined in the cabin, the man at the helm cried out, A boat! which brought my dream that instant into my mind. I was the first man that jumped on the deck; and, looking from the shrouds onward, according to my dream, I descried a little boat at some distance; but, as the waves were high, it was as much as we could do sometimes to discern her; we however stopped the ship's way, and the boat, which was extremely small, came alongside with eleven miserable men, whom we took on board immediately. To all human appearance, these people must have perished in the course of one hour or less, the boat being small, it barely contained them. When we took them up they were half drowned, and had no victuals, compass, water, or any other necessary whatsoever, and had only one bit of an oar to steer with, and that right before the wind; so that they were obliged to trust entirely to the mercy of the waves. As soon as we got them all on board, they bowed themselves on their knees, and, with hands and voices lifted up to heaven, thanked God for their deliverance; and I trust that my prayers were not wanting amongst them at the same time. This mercy of the Lord quite melted me, and I recollected his words, which I saw thus verified in the 107th Psalm 'O give thanks unto the Lord,

4. 2 Corinthians 6.17.
5. One of the ropes leading from the ship's masthead.

for he is good, for his mercy endureth for ever. Hungry and thirsty, their souls fainted in them. They cried unto Lord in their trouble, and he delivered them out of their distresses. And he led them forth by the right way, that they might go to a city of habitation. O that men would praise the Lord for his goodness and for his wonderful works to the children of men! For he satisfieth the longing soul, and filleth the hungry soul with goodness.

'Such as sit in darkness and in the shadow of death:

'Then they cried unto the Lord in their trouble, and he saved them out of their distresses. They that go down to the sea in ships; that do business in great waters: these see the works of the Lord, and his wonders in the deep. Whoso is wise and will observe these things, even they shall understand the loving kindness of the Lord.'

The poor distressed captain said, 'that the Lord is good; for, seeing that I am not fit to die, he therefore gave me a space of time to repent.' I was very glad to hear this expression, and took an opportunity when convenient of talking to him on the providence of God. They told us they were Portuguese, and were in a brig loaded with corn, which shifted that morning at five o'clock, owing to which the vessel sunk that instant with two of the crew; and how these eleven got into the boat (which was lashed to the deck) not one of them could tell. We provided them with every necessary, and brought them all safe to London: and I hope the Lord gave them repentance unto life eternal.

I was happy once more amongst my friends and brethren, till November, when my old friend, the celebrated Doctor Irving, bought a remarkable fine sloop, about 150 tons. He had a mind for a new adventure in cultivating a plantation at Jamaica and the Musquito Shore[6]; asked me to go with him, and said that he would trust me with his estate in preference to any one. By the advice, therefore, of my friends, I accepted of the offer, knowing that the harvest was fully ripe in those parts, and hoped to be the instrument, under God, of bringing some poor sinner to my well beloved master, Jesus Christ. Before I embarked, I found with the Doctor four Musquito Indians, who were chiefs in their own country, and were brought here by some English traders for some selfish ends. One of them was the Musquito king's son; a youth of about eighteen years of age; and whilst he was here he was baptized by the name of George. They were going back at the government's expense, after having been in England about twelve months, during which they learned to speak pretty good English. When I came to talk to them about eight days before we sailed, I was very much mortified in finding that they had not frequented any churches since they were here, to be baptized, nor was any attention paid to

6. Or Musquito. Named after the Miskito Indians and Zambo-Mosquito people living on the Caribbean coast of modern-day Nicaragua and Honduras. Britain allied with them against Spain.

their morals. I was very sorry for this mock Christianity, and had just an opportunity to take some of them once to church before we sailed. We embarked in the month of November 1775, on board of the sloop Morning Star, Captain David Miller, and sailed for Jamaica. In our passage, I took all the pains that I could to instruct the Indian prince in the doctrines of Christianity, of which he was entirely ignorant; and, to my great joy, he was quite attentive, and received with gladness the truths that the Lord enabled me to set forth to him. I taught him in the compass of eleven days all the letters, and he could put even two or three of them together and spell them. I had Fox's Martyrology[7] with cuts, and he used to be very fond of looking into it, and would ask many questions about the papal cruelties he saw depicted there, which I explained to him. I made such progress with this youth, especially in religion, that when I used to go to bed at different hours of the night, if he was in his bed, he would get up on purpose to go to prayer with me, without any other clothes than his shirt; and before he would eat any of his meals amongst the gentlemen in the cabin, he would first come to me to pray, as he called it. I was well pleased at this, and took great delight in him, and used much supplication to God for his conversion. I was in full hope of seeing daily every appearance of that change which I could wish; not knowing the devices of satan, who had many of his emissaries to sow his tares[8] as fast as I sowed the good seed, and pull down as fast as I built up. Thus we went on nearly four fifths of our passage, when satan at last got the upper hand. Some of his messengers, seeing this poor heathen much advanced in piety, began to ask him whether I had converted him to Christianity, laughed, and made their jest at him, for which I rebuked them as much as I could; but this treatment caused the prince to halt between two opinions. Some of the true sons of Belial,[9] who did not believe that there was any hereafter, told him never to fear the devil, for there was none existing; and if ever he came to the prince, they desired he might be sent to them. Thus they teazed the poor innocent youth, so that he would not learn his book any more! He would not drink nor carouse with these ungodly actors, nor would he be with me, even at prayers. This grieved me very much. I endeavoured to persuade him as well as I could, but he would not come; and entreated him very much to tell me his reasons for acting thus. At last he asked me, 'How comes it that all the white men on board who can read and write, and observe the sun, and know all things, yet swear, lie, and get drunk, only excepting yourself?' I answered him, the reason was, that they did not fear God; and that if any one of them died so they could not go to, or

7. John Fox (1517–1587) published his famous Book of Martyrs in 1558. Many editions were illustrated with "cuts," others were abridged.
8. Noxious weeds. An allusion to Christ's parable in Matthew 13:36–43.
9. One of the fallen angels in Milton's Paradise Lost.

be happy with God. He replied, that if these persons went to hell he
would go to hell too. I was sorry to hear this; and, as he sometimes had
the tooth-ach, and also some other persons in the ship at the same
time, I asked him if their toothach made his easy: he said, No. Then I
told him if he and these people went to hell together, their pains would
not make his any lighter. This answer had great weight with him: it
depressed his spirits much; and he became ever after, during the passage, fond of being alone. When we were in the latitude of Martinico,
and near making the land, one morning we had a brisk gale of wind,
and, carrying too much sail, the main-mast went over the side. Many
people were then all about the deck, and the yards, masts, and rigging,
came tumbling all about us, yet there was not one of us in the least
hurt, although some were within a hair's breadth of being killed: and,
particularly, I saw two men then, by the providential hand of God,
most miraculously preserved from being smashed to pieces. On the
fifth of January we made Antigua and Montserrat, and ran along the
rest of the islands: and on the fourteenth we arrived at Jamaica. One
Sunday while we were there I took the Musquito Prince George to
church, where he saw the sacrament administered. When we came out
we saw all kinds of people, almost from the church door for the space
of half a mile down to the waterside, buying and selling all kinds of
commodities: and these acts afforded me great matter of exhortation
to this youth, who was much astonished. Our vessel being ready to sail
for the Musquito shore, I went with the Doctor on board a Guinea-
man, to purchase some slaves to carry with us, and cultivate a plantation; and I chose them all my own countrymen. On the twelfth of
February we sailed from Jamaica, and on the eighteenth arrived at the
Musquito shore, at a place called Dupeupy.[1] All our Indian guests now,
after I had admonished them and a few cases of liquor given them by
the Doctor, took an affectionate leave of us, and went ashore, where
they were met by the Musquito king, and we never saw one of them
afterwards. We then sailed to the southward of the shore, to a place
called Cape Gracias a Dios,[2] where there was a large lagoon or lake,
which received the emptying of two or three very fine large rivers, and
abounded much in fish and land tortoise. Some of the native Indians
came on board of us here; and we used them well, and told them we
were come to dwell amongst them, which they seemed pleased at. So
the Doctor and I, with some others, went with them ashore; and they
took us to different places to view the land, in order to choose a place
to make a plantation of. We fixed on a spot near a river's bank, in a
rich soil; and, having got our necessaries out of the sloop, we began to
clear away the woods, and plant different kinds of vegetables, which
had a quick growth. While we were employed in this manner, our vessel

1. Unidentified town in southern Honduras.
2. Or Cabo Gracias à Dios, in present-day Nicaragua, on the Honduras border.

went northward to Black River to trade. While she was there, a Spanish guarda costa[3] met with and took her. This proved very hurtful, and a great embarrassment to us. However, we went on with the culture of the land. We used to make fires every night all around us, to keep off wild beasts, which, as soon as it was dark, set up a most hideous roaring. Our habitation being far up in the woods, we frequently saw different kinds of animals; but none of them ever hurt us, except poisonous snakes, the bite of which the Doctor used to cure by giving to the patient, as soon as possible, about half a tumbler of strong rum, with a good deal of Cayenne pepper in it. In this manner he cured two natives and one of his own slaves. The Indians were exceedingly fond of the Doctor, and they had good reason for it; for I believe they never had such an useful man amongst them. They came from all quarters to our dwelling; and some *woolwow*,[4] or flat-headed Indians, who lived fifty or sixty miles above our river, and this side of the South Sea, brought us a good deal of silver in exchange for our goods. The principal articles we could get from our neighbouring Indians, were turtle oil, and shells, little silk grass, and some provisions; but they would not work at any thing for us, except fishing; and a few times they assisted to cut some trees down, in order to build us houses; which they did exactly like the Africans, by the joint labour of men, women, and children. I do not recollect any of them to have had more than two wives. These always accompanied their husbands when they came to our dwelling; and then they generally carried whatever they brought to us, and always squatted down behind their husbands. Whenever we gave them any thing to eat, the men and their wives ate it separate. I never saw the least sign of incontinence amongst them. The women are ornamented with beads, and fond of painting themselves; the men also paint, even to excess, both their faces and shirts: their favourite colour is red. The women generally cultivate the ground, and the men are all fishermen and canoe makers. Upon the whole, I never met any nation that were so simple in their manners as these people, or had so little ornament in their houses. Neither had they, as I ever could learn, one word expressive of an oath. The worst word I ever heard amongst them when they were quarreling, was one that they had got from the English, which was, 'you rascal.' I never saw any mode of worship among them; but in this they were not worse than their European brethren or neighbours: for I am sorry to say that there was not one white person in our dwelling, nor any where else that I saw in different places I was at on the shore, that was better or more pious than those unenlightened Indians; but they either worked or slept on Sundays: and, to my sorrow, working was too much Sunday's employment with ourselves; so much so, that in some length of time we really did not know one day from

3. Coast guard vessel.
4. Woolwa or Ulua Indians lived in the interior of present-day Nicaragua.

another. This mode of living laid the foundation of my decamping at last. The natives are well made and warlike; and they particularly boast of having never been conquered by the Spaniards. They are great drinkers of strong liquors when they can get them. We used to distil rum from pine apples, which were very plentiful here; and then we could not get them away from our place. Yet they seemed to be singular, in point of honesty, above any other nation I was ever amongst. The country being hot, we lived under an open shed, where we had all kinds of goods, without a door or a lock to any one article; yet we slept in safety, and never lost any thing, or were disturbed. This surprised us a good deal; and the Doctor, myself, and others, used to say, if we were to lie in that manner in Europe we should have our throats cut the first night. The Indian governor goes once in a certain time all about the province or district, and has a number of men with him as attendants and assistants. He settles all the differences among the people, like the judge here, and is treated with very great respect. He took care to give us timely notice before he came to our habitation, by sending his stick as a token, for rum, sugar, and gunpowder, which we did not refuse sending; and at the same time we made the utmost preparation to receive his honour and histrain [his train]. When he came with his tribe, and all our neighbouring chieftains, we expected to find him a grave reverend judge, solid and sagacious; but instead of that, before he and his gang came in sight, we heard them very clamorous; and they even had plundered some of our good neighbouring Indians, having intoxicated themselves with our liquor. When they arrived we did not know what to make of our new guests, and would gladly have dispensed with the honour of their company. However, having no alternative, we feasted them plentifully all the day till the evening; when the governor, getting quite drunk, grew very unruly, and struck one of our most friendly chiefs, who was our nearest neighbour, and also took his gold-laced hat from him. At this a great commotion taken place; and the Doctor interfered to make peace, as we could all understand one another, but to no purpose; and at last they became so outrageous that the Doctor, fearing he might get into trouble, left the house, and made the best of his way to the nearest wood, leaving me to do as well as I could among them. I was so enraged with the Governor, that I could have wished to have seen him tied fast to a tree and flogged for his behaviour; but I had not people enough to cope with his party. I therefore thought of a stratagem to appease the riot. Recollecting a passage I had read in the life of Columbus, when he was amongst the Indians in Mexico or Peru, where, on some occasion, he frightened them, by telling them of certain events in the heavens, I had recourse to the same expedient; and it succeeded beyond my most sanguine expectations. When I had formed my determination, I went in the midst of them; and, taking hold of the Governor, I pointed up to the heavens. I menaced him and the rest: I told them God lived there, and that he was angry with them, and they must not quarrel so; that they were all brothers, and if they did not leave off, and go away quietly, I would take the book (pointing to the Bible), read, and *tell* God to make them dead. This was something like magic. The clamour immediately ceased, and I gave them some rum and a few other things; after which they went away peaceably; and the Governor afterwards gave our neighbour, who was called Captain Plasmyah, his hat again. When the Doctor returned, he was exceedingly glad at my success in thus getting rid of our troublesome guests. The Musquito people within our vicinity, out of respect to the Doctor, myself and his people, made entertainments of the grand kind, called in their tongue *tourrie* or *dryckbot*. The English of this expression is, a feast of drinking about, of which it seems a corruption of language. The drink consisted of pine apples roasted, and casades[5] chewed or beaten in mortars; which, after lying some time, ferments, and becomes so strong as to intoxicate, when drank in any quantity. We had timely notice given to us of the entertainment. A white family, within five miles of us, told us how the drink was made, and I and two others went before the time to the village, where the mirth was appointed to be held; and there we saw the whole art of making the drink, and also the kind of animals that were to be eaten there. I cannot say that the sight of either the drink or the meat were enticing to me. They had some thousands of pine apples roasting, which they squeezed, dirt and all, into a canoe they had there for the purpose. The casade drink was in beef barrels and other vessels, and looked exactly like hog-wash. Men, women, and children, were thus employed in roasting the pine apples, and squeezing them with their hands. For food they had many land torpins or tortoises, some dried turtle, and three large alligators alive, and tied fast to the trees. I asked the people what they were going to do with these alligators; and I was told they were to be eaten. I was much surprised at this, and went home, not a little disgusted at the preparations. When the day of the feast was come, we took some rum with us, and went to the appointed place, where we found a great assemblage of these people, who received us very kindly. The mirth had begun before we came; and they were dancing with music: and the musical instruments were nearly the same as those of any other sable people; but, as I thought, much less melodious than any other nation I ever knew. They had many curious gestures in dancing, and a variety of motions and postures of their bodies, which to me were in no wise attracting. The males danced by themselves, and the females also by themselves, as with us. The Doctor shewed his people the example, by immediately joining the women's party, though not by their choice. On perceiving the women disgusted,

5. Or cassava. A tropical shrub with thick roots from which edible starch is obtained.

he joined the males. At night there were great illuminations, by setting
fire to many pine trees, while the dryckbot went round merrily by calabashes or gourds: but the liquor might more justly be called eating
than drinking. One Owden, the oldest father in the vicinity, was
dressed in a strange and terrifying form. Around his body were skins
adorned with different kinds of feathers, and he had on his head a very
large and high head-piece, in the form of a grenadier's cap, with prickles
like a porcupine; and he made a certain noise which resembled the cry
of an alligator. Our people skipped amongst them out of complaisance,
though some could not drink of their tourrie; but our rum met with
customers enough, and was soon gone. The alligators were killed and
some of them roasted. Their manner of roasting is by digging a hole
in the earth, and filling it with wood, which they burn to coal, and
then they lay sticks across, on which they set the meat. I had a raw
piece of the alligator in my hand: it was very rich: I thought it looked
like fresh salmon, and it had a most fragrant smell, but I could not eat
any of it. This merry-making at last ended without the least discord in
any person in the company, although it was made up of different
nations and complexions. The rainy season came on here about the
latter end of May, which continued till August very heavily; so that the
rivers were overflowed, and our provisions then in the ground were
washed away. I thought this was in some measure a judgment upon us
for working on Sundays, and it hurt my mind very much. I often wished
to leave this place and sail for Europe; for our mode of procedure and
living in this heathenish form was very irksome to me. The word of
God faith, 'What does it avail a man if he gain the whole world, and
lose his own soul?'[6] This was much and heavily impressed on my mind;
and, though I did not know how to speak to the Doctor for my discharge, it was disagreeable for me to stay any longer. But about the
middle of June I took courage enough to ask him for it. He was very
unwilling at first to grant my request; but I gave him so many reasons
for it, that at last he consented to my going, and gave me the following
certificate of my behaviour:

> The bearer, Gustavus Vassa, has served me several years with
> strict honesty, sobriety, and fidelity. I can, therefore, with justice
> recommend him for these qualifications; and indeed in every
> respect I consider him as an excellent servant. I do hereby certify
> that he always behaved well, and that he is perfectly trust-worthy.
>   CHARLES IRVING.
> *Musquito Shore, June* 15, 1767.

Though I was much attached to the doctor, I was happy when he
consented. I got every thing ready for my departure, and hired some
Indians, with a large canoe, to carry me off. All my poor countrymen,

6. Matthew 16:26.

the slaves, when they heard of my leaving them, were very sorry, as I had always treated them with care and affection, and did everything I could to comfort the poor creatures, and render their condition easy. Having taken leave of my old friends and companions, on the 18th of June, accompanied by the doctor, I left that spot of the world, and went southward above twenty miles along the river. There I found a sloop, the captain of which told me he was going to Jamaica. Having agreed for my passage with him and one of the owners, who was also on board, named Hughes, the doctor and I parted, not without sheding tears on both sides. The vessel then sailed along the river till night, when she stopped in a lagoon within the same river. During the night a schooner belonging to the same owners came in, and, as she was in want of hands, Hughes, the owner of the sloop, asked me to go in the schooner as a sailor, and said he would give me wages. I thanked him; but I said I wanted to go to Jamaica. He then immediately changed his tone, and swore, and abused me very much, and asked how I came to be freed. I told him, and said that I came into that vicinity with Dr. Irving, whom he had seen that day. This account was of no use; he still swore exceedingly at me, and cursed the master for a fool that sold me my freedom, and the doctor for another in leting me go from him. Then he desired me to go in the schooner, or else I should not go out of the sloop as a free-man. I said this was very hard, and begged to be put on shore again; but he swore that I should not. I said I had been twice amongst the Turks, yet had never seen any such usage with them, and much less could I have expected any thing of this kind amongst Christians. This incensed him exceedingly; and, with a volley of oaths and imprecations; he replied, 'Christians! Damn you, you are one of St. Paul's men;[7] but by G—, except you have St. Paul's or St. Peter's faith, and walk upon the water to the shore, you shall not go out of the vessel; which I now found was going amongst the Spaniards towards Carthagena,[8] where he swore he would sell me. I simply asked him what right he had to sell me? but, without another word, he made some of his people tie ropes round each of my ancles, and also to each wrist, and another rope round my body, and hoisted me up without letting my feet touch or rest upon any thing. Thus I hung, without any crime committed, and without judge or jury; merely because I was a free man, and could not by the law get any redress from a white person in those parts of the world. I was in great pain from my situation, and cried and begged very hard for some mercy; but all in vain. My tyrant, in a great rage, brought a musquet out of the cabin, and loaded it before me and the crew, and swore that he would shoot me if I cried any more. I had now no alternative; I therefore remained silent, seeing

7. Galatians 3.28 and Philemon 16. "St Paul's Men" may also mean tricksters who gather at St Paul's Cathedral in London.
8. Or Cartagena: city in present-day Colombia.

not one white man on board who said a word on my behalf. I hung in that manner from between ten and eleven o'clock at night till about one in the morning; when, finding my cruel abuser fast asleep, I begged some of his slaves to slack the rope that was round my body, that my feet might rest on something. This they did at the risk of being cruelly used by their master, who beat some of them severely at first for not tying me when he commanded them. Whilst I remained in this condition, till between five and six o'clock next morning, I trust I prayed to God to forgive this blasphemer, who cared not what he did, but when he got up out of his sleep in the morning was of the very same temper and disposition as when he left me at night. When they got up the anchor, and the vessel was getting under way, I once more cried and begged to be released; and now, being fortunately in the way of their hoisting the sails, they released me. When I was let down, I spoke to one Mr. Cox, a carpenter, whom I knew on board, on the impropriety of this conduct. He also knew the doctor, and the good opinion he ever had of me. This man then went to the captain, and told him not to carry me away in that manner; that I was the doctor's steward, who regarded me very highly, and would resent this usage when he should come to know it. On which he desired a young man to put me ashore in a small canoe I brought with me. This sound gladdened my heart, and I got hastily into the canoe and set off, whilst my tyrant was down in the cabin; but he soon spied me out, when I was not above thirty or forty yards from the vessel, and, running upon the deck with a loaded musket in his hand, he presented it at me, and swore heavily and dreadfully, that he would shoot me that instant, if I did not come back on board. As I knew the wretch would have done as he said, without hesitation, I put back to the vessel again; but, as the good Lord would have it, just as I was alongside he was abusing the captain for letting me go from the vessel; which the captain returned, and both of them soon got into a very great heat. The young man that was with me now got out of the canoe; the vessel was sailing on fast with a smooth sea: and I then thought it was neck or nothing,[9] so at that instant I set off again, for my life, in the canoe, towards the shore; and fortunately the confusion was so great amongst them on board, that I got out of the reach of the musquet shot unnoticed, while the vessel sailed on with a fair wind a different way; so that they could not overtake me without tacking:[1] but even before that could be done I should have been on shore, which I soon reached, with many thanks to God for this unexpected deliverance. I then went and told the other owner, who lived near that shore (with whom I had agreed for my passage) of the usage I had met with. He was very much astonished, and appeared very sorry for it. After treating me with kindness, he gave me some refreshment,

9. All or nothing.
1. Going in a zigzag course, sailing against the wind.

and three heads of roasted Indian corn, for a voyage of about eighteen miles south, to look for another vessel. He then directed me to an Indian chief of a district, who was also the Musquito admiral, and had once been at our dwelling; after which I set off with the canoe across a large lagoon alone (for I could not get any one to assist me), though I was much jaded,[2] and had pains in my bowels, by means of the rope I had hung by the night before. I was therefore at different times unable to manage the canoe, for the paddling was very laborious. However, a little before dark I got to my destined place, where some of the Indians knew me, and received me kindly. I asked for the admiral; and they conducted me to his dwelling. He was glad to see me, and refreshed me with such things as the place afforded; and I had a hammock to sleep in. They acted towards me more like Christians than those whites I was amongst the last night, though they had been baptized. I told the admiral I wanted to go to the next port to get a vessel to carry me to Jamaica; and requested him to send the canoe back which I then had, for which I was to pay him. He agreed with me, and sent five able Indians with a large canoe to carry my things to my intended place, about fifty miles; and we set off the next morning. When we got out of the lagoon and went along shore, the sea was so high that the canoe was oftentimes very near being filled with water. We were obliged to go ashore and drag across different necks of land; we were also two nights in the swamps, which swarmed with musquito flies, and they proved troublesome to us. This tiresome journey of land and water ended, however, on the third day, to my great joy; and I got on board of a sloop commanded by one Captain Jenning. She was then partly loaded, and he told me he was expecting daily to sail for Jamaica; and having agreed with me to work my passage, I went to work accordingly, I was not many days on board before we sailed; but to my sorrow and disappointment, though used to such tricks, we went to the southward along the Musquito shore, instead of steering for Jamaica. I was compelled to assist in cutting a great deal of mahogany wood on the shore as we coasted along it, and load the vessel with it, before she sailed. This fretted me much; but, as I did not know how to help myself among these deceivers, I thought patience was the only remedy I had left, and even that was forced. There was much hard work and little victuals on board, except by good luck we happened to catch turtles. On this coast there was also a particular kind of fish called manatee,[3] which is most excellent eating, and the flesh is more like beef than fish; the scales are as large as a shilling, and the skin thicker than I ever saw that of any other fish. Within the brackish waters along shore there were likewise vast numbers of alligators, which made the fish scarce. I was on board this sloop sixteen days, during which, in our coasting, we

2. Exhausted.
3. Sea cow.

came to another place, where there was a smaller sloop called the
Indian Queen, commanded by one John Baker. He also was an Englishman, and had been a long time along the shore trading for turtle
shells and silver, and had got a good quantity of each on board. He
wanted some hands very much; and, understanding I was a free man,
and wanted to go to Jamaica, he told me if he could get one or two,
that he would sail immediately for that island: he also pretended to
me some marks of attention and respect, and promised to give me
forty-five shillings sterling a month if I would go with him. I thought
this much better than cutting wood for nothing. I therefore told the
other captain that I wanted to go to Jamaica in the other vessel; but
he would not listen to me: and, seeing me resolved to go in a day or
two, he got the vessel to sail, intending to carry me away against my
will. This treatment mortified me extremely. I immediately, according
to an agreement I had made with the captain of the Indian Queen,
called for her boat, which was lying near us, and it came alongside;
and, by the means of a north-pole shipmate which I met with in the
sloop I was in, I got my things into the boat, and went on board of the
Indian Queen, July the 10th. A few days after I was there, we got all
things ready and sailed: but again, to my great mortification, this vessel
still went to the south, nearly as far as Carthagena, trading along the
coast, instead of going to Jamaica, as the captain had promised me:
and, what was worst of all, he was a very cruel and bloody-minded man,
and was a horrid blasphemer. Among others he had a white pilot, one
Stoker, whom he beat often as severely as he did some negroes he had
on board. One night in particular, after he had beaten this man most
cruelly, he put him into the boat, and made two negroes row him to a
desolate key, or small island; and he loaded two pistols, and swore
bitterly that he would shoot the negroes if they brought Stoker on
board again. There was not the least doubt but that he would do as
he said, and the two poor fellows were obliged to obey the cruel mandate; but, when the captain was asleep, the two negroes took a blanket
and carried it to the unfortunate Stoker, which I believe was the means
of saving his life from the annoyance of insects. A great deal of entreaty
was used with the captain the next day, before he would consent to
let Stoker come on board; and when the poor man was brought on
board he was very ill, from his situation during the night, and he
remained so till he was drowned a little time after. As we sailed southward we came to many uninhabited islands, which were overgrown with
fine large cocoa nuts. As I was very much in want of provisions, I
brought a boat load of them on board, which lasted me and others for
several weeks, and afforded us many a delicious repast in our scarcity.
One day, before this, I could not help observing the providential hand
of God, that ever supplies all our wants, though in the ways and manner
we know not. I had been a whole day without food, and made signals

for boats to come off, but in vain. I therefore earnestly prayed to God for relief in my need; and at the close of the evening I went off the deck. Just as I laid down I heard a noise on the deck; and, not knowing what it meant, I went directly on the the deck again, when what should I see but a fine large fish about seven or eight pounds, which had jumped aboard! I took it, and admired, with thanks, the good hand of God; and, what I considered as not less extraordinary, the captain, who was very avaricious, did not attempt to take it from me, there being only him and I on board; for the rest were all gone ashore trading. Sometimes the people did not come off for some days: this used to fret the captain, and then he would vent his fury on me by beating me, or making me feel in other cruel ways. One day especially, in his wild, wicked, and mad career, after striking me several times with different things, and once across my mouth, even with a red burning stick out of the fire, he got a barrel of gunpowder on the deck, and swore that he would blow up the vessel. I was then at my wit's end, and earnestly prayed to God to direct me. The head was out of the barrel; and the captain took a lighted stick out of the fire to blow himself and me up, because there was a vessel then in sight coming in, which he supposed was a Spaniard, and he was afraid of falling into their hands. Seeing this I got an axe, unnoticed by him, and placed myself between him and the powder, having resolved in myself as soon as he attempted to put the fire in the barrel to chop him down that instant. I was more than an hour in this situation; during which he struck me often, still keeping the fire in his hand for this wicked purpose. I really should have thought myself justifiable in any other part of the world if I had killed him, and prayed to God, who gave me a mind which rested solely on himself. I prayed for resignation, that his will might be done; and the following two portions of his holy word, which occurred to my mind, buoyed up my hope, and kept me from taking the life of this wicked man. 'He hath determined the times before appointed, and set bounds to our habitations,' Acts xvii. 26. And, 'Who is there amongst you that feareth the Lord, that obeyeth the voice of his servant, that walketh in darkness and hath no light? let him trust in the name of the Lord, and stay upon his God,' Isaiah I. 10. And thus by the grace of God I was enabled to do. I found him a present help in the time of need, and the captain's fury began to subside as the night approached: but I found,

> That he who cannot stem his anger's tide
> Doth a wild horse without a bridle ride.[4]

The next morning we discovered that the vessel which had caused such a fury in the captain was an English sloop. They soon came to an

4. Adapted from the play *Love's Last Shift*, II:7, by Colley Cibber (1671–1757).

anchor where we were, and, to my no small surprise, I learned that
Doctor Irving was on board of her on his way from the Musquito shore
to Jamaica. I was for going immediately to see this old master and
friend, but the captain would not suffer me to leave the vessel. I then
informed the doctor, by letter, how I was treated, and begged that he
would take me out of the sloop: but he informed me that it was not
in his power, as he was a passenger himself; but he sent me some rum
and sugar for my own use. I now learned that after I had left the estate
which I managed for this gentleman on the Musquito shore, during
which the slaves were well fed and comfortable, a white overseer had
supplied my place: this man, through inhumanity and ill-judged avarice, beat and cut the poor slaves most unmercifully; and the consequence was, that every one got into a large Puriogua canoe, and
endeavoured to escape; but not knowing where to go, or how to manage
the canoe, they were all drowned; in consequence of which the doctor's
plantation was left uncultivated, and he was now returning to Jamaica
to purchase more slaves and stock it again. On the 14th of October
the Indian Queen arrived at Kingston in Jamaica. When we were
unloaded I demanded my wages, which amounted to eight pounds and
five shillings sterling; but Captain Baker refused to give me one farthing, although it was the hardest-earned money I ever worked for in
my life. I found out Doctor Irving upon this, and acquainted him of
the captain's knavery. He did all he could to help me to get my money;
and we went to every magistrate in Kingston (and there were nine),
but they all refused to do any thing for me, and said my oath could
not be admitted against a white man. Nor was this all; for Baker threatened that he would beat me severely if he could catch me for attempting to demand my money; and this he would have done, but that I
got, by means of Dr. Irving, under the protection of Captain Douglas
of the Squirrel man of war. I thought this exceedingly hard usage;
though indeed I found it to be too much the practice there to pay free
men for their labour in this manner. One day I went with a free negroe
taylor, named Joe Diamond, to one Mr. Cochran, who was indebted
to him some trifling sum; and the man, not being able to get his money,
began to murmur. The other immediately took a horse-whip to pay
him with it; but, by the help of a good pair of heels, the taylor got off.
Such oppressions as these made me seek for a vessel to get off the
island as fast as I could; and by the mercy of God I found a ship in
November bound for England, when I embarked with a convoy, after
having taken a last farewell of Doctor Irving. When I left Jamaica he
was employed in refining sugars; and some months after my arrival in
England I learned, with much sorrow, that this my amiable friend was
dead, owing to his having eaten some poisoned fish. We had many
very heavy gales of wind in our passage; in the course of which no
material incident occurred, except that an American privateer, falling

in with the fleet, was captured and set fire to by his Majesty's ship the Squirrel. On January the seventh, 1777, we arrived at Plymouth. I was happy once more to tread upon English ground; and, after passing some little time at Plymouth and Exeter among some pious friends, whom I was happy to see, I went to London with a heart replete with thanks to God for all past mercies.

Chap. XII.

Different transactions of the author's life till the present time—His application to the late Bishop of London to be appointed a missionary to Africa—Some account of his share in the conduct of the late expedition to Sierra Leona—Petition to the Queen—Conclusion.

Such were the various scenes which I was a witness to, and the fortune I experienced until the year 1777. Since that period my life has been more uniform, and the incidents of it fewer, than in any other equal number of years preceding; I therefore hasten to the conclusion of a narrative, which I fear the reader my think already sufficiently tedious.

I had suffered so many impositions in my commercial transactions in different parts of the world, that I became heartily disgusted with the seafaring life, and I was determined not to return to it, at least for some time. I therefore once more engaged in service shortly after my return, and continued for the most part in this situation until 1784.

Soon after my arrival in London, I saw a remarkable circumstance relative to African complexion, which I thought so extraordinary, that I beg leave just to mention it: A white negro woman, that I had formerly seen in London and other parts, had married a white man, by whom she had three boys, and they were every one mulattoes, and yet they had fine light hair. In 1779 I served Governor Macnamara, who had been a considerable time on the coast of Africa. In the time of my service, I used to ask frequently other servants to join me in family prayers; but this only excited their mockery. However, the Governor, understanding that I was of a religious turn, wished to know of what religion I was; I told him I was a protestant of the church of England, agreeable to the thirty-nine articles[1] of that church, and that whomsoever I found to preach according to that doctrine, those I would hear. A few days after this, we had some more discourse on the same subject: the Governor spoke to me on it again, and said that he would, if I chose, as he thought I might be of service in converting my countrymen to the Gospel faith, get me sent out as a missionary to Africa. I at first refused going, and told him how I had been served on a like occasion

1. The creed of the Church of England, published in 1563.

by some white people the last voyage I went to Jamaica, when I attempted (if it were the will of God) to be the means of converting the Indian prince; and I said I supposed they would serve me worse than Alexander the coppersmith did St. Paul,[2] if I should attempt to go amongst them in Africa. He told me not to fear, for he would apply to the Bishop of London to get me ordained. On these terms I consented to the Governor's proposal to go to Africa, in hope of doing good if possible amongst my countrymen; so, in order to have me sent out properly, we immediately wrote the following letters to the late Bishop of London:

> To the Right Reverend Father in God, ROBERT, Lord Bishop of London:
>
> The MEMORIAL[3] of GUSTAVUS VASSA
>
> SHEWETH,
>
> That your memorialist is a native of Africa, and has a knowledge of the manners and customs of the inhabitants of that country.
>
> That your memorialist has resided in different parts of Europe for twenty-two years last past, and embraced the Christian faith in the year 1759.
>
> That your memorialist is desirous of returning to Africa as a missionary, if encouraged by your Lordship, in hopes of being able to prevail upon his countrymen to become Christians; and your memorialist is the more induced to undertake the same, from the success that has attended the like undertakings when encouraged by the Portuguese through their different settlements on the coast of Africa, and also by the Dutch: both governments encouraging the blacks, who, by their education are qualified to undertake the same, and are found more proper than European clergymen, unacquainted with the language and customs of the country.
>
> Your memorialist's only motive for soliciting the office of a missionary is, that he may be a means, under God, of reforming his countrymen and persuading them to embrace the Christian religion. Therefore your memorialist humbly prays your Lordship's encouragement and support in the undertaking.
>
> GUSTAVUS VASSA.
>
> At Mr. Guthrie's, taylor,
> No. 17, Hedge-lane.

MY LORD,

I have resided near seven years on the coast of Africa, for most part of the time as commanding officer. From the knowledge I have of the country and it's inhabitants, I am inclined to think that the within plan will be attended with great success, if coun-

2. See 1 Timothy 1.18–20, 2 Timothy 4.14.
3. Written statement; memorandum.

tenanced by your Lordship. I beg leave further to represent to your Lordship, that the like attempts, when encouraged by other governments, have met with uncommon success; and at this very time I know a very respectable character a black priest[4] at Cape Coast Castle. I know the within named Gustavus Vassa, and believe him a moral good man.

I have the honour to be,
My Lord,
Your Lordship's
Humble and obedient servant,
MATT. MACNAMARA.

Grove, 11th March 1779.

This letter was also accompanied by the following from Doctor Wallace, who had resided in Africa for many years, and whose sentiments on the subject of an African mission were the same with Governor Macnamara's.

March 13, 1779.

MY LORD,

I have resided near five years on Senegambia[5] on the coast of Africa, and have had the honour of filling very considerable employments in that province. I do approve of the within plan, and think the undertaking very laudable and proper, and that it deserves your Lordship's protection and encouragement, in which case it must be attended with the intended success.

I am,
My Lord,
Your Lordship's
Humble and obedient servant,
THOMAS WALLACE.

With these letters, I waited on the Bishop by the Governor's desire, and presented them to his Lordship. He received me with much condescension[6] and politeness; but, from some certain scruples of delicacy, declined to ordain me.

My sole motive for thus dwelling on this transaction, or inserting these papers, is the opinion which gentlemen of sense and education, who are acquainted with Africa, entertain of the probability of converting the inhabitants of it to the faith of Jesus Christ, if the attempt were countenanced by the legislature.

Shortly after this I left the Governor, and served a nobleman in the Devonshire militia, with whom I was encamped at Coxheath for some

---

4. Philip Quaque, brought to England and educated, served as Chaplain at Cape Coast for many years.
5. Region in West Africa between the Senegal and Gambia Rivers, in present-day Senegal, Mali, and Gambia.
6. Gracious, considerate, or submissive deference shown to another; complaisance.

time; but the operations there were too minute and uninteresting to make a detail of.

In the year 1783, I visited eight counties in Wales, from motives of curiosity. While I was in that part of the country I was led to go down into a coal-pit in Shropshire, but my curiosity nearly cost me my life; for while I was in the pit the coals fell in, and buried one poor man, who was not far from me: upon this I got out as fast as I could, thinking the surface of the earth the safest part of it.

In the spring 1784 I thought of visiting old ocean again. In consequence of this I embarked as steward on board a fine new ship called the London, commanded by Martin Hopkin, and sailed for New-York. I admired this city very much; it is large and well-built, and abounds with provisions of all kinds. While we lay here a circumstance happened which I thought extremely singular:—One day a malefactor was to be executed on a gallows; but with a condition that if any woman, having nothing on but her shift, married the man under the gallows, his life was to be saved. This extraordinary privilege was claimed; a woman presented herself; and the marriage ceremony was performed. Our ship having got laden we returned to London in January 1785. When she was ready again for another voyage, the captain being an agreeable man, I sailed with him from hence in the spring, March 1785, for Philadelphia. On the fifth of April we took our departure from the Land's-end, with a pleasant gale; and about nine o'clock that night the moon shone bright, the sea was smooth, while our ship was going free by the wind, at the rate of about four or five miles an hour. At this time another ship was going nearly as fast as we on the opposite point, meeting us right in the teeth, yet none on board observed either ship until we struck each other forcibly head and head, to the astonishment and consternation of both crews. She did us much damage, but I believe we did her more; for when we passed by each other, which we did very quickly, they called to us to bring to, and hoist out our boat, but we had enough to do to mind ourselves; and in about eight minutes we saw no more of her. We refitted as well as we could the next day, and proceeded on our voyage, and in May arrived at Philadelphia. I was very glad to see this favourite old town once more; and my pleasure was much increased in seeing the worthy quakers freeing and easing the burthens of many of my oppressed African brethren. It rejoiced my heart when one of these friendly people took me to see a free-school[7] they had erected for every denomination of black people, whose minds are cultivated here and forwarded to virtue; and thus they are made useful members of the community. Does not the success of this practicc [practice] say loudly to the planters in the language of scripture—"Go ye and do likewise?"[8]

7. School founded by Anthony Benezet.
8. Luke 10.37.

In October 1785 I was accompanied by some of the Africans, and presented this address of thanks to the gentlemen called Friends or Quakers, in Gracechurch-Court Lombard-Street:

GENTLEMEN,

By reading your book, entitled a Caution to Great Britain and her Colonies, concerning the Calamitous State of the enslaved Negroes:[9] We the poor, oppressed, needy, and much-degraded negroes, desire to approach you with this address of thanks, with our inmost love and warmest acknowledgment; and with the deepest sense of your benevolence, unwearied labour, and kind interposition, towards breaking the yoke of slavery, and to administer a little comfort and ease to thousands and tens of thousands of very grievously afflicted, and too heavy burthened negroes.

Gentlemen, could you, by perseverance, at last be enabled, under God, to lighten in any degree the heavy burthen of the afflicted, no doubt it would, in some measure, be the possible means, under God, of saving the souls of many of the oppressors; and, if so, sure we are that the God, whose eyes are ever upon all his creatures, and always rewards every true act of virtue, and regards the prayers of the oppressed, will give to you and yours those blessings which it is not in our power to express or conceive, but which we, as a part of those captived, oppressed, and afflicted people, most earnestly wish and pray for.

These gentlemen received us very kindly, with a promise to exert themselves on behalf of the oppressed Africans, and we parted.

While in town I chanced once to be invited to a quaker's wedding. The simple and yet expressive mode used at their solemnizations is worthy of note. The following is the true form of it:

After the company have met they have seasonable exhortations by several of the members; the bride and bridegroom stand up, and, taking each other by the hand in a solemn manner, the man audily declares to this purpose:

"Friends, in the fear of the Lord, and in the prefence of this assembly, whom I desire to be my witnesses, I take this my friend, M. N. to be my wife; promising, through divine assistance, to be unto her a loving and faithful husband till death separate us:" and the woman makes the like declaration. Then the two first sign their names to the record, and as many more witnesses as have a mind. I had the honour to subscribe mine to a register in Gracechurch-Court, Lombard-Street.

We returned to London in August; and our ship not going immediately to sea, I shipped as a steward in an American ship called the Harmony, Captain John Willet, and left London in March 1786, bound to Philadelphia. Eleven days after sailing we carried our foremast away.

9. A *Caution and Warning to Great Britain and Her Colonies*, published by Anthony Benezet in 1766.

We had a nine weeks passage, which caused our trip not to succeed well, the market for our goods proving bad; and, to make it worse, my commander began to play me the like tricks as others too often practise on free negroes in the West Indies. But I thank God I found many friends here, who in some measure prevented him. On my return to London in August I was very agreeably surprised to find that the benevolence of government had adopted the plan of some philanthropic individuals to send the Africans from hence to their native quarter; and that some vessels were then engaged to carry them to Sierra Leone; an act which redounded to the honour of all concerned in its promotion, and filled me with prayers and much rejoicing. There was then in the city a select committee of gentlemen for the black poor, to some of whom I had the honour of being known; and, as soon as they heard of my arrival they sent for me to the committee. When I came there they informed me of the intention of government; and as they seemed to think me qualified to superintend part of the undertaking, they asked me to go with the black poor to Africa. I pointed out to them many objections to my going; and particularly I expressed some difficulties on the account of the slave dealers, as I would certainly oppose their traffic in the human species by every means in my power. However these objections were over-ruled by the gentlemen of the committee, who prevailed on me to go, and recommended me to the honourable Comssimioners [Commissioners] of his Majesty's Navy as a proper person to act as commissary for government in the intended expedition; and they accordingly appointed me in November 1786 to that office, and gave me sufficient power to act for the government in the capacity of commissary, having received my warrant and the following order.

> *By the principal Officers and Commissioners*
> *of his Majesty's Navy.*

WHEREAS you were directed, by our warrant of the 4th of last month, to receive into your charge from Mr. Irving the surplus provisions remaining of what was provided for the voyage, as well as the provisions for the support of the black poor, after the landing at Sierra Leone, with the cloathing, tools, and all other articles provided at government's expense; and as the provisions were laid in at the rate of two months for the voyage, and for four months after the landing, but the number embarked being so much less than was expected, whereby there may be a considerable surplus of provisions, cloathing, &c. These are, in addition to former orders, to direct and require you to appropriate or dispose of such surplus to the best advantage you can for the benefit of government, keeping and rendering to us a faithful account of what you do herein. And for your guidance in preventing any white persons going, who are not intended to have the indulgence of being carried thither, we send you herewith a list of those recommended by the Committee for the black poor as proper persons to be permitted to embark, and acquaint you that you are not to suffer any others to go who do not produce a certificate from the committee for the black poor, of their having their permission for it. For which this shall be your warrant. Dated at the Navy Office, January 16, 1787.

J. HINSLOW,
GEO. MARSH,
W. PALMER.

To Mr. Gustavus Vassa, Commissary of Provisions and Stores for the Black Poor going to Sierra Leone.

I proceeded immediately to the execution of my duty on board the vessels destined for the voyage, where I continued till the March following.

During my continuance in the employment of government, I was struck with the flagrant abuses committed by the agent, and endeavored to remedy them, but without effect. One instance, among many which I could produce, may serve as a specimen. Government had ordered to be provided all necessaries (slops,[1] as they are called, included) for 750 persons; however, not being able to muster more than 426, I was ordered to send the superfluous slops, &c. to the king's stores[2] at Portsmouth; but, when I demanded them for that purpose from the agent, it appeared they had never been bought, though paid for by government. But that was not all, government were not the only objects of peculation;[3] these poor people suffered infinitely more; their accommodations were most wretched; many of them wanted beds, and many more cloathing and other necessaries. For the truth of this, and much more, I do not seek credit from my own assertion. I appeal to the testimony of Capt. Thompson, of the Nautilus, who convoyed us, to whom I applied in February 1787 for a remedy, when I had remonstrated to the agent in vain, and even brought him to be a witness of the injustice and oppression I complained of. I appeal also to a letter written by these wretched people, so early as the beginning of the preceding January, and published in the Morning Herald of the 4th of that month, signed by twenty of their chiefs.

I could not silently suffer government to be thus cheated, and my countrymen plundered and oppressed, and even left destitute of the necessaries for almost their existence. I therefore informed the Commissioners of the Navy of the agent's proceeding; but my dismission

1. The clothes and bedding of a sailor.
2. The royal naval storehouses.
3. Embezzlement.

was soon after procured, by means of a gentleman in the city, whom the agent, conscious of his peculation, had deceived by letter, and whom, moreover, empowered the same agent to receive on board, at the government expense, a number of persons as passengers, contrary to the orders I received. By this I suffered a considerable loss in my property: however, the commissioners was satisfied with my conduct, and wrote to Capt. Thompson, expressing their approbation of it.

Thus provided, they proceeded on their voyage; and at last, worn out by treatment, perhaps not the most mild, and wasted by sickness, brought on by want of medicine, cloaths, bedding, &c. they reached Sierra Leone just at the commencement of the rains. At that season of the year it is impossible to cultivate the lands; their provisions therefore were exhausted before they could derive any benefit from agriculture; and it is not surprising that many, especially the lascars,[4] whose constitutions are very tender, and who had been cooped up in the ships from October to June, and accommodated in the manner I have mentioned, should be so wasted by their confinement as not long to survive it.

Thus ended my part of the long-talked-of expedition to Sierra Leone; an expedition which, however unfortunate in the event, was humane and politic in its design, nor was its failure owing to government: every thing was done on their part; but there was evidently sufficient mismanagement attending the conduct and execution of it to defeat its success.

I should not have been so ample in my account of this transaction, had not the share I bore in it been made the subject of partial animadversion, and even my dismission from my employment thought worthy of being made by some a matter of public triumph.[5] The motives which might influence any person to descend to a petty contest with an obscure African, and to seek gratification by his depression, perhaps it is not proper here to inquire into or relate, even if its detection were necessary to my vindication; but I thank Heaven it is not. I wish to stand by my own integrity, and not to shelter myself under the impropriety of another; and I trust the behavior of the Commissioners of the Navy to me entitle me to make this assertion; for after I had been dismissed, March 24, I drew up a memorial thus:

> To the Right Honourable the Lords Commissioners of his Majesty's
>   Treasury:
> The Memorial and Petition of GUSTAVUS VASSA a black Man, late
>   Commissary to the black Poor going to AFRICA.
> HUMBLY SHEWETH,
>   That your Lordships' memorialist was, by the Honourable the

4. Soldiers.
5. See the Public Advertiser, July 14, 1787 [Equiano's note].

Commissioners of his Majesty's Navy, on the 4th of December last, appointed to the above employment by warrant from that board;

That he accordingly proceeded to the execution of his duty on board of the Vernon, being of the ships appointed to proceed to Africa with the above poor;

That your memorialist, to his great grief and astonishment, received a letter of dismission from the Honourable Commissioners of the Navy, by your Lordships' orders;

That, conscious of having acted with the most perfect fidelity and the greatest assiduity in discharging the trust reposed in him, he is altogether at a loss to conceive the reasons of your Lordships' having altered the favourable opinion you were pleased to conceive of him, sensible that your Lordships would not proceed to so severe a measure without some apparent good cause; he therefore has every reason to believe that his conduct has been grossly misrepresented to your Lordships; and he is the more confirmed in his opinion, because, by opposing measures of others concerned in the same expedition, which tended to defeat your Lordships' humane intentions, and to put the government to a very considerable additional expense, he created a number of enemies, whose misrepresentations, he has too much reason to believe, laid the foundation of his dismission. Unsupported by friends, and unaided by the advantages of a liberal education, he can only hope for redress from the justice of his cause, in addition to the mortification of having been removed from his employment, and the advantage which he reasonably might have expected to have derived therefrom. He has had the misfortune to have sunk a considerable part of his little property in fitting himself out, and in other expenses arising out of his situation, an account of which he here annexes. Your memorialist will not trouble your Lordships with a vindication of any part of his conduct, because he knows not of what crimes he is accused; he, however, earnestly entreats that you will be pleased to direct an inquiry into his behaviour during the time he acted in the public service; and, if it be found that his dismission arose from false representations, he is confident that in your Lordships' justice he shall find redress.

Your petitioner therefore humbly prays that your Lordships will take his case into consideration, and that you will be pleased to order payment of the above referred-to account, amounting to 32£ 4s. and also the wages intended, which is most humbly submitted.

London, May 12, 1787.

The above petition was delivered into the hands of their Lordships, who were kind enough, in the space of some few months afterwards, without hearing, to order me 50£ sterling—that is, 18£ wages for the time (upwards of four months) I acted a faithful part in their service. Certainly the sum is more than a free negro would have had in the western colonies!!!

March the 21st, 1788, I had the honour of presenting the Queen with a petition on behalf of my African brethren, which was received most graciously by her Majesty:[6]

To the QUEEN's most Excellent Majesty.
MADAM,

Your Majesty's well known benevolence and humanity emboldens me to approach your royal presence, trusting that the obscurity of my situation will not prevent your Majesty from attending to the sufferings for which I plead.

Yet I do not solicit your royal pity for my own distress; my sufferings, although numerous, are in a measure forgotten. I supplicate your Majesty's compassion for millions of my African countrymen, who groan under the lash of tyranny in the West Indies.

The oppression and cruelty exercised to the unhappy negroes there, have at length reached the British legislature, and they are now deliberating on its redress; even several persons of property in slaves in the West Indies, have petitioned parliament against its continuance, sensible that it is as impolitic as it is unjust— and what is inhuman must ever be unwise.

Your Majesty's reign has been hitherto distinguished by private acts of benevolence and bounty; surely the more extended the misery is, the greater claim it has to your Majesty's compassion, and the greater must be your Majesty's pleasure in administering to its relief.

I presume, therefore, gracious Queen, to implore your interposition with your royal consort, in favour of the wretched Africans; that, by your Majesty's benevolent influence, a period may now be put to their misery; and that they may be raised from the condition of brutes, to which they are at present degraded, to the rights and situation of freemen, and admitted to partake of the blessings of your Majesty's happy government; so shall your Majesty enjoy the heart-felt pleasure of procuring happiness to millions, and be rewarded in the grateful prayers of themselves, and of their posterity.

And may the all-bountiful Creator shower on your Majesty, and the Royal Family, every blessing that this world can afford, and every fulness of joy which divine revelation has promised us in the next.

6. At the request of some of my most particular friends, I take the liberty of inserting it here [Equiano's note].

I am your Majesty's most dutiful and devoted servant to command,

GUSTAVUS VASSA,
The Oppressed Ethiopean.

No. 53, Baldwin's Gardens.

The negro consolidated act,[7] made by the assembly of Jamaica last year, and the new act of amendment now in agitation there, contain a proof of the existence of those charges that have been made against the planters relative to the treatment of their slaves.

I hope to have the satisfaction of seeing the renovation of liberty and justice resting on the British government, to vindicate the honour of our common nature. These are concerns which do not perhaps belong to any particular office: but, to speak more seriously to every man of sentiment, actions like these are the just and sure foundation of future fame; a reversion, though remote, is coveted by some noble minds as a substantial good. It is upon these grounds that I hope and expect the attention of gentlemen in power. These are designs consonant to the elevation of their rank, and the dignity of their stations: they are ends suitable to the nature of a free and generous government; and, connected with views of empire and dominion, suited to the benevolence and solid merit of the legislature. It is a pursuit of substantial greatness.—May the time come—at least the speculation to me is pleasing—when the sable people shall gratefully commemorate the auspicious era of extensive freedom. Then shall those persons[8] particularly be named with praise and honour, who generously proposed and stood forth in the cause of humanity, liberty, and good policy; and brought to the ear of the legislature designs worthy of royal patronage and adoption. May Heaven make the British senators the dispersers of light, liberty, and science, to the uttermost parts of the earth: then will be glory to God on the highest, on earth peace, and good-will to men: —Glory, honour, peace, &c. to every soul of man that worketh good, to the Britons first, (because to them the Gospel is preached) and also to the nations. 'Those that honour their Maker have mercy on the poor.' 'It is righteousness exalteth a nation; but sin is a reproach to any people; destruction shall be to the workers of iniquity, and the wicked shall fall by their own wickedness.'[9] May the blessings of the Lord be upon the heads of all those who commiserated the cases of the oppressed negroes, and the fear of God prolong their days; and may

7. The Jamaica Consolidated Act, passed in 1787, mandated that slave-owners provide slaves with land for their maintenance, sufficient time to maintain themselves, proper clothing, and religious instruction.
8. [Granville] Sharp, Esq; the Reverend Thomas Clarkson; the Reverend James Ramsay; our approved friends, men of virtue, are an honour to their country, ornamental to human nature, happy in themselves, and benefactors to mankind! [Equiano's note].
9. Proverbs 14.31, 14.34, 10.28, and 11.5.

their expectations be filled with gladness! 'The liberal devise liberal things, and by liberal things shall stand,' Isaiah xxxii. 8. They can say with pious Job, 'Did not I weep for him that was in trouble? was not my soul grieved for the poor?' Job xxx. 25.

As the inhuman traffic of slavery is to be taken into the consideration of the British legislature, I doubt not, if a system of commerce was established in Africa, the demand for manufactures would most rapidly augment, as the native inhabitants will insensibly adopt the British fashions, manners, customs, &c. In proportion to the civilization, so will be the consumption of British manufactures.

The wear and tear of a continent, nearly twice as large as Europe, and rich in vegetable and mineral productions, is much easier conceived than calculated.

A case in point.—It cost the Aborigines of Britain little or nothing in clothing, &c. The difference between their forefathers and the present generation, in point of consumption, is literally infinite. The supposition is most obvious. It will be equally immense in Africa—The same cause, viz. civilization, will ever have the same effect.

It is trading upon safe grounds. A commercial intercourse with Africa opens an inexhaustible source of wealth to the manufacturing interests of Great Britain, and to all which the slave trade is an objection.

If I am not misinformed, the manufacturing interest is equal, if not superior, to the landed interest, as to the value, for reasons which will soon appear. The abolition of slavery, so diabolical, will give a most rapid extension of manufactures, which is totally and diametrically opposite to what some interested people assert.

The manufacturers of this country must and will, in the nature and reason of things, have a full and constant employ by supplying the African markets.

Population, the bowels and surface of Africa, abound in valuable and useful returns; the hidden treasures of centuries will be brought to light and into circulation. Industry, enterprize, and mining, will have their full scope, proportionably as they civilize. In a word, it lays open an endless field of commerce to the British manufactures and merchant adventurer. The manufacturing interest and the general interests are synonymous. The abolition of slavery would be in reality an universal good.

Tortures, murder, and every other imaginable barbarity and iniquity, are practised upon the poor slaves with impunity. I hope the slave trade will be abolished. I pray it may be an event at hand. The great body of manufacturers, uniting in the cause, will considerably facilitate and expedite it; and, as I have already stated, it is most substantially their interest and advantage, and as such the nation's at large, (except those persons concerned in the manufacturing neck-yokes, collars, chains, hand-cuffs, leg-bolts, drags, thumbscrews, iron muzzles, and coffins; cats,[1] scourges, and other instruments of torture used in the slave trade). In a short time one sentiment alone will prevail, from motives of interest as well as justice and humanity. Europe contains one hundred and twenty millions of inhabitants. Query—How many millions doth Africa contain? Supposing the Africans, collectively and individually, to expend 5£ a head in raiment and furniture yearly when civilized, &c. an immensity beyond the reach of imagination!

This I conceive to be a theory founded upon facts, and therefore an infallible one. If the blacks were permitted to remain in their own country, they would double themselves every fifteen years. In proportion to such increase will be the demand for manufactures. Cotton and indigo grow spontaneously in most parts of Africa; a consideration this of no small consequence to the manufacturing towns of Great Baitain [Britain]. It opens a most immense, glorious, and happy prospect—the clothing, &c. of a continent ten thousand miles in circumference, and immensely rich in productions of every denomination in return for manufactures.

I have only therefore to request the reader's indulgence and conclude. I am far from the vanity of thinking there is any merit in this narrative: I hope censure will be suspended, when it is considered that it was written by one who was as unwilling as unable to adorn the plainness of truth by the colouring of imagination. My life and fortune have been extremely chequered, and my adventures various. Even those I have related are considerably abridged. If any incident in this little work should appear uninteresting and trifling to most readers, I can only say, as my excuse for mentioning it, that almost every event of my life made an impression on my mind and influenced my conduct. I early accustomed myself to look for the hand of God in the minutest occurrence, and to learn from it a lesson of morality and religion; and in this light every circumstance I have related was to me of importance. After all, what makes any event important, unless by its observation we become better and wiser, and learn 'to do justly, to love mercy, and to walk humbly before God?'[2] To those who are possessed of this spirit, there is scarcely any book or incident so trifling that does not afford some profit, while to others the experience of ages seems of no use; and even to pour out to them the treasures of wisdom is throwing the jewels of instruction away.

THE END.

1. Cat-o'-nine-tails; whips consisting of nine knotted pieces of cord fastened to a thick rope. *Drags*: weights impeding motion.
2. Micah 6.8.

Note on the Text

In Equiano's lifetime, the *Narrative* went through nine English editions; one American printing; and Dutch, German, and Russian translations. From 1797, the year Equiano died, until 1837, several other editions followed, including reprints bound together with Phillis Wheatley's poems, and an abridged edition.

In his authoritative introduction to the 1969 facsimile of the first edition, Paul Edwards has offered a detailed description of the eight editions he inspected (he did not see the ninth), and later editors have added to his account. Adam Potkay, who reprinted a part of the 1814 edition, has provided a helpful overview of the various "editions," some of which "may represent conflations or multiple copies of one issue." Henry Louis Gates, Jr., reprinted the 1814 Leeds imprint; and Robert J. Allison re-edited the first American printing of 1791.

Vincent Carretta, in his awe-inspiring reprint, accompanied by a total of more than seven hundred endnotes, considered all posthumous editions untrustworthy and the American editions unauthorized and therefore chose the ninth edition as copy text because "it contains Equiano's final changes." This choice has made widely available the previously rare ninth edition (it was the one used by Henri Grégoire and is preserved at the University of California, Riverside; the University of Maryland; and the Bayerische Staatsbibliothek München). I have chosen to follow the text of the first edition, which has not been reprinted since the Edwards edition and which had a wider circulation in Equiano's lifetime than did the ninth. Many of the textual differences among the various editions are minor (slight stylistic revisions, changes in paragraphing, and typographical variations), which is why Potkay states accurately that, unlike that of many other eighteenth-century works, "Equiano's text remains remarkably consistent over time." However, as Carretta puts it equally correctly, Equiano did make "substantive changes" in each edition.

The present edition is reprinted from the original first edition, printed for the author in London, 1789. This edition does not reproduce features of eighteenth-century typography, such as the long "s" and the use of quotation marks at the beginning of every line from a quoted passage, but typographical errors are corrected in brackets.

Equiano's use of the lower-case l. for pound has been regularized by substituting the sign £ throughout. No further editorial changes have been made in the text, but some of the more significant variants that differentiate later printings from the first edition are listed on the following pages. The first section gives the full text of selected passages that Equiano added to the *Narrative* after the first edition. The second section glosses some representative smaller differences between the first and ninth editions. The title page and frontispieces of both volumes have been reproduced from the ninth edition by permission of the Bayerische Staatsbibliothek.

Selected Variants

ADDITIONS

Appendix A

[The note "To The Reader" and the letters on the *Oracle* article first appeared in the fifth edition of 1792.]

To The Reader.

An invidious falsehood having appeared in the Oracle of the 25th, and the Star of the 27th of April 1792, with a view to hurt my character,[1] and to discredit and prevent the sale of my Narrative, asserting, that I was born in the Danish island of Santa Cruz, in the West Indies,[2] it is necessary that, in this edition, I should take notice thereof, and it is only needful for me to appeal to those numerous and respectable persons of character who knew me when I first arrived in England, and could speak no language but that of Africa.[3]

Under this appeal, I now offer this edition of my Narrative to the

1. ————"Speak of me as I am,
   Nothing extenuate, nor set down aught
   In malice."————[Equiano's note].
2. I may now justly say,
   There is a lust in man no charm can tame,
   Of loudly publishing his neighbour's shame;
   On eagles wings immortal scandals fly,
   But virtuous actions are but born and die."‡
   ‡*London*. The County Chronicle, and Weekly Advertiser for Esssex, Herts, Kent, Surry, Middlesex, &c. Tuesday, February 19th, 1788. (Postscript).
   "We are sorry the want of room prevents us from giving place to the favors of Gustavus Vassa on the Slave Trade. The zeal of this worthy African, in favour of this brethren, would do honour to any colour, or to any cause" [Equiano's note].
3. My friend Mrs. Baynes, formerly Miss Guerin, at
   Southampton, and many others of her friends.
   John Hill, Esq. Custom-house, Dublin.
   Admiral Affleck:
   Admiral George Balfour, Portsmouth.
   Captain Gallia, Greenock.
   Mrs. Shaw, James-street, Covent-Garden, London, [Equiano's note].

candid reader, and to the friends of humanity, hoping it may still be the means, in its measure, of showing the enormous cruelties practised on my sable brethren, and strengthening the generous emulation now prevailing in this country, to put a speedy end to a traffic both cruel and unjust.

Edinburgh, June 1792.

Letter of Alexander Tillock to John Montieth, ESQ. Glasgow.

DEAR SIR,

Your note of the 30th ult. I would have answered in course; but wished first to inform you what paper we had taken the article from which respected GUSTAVUS VASSA. By this day's post, have sent you a copy of the Oracle of Wednesday the 25th—in the last column of the 3rd page, you will find the article from which we inserted the one in the Star of the 27th ult.—If it be erroneous, you will see it had not its origin with us. As to G. V. I know nothing about him.

After examining the paragraph in the Oracle, which immediately follows the one in question, I am inclined to believe that the one respecting G. V. 'may have been fabricated by some of the advocates for continuing the Slave-trade, for the purpose of weakening the force of the evidence brought against that trade; for, I believe, if they could, they would stifle the evidence altogether.

Having sent you the Oracle, we have sent all that we can say about the business. I am,

> Dear Sir,
> Your most humble Servant,
> ALEX. TILLOCH.

Star Office, 5th May, 1792.

Letter
From the Rev. Dr. J. Baker, of May Fair Chapel, London, to
Mr. Gustavus Vassa, at David Dale's, Esq. Glasgow.
DEAR SIR,

I went after Mr. Millan (the printer of the Oracle), but he was not at home. I understood that an apology would be made to you, and I desired it might be a proper one, such as would give fair satisfaction, and take off any disadvantageous impressions which the paragraph alluded to may have made. Whether the matter will bear an action or not, I do not know, and have not inquired whether you can punish by law; because I think it is not worth while to go to the expence of a law-suit, especially if a proper apology is made; for, can any man that reads your Narrative believe that you are not a native of Africa—I see

therefore no good reason for not printing a fifth edition, on account
of a scandalous paragraph in a newspaper.

I remain.

DEAR SIR,

Your sincere friend,

J. BAKER.

Grosvenor-street, May 14, 1792.

Appendix B

[Letters of recommendation appear in all editions from 1791 to 1794, but
accumulate in number.]

*To the CHAIRMAN of the COMMITTEES for the ABOLITION
of the SLAVE TRADE.*
Magdalen College, Cambridge, May 26, 1790.

GENTLEMEN,

I take the liberty, as being joined with you in the same laudable
endeavours to support the cause of humanity in the abolition of the
Slave Trade, to recommend to your protection the bearer of this note
GUSTAVUS VASSA, an African; and to beg the favour of your assistance
to him in the sale of this book.

I am, with great respect,

GENTLEMEN,

Your most obedient servant,

P. PECKARD,

Manchester, July 23, 1790.

Thomas Walker has great pleasure in recommending the sale of the
NARRATIVE of Gustavus Vassa to the friends of justice and humanity,
he being well entitled to their prótection and support, from the united
testimonies of the Rev. T. Clarkson, of London; Dr. Peckard, of Cambridge; and Sampson and Charles Lloyd, Esqrs. of Birmingham.

Sheffield, August 20, 1790.

In consequence of the recommendation of Dr. Peckard, of Cam-
bridge; Messrs. Lloyd, of Birmingham; the Rev. T. Clarkson, of
London; Thomas Walker, Thomas Cooper, and Isaac Moss, Esqrs, of
Manchester, we beg leave also to recommend the sale of the NARRA-
TIVE of GUSTAVUS VASSA to the friends of humanity in the town and
neighbourhood of Sheffield.

Dr. Brown,	Rev. Ja. Wilkinson,
Wm. Shore, Esq,	Rev Edw. Goodwin,
Samuel Marshall,	John Barlow

Nottingham, January 17, 1791.

In consequence of the respectable recommendation of several gentlemen of the first character, who have born testimony to the good sense, intellectual improvements, and integrity of GUSTAVUS VASSA, lately of that injured and oppressed class of men, the injured Africans; and further convinced of the justice of his recommendations, from our own personal interviews with him, we take the liberty also to recommend the said GUSTAVUS VASSA to the protection and assistance of the friends of humanity.

Rev. G. Walker,	F Wakefield,
John Morris,	T. Bolton,
Joseph Rigsby, Rector, St. Peter's,	
Samuel Smith,	Thomas Hawksley,
John Wright,	S. White, M.D.
	J. Hancock.

Letter
To Mr. O'Brien, Carrrickfergus.
(Per favour of Mr. Gustavus Vassa.)

Belfast, December 25, 1791.

DEAR SIR,

The bearer of this, Mr. GUSTAVUS VASSA, an enlightened African, of good sense, agreeable manners, and of an excellent character, and who comes well recommended to this place, and noticed by the first people here, goes to-morrow for your town, for the purpose of vending some books, written by himself, which is a Narrative of his own Life and Sufferings, with some account of his native country and its inhabitants. He was torn from his relatives and country (by the more savage white men of England) at an early period in life; and during his residence in England, at which time I have seen him, during my agency for the American prisoners, with Sir William Dolben, Mr. Granville Sharp, Mr. Wilkes, and many other distinguished characters; he supported an irreproachable character, and was a principal instrument in bringing about the motion for a repeal of the Slave-act. I beg leave to introduce him to your notice and civility and if you can spare the time, your introduction of him personally to your neighbours may be of essential benefit to him.

I am,
SIR,
Your obedient humble servant,
THOS. DIGGES..

Letter
To Rowland Webster, Esq. Stockton.
(Per favour of *Mr. Gustavus Vassa.)*

DEAR SIR,

I take the liberty to introduce to your knowledge Mr. GUSTAVUS VASSA, an African of distinguished merit. He has recommendations to Stockton, and I am happy in adding to the number. To the principal supporters of the Bill for the Abolition of the Slave-trade he is well known; and he has, himself, been very instrumental in promoting a plan so truly conducive to the interests of Religion and Humanity. Mr. VASSA has published a Narrative which clearly delineates the iniquity of that unnatural and destructive commerce; and I am able to assert, from my own experience, that he has not exaggerated in a single particular. This work has been mentioned in very favourable terms by the Reviewers, and fully demonstrate that genius and worth are not limited to country or complexion.—He has with him some copies for sale and if you can conveniently assist him in the disposal thereof, you will greatly oblige,

Dear SIR,
Your friend and servant,
WILLIAM EDDIS.

Durham, October 25, 1792.

Hull, November 12, 1792.

The bearer hereof, Mr. GUSTAVUS VASSA, an African, is recommended to us by the Rev. Dr. Peckard, Dean of Peterborough, and by many other very respectable characters, as an intelligent and upright man; and as we have no doubt but the accounts we have received are grounded on the best authority, we recommend him to the assistance of the friends of humanity in this town, in promoting subscriptions to an interesting Narrative of his Life.

John Sykes, Mayor,   R. A. Harrison, Esq.
Thomas Clarke, Vicar,   Jos. R. Pease, Esq.
William Hornby, Esq. of Gainsborough.

Letter
To William Hughes, Esq. Devizes.

DEAR SIR,

Whether you will consider my introducing to your acquaintance the bearer of this letter, OLAUDAH EQUIANO, the enlightened African, (or GUSTAVUS VASSA) as a liberty or a favour, I shall not anticipate.

He came recommended to me by men of distinguished talents and exemplary virtue, as an honest and benevolent man; and his conversation and manners as well as his book do more than justice to the recommendation.

The active part he took in bringing about the motion for a repeal of the Slave act, has given him much celebrity as a public man; and, in all the varied scenes of chequered life, through which he has passed, his private character and conduct have been irreproachable.

His *business* in your part of the world is to promote the sale of his book, and it is a part of *my business* as a friend to the cause of humanity, to do all the little service that is in my poor power to a man who is engaged in so noble a cause as the freedom and salvation of his enslaved and unenlightened countrymen.

The simplicity that runs through his Narrative is singularly beautiful, and that beauty is heightened by the idea that it is *true*; this is all I shall say about this book, save only that I am sure those who buy it will not regret that they have laid out the price of it in the purchase.

Your notice, civility, and personal introduction of this fair-minded black man, to your friends in Devizes, will be gratifying to your own feelings, and laying a considerable weight of obligation on

DEAR SIR,

Your most obedient and obliged servant,

WILLIAM LANGWORTHY.

Bath, October 10th, 1793.

* * *

N.B. These letters * * * would not have appeared in the Narrative, were it not on the account of the false assertions of my enemies.

The kind reception which this Work has met with from many hundred persons, of all denominations, demands the Author's most sincere thanks to his numerous friends; and he most respectfully solicits the favour and encouragement of the candid, and unprejudiced friends of the Africans.

Appendix C

[This paragraph is absent from the first edition but is printed in the second and all subsequent editions. It was inserted after the phrase "woman of her species" (Vol. I, p. 207, in the first edition; p. 78 in this edition).]

One Mr. D— told me that he had sold 41,000 negroes, and that he once cut off a negro man's leg for running away—I asked him if the man had died in the operation, how he, as a Christian, could answer for the horrid act before God? and he told me, answering was a thing of another world, what he thought and did were policy. I told him that the Christian doctrine taught us to do unto others as we would that others should do unto us. He then said that his scheme had the desired effect—it cured that man and some others of running away.

Appendix D

[This paragraph is absent from the first edition but is printed in the second and all subsequent editions. It was inserted after the phrase "in the western colonies!!!" (Vol. II, p. 243, in the first edition; see p. 175 above).]

From that period to the present time my life has passed in an even tenor, and great part of my study and attention has been to assist in the cause of my much injured countrymen.

Appendix E

[This note is absent from the first edition but is printed in the ninth edition. It was keyed to the phrase "interests of Great Britain." (Vol. II, p. 251, in the first edition; see p. 177 above).]

In the ship Trusty, lately for the new settlement of Sierra Leone, in Africa, were 1300 pairs of shoes (an article hitherto scarcely known to be exported to that country) with several others equally new, as articles of export.—Thus will it not become the interest as well as the duty of every artificer, mechanic, and tradesman, publicly to enter their protest against this traffic on the human species? What a striking—what a beautiful contrast is here presented to view, when compared to the cargo of a slaveship! Every feeling heart indeed sensibly participates of the joy, and with a degree of rapture reads barrels of *flour* instead of *gunpowder—biscuits and bread* instead of *horsebeans—implements of husbandry* instead of *guns* for destruction, rapine and murder—and various articles of ussefulness are the pleasing substitutes for the *torturing thumb-screw* and the *galling chain*, &.

Appendix F

[This additional paragraph appears in the sixth and subsequent editions. It was inserted after the phrase "in return for manufactures" (Vol. II, p. 254 in the first edition; see p. 178 above).]

Since the first publication of my Narrative, I have been in a great variety of scenes in many parts of Great Britain, Ireland and Scotland, an account of which might well be added here;[4] but this would swell

4. Viz. Some curious adventures beneath the earth, in a river in Manchester,—and a most astonishing one under the Peak of Derbyshire—and in Sept. 1792, I went 90 fathoms down St. Anthony's Colliery, at Newcastle, under the river Tyne, some hundreds of yards on Durham side [Equiano's note].

the volume too much, I shall only observe in general, that, in May 1791, I sailed from Liverpool to Dublin where I was very kindly received, and from thence to Cork, and then travelled over many counties in Ireland. I was every where exceedingly well treated, by persons of all ranks. I found the people extremely hospitable, particularly in Belfast where I took my passage on board of a vessel for Clyde, on the 29th of January, and arrived at Greenock on the 30th. Soon after I returned to London, where [I] found persons of note from Holland and Germany, who requested of me to go there; and I was glad to hear that an edition of my Narrative had been printed in both places, also in New York. I remained in London till I heard the debate in the House of Commons on the Slave Trade, April the 2d and 3d. I then went to Soham in Cambridgeshire, and was married on the 7th of April to Miss Cullen, daughter of James and Ann Cullen, late of Ely.[5]

5. See Gentleman's Magazine for April 1792, Literary and Biographical Magazine and British Review for May 1792, and the Edinburgh Historical Register or Monthly Intelligencer for April 1792 [Equiano's note].

SELECTED TEXTUAL DIFFERENCES
BETWEEN THE FIRST AND
NINTH EDITIONS†

Vol. I, p. 34 [28] virgin] young woman

Vol. I, p. 38 [30] sprung from the other.] sprung from the other.*

*See 1 Chron. 1.33. Also John Brown's *Dictionary of the Bible* on the same verse.

Vol. I, p. 70 [38] into terror when] into terror, which I am yet at a loss to describe, nor the feelings of my mind. When

Vol. I, p. 85 [42] from those in Africa] from those I have seen in Africa

Vol. I, p. 110 [49] Immediately afterwards the press-gang] Immediately the press-gang

Vol. I, p. 131 [56] It was now between two and three years] It was now between three and four years

Vol. II, p. 117 [135] among the quakers, where the word of God was neither read nor preached, so that I remained] among the people called Quakers, whose meeting at times was held in silence, and I remained

Vol. II, p. 154 [146] Mr. G——S——] Mr. G. Smith

Vol. II, p. 156 [147] lost from God] lost to good

Vol. II, p. 157 [147] spared, nigh to hell] spar'd, when nigh to hell

Vol. II, p. 157 [148] I mused, nigh despair] I mus'd, and nigh despair

Vol. II, p. 224 [169] of all kinds. While we lay here a circumstance happened which I thought extremely singular:—One day a malefactor was to be executed on a gallows; but with a condition that if any woman, having nothing on but her shift, married the man under the gallows, his life was to be saved. This extraordinary privilege was claimed; a woman presented herself; and the marriage ceremony was performed. Our ship] of all kinds. Our ship

Vol. II, p. 229 [170] a register in Gracechurch-Court, Lombard-Street.] a certificate in Whiteheart-Court, Lombard-Street. This mode I highly recommend.

†Bracketed page numbers refer to this Norton Critical Edition.

CONTEXTS

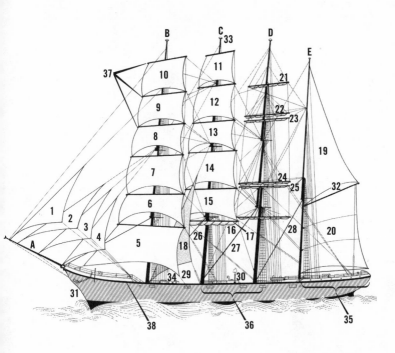

A. Bowsprit	10. Fore royal	24. Mizzen upper topsail yard
B. Foremast	11. Main royal	25. Mizzen lower topsail yard
C. Mainmast	12. Main upper topgallant sail	26. Main stay
D. Mizzen mast	13. Main lower topgallant sail	27. Mizzen stay
E. Jigger mast	14. Main upper topsail	28. Jigger stay
1. Flying jib	15. Main lower topsail	29. Fore sheet
2. Outer jib	16. Mainsail (shown hauled	30. Galley
3. Inner jib	up in its gear)	31. Cutwater
4. Fore topmast staysail	17. Mainyard	32. Gaff
5. Foresail	18. Main topsail staysail	33. Main truck
6. Fore lower topsail	19. Gaff topsail	34. Forecastle
7. Fore upper topsail	20. Spanker	35. Quarter deck
8. Fore lower topgallant sail	21. Mizzen royal yard	36. Waist
9. Fore upper topgallant sail	22. Mizzen upper topgallant yard	37. Yardarm
	23. Mizzen lower topgallant yard	38. Gunwale or gunnel

Illustration of Nautical Terms

Related Public Writings

JAMES TOBIN

From Cursory Remarks [upon James Ramsay's Antislavery Writing]†

[James Tobin was a onetime West India planter and member of the Council of Nevis who, in defense of slavery, attacked abolitionist James Ramsay (1733–1789), a personal friend of Equiano's. In his *Cursory Remarks upon the Reverend Mr. Ramsay's Essay* (1785), Tobin always proceeds from a specific page in Ramsay's antislavery work, *Essay on the Treatment and Conversion of African Slaves in the Sugar Colonies* (1784), and then launches his attempted refutation.]

* * *

Page 17.—He calls slavery, an artificial servitude, *"unprofitable to the public,"* &c. Yet (in pages 109, 112, &c.) he proves, by what he esteems an accurate calculation, that the labour of the slaves in the English West India colonies, brings a clear annual income to the exchequer of near *two millions* sterling; and that, during the late war, a *sixth part of the whole national revenue* was supplied from that source alone. If this is not making slavery *tolerably profitable to the public*, language has no meaning!

Page 18.—"Slavery being the negation of law, cannot arise from law, or be compatible with it." As much depends on the particular sense in which the word *law* is here used, this is a position, I shall leave to be argued by the sages of that intricate profession; observing only, as facts, that many acts of parliament made in England, have taken the liberty to countenance slavery in particular cases; and that all the colonial laws in being, for the regulation, good government, &c. of slaves, have invariably received the sanction of the executive branch of the British legislature.

Page 20.—"By some of our colonial laws, the evidence of a free African will not be taken against a white man." Mr. Ramsay should have

† From James Tobin, *Cursory Remarks upon the Reverend Mr. Ramsay's Essay on the Treatment and Conversion of African Slaves in the Sugar Colonies* (London: G. and T. Wilkie, 1785), pp. 10–11 and 37–38.

said here, "By the laws of *some of our colonies*," for in many of the islands (and if I mistake not, in the very island where he was so long resident) a free African is as free, to all intents and purposes, as the fairest member of the community; and his oath, if a christian, equally admissable in the several courts of judicature; the weight of his testimony will indeed there, and so it would in Great Britain, depend much on his good or bad character.

* * *

Page 59.—"From these circumstances, and from their manners being more communicative, the French in the colonies live more in a family way, among their slaves, than our planters, &c."—That the French planters do certainly live more in a *family way* among their negroes than the English, I have already allowed: but if such *family intercourse* is really any advantage to their slaves, it is notoriously a depreciation of their own characters, and consequence in life. It may here be noticed, as a little singular, that although the author takes several opportunities of exposing, in the most glaring colours, the promiscuous commerce too common between the English managers and overseers, and the female slaves under their charge, he is entirely silent as to any such practice in the French islands, where (as well as in the Spanish settlements) it is, notwithstanding, openly carried to the most notorious and extravagant excess, not merely by young, raw managers and overseers, but even in families of the first rank, opulence, and distinction.[1]

* * *

GUSTAVUS VASSA

Letter to James Tobin†

To J. T [James Tobin] Esq; Author of the BOOKS called CURSORY REMARKS & REJOINDER.

Sir,
    That to love mercy and judge rightly of things is an honour to man, no body I think will deny; but "if he understandeth not, nor sheweth

1. This family intimacy between the French planters and their slaves produces such a number of Mulattoes, Meztizes, and other shades of complexion, that their owners cannot find employment for half their mixed breed about their houses, which occasions many slaves, nearly as fair as their sallow masters, to be met with at work in the common fields; and I have frequently seen, the whip of a French overseer laid over a pair of naked shoulders much whiter than his own. In the English islands, even a Mulatto is seldom or ever found in the field, or at other common hard labour [Tobin's note].
† From *The Public Advertiser*, January 28, 1788.

compassion to the sufferings of his fellow-creatures, he is like the beasts that perish." Psalm lix verse 20.

Excuse me, Sir, if I think you in no better predicament than that exhibited in the latter part of the above clause; for can any man less ferocious than a tiger or a wolf attempt to justify the cruelties inflicted on the negroes in the West Indies? You certainly cannot be susceptible of human pity to be so callous to their complicated woes! Who could but the Author of the Cursory Remarks so debase his nature, as not to feel his keenest pangs of heart on reading their deplorable story? I confess my cheek changes colour with resentment against your unrelenting barbarity, and wish you from my soul to run the gauntlet of Lex Talionis[1] at this time; for as you are so fond of flogging others, it is no bad proof of your deserving a flagellation yourself. Is it not written in the 15th chapter of Numbers, the 15th and 16th verses, that there is the same law for the stranger as for you?

Then, Sir, why do you rob him of the common privilege given to all by the Universal and Almighty Legislator? Why exclude him from the enjoyment of benefits which he has equal right to with yourself? Why treat him as if he was not of like feeling? Does civilization warrant these incursions upon natural justice? No.—Does religion? No.— Benevolence to all is its essence, and do unto others as we would others should do unto us, its grand precept—to Blacks as well as Whites, all being the children of the same parent. Those, therefore, who transgress those sacred obligations, and here, Mr. Remarker, I think you are caught, are not superior to brutes which understandeth not, nor to beasts which perish.

From your having been in the West Indies, you must know that the facts stated by the Rev. Mr. Ramsay are true; and yet regardless of the truth, you controvert them. This surely is supporting a bad cause at all events, and brandishing falsehood to strengthen the hand of the oppressor. Recollect, Sir, that you are told in the 17th verse of the 19th chapter of Leviticus, "You shall not suffer sin upon your neighbour"; and you will not I am sure, escape the upbraidings of your conscience, unless you are fortunate enough to have none; and remember also, that the oppressor and the oppressed are in the hands of the just and awful God, who says, Vengeance is mine and I will repay—repay the oppressor and the justifier of the oppression. How dreadful then will your fate be? The studied and torturing punishments, inhuman, as they are, of a barbarous planter, or a more barbarous overseer, will be tenderness compared to the provoked wrath of an angry but righteous God! who will raise, I have the fullest confidence, many of the sable race to the joys of Heaven, and cast the oppressive white to that doleful place, where he will cry, but will cry in vain, for a drop of water!

---

1. Law of punishment that exacts a penalty just like the crime; an eye for an eye.

Your delight seems to be in misrepresentation, else how could you in page 11 of your Remarks, and in your Rejoinder, page 35, communicate to the public such a glaring untruth as that the oath of a free African is equally admissible in several courts with that of a white person? The contrary of this I know is the fact at every one of the islands I have been, and I have been at no less than fifteen. But who will dispute with such an invective fibber? Why nobody to be sure; for you'll tell, I wish I could say truths, but you oblige me to use ill manners, you lie faster than Old Nick can hear them. A few shall stare you in the face:

What is your speaking of the laws in favour of the Negroes?

Your description of the iron muzzle?

That you never saw the infliction of a severe punishment, implying thereby that there is none?

That a Negro has every inducement to wish for a numerous family?

That in England there are no black labourers?

That those who are not servants, are in rags or thieves?

In a word, the public can bear testimony with me that you are a malicious slanderer of an honest, industrious, injured people!

From the same source of malevolence the freedom of their inclinations is to be shackled—it is not sufficient for their bodies to be oppressed, but their minds must also? Iniquity in the extreme! If the mind of a black man conceives the passion of love for a fair female, he is to pine, languish, and even die, sooner than an intermarriage be allowed, merely because the complexion of the offspring should be tawney—A more foolish prejudice than this never warped a cultivated mind—for as no contamination of the virtues of the heart would result from the union, the mixture of colour could be of no consequence. God looks with equal good-will on all his creatures, whether black or white—let neither, therefore, arrogantly condemn the other.

The mutual commerce of the sexes of both Blacks and Whites, under the restrictions of moderation and law, would yield more benefit than a prohibition—the mind free—would not have such a strong propensity toward the black females as when under restraint: Nature abhors restraint, and for ease either evades or breaks it. Hence arise secret amours, adultery, fornication and all other evils of lasciviousness! hence that most abandoned boasting of the French Planter, who, under the dominion of lust, had the shameless impudence to exult at the violations he had committed against Virtue, Religion, and the Almighty—hence also spring actual murders on infants, the procuring of abortions, enfeebled constitution, disgrace, shame, and a thousand other horrid enormities.

Now, Sir, would it not be more honour to us to have a few darker visages than perhaps yours among us, than inundation of such evils? and to provide effectual remedies, by a liberal policy against evils which may be traced to some of our most wealthy Planters as their fountain, and which may have smeared the purity of even your own chastity?

As the ground-work, why not establish intermarriages at home, and in our Colonies? and encourage open, free, and generous love upon Nature's own wide and extensive plan, subservient only to moral rectitude, without distinction of the colour of a skin?

That ancient, most wise, and inspired politician, Moses, encouraged strangers to unite with the Israelites, upon this maxim, that every addition to their number was an addition to their strength, and as an inducement, admitted them to most of the immunities of his own people. He established marriage with strangers by his own example— The Lord confirmed them—and punished Aaron and Miriam for vexing their brother for marrying the Ethiopian—Away then with your narrow impolitic notion of preventing by law what will be a national honour, national strength, and productive of national virtue—Intermarriages!

Wherefore, to conclude in the words of one of your selected texts, "If I come, I will remember the deeds which he doeth, prating against us with malicious words."

I am Sir,
Your fervent Servant,
GUSTAVUS VASSA, the Ethiopian and the King's late Commissary
   for the African Settlement.
Baldwin's Garden, Jan. 1788

SAMUEL JACKSON PRATT

From Humanity; or, the Rights of Nature†

[Samuel Jackson Pratt (1749–1814) was a prolific writer who published novels, plays, travel narratives, and poems, among them this long antislavery poem *Humanity; or, the Rights of Nature* (1788), to which Equiano published a response.]

I

* * *

O native Britons! here assert your claim,
Boast of your ISLE and justify her fame!

---

† From Samuel Jackson Pratt, *Humanity; or, the Rights of Nature: A Poem in Two Books* (London: T. Cadell, 1788), pp. 9, 11–12, 13, 14–15, 84–87. Equiano wrote a letter (see p. 203) in praise of Pratt's poem. All notes are by the editor of this Norton Critical Edition.

* * *

Just is the boast! yet why to *home* confin'd
Are the soft mercies of thy Albion's[1] mind?
Why, at her bidding, rolls the crimson flood,
To deluge AFRIC in her children's blood?
Why torn from Sire, from children, and from wife,
Dragg'd at her wheels, are captives chain'd for life;
And why do hecatombs[2] each day expire,
Smote by her mangling whip and murderous fire?
Those stripes, those yielding shrieks that rend the air,
Ill fated AFRICA, thy wrongs declare?

   Blush, Britain blush, for thou, 'tis thou has sold
A richer gem than India's mines can hold;
Traffic'd thy soft HUMANITY away,
And turn'd her strongest objects into prey!
Thy generous sons upon that fatal shore,
Their nature lose, and harden into ore:
There greedy avarice, rears his venal throne,
'Midst seas of blood that float the sultry zone;
With wiry lash and iron rod he sways,
The tyrant orders, and the slave obeys;
Havoc and horror rage at his command,
And Desolation covers all the land!
   O! that my Muse could mount on Nature's wing,
Soar like her "darling," her lov'd Shakespeare, sing!

* * *

Ne'er did thy eyes such marks of horror trace,
As hourly agonize the *Negro race*!

* * *

   Wouldst thou the map of slavery survey,
And the dire circuit of the trade display,
Dart thy astonish'd eye o'er distant lands,
From Senegal to Gambia's burning sands,
Pursue the blushing lines to Congo's shore,
Then traverse many a league, Benguela[3] o'er,

1. Britain's.
2. Hundreds.
3. Port in Angola.

Career immense! o'er which the merchant reigns,
And drags reluctant MILLIONS in his chains!

   COMMERCE! thou sailest on a sanguine flood,
On a red sea of Man's devoted blood;
Thy pompous robe, tho' gemm'd as India's shore,
Proud, tho' it flows, is dy'd in human gore.
The tears of millions bathe thy fatal cane,
And half thy treasure springs from human pain,
And not an idol on thy altars shine
But human victims stain the crimson shrine!

* * *

II

   Survey the triple horrors of their state,
Doom'd in each change to be the sport of fate,
Torn from their native land at first they come,
And then are thrown into the sailing tomb,
In wat'ry dens like coupled beasts they lie,
And beg the mournful privilege to die;
Than Man, more kind, but Death oft brings relief,
Releases one, while one survives to grief;
The living wretch his dead associate sees,
The body clasps and drinks the putrid breeze,
Chain'd to the noxious corpse till rudely thrown,
In the vex'd sea, then left a slave alone.
Ah! wretch forlorn! *thy* lot the most severe,
Assassination would be mercy here!
Methinks I hear thee cry, "Ah! give me death,
Give the last blow and stop this hated breath,
To arm this hand were holy innocence,
I call on suicide as self defence,
Oh! for a sword to waft me to the shore,
Where never Christian White may torture more,
Curse, curse me not with Being, instant throw
This loathsome body to the waves below!"
His prayer deny'd, comdemn'd 'midst slaves to groan,
The cruel Merchant marks him for his own,
The scar by Christian cruelty imprest,
Smoaks on his arm, or blackens on his breast,
The wattled oziers[4] form his rugged bed,

---

4. Or osiers, willows.

And daily anguish earns his daily bread;
Short food, and shorter rest, and endless toil,
Above the scourage, below the burning soil.

   Soon with his sable Brothers must he go,
"Doom'd to a sad variety of woe,"
Like harness'd Mules o'er Afric's dreadful sand,
In slow progression moves the mournful band,
The length'ning files begin their circuit wide,
While on their limbs are galling braces ty'd;
Fraught with coarse viands, see the straining throng,
Drag the oppressive caravan along,
The massy iron and the direful log,
Their naked bodies ev'n in slumber clog,
An iron collar o'er each neck is past,
And iron rivets hold the collar fast;
A tighten'd chain across each shoulder goes,
While the dark driver takes his own repose;
At length arriv'd, the miserable band
Like the stall'd oxen pass from hand to hand.

   Ye friends of Man! whose souls with mercy glow,
Swell not your bosoms with this weight of woe?
Fires not the social blood within your veins,
To make the White Man feel the Negro's pains?
Beat not your hearts the miscreant arms to bind,
Of the proud Christian with a savage mind?
Dost thou not pant to snap the impious chain,
And rush to succour the insulted train?
From servile bondage, to free the hapless race,
And fix the haughty tyrants in their place?
Make *them* the weight of Slav'ry to know,
Till their hard natures melt at social woe,
Nor till they humanize to social men,
Would ye restore them to their rights again!

* * *

GUSTAVUS VASSA

Letter to the Author of the *Poem on Humanity*†

To the Author of the POEM ON HUMANITY.
Worthy Sir,

In the name of the poor injured Africans, I return you my innate thanks; with prayers to my God ever to fill you with the spirit of philanthropy here, and hereafter receive you into glory. During time may you exert every endeavour in aiding to break the accursed yoke of slavery, and ease the heavy burthens of the oppressed Africans. Sir, permit me to say, "Those that honour their Maker have mercy on the poor";[1] and many blessings are upon the heads of the Just. May the fear of the Lord prolong your days, and cause your memory to be blessed, and your expectations filled with gladness, for commiserating the poor Africans, who are counted as beasts of burthen by base-minded men. May God ever enable you to support the cause of the poor and the needy. The liberal devise liberal things, and by liberal things shall stand;[2] and may you ever say with the pious Job, "Did not I weep for him that was in trouble? Was not my soul grieved for the poor?"[3] May the all-seeing God hear my prayers for you and crown your works with abounding success! pray you excuse what you here see amiss. I remain with thanks and humble respect.

Yours to Command,
GUSTAVUS VASSA,
The Oppressed African.
Now at No. 13, Tottenham-Street,
Wednesday June 25, 1788.

Editorial Note:

We cannot but think the letter a strong argument in favour of the *natural abilities*, as well as *good feelings*, of the Negro Race, and a solid answer in their favour, though manifestly written in haste, and we print it exactly from the original. As to the question of their *stupidity*, we are sincere friends to *commerce*, but we would have it flourish without *cruelty*.

---

† From *The Morning Chronicle and London Advertiser*, June 27, 1788. All notes are by the editor of this Norton Critical Edition.
1. Proverbs 14.31.
2. Isaiah 32.8.
3. Job 30.25.

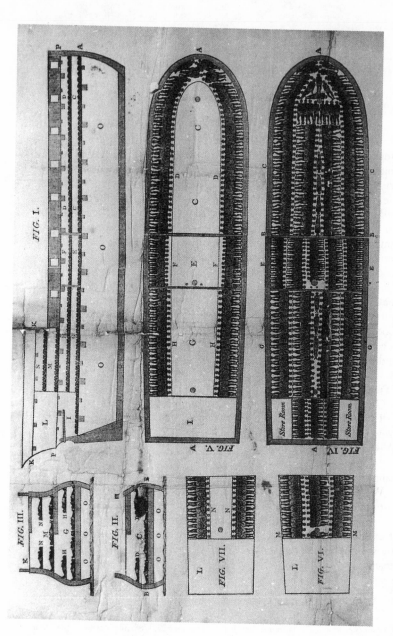

"Description of a Slave Ship." James Phillips, London printer, 1789. Derived from the frequently reproduced "Cross section of the Slave Ship Brookes (1786)," an illustration accompanying various works by Thomas Clarkson and also distributed separately by abolitionists

GUSTAVUS VASSA

Letter to the Committee for the Abolition of the Slave Trade†

To the Committee for the Abolition of the Slave Trade at Plymouth.

Gentlemen,

Having seen a plate representing the form in which Negroes are stowed on board the Guinea ships, which you are pleased to send to the Rev. Mr. Clarkson, a worthy friend of mine, I was filled with love and gratitude towards you for your humane interference on behalf of my oppressed countrymen. Surely this case calls aloud for redress! May this year bear record of acts worthy of a British Senate, and you have the satisfaction of seeing the completion of the work you have so humanely assisted us. With you I think it the indispensable duty of every friend of humanity, not to suffer themselves to be led away with the specious but false pretext drawn from the supposed political benefits this kingdom derives from the continuance of this iniquitous branch of commerce. It is the duty of every man, every friend to religion and humanity, to assist the different Committees engaged in this pious work; reflecting that it does not often fall to the lot of individuals to contribute to so important a moral and religious duty as that of putting an end to a practise which may, without exaggeration, be stiled one of the greatest evils now existing on earth.—The wise man saith, "Righteousness exalteth a nation, but sin is reproach to any people." Prov xiv. 34.

Permit me, Gentlemen, on behalf of myself and my brethren, to offer you the warmest effusions of hearts over flowing with gratitude for your pious efforts, which it is my constant prayer may prove successful

With the best wishes for health and happiness,
I am, Gentlemen,
Your obedient, humble Servant,
GUSTAVUS VASSA, the African.

Feb. 7, 1789, No. 10, Union Street,
Middlesex Hospital.

† From *The Public Advertiser*, February 14, 1789.

General Background

JEAN-JACQUES ROUSSEAU

From A Discourse upon the Origin and Foundation of the Inequality among Mankind†

[Jean-Jacques Rousseau (1712–1778), the Geneva-born philosopher, achieved wide renown for his *Confessions* (1782). In his influential philosophical writings, he developed the paradox of the superiority of the savage state and reacted against the artificiality of social customs. The following excerpts suggest Rousseau's fundamental significance for the abolitionists' view of Africa and for revolutionary thinking in general.]

* * *

Let us therefore beware of confounding savage Man with the Men, whom we daily see and converse with. Nature behaves towards all Animals left to her Care with a Predilection, that seems to prove how jealous she is of that Prerogative. The Horse, the Cat, the Bull, nay the Ass itself, have generally a higher Stature, and always a more robust Constitution, more Vigour, More Strength and Courage in the Forests than in our Houses; the lose half there Advantages by becoming domestic Animals; it looks as if all our Attention to treat them kindly, and to feed them well, served only to bastardize them. It is thus with Man himself. In proportion as he becomes sociable and a Slave to others, he becomes weak, fearful, mean-spirited, and his soft and effeminate Way of Living at once completes the Enervation of his Strength and of his Courage. We may add, that there must be still a wider Difference between Man and Man in a savage and domestic Condition, than between Beast and Beast; for as Men and Beasts have been treated alike by Nature, all the Conveniencies with which Men indulge themselves more than they do the Beasts tamed by them, are so many par-

† From John James Rousseau, A *Discourse upon the Origin and Foundation of the Inequality among Mankind* (London: R. & J. Dodsley, 1761), pp. 29–31, 33, 64–65, 76–77, 97, 114, 178–79. [Transl. of *Discours sur l'origine et les fondements de l'inégalité parmi les hommes* (Amsterdam, 1755)].

ticular Causes which make them degenerate more sensibly.

Nakedness therefore, the want of Houses, and of all these Unnecessaries, which we consider as so very necessary, are not such mighty Evils in respect to these primitive Men, and much less still any Obstacle to their Preservation. His Sight, his Hearing, and his Smelling equally subtile: such is the animal State in general, and accordingly, if we may believe Travellers, it is that of most Savage Nations. We must not therefore be surprised, that the *Hottentots* of the Cape of *Good Hope*, distinguish with their naked Eyes Ships on the Ocean, at as great a Distance as the *Dutch* can discern them with their Glasses.

* * *

Authors, I know, are continually telling us, that in this State Man would have been a most miserable Creature; and if it is true, as I fancy I have proved it, that he must have continued many Ages without either the Desire or the Opportunity of emerging from such a State, this their Assertion could only serve to justify a Charge against Nature, and not any against the Being which Nature had thus constituted; but, if I thoroughly understand this Term *miserable*, it is a Word, that either has no Meaning, or signifies nothing but a Privation attended with Pain, and a suffering State of Body or Soul: now I would fain know what kind of Misery can be that of a free Being, whose Heart enjoys perfect Peace, and Body perfect Health? and which is aptest to become insupportable to those who enjoy it, a Civil or a Natural Life? In Civil Life we can scarcely meet a single Person who does not complain of his Existence; many even throw away as much of it as they can, and the united Force of Divine and Human Laws can hardly put bounds to this Disorder. Was ever any free Savage known to have been so much as tempted to complain of Life, and lay violent Hands on himself? Let us therefore judge with less Pride on which side real Misery is to be placed.

It is therefore certain that Pity is a natural Sentiment, which, by moderating in every Individual the Activity of Self-love, contributes to the mutual Preservation of the whole Species. It is this Pity which hurries us without Reflection to the Assistance of those we see in Distress; it is this Pity which, in a State of Nature, stands for Laws, for Manners, for Virtue, with this Advantage, that no one is tempted to disobey her sweet and gentle Voice: it is this Pity which will always hinder a robust Savage from plundering a feeble Child, or infirm old Man, of the Subsistence they have acquired with Pain and Difficulty, if he has but the least Prospect of providing for himself by any other Means: it is this Pity which, instead of that sublime Maxim of argumentative Justice, *Do to others as you would have others do to you*, inspires all Men with that other Maxim of natural Goodness a great deal less perfect, but perhaps more useful, *Consult your own Happiness with as little Prejudice as you can to that of others*.

* * *

II

[PROPERTY]

The first Man, who, after enclosing a Piece of Ground, took it into his Head to say, *This is mine*, and found People simple enough to believe him, was the true Founder of civil Society. How many Crimes, how many Wars, how many Murders, how many Misfortunes and Horrors, would that Man have saved the Human Species, who pulling up the Stakes or filling up the Ditches should have cried to his Fellows: Be sure not to listen to this Impostor; you are lost, if you forget that the Fruits of the Earth belong equally to us all, and the Earth itself to nobody!

* * *

[VALUE]

Public Esteem acquires a Value. He who sings or dances best; the handsomest, the strongest, the most dexterous, the most eloquent, comes to be the most respected: this was the first Step towards Inequality, and at the same time towards Vice. From these first Preferences there proceeded on one side Vanity and Contempt, on the other Envy and Shame; and the Fermentation raised by these new Levains at length produced Combinations fatal to Happiness and Innocence.

* * *

Savage Man and civilized Man differ so much at bottom in point of Inclinations and Passions, that what constitutes the supreme Happiness of the one would reduce the other to despair. The first sighs for nothing but Repose and Liberty; he desires only to live, and to be exempt from Labour; nay, the Ataraxy[1] of the most confirmed Stoic falls short of his consummate Indifference for every other Object. On the contrary, the Citizen always in Motion, is perpetually sweating and toiling, and racking his Brains to find out Occupations still more laborious: He continues a Drudge to his last Minute; nay, he courts Death to be able to live, or renounces Life to acquire Immortality. He cringes to Men in Power whom he hates, and to rich Men whom he despises; he sticks at nothing to have the Honour of serving them; he is not

---

1. Calmness of mind [*Editor*].

ashamed to value himself on his own Weakness and the Protection they afford him; and proud of his Chains, he speaks with Disdain of those who have not the Honour of being the Partner of his Bondage. What a Spectacle must the painful and envied Labours of an *European* Minister of State form in the Eyes of a *Caribbean*! How many cruel Deaths would not this indolent Savage prefer to such a horrid Life, which very often is not even sweetened by the Pleasure of doing good?

* * *

Historical Background

EVA BEATRICE DYKES

[Humanitarianism, John Wesley, and Gustavus Vassa]†

[Humanitarianism]

One of the salient features of the "Romantic Movement" of the latter eighteenth and early nineteenth centuries was the love of freedom. Whether this love was coloured by an increasing conservatism and limited more or less by an adherence to traditional forms and conventions, as was the case with Wordsworth, Southey, and Coleridge, or whether it was heightened by an intense hostility toward existing conventions and the restrictions of church, society, and state, as was the case with Byron and Shelley, it is not surprising to find among these men and their forerunners a deep sympathy for the oppressed of any race and especially for the Negro.

During the eighteenth century the slave trade of England, fostered and encouraged by the British legislature, was one of the most productive sources of revenue. "The growth of the sugar islands, the cultivation of tobacco in Virginia and of rice and cotton in the Carolinas, the development of the Spanish mines, the increasing needs of Brazil, where Pombal made the freedom of the Indians a reality, all contributed to enlarge the demand for Negroes, until, in occasional years towards the end of the century, the total export from Africa might exceed 100,000 though the annual average was certainly much less. The English alone, at a low estimate, carried over two million Negroes to America in the period between 1680 and 1786. They generally enjoyed the largest share of the trade, but no one of the colonizing nations kept its hands entirely clean."[1] So important and productive was this industry that it received from England "not only national regulation and protection but also a national subsidy."[2]

† From *The Negro in English Romantic Thought* (Washington, D.C.: Associated Publishers, 1942), pp. 1–3, 23–25, 60–61.
1. *The Cambridge Modern History*, ed. A. W. Ward, G. W. Prothero, and Stanley Leathes (New York, 1909), Vol. 6, p. 187.
2. *Ibid.*

The eighteenth century, however, witnessed an ever increasing humanitarian spirit, which had as its aim the happiness of all mankind. Among the many factors contributing to this spirit may be mentioned five. In the first place, there was the theory of moralists like Dr. Samuel Clarke, Shaftesbury, Butler, and Hume, who advocated interest in one's fellowmen. For example, in 1705 Clarke advanced the theory in his *Boyle Lectures* "that we so deal with every man as in like circumstances we could reasonably expect that he should deal with us."[3] In 1711 Shaftesbury through his *Characteristics* emphasized the fact that man is naturally a virtuous being.[4] Butler in his *Sermons on Human Nature* (1726) said that within man is a principle which impels him to seek the good of all. Again, the welfare of the public is emphasized in Hume's *Treatise on Human Nature* (1793).[5]

In the second place, the activities of the Quakers were to a large extent responsible for sympathy for the Negro. The Quakers were the earliest religious group to protest effectively against the slave system. As early as 1671 George Fox, their founder, wrote: "Respecting the Negroes, I desired them [i.e. the 'Friends'] to endeavor to train them up in the fear of God, as well those that were bought with their money as those that were born in their families. . . . I desired also that they would cause their overseers to deal mildly and gently with their Negroes, and not use cruelty toward them as the manner of some hath been and is, and that after certain years of servitude they should set them free."[6] The humane attitude became a tradition with the followers of Fox in the eighteenth and nineteenth centuries.

In the third place, the Deist movement starting in England in the latter part of the seventeenth century comes in for its contribution to sympathy for the oppressed. Lord Herbert of Cherbury, Toland, Collins, Woolston, Bolingbroke, and Tindall were the chief exponents of this phase of English thought. These men inspired Voltaire and the later rationalists of France and England to stress the perfectibility of man.

As a direct protest against that scepticism which inevitably resulted from extreme rationalism, John Wesley with his group came on the scene and thereby contributed to the tide of humanitarianism. He advanced the doctrine that real conversion meant an overwhelming desire to lead all one's fellowmen to Christ by virtue of the fact that in God's sight all men are equal and are bound together by an

---

3. George T. Coleman, *Certain Movements in England and America Which Influenced the Transition from the Ideals of Personal Righteousness of the Seventeenth Century to the Modern Ideals of Social Service* (Menasha, Wisconsin, 1917), p. 38.
4. Frank K. Klingberg, *The Anti-Slavery Movement in England* (New Haven and London, 1926), p. 26.
5. Colman, *op. cit.*, p. 40.
6. S. H. Swinny, "The Humanitarianism of the Eighteenth Century and Its Results," in *The Western Races and the World*, ed. F. S. Marvin (London and New York, 1922), p. 128.

indissoluble bond of affection. Such a belief would naturally take into consideration the Negro as one link in humanity's chain. A close study of eighteenth century Methodism reveals that this movement contributed much to that sympathy for the Negro which reached its climax in England in the nineteenth century.

Finally there arose an increasing interest in the "noble savage," who because of his innocence, his freedom from the corruptions of civilization, and his proximity to nature was considered the ideal person and the epitome of perfection. As early as 1732 there appeared in England an anonymous poem, "The Happy Savage," extolling man in his natural state. The poem begins:

> Oh, happy he who never saw the face
> Of man, nor heard the sound of human voice!
> But soon as born was carried and exposed
> In some vast desert. . . .

where, suckled by the wolf or bear, he lives a life free from deceit and worry.

> Sweet are his slumbers; of all human arts
> Happily ignorant, nor taught by wisdom
> Numberless woes, nor polished into torment.[7]

At first, American Indians and savages of the South Sea Islands and other heathen climes were regarded as noble savages. Eventually the Negro was included in this category. Fairchild says it was Mungo Park who "helped to establish the Negro as a Noble Savage."[8] That lack of social distinctions which characterized primitive man and his freedom from restraint were considered as desirable goals for all men of the eighteenth century.

From these various avenues, then, came those impulses which eventually culminated in the abolition of the slave trade and the subsequent emancipation of the slaves throughout the British Dominions.

*   *   *

[John Wesley]

The founder of Methodism, John Wesley, was a staunch crusader against slavery. In 1735 he and his brother Charles went to Georgia as missionaries while James Oglethorpe was governor. His experiences with the Negroes in America are mentioned in many passages in his journal and letters. In 1736 Wesley's protests against the injustices and abuses perpetrated on the Negroes in Carolina, Georgia, and Florida

7. Ernest Bernbaum, ed., *English Poets of the Eighteenth Century* (New York, etc., 1918), p. 121.
8. Hoxie N. Fairchild, *The Noble Savage: A Study in Romantic Naturalism* (New York, 1928), p. 119.

incurred much animosity.[9] Although there were no slaves at this time in Georgia since the Trustees would not countenance slavery, there was what Wesley calls a system of self-apprenticeship or self-hiring out over a period of years, which the Trustees, were powerless to prevent. Unlike Whitefield, Wesley courageously upheld the Trustees in their condemnation of slavery. An entry for August 20, 1736, shows that he had read "The Negro's Advocate." To him the spiritual and intellectual condition of the Negro was a matter of deep concern. In America he spoke frequently to the Negroes about their salvation and was impressed with their willingness to respond.[1] An entry under "Sunday 29" for June 29, 1740, shows that he had collected money for a Negro school.[2]

When Wesley returned to England, his interest in the American Negro did not wane. He was particularly pleased to receive letters from a friend and minister, Samuel Davis, concerning progress in promoting the conversion of many slaves in Virginia. Davis writes of their joy and gratitude for receiving the Psalms and Hymns sent to them from England. So intense was their delight that in many instances they would pass whole nights in singing hymns of praise. He cannot help observing that the Negroes, "above all of the human species I ever knew, have the nicest ear for music."[3] In January, 1758, we see Wesley preaching in Wandworth, England, at the home of a Mr. Gilbert. On this occasion two Negroes and a mulatto seemed deeply impressed.[4] In December, 1758, he baptized two Negroes belonging to Mr. Gilbert, one of whom was the first African Christian he had known.[5] When he preached at Whitehaven in May, 1780, he was pleased at the excellent testimony given by a Negro woman. Her speech was so refined and showed such a choice selection of words as he had never "heard, either in England or America" from any "Negro speaker (man or woman) before."[6] In February, 1788, he preached on slavery to a crowded house.[7]

Sixteen years before, Wesley had written February 11, 1772, that he had read Sterne's *Sentimental Journey*, which he condemned for its oddity and uncouthness.[8] Unlike this book is another one published by a Quaker "on that execrable sum of all villainies, commonly called

---

9. John Wesley, *Journal*, ed. Nehemiah Curnock (London, 1909), Vol. 1, p. 181, Note 2, and p. 244, Note 1.
1. *Ibid.*, pp. 350, 352.
2. *Ibid.*, Vol. 2, p. 362.
3. *Ibid.*, Vol. 4, pp. 125, 149, 194, 195.
4. *Ibid.*, pp. 247, 248.
5. *Ibid.*, p. 292.
6. *Ibid.*, Vol. 6, pp. 277, 278. See also Vol. 7, p. 144, where Wesley records the baptism of a young Negro.
7. *Ibid.*, Vol. 7, p. 359.
8. *Ibid.*, Vol. 5, p. 445.

the Slave-trade." Wesley says, "I read of nothing like it in the heathen world, whether ancient or modern; and it infinitely exceeds, in every instance of barbarity, whatever Christian slaves suffer in Mahometan countries."[9]

The letters of Wesley afford further glimpses of his humanitarian interest in the slave. He wrote letters of encouragement to English abolitionists and sent contributions to periodicals, which, certainly, must have molded public opinion in favour of the Negro. For example, he sent in 1774 to the *Monthly Review* a letter with two clippings from newspapers of Virginia and North Carolina. These clippings were advertisements of runaway slaves. One owner offered as a reward a certain amount for the head severed from the bodies and less if the Negro should be brought home alive.[1] In November, 1783, Wesley wrote to Captain Richard Williams, who had sent him some lines on slavery, "I think the lines on Slavery will do well! They are both sensible and poetical."[2] Again in December Wesley wrote him that he was sending the poem to the *General Post*, a Bristol newspaper.[3] When the Abolition Committee met in August and October, 1787, Wesley sent letters of encouragement.[4] He wrote Granville Sharp October 11, 1787, a letter expressing his "perfect detestation of the horrid Slave Trade" and recommending a "more honorable" means of securing information than the hiring and paying of informers and commends him and his "glorious Cause" to God.[5] By November 24, 1787, Wesley had printed a large edition of *Thoughts up on Slavery* and sent copies to every section in England. Though he expected much opposition from slave-holders and slave-merchants, he was not discouraged; for God is mightier than they.[6] His fervor is again manifest in a letter to Henry Moore from Bristol in March, 1790, when he stated that he would do anything in his power "toward the extirpation of that trade which is a scandal not only to Christianity but humanity."[7]

Wesley's famous letter to Wilberforce was probably occasioned by his reading of the life of Gustavus Vassa. He records in his *Journal* for February 23 1791,[8] that he has read *Gustavus Vassa*. In the letter to Wilberforce, February 24, 1791, he emboldens him, "Go on, in the name of God and in the power of His might, till even American slavery (the vilest that ever saw the sun) shall vanish away before it." In the same letter he refers to a "tract wrote by a poor African," who states

9. *Ibid.*, pp. 445, 446.
1. Wesley, *Letters*, ed. John Telford (London, 1931), Vol. 6, pp. 126, 127.
2. *Ibid.*, Vol. 7, p. 195.
3. *Ibid.*, p. 201.
4. *Ibid.*, Vol. 8, p. 6.
5. *Ibid.*, p. 17.
6. *Ibid.*, p. 23.
7. *Ibid.*, p. 307.
8. *Journal*, Vol. 8, p. 128.

that in the colonies the oath of a black placed against that of a white is of no import.[9]

The essay, *Thoughts upon Slavery*, which Wesley mentions frequently in his letters, was first published in 1774. Much of the information was secured from Thomas Philip's account of a voyage to Guinea and accounts of other travellers. This protest closes with a prayer that God may heed the cries of the slaves:

> The servile progeny of *Ham*
>> Seize as the purchase of thy blood!
> Let all the heathen know thy name:
>> From idols to the living God
> The dark *Americans convert*,
> And shine in every pagan heart![1]

* * *

[*Gustavus Vassa*]

Negroes did not fail to plead their own cause. We have mentioned John Wesley's reference in his journal to having read "Gustavus Vasa."[2] In 1787 there appeared *The Interesting Narrative of the Life of Olaudah Equiano or Gustavus Vassa Written by Himself*. This work was dedicated to the British Houses of Parliament and written to excite in their "august assemblies a sense of compassion for the miseries which the Slave Trade" had entailed on the writer's "unfortunate countrymen." We learn from the narrative that the author was born in 1745 in Africa of well-born parents. He was kidnapped and sold as a slave in Barbados whence he was taken to Virginia. From here his master sent him to England in 1757. On this voyage the captain of the ship gave him the name of "Gustavus Vassa." Following the custom of the period, he was baptized in 1759 in St. Margaret's, Westminster. Having received his freedom, he exerted his efforts in behalf of his fellow countrymen in slavery. On March 21, 1788, he presented to the Queen a petition, part of which reads, "Your Majesty's well known benevolence and humanity embolden me to approach your royal presence, trusting that the obscurity of my situation will not prevent your Majesty from attending to the sufferings for which I plead.

"Yet I do not solicit your royal pity for my own distress; my sufferings, although numerous, are in a measure forgotten. I supplicate your Majesty's compassion for millions of my African countrymen, who

9. *Letters*, Vol. 8, p. 265. The "poor African" to whom Wesley refers is Olaudah Equiano or Gustavus Vassa, who wrote an account of his life. [See below, pp. 281–82. *Editor*.]
1. *Thoughts upon Slavery* (London, printed; reprinted in Philadelphia, 1774), p. 57.
2. See above.

groan under the lash of tyranny in the West Indies." The petition is
signed "Gustavus Vassa, The Oppressed Ethiopian."[3]

WYLIE SYPHER

[The Nature of the Protest] †

* * *

Although the Abolition Committee determined to attack not the
institution of slavery but the slave-trade, the literary crusaders ignored
the distinction; they were devoted to their "ideology." One may
therefore speak of "anti-slavery" writing rather than "anti-slave trade"
writing. More remarkable, they seem to have been indifferent to "ori-
ental" slavery in the Near East, and to the thriving commerce in men
along the eastern coast of Africa. "Slavery" meant, rather, the traffic
between western Africa and the islands of the Caribbean.

Even though dealing in propaganda, British anti-slavery writers contribute to the literary traditions of the eighteenth century: the noble
Negro himself, living in an Africa that is at once Theocritean[1] and
Rousseauistic; the "character" of the oppressor, the heartless "Creole"
or West Indian; the bursts of savage eloquence condemning the sordid
interests of commerce; the gratuitous horror and equally gratuitous
pathos of scenes on West-Indian plantations—all are symptomatic of
an age.

The literary campaign falls into five stages that are reasonably distinct:

1.—First, there is the period before 1725. Far back in the seventeenth
century are objectors against slavery, usually religious writers. At the
same time, Mrs. Behn and Thomas Southerne establish the tradition
of the noble Negro. Most of the religious writers, like Morgan Godwyn,
plead rather for mild treatment of slaves and for their religious instruction, than for the abolition of slavery itself, or even of the slave-trade.

2.—During the years from 1725 to 1773, the benevolistic and religious
objections to slavery gather force. In France Montesquieu is writing
his celebrated chapter in the *Spirit of the Laws*, a chapter which has
repercussions in England. Among the Quakers there are vigorous protests, especially in America.

3.—The years from 1773 to 1787 mark the onset of active opposition
to slavery and the slave-trade. In 1773 appears the *Dying Negro*,[2] by

---

3. Wilson Armistead, A *Tribute for the Negro* (London and New York, 1848), pp. 236, 237.
† From *Guinea's Captive Kings: British Anti-Slavery Literature of the XVIIIth Century* (Chapel
  Hill: University of North Carolina Press, 1942), pp. 9–10. Copyright © 1942 by the University
  of North Carolina Press, renewed 1970 by Wylie Sypher. Used by permission of the publisher.
1. In the style of the Greek poet Theocritus; pastoral, idyllic [*Editor*].
2. See excerpt below, pp. 288–91 [*Editor*].

Bicknell and Day, provoked by the widely publicized Somerset case of 1772. In this period religious, benevolistic, and "noble Negro" currents meet and mingle with a great stream of egalitarian theory.

4.—From 1787 to 1791 the tide of literary anti-slavery rises highest. The foundation of the Abolition Society calls forth many occasional verses, and popular interest is caught by the researches of Clarkson and the parliamentary activity of Wilberforce. The outbreak of the French Revolution, however, not only diverts occasional poetry to new themes, but also cools some of the ardor.

5.—From 1791 to 1800 there is a decisive ebb in anti-slavery writing, except in doctrinaire prose fiction. Defenders of slavery become active, and the new generation is not much concerned with the sorrows of the Negro. Events in France are too momentous.

CHARLES H. NICHOLS

From Many Thousand Gone: The Ex-Slaves' Account of Their Bondage and Freedom†

*   *   *

Slaves were bartered for a few yards of calico, a couple of barrels of rum, or a keg of gunpowder, and it is very likely that the chiefs and kings of Africa felt they got the better of the bargain. After all, what commodity could be more expendable than an enemy? A slaver made contacts with a designated trading post and quickly learned the elaborate protocol for softening up the local ruler. It was not an easy job. A European unfamiliar with native customs and habits alienated the chiefs and spoiled his prospects. These kings not only expected gifts and payment for their chattels; they also exacted a "duty" for slaves taken away.

Groups of slaves were often made up of widely different and hostile nations, and their desperate circumstances were certainly not calculated to make them cooperative. Hence a trader was bound to be a vicious and coercive man: violence stalked him. MacKenzie-Grieve tells of Captain Messervy, who "being on the Forecastle of the ship, among the Men-negroes when they were eating their victuals, they laid hold on him, and beat out his brains with the little Tubs out of which they eat their boiled rice."[1] No attempt was made to keep the crew from

† From *Many Thousand Gone: The Ex-Slaves' Account of Their Bondage and Freedom* (Leiden: E. J. Brill, 1963, pp. 8–13. Reprinted with the permission of E. J. Brill.
1. Averil MacKenzie-Grieve, *Last Years of the English Slave Trade, Liverpool 1750–1807* (London: Putnam & Co. Ltd., [1941]), p. 131.

enjoying the slave women, but a man had to be alert on the after-deck. Many a lecher was attacked and beaten. Even if the whites succeeded in assuring their supremacy by subduing their cargo with whips and chains, there was often fighting among the slaves themselves. They had to be prevented from inflicting injuries which rendered them useless to the trade. "The slaves of New Calabar," wrote one Captain, "are a strange sort of brutish creatures, very weak and slothful; but cruel and bloody in their temper, always quarreling, biting and fighting and sometimes choaking and murdering one another without mercy, as happened to several aboard our ship."[2] Chained together in twos by the ankles and wrists and stuffed below the decks, the slaves fought to get near the grating for a breath of fresh air. They fought over food and trinkets. "The men linked together often fight, when one wants to obey the calls of nature, and the other is unwilling to go . . . with him." Indeed a sick Negro often made no attempt to reach the sewage buckets and his indignant neighbors began a new fracas.

The conditions of the Middle Passage are now pretty well known. Vessels the size of small coastal schooners might carry over 700 blacks, packed as tightly as kippers in a can. The men were stacked between the decks, lying on their sides, huddled together spoon fashion, the knees of each one in the back of his fellow. The women and children thronged the cabin and the after deck. Obviously the niceties of sanitation and cleanliness were impossible. We can hardly credit the claim of the owners that slaving vessels were kept clean. We have the testimony of a British seaman that one could smell a slaver "five miles downwind." Each ship had its surgeon whose duty it was to inspect the blacks daily. Slaves were permitted on deck every day in fair weather. But the voyage from the Bight of Benin to the West Indies lasted from seven weeks to two months, and the overcrowding, sickness and storms made the Middle Passage a nightmare. One 235 ton Liverpool ship described by Falconbridge carried between six and seven hundred slaves. According to MacKenzie-Grieve "Her width across the beam twenty-five feet, and she measured ninety-two feet in length between decks. The space was divided into four rooms of which one was a store room. The male slaves' room was approximately forty-five feet long, that of the women ten feet, and that of the boys twenty-two feet. Each room was divided by a platform. The slaves were obliged to lie one on top of the other since there was no space to lie on their sides. Fifteen died before they left Bonny river, and three hundred during the Middle Passage."[3] Ordinarily the space regulations called for five feet six inches in length, sixteen inches in width, and four feet,

2. Elizabeth Donnan, *Documents Illustrative of the Slave Trade to America*, 4 vols. (Washington, D.C.: Carnegie Institute, 1930–1925), Vol. II., p. 15.
3. *Last Years*, pp. 128–129.

four inches in height for each slave. On June 30, 1788 the British parliament passed an act to regulate the carrying of slaves, limiting the number of slaves to five for every three tons of the burden of a ship of a 200 tons and requiring at least four feet, four inches between decks. The very existence of the law suggests that even these meager specifications were ignored by many owners.

Each voyage produced some new outrage. Granville Sharp, an 18th Century Englishman indefatigable in his effort to end the slave trade, recorded in his memoirs:

> March 9, 1783. Gustavus Vassa called on me with an account of 132 Negroes being thrown alive into the sea, from on board an English slave ship.

The master of the ship was taking 440 slaves from Africa to Jamaica when an epidemic broke out among the Negroes. The officers of the ship decided that if these sick slaves died a natural death, "the loss would fall to the owners of the ship; but if they were thrown alive into the sea on any sufficient pretext of necessity for the safety of the ship, it would be the loss of the underwriters."[4] This case became a *cause celebre* and probably rang the death knell of the English slave trade. The Captain involved was Luke Collingwood who years before had brought Venture from Guinea to Barbados. On September 6, 1781 he and the crew of the *Zong* sailed from Africa and made for Jamaica. By November 29 they had been at sea for over two months. Fever and dysentery decimated the Negroes and the crew; sixty slaves and seven whites had died. Food and water were scarce. Below the decks were 132 blacks afflicted with dysentery; the noisome stench was all about them like a thick fog. Collingwood paced the deck, dogged at every step by thoughts of bankruptcy. Finally he arrived at this inhuman solution to his problem: why not jettison his black cargo and let the underwriters pay the bill? The miserable slaves were dragged up through the hatches and, in spite of their struggles and cries of horror, hurled overboard. Ironed and chained as they were, they sank each on like an anchor, without hope of rescue. The ship returned to Liverpool. Here the infamous Collingwood soon was disabused of the naive hope that the underwriters would accept his explanation. They refused to pay the insurance. The case was heard in the court of the King's Bench, and it was shown that there was not sufficient necessity for the drowning of the sick slaves. Granville Sharp, alerted by Gustavus Vassa, publicized the case and warned the Duke of Portland, "there is an absolute necessity to abolish the slave trade."[5]

Yet even though great losses were sustained—slaves thrown over-

4. *Ibid.*, pp. 137–142.
5. *Ibid.*, p. 139.

board, or wiped out by disease, or killed in abortive mutiny—the slave trader made a generous profit. John Hope Franklin points out that in the late eighteenth century it was possible for a ship captain to make a commission of 360 pounds on the sale of 307 slaves and for the trader to earn 465 pounds on the same sale.[6] It was not unusual for a ship carrying 250 slaves to net as much as 7,000 pounds on one voyage. "Profits of one hundred per cent were not uncommon for Liverpool merchants."[7] One trader arrived at Barbados with 372 of his original cargo of 700 slaves. The loss of half of a cargo in transit was not uncommon. It is odd that it never seems to have occurred to them that, had they started out with fewer chattels they might have arrived with more! But their cupidity knew no bounds. The imagination is staggered by the number of human beings involved, for few records of the exact number of Africans sold exist. Dunbar estimated that 900,000 Negroes were imported in the sixteenth century, 2,750,000 in the seventeenth, 7,000,000 in the eighteenth, and 4,000,000 in the nineteenth century.[8] This is probably a very conservative estimate.

The rapid exploitation of the European colonies in the new world— in the West Indies and on the North and South American continents—created this insatiable demand for labor to work on sugar, rice and cotton plantations. The traffic in Negroes was itself the very basis of colonial industry and commerce in the eighteenth century. As Elizabeth Donnan points out, it determined the relations between Europe and the colonies; it was the most important factor in the century's wars. Indeed the slave trade was undoubtedly the main source of wealth among the colonial powers in this period.

Hence the Dutch man-o'-war that brought a cargo of twenty Negroes to Jamestown, Virginia in 1619 was followed by a large number of slave ships. The African was imported slowly at first and with considerable misgivings, but the demand for cheap labor grew, and the trade became enormously profitable. In 1650 there were only 300 Negroes in Virginia. There were 2000 in 1671. By 1721 they comprised more than half of Virginia's population. This growth characterized nearly all the colonies so that there were 250,000 slaves in the American colonies in 1750, and the number doubled by 1776.

Early opposition to the introduction of slaves was not based on any moral scruple but rather on the fear of rebellion. However, the need for labor was so great, cotton culture, especially after the invention of the cotton gin, so lucrative that the trade flourished. At the constitutional convention of 1787 Congress was given full control over the

6. See n. 2, p. 50 [*Editor*].
7. John Hope Franklin, *From Slavery to Freedom*, 2nd. ed., rev. & enl. (New York: Knopf, 1956), p. 57.
8. *Ibid.*, pp. 57–58.

colonies' international commerce, except that they were not to restrict the foreign slave trade until after 1808. This arrangement suited all the economic interests concerned. It made it possible for the Carolinas and Georgia to stock up on Negroes. Slaveholders of Maryland and Virginia, on the other hand, enjoyed the hope (to be fulfilled after 1808) that the value of their Negroes would rise. Still the foreign traffic continued sporadically after 1808, for there is plenty of evidence of smuggling. On August 27, 1825, for example, the following official notice appeared in the St. Francisville, Louisiana *Journal*:

> Seventeen Negroes and one mulatto, shipped at Havana as slaves in a vessel under the American flag, were secretly brought in the same vessel into the Mississippi on the 23rd of June last, and afterwards put on shore in the night between Fort St. Philip and the English Turn. On the 2d July instant, three of those negroes were seized by the Inspector of Revenue, on duty near the place and secured to await the result of the prosecution now pending against the vessel. Several others of them, making in all the number originally brought in, have since been detected in various places of concealment and secured with the like object.[9]

These seventeen smuggled Negroes, originally from Jamaica, had been taken to Havana. Those responsible for smuggling them into Louisiana were liable to prosecution under the 1818 act of Congress which provided for a penalty of from $1,000 to $10,000 in fines and imprisonment from three to seven years.

Why this distaste for the foreign slave trade on the part of the slavocracy? The answer is that by the early years of the nineteenth century the domestic traffic in Negroes had become so thriving an enterprise that few owners or traders wished to see prices reduced by competition with the foreign market. Maryland and Virginia had large stocks of slaves, and one of their main sources of income was derived from the traffic with the deep South. Though few of the narrators were involved in the international traffic, many have left us their experiences in the domestic slave trade.

*   *   *

9. A *Documentary History of American Industrial Society*, ed. by John R. Commons, Ulrich B. Phillips, Eugene A. Gilmore, Helen L. Sumner, and John B. Andrews (Cleveland, The A. H. Clark Company, 1910–11), Vol. II, pp. 53–54.

NATHAN I. HUGGINS

[The Rupture and the Ordeal] †

* * *

Thinking back on the African's capture and forced migration to America, we tend to focus on the pain and brutality, the great physical suffering, captives must have undergone. There is testimony enough to credit our wildest fantasies about the horrors and inhumanity of the slave trade—the cross-country coffles, the infamous middle passage. Or we think about the loss of freedom that defined the slave's status, imagining people, once free, who through the agency of the slaver were placed in bondage.

We are thus distracted from what is more profound and personal in the experience. We tend to see only the surface of what was, perhaps, the most traumatizing mass human migration in modern history. Pain, suffering, and brutality, much as they are feared and avoided, are part of the imagined possibilities of everyone, everywhere. Any normal social context has within it the potential for misfortune, pain, oppression, and victimization. One sees around oneself those who have fallen victim to disease or crippling accident or criminality or impoverishment. Normal existence makes one conscious of such possibilities, and therefore we become conditioned to living with such personal disaster without questioning the fundamental ground on which we stand.

But what of that catastrophe that spins one outside the orbit of the known universe, that casts one into circumstances where experience provides neither wisdom nor solace? What if the common ground one shared with the sound and the infirm, the rich and the poor, the clever and the dull, the quick and the dead, fell away and one were left isolated in private pain with no known point of reference? Would not, then, the pain itself be the slightest of miseries?

Similarly, to be unfree would of itself amount to little more than misfortune if the terms by which one lived with one's fellow men and the calculus by which one was valued remained unchanged. After all, freedom, as we think of it, is a modern and Western notion—somewhat a fiction even so—and neither European nor African involved in the slave trade would have presumed freedom to have been the natural state of man. The African, certainly, and probably the European, would have questioned the desirability of a freedom that described an independent person having slight social and political restraints and respon-

† From *Black Odyssey: The Afro-American Ordeal in Slavery* (New York: Pantheon, 1997), pp. 25–27, 38–43, 114–15. Copyright © 1977 by Nathan I. Huggins. Reprinted by permission of Pantheon Books, a division of Random House, Inc.

sibilities. Unfreedom, and even slavery, was conceivable to the African as a normal state of mankind. The African had even seen slaves about him, those of his father and of other men. At the worst, it was a misfortune, or sometimes a circumstance that a clever slave could work to his advantage. But the transatlantic slave trade was outside that experience; it was something radically new and unimaginable. In a process that could only be related to a witch's spell, one was transformed from person to thing.

Two edges of the slave trade—the rupture of the African from the social tissue that held all meaning for him and his conversion into a marketable object—cut the deepest and touched each to the quick. All other horrors attending to the trade were merely external and superficial cruelties. With luck they might abate in time or be mitigated by circumstance. But these two shocks reverberated to the very foundation of the African's being, changing forever the framework of his life. Thus, those few who suffered these shocks but somehow managed to escape the Atlantic crossing were so altered by the experiences, so set adrift, that they could never find their way back into the world from which they had been torn.

Such experiences do not happen with a single blow. Certainly the mind cannot take in, whole, such devastating events. Rather, as in an earthquake, which begins with tremors, building to catastrophe, each shock deeper and broader than the last, one is finally left alone among other moving creatures, stunned, wounded, and isolated amid the shambles of the known world. In such a disaster, it is impossible for the survivor to fix the point of the most telling blow and to completely rediscover himself after its enormity has passed. So, too, the African was engulfed in a process, the end of which was impossible to see from its onset and its precise beginnings lost forever to recall.

*   *   *

The conditions of transoceanic travel were never good during the Atlantic slave trade. The ships were small, seldom larger than 350 tons. During most of the period, the general understanding of navigation and the technology of sailing were skimpy enough to make all voyages risky. The crews of ships, mainly drawn from the margins of European life, were themselves working under duress and suffering conditions of work little better than the captives in the holds. Under the best of circumstances, therefore, these ships sailed close to the edge of peril. There were, of course, the standard hazards of sailing vessels: storms and calms. There was also, particularly during the years of the most intense mercantile competition, the risk that a vessel, with its slave cargo, might fall into the hands of hostile adventurers. Alternately, the densely packed ships might be swept with disease—aggravated and intensified by overlong delays due to calms or misadventure. In either case, much of the human cargo would be thrown into the sea to prevent capture or disease.

For those who ventured their lives and capital in the slave trade, it was a risky enterprise that exacted a heavy toll in money and lives, European as well as African. It offered, however, substantial wealth to those who profited. There would be many a family fortune and industrial empire whose foundations in capital accumulation would rest on the trade in slaves. At the height of the trade, healthy young African men could be bought for as low as ten dollars in Africa and sold for as much as six hundred dollars in America. While these figures represent extremes, they illustrate the magnitude of profit that could be gained from a cargo of two or three hundred captives.

Those Europeans who remained in Bristol or Liverpool, Brest or Amsterdam, Salem or Boston or Newport, might hazard only money and ships. Those who, by choice or compulsion, manned the ships or administered the trade from Africa, placed in jeopardy their health and their lives. Navigational risks were standard to all trade, but the special nature of this merchandise also introduced the possibilities of slave uprisings and contagion due to epidemic disease spawned in congested holds.

Wherever Europeans and Africans met, they exchanged diseases. European sailors brought gonorrhea and syphilis and measles, while Africans carried various forms of fevers, including yellow fever and malaria, amoebic dysentery, and other tropical ills. The immunities and defenses against known microorganisms were of little avail against new strains. Within the slave-ship incubators, microbes, viruses, and parasites survived better than men and women. A voyage of normal length could be expected to take its human toll, but when there was mischance or delays, short rations reduced human resistance even further. The losses could be devastating.

To the ship's captain (often an investor), the problems were clear enough, even if the solutions were not. He would be certain, even in a problemless crossing, to lose some slaves. Would it be better to take on as many slaves as his ship could hold or to find some optimum capacity that would calculate profit on a greater rate of survival? On the one hand, the captain would be willing to risk a high percentage of loss on the assumption that the numbers actually landed alive would more than make up for those who perished. On the other hand, he could assume that a less packed vessel and more tolerable conditions would reduce to a negligible figure the loss in middle passage, making the voyage more efficient. From the captain's point of view, it was risky either way, but the odds tended to favor those who chose to cover every available inch of space with human merchandise. This was especially true since much of the loss at sea could be recompensed to the investors by insurance, whereas there would be no return for the space that was not filled at the outset.

In addition to the general practice of filling all available space, attempts were made to create room where none had existed before. Thus, Africans were shackled and made to lie "spoonlike" on platforms built in the holds of small ships. The holds were about five feet from deck to overhead, with six-foot-wide platforms dividing the space. A ship's capacity was a matter of ingenuity and callous inhumanity. The English Parliament in 1788, attempting to reform practices of overcrowding, restricted the capacity to three slaves for every two tons of ship. In the celebrated illustration of the *Brookes*,[1] we get a sense of what those proportions meant, when 451 slaves would be packed on a ship weighing 320 tons.

Unlike the experience of the European immigrants crossing the Atlantic, time and technology did not serve to make the African's passage easier. The British decision in 1807 to outlaw the slave trade and to patrol the African coast coincided with the end of the legal importation of slaves into the United States. But these curtailments only added more problems for those few whites still drawn into the trade and greater dangers for the men and women who became their illegal cargoes. Slavers shifted to the sleek-lined, heavily sailed sloops and clippers of American design, which could outsail any British patrol ship. What they gained in speed, they gave up in space. Unwilling, however, to lose trade, the captains packed these ships with slaves so that, if anything, their conditions were more intolerable than those of the earlier slower vessels. In time, also, many captains—enterprising Yankee skippers often enough—rounded the Cape of Good Hope and traded with the Arab slavers of Zanzibar and East Africa, thereby extending the length of passage to the New World.

All the risks to lives and capital were dependent on the time spent at sea. The shorter the voyage, the less likelihood disease or disaster would strike. If the trip were merely from the Gambia River to the West Indies under the most favorable conditions, the crossing could be made in as little as three weeks. A longer voyage, say from the Congo to Virginia, with trouble at sea, could take more than three months.

Problems of raging winds and heavy seas were the main concerns, for they could send a small craft far off its course, wasting weeks. Or worse, the craft could be tossed like matchwood in the towering waves, swamped by mountainous seas, or spun off into oblivion by hurricane winds. Or, the other curse of sailors, the craft might be reduced to immobility for days on end—becalmed in doldrums—the sails yawning for the slightest breeze that might pick them up again. With time lost, troubles multiplied. Rations had to be made to stretch. Meager at best

1. See p. 204 [*Editor*].

(salt beef and hardtack for the crew; rice, stewed yams, or plantains for slaves, and a pint of water served twice a day), they became half-rations or quarter-rations or less if need be. Storms brought additional problems because the hatches had to be covered; and, as they were the only source of air to the densely packed hold, when the hatches were reopened, many captives would have died from suffocation and would be thrown into the sea.

Those Europeans who would jeopardize their wealth and lives in the slave trade had to take all these risks into account. From one point of view, these calculations were no different from those one would make in any hazardous business venture with any other species of merchandise. Certainly, they would prefer to think so, abjuring such moral and sentimental considerations as might be raised about trading in human beings. So long as such scruples did not weaken resolve, with enterprise, daring, and luck, enormous profits were to be made from this trade. One needed merely to understand that the object of shipping was to get as much acceptable cargo to port as one could at the lowest possible cost.

Even slaves who were sick or dying, like any other damaged merchandise, could be expected to bring some price. And those who were too far gone, if detected soon enough, could be jettisoned so that they would not continue to drain food and water. That, too, was a judgment one could make with any species of cargo that proved more costly to transport than would be realized in sale or auction. All such decisions were simple enough to come by as long as one was ruthless in insisting on the analogy between human beings and other items of commerce.

But the humanity of the Africans was a fact and could not be gainsaid by any "hard-headed" calculations. That fact made them different from all other forms of cargo, and all who trafficked in slaves had to come to know it.

Because they were human, the crew could find among the women release for their sexual hungers. That was common enough, the women being separate from the men, the voyages being long, and the women having no choice in the matter.

Because they were intelligent human beings, the captives could calculate, too, and might take their own desperate risks to break out of their oppression. They could frustrate the entire enterprise with a slave mutiny. Or individuals might take themselves out of their captors' hands by suicide. Such possibilities were constant reminders that an irreducible human quality made the forced transport and sale of Africans in the New World something different from the trade in tea and spices.

The slave trade for Europeans remained an enterprise of calculable risks. Not so for Africans. The dungeons or barracoons of the coast had been only other way stations, like the rest in the African's journey, carrying him into unknown worlds where the mind and spirit were twisted through anguish unimaginable except in fantasies of the nether world. Already the deep ruptures with self and place had occurred. One was like the dust and grasses, blown and swirled by the capricious spirits in the winds; like leaves and twigs caught up by the willful grasp of the river spirits, drawn relentlessly to the sea. Ties that had held them fast had been severed, and they were in the sway of irresistable forces. Whoever the demons possessing them, they were not done yet.

* * *

To the African mind, unfreedom was no outlandish condition. Freedom was not much thought about in the Old World. One always belonged to a place and a people, having ties and obligations going far beyond the will of a single person to change. Imagining a state of freedom—meaning to be unfettered by wills, judgments, and determinations not one's own—would have been a frightening vision, like being a plant with roots in the earth too shallow to hold fast, like being free to move in the wind but having no place and no way to draw sustenance.

American slavery, however, required a radical transformation of personal meaning. In the New World, one asked, "What is a person worth? What is his value?" That would have been a strange question to Africans before the slave trade. To them, a person was, he belonged, he had meaning–be he powerful or weak, quick or slow. But they would have been at a loss to discover a quantitative value to stand for a man or woman. That is not to claim that the African held individual human life in higher esteem than did Europeans. There was human sacrifice, of course, and the close margins of life and death served to inure them to personal loss. It was, merely, that the estimate of human quality would not have been calculated in money, goods, or as capital assets.

But, in essence, that was what American slavery was all about. It began in the African slave markets, and Afro-American generations to come would know the market to be the social test of their value. To be felt and inspected, talked of as a thing, transferred from place to place, bought and sold—that was the common pulse of the slave experience through two and one half centuries of Afro-American history.

Even those few fortunate enough never to hear the auctioneer chant their qualities would know the slave market as the basic symbol of their condition. Boys of a certain age went for so much, able-bodied, mature men for another amount. Acquired skills added to the price; marks from the lash took value away. Strong-bodied women who could fell trees and plow commanded one price; frail or sickly ones brought less. A comely young woman in the flush of youth might send prices beyond reasonable bounds. Did a woman have children? Would she have more? There was money in that. Did a man have the marks from small-pox? That was value to the discerning eye.

To be chattel property meant one could be traded and transferred as any other object of value. A master who wanted to set his children up on their own normally did so with a gift from among his own slaves, often breaking black kinship ties as a result. In fact, in the antebellum United States, which lacked a national monetary system, where state and private bank notes were insecure and lost value at a distance from place of issue, slaves were a convenient way to move wealth from one state to another.

* * *

DAVID DABYDEEN

Eighteenth-Century English Literature on Commerce and Slavery†

Eighteenth-century Britain experienced a rapid expansion of commerce, with the growth of colonies, the spread of empire and British domination of the trade in African slaves. 'There was never from the earliest ages', Samuel Johnson wrote, 'a time in which trade so much engaged the attention of mankind, or commercial gain was sought with such general emulation'. One writer in the *Craftsman* of 1735 described the 'Torrent of Riches, which has been breaking in upon us, for an Age or two past'. John Brown wrote of 'The Spirit of Commerce, now predominant', and Revd. Catcott preached breathlessly on the commercial supremacy of Britain:

> In a word, the whole earth is the market of Britain; and while we remain at home safe and undisturbed, have all the products and commodities of *the eastern* and *western Indies* brought to us in our ships and delivered into our hands . . . Our island has put on quite a different face, since the increase of commerce among us . . . In a word, commerce is the first mover, the main spring in the political machine, and that which gives life and motion to the whole, and sets all the inferior wheels to work.[1]

---

† From *The Black Presence in English Literature*, ed. David Dabydeen (Manchester, Engl.: University of Manchester Press, 1985), pp. 26–49. Permission of David Dabydeen.

1. Samuel Johnson, cited by L. Whitney: *Primitivism And The Idea Of Progress* (Baltimore, 1934), p. xviii; *Craftsman* of 1735 reproduced in *The Gentleman's Magazine*, Vol. 5, 1735, pp. 717–18; John Brown: *An Estimate Of The Manners And Principles Of The Times* (2nd ed., London, 1757), p. 22; A. S. Catcott: *The Antiquity and Honourableness of the Practice of Merchandize. A Sermon* (Bristol, 1744), pp. 13, 14, 15.

Addison some three decades earlier had described London as 'a kind of *Emporium* for the whole Earth' (*Spectator*, 69), a view echoed, on a national level, in Defoe's A *Tour Thro' the whole Island of Great Britain* (1724–6) with its sense of unbounded progress, agricultural, commercial and industrial.

The age therefore, whilst being one of 'high culture' (the rise of British art, the establishment of tastes for Italianate music and architecture, and a general cultivation of 'civilised' values) was to a greater extent an age of commercial achievements. As J. A. Doyle puts it, 'if the eighteenth century was the age of Addison and Horace Walpole, it was in a far more abiding sense the age of Chantham and Wolfe and Clive'.[2] The great trading companies established in the previous century flourished and there was a general sense of the manifold possibilities of money-making, of financial development through international trade and commerce with the colonies. Schemes for making money by taking out patents on new inventions abounded, as did speculation in the stock of all kinds of companies, the mood of financial adventurism reaching a giddy height in the South Sea period of 1720, the South Sea disaster being the first great crisis in British capitalism.

'It is money that sells all, money buys all, money pays all, money makes all, money mends all, and money mars all'; ' 'tis Money makes the Man'; All Things are to be had for Money'; 'Money, th' only Pow'r ... the last Reason of all Things'; 'Money answers all Things': these are the often repeated maxims of the age.[3] The greater proportion of this money was derived from the traffic in human beings, the buying and selling of African peoples and the enforced labour of these people. The slave trade was of vast economic importance to the financial existence of Britain. It was the revenue derived from slavery and the slave trade which greatly helped to finance the industrial revolution.[4] In seventeenth and eighteenth century opinion blacks were 'the strength and sinews of this western world', the slave trade 'the spring and parent whence the others flow', 'the first principle and foundation of all the rest, the mainspring of the machine which sets every wheel in motion',

---

2. J. A. Doyle cited by A. A. Ettinger: *James Edward Oglethorpe. Imperial Idealist* (Oxford, 1936), p. 110; T. Seymour: *Literature And The South Sea Bubble* (unpublished PhD diss., Chapel Hill, 1955), p. 12.

3. *Maxims of Wisdom for Gaining Wealth* (London, 1788), p. 20; *Put Money in your Purse* (London, 1754), p. 321; *The Universal Merchant: Containing The Rationale of Commerce, in Theory and Practice* (London, 1753), p. 6; *A Trip To Leverpoole By Two of Fate's Children In Search of Fortunatus's Purse. A Satyr* (London, 1706), title-page quoting from Butler's *Hudibras*; J. Vanderlint: *Money answers all Things* (London, 1734).

4. Eric Williams in *Capitalism & Slavery* (Chapel Hill, 1944), p. 52, has written that 'the profits obtained provided one of the main streams of that accumulation of capital in England which financed the Industrial Revolution'. James Walvin in *The Black Presence: A Documentary History of the Negro in England, 1555–1860* (London, 1971), p. 8, states that such commerce 'underpinned Britain's transition towards an industrial society'.

'the Hinge on which all the Trade of this Globe moves on' and 'the best traffick the kingdom hath'.[5] The profits from the slave trade were seen as benefiting the whole British nation without exception: as one writer in 1730 stated, *there is not a Man in this Kingdom, from the highest to the lowest, who does not more or less partake of the Benefits and Advantages of the* Royal African Company's *FORTS and CASTLES in Africa.*' Other writers told of the 'immensely great' profits made by sugar planters who have 'remitted over their Effects, and purchas'd large Estates in England', of the 'many private Persons in England [who] daily gain great Estates in every Branch of the Trade' and of investors in the African Company who have 'for Sixty Years past, got great Estates out of the Subscription'.[6] West Indian merchants and planters educated their children in Britain and supported them in a state of opulence; thousands of black slaves were also brought to Britain by returning merchants and planters.[7]

The trade in black people was at the time justified on economic and moral grounds. Slavery was right and allowable, the argument ran, because it was profitable and therefore 'necessary'. According to Defoe '[It is] an Advantage to our Manufacturers, an encreasing the Employment of the Poor, a Support to our General Commerce, and an Addition to the General Stock of the Nation'. Grosvenor in parliament admitted euphemistically that the slave trade 'was an unamiable one' but added with no recognition of the callousness of his comparison that 'So also were many others: the trade of a butcher was an unamiable trade, but it was a very necessary one, not withstanding'.[8] The term 'necessity' appears again and again in works excusing the slave trade. William Bosman for instance, writing in 1705, admits that 'I doubt not but this Trade seems very barbarous to you, but since it is followed

5. Williams, *Capitalism and Slavery*, pp. 30, 51; J. Houstoun: *Some New and Accurate Observations . . . Of the Coast of Guinea* (London, 1725), p. 43; Peter Hogg: *Slavery: The Afro-American Experience* (British Library Publication, London, 1979), p. 3.
6. *The Case Of The Royal African Company of England* (London, 1730), p. 31; *The Dispute between the Northern Colonies and the Sugar Islands, set in a Clear View* (1731 broadside, in *The Goldsmiths Library's Collection of Broadsides* IV, no. 343.3, Senate House Library, London University); *A Letter To The Right Reverend The Lord Bishop of London From An Inhabitant Of His Majesty's Leeward-Caribbee-Islands* (London, 1730), p. 14; *Some Matters of Fact Relating to the Present State of the African Trade* (n.p., 1720), p. 1.
7. By 1768 the estimate of the number of blacks in Britain was 20,000 (F. Shyllon: *Black People in Britain 1555–1833*, Oxford, 1977, p. 102). The figure may have been higher—the *London Chronicle* of 1756 gave a number of 30,000 (D. A. Lorimer: *Colour, Class and the Victorians*, London, 1978, p. 25). *The Daily Journal* of 5 April 1723 reported that 'Tis said there is a great Number of Blacks come daily into this City, so that 'tis thought in a short Time, if they be not suppress'd, the City will swarm with them'.
8. Daniel Defoe: *A Brief Account Of The Present State Of The African Trade* (London, 1713), p. 55; *Review* (ed. A. W. Secord. New York, 1938), IX, p. 82. Defoe also declares that the British plantations 'can no more subsist without Negroes, than *England* could without Horses'—see R. P. Kaplan: *Daniel Defoe's Views on Slavery And Racial Prejudice* (unpublished PhD diss., New York Univ., 1970), p. 120. For Grosvenor statement, see *Report of the Debate on a Motion For the Abolition of the Slave Trade in the House of Commons on Monday and Tuesday, April 18th and 19th, 1791* (London, 1791), p. 47.

by meer necessity it must go on'. William Snelgrave some thirty years afterwards echoed Bosman's sentiments:

> Tho' to traffic in human Creatures, may at first sight appear barbarous, inhuman and unnatural; yet the Traders herein have as much to plead in their own Excuse, as can be said for some other Branches of Trade, namely, the *Advantage* of it.[9]

Such a brutal economic rationale was indicative of the materialist mood of the age, one which saw profit as the main criterion of behaviour, and morality only as a secondary consideration.

The moral justification of the slave trade ranged from the argument that the trade was 'benevolent' in that it provided poor white people with employment, to the argument that the slave trade saved Africans from the bloody tyranny of their own countrymen and from being eaten by their fellow cannibals. As John Dunton put it, 'they must either be *killed* or *eaten*, or both, by their barbarous conquering enemy'. James Grainger, James Boswell, Edward Long and others were all agreed on the compassionate nature of slavery, using exact arguments as Dunton's.[1] One writer in 1740 spoke not of 'enslaving' blacks but of 'rather ransoming the Negroes from their national Tyrants' by transplanting them to the colonies where 'under the benign Influences of the Law, and Gospel, they are advanced to much greater Degrees of Felicity, tho' not to absolute Liberty'.[2]

Viewing the African as a primitive, sub-human creature was necessary to the whole business of slavery since it avoided or made easy any problems of morality: Christians were not enslaving human beings, for blacks were not fully human. Africans embodied all the qualities that Lord Chesterfield, a self-conscious gentleman of taste and culture, abhorred. According to Chesterfield Africans were 'the most ignorant and unpolished people in the world, little better than lions, tigers, leopards, and other wild beasts, which that country produces in great numbers.' It was thus morally acceptable 'to buy a great many of them to sell again to advantage in the West Indies'.[3] An indication of the primitivism of the African was the supposed absence of manufactures,

---

9. *A New and Accurate Description of Guinea* . . . (London, 1705), cited by M. Craton, J. Walvin and D. Wright: *Slavery, Abolition and Emancipation* (London, 1976), p. 220; William Snelgrave: *A New Account of Some Parts of Guinea, And the Slave-Trade* (London, 1734), p. 160.

1. *The Athenian Mercury*, VIII, no. 30 (1691). See C. A. Moore's *Backgrounds of English Literature* (Minneapolis, 1953), p. 153. Edward Long's views are cited by O. Wali: *The Negro in English Literature* (unpublished PhD diss., North Western Univ., 1967), pp. 391–2. For Grainger's and Boswell's views see Wylie Sypher: *Guinea's Captive Kings* (Chapel Hill, 1944), pp. 169f.; p. 59.

2. 'The African Slave Trade defended', in *The London Magazine*, IX, 1740, pp. 493–4; cited by E. Donnan: *Documents Illustrative Of The History Of The Slave Trade To America* (4 vols, Washington, 1930–5), II, p. 470.

3. *The Letters Of The Earl of Chesterfield To His Son* (ed. C. Strachey, with notes by A. Calthrop, 3rd ed., London, 1932), p. 116.

sciences, arts, and systems of commerce within African society. It was repeatedly asserted that blacks were ignorant, unskilled and undeveloped creatures, their lack of scientific, industrial and commercial knowledge accounting for their savage morality.[4]

The literary response: commerce and civilisation

Many eighteenth century men of letters were directly involved in the business world, holding prominent government posts, holding investments in financial schemes and companies, or writing on money matters. Addison, Defoe, Cleland, Steele, Swift, Pope, Prior and Smollett, among others, were in one way or another connected with the world of commerce. Addison for instance was a commissioner of land tax and plantations; Cleland, a commissioner of land tax and house duties; Smollett, once a surgeon on a slave-ship, married a colonial, slave-owning heiress. Inevitably, perhaps, a great deal of eighteenth century literature concerned itself with financial matters. As T. K. Meier has written,

> literary men of the seventeenth and eighteenth centuries, including Dryden, Pope, Steele, Thomson, most of the georgic poets, and a number of lesser dramatists, essayists, and poets did heap high praise upon both the concept of capitalistic business enterprise and upon businessmen who practiced it . . . Commerce and industry had caught the literary imagination of the period and represented for a time at least, the progressive hope of the future.

Bonamy Dobrée in discussing eighteenth century poetry has described commerce as 'the great theme that calls forth the deepest notes from poets of the period'. No other theme, Dobrée writes, 'can compare in volume, in depth, in vigour of expression, in width of imagination, with the full diapason of commerce'.[5]

Poets like James Thomson, Richard Glover, Edward Young, James Gaugh, George Cockings and John Dyer celebrated commerce as the catalyst of social, cultural and economic progress. Thomson's *The Castle of Indolence* (1748) views urban development, the establishment of empire and the expansion of markets as laudable ideals; his 'Knight of Industry' is an imperialist and property developer, creating a city out

---

4. For a sample of such opinions see *A Brief Discovery . . . of . . . The Island of Madagascar*, in *A Collection of Voyages and Travels* (London, 1745), II, p. 633; *A True Relation Of The Inhuman and Unparalleled Actions And Barbarous Murders, Of Negroes or Moors ibid.*, II, p. 515. The first writes that there are 'no ingenious manufactures . . . no arts, no sciences' among the Negroes, that they show no 'symptoms of ingenuity'; the second and third writers describe blacks as 'idle, sluggish, . . . free from having any tillage whatsoever'; 'they make little use of labour or manufactures'.

5. Tom K. Meier: *Defoe And The Defense of Commerce* (unpublished PhD diss., Columbia Univ., 1971), pp. 1, 18. Bonamy Dobrée: 'The theme of patriotism in the poetry of the early eighteenth century', in *Proceedings Of The British Academy* XXXV, 1949, p. 60.

of undeveloped land, just as Defoe's Crusoe transforms his desert
island into a flourishing town:

> Then towns he quickened by mechanic arts,
> And bade the fervent city flow with toil;
> Bade social commerce raise renownèd marts,
> Join land to land, and marry soil to soil,
> Unite the poles, and without bloody spoil
> Bring home of either Ind the gorgeous stores.
>
> (Canto II, 20)

In *The Seasons—Autumn* (1730; ll. 22–150) Thomson traces approv-
ingly the long historical process whereby the city rises out of the wilderness, with the evolution of man from the horrors of a primitive
existence into a blissful state of commercial and scientific activity.
Glover's *London: Or, the Progress of Commerce* (4th ed., 1739) celebrates, in a similar vein, the development of nature and the growth of
the city through commerce:

> . . . She in lonely sands
> Shall bid the tow'r-encircled city rise,
> The barren sea shall people, and the wilds
> Of dreary nature shall with plenty cloath. (ll. 127–30)

It is commerce that has awakened the whole world from its primitive
slumber, bringing development, progress and civilisation:

> thou beganst
> Thy all-enlivening progress o'er the globe
> Then rude and joyless . . . (1.173f.)

Urban development is the theme too in poems like Cockings' *Arts,
Manufacture, And Commerce*(c.1769), Gaugh's *Britannia* (1767) and
Young's *The Merchant* (1741). The sense of the limitless possibilities
of expansion and gain is given perfect expression by Young as he urges
Englishmen to seize the present opportunities of commerce:

> Rich *Commerce* ply with Warmth divine
> By *Day*, by *Night*; the *Stars* are Thine
> Wear out the Stars in *Trade*! Eternal run
> From Age to Age, the noble Glow,
> A Rage to gain, and to *bestow*,
> Whilst Ages last! In *Trade* burn out the Sun! (Strain IV, 19)

In this poem Young's model of the world is a purely economic one,
the relationship between earth, sea and air seen as a series of commercial transactions:

> *Earth's* Odours *pay* soft *Airs* above,
> That o'er the teeming Field *prolific* range;

> *Planets* are Merchants, take, return
> Lustre and Heat; by Traffic burn;
> The whole *Creation* is one vast *Exchange*. (Strain III, 26)

The kindling of commercial activity is compared to natural awakenings, to the rain from heaven which cheers the glebe, activates the bees and rouses the flowers. Blake may have seen 'a Heaven in a Wild Flower' (*Auguries of Innocence*, 1.2), but Young is more down-to-earth. Such a commercial response to nature is a distinguishing feature of much of eighteenth century literature. Trees existed to be cut down and fashioned into merchant ships. When one writer described 'beautiful forests', he meant not their aesthetic qualities but their commercial potential: 'The farther one advances into the country, the more beautiful Forests are found, full of Gummy Trees, fit to make Pitch for Ships; as also infinite Store of Trees fit for Masts.'[6]

The consensus of opinion in many pieces of eighteenth century literature is that commerce is a wonderful activity, creative of progress, culture and civilisation. Glover writes of the mathematics, philosophy, poetry and laws that result from commerce:

> Barbarity is polish'd, infants arts
> Bloom in the desert, and benignant peace
> With hospitality, begin to soothe
> Unsocial rapine, and the thirst of blood.
> (*London*, ll. 209–12)

Young makes similar claims for the civilising power of commerce:

> Commerce gives Arts, as well as *Gain*;
> By Commerce wafted o'er the Main,
> *They* barbarous Climes enlighten as they run;
> *Arts* the rich Traffic of the Soul!
> May travel *thus*, from Pole to Pole,
> And gild the World with Learning's *brighter* Sun.
> (*Merchant*, Strain II, 1)

The contact between men as a result of mutual trade is seen as conducive to tolerance, morality and culture. The merchant, the agent of commerce, was also celebrated as the agent of progress and civilisation, the embodiment of civilised standards derived from his commercial experience. No praise was great enough to lavish upon him, all poetic eulogies fell short of their mark:

> Is *Merchant* an inglorious Name?
> No; fit for *Pindar* such a Theme,
> Too great for Me; I pant beneath the Weight!
> If loud, as *Ocean's* were my Voice,

---

6. *The Four Kings of Canada* (London, 1710), p. 46.

> If Words and Thoughts to court my Choice
> Out-number'd *Sands*, I could not reach its Height.
> (*Merchant*, Strain III, 24)

The merchant was also seen as a force for liberty, 'liberty' being a key word in literature celebrating commerce. Commerce meant the rise of the middle class which, as it gained political influence, sought protection from the tyranny and arbitrary laws of the aristocratic class, its main ambition being the legal protection of property. Hence Young's verse:

> *Trade*, gives fair *Virtue* fairer still to shine;
> Enacts those Guards of Gain, the *Laws*;
> *Exalts* even *Freedom's* glorious Cause. (*Merchant*, Strain IV, 14)

There was, as C. A. Moore has said, 'one dark blot' in this bright picture of progress, civilisation and liberty through commerce: 'The one detail out of moral keeping was the slave traffic'.[7] Slavery was such an undeniably crucial aspect of colonial and international commerce that the men of letters could not avoid touching on the subject. Their problem was how to reconcile their belief in the civilising effects of commerce to the barbaric realities of the slave trade. Cornelius Arnold and John Dyer provided one way out of the dilemma. Arnold interrupts briefly his eulogy on commerce to express perfunctory regret at the fact of African slavery, but he blames the Africans for the existence of the slave trade, the argument being that Africans, in their civil wars, capture their fellow countrymen and sell them into slavery:

> . . . Onward they [i.e. British merchants] steer their Course,
> To *Afric's* parched Clime, whose sooty Sons,
> Thro' Rage of civil Broils . . . hard Destiny!
> Forc'd from their native Home to *Western Ind*,
> In Slavery drag the galling Chain of Life.[8]

Dyer's *Fleece* (1757) contains a similar perfunctory pity for the condition of the black, Dyer not wishing to appear inhumane and uncivilised; nevertheless the black is shouldered with the blame for slavery:

> On Guinea's sultry strand, the drap'ry light
> Of Manchester or Norwich is bestow'd
> For clear transparent gums, and ductile wax,
> And snow-white iv'ry; yet the valued trade,
> Along this barb'rous coast, in telling, wounds
> The gen'rous heart, the sale of wretched slaves;

7. Moore, *Backgrounds*, p. 133.
8. Cornelius Arnold: *Commerce* (1751), in *Poems On Several Occasions* (London, 1757), p. 129. The truth was that the European actively encouraged Africans to fight against and enslave each other by the bribery of tribal leaders—see W. Rodney: *A History Of The Upper Guinea Coast 1545–1800* (Oxford, 1970), pp. 102–6, 113, etc.

> Slaves, by their tribes condemn'd, exchanging death
> For life-long servitude; severe exchange!
>> (Book IV, 1.189 f)

Young and Glover deal with the problem of slavery in different ways. There is in Young's poem a brief, scornful reference to blacks, describing, of all things, their laziness:

> *Afric's* black, lascivious, slothful Breed,
>   To clasp their *Ruin*, fly from *Toil* . . .
>> (*Merchant*, Strain V, 20)

Africa is attacked because it does not practise the principles of capitalist development which Young celebrates, the African is seen as being ignorant of the principles of science and commerce:

> Of *Nature's* Wealth from *Commerce* rent,
> *Afric's* a glaring Monument:
> Mid *Citron* Forests and *Pomgranate* Groves
> (Curs'd in a Paradise!) she pines;
> O'er *generous* Glebe, o'er *golden* Mines
> Her *begger'd*, *famish'd*, Tradeless Natives roves.
>> (*Merchant*, Strain V, 21)

Young, in an indirect way, is saying that slavery is a benevolent institution, since it teaches the African the virtues of labour. Glover, though equally deceitful, is not so breathtakingly perverse; his poem (*London*, *op. cit.*) attacks the Spanish for enslaving and destroying the Indian natives but he makes no reference to the British participation in slavery and British treatment of the Africans—his poem was written in 1739 when anti-Spanish sentiment was running high in Britain, British traders angry at the liberties taken by Spanish merchants and jealous of Spanish commercial rivalry, a rivalry that erupted into war in 1739 (the 'War of Jenkins' Ear'). Glover's reference to slavery, and Indian slavery at that, is merely political therefore.

Another way of reckoning with slavery whilst being faithful to the ethic of commerce was to minimise the brutality of the trade through careful choice of diction. James Grainger for example, in his poem *The Sugar-Cane* (1764) strives to reduce the horror of slavery by 'wrapping it up in a napkin of poetic diction'. *The Sugar-Cane* is as good an example as any of the way in which 'the raw materials of human experience were habitually transmuted in eighteenth-century poetry'.[9] Instead of 'slave-owner', Grainger prefers to use the term 'Master-Swain'; he prefers 'Assistant Planter' to the term 'slave'. The use of poetical phrases such as 'Afric's sable progeny' to describe the black slaves further softens the stark realities of their actual condition. It is

---

9. I borrow James Sutherland's words from a different context: *A Preface To Eighteenth Century Poetry* (Oxford, 1948), p. 89.

such callous abstractions that provoked Samuel Johnson's attack on Grainger's acceptance of slavery.

Picturesque descriptions of slave labour and the slave environment was another feature of pro-commerce literature. Grainger's *The Sugar-Cane* contained idyllic descriptions of the golden cane-fields with their contentedly laborious black swains,

> Well-fed, well-cloath'd, all emulous to gain
> Their master's smile, who treated them like men.
> (Book I, II. 611–12)

The author of *The Pleasures of Jamaica* written some three decades before, presented a view of slave plantations that was similarly picturesque:

> Hither retiring, to avoid the heat,
> We find refreshment in a cool retreat;
> Each rural object gratifies the sight,
> And yields the mind and innocent delight;
> Greens of all shades the diff'rent plats adorn,
> Here the young cane, and there the growing corn;
> In verdant pastures interspers'd between,
> The lowing herds, and bleating flocks are seen:
> With joy his lord the faithful Negro sees,
> And in his way endeavours how to please;
> Greets his return with his best country song,
> The lively dance, and tuneful merry-wang.
> When nature by the cane has done her part,
> Which ripen'd now demands the help of art,
> How pleasant are the labours of the mill,
> While the rich streams the boiling coppers fill.

As one of the characters in La Valée's anti-slavery novel explains to the African, avarice 'borrows the voice and colours of fiction. Fiction gilds your chains . . .'.[1] The same 'fiction' was being employed to describe the condition of England's peasants and workers—hence the masses of eighteenth century pastoral verse which romanticised agricultural labour, erasing from it any notion of toil and exploitation. And if, as in *The Pleasures of Jamaica*, the African slaves trip over each other in their joyful haste to greet their returning master, so in Addison's version of country life are the English peasants gladdened by the approach of their squire Sir Roger:

> I could not but observe with a great deal of Pleasure the Joy that appeared in the Countenances of these ancient Domesticks upon my Friend's Arrival at his Country-Seat. Some of them could not

---

1. Poem in *The Gentleman's Magazine* VIII, 1738, p. 158. Joseph La Valée: *The Negro Equalled By Few Europeans* (Dublin, 1791), I, pp. 81–2.

> refrain from tears at the Sight of their old Master; every one of
> them press'd forward to do something for him, and seemed *dis-
> couraged if they were not employed*. (*Spectator* 106; my italics)

It is no wonder that abolition pamphleteers made frequent appeals to
English workers, urging them to recognise in the servitude and distress
of blacks the conditions of their own existence.

The fact is that many of the pro-commerce writers who either justified slavery or minimised its inhumanity were in one way or another
involved in the profits to be made from slavery. Glover, for instance,
was the son of a merchant, and also a member of parliament, noted
for his defence of West India merchants before parliament. In 1742,
a petition drawn up by Glover and signed by 300 merchants complaining of the inadequate protection of English trade, was presented to
parliament. Glover afterwards attended to sum up their evidence
before the house of commons. In 1775 he received a plate worth £300
from West India merchants in acknowledgement of his services to
them. His will mentions property in the City of London and in South
Carolina. Cornelius Arnold was in later life beadle to the Distillers
Company with its interests in West India sugar. Grainger, who died in
St Christopher in 1766 was married to the daughter of a Nevis planter,
and took charge of his wife's uncle's plantations; he invested his savings
in the purchase of slaves.[2]

The involvement in the economic benefits of slavery meant a warped
ethical response to it. We catch the sense of wealth beyond the dreams
of avarice in William Goldwin's poem *Great Britain: Or, The Happy
Isle* (1705), specifically in the compounded descriptive phrases like
'Massy heaps of shining Treasure':

> See! How the Busie Merchant Ploughs the Main
> In Vessels big with weighty Heaps of Gain; . . .
> Huge Loads of Wealth, the distant World's Encrease (p. 5)

The feeling of great wealth is carried over in Goldwin's *Poetical Description of Bristol* (1712) in which the sole reference to slavery is an indirect
one—'Jamaica's Growth, or Guinea's Golden-dust'; also in R. J.
Thorn's *Bristolia* (1794)

> Around the quays, in countless heaps appear,
> Bales pil'd on bales, and loads of foreign ware.

The alternative response to commerce

The alternative response to the wealth pouring into society took
many forms. To begin with there was a sense of the physical ugliness

---

2. Details from *The Dictionary of National Biography*.

and the despoilation of the landscape resulting from commercial and industrial activity. Goldwin's response to the growing signs of industrialisation, for example, is more ambivalent than Dyer's or Thorne's. In Dyer's *Fleece*, the smoke rising over Leeds was described as 'incense' and praised as a sign of industrial activity. Thorn's poem on Bristol was also optimistic about industrial fumes—standing upon Brandon Hill like a latterday Moses upon Pisgah, he surveyed the promised land of money and machinery:

> Here, whilst I stand, what clouds of smoke appear
> From different work-shops, and dissolve in air!

Goldwin, in his *Poetical Description of Bristol*, whilst celebrating the city's commercial and manufacturing wealth, rejects the accompanying destruction of nature, the uprooting of Kingswood Forest and the rape of the earth as miners tear 'Magazines of Coals from Nature's Bowel'. The mine and miners present a 'horrid' sight to the eye. He launches into an attack on the ugliness and pollution of a glass manufacturing works:

> Thick dark'ning Clouds in curling smoky Wreaths
> Whose sooty Stench the Earth and Sky annoys,
> And Nature's blooming Verdure half destroys.

The sulphur emitted from the factory's chimney 'blasts the Fruit of fair Sicilia's Fields'. Goldwin's poem ends with a paeon on natural beauty, the 'Grotesque' rocks and cliffs along the river which 'afright the climbing Eye' in a different way from the 'horrid' sight of the coalmine. Goldwin's anxieties about progress accumulate throughout the eighteenth century, culminating in the next in Mrs Gaskell's polluted Milton in *North and South* and Dickens' Coketown in *Hard Times*, a pessimism about progress perfectly expressed in Hopkins' *God's Grandeur*.

Bound up with the disgust at the physical pollution created by 'progress' was a sense of the city as a hideous, dirty, chaotic phenomenon. The pro-commerce writers may have celebrated the evolution of the city from the barren wilderness as a sign of civilisation, but others— Pope, Swift, Gay, Smollett—depicted the city as corrupt, putrid and anarchic to the point of insanity. London is depicted as a gigantic Bedlam riddled with crime and disease, as Max Byrd in his recent study of the image of the city in eighteenth century literature has shown.[3]

If the spirit of commerce was seen as having stimulated crime it was also seen as having created inhumane attitudes in people, a selfishness and hardness of heart. R. Lovell, in *Bristol. A Satire* (1794), described

3. Max Byrd: *London Transformed. Images of the City in the Eighteenth Century* (New Haven and London, 1978).

the soullessness of Bristolians who are motivated only by 'sordid wealth':

> Foul as their streets, triumphant meanness sways,
> And groveling as their mud-compelling drays.

Bristolians have become mere emblems of money, devoid of 'the nobler cares of mind', 'soft humanities', 'mild urbanity' and 'sympathetic feeling':

> In all his sons the mystic signs we trace;
> Pounds, shillings, pence, appear in every face.

Another eighteenth-century observer of Bristolians described how 'Their Souls are engrossed by lucre', with the more gentle qualities of mind 'banished from their republic as a contagious disease'. Samuel Johnson noted the same quality in Bristolians: according to Johnson, Richard Savage's rejection at Bristol was because his wit, culture and conversation were not valued in this 'place of commerce', the traders more conscious of 'solid gain'.[4]

Both Dyer and Thomson in their eulogies on commerce had asserted its benevolent effect upon the labouring classes in raising their standard of living to glorious levels. According to Thomson, commerce fuelled by the spirit of liberty has enriched the whole nation—'The poor man's lot with milk and honey flows' (*Liberty*), V, 1. 6). Although the principle of subordination still holds sway in society, the wealth derived from commerce is equally enjoyed, Thomson claimed. Dyer similarly described the national benefits of industry which 'lifts the swain,/And the straw cottage to a palace turns' (*Fleece*, book III, 1. 332). Other writers were more realistic than Thomson and Dyer, recognising an unequal distribution of wealth and a stark division in society between the haves and have-nots. 'Under the present Stage of Trade', John Brown wrote,

> the Increase of Wealth is by no means equally or proportionally diffused. The Trader reaps the main Profit: after him, the Landlord, in a lower Degree: But the common Artificer, and still more the common Labourer, gain little by the exorbitant Advance of Trade. (*Estimate, op. cit.*, p. 192)

Thomas Bedford, in a sermon bitterly attacking commerce, colonisation and slavery, observed that because trade and commerce had introduced inflation in Britain and a more expensive manner of living, 'the

---

4. P. T. Marcy: *Eighteenth Century Views Of Bristol And Bristolians* (Bristol, 1966), p. 13; S. Johnson: *Lives of the Poets* (2 vols., Oxford, 1975), II, p. 168.

bulk of its people may still continue poor, in the midst of a thousand like advantages'.[5]

Those who attacked commerce as a force for squalor and degradation focused increasingly on slavery for the substance of their views. The bulk of British anti-slavery literature was written in the latter part of the century, spurred on by the propaganda of the abolition movement, but by 1750 there was already considerable public awareness of the brutality of the slave trade. Hence Postlethwayt in 1746 produced a tract in defence of slavery, to counter the 'Many [who] are prepossessed against this Trade, thinking it *a barbarous, inhuman, and unlawful Traffic for a Christian Country to Trade in Blacks'*. The 'many' in the first half of the century included the Quakers, John Dunton, Ralph Sandiford, Jonathan Swift, Samuel Johnson, Charles Gildon, Joseph Warton, Richard Savage, and others. Even Defoe had at one time written anti-slavery verse, denouncing the slavetraders and their brand of Christianity.[6] Major poets like Wordsworth, Blake, Southey and Cowper were later to make similar protests against slavery. William Blake, in addition to poems like *The Little Black Boy*, created some powerful engravings of slave abuses as illustrations for John Stedman's 1796 *Narrative of a five year's expedition against the revolted Negroes of Surinam* (Figs. 9 and 10). The production of poetry was spurred on by the formation of the Abolition Society in 1787, and the relationships that leading social crusaders sought to forge with eminent writers. The Revd. John Newton for instance, an ex-Guinea merchant turned penitent, urged Cowper to put his pen to the service of black humanity. Cowper responded with some anti-slavery ballads which were instantly popular and distributed in their thousands throughout the country. Wordsworth's contact with William Wilberforce and Thomas Clarkson (the former a close acquaintance of his uncle, the latter a fellow resident in the Lake District) led to verse supportive of their campaigns, such as the 1807 sonnet on Clarkson's Abolition Bill. Such poets, however, were merely being perfunctory in their anti-slavery productions—the triteness and laboured sentiments of their expressions betray an absence of deep, personal involvement or vision.[7] Indeed

---

5. Thomas Bedford: *The Origin Of our Grievances: A sermon* (London, 1770), p. 14.
6. M. Postlethwayt: *The National and Private Advantages Of The African Trade Considered* (London, 1746), p. 4. The Quakers declared against slavery in 1727—see T. Clarkson: *An Essay On The Slavery And Commerce Of The Human Species, Particularly The African* (London, 1786), p. viii; for Dunton's change of heart about slavery see Moore, *Backgrounds*, p. 135; R. Sandiford: *The Mystery of Iniquity* (2nd ed., London, 1730); J. Swift: *Guilliver's Travels* (Oxford, 1956), pp. 293, 352; *Boswell's Life of Johnson* (ed. G. B. Hill, 6 vols., Oxford, 1934), II, pp. 476–7; Charles Gildon: *The Life And Strange Surprizing Adventures of Mr. D——De F——* (2nd ed., London, 1719), p. 14; J. Warton: 'Ode to Liberty', in *The Works Of The British Poets* (ed. Thomas Park, London, 1808, XXXVII, p. 15); R. Savage: *Of Public Spirit in Regard To Public Works*, l. 301f., in *Poetical Works* (ed. C. Tracy, Cambridge, 1962), p. 233; D. Defoe: *Reformation of Manners, A Satire* (n.p.; 1702), p. 17.
7. See Sypher: *Guinea's Captive Kings*, pp. 186–9; 215–17.

I. Cruikshank, The Abolition of the Slave Trade, or the Inhumanity of dealers in human flesh exemplified in Captn. Kimber

William Blake, A *Negro Hung Alive by the Ribs to a Gallow* (1796). Courtesy of Karen C. F. Dalton and Image of the Black in Western Art Research Project and Photo Archive, Harvard University.

William Blake, *Flagellation of a Female Samboe Slave (1796)*. Courtesy of Karen C. F. Dalton and Image of the Black in Western Art Research Project and Photo Archive, Harvard University.

Anonymous, *The Execution of Breaking on the Rack* (1796). Courtesy of Karen C. F. Dalton and Image of the Black in Western Art Research Project and Photo Archive, Harvard University.

Cowper in a letter of 1788 admitted that 'the subject, as a subject for song, did not strike me much' and Wordsworth in a passage in the Prelude dealing with abolition agitation confessed that

> For me that strife had ne'er
> Fasten'd on my affections, nor did now
> Its unsuccessful issue much excite
> My sorrow . . . (A-version, Book. X, ll. 202 ff.)

The French revolution, being a white affair and closer to home, excited more profound and lasting interest than the Haitian revolution of the identical period. There were indeed a scattering of verse and pamphlets singing the courage and genius of Toussaint L'Ouverture, but it took nearly one hundred and fifty years, with the appearance of C. L. R. James' *The Black Jacobins*, before a full assessment of the profundity of the Haitian revolution was made. James is, significantly, a black West Indian: given the established and enduring European belief that black people have no history to speak of,[8] the burden of revelation has fallen on black scholars and slave-descendants like James.

The lack of integrity on the part of English eighteenth-century writers can be startlingly glimpsed in Coleridge's attitude to blacks. His first major poem was a Greek ode against the slave trade which earned him the Browne Gold Medal at Cambridge University.[9] He was to write that 'my Greek ode is, I think, my *chef d'oeuvre* in poetical composition'. Coleridge's interest however lay more in the exercise of scholarship than in the plight of blacks: slaves were mere fodder for conceptualisation and poetical practice conducted in Greek with the aim of winning a coveted prize. His real attitude to blacks is revealed in his nausea at Othello's embrace of Desdemona. It was one thing to sympathise spaciously and within the elegant, classical boundaries of a Greek ode with blacks, but quite another thing to have them marrying into the family. Similar hypocrisy can be imputed to other English writers. From the 1770s onwards England was deluged with anti-slavery verse, the sheer bulk of it, and the bewildering variety of poetical expression (odes, pastorals, eclogues, sonnets, doggerel, even creole jingles) being an overwhelming aspect of the literary history of the period. There is little evidence though to suggest that any of these poets devoted any personal time or effort, or dug deep into their pockets, to support the abolition cause. Indeed, it is more probable that the theme of slavery fed them, providing an opportunity for grubs and hacks to indulge in sentiment, to try out verse techniques, and to make some money by either capitalising on popular feeling or else by cashing

8. See Peter Fraser's 'Introduction' to the *Africa Beyond Africa* catalogue, published by the Commonwealth Institute (London, 1984).
9. E. B. Dykes: *The Negro in English Romantic Thought* (Washington, 1942), p. 75.

in on the latest sensational revelation in the newspapers of West Indian brutalities.

Unlike the black writers of the eighteenth century (Equiano for instance, who trudged all over England organising anti-slavery rallies and publicising his slave autobiography) whose finances and very lives were bound up with their literary productions, English writers merely exploited the slave theme for their own gain and recognition. For Swift, the theme provided an opportunity for the exercise of wit and display of satirical prowess. He thunders against the brutishness and hypocrisy of the business of colonisation:

> Ships are sent out with the first opportunity, the natives driven out or destroyed, their princes tortured to discover their gold, a free licence given to all acts of inhumanity and lust, the earth reeking with the blood of its inhabitants: and this execrable crew of butchers employed in so pious an expedition, is a *modern colony* sent to convert and civilise an idolatrous and barbarous people. (Bk. 4, Ch. 12)

Yet Swift was quite happy to invest hundreds of pounds, in 1720, in the South Sea Company whose sole business at the time was to ferry African slaves to the Spanish colonies. In 1713, by the Treaty of Utrecht, Britain had gained the 'Asiento' privelege of supplying the Spanish colonies with slaves, and this monopoly was granted to the South Sea Company. The 'Asiento' privelege was considered at the time to be the 'jewel' clause of the Treaty. Alexander Pope published his *Windsor Forest* in 1713 to celebrate the Treaty, a poem in praise of the values of liberty and civilisation: English liberty and civilisation that is, for apart from the odd jejeune pastoral expression of hope that the 'freed Indians' would eventually be able to 'woo their sable loves' in the liberty and civilisation of 'their native groves', there is no hint of the real barbarity of the 'Asiento' monopoly. In 1720, Pope, like Swift, was busily investing capital in the South Sea Company in the hope of a quick killing.[1]

The profits to be made from slavery, then, conditioned or compromised the literary expressions of both pro-commerce and anti-slavery writers. As C. A. Moore puts it, 'the conscience of the public was so blinded to the moral issue by the widespread participation in dividends that it was very difficult to bring independent judgment or sentiment to bear upon the subject'.[2] The dilemma over the slave trade—the recognition of its immorality, and yet at the same time its profitability—was one aspect of the general dilemma of the age in its attempt

---

1. The names of Pope and Swift are to be found in the company's subscription books which are now kept in the House of Lords Records Office.
2. Moore, *Backgrounds*, p. 133.

to reconcile the moral with the economic. 'Religion is one thing, trade is another'—it is this separation between the two, or, as Anderson puts it, 'the withdrawal of economic affairs from the jurisdiction of morality', which posed crucial, central problems at the time to many writers on economic matters. These problems lay at the very core of Britain's commercial existence; indeed they provoked questions about the country's very survival as a world power. Davenant for instance recognised the evils resulting from trade but also its 'necessity' in terms of Britain's continued supremacy over its rivals and competitors:

> Trade, without doubt, is in its nature a pernicious thing: it brings in that Wealth which introduces Luxury; it gives a rise to Fraud and Avarice, and extinguishes Virtue and Simplicity of Manners; it depraves a People and makes for that Corruption which never fails to end in Slavery, Foreign or Domestick. *Licurgus*, in the most perfect Model of Government that was ever fram'd, did banish it from his Commonwealth. But, the Posture and Condition of other Countries consider'd, 'tis become with us a necessary Evil.

Some fifty years later John Brown came up against the same hurdle—he rails against the luxury and immorality created by the wealth from commerce, but realises that to discourage or curtail such commerce would lead to national decline with rival countries overtaking Britain in economic and military might. 'Thus are we fallen into a kind of Dilemma', Brown muses, uncertain of the solution.[3] The dilemma was also faced by some pro-slavery writers, particularly on the issue of baptising and christianising blacks. Slave-owners, one apologist pointed out in 1730,[4] were reluctant to educate their slaves to the christian gospel because of the economic costs. The slaves would have to be given time off work to attend Bible classes which would mean a loss in production. This would be 'too great an Invasion on the property of the Masters'. If for instance, the writer calculates, a planter were to allow one-fifth of his total collection of one hundred slaves to be educated once a fortnight in the gospel, and estimating that each slave made six pence profit per day for his owner, then the owner would lose a whole £13 *per annum*, and £65 *per annum* if he let all his blacks be educated; to educate all the hundred thousand blacks in the West Indies would cost a massive sum of £65,000. As to the morality of the slave trade itself the writer does not deny that 'Millions of Lives it destroys', but stresses that it is still 'absolutely necessary' for reasons of national supremacy—Britain, France, Spain, Holland and Portugal are all involved in the slave trade and

3. Hans H. Anderson: *Daniel Defoe: A Study of The Conflict Between Commercialism And Morality In The Early Eighteenth Century* (unpublished PhD diss., Univ. of Chicago, 1930), p. 107; Charles Davenant: *An Essay Upon The Probable Methods Of making a People Gainers In The Ballance of Trade* (London, 1699), pp. 154–5; John Brown, *op. cit.*, p. 217.
4. *A Letter To The Right Reverend The Lord Bishop Of London*, p. 15.

were any of them to break it off on the Topick of Unlawfulness, they would soon lose their Share in the Profits arising from it, which is hardly to be expected from them unlelss their Neighbours could be prevail'd to drop theirs too.

Because of this international competition, the writer concludes, it is unlikely that the slave trade will decline, unless God personally intervenes! God of course did not intervene, but the black slaves themselves did. Whenever opportunity presented itself they revolted—in the slave factories on the West African coast, on board the slaveships taking them to the colonies, and on the plantations. These revolts, and the bloodletting and barbarities they unleashed, made more impact on the dismantling of slavery than the poems issued by English writers. The sword was mightier than the pen: the irrationality of whites, their refusal to be persuaded by reasoned and moral arguments, forced blacks into violent behaviour. This legacy of the 'criminalisation' of blacks is, according to contemporary opinion, still a distinguishing feature of the racial encounter between blacks and whites. As Joe Harte, a black British political campaigner put it, in writing about the Brixton riots of 1981, 'our community the world over resents the burden imposed on us by white society to dramatize our grievances before they are met.'[5]

5. *Team Work* (Journal of the West Indian Standing Conference), I, October 1984.

Travel and Scientific Literature

ANTHONY BENEZET

From Some Historical Account of Guinea†

* * *

Negroes * * * enjoy a good state of health,[1] and are able to procure to themselves a comfortable subsistence, with much less care and toil than is necessary in our more northern climate; which last advantage arises not only from the warmth of the climate, but also from the overflowing of the rivers, whereby the land is regularly moistened, and rendered extremely fertile; and being in many places improved by culture, abounds with grain and fruits, cattle, poultry, &c. The earth yields all the year a fresh supply of food: Few cloaths are requisite, and little art necessary in making them, or in the construction of their houses, which are very simple, principally calculated to defend them from the tempestuous seasons and wild beasts; a few dry reeds covered with matts serve for their beds. The other furniture, except what belongs to cookery, gives the women but little trouble; the moveables of the greatest among them amounting only to a few earthen pots, some wooden utensils, and gourds or calabashes; from these last, which grow almost naturally over their huts, to which they afford an agreeable shade, they are abundantly stocked with good clean vessels for most household uses, being of different sizes, from half a pint to several gallons.

That part of Africa from which the Negroes are sold to be carried into slavery, commonly known by the name of Guinea, extends along the coast three or four thousand miles. Beginning at the river Senegal,

---

† From *Some Historical Account of Guinea: Its Situation, Produce, and the General Disposition of Its Inhabitants with an Inquiry into the Rise and Progress of the Slave-Trade, Its Nature and Lamentable Effects* (Philadelphia: Crukshank, 1771), Ch. I, pp. 5–6, 15–17; Ch. VII, pp. 72–74, 80–81. Benezet's widely circulating digest drew on many sources, the most important for Equiano being Michel Adanson's *Voyage to Senegal* (Engl., transl. 1759).

1. James Barbot, agent general to the French African company, in his account of Africa, page 105, says, "The natives are seldom troubled with any distempers, being little affected with the unhealthy air. In tempestuous times they keep much within doors; and when exposed to the weather, their skins being suppled, and pores closed by daily anointing with palm oil, the weather can make but little impression on them."

situate about the 17th degree of North latitude, being the nearest part of Guinea, as well to Europe as to North America; from thence to the river Gambia, and in a southerly course to Cape Sierra Leona, comprehends a coast of about seven hundred miles; being the same tract for which Queen Elizabeth granted charters to the first traders to that coast. From Sierra Leona, the land of Guinea takes a turn to the eastward, extending that course about fifteen hundred miles.

*   *   *

[From Michel Adanson] "Which way soever I turned my eyes on this pleasant spot, I beheld a perfect image of pure nature, an agreeable solitude, bounded on every side by charming landscapes: the rural situation of cottages in the midst of trees; the ease and indolence of the *Negroes*, reclined under the shade of their spreading foliage; the simplicity of their dress and manners; the whole revived in my mind the idea of our first parents, and I seemed to contemplate the world in its primitive state. They are generally speaking, very good-natured, sociable, and obliging. I was not a little pleased with this my first reception; it convinced me, that there ought to be a considerable abatement made in the accounts I had read and heard every where of the savage character of the Africans. I observed both in Negroes and Moors, great humanity and sociableness, which gave me strong hopes that I should be very safe amongst them, and meet with the success I desired in my enquiries after the curiosities of the country."[2] He[3] was agreeably amused with the conversation of the Negroes, their *fables, dialogues,* and *witty stories* with which they entertain each other alternately, according to their custom. Speaking of the remarks which the natives made to him, with relation to the *stars* and *planets,* he says, "It is amazing, that such a rude and illiterate people, should reason so pertinently in regard to those heavenly bodies; there is no manner of doubt, but that with proper instruments, and a good will, they would become *excellent astronomers.*"

*   *   *

That celebrated civillian Montesquieu,[4] in his treatise *on the spirit of laws,* on the article of slavery says, "*It is neither useful to the master nor slave; to the slave, because he can do nothing through principle (or virtue,) to the master because he contracts with his slave all sorts of bad*

---

2. Adanson, [*Voyage to Senegal*], page 252.
3. Benezet is referring to Adanson [*Editor*].
4. Charles-Louis de Secondat Montesquieu (1689–1755), the Bordeaux-born philosopher, is best known for his *Persian Letters* (1722), in which he satirized French civilization through the eyes of two imaginary Persian travelers, and for his theory of the division of executive, legislative, and judicial powers. The excerpts quoted here are from his most important work, *De l'Esprit des Lois* (1748), and illustrate Montesquieu's significance for antislavery thinking [*Editor*].

habits, insensibly accustoms himself to want all moral virtues, becomes, haughty, hasty, hard hearted, passionate, voluptuous and cruel." The lamentable truth of this assertion was quickly verified in the English plantations. When the practice of slave keeping was introduced, it soon produced its natural effects; it reconciled men of otherwise good dispositions to the most hard and cruel measures. It quickly proved what under the law of Moses was apprehended would be the consequence of unmerciful chastisements. Deut. xxv. 2. *"And it shall be if the wicked man be worthy to be beaten, that the judge shall cause him to lie down, and to be beaten before his face, according to his fault, by a certain number; forty stripes he may give him and not exceed."* And the reason rendered is out of respect to human nature, viz. *"Lest if he should exceed and beat him above these with many stripes, then thy brother should seem vile unto thee."* As this effect soon followed the cause, the cruelest measures were adopted, in order to make the most of the poor *wretches* labour; and in the minds of the masters such an idea was excited of inferiority in the nature of these their unhappy fellow creatures, that they soon esteemed and treated them as beasts of burden: pretending to doubt, and some of them, even presuming to deny, the efficacy of the death of Christ extended to them.

*   *   *

This is confirmed in a *History of Jamaica* wrote in thirteen letters, about the year 1740, by a person then residing in that island who writes, as follows, "I shall not now enter upon the question whether the slavery of the Negroes be agreeable to the laws of nature or not though it seems extreamly hard they should be reduced to serve and toil for the benefit of others, without the least advantage to themselves. Happy Britannia where slavery is never known; where liberty and freedom chears every misfortune here (*says the author,*) we can boast of no such blessing; we have at least ten slaves to one freeman. I incline to touch the hardships which these poor creatures suffer, in the tenderest manner, from a particular regard which I have to many of their masters; but I cannot conceal their sad circumstances intirely: the most trivial error is punished with terrible whipping. I have seen some of them treated in that cruel manner, for no other reason but to satisfy the brutish pleasure of an overseer, who has their punishment mostly at his discretion. I have seen their bodies all in a gore of blood, the skin torn off their backs with the cruel whip; beaten pepper and salt rubbed in the wounds, and a large stick of sealing wax dropped leisurely upon them. It is no wonder, if the horrid pain of such inhuman tortures incline them to rebel. Most of these slaves are brought from the coast of Guinea: When they first arrive, it's observed they are simple and very innocent creatures; but soon turn to be roguish enough: And when they come to be whipt, urge the example of the whites for an excuse of their faults."

These accounts of the deep depravity of mind attendant on the practice of slavery, verify the truth of Montesquieu's remarks of its pernicious effects. And altho' the same degree of opposition to instructing the Negroes may not now appear in the islands as formerly; especially since the society appointed for propagating the Gospel have possessed a number of Negroes in one of them; nevertheless the situation of these oppressed people is yet dreadful, as well to themselves as in its consequences to their hard task-masters, and their offspring, as must be evident to every impartial person who is acquainted with the treatment they generally receive, or with the laws which from time to time have been made in the colonies, with respect to the Negroes; some of them being absolutely inconsistant with reason, and shocking to humanity.

* * *

JOHN MATTHEWS

From A Voyage to the River Sierra-Leone†

Letter VI.

Voltaire, in his preliminary discourse, mentions a race of people inhabiting the interior parts of Africa, whom he calls Albinos, and represents them as being of a milky white colour, and diminutive stature. I have made the most diligent inquiry of the natives, and travelling black merchants, but never could gain the least information that such a people existed. But I have seen several white negroes in different parts of Africa of a milky, or chalky whiteness, and white wool; but these do not propagate their likeness, but have black children, and are only considered as *lusus naturæ*.[1] I remember to have seen one of the same kind in Georgia, South Carolina, and one in England, they were both females.

* * *

Almost every married woman has, according to the country custom, her *yangeé cameé*, or cicisbeo, whom she first solicits. This connexion

† A Voyage to the River Sierra-Leone, or the Coast of Africa* * * with an Additional Letter on the Subject of the African Slave Trade (1788; repr. London: White and Son, 1791), Letter VI, pp. 95, 120–25.
1. A sport or game of nature [*Editor*].

she is at little or no pains to conceal, and her husband is often obliged to be silent, as otherwise he would have reason to dread worse consequences; for although the laws of the country are severe against adultery, it requires the arm of power, even among themselves, to put them in force. But it should be observed that it is among the great who keep a number of wives, that this practice more particularly prevails. The common people are in general contented with one, or at most with two wives. Yet there is one singular circumstance which should not pass unnoticed respecting their women's private amours.—They never attempt to impose on their husbands by introducing a spurious offspring into his family, but always declare before they are delivered who is the father. But if the husband wishes to have children by a favourite woman, he obliges her, though it is sometimes done voluntarily, to make a vow, that she will not for a certain time go astray; and should she during that period be induced either by force or persuasion to break her vow, she immediately tells her husband, and both the offending parties undergo a most shameful punishment, and are ever after reckoned infamous, and held in contempt.

They deposit their dead in the ground in the European manner, and generally either in the evening or morning; but the ceremony of interrogating the corpse is curious, and deserves a particular description.

When the deceased is designed for interment, the corpse is laid upon an open bier, decently wrapped in a white cloth, and born upon the heads of six young people, either male or female; for that is a matter left entirely to the choice of the corpse, who signifies his approbation or disapprobation of the bearers, by his inclination or disinclination to move (which they firmly believe it is capable of exerting) to the place of burial. This place is always in the bush out of the town. When arrived there a person, who is generally a relation or friend of the deceased, places himself five or six paces before the bier, with a green bough in his hand, and addresses the deceased in this manner—"You are now a dead man—you know you are no longer alive and as one of us—you know you are placed upon the sticks (i.e. the bier) of God Almighty, and that you must answer truth,"—And then he asks him what made him die—whether he knew of his own death, or whether it was caused by witchcraft or poison; for it is a firm and universal belief among them, that no person dies without having a previous knowledge of his death, except his death be caused by witchcraft or poison, or the more powerful charms of another person over those he wears.

If the corpse answers in the affirmative to any of the questions proposed, it is signified by forcibly impelling the bearers several paces forward, by a power which they say they are unable to resist—if, on the contrary, it is signified by a rolling motion, which they also say they cannot prevent.—If, by the sign given, a suspicion arises that the death of the party was occasioned by poison or witchcraft, they proceed to question him who was the person, and name several people to whom they suppose he was not attached in his life time; but they first begin with his relations. If it should happen to be any of them the corpse remains silent for some time, as if ashamed to accuse his own kindred, but at last is obliged to answer. He is then more particularly questioned whether he is certain of the person; if he is, it is requested that he will strike that hand which holds the bough, (the person before the corpse holding the bough up in his hand). Upon this the corpse immediately impels the bier forwards, and strikes the bough. In order to convince the spectators, they repeat this two or three times.

The culprit is then seized, and if a witch sold without further ceremony: and it frequently happens if the deceased were a great man, and the accused poor, not only he himself but his whole family are sold together. But if the death of the deceased was caused by poison, the offender is reserved for a further trial; from which, though it is in some measure voluntary, he seldom escapes with life.

After depositing the corpse in the grave, which is hung round with mats, and his most valued clothes and necessaries put in with him.— They confine the accused in such a manner that he can release himself; which signifies to him he has transgressed the laws of his country, and is no longer at liberty. As soon as it is dark he escapes to the next town, and there claims the protection of the head man, who is supposed to be an impartial person; informs him that the corpse of such a person has accused him of causing his death by poison; that he is innocent, and desires that to prove it he may drink red water. This request is always allowed, and the friends of the deceased are sent for to be witnesses.

At the time appointed the accused is placed upon a kind of high chair, stripped of his common apparel, and a quantity of plantain leaves are wrapped round his waist. Then in presence of the whole town, who are always assembled upon these occasions, he first eats a little colá or rice, and then drinks the poisoned water.

* * *

JOHN MITCHELL

From Essay on the Causes of the Different Colours of People in Different Climates†

* * *

There is no doubt, but that Noah and his sons were of a complexion suitable to the climate where they resided, as well as all the rest of mankind; which is the colour of the southern Tartars of Asia, or northern Chinese, at this day perhaps, which is a dark swarthy, a medium between black and white: from which primitive colour the Europeans degenerated as much on one hand, as the Africans did on the other; the Asiatics, unless, perhaps, where mixed with the whiter Europeans, with most of the Americans, retaining the primitive and original complexion. The grand obstacle to the belief of this relation between white and black people is, that, on comparing them together, their colours seem to be so opposite and contrary, that it seems impossible that one should ever have been descended from the other. But, besides the falsity of this supposed direct contrariety of their colours, they being only different, though extreme degrees of the same sort of colour, as we have above proved; besides this, that is not a right state of the question; we do not affirm that either blacks or whites were originally descended from one another, but that both were descended from people of an intermediate tawny colour; whose posterity became more and more tawny, i.e. black, in the southern regions, and less so, or white, in the northern climes; while those who remained in the middle regions, where the first men resided, continued of their primitive tawny complexions; which we see confirmed by matter of fact, in all the different people in the world. Agreeably to this, we see, that the heat of the sun will tan, as the saying is, the fairest skin, of a dark swarthy, even at this day; in which there is some degree of blackness; or at least this may well be said to be a tendency to their primitive swarthy complexions. So that if the heat of the sun will turn a white skin swarthy, as nobody in hot countries can doubt, the same cause might turn the swarthy and tawny black; for the effect seems to be the same in one as in the other, and may therefore be produced by one and the same cause. As for the black people recovering, in the same manner, their primitive swarthy colours of their fore-fathers, by removing from their intemperate scorching regions, it must be observed, that there is a great difference in the different ways of

---

† From "Essay on the Causes of the Different Colours of People in Different Climates," Royal Society, *Philosophical Transactions* 1744, vol. 9 (London: C. R. Baldwin, 1809), pp. 65–67.

changing colours to one another: thus dyers can very easily dye any white cloth black, but cannot so easily discharge that black, and bring it to its first colour: and thus, though the skins of white, or even swarthy people, are easily affected by the greater power of the sun's beams than what they have been used to, and thereby become black; yet they are thereby rendered so thick and hard, or tough and callous, as not to be so easily affected, or readily wrought on, to render them again of their original swarthy or pale colour, by any of those causes, as the absence of the sun, coldness of the climate, or ways of life in it, which we have supposed to be the causes of the fair complexions of the Europeans; though probably it has never been tried what effect these luxurious customs, or soft and effeminate lives, which we have supposed to be the causes of mankind's turning to so tender and delicate complexions as the Europeans have, and to be the cause of all whiteness in the complexions of men, or changes from a dark to a fairer complexion, might have on the colour of negroes; but this we are assured of, that they are not of so deep a black, in cold northern, as in the hotter southerly regions. Besides, we want not some convincing instances, from the gleanings of a few historians, to show that such changes have happened in the memory of men, and within the compass of those records we have of time; for we could not suppose it to have happened all at once: thus Herodotus tells us, that the Colchi[1] were formerly black, with frizzled hair; which he says he relates rather as a thing well know before, than a bare report; but there is no sign of any blackness in the complexions of their descendants, they being rather, especially about Circassia,[2] reckoned some of the fairest people in the world at this day. Captain Smith tells us, that, even in Virginia, an Englishman, by living only 3 years among the Indians, became "so like an Indian, in habit and complexion, that he knew him only by his tongue:" and what might his children have turned to in a succession of many generations, by these same ways of life, which had so altered him in 3 years? The Moors and Lybians, being driven out of Africa, on the Turkish conquests, retired to the land of the negroes; but are no more to be found there of their original tawny colour. The king of Gualata is supposed to be lineally descended from these tawny Moors, but is even blacker than the original negroes. The Abessines, who came from Arabia originally, are no longer of their swarthy complexion, but have got the black complexion of the Ethiopians, whose country they possess. The Mosemleeks of Canada, who wear clothes, and are more civilized than the other savages their neighbours, who go quite naked, are so much more refined in their complexions by this usage, as to be taken for Spaniards, and not Indians. Nay the

1. People from Colchis, an Asian country famous as the home of Medea [*Editor*].
2. A Russian district on the Black Sea [*Editor*].

Spaniards themselves, who have inhabited America under the torrid zone for any time, are become as dark coloured as our native Indians of Virginia: and were they not to intermarry with the Europeans, but lead the same rude and barbarous lives with the Indians, it is very probable, that, in a succession of many generations, they would become as dark in complexion.

Eighteenth-Century Authors of African Ancestry

Among Equiano's contemporaries were several authors of African birth or background. In 1773, Phillis Wheatley's *Poems on Various Subjects, Religious and Moral* appeared in London; it was the first English-language book published by an African. In 1782, the published *Letters of the Late Ignatius Sancho, an African, to Which are Prefixed Memoirs of His Life* generated much attention.

The three Anglo-African writers excerpted here shared with Equiano a Christian outlook and an interest in scenes representing the almost magical encounter with books that would not "talk." James Albert Ukawsaw Gronniosaw (b. 1710?) was born in Bornu (in the northeast of present-day Nigeria), sold into slavery, and owned by a Dutch family in New York. Like Equiano, he witnessed naval action in the Seven Years' War and later settled in England and married an Englishwoman. John Marrant (1755–1791) was a freeborn New Yorker who became an Indian missionary, served England in the Revolutionary War, and later lived in Boston and London. Quobna Ottobah Cugoano (b. 1757?) was born in Ajumako (in present-day Ghana), enslaved in Grenada, and then lived in London, where he was a friend and "Son of Africa" associate of Equiano's.

JAMES ALBERT UKAWSAW GRONNIOSAW

[*From* A Narrative]†

An Account of James Albert, &c.

I was born in the city of *Baurnou*, my mother was the eldest daughter of the reigning King there. I was the youngest of six children, and particularly loved by my mother; and my grand-father almost doated on me.

---

† From A *Narrative of the Most Remarkable Particulars in the Life of James Albert Ukawsaw Gronniosaw, An African Prince, Written by Himself* (1770, 1774). From Adam Potkay and Sandra Burr, eds., *Black Atlantic Writers of the 18th Century* (New York: St Martin's Press, 1995), pp. 28–34.

I had, from my infancy, a curious turn of mind; was more grave and reserved, in my disposition, than either of my brothers and sisters, I often teazed them with questions they could not answer; for which reason they disliked me, as they supposed that I was either foolish or insane. Twas certain that I was, at times, very unhappy in myself: It being strongly impressed on my mind that there was some GREAT MAN of power which resided above the sun, moon and stars, the objects of our worship.—My dear, indulgent mother would bear more with me than any of my friends beside.—I often raised my hand to heaven, and asked her who lived there? Was much dissatisfied when she told me the sun, moon and stars, being persuaded, in my own mind, that there must be some SUPERIOR POWER.—I was frequently lost in wonder at the works of the creation: Was afraid, and uneasy, and restless, but could not tell for what. I wanted to be informed of things that no person could tell me; and was always dissatisfied.— These wonderful impressions began in my childhood, and followed me continually till I left my parents, which affords me matter of admiration and thankfulness.

To this moment I grew more and more uneasy every day, insomuch that one Saturday (which is the day on which we kept our sabbath) I laboured under anxieties and fears that cannot be expressed; and, what is more extraordinary, I could not give a reason for it.—I rose, as our custom is, about three o'clock (as we are obliged to be at our place of worship an hour before the sun rise) we say nothing in our worship, but continue on our knees with our hands held up, observing a strict silence till the sun is at a certain height, which I suppose to be about 10 or 11 o'clock in *England*: When at a certain sign made by the Priest, we get up (our duty being over) and disperse to our different houses.— Our place of meeting is under a large palm tree; we divide ourselves into many congregations; as it is impossible for the same tree to cover the inhabitants of the whole city, though they are extremely large, high and majestic; the beauty and usefulness of them are not to be described; they supply the inhabitants of the country with meat, drink and clothes; the body of the palm tree is very large; at a certain season of the year they tap it, and bring vessels to receive the wine, of which they draw great quantities, the quality of which is very delicious: The leaves of this tree are of a silky nature; they are large and soft; when they are dried and pulled to pieces, it has much the same appearance as the English flax, and the inhabitants of BOURNOU manufacture it for clothing, &c. This tree likewise produces a plant, or substance, which has the appearance of a cabbage, and very like it, in taste almost the same: It grows between the branches. Also the palm tree produces a nut, something like a cocoa, which contains a kernel, in which is a large quantity of milk, very pleasant to the taste: The shell is of a hard substance, and of a very beautiful appearance, and serves for basons, bowls, &c.

I hope this digression will be forgiven.—I was going to observe, that after the duty of our sabbath was over (on the day in which I was more distressed and afflicted than ever) we were all on our way home as usual, when a remarkable black cloud arose and covered the sun; then followed very heavy rain and thunder, more dreadful than ever I had heard: The heavens roared, and the earth trembled at it: I was highly affected and cast down; insomuch that I wept sadly, and could not follow my relations & friends home.—I was obliged to stop, and felt as if my legs were tied, they seemed to shake under me: So I stood still, being in great fear of the MAN of POWER, that I was persuaded, in myself, lived above. One of my young companions (who entertained a particular friendship for me, and I for him) came back to see for me: He asked me why I stood still in such very hard rain? I only said to him that my legs were weak, and I could not come faster: He was much affected to see me cry, and took me by the hand, and said he would lead me home, which he did. My mother was greatly alarmed at my tarrying out in such terrible weather; she asked me many questions, such as what I did so for? And if I was well? My dear mother, says I, pray tell me who is the GREAT MAN of POWER that makes the thunder? She said, there was no power but the sun, moon and stars; that they made all our country.—I then inquired how all our people came? She answered me, from one another; and so carried me to many generations back.—Then says I, who made the *first man?* And who made the first cow, and the first lion, and where does the fly come from, as no one can make him? My mother seemed in great trouble; she was apprehensive that my senses were impaired, or that I was foolish. My father came in, and seeing her in grief asked the cause, but when she related our conversation to him he was exceedingly angry with me, and told me he would punish me severely if ever I was so troublesome again; so that I resolved never to say any thing more to him. But I grew very unhappy in myself; my relations and acquaintance endeavoured, by all the means they could think on, to divert me, by taking me to ride upon goats (which is much the custom of our country) and to shoot with a bow and arrow; but I experienced no satisfaction at all in any of these things; nor could I be easy by any means whatever: My parents were very unhappy to see me so dejected and melancholy.

About this time there came a merchant from the *Gold Coast* (the third city in GUINEA) he traded with the inhabitants of our country in ivory, &c. he took great notice of my unhappy situation, and inquired into the cause; he expressed vast concern for me, and said, if my parents would part with me for a little while, and let him take me home with him, it would be of more service to me than any thing they could do for me.—He told me that if I would go with him I should see houses with wings to them walk upon the water, and should also see the white folks; and that he had many sons of my age, which should be my companions; and he added to all this that he would bring me safe back again soon.—I was highly pleased with the account of this strange place, and was very desirous of going.—I seemed sensible of a secret impulse upon my mind, which I could not resist, that seemed to tell me I must go. When my dear mother saw that I was willing to leave them, she spoke to my father and grandfather and the rest of my relations, who all agreed that I should accompany the merchant to the Gold Coast. I was the more willing as my brothers and sisters despised me, and looked on me with contempt on the account of my unhappy disposition; and even my servants slighted me, and disregarded all I said to them. I had one sister who was always exceeding fond of me, and I loved her entirely; her name was LOGWY, she was quite white, and fair, with fine light hair, though my father and mother were black.—I was truly concerned to leave my beloved sister, and she cry'd most sadly to part with me, wringing her hands, and discovered every sign of grief that can be imagined. Indeed if I could have known when I left my friends and country that I should never return to them again my misery on that occasion would have been inexpressible. All my relations were sorry to part with me; my dear mother came with me upon a camel more than three hundred miles, the first of our journey lay chiefly through woods: At night we secured ourselves from the wild beasts by making fires all around us; we and our camels kept within the circle, or we must have been torn to pieces by the lions, and other wild creatures, that roared terribly as soon as night came on, and continued to do so till morning.—There can be little said in favour of the country through which we passed; only a valley of marble that we came through which is unspeakably beautiful.—On each side of this valley are exceedingly high and almost inaccessible mountains—Some of these pieces of marble are of prodigious length and breadth but of different sizes and colour, and shaped in a variety of forms, in a wonderful manner.—It is most of it veined with gold mixed with striking and beautiful colours; so that when the sun darts upon it, it is as pleasing a sight as can be imagined.—The merchant that brought me from BOURNOU was in partnership with another gentleman who accompanied us; he was very unwilling that he should take me from home, as, he said, he foresaw many difficulties that would attend my going with them.—He endeavoured to prevail on the merchant to throw me into a very deep pit that was in the valley, but he refused to listen to him, and said, he was resolved to take care of me: But the other was greatly dissatisfied; and when we came to a river, which we were obliged to pass through, he purposed throwing me in and drowning me; but the merchant would not consent to it, so that I was preserved.

We travel'd till about four o'clock every day, and then began to make preparations for night, by cutting down large quantities of wood, to make fires to preserve us from the wild beasts.—I had a very unhappy and discontented journey, being in continual fear that the people I was with would murder me. I often reflected with extreme regret on the kind friends I had left, and the idea of my dear mother frequently drew tears from my eyes. I cannot recollect how long we were in going from *Bournou* to the *Gold Coast*; but as there is no shipping nearer to *Bournou* than that city, it was tedious in travelling so far by land, being upwards of a thousand miles.—I was heartily rejoiced when we arrived at the end of our journey: I now vainly imagined that all my troubles and inquietudes would terminate here; but could I have looked into futurity, I should have perceived that I had much more to suffer than I had before experienced, and that they had as yet but barely commenced.

I was now more than a thousand miles from home, without a friend or any means to procure one. Soon after I came to the merchant's house I heard the drums beat remarkably loud, and the trumpets blow—the persons accustom'd to this employ, are oblig'd to go upon a very high structure appointed for that purpose, that the sound might be heard at a great distance: They are higher than the steeples are in *England.* I was mightily pleased with sounds so entirely new to me, and was very inquisitive to know the cause of this rejoicing, and asked many questions concerning it; I was answered that it was meant as a compliment to me, because I was grandson to the King of *Bournou.*

This account gave me a secret pleasure; but I was not suffered long to enjoy this satisfaction, for, in the evening of the same day, two of the merchant's sons (boys about my own age) came running to me, and told me, that the next day I was to die, for the King intended to behead me.—I reply'd, that I was sure it could not be true, for that I came there to play with them, and to see houses walk upon the water, with wings to them, and the white folks; but I was soon informed that their King imagined I was sent by my father as a spy, and would make such discoveries, at my return home, that would enable them to make war with the greater advantage to ourselves; and for these reasons he had resolved I should never return to my native country.—When I heard this, I suffered misery that cannot be described.—I wished, a thousand times, that I had never left my friends and country.—But still the Almighty was pleased to work miracles for me.

The morning I was to die, I was washed and all my gold ornaments made bright and shining, and then carried to the palace, where the King was to behead me himself (as is the custom of the place).—He was seated upon a throne at the top of an exceeding large yard, or court, which you must go through to enter the palace, it is as wide and spacious as a large field in *England.*—I had a lane of life-guards to go through.—I guessed it to be about three hundred paces.

I was conducted by my friend, the merchant, about half way up; then he durst proceed no further: I went up to the King alone—I went with an undaunted courage, and it pleased God to melt the heart of the King, who sat with his scymitar in his hand ready to behead me; yet, being himself so affected, he dropped it out of his hand, and took me upon his knee and wept over me. I put my right hand round his neck, and prest him to my heart.—He set me down and blest me; and added that he would not kill me, and that I should not go home, but be sold for a slave, so then I was conducted back again to the merchant's house.

The next day he took me on board a French brig; the Captain did not chuse to buy me: He said I was too small; so the merchant took me home with him again.

The partner, whom I have spoken of as my enemy, was very angry to see me return, and again purposed putting an end to my life; for he represented to the other, that I should bring them into troubles and difficulties, and that I was so little that no person would buy me.

The merchant's resolution began to waver, and I was indeed afraid that I should be put to death: But however he said he would try me once more.

A few days after a *Dutch* ship came into the harbour, and they carried me on board, in hopes that the Captain would purchase me.—As they went, I heard them agree, that, if they could not sell me *then*, they would throw me overboard.—I was in extreme agonies when I heard this; and as soon as ever I saw the *Dutch* Captain, I ran to him, and put my arms round him, and said, "Father save me." (for I knew that if he did not buy me I should be treated very ill, or, possibly murdered) And though he did not understand my language, yet it pleased the Almighty to influence him in my behalf, and he bought me *for two yards of check*, which is of more value *there*, than in *England*.

When I left my dear mother I had a large quantity of gold about me, as is the custom of our country, it was made into rings, and they were linked into one another, and formed into a kind of chain, and so put round my neck, and arms and legs, and a large piece hanging at one ear almost in the shape of a pear. I found all this troublesome, and was glad when my new master took it from me.—I was now washed, & clothed in the *Dutch* or *English* manner.—My master grew very fond of me, and I loved him exceedingly. I watched every look, was always ready when he wanted me, and endeavoured to convince him, by every action, that my only pleasure was to serve him well.—I have since thought that he must have been a serious man. His actions corresponded very well with such a character.—He used to read prayers in public to the ship's crew every sabbath day; and when first I saw him read, I was never so surprised in my whole life as when I saw the book talk to my master; for I thought it did, as I observed him to look upon it, and move his lips.—I wished it would do so to me.—As soon as my master had done reading I follow'd him to the place where he put the book, being mightily delighted with it, and when nobody saw me, I open'd it and put my ear down close upon it, in great hope that it would say something to me; but was very sorry and greatly disappointed when I found it would not speak, this thought immediately presented itself to me, that every body and every thing despised me because I was black.

* * *

JOHN MARRANT

[A Captive of the Cherokees]†

* * *

By constant conversation with the hunter [an Indian whom Marrant met and befriended earlier], I acquired a fuller knowledge of the Indian tongue: This, together with the sweet communion I enjoyed with God, I have since considered as a preparation for the great trial I was soon after to pass through.

The hunting season being now at an end, we left the woods, and directed our course towards a large Indian town, belonging to the Cherokee nation; and having reached it, I said to the hunter, they will not suffer me to enter in. He replied, as I was with him, nobody would interrupt me.

There was an Indian fortification all round the town, and a guàrd placed at each entrance. The hunter passed one of these without molestation, but I was stopped by the guard and examined. They asked me where I came from, and what was my business there? My companion of the woods attempted to speak for me, but was not permitted; he was taken away, and I saw him no more I was now surrounded by about fifty men, and carried to one of their principal chiefs and Judge to be examined by him. When I came before him, he asked me what was my business there? I told him I came there with a hunter, whom I met with in the woods. He replied, "Did I not know that whoever came there without giving a better account of themselves than I did, was to be put to death?" I said I did not know it. Observing that I

† From A Narrative of the Lord's Wonderful Dealings with John Marrant, a Black (Now Going to Preach the Gospel in Nova-Scotia) Born in New-York, in North-America (1785). From Adam Potkay and Sandra Burr, eds., Black Atlantic Writers of the 18th Century (New York: St. Martin's Press, 1995), pp. 82–87.

answered him so readily in his own language, he asked me where I learnt it? To this I returned no answer, but burst out into a flood of tears, and calling upon my Lord Jesus. At this he stood astonished, and expressed a concern for me, and said I was young. He asked me who my Lord Jesus was?—To this I gave him no answer, but continued praying and weeping. Addressing himself to the officer who stood by him, he said he was sorry; but it was the law, and it must not be broken. I was then ordered to be taken away, and put into a place of confinement. They led me from their court into a low dark place, and thrust me into it, very dreary and dismal; they made fast the door, and set a watch. The judge sent for the executioner, and gave him his warrant for my execution in the afternoon of the next day. The executioner came, and gave me notice of it, which made me very happy, as the near prospect of death made me hope for a speedy deliverance from the body: And truly this dungeon became my chapel, for the Lord Jesus did not leave me in this great trouble, but was very present, so that I continued blessing him, and singing his praises all night without ceasing: The watch hearing the noise, informed the executioner that somebody had been in the dungeon with me all night; upon which he came in to see and to examine, with a great torch lighted in his hand, who it was I had with me; but finding nobody, he turned round, and asked me who it was? I told him it was the Lord Jesus Christ; but he made no answer, turned away, went out, and fastened the door. At the hour appointed for my execution I was taken out, and led to the destined spot, amidst a vast number of people. I praised the Lord all the way we went, and when we arrived at the place I understood the kind of death I was to suffer, yet blessed be God, at that instant none of those things moved me.

When the executioner shewed me a basket of turpentine wood, stuck full of small pieces like skewers; he told me I was to be stripped naked, and laid down on one side by the basket, and these sharp pegs were to be stuck into me, and then set on fire, and when they had burnt to my body,[1] I was to be turned on the other side, and served in the same manner, and then to be taken by four men and thrown into the flame, which was to finish the execution; I burst into tears, and asked what I had done to deserve so cruel a death? To this he gave me no answer. I cried out, Lord, if it be thy will that it should be so, thy will be done:[2] I then asked the executioner to let me go to prayer; he asked me to whom? I answered, to the Lord my God; he seemed surprized, and asked me where he was? I told him he was present; upon which he gave me leave. I desired them all to do as I did, so I fell down upon my knees, and mentioned to the Lord his delivering of the three

1. These Pegs were to be kindled at the opposite end from the Body [Marrant's note].
2. Matthew 6.10.

children in the fiery furnace, and of Daniel in the Lion's den,[3] and had close communion with God. I prayed in English a considerable time, and about the middle of my prayer, the Lord impressed a strong desire upon my mind to turn into their language, and pray in their tongue. I did so, and with remarkable liberty, which wonderfully affected the people. One circumstance was very singular, and strikingly displays the power and grace of God. I believe the executioner was savingly converted to God. He rose from his knees, and embracing me round the middle was unable to speak for about five minutes; the first words he expressed, when he had utterance, were, "No man shall hurt thee till thou hast been to the king."[4]

I was taken away immediately, and as we passed along, and I was reflecting upon the deliverance which the Lord had wrought out for me, and hearing the praises which the executioner was singing to the Lord, I must own I was utterly at a loss to find words to praise him. I broke out in these words, what can't the Lord Jesus do! and what power is like unto his! I will thank thee for what is past, and trust thee for what is to come. I will sing thy praise with my feeble tongue whilst life and breath shall last, and when I fail to sound thy praises here, I hope to sing them round thy throne above: And thus with unspeakable joy, I sung two verses of Dr. Watts's hymns:

> "My God, the spring of all my joys
>   The life of my delights;
> The glory of my brightest days,
>   And comfort of my nights.
> In darkest shades, if thou appear
>   My dawning is begun;
> Thou art my soul's bright morning star,
>   And thou my rising sun."

Passing by the judge's door, who had before examined and condemned me, he stopped us, and asked the executioner why he brought me back? The man fell upon his knees, and begged he would permit me to be carried before the king, which being granted, I went on, guarded by two hundred men with bows and arrows. After many windings I entered the king's outward chamber, and after waiting some time he came to the door, and his first question was, how came I there? I answered, I came with a hunter whom I met with in the woods, and who persuaded me to come there. He then asked me how old I was? I told him not fifteen. He asked me how I was supported before I met with this man? I answered, by the Lord Jesus Christ, which seemed to

---

3. Daniel 3.17 and Daniel 6.16–23.
4. The Office of the Executioner there, in many respects resembles that of a High Sheriff in this country [Marrant's note].

confound him. He turned round, and asked me if he lived where I came from? I answered, yes, and here also. He looked about the room, and said he did not see him; but I told him I felt him. The executioner fell upon his knees, and intreated the king in my behalf, and told him what he had felt of the same Lord. At this instant the king's eldest daughter came into the chamber, a person about nineteen years of age, and stood at my right hand. I had a Bible in my hand, which she took out of it, and having opened it, she kissed it, and seemed much delighted with it. When she had put it into my hand again, the king asked me what it was? And I told him the name of my God was recorded there; and after several questions, he bid me read it, which I did, particularly the fifty-third chapter of Isaiah, in the most solemn manner I was able; and also the twenty-sixth chapter of Matthew's Gospel; and when I pronounced the name of Jesus, the particular effect it had upon me was observed by the king. When I had finished reading, he asked me why I read those names[5] with so much reverence? I told him, because the Being to whom those names belonged made heaven and earth, and I and he; this he denied. I then pointed to the sun, and asked him who made the sun, and moon, and stars, and preserved them in their regular order; He said there was a man in their town that did it. I laboured as much as I could to convince him to the contrary. His daughter took the book out of my hand a second time; she opened it, and kissed it again; her father bid her give it to me, which she did; but said, with much sorrow, the book would not speak to her. The executioner then fell upon his knees again, and begged the king to let me go to prayer, which being granted, we all went upon our knees, and now the Lord displayed his glorious power. In the midst of the prayer some of them cried out, particularly the king's daughter, and the judge who ordered me to be executed, and several others seemed under deep conviction of sin: This made the king very angry; he called me a witch, and commanded me to be thrust into the prison, and to be executed the next morning. This was enough to make me think, as old Jacob once did, "All these things are against me;" for I was dragged away, and thrust into the dungeon again with much indignation;[6] but God, who never forsakes his people, was with me. Though I was weak in body, yet I was strong in spirit:[7] The executioner went to the king, and assured him, that if he put me to death, his daughter would never be well. They used the skill of all their doctors that afternoon and night; but physical prescriptions were useless. In the morning the executioner came to me, and, without opening the prison door, called to me, and hearing me answer, said, "Fear not, thy God who delivered thee yester-

5. Or what those parts were which seemed to affect so much, not knowing what I read, as he did not understand the English language [Marrant's note].
6. See Genesis 42.36
7. 2 Corinthians 12.10.

day, will deliver thee to-day." This comforted me very much, especially to find he could trust the Lord. Soon after I was fetched out; I thought it was to be executed; but they led me away to the king's chamber with much bodily weakness, having been without food two days. When I came into the king's presence, he said to me, with much anger, if I did not make his daughter and that man well, I should be laid down and chopped into pieces before him. I was not afraid, but the Lord tried my faith sharply. The king's daughter and the other person were brought out into the outer chamber, and we went to prayer; but the heavens were locked up to my petitions. I besought the Lord again, but received no answer: I cried again, and he was intreated. He said, "Be it to thee even as thou wilt;"[8] the Lord appeared most lovely and glorious; the king himself was awakened, and the others set at liberty. A great change took place among the people; the king's house became God's house; the soldiers were ordered away, and the poor condemned prisoner had perfect liberty, and was treated like a prince. Now the Lord made all my enemies to become my great friends. I remained nine weeks in the king's palace, praising God day and night. I was never out but three days all the time. I had assumed the habit of the country, and was dressed much like the king, and nothing was too good for me. The king would take off his golden ornaments, his chain and bracelets, like a child, if I objected to them, and lay them aside. Here I learnt to speak their tongue in the highest stile.

* * *

QUOBNA OTTOBAH CUGOANO

[Reflections and Memories]†

* * *

No necessity, or any situation of men, however poor, pitiful and wretches they may be, can warrant them to rob others, or oblige them to become thieves, because they are poor, miserable and wretched: But the robbers of men, the kid-nappers, ensnarers and slave-holders, who take away the common rights and privileges of others to support and enrich themselves, are universally those pitiful and detestable wretches; for the ensnaring of others, and taking away their liberty by

8. Matthew 26.39.
† From *Thoughts and Sentiments on the Evil and Wicked Traffic of the Slavery and Commerce of the Human Species, Humbly Submitted to the Inhabitants of Great-Britain, by Ottobah Cugoano, a Native of Africa* (1787). From Adam Potkay and Sandra Burr, eds., *Black Atlantic Writers of the 18th Century* (New York: St. Martin's Press, 1995), pp. 131–137; and retyped edition, pp. 80–81.

slavery and oppression, is the worst kind of robbery, as most opposite to every precept and injunction of the Divine Law, and contrary to that command which enjoins that *all men should love their neighbours as themselves*,[1] and *that they should do unto others, as they would that men should do to them.*[2] As to any other laws that slave-holders may make among themselves, as respecting slaves, they can be of no better kind, nor give them any better character, than what is implied in the common report—that there may be some honesty among thieves. This may seem a harsh comparison, but the parallel is so coincident that, I must say, I can find no other way of expressing my Thoughts and Sentiments, without making use of some harsh words and comparisons against the carriers on of such abandoned wickedness. But, in this little undertaking, I must humbly hope the impartial reader will excuse such defects as may arise from want of better education; and as to the resentment of those who can lay their cruel lash upon the backs of thousands, for a thousand times less crimes than writing against their enormous wickedness and brutal avarice, is what I may be sure to meet with.

However, it cannot but be very discouraging to a man of my complexion in such an attempt as this, to meet with the evil aspersions of some men, who say, "That an African is not entitled to any competent degree of knowledge, or capable of imbibing any sentiments of probity; and that nature designed him for some inferior link in the chain, fitted only to be a slave." But when I meet with those who make no scruple to deal with the human species, as with the beasts of the earth, I must think them not only brutish, but wicked and base; and that their aspersions are insidious and false: And if such men can boast of greater degrees of knowledge, than any African is entitled to, I shall let them enjoy all the advantages of it unenvied, as I fear it consists only in a greater share of infidelity, and that of a blacker kind than only skin deep. And if their complexion be not what I may suppose, it is at least the nearest in resemblance to an infernal hue. A good man will neither speak nor do as a bad man will; but if a man is bad, it makes no difference whether he be a black or a white devil.

By some of such complexion, as whether black or white it matters not, I was early snatched away from my native country, with about eighteen or twenty more boys and girls, as we were playing in a field. We lived but a few days journey from the coast where we were kidnapped, and as we were decoyed and drove along, we were soon conducted to a factory, and from thence, in the fashionable way of traffic, consigned to Grenada. Perhaps it may not be amiss to give a few remarks, as some account of myself, in this transposition of captivity.

I was born in the city of Agimaque, on the coast of Fantyn; my father

1. See Matthew 19.19 or Mark 12.31.
2. The "golden rule" of Matthew 7.12.

was a companion to the chief in that part of the country of Fantee, and when the old king died I was left in his house with his family; soon after I was sent for by his nephew, Ambro Accasa, who succeeded the old king in the chiefdom of that part of Fantee known by the name of Agimaque and Assinee. I lived with his children, enjoying peace and tranquillity, about twenty moons, which, according to their way of reckoning time, is two years. I was sent for to visit an uncle, who lived at a considerable distance from Agimaque. The first day after we set out we arrived at Assinee, and the third day at my uncle's habitation, where I lived about three months, and was then thinking of returning to my father and young companion at Agimaque; but by this time I had got well acquainted with some of the children of my uncle's hundreds of relations, and we were some days too ventursome in going into the woods to gather fruit and catch birds, and such amusements as pleased us. One day I refused to go with the rest, being rather apprehensive that something might happen to us; till one of my play-fellows said to me, because you belong to the great men, you are afraid to venture your carcase, or else of the *bounsam*, which is the devil. This enraged me so much, that I set a resolution to join the rest, and we went into the woods as usual; but we had not been above two hours before our troubles began, when several great ruffians came upon us suddenly, and said we had committed a fault against their lord, and we must go and answer for it ourselves before him.

Some of us attempted in vain to run away, but pistols and cutlasses were soon introduced, threatening, that if we offered to stir we should all lie dead on the spot. One of them pretended to be more friendly than the rest, and said, that he would speak to their lord to get us clear, and desired that we should follow him; we were then immediately divided into different parties, and drove after him. We were soon led out of the way which we knew, and towards the evening, as we came in sight of a town, they told us that this great man of theirs lived there, but pretended it was too late to go and see him that night. Next morning there came three other men, whose language differed from ours, and spoke to some of those who watched us all the night, but he that pretended to be our friend with the great man, and some others, were gone away. We asked our keepers what these men had been saying to them, and they answered, that they had been asking them, and us together, to go and feast with them that day, and that we must put off seeing the great man till after; little thinking that our doom was so nigh, or that these villains meant to feast on us as their prey. We went with them again about half a day's journey, and came to a great multitude of people, having different music playing; and all the day after we got there, we were very merry with the music, dancing and singing. Towards the evening, we were again persuaded that we could not get back to where the great man lived till next day; and when bed-time came, we were separated into different houses with different people. When the next morning came, I asked for the men that brought me there, and for the rest of my companions; and I was told that they were gone to the sea side to bring home some rum, guns and powder, and that some of my companions were gone with them, and that some were gone to the fields to do something or other. This gave me strong suspicion that there was some treachery in the case, and I began to think that my hopes of returning home again were all over. I soon became very uneasy, not knowing what to do, and refused to eat or drink for whole days together, till the man of the house told me that he would do all in his power to get me back to my uncle; then I eat a little fruit with him, and had some thoughts that I should be sought after, as I would be then missing at home about five or six days. I enquired every day if the men had come back, and for the rest of my companions, but could get no answer of any satisfaction. I was kept about six days at this man's house, and in the evening there was another man came and talked with him a good while, and I heard the one say to the other he must go, and the other said the sooner the better; that man came out and told me that he knew my relations at Agimaque, and that we must set out to-morrow morning, and he would convey me there. Accordingly we set out next day, and travelled till dark, when we came to a place where we had some supper and slept. He carried a large bag with some gold dust, which he said he had to buy some goods at the sea side to take with him to Agimaque. Next day we travelled on, and in the evening came to a town, where I saw several white people, which made me afraid that they would eat me, according to our notion as children in the inland parts of the country.[3] This made me rest very uneasy all the night, and next morning I had some victuals brought, desiring me to eat and make haste, as my guide and kid-napper told me that he had to go to the castle with some company that were going there, as he had told me before, to get some goods. After I was ordered out, the horrors I soon saw and felt, cannot be well described; I saw many of my miserable countrymen chained two and two, some hand-cuffed, and some with their hands tied behind. We were conducted along by a guard, and when we arrived at the castle, I asked my guide what I was brought there for, he told me to learn the ways of the *browfow*, that is the white faced people. I saw him take a gun, a piece of cloth, and some lead for me, and then he told me that he must now leave me there, and went off. This made me cry bitterly, but I was soon conducted to a prison, for three days, where I heard the groans and cries of many, and saw some of my fellow-captives. But when a vessel arrived to conduct us away to the ship, it was a most horrible scene; there was nothing to be heard but rattling

---

3. See John Matthews, *Voyage to the River Sierra-Leone* (1788), and Equiano's *Narrative*, above, p. 39 [*Editor*].

of chains, smacking of whips, and the groans and cries of our fellow-men. Some would not stir from the ground, when they were lashed and beat in the most horrible manner. I have forgot the name of this infernal fort; but we were taken in the ship that came for us, to another that was ready to sail from Cape Coast. When we were put into the ship, we saw several black merchants coming on board, but we were all drove into our holes, and not suffered to speak to any of them. In this situation we continued several days in sight of our native land; but I could find no good person to give any information of my situation to Accasa at Agimaque. And when we found ourselves at last taken away, death was more preferable than life, and a plan was concerted amongst us, that we might burn and blow up the ship, and to perish all together in the flames; but we were betrayed by one of our own countrywomen, who slept with some of the head men of the ship, for it was common for the dirty filthy sailors to take the African women and lie upon their bodies; but the men were chained and pent up in holes. It was the women and boys which were to burn the ship, with the approbation and groans of the rest; though that was prevented, the discovery was likewise a cruel bloody scene.

But it would be needless to give a description of all the horrible scenes which we saw, and the base treatment which we met with in this dreadful captive situation, as the similar cases of thousands, which suffer by this infernal traffic, are well known. Let it suffice to say, that I was thus lost to my dear indulgent parents and relations, and they to me. All my help was cries and tears, and these could not avail; nor suffered long, till one succeeding woe, and dread, swelled up another. Brought from a state of innocence and freedom, and, in a barbarous and cruel manner, conveyed to a state of horror and slavery: This abandoned situation may be easier conceived than described. From the time that I was kid napped and conducted to a factory, and from thence in the brutish, base, but fashionable way of traffic, consigned to Grenada, the grievous thoughts which I then felt, still pant in my heart; though my fears and tears have long since subsided. And yet it is still grievous to think that thousands more have suffered in similar and greater distress, under the hands of barbarous robbers, and merciless task-masters; and that many even now are suffering in all the extreme bitterness of grief and woe, that no language can describe[.] The cries of some, and the sight of their misery, may be seen and heard afar; but the deep sounding groans of thousands, and the great sadness of their misery and woe, under the heavy load of oppressions and calamities inflicted upon them, are such as can only be distinctly known to the ears of Jehovah Sabaoth.[4]

This Lord of Hosts, in his great Providence, and in great mercy to

4. God of armies. See Romans 9.29 and James 5.4.

me, made a way for my deliverance from Grenada.—Being in this dreadful captivity and horrible slavery, without any hope of deliverance, for about eight or nine months, beholding the most dreadful scenes of misery and cruelty, and seeing my miserable companions often cruelly lashed, and as it were cut to pieces, for the most trifling faults; this made me often tremble and weep, but I escaped better than many of them. For eating a piece of sugar-cane, some were cruelly lashed, or struck over the face to knock their teeth out. Some of the stouter ones, I suppose often reproved, and grown hardened and stupid with many cruel beatings and lashings, or perhaps faint and pressed with hunger and hard labour, were often committing trespasses of this kind, and when detected, they met with exemplary punishment. Some told me they had their teeth pulled out to deter others, and to prevent them from eating any cane in future. Thus seeing my miserable companions and countrymen in this pitiful, distressed and horrible situation, with all the brutish baseness and barbarity attending it, could not but fill my little mind with horror and indignation. But I must own, to the shame of my own countrymen, that I was first kid-napped and betrayed by some of my own complexion, who were the first cause of my exile and slavery; but if there were no buyers there would be no sellers. So far as I can remember, some of the Africans in my country keep slaves, which they take in war, or for debt; but those which they keep are well fed, and good care taken of them, and treated well; and, as to their cloathing, they differ according to the custom of the country. But I may safely say, that all the poverty and misery that any of the inhabitants of Africa meet with among themselves, is far inferior to those inhospitable regions of misery which they meet with in the West-Indies, where their hard-hearted overseers have neither regard to the laws of God, nor the life of their fellow-men.

Thanks be to God, I was delivered from Grenada, and that horrid brutal slavery.—A gentleman coming to England, took me for his servant, and brought me away, where I soon found my situation more agreeable. After coming to England, and seeing others write and read, I had a strong desire to learn, and getting what assistance I could, I applied myself to learn reading and writing, which soon became my recreation, pleasure, and delight; and when my master perceived that I could write some, he sent me to a proper school for that purpose to learn. Since, I have endeavoured to improve my mind in reading, and have sought to get all the intelligence I could, in my situation of life, towards the state of my brethren and countrymen in complexion, and of the miserable situation of those who are barbarously sold into captivity, and unlawfully held in slavery.

But, among other observations, one great duty I owe to Almighty God, (the thankful acknowledgement I would not omit for any consideration) that, although I have been brought away from my native country, in that torrent of robbery and wickedness, thanks be to God fo[r] his good providence towards me; I have both obtained liberty, and acquired the great advantages of some little learning, in being able to read and write, and, what is still infinitely of greater advantage, I trust, to know something of HIM *who is that God whose providence rules over all, and who is the only Potent One that rules in the nations over the children of men. It is unto Him, who is the Prince of the Kings of the earth, that I would give all thanks.* And, in some manner, I may say with Joseph, as he did with respect to the evil intention of his brethren, when they sold him into Egypt, that whatever evil intentions and bad motives those insidious robbers had in carrying me away from my native country and friends, I trust, was what the Lord intended for my good. In this respect, I am highly indebted to many of the good people of England for learning and principles unknown to the people of my native country. But, above all, what have I obtained from the Lord God of Hosts, the God of the Christians! in that divine revelation of the only true God, and the Saviour of men, what a treasure of wisdom and blessings are involved? How wonderful is the divine goodness displayed in those invaluable books the Old and New Testaments, that inestimable compilation of books, the Bible? And, O what a treasure to have, and one of the greatest advantages to be able to read therein, and a divine blessing to understand!

*   *   *

[A silent book]

This strange harangue, unfolding deep mysteries and alluding to such unknown facts, of which no power of eloquence could translate, and convey, at once, if a distinct idea to an American that its general tenor was altogether incomprehensible to Atahualpa. Some parts in it, as more obvious than the rest, filled him with astonishment and indignation. His reply, however, was temperate, and as suitable as could be well expected. He observed that he was Lord of the dominions over which he reigned by hereditary successions; and, said, that he could not conceive how a foreign priest should pretend to dispose of territories which did not belong to him, and that if such a preposterous grant had been made, he, who was the rightful possessor, refused to confirm, it; that he had no inclination to renounce the religious institutions established by his ancestors; nor would he forsake the service of the Sun, the immortal divinity whom he and his people revered, in order to worship the God of the Spaniards, who was subject to death; and that with respect to other matters, he had never heard of them before, and did not then understand their meaning. And he desired to know where Valverde had learned things so extraordinary. In this book, replied the fanatic Monk, reaching out his breviary. The Inca opened it eagerly, and turning over the leaves, lifted it to his ear: This, says he, is silent; it tells me nothing; and threw it with disdain to the ground. The enraged father of ruffians, turning towards his countrymen, the assassinators, cried out, To arms, Christians, to arms; the word of God is insulted; avenge this profanation on these impious dogs.

At this the Christian desperadoes impatient in delay, as soon as the signal of assault was given their martial music began to play, and their attack was rapid, rushing suddenly upon the Peruvians, and with their hell-invented enginery of thunder, fire and smoke, they soon put them to flight and destruction.

* * *

The English Debate about the Slave Trade

THOMAS CLARKSON

From An Essay on the Slavery and Commerce of the Human Species, Particularly the African†

*   *   *

The present age has also produced some zealous and able opposers of the *colonial* slavery. For about the middle of the present century, *John Woolman* and *Anthony Benezet*, two respectable members of the religious society called Quakers, devoted much of their time to the subject. The former travelled through most parts of *North America* on foot, to hold conversations with the members of his own sect, on the impiety of retaining those in a state of involuntary servitude, who had never given them offence. The latter kept a school at *Philadelphia*, for the education of black people. He took every opportunity of pleading in their behalf. He published several treatises against slavery,[1] and gave an hearty proof of his attachment to the cause, by leaving the whole of his fortune in support of that school, to which he had so generously devoted his time and attention when alive.

Till this time it does not appear, that any bodies of men had collectively interested themselves in endeavouring to remedy the evil. But in the year 1754, the religious society, called Quakers, publickly testified their sentiments upon the subject,[2] declaring, that "to live in ease and plenty by the toil of those, whom fraud and violence had put

---

† From *Translated from a Latin Dissertation Which Was Honoured with the First Prize in the University of Cambridge, for the Year 1785* (London: J. Phillips, 1786), pp. vi–vii, 56–57, 128–32, 128–32, 186–88, 207–08, 246–48. Clarkson's famous and frequently cited brief against the slave trade also included excerpts from Mitchell's essay on colors (see pp. 256–58 above). Equiano quotes Clarkson (see p. 30 above).

1. A Description of Guinea, with an Inquiry into the Rise and Progress of the Slave Trade, &c.——A Caution to Great Britain and her Colonies, in a short Representation of the calamitous State of the enslaved Negroes in the British Dominions. Besides several smaller pieces.
2. They had censured the *African Trade* in the year 1727, but had taken no publick notice of the *colonial* slavery till this time.

into their power, was neither consistent with Christianity nor common
justice."

Impressed with these sentiments, many of this society immediately
liberated their slaves.

*   *   *

It appears that mankind were originally free, and that they possessed
an equal right to the soil and produce of the earth. For proof of this,
we need only appeal to the divine writings; to the *golden age* of the
poets, which, like other fables of the times had its origin in truth; and
to the institution of the *Saturnalia*, and of other similar festivals; all
of which are so many monuments of this original equality of men.
Hence then there was no rank, no distinction, no superiour. Every man
wandered where he chose, changing his residence, as a spot attracted
his fancy, or suited his convenience, uncontrouled by his neighbour,
unconnected with any but his family. Hence also (as every thing was
common) he collected what he chose without injury, and enjoyed without injury what he had collected. Such was the first situation of mankind,[3] a state of *dissociation* and *independence*.

*   *   *

When the African slaves, who are collected from various quarters,
for the purposes of sale, are delivered over to the *receivers*, they are
conducted in the manner above described to the ships. Their situation
on board is beyond all description; for here they are crouded, hundreds
of them together, into such a small compass as would scarcely be
thought sufficient to accommodate twenty, if considered as *free men*.
This confinement soon produces an effect, that may be easily imagined. It generates a pestilential air, which, co-operating with bad provisions, occasions such a sickness and mortality among them, that
not less than[4] *twenty thousand* are generally taken off in every yearly
transportation.

Thus confined in a pestilential prison, and almost entirely excluded
from the chearful face of day, it remains for the sickly survivors to linger
out a miserable existence, till the voyage is finished. But are no farther
evils to be expected in the interim, particularly if we add to their
already wretched situation the indignities that are daily offered them,
and the regret which they must constantly feel, at being for ever forced

3. This conclusion concerning the dissociated state of mankind, is confirmed by all the early
writers, with whose descriptions of primitive times no other conclusion is reconcilable.
4. It is universally allowed, that at least one fifth of the exported negroes perisht in the passage.
This estimate is made from the time in which they are put on board, to the time when they
are disposed of in the colonies. The French are supposed to lose the greatest number in the
voyage, but 'particularly from this circumstance, because their slave ships are in general so
very large, that many of the slaves that have been put on board sickly, die before the cargo
can be completed.

from their connexions? These evils are but too apparent. Some of them have resolved, and, notwithstanding the threats of the *receivers*, have carried their resolves into execution, to starve themselves to death. Others, when they have been brought upon deck for air, if the least opportunity has offered, have leaped into the sea, and terminated their miseries at once. Others, in a fit of despair, have attempted to rise, and regain their liberty. But here what a scene of barbarity has constantly ensued. Some of them have been instantly killed upon the spot; some have been bruised and mutilated in the most barbarous and shocking manner, and have been returned bleeding to their companions, as a sad example of resistance; while others, tied to the ropes of the ship, and mangled alternately with the whip and knife, have been left in that horrid situation, till they have expired.

But this is not the only inhuman treatment which they are frequently obliged to undergo; for if there should be any necessity, from tempestuous weather, for lightening the ship; or if it should be presumed on the voyage, that the provisions will fall short before the port can be made, they are, many of them, thrown into the sea, without any compunction of mind on the part of the *receivers*, and without any other regret for their loss, than that which *avarice* inspires. Wretched survivors! what must be their feelings at such a sight! how must they tremble to think of that servitude which is approaching, when the very *dogs* of the *receivers* have been retained on board, and preferred to their unoffending countrymen. But indeed so lightly are these unhappy people esteemed, that their lives have been even taken away upon speculation: there has been an instance,[5] within the last five years, of *one hundred and thirty two* of them being thrown into the sea, because it was supposed that, by this *trick*, their value could be recovered from the insurers.

*   *   *

We shall therefore declare our sentiments, by asserting that they are true, and that all mankind, however various their appearance, are derived from the same stock.

To prove this, we shall not produce those innumerable arguments, by which the scriptures have stood the test of ages, but advert to a single fact. It is an universal law, observable throughout the whole creation, *that if two animals of a different species propagate, their off-*

---

5. This instance happened in a ship, commanded by one Collingwood. On the 29th of November, 1781, fifty-four of them were thrown into the sea alive; on the 30th forty-two more; and in about three days afterwards, twenty-six. Ten others, who were brought upon the deck for the same purpose, did not wait to be hand-cuffed, but bravely leaped into the sea, and shared the fate of their companions. It is a fact, that the people on board this ship had not been put upon short allowance. The excuse which this execrable wretch made on board for his conduct, was the following, *"that if the slaves, who were then sickly, had died a natural death, the loss would have been the owners; but as they were thrown alive into the sea, it would fall upon the underwriters."*

spring is unable to continue its own species. By this admirable law, the different species are preserved distinct; every possibility of confusion is prevented, and the world is forbidden to be over-run by a race of monsters. Now, if we apply this law to those of the human kind, who are said to be of a distinct species from each other, it immediately fails. The *mulattoe* is as capable of continuing his own species as his father; a clear and irrefragable proof, that the[6] scripture account of the creation is true, and that "God, who hath made the world, hath made of[7] one blood all the nations of men that dwell on all the face of the earth."

*   *   *

It can be shewn, that the members of the *very same family*, when divided from each other, and removed into different countries, have not only changed their family complexion, but that they have changed it to *as many different colours* as they have gone into *different regions of the world*. We cannot have, perhaps, a more striking instance of this, than in the *Jews*. These people are scattered over the face of the whole earth. They have preserved themselves distinct from the rest of the world by their religion; and, as they never intermarry with any but those of their own sect, so they have no mixture of blood in their veins, that they should differ from each other: and yet nothing is more true, than that the[8] *English Jew* is white, the *Portuguese* swarthy, the *Armenian* olive, and the *Arabian* copper; in short, that there appear to be as many different species of *Jews*, as there are countries in which they reside.

*   *   *

It is said again, that Christianity, among the many important precepts which it contains, does not furnish us with one for the abolition of slavery. But the reason is obvious. Slavery at the time of the introduction of the gospel was universally prevalent, and if Christianity had abruptly declared, that the millions of slaves should have been made free, who were then in the world, it would have been universally rejected, as containing doctrines that were dangerous, if not destructive, to society. In order therefore that it might be universally received, it never meddled, by any positive precept, with the civil institutions of

---

6. When America was first discovered, it was thought by some, that the scripture account of the creation was false, and that there were different species of men, because they could never suppose that people, in so rude a state as the Americans, could have transported themselves to that continent from any parts of the known world. This opinion however was refuted by the celebrated Captain Cooke, who shewed that the traject between the continents of Asia and America, was as short as some, which people in as rude a state have been actually known to pass. This affords an excellent caution against an ill-judged and hasty censure of the divine writings, because every difficulty which may be started, cannot instantly be cleared up.
7. The divine writings, which assert that all men were derived from the *same stock* shew also in the same instance of *Cush* * * * that some of them had changed their original complexion.
8. We mean such only as are *natives* of the countries which we mention, and whose ancestors have been settled there for a certain period of time.

the times: but though it does not expressly say, that "you shall neither buy, nor sell, nor possess a slave," it is evident that, in its general tenour, it sufficiently militates against the custom.

The first doctrine which it inculcates, is that of *brotherly love*. It commands good will towards men. It enjoins us to love our neighbours as ourselves, and to do unto all men, as we would that they should do unto us. And how can any man fulfil this scheme of universal benevolence, who reduces an unfortunate person *against his will*, to the *most insupportable* of all human conditions; who confiders him as his *private property*, and treats him, not as a brother, nor as one of the same parentage with himself, but as an *animal of the brute creation?*

*   *   *

JOHN WESLEY

Letter to William Wilberforce Commenting on Gustavus Vassa †

[John Wesley (1703–1791), the founder of English Methodism, was moved by John Woolman's and Anthony Benezet's writings (including especially Michel Adanson's description of Africa) to publish his immensely influential *Thoughts upon Slavery* (1774). Its appearance prompted 229,000 English Methodists to petition Parliament against slavery. Near the end of his life, Wesley, who was one of the subscribers to Equiano's *Narrative*, mentioned Equiano's book in the following letter to William Wilberforce (1759–1833), the Member of Parliament from Hull who led the parliamentary battle to curb the slave trade and whose 1789 speech is excerpted below, pp. 282–83. See also the 1791 debate in the House of Commons, pp. 283–87, and Eva B. Dykes's account of John Wesley, pp. 210–16.]

Balam, *February* 24, 1791.

DEAR SIR,—Unless the divine power has raised you up to be as *Athanasius contra mundum*,[1] I see not how you can go through your glorious enterprise in opposing that execrable villany, which is the scandal of religion, of England, and of human nature. Unless God has raised you up for this very thing, you will be worn out by the opposition of men and devils. But if God be for you, who can be against you? Are all of them together stronger than God? O be not weary of well doing!

† John Wesley, Letter to William Wilberforce, February 24, 1791, in *Letters*, ed. John Telford (London: Epworth Press, 1931), vol. 8, 264–65.
1. Athanasius against the world [Telford]. Saint Athanasius (ca. 293–373) was at times the sole defender of Christian orthodoxy against the heresy of Arianism, according to which Christ was a lesser being than God [*Editor*].

Go on, in the name of God and in the power of His might, till even American slavery (the vilest that ever saw the sun) shall vanish away before it.

Reading this morning a tract wrote by a poor African, I was particularly struck by that circumstance, that a man who has a black skin, being wronged or outraged by a white man, can have no redress; it being a *law* in all our Colonies that the *oath* of a black against a white goes for nothing. What villany is this!

That He who has guided you from youth up may continue to strengthen you in this and all things is the prayer of, dear sir,

Your affectionate servant.

WILLIAM WILBERFORCE

From Speech in the House of Commons†

* * *

When we consider the vastness of the Continent of Africa; when we reflect how all other countries have for some centuries past been advancing in happiness and civilization; when we think how in this same period all improvement in Africa has been defeated by her intercourse with Britain; when we reflect how it is we ourselves that have degraded them to that wretched brutishness and barbarity which we now plead as the justification of our guilt; how the Slave Trade has *enslaved their minds*, blackened their character and sunk them so low in the scale of animal beings, that some think the very apes are of a higher class, and fancy the *Ourang Outang* has given them the go-by.— What a mortification must we feel at having so long neglected to think of our guilt, or to attempt any reparation: It seems, indeed, as if we had determined to forbear from all interference until the measure of our folly and wickedness was so full and complete; until the impolicy which eventually belongs to vice, was become so plain and glaring, that not an individual in the country should refuse to join in the abolition: It seems as if we had waited until the persons most interested should be tired out with the folly and nefariousness of the trade, and should unite in petitioning against it.

Let us then make such amends as we can for the mischiefs we have done to that unhappy Continent: Let us recollect what Europe itself was no longer ago than three or four centuries. What if I should be able to shew this House that in a civilized part of Europe, in the time

† From *The Speech of William Wilberforce, Esq., Representative of York, on Wednesday the 13th of May, 1789, on the Question of the Abolition of the Slave Trade* (London: Logographic Press, n.d.), pp. 47–50.

of our Henry II, there were people who actually sold their own children? what, if I should tell them, that England itself was that country? what if I should point out to them that the very place where this inhuman traffic was carried on was *the City of Bristol?* Ireland at that time used to drive a considerable trade in slaves, with these neighbouring barbarians; but a great plague having infested the country, the Irish were struck with a panic, suspected (I am sure very properly) that the plague was a punishment sent from Heaven, for the sin of the Slave Trade, and therefore abolished it. All I ask, therefore, of the people of Bristol, is, that they would become as civilized now, as Irishmen were four hundred years ago. Let us put an end at once to this inhuman traffic,— let us stop this effusion of human blood. The true way to virtue is by withdrawing from temptation;—let us then withdraw from these wretched Africans, those temptations to fraud, violence, cruelty, and injustice, which the Slave Trade furnishes. Wherever the sun shines, let us go round the world with him diffusing our beneficence; but let us not traffic, only that we may set Kings against their Subjects, Subjects against their Kings, sowing discord in every village, fear and terror in every family, setting millions of our fellow creatures a hunting each other for slaves, creating fairs and markets for human flesh, through one whole continent of the world, and under the name of policy, concealing from ourselves all the baseness and iniquity of such a traffic.

Why may we not hope, ere long, to see Hans-towns[1] established on the coast of Africa, as they were on the Baltic?

*   *   *

From The 1791 Debate in the House of Commons on the Abolition of the Slave Trade†

*   *   *

The idea of abolishing the slave trade in Britain, suggested first by the society of Quakers, was quickly communicated to different societies of men, who united in the formation of societies for effecting that purpose. Petitions for the abolition of the slave trade were presented and agitated in the House of Commons so early as the sessions of parliament 1788: a very full and elaborate enquiry into the subject was instituted by the privy council; and a great body of evidence collected respecting the nature and extent of the trade in negroes on the African

---

1. Free towns in the medieval Hanseatic League of northern Germany and neighboring countries, formed for economic advancement and protection [*Editor*].

† From *The Annual Register, or a View of the History, Politics, and Literature for the Year 1791* (London: Dodsley's Annual Register), 243–246. The movement for the abolition of the slave trade succeeded only in 1807, ten years after Equiano's death.

coast,—their passages thence to the West India islands,—their treatment and condition in the plantations,—and the consequences that might be expected to result from an abolition or regulation of the trade in the different islands which it supplied with slaves. An act was passed in the last parliament, for regulating the transportation of slaves from Africa to the West Indies, in which various provisions were made for their accommodation during the voyage, and premiums granted for the encouragement of captains and surgeons of slave-ships, to be attentive to the health and safety of those whom they transported. A set of resolutions were also carried in the House of Commons declaratory of the manifold abuses of the slave trade, and intended as preparatory to a bill for its total abolition: and a variety of additional evidence was taken on both sides of the question during the remainder of that parliament, by a select committee.

The House being in possession of these documents, Mr. Wilberforce, member for Yorkshire, a man of talents and eloquence, as of religious impressions and habits of virtue, and who had stood forth from the beginning, the active and unwearied leader in this humane cause, moved in a committee of the whole House of Commons on the 18th of April, "that the chairman be instructed to move for leave to bring in a bill to prevent the farther importation of slaves into the British colonies in the West Indies." This motion Mr. Wilberforce prefaced by a very animated and affecting account of the slave trade. He set out with an accurate detail of the unfair means by which slaves are obtained on the coast of Africa. He specified many acts of the most flagrant cruelty; and exposed all the mean and inhuman devices of those unfeeling men who were concerned in this bloody traffic. Different tribes of the Indians, he said, were encouraged to make war on each other for the sake of making prisoners, and of thus providing the market with slaves. The administration of justice in most parts of Africa was converted into an engine of oppression; and every fraud and violence practised that low cunning and brutal ferocity could suggest. Having stated several shocking examples of these, he described the unparalleled suffering of the slaves under the horrors of the middle passage, and after their arrival in the slave-market. He next contended, that the abolition of the trade would not operate to the detriment of our West India islands: notwithstanding the barbarous treatment which the negroes have long experienced, their numbers had not on the whole decreased, but in some islands had lately been on the increase: whence he argued, that when the planter should be deprived of all prospect of a future market, he would be induced to pay a proper attention to the health, morals, and comfort of his slaves; and by thus considerably augmenting not only their happiness, but their numbers, would render continual supplies from Africa unnecessary. With regard to the probable effects of the abolition recommended, on the marine, the Guinea trade, he said, instead of being a nursery of seamen, was, in his opinion, their grave. It appeared, from the Liverpool and muster-rolls, that in 350 slave ships, having on board 12,263 persons, there were lost 2,645 in twelve months. All attempts to meliorate the condition of the negroes, without the total abolition of slavery, he considered likely to prove not only inefficacious, but not safe. As to the advantages of the trade in a commercial view, he deemed it almost an unbecoming condescension to discuss them. But, could its advocates prove, what he knew never could be proved, that it was of considerable importance to this country, either in its immediate separation or remote effects, still he should exclaim, "still there is a smell of blood, which all the perfumes of Arabia cannot remove." He concluded by moving, That the chairman be instructed to bring in a bill to prevent the further importation of slaves into the British colonies in the West Indies.

The propriety of continuing the slave trade, was, on the other hand, very ably supported on the grounds of justice, policy, and what may at first sight seem paradoxical, even of humanity. A very great diversity of ranks of life, it was said, was established, by a beneficent providence, in civil society; and a great portion of the human race had, at all times, existed in the condition of slaves. Captives taken in war in all nations in former times, and in many at present, have no alternative but slavery or death. The prayers of so many warriors in Homer, when overpowered by their adversaries, to be taken alive, shew how ardently human nature pants after a continuance of existence, though at the expence of liberty. The purchaser of slaves taken in war does them no wrong, though he does not better their condition: nay, by purchasing them, he does them a kindness; for their ferocious conquerors would give way to the savage gratification of animal rage and cruelty, if the thirst of blood were not transmuted into that of gain. As the justice and even humanity of the slave trade were thus supported by abstracted principles, so would the abolition appear manifest from the long sanction given to it by parliament. On the faith of parliament, property to a very great amount had been embarked in this trade; the total loss of which would immediately follow its sudden abolition.

With regard to the political wisdom of tolerating the slave trade, it was maintained, in opposition to Mr. Wilberforce's assertion of its being the grave, that it was an important nursery for seamen. Lord Rodney had declared that our being enabled to obtain from the Guinea ships so numerous a body of men enured to the climate, whenever we wished to send a fleet to the West Indies on the breaking out of a war, was, in his opinion, a consideration of great moment. His Lordship's authority was urged on the present occasion; and his opinion illustrated and confirmed by other concurring testimonies and observations. The policy of the slave trade was farther urged, from the consideration of its importance to the revenue. The exports to Africa were estimated at 800,000£, to which might be added the imports of the West India trade, to the amount of at least 6,000,000 a year: a trade not only very liable to be materially affected by the abolition proposed, but perhaps, even completely ruined. The evidences adduced to prove the horrid cruelties practised upon slaves, were represented to be in some instances false, in many partial, in almost all exaggerated. The defenders of the slave trade, in farther reasoning on this subject, urged the following dilemma:—Either our abolition of that trade would annihilate slavery in the West Indies, or it would not. If it did, our West India islands would be ruined for want of proper hands to cultivate them: if it did not, and this was the most probable case, what good purpose would be served by our giving up the trade, if other nations should immediately take up the lucrative traffic on our abandoning it?

To the argument in favour of both the justice and humanity of the slave trade, drawn from the wretched condition of captives taken in war, and devoted, if not to slavery, to death, it was answered, that it was the slave market that was in many instances the only source of that miserable condition: not only were crimes continually committed, but wars begun and pursued to a great extent, for the sole purpose of supplying us with slaves. A few prisoners of war might possibly be murdered, if not sold to our dealers: still death would be preferable to a life of slavery; often embittered by a treatment the most cruel and inhuman. These manifold instances of barbarity were painted with a shocking and disgusting minuteness, although the bare recital of them was more than sufficiently painful for the purpose of exciting condemnation and abhorrence. On a constant and close investigation of this subject, which appeared to us to involve a very interesting question concerning our common nature, we have found for certain, that, although not a few of the barbarities said to have been committed were exaggerated and sometimes distorted into shapes very different from their original and natural appearances, yet enough of reality remained to prove how largely human beings participate in the ferocity of animal nature! and what tygers they quickly become when freed from the muzzle of the law! Among British planters, but oftener overseers, and above all among Dutch planters and overseers, it fully appears, that cruelties are sometimes carried far beyond the original point of punishment, either as an example, or a gratification of resentment; and degenerate into a kind of horrid and relentless triumph over all that can be urged in commiseration of the tortured victim, either by the compassion of the spectators, or the still voice of conscience in the tormentor's own breast.

With regard to the inefficacy of our abolition of the slave trade to any substantial purpose of humanity, it was admitted that other nations might pursue the trade if we abandoned it. From this, however, they might, in a great measure, be restrained by proper regulations: at the worst, we should have the satisfaction of reflecting that the guilt would not rest on our heads.

In answer to the objection that the intended abolition would prove the ruin of our colonies, it was confidently asserted, that the stock of slaves which they at present contained, if well managed and mildly treated, would be fully competent to all the requisite labour, and furnish a sufficient supply for future exigencies.

Mr. Wilberforce's motion, after a debate of two days, was negatived by a majority of 163 to 88.

Antislavery Verse

THOMAS DAY AND JOHN BICKNELL

From The Dying Negro†

*   *   *

Swift round the globe, by earth nor heav'n controul'd,
Fly proud oppression and dire lust of gold.
Wheree'er the thirsty hell-hounds take their way,
Still nature bleeds, and man becomes their prey.
In the wild wastes of Afric's sandy plain,
Where roars the lion through his drear domain,
To curb the savage monarch in the chace,
There too Heav'n planted man's majestic race;
Bade reason's sons with nobler titles rise,
Lift high their brow sublime, and scan the skies.[1]
What tho' the sun in his meridian blaze
On their scorch'd bodies dart his fiercest rays?
What tho' no rosy tints adorn their face,
No silken ringlets shine with flowing grace?
Yet of etherial temper are their souls,
And in their veins the tide of honour rolls;
And valour kindles there the hero's flame,
Contempt of death, and thirst of martial fame.
And pity melts the sympathizing breast,
Ah! fatal virtue!—for the brave distrest.

    My tortur'd breast, O sad remembrance spare!
Why dost thou plant thy keenest daggers there,

† From *The Dying Negro, A Poetical Epistle, Supposed to Be Written by a Black (Who lately Shot Himself on Board a Vessel in the River Thames;) to His Intended Wife* (London: W. Flexney, 1773), pp. 7–13. This immensely popular poem from which Equiano quotes (see p. 72) apparently by memory, also includes footnotes to Michel Adanson's *Voyage to Senegal*, which Benezet (see above, pp. 250–53) helped to popularize.

1. "It is amazing, that such a rude and illiterate people should reason so pertinently in regard to the Heavenly Bodies; there is no doubt but that with proper instruments, and a good will, they would become excellent Astronomers." *M. Adanson's Voyage to Senegal, &c.*

And shew me what I was, and aggravate despair?
Ye streams of Gambia, and thou sacred shade!
Where, in my youth's first dawn I joyful stray'd,
Oft have I rouz'd amid your caverns dim,
The howling tiger, and the lion grim,
In vain they gloried in their headlong force,
My javelin pierc'd them in their raging course.
But little did my boding mind bewray,[2]
The victor and his hopes were doom'd a prey
To human beasts more fell, more cruel far than they.
Ah! what avails it that in every plain,
I purchas'd glory with my blood in vain?
Ah! what avails the conqu'ror's laurel meed,[3]
The generous purpose or the dauntless deed?
Fall'n are my trophies, blasted is my fame,
Myself become a thing without a name,
The sport of haughty Lords and ev'n of slaves the shame

   Curst be the winds, and curst the tides that bore
These European robbers to our shore!
O be that hour involv'd in endless night,
When first their streamers met my wond'ring sight,
I call'd the warriors from the mountain's steep,
To meet these unknown terrors of the deep;
Rouz'd by my voice, their generous bosoms glow,
They rush indignant, and demand the foe,
And poize the darts of death and twang the bended bow.
When lo! advancing o'er the sea-beat plain,
I mark'd the leader of a warlike train.
Unlike his features to our swarthy race.
And golden hair play'd round his ruddy face.
While with insidious smile and lifted hand,
He thus accosts our unsuspecting band.
"Ye valiant chiefs, whom love of glory leads
To martial combats, and heroic deeds;
No fierce invader your retreat explores,
No hostile banner waves along your shores.
From the dread tempests of the deep we fly,
Then lay, ye chiefs, these pointed terrors by.
And O, your hospitable cares extend,
So may ye never need the aid ye lend!
So may ye still repeat to every grove
The songs of freedom, and the strains of love!"
Soft as the accents of the traitor flow,

2. Betray, reveal [*Editor*].
3. Reward [Editor].

We melt with pity, and unbend the bow;
With lib'ral hand our choicest gifts we bring,
And point the wand'rers to the freshest spring.
Nine days we feasted on the Gambian strand,
And songs of friendship echo'd o'er the land.[4]
When the tenth morn her rising lustre gave,
The chief approach'd me by the sounding wave.
"O, youth," he said, "what gifts can we bestow,
Or how requite the mighty debt we owe?
For lo! propitious to our vows, the gale
With milder omens fills the swelling sail.
To-morrow's sun shall see our ships explore
These deeps, and quit your hospitable shore.
Yet while we linger, let us still employ
The number'd hours in friendship and in joy;
Ascend our ships, their treasures are your own,
And taste the produce of a world unknown."

He spoke; with fatal eagerness we burn,
Ah! wretches, destin'd never to return!
The similing traitors with insidious care,
The goblet proffer, and the feast prepare,
'Till dark oblivion shades our closing eyes,
And all disarm'd each fainting warrior lies,
O wretches! to your future evils blind!
O morn for ever present to my mind!
When bursting from the treach'rous bands of sleep,
Rouz'd by the murmers of the dashing deep,
I woke to bondage, and ignoble pains,
And all the horrors of a life in chains.[5]

4. Which way soever I turned my eyes on this pleasant spot, I beheld a perfect image of pure nature, an agreeable solitude bounded on every side by charming landscapes; the rural situation of cottages in the midst of trees; the ease and indolence of the Negroes, reclined under the shade of their spreading foliage; the simplicity of their dress and manners; the whole revived in my mind the idea of our first parents, and I seemed to contemplate the world in its primitive state. They are, generally speaking, very good-natured, sociable, and obliging. I was not a little pleased with this, my first reception; it convinced me that there ought to be considerable abatement made in the accounts I had read and heard of the savage characters of the Africans. M. Adanson's *Voyage to Senegal, &c.*

5. "As we past along the coast, we very often lay before a town, and fired a gun for the natives to come off, but no soul came near us; at length we learnt by some ships that were trading down the coast, that the natives came seldom on board an English ship, for fear of being detained or carried off; yet at last some ventured on board; but if these chanced to spy any arms, they would all immediately take to their canoes, and make the best of their way home." Smith's *Voyage to Guinea.*

"It is well known that many of the European nations, have, very unjustly and inhumanly, without any provocation, stolen away, from time to time, abundance of the people, not only on this coast, but almost every where in Guinea, who have come on board their ships, in a harmless and confiding manner; these they have in great numbers carried away, and sold in the plantations." J. Barbot's *Description of Guinea.*

Where were your thunders in that dreadful hour,
Ye Gods of Afric! where your heavenly power?
Did not my prayers, my groans, my tears invoke
Your slumb'ring justice to direct the stroke?

*   *   *

CRITICISM

Early Reviews and Assessments

From the *Monthly Review* (June 1789)†

We entertain no doubt of the general authenticity of this very intelligent African's story, though it is not improbable that some English writer has assisted him in the compilement, or, at least, the correction of his book; for it is sufficiently well-written. The Narrative wears an honest face; and we have conceived a good opinion of the man, from the artless manner in which he has detailed the variety of adventures and vicissitudes which have fallen to his lot. His publication appears very seasonable, at a time when negroe-slavery is the subject of public investigation; and it seems calculated to increase the odium that has been excited against the West-India planters, on account of the cruelties that some are said to have exercised on their slaves, many instances of which are here detailed.

The sable author of this volume appears to be a very sensible man; and he is, surely, not the less worthy of credit from being a convert to Christianity. He is a Methodist, and has filled many pages towards the end of this work, with accounts of his dreams, visions, and divine influences; but all this, supposing him to have been under any delusive influence, only serves to convince us that he is guided by principle, and that he is not one of those poor converts, who having undergone the ceremony of baptism, have remained content with that portion only of the Christian religion; instances of which are said to be almost innumerable in America and the West Indies.

GUSTAVUS VASSA appears to possess a very different character; and, therefore, we heartily wish success to his publication, which we are glad to see has been encouraged by a very respectable subscription.

---

† June 1789: 551. Equiano included this review in his fifth through ninth editions.

From *General Magazine and Impartial Review* (July 1789)[†]

This is "a round unvarnished tale" of the chequered adventures of an African, who early in life, was torn from his native country, by those savage dealers in a traffic disgraceful to humanity, and which has fixed a stain on the legislature of Britain. The Narrative appears to be written with much truth and simplicity. The author's account of the manners of the natives of his own province (Eboe) is interesting and pleasing; and the reader, unless perchance he is either a West-India planter, or Liverpool merchant, will find his humanity often severely wounded by the shameless barbarity practised towards the author's hapless country-men in all our colonies; if he feel, as he ought, the oppressed and the oppressors will equally excite his pity and indignation. That so unjust, so iniquitous a commerce may be abolished, is our ardent wish; and we heartily join in our author's prayer, "That the God of Heaven may inspire the hearts of our Representatives in Parliament, with peculiar benevolence on that important day when so interesting a question is to be discussed; when thousands in consequence of their determination, are to look for happiness or misery!"

"W."

[Review of *The Interesting Narrative*][‡]

* * *

The life of an African, written by himself, is certainly a curiosity, as it has been a favourite philosophic whim to degrade the numerous nations, on whom the sun-beams more directly dart, below the common level of humanity, and hastily to conclude that nature, by making them inferior to the rest of the human race, designed to stamp them with a mark of slavery. How they were shaded down, from the fresh colour of northern rustics, to the sable hue seen on the African sands, is not our task to inquire, nor do we intend to draw a parallel between the abilities of a negro and European mechanic; we shall only observe, that if these volumes do not exhibit extraordinary intellectual powers, sufficient to wipe off the stigma, yet the activity and ingenuity, which conspicuously appear in the character of Gustavus, place him on a par

† July 1789: n.p. Equiano included this review in his third through ninth editions.
‡ "W." was identified by Vincent Carretta as Mary Wollstonecraft. *From Analytical Review, or History of Literature, Domestic and Foreign*, vol. 4 (London: J. Johnson, 1789), pp. 27–28.

with the general mass of men, who fill the subordinate stations in a more civilized society than that which he was thrown into at his birth.

The first volume contains, with a variety of other matter, a short description of the manners of his native country, an account of his family, his being kidnapped with his sister, his journey to the sea coast, and terror when carried on shipboard. Many anecdotes are simply told, relative to the treatment of male and female slaves, on the voyage, and in the West Indies, which make the blood turn its course; and the whole account of his unwearied endeavours to obtain his freedom, is very interesting. The narrative should have closed when he once more became his own master. The latter part of the second volume appears flat; and he is entangled in many, comparatively speaking, insignificant cares, which almost efface the lively impression made by the miseries of the slave. The long account of his religious sentiments and conversion to methodism, is rather tiresome.

Throughout, a kind of contradiction is apparent: many childish stories and puerile remarks, do not agree with some more solid reflections, which occur in the first pages. In the style also we observed a striking contrast: a few well written periods do not smoothly unite with the general tenor of the language.

* * *

RICHARD GOUGH

From *Gentleman's Magazine* (June 1789)†

* * *

Among other contrivances (and perhaps one of the most innocent) to interest the national humanity in favour of the Negro slaves, one of them here writes his own history, as formerly another of them published his correspondence * * *. These memoirs, written in a very unequal style, place the writer on a par with the general mass of men in the subordinate stations of civilised society, and prove that there is no general rule without an exception. The first volume treats of the manners of his countrymen, and his own adventures till he obtained his freedom; the second, from that period to the present, is uninteresting; and his conversion to methodism oversets the whole.

† June 1789: 539.

HENRI GRÉGOIRE

Vassa†

Olaudah Equiano, better known by the name of Gustavus Vassa, was born in 1746 [sic], at Essaka, a beautiful and charming valley far distant from the coast and capital of Benin. It is considered a part of Benin, although it is largely self-governing under the authority of elders or chiefs, one of whom was his father.

At the age of eleven, Vassa was carried off together with his sister, by robbers who stole children to take them into slavery. These barbarians soon deprived him even of the consolation of mingling his tears with those of his sister. He was forever separated from her and thrown into a slave ship. After his passage across the ocean, under terrible conditions which he relates, he was sold in Barbados, and resold to a lieutenant commander of a vessel who brought him to England. He accompanied him to Guernsey, to the siege of Louisbourg in Canada by Admiral Bascaven [Boscawen], in 1758, and to the siege of Belle-isle, in 1761.

When events brought him back to the New World he was, through treachery, again put in irons. Sold into slavery in Montserrat, Vassa became the plaything of fortune, sometimes free, sometimes a slave or a domestic servant. He made many voyages to most of the Antilles and to different points on the American continent. He often returned to Europe, visited Spain, Portugal, Italy, Turkey, and Greenland. The love of freedom, whose first fruits he had tasted in his childhood, increasingly tormented his mind because of the obstacles that prevented him from recovering freedom. He hoped in vain that a consistent zeal for the interests of his masters would be a sure means to this end. Justice would have found in his zeal another reason for breaking his chains, but for greed it was a motive for riveting them tighter. He saw that with men possessed by the thirst for gold he had to have recourse to other means. Then he forced himself to live as economically as possible, and with three pence he began small trade that brought him a modest nest egg, in spite of the many losses he sustained through the thievery of the whites. Finally in 1781, having escaped the dangers of the sea and several shipwrecks, and having survived the cruelty of his masters, one of whom, in Savannah, almost murdered him, Vassa, after thirty years of a wandering and stormy life, was restored to liberty and

† From *On the Cultural Achievements of Negroes*, (orig. 1808), transl. with notes and introduction by Thomas Cassirer and Jean-François Brière (Amherst: University of Massachusetts Press, 1996), pp. 102–5. Copyright © 1996 by Thomas Cassirer and Jean-François Brière. Reproduced by permission of the publisher.

settled in London, where he married and published his memoirs,[1] which have been reprinted several times in both hemispheres. It is proven by the most respectable testimony that he was the Author. This precaution is necessary against a class of individuals who are always disposed to slander the Negroes in order to extenuate the crimes of their oppressors.

The book is written with the naïveté, (I could almost say the roughness) of a man of nature. His manner is that of Daniel Defoe in his *Robinson Crusoe*, or that of Jamerai Duval, who rose from a cowherd to hermit to librarian of Emperor Francis I, and whose unpublished memoirs, so worthy of publication, are in the hands of Ameilhon.[2]

We share the feelings of surprise that Vassa experienced at the shock of an earthquake, the appearance of snow, a painting, a watch, and a quadrant, and we follow him as he questions his reason about the use of those instruments. The art of navigation had an inexpressible attraction for him: He also saw it as a way of one day escaping from slavery. He made an agreement with the captain of a vessel to give him lessons. They were often interrupted, but his initiative and intelligence made up for this. While he was a servant to Dr. Irving, he learned from him the method of desalting sea water by distillation. Some time afterward Vassa was a member of an expedition to find a passage to the North. When the expedition found itself in distress he used the doctor's procedure to provide drinking water for the crew.

Although he was taken from his country when he was quite young, he retained a rich store of recollections, thanks to his affection for his family and a good memory. We read with interest the description he has given of his country, where luxuriant nature has been prodigal of her bounties. Agriculture is the principal occupation of the inhabitants, who are very industrious, although they are passionately fond of poetry, music, and dancing. Vassa remembers clearly that the physicians of Benin drew blood by means of cupping glasses, and that they excel in the art of healing wounds and overcoming the effect of poisons. He draws an interesting picture of the superstitions and customs of his country, which he contrasts with those of countries where he has traveled. Thus, in Smyrna he finds that the Greeks have dances that are common in Benin; he compares the customs of the Jews and those of his fellow countrymen, among whom circumcision is generally practiced. In his country anyone who touches a dead body is considered to have become impure, according to law, and the women are subject to the same purifying rites as among the Hebrews.

1. *The interesting Narrative of the life of Olaudah Equiano, or Gustavus Vassa, the African, written by himself,* 9th ed., 8vo. (London, 1794), with the portrait of the Author.
2. The two volumes that have been published constitute the smaller and less interesting part of his writings. (Hubert Pascal Ameilhon [1730–1811] published books on Egyptian hieroglyphs and commerce. [*Editor*].)

Adversity often has the effect of strengthening religious sentiment. When we are struck by misfortune and abandoned on earth by our fellow men, we turn our eyes toward Heaven where we seek consolation and a father. Such was the case with Vassa; he did not sink under the unending load of evils that pressed upon him. Imbued with the presence of the Supreme Being, he directed his view beyond the bounds of life, toward a new land.

He hesitated a long time on his choice of a faith, and he gives a striking description of his anguish in a poem of 112 lines, written in English, that he inserted into his memoirs. He was shocked to see that in all Christian groups there were so many individuals whose actions are in direct opposition to their principles and who blaspheme the name of God, whom they profess to worship. For example, he felt indignant that the king of Naples and his court went every Sunday to the opera. He saw that some observed four precepts of the ten commandments, others six or seven, and he could not conceive how anyone could be half-virtuous. He did not realize that, in the words of Nicole,[3] we cannot deduce the doctrine from conduct, nor conduct from the doctrine. He was baptized in the Anglican church and, after a long period of uncertainty, turned Methodist and was almost sent as missionary to Africa. In the school of adversity Vassa had become very sensitive to the misfortunes of others, and no one could more justifiably claim the maxim of Terence (*Homo sum: nil humani alienum mihi puto*, I am a man and consider nothing human foreign to me, *Heautontimoroumenos*, line 77. *Cassirer and Brière*). He deplored the fate of the Greeks, who were treated by the Turks in almost the same manner as the Negroes by the colonists. He even felt pity for the galley slaves of Genoa, because their punishment went beyond the bounds of justice.

He saw his African countrymen fall victim to all the tortures that greed and rage could invent. He contrasted this cruelty with its antithesis, the morality of the Gospel. He proposed a plan of commerce between Europe and Africa, which at the least would not wound justice. In 1789 he presented to the Parliament of England a petition for the suppression of the slave trade. If Vassa is still living, the bill that was lately passed, must be a consolation to his heart and to his old age. Anyone is to be pitied, for sure, who does not feel affection for Vassa, after reading his memoirs.

3. Pierre Nicole (1625–1695) was a French Catholic theologian who represented the reform movement known as Jansenism [*Editor*].

LYDIA MARIA CHILD

[Olaudah Equiano]†

* * *

Olaudah Equiano, better known by the name of Gustavus Vasa, was stolen in Africa, at twelve years old, together with his sister. They were torn from each other; and the brother, after a horrible passage in a slave ship, was sold at Barbadoes. Being purchased by a lieutenant, he accompanied his new master to England, Guernsey, and the siege of Louisbourg. He afterwards experienced great changes of fortune, and made voyages to various parts of Europe and America. In all his wanderings, he cherished an earnest desire for freedom. He hoped to obtain his liberty by faithfulness and zeal in his master's service; but finding avarice stronger than benevolence, he began trade with a capital of three pence, and by rigid economy was at last able to purchase—*his own body and soul*; this, however, was not effected, until he had endured much oppression and insult. He was several times shipwrecked, and finally, after thirty years of vicissitude and suffering, he settled in London and published his Memoirs. The book is said to be written with all the simplicity, and something of the roughness, of uneducated nature. He gives a *naïve* description of his terror at an earthquake, his surprise when he first saw snow, a picture, a watch, and a quadrant.

He always had an earnest desire to understand navigation, as a probable means of one day escaping from slavery. Having persuaded a sea-captain to give him lessons, he applied himself with great diligence, though obliged to contend with many obstacles, and subject to frequent interruptions. Doctor Irving, with whom he once lived as a servant, taught him to render salt water fresh by distillation. Some time after, when engaged in a northern expedition, he made good use of this knowledge, and furnished the crew with water they could drink.

His sympathies were, very naturally, given to the weak and the despised, wherever he found them. He deplores the fate of modern Greeks, nearly as much degraded by the Turks as the negroes are by their white brethren. In 1789, Vasa presented a petition to the British parliament, for the suppression of the slave trade.

* * *

---

† From *An Appeal in Favor of That Class of Americans Called Africans*, ed. Carolyn L. Karcher (1833; repr. Amherst: University of Massachusetts Press, 1996), pp. 151–52.

Modern Criticism

PAUL EDWARDS

From Introduction to *The Life of Olaudah Equiano*†

Olaudah Equiano was born around the year 1745, probably rather to the east of the modern Nigerian city of Onitsha.[1] There are slight inconsistencies in his account of his age. He says that he was turned eleven when captured (I. 47) [32] and that his journey to the coast took six or seven months, which would have made him almost twelve when he left Africa. But he speaks of himself as "near twelve years of age" on his arrival in England about a year later (I. 103) [48]. All the same, we can take it that the date he gives for his birth is approximately right, within about a year.

He was taken by slave-ship first to Barbados, then to Virginia, where he was purchased by a Lieutenant Pascal of the British navy. He served in the Seven Years War with General Wolfe in Canada and Admiral Boscawen in the Mediterranean. Captain Pascal re-sold him into slavery, and he worked for some time aboard the ships of Robert King, a Quaker merchant of Philadelphia who helped him purchase his freedom. His subsequent adventures included voyages to the Arctic with the Phipps expedition of 1772–3, a grand tour of the Mediterranean as personal servant to an English gentleman, and six months amongst the Miskito Indians of Central America. He was appointed Commissary for Stores to the 1787 expedition to re-settle freed slaves in Sierra Leone, but was dismissed after disagreements with the leaders of the expedition, and so never returned to Africa.

In 1792 he married Susanna Cullen, whose family lived in Ely, at Soham Church, Cambridgeshire. The marriage is recorded in the *Gentleman's Magazine* (1792, Part I, p. 384) and in an entry in Soham Church register for April 7th 1792. * * * In his will of May 1796 Equiano indicates that his wife, Susanna, had pre-deceased him, and refers

---

† From *The Life of Olaudah Equiano, or Gustavus Vassa, the African* (London: Dawsons of Pall Mall, 1969), pp. v–lxxii. The Colonial History Series. Bracketed page numbers refer to this Norton Critical Edition.
1. For a discussion of Equiano's birthplace, see below, pp. 308–14.

to his daughters Ann Maria and Johanna. On a slip of paper in the Royal Commonwealth Society Library copy of the 1814 Leeds edition of Equiano, there is the following note:

> Near this place lies interred
> Ann Maria Vassa
> Daughter of Gustavus Vassa
> the African she died July 21
> 1797 aged 4 years.
> Should simple village rhymes attract thine eye
> Strangers as thoughtfully as thou passest by
> Know that there lies beside this humble stone
> A child of colour haply not thine own
> Her father born of Afric's sun burnt race
> Torn from his native fields, oh foul disgrace
> Through various toils at length to britain came
> Espoused, so heaven ordained an English dame
> And follow'd Christ, their hope to infants dear
> But one a hapless orphan slumbers here
> To bury her the village children came
> And droped choice flowers and lisped her only fame
> And some that loved her most as if unblesed
> Bedewed with tears the white wreaths on their breast
> but she is gone and dwells in that abode
> were [sic] some of every clime shall join in God

As this has only recently come to light, it has not yet been possible to identify the source of the poem, which is presumably a memorial tablet inscription. The reference to "village children" would indicate, however, that the child's death did not take place in London, where her father had died three months earlier on March 31st, 1797.[2] It may be that Equiano's widow had returned after his death either to her father's home at Ely, or possibly to the village of Soham, where she had been married, though there is no sign of this inscription at Soham parish church.

*   *   *

The Authorship of the Narrative

There is a long history of doubt as to whether, in fact, Equiano was the sole author of the *Narrative*. Not long after its publication the *Monthly Review* wrote:

> . . . it is not improbable that some English writer has assisted him in the compilement, or at least the correction of his book; for it is sufficiently well written.[3]

2. The *Gentleman's Magazine*, Vol. 67, p. 356.
3. The *Monthly Review*, June 1789, p. 551. [See p. 295 of this NCE. *Editor.*]

More recently, G. I. Jones has written that "the style is far too close to the literary standards of the period to have been entirely his own work".[4] These doubts are reasonable in view of precedents for the "ghosting" or revision of other 18th century works by Africans living in England. Gronniosaw's A *Narrative of the most remarkable particulars in the Life of James Albert Ukawsaw Gronniosaw* (Bath, 1770?) was, according to its preface, "taken from his own mouth and committed to paper by the elegant pen of a young lady of the town of Leominster". Christopher Fyfe[5] has suggested reasons for doubting the authenticity of the book by Equiano's friend, Ottobah Cugoano, *Thoughts and Sentiments on the Evil and Wicked Traffic of . . . Slavery* (London, 1787). Even the letter written by Ignatius Sancho to Lawrence Sterne in 1766 was "improved" by Sterne despite its excellent English, presumably with a view to its publication amongst his own papers.[6]

At the same time it must be remembered that Equiano had a considerable amount of schooling, both formal and informal, after his enslavement. Equiano's first teacher was Richard Baker, whom he met on the voyage from the American plantations to England in 1757, a long passage of thirteen weeks (I. 103) [47] during which Dick showed him "a great deal of partiality and attention", helping him with his English. "For the space of two years", Equiano tells us, "he was of very great use to me, and was my constant companion and instructor." Equiano stayed with an English family for six months on his arrival in England, and the mother of his playmate Mary, he says, "behaved to me with great kindness [* * *] and taught me every thing in the same manner as she did her own child, and, indeed, in every respect, treated me as such". (I. 109) [49] The following year, he tells us,

> I could now speak English tolerably well, and I perfectly understood every thing that was said. I now not only felt myself quite easy with these new countrymen, but relished their society and manners. I no longer looked upon them as spirits, but as men superior to us; and I therefore had the stronger desire to resemble them; to imbibe their spirit, and imitate their manners. * * * I therefore embraced every occasion of improvement; and every new thing that I observed I treasured up in my memory. I had long wished to be able to read and write; and for this purpose I took every opportunity to gain instruction, but had made as yet very little progress. However, when I went to London with my master, I had soon an opportunity of improving myself, which I gladly embraced. Shortly after my arrival, he sent me to wait upon

4. In Philip Curtin (ed.), *Africa Remembered*, University of Wisconsin Press, 1967, p. 69.
5. Christopher Fyfe, *History of Sierra Leone*, OUP, 1962, p. 13. See also Paul Edwards (ed.), Cugoano's *Thoughts and Sentiments*, etc., Dawsons, 1968, pp. vii–xi, for evidence against Cugoano's authorship.
6. L. P. Curtis (ed.), *Letters of Lawrence Sterne*, OUP, 1935, pp. 285–7.

the Miss Guerins, who had treated me with such kindness when I was there before; and they sent me to school. (I. 132–3) [56]

Schooling did not end when he went to sea. On the fireship, *Aetna*, he says,

I had leisure to improve myself in reading and writing. The latter I had learned a little of before I left the Namur, as there was a school on board. (I. 151–2) [62]

The *Namur* was the ship he had gone to immediately after leaving the house of the Misses Guerin, in 1759, at about the age of fourteen or fifteen. Seven years later he was to get his freedom, after which he spent much of his life in the company of educated Englishmen, as a valet and hairdresser, a doctor's assistant, and the associate of many of the leading abolitionists. Since he did not publish his book until the age of forty four, it need not be so surprising that by this time he had achieved a considerable mastery of the language.

Further evidence for the authenticity of the *Narrative* is the occurrence of a high proportion of West African English rhymes in a poem included in the text (II. 155–9) [146–49]. Such rhymes as *sin/between*, *relieve/give*, and *sin/clean* are distinctive of the characteristic merging, in West African English speech, of the vowels [i] and [i:]. Others, like *been/pain*, *word/Lord*, *do/woe*, *good/showed*, and *please/release*, might all be rhymed occasionally in 18th century verse, but are strongly indicative of a West African author, in view of the context in which they appear and the cluster they form. Since it is virtually certain that these lines were written by a West African there seems no reason to doubt that they were written by Equiano himself. The poem is not a good one, but it is far from being incompetent, and better, indeed, than many verses written by native speakers of English. It seems likely, too, that had Equiano's *Narrative* been very extensively revised by a native speaker of English, these rhymes would have been revised in the process. In the circumstances, then, the evidence points strongly to the *Narrative* being Equiano's own work, though one might have reservations about some of the more rhetorical episodes, which perhaps show traces of a reviser's hand.

The strongest evidence, however, is a manuscript letter by Equiano in the Hornby Collection in Liverpool City Library, addressed to "The Revd. G. Walker, at Nottingham". The letter reads:

London Feby the 27.th—1792
Dr. Revd. & Worthy friends &c.
This with my Best of Respects to you and wife with many Prayers that you both may ever be Well in Souls and Bodys—& also your Little Lovely Daughter—I thank you

for all kindnesses which you[7] was please to
show me, may God ever Reward you for
it—Sir, I went to Ireland & was there
8½ months—& sold 1900 copies of my
narrative. I came here on the 10th inst.—&
I now mean as it seem Pleasing to my Good
God!—to leave London in about 8—or 10
Days more, & take me a Wife–(one Miss
Cullen—) of Soham in Cambridge shire—
& when I have given her about 8 or 10 Days
Comfort, I mean Directly to go to Scotland
—and sell my 5th. Editions—I Trust that
my going about has been of much use to the
Cause of the Abolition of the accused Slave
Trade—a Gentleman of the Committee the
Revd. Dr. Baker has said that I am more
use to the Cause than half the People in the
Country—I wish to God, I could be so. a
noble Earl of Stanhope has Lately Con-
sulted me twice about a Bill which his
Ld.ship now mean to bring in to the House
to allow the sable People of the wt. Indias
the Rights of taking an oath against any
White Person—I hope it may Pass, tis high
time—& will be of much use.—May the
Lord Bless all the friends of Humanity.
Pray Pardon what ever you here[8] see
amiss—I will be Glad to see you at my
Wedg.—Pray give my best Love To the
Worthy & Revd. Mr. Robinson, & his—
also to my friends Coltman—& Mr. & Mrs.
Buxton—I Pray that the Good Lord may
make all of that family Rich in faith as in
the things of this World[9]—I have Great
Deal to say if I ever have the Pleasure to see
you again—I have been in the uttermust
hurry[1] ever since I have being in this
wickd. Town—& I only came now to save
if I can, £.232, I Lent to a man, who now
Dying. Pray Excuse have[2]—will be Glad
to hear from you—& do very much beg

7. was] *intercalated.*
8. here] *intercalated.*
9. as in the things of this World] *added at foot of page.*
1. hurry] *above* hast *deleted.*
2. have] haste?

your Prayers as you ever have mine—& if
I see you no more here Below may I see you
all at Last at Gods Right Hand—where
parting will be no more—Glory to God
that J. Christ is yet all, & in all, to my Poor
Soul—
    I am with all Due Respects
      yours to Command—
         Gustavus Vassa
         The African
      —————at Mr. Hardys No. 4 Taylors
Building Chandos street, Covent Garden
[*Reverse side*]
P.S. you see how I am confused—Pray
excuse this mistake of the frank—
for Mr. Housman
Pray mind the Africans from the Pulpits—

On one hand, this letter shows Equiano to have been fluent and articulate in English, and fully capable of writing an account of his life. On the other, it contains occasional lapses in spelling and grammar which do not occur in the *Narrative*, and so appear to suggest the likelihood of some revision, though not of "ghosting". However, the spelling errors are trivial—*accused* for *accursed* (line 20) and *uttermust* for *uttermost* (line 42); *bodys* (line 5) is an occasional eighteenth-century spelling. Nor can the rather erratic punctuation be taken as evidence of anything more than carelessness through haste, particularly since it is a feature of a great deal of eighteenth-century casual writing. That the letter was in fact written at speed is indicated by several references to this in the text. The handwriting also suggests great haste, for we can compare it with a sample of Equiano's best hand on a flyleaf taken from one of his books—this flyleaf is also in the Hornby collection at Liverpool, and reads as follows:

         Gustavus V.
    His Book.—————
         Given to him
By that Truly Pious,
And Benevolent man
Mr. Granville Sharp.
    April the 13th 1779.
      London—————

This is written in a most elegant, flowing hand though clearly Equiano's from the signature, being in the same hand as that of the hastily scrawled letter.

    Certain of the errors in the letter are simply those of carelessness—

the word *have* for *haste* (line 46) is an obvious example. Two errors are the result of missing words, *Great Deal* for *a Great Deal* (lines 40–41) and *who now Dying* for *who is now Dying* (lines 45–46). Two more are caused by faulty verb endings, *please* for *pleased* (line 7) and *mean* for *means* (line 27). Yet in each of these cases, the correct form appears at some other point in the letter, again showing that haste, not ignorance, was the cause of the mistake—incidentally, each of these four mistakes is common in British students' examination papers. *You was please(d)* (line 7) is not a mistake, but a fairly common eighteenth-century form. There is one mistake which may well originate in pronunciation (I think probably West African, though this could also be a native pronunciation error), *since I have being* for *since I have been* (line 43); but again we see that Equiano knows the correct form, for in the same sentence we have *I have been in the utterm(o)st hurry*. Finally, there is the use of the indefinite article in *a Noble Earl of Stanhope has Lately Consulted me* (lines 25–26). But it seems probable that Equiano intended to write *a noble Earl has lately consulted me*, and carelessly completed the Earl's title without changing the article. Elsewhere in the letter he knows the correct use of the article—*a Gentleman of the Committee* (line 21), *my best Love To the Worthy and Revd. Mr. Robinson* (lines 35–36).

It would be reasonable to conclude from this letter, then, that Equiano's English was fluent enough for him to have written his autobiography without any assistance. Occasional lapses in the letter might suggest that someone would, perhaps, have been required to make minor corrections on reading the manuscript or proofs of the autobiography. At the same time, since Equiano clearly knows the correct form even when his letter is in error, there is no reason to think him incapable of correcting his own manuscript and proofs.

Equiano's Description of Africa

I

It is impossible to locate Equiano's birthplace, Essaka, with any great precision, and suggestions have been made placing it to both east and west of the Niger. However, the few words of his native language recorded in the *Narrative* leave no doubt that Equiano was an Ibo. The word for year, "Ah-affoe", is clearly the modern Ibo word *afo*; and though his word for "calculators or yearly men", recorded as "Ah-affoe-way-cah", does not exist in modern Ibo, in addition to "affoe" it contains the word *ka*, one meaning of which is "to fix a date" (i.e. for festivals). The word "Embrenché" signifying "a mark of grandeur" is the modern *mgburichi*, the name given to those who either receive or make the *ichi* facial scars, the mark of a titled man. The word is recorded by other early writers: John Adams notes that the Ibo word for a gentleman is *Breeché*[3] and J. Africanus Horton, describing markings made at Isuama, says that "the people so tattooed are called Mbritshi or Itshi".[4] It is significant in any attempt to locate Essaka that such markings are unknown west of the Niger and are characteristic of the Nri-Awka area, to the east of Onitsha. G. I. Jones[5] suggests that the *ichi* scarification may have been used to the west of the Niger in the 18th century, believing as he does that Equiano was a Western Ibo. But I shall argue below that Equiano probably came from east of the Niger, and his mention of *mgburichi* serves to reinforce this view.

Finally there is the word "Oye-Eboe", the "red men living at a distance!" This can hardly be *oyibo*, white man, a late Ibo borrowing from Yoruba; Chinua Achebe[6] thinks that "Oye-Eboe could mean *onye Igbo*, Ibo man—in the past Igbo was applied to the next clan." But he makes an even more striking suggestion, that "if the large river is the Niger, the 'Oye-Eboe' could well be the people from Aboh (*onye Aboh*). These riverain people are reputed to be light skinned." Aboh, on the Niger to the south of Onitsha, is sometimes called "Ebo" by earlier writers.[7] The rulers of Aboh drew their authority from the Kings of Benin, and only a few years before the birth of Equiano "two claimants to the stool at Ebo (Aboh) appealed to the Oba (i.e. of Benin) as their overlord to decide who was the rightful heir".[8]

If the "Oye-Eboe" were in fact Aboh-men, this might well help to explain Equiano's statement about the "nominal" subjection of Essaka to the King of Benin. At first sight, this statement seems to indicate a western location for Essaka, as G. I. Jones argues; but we should not ignore "the powerful influence which this kingdom exerted over the imagination of her neighbours, particularly in south-eastern Nigeria, where her power was felt by Ibo and Ibo-speaking peoples east of the Niger".[9] It would be by such people as Benin-dominated Aboh traders that the almost fabulous reputation of Benin would be spread amongst the eastern Ibo.

In arguing the case for a western location of Essaka, Jones claims that the name Equiano is "Ekwuno . . . a common Ika and riverain Ibo name." On the other hand, names similar to Equiano are found east of the Niger: I have been told of *ekwuano*, meaning "When they speak others attend", and Achebe writes of two occurrences of the name *ekweano*, meaning "If they agree I shall stay" near the Onitsha-Orlu boundary. Jones speaks of the dominance of Benin to the west of the

---

3. John Adams, *Sketches Taken during Ten Voyages*, etc., London, 1822, pp 41–2.
4. James Africanus Horton, *West African Countries and Peoples*, London, 1868, p. 178.
5. See Philip D. Curtin (ed.), *Africa Remembered*, University of Wisconsin Press, 1967, pp. 60–9.
6. All suggestions by Chinua Achebe were made in personal communications.
7. Achebe writes: "*Onye Ebo* is the way a native speaker refers to himself in the Aboh dialect."
8. J. E. Egharevba, *A Short History of Benin*, Ibadan, 1960, p. 41.
9. K. Dike, *Trade and Politics in the Niger Delta*, OUP, 1956, p. 21.

Niger, but as we have seen this is not conclusive evidence, as Equiano remarks that "our subjection to the King of Benin was little more than nominal". Jones acknowledges that the description of Essaka houses resembles the eastern Nri-Awka Ibo rather than the western Ika, which "conform to the Benin pattern", but makes the assumption, similar to the one he makes about *mgburichi*, that in the 18th century western Ibo houses may have followed the present eastern Ibo pattern. The same argument is again put forward about the "small pieces of coin . . . something like an anchor" which Equiano says were used in Essaka (I. 18) [24]. Jones observes, "it would seem, from Olaudah's description, that this sort also existed west of the Niger". In fact currency of this kind has only been found to the east of the Niger, the "*umumu* currency consisting of tiny arrow shaped pieces of iron" noted by Forde and Jones[1] as still found in the eastern Onitsha region. Basden[2] writes about these coins as follows: "In the area between Awka and Enugu, a novel currency was discovered . . . formed of tiny pieces of thin flat iron, half an inch in length, with one end barbed, resembling a miniature arrow-head. . . . Awka men, in former days, used the 'umumu' extensively for the purchase of slaves from the people of Umu-Mba." Jones points out that cotton-growing and indigo-dyeing are largely confined to the west of the Niger, though in the case of the latter it is not clear whether the blue dye mentioned by Equiano (I. 12) [22] was in fact obtained from indigo, since this comes from the leaves of the plant whereas Equiano's dye came from the berries. In any case, this has to be set against a very great deal that indicates an eastern location, or at least leaves the question open. And if we turn to Equiano's account of his journey to the coast, we find once more firm pointers towards the east bank of the Niger.

To begin with, Equiano tells us that the Oye-Eboe lived to the south-west of his home, and we have seen evidence pointing to Aboh as the possible home of the Oye-Eboe. Equiano tells us that he was particular to note the direction he was travelling in, which would be likely to remain firmly fixed in his memory, since it would have been a matter of the greatest importance to him:

> I had also remarked where the sun rose in the morning and set in the evening, as I had travelled along; and I had observed that my father's house was towards the rising of the sun (I. 52–3) [33].

Had he set out from the west of the Niger, to travel east like this would be to move away from the general direction of the great slave ports of the Niger Delta.[3] More plausible would be a journey from the east,

1. Daryll Forde and G. I. Jones, *The Ibo and Ibibio-speaking Peoples of South-Eastern Nigeria*, OUP, 1950, p. 15.
2. G. T. Basden, *Niger Ibos*, London, 1938, p. 339.
3. Jones ignores Equiano's statement that the Oye-Eboe lived to the south-west, and speaks of them as coming from "east of the Niger" (p. 62), which would be impossible if Essaka were

westward towards the Niger, the "large river", or one of the delta rivers, and from there a passage by boat to the slave port.

Now one should not insist on too literal a reading of Equiano's journey, since it is unlikely that a man in his mid-forties would be able to recall with total accuracy such a catastrophic experience of his childhood. Even so, Equiano's account squares well with the description of these slave routes given by John Adams and Hugh Crow. The tribe living in boats who spoke a different language and terrified Equiano so much may very well have been Ibibio. Certainly the Ibos at this time, and later, were afraid of them and the boat-dwellers bear a distinct resemblance, as Equiano describes them, to the Ibibios of Adams and Crow. Adams wrote of them:

> To this nation the Heebos express a very strong aversion and call them cannibals. They certainly have a ferocious aspect . . . very black skins and their teeth filed so as to resemble a saw.[4]

Crow gives this description of the Ibibios living to the north of Bonny, the Creek-men as he calls them:

> When they attain the age of seven or eight years their teeth are sharpened with a file, and they do not hesitate to acknowledge that they devour each other when the occasion offers. They live almost constantly in their canoes, in creeks and corners, and procure a precarious subsistence by marauding and plundering.[5]

Adams gives an account of the last stages of the slave journey down the Niger to Bonny which resembles closely Equiano's record of his experience:

> Fairs, where the slaves of the Heebo nation are obtained, are held every five or six weeks at several villages, which are situated upon the banks of rivers and creeks of the interior, and to which the traders of Bonny resort to purchase them . . . Large canoes, capable of carrying 120 persons are launched and stored for the voyage. . . . At the expiration of the sixth day they generally return, bringing with them 1,500 or 2,000 slaves, who are sold to Europeans the evening after their arrival, and taken on board the ships.[6]

Up to the time that he met these people, Equiano tells us that "all the nations and people . . . resembled our own in their manner, customs

---

west of the Niger. He recognises, Ibo being spoken all the way to the coast, that the slave port from which Equiano sailed was most likely to have been one of the delta ports—Brass, Kalabari or Bonny (Curtin, *op. cit.*, p. 69)—which would not fit at all the account Equiano gives of his journey had it begun west of the Niger. The figures of the numbers of slaves taken from various West African ports in E. Donnan, *Documents Illustrative of the History of the Slave Trade to America*, Washington D.C., 1931, Vol. II, pp. 496 f., make it clear that Bonny and Calabar handled slaves on a far larger scale than ports further west.

4. Adams, *op. cit.*, pp. 40–1. Of course, as Jones points out, the filing of teeth is common.
5. Hugh Crow, *Memoirs*, London, 1830, p. 143.
6. Hugh Crow, *op. cit.*, pp. 38–9.

and language" (I. 66) [37]. He also says that "from the time I left my own nation I always found somebody that understood me till I came to the sea coast" (I. 59) [35] so that the "various languages" he acquired, which did not "totally differ", were presumably dialects of Ibo. There would, of course, have been Ibos living all the way down the slave route to the coast.

Clearly the precise location of Essaka is open to doubt, but the evidence seems to indicate most strongly an area to the east of Onitsha and some distance away from the Niger. Achebe suggests the village of Iseke, on the Onitsha-Orlu boundary, as a very likely spot. My own feeling is that in general the evidence points further north, to the area round Awka, and indeed the name Awka might be the second element of Essaka, which could be an anglicized form of some such name as Ezi-Awka. In the end, however, it seems too ambitious to try to identify Essaka as exactly as this.

II

The description of Ibo life and society given by Equiano conforms closely in most respects to present day practice. The religious practices—the belief in transmigration, the cult of ancestors, the worship of a supreme deity—are all recognizable. Equiano's "one Creator" who lives in the sun is Chukwu, who is often said to live in the sun or is identified with the Sun, Anyanwu.[7]

The wearing of a belt "that he may never eat or drink" may reflect the comparative rarity of direct sacrifices to Chukwu in parts of Ibo.[8] The fastidiousness over touching the dead or menstruating women (I. 32) [28] is still common,[9] and Equiano's descriptions of dancing, marriage ceremonies, musical instruments, blood letting, swearing, and the fear of poison are close to modern custom and belief. One peculiarity however is his description of the women warriors (I. 25–6) [26]. At first sight this seems highly unlikely since the women of the Ibo are traditionally the peacemakers—"in war it is the function of the women to override the fighting of the men and make peace . . . the female principle seems to be, in general, associated with a cooling, pacifying influence".[1] Equiano tells us, however, that not only did the women of Essaka fight, but wherever he travelled from his home to the coast, women were "trained in the arts of war" (I. 70) [38]. Jones notes this as puzzling[2] but adds that "there are recorded cases . . . of Isuama Ibo

7. See C. K. Meek, *Law and Authority in a Nigerian Tribe*, OUP, 1937, p. 21; Talbot, *op. cit.*, II, 43; Forde and Jones, *op. cit.*, p. 25.
8. See Meek, *op. cit.*, p. 20; Forde and Jones, *op. cit.*, p. 25. For details of transmigration and the ancestor cult see Meek, *op. cit.*, pp. 54–5 and 61–79.
9. See Meek, *op. cit.*, pp. 308 and 279 n.
1. M. M. Green, *Ibo Village Affairs*, Sidgwick and Jackson, 1947, p. 177.
2. See Curtin, *op. cit.*, p. 66.

villages which were smaller than their neighbours and which made up for their deficient manpower by encouraging their womenfolk to fight alongside their husbands in defence of their farmlands". And in the 1929 women's riots, the women of the Ibo displayed a frightening degree of aggressiveness. It may have been that in the past Ibo women were called upon more often to help their men in this way, and indeed, there is an Ibo legend that tells how God decided not to allow women to fight in war because they were so fierce they could have destroyed the whole world. Horton[3] quotes Samuel Crowther as recording that the Ibo women follow their men into battle "and are employed in removing the dead and wounded out of the way". In fact, it may well be that Equiano's information, however surprising, is perfectly accurate.

There are one or two instances in which Equiano's memory may have let him down, though these are all of them minor. He describes the Ibo tobacco pipes as enormously long, whereas they were probably short, as they are today. Jones suggests that Equiano is confusing these with pipes that he saw in the Levant.[4] And in referring to the pipe's being carried "out of grandeur by two boys", Equiano may have been influenced by his friend Cugoano, a Fanti. Writing of the Fanti, Adams refers to "the boy who carried the smoking apparatus belonging to a gentleman",[5] and no doubt Equiano, talking over his childhood with other Africans, or reading about their experiences, might sometimes confuse the two. There is at least one instance in the *Narrative* where this has happened.[6] Equiano's statement that he never saw anyone intoxicated with palm-wine (I. 14) [23] could be a consequence of wishful thinking, brought about by his Methodism and his desire to present his own people in a favourable light; but it is true that fresh palm-wine is not intoxicating, and that traditionally, the Ibos have not shown great interest in strong drink. Basden remarks that in early days "the Ibos were not acquainted with any method of brewing intoxicating liquor. . . . Comparatively few of the old men could be designated drunkards. In any case, it is not a common weakness and the Ibos generally can be classed as a sober people."[7] The computing of the year from "the day on which the sun crosses the line" (I. 29) [27] does not appear to be accurate, since the Ibo year is calculated in terms of 13 lunar months. But the festival sounds like "Aro-Ichu-Aja, sometimes known as 'Igu-Aro'—the counting of the year. . . . During the late afternoon and evening there is much firing of guns. The feast follows, the women bringing what they have prepared . . . After all have partaken,

---

3. James Africanus Horton, *op. cit.*, p. 179.
4. Curtin, *op. cit.*, p. 73n.
5. Adams, *op. cit.*, p. 8.
6. See below, p. 323–24, for a discussion of a borrowing from Gronniosaw.
7. Basden, *op. cit.*, p. 125.

more gun firing follows. . . ."[8] There is a slight confusion over the "crowing snake" (I. 37) [29] which Equiano says is harmless. In fact this snake, called *ubi*, which is still commonly believed to crow, is dangerous, and the harmless domesticated snake was probably the python (*eke*). The powdered wood (I. 15) [23] which Equiano says was mixed with oil and used to perfume the body, is presumably camwood, but this does not have the "delicious fragrance" Equiano ascribes to it. Nor are locusts considered a pest by the Ibos, who commonly eat them as a delicacy when they swarm.[9] Equiano's memories seem to have been distorted here by his biblical reading. Lastly, his claim that Benin "seems only terminated at length by the empire of Abyssinia, near 1,500 miles from its beginning" (I. 4) [20] reflects the ignorance of most people at this time of the interior of Africa, about which Swift rhymed his well-known remarks on "Afric maps".

But all in all, in spite of its sketchiness, the closeness of Equiano's account to modern Ibo practice is strong testimony in favour of the reliability of his observation in other respects. There is hardly any imposition of the popular primitivist view of noble savagery, which a more sentimental writer might have been tempted to adopt. His errors appear to be minor lapses or misunderstandings[1] and indeed it would be surprising if Equiano had achieved a totally accurate recall of a society he had left over thirty years before at the age of eleven.

Equiano's Appointment as Commissary for Stores

In November 1786, Equiano was appointed Commissary for Stores for the Black Poor going to Sierra Leone, but after he had quarrelled constantly with the Agent, Joseph Irwin, his appointment was terminated in March 1787, before the expedition left Plymouth for Sierra Leone.

The proposal to found a colony in Sierra Leone for freed slaves was made by Henry Smeathman in 1786. Smeathman was a botanist who had lived some years in Sierra Leone. A year before his proposals for the settlement of freed slaves he had given evidence before a commission that the climate of Sierra Leone would kill off a hundred convicts a month should a convict station be established there. But in 1786 he had plans of his own for the new colony, and so described its climate

---

8. *ibid.*, p. 71.
9. See, for example, Chinna Achebe, *Things Fall Apart*, Heinemann, 1958, pp. 48–9.
1. He appears to be in error on at least two other points in his narrative. Firstly, he says (II. 5)[102] that he heard George Whitefield preach in Pennsylvania early in 1766. Whitefield in fact arrived in England from America on July 7th 1765, and did not leave England again until September 16th 1768. Secondly Equiano claims to have seen Vesuvius in violent eruption in 1770, but records show that paroxysms occurred in 1766 and 1779, between which dates it was comparatively quiescent. It is nevertheless possible that he witnessed a minor eruption.

and fertility with enthusiasm. The Treasury and the Committee for the Relief of the Black Poor accepted his opinions about the suitability of Sierra Leone, but further investigations by the Committee revealed that Smeathman intended to set up estates there using local slave labour, and it looked as though the plans might be dropped. But Smeathman died, and the freed slaves themselves were eager to go to Sierra Leone, choosing Smeathman's friend Irwin themselves as his successor.

However, as the time approached for the sailing, doubts arose in the minds of the intending settlers. Some of them feared that they were being sent to a penal colony, others that they would be sold again as slaves. Ottobah Cugoano, a Fanti and former slave, writing in 1787, summarized their doubts and fears in his *Thoughts and Sentiments on the Evil of Slavery*:

> This prospect of settling of a free colony to Great Britain in a peaceable alliance with the inhabitants of Africa at Sierra Leone, has neither altogether met with the credulous approbation of the Africans here, nor yet been sought after with any prudent and right plan by the promoters of it.

Cugoano complains that no treaty had been made with the African inhabitants of Sierra Leone about the territory of the Colony, that the arrangements had been too hasty up to the time the settlers went aboard, and that there had been too much delay since, resulting in sickness. He also complains that many of the best men among the London Africans had been prevented from going with the expedition "by means of some disagreeable jealousy of those who were appointed as governors". Indeed, many of the Africans in Britain feared to return to Africa, since "a burnt child dreads the fire" and they were insufficiently persuaded of their security and freedom once they would have reached Sierra Leone:

> For it seemed prudent and obvious to many of them taking heed of that sacred enquiry, *Doth a fountain send forth at the same place sweet water and bitter?* They were afraid that their doom would be to drink of the bitter water. For can it readily be conceived that government would establish a free colony for them nearly on the spot, while it supports its forts and garrisons, to ensnare merchandize, and to carry others into captivity and slavery?
> (*Thoughts and Sentiments etc.* pp. 139–142).

Consequently, though a large number had agreed to sail, comparatively few were now prepared to do so and the three ships had to be filled with anyone who could be persuaded to go aboard, including a number of white prostitutes. It may be that these were the passengers "taken on contrary to my orders" about whom Equiano complained in a letter to the *Public Advertiser* of July 14th 1787, and to whom he refers (II. 236) [173] in the *Narrative*; though there is no evidence that the other settlers were against these women being taken aboard, there being a shortage of women amongst them. Matters were further complicated by sickness and bad weather. A delay in Portsmouth for the sickness to clear up was followed by another in Plymouth while storm damage was repaired. Conditions on board were poor and tempers became strained as a result of the delays. Equiano's quarrels with Irwin came to a head when he accused Irwin of embezzling funds and ill-treating the black passengers, and was in turn himself accused of insolent and insubordinate conduct towards the leaders of the expedition.

Equiano wrote a letter on the subject to his friend Cugoano, (often called John Stewart) and this was published in the *Public Advertiser* on April 4th 1787:

> We are sorry to find that his Majesty's Commissary for the African Settlement has sent the following letter to Mr. John Stewart, Pall Mall:

> "At Plymouth, March 24, 1787.
>
> Sir,
>
> These with my respects to you. I am sorry you and some more are not here with us. I am sure Irwin, [*The Agent for Africa*] and Fraser the parson, are great villains, and Dr. Currie. I am exceeding much aggrieved at the conduct of those who call themselves gentlemen. They now mean to serve (or use) the blacks the same as they do in the West Indies. For the good of the settlement I have borne every affront that could be given, believe me, without giving the least occasion, or ever yet resenting any.

> By Sir Charles Middleton's letter to me, I now find Irwin and Fraser have wrote to the Committee and the Treasury, that I use the white people with arrogance, and the blacks with civility, and stir them up to mutiny: which is not true, for I am the greatest peace-maker that goes out. The reason of this lie is, that in the presence of these two, I acquainted Captain Thompson of the Nautilus sloop, our convoy, that I would go to London and tell of their roguery; and further insisted on Captain Thompson to come on board of the ships, and see the wrongs done to me and the people: so Captain Thompson came and saw it, and ordered the things to be given according to contract—which is not yet done in many things—and many of the black people have died for want of their due. I am grieved in every respect. Irwin never meant well to the people, but self-interest has ever been his end: twice this week they have taken him, bodily, to the Captain, to complain of him, and I have done it four times.

> I do not know how this undertaking will end; I wish I had never

been involved in it; but at times I think the Lord will make me very useful at last.

I am, dear Friend,
With respect, your's,
'G. VASA.'
The Commissary for
the Black Poor."

An extract from a letter by another educated African, A. E. Griffith, who was to become secretary to the Timne Chief, Naimbauna, was printed in the same issue of the *Public Advertiser*. "The people, in general, are very sickly", he wrote, "and die very fast indeed, for the doctors are very neglectful of the people, very much so." Two days later, the *Public Advertiser* of April 6th 1787 gave the following account of a report sent up from Plymouth by the dissatisfied settlers, quite likely to have been written by Equiano as their principal spokesman. Curiously, several expressions in this report closely resemble the passage already quoted from Cugoano's *Thoughts and Sentiments*, and could be considered as evidence to support the view that Equiano may have had a hand in writing or revising Cugoano's book.[2] Here is the editorial report:

We find his Majesty's servants have taken away the Commissary's commission from Mr. Vasa—He came up from Plymouth to complain, and is now gone back again to take his effects on shore. The memorials of all the Black peoples which they have sent up from Plymouth, represent that they are much wronged, injured and oppressed natives of Africa, and under various pretences and different manners have been dragged away from London, and carried captives from Plymouth, where they have nothing but slavery before their eyes, should they proceed to Africa or the West Indies under the command of the persons who have the charge of them—That many of them served under Lord Dunmore, and other officers in America, in the British Army—Also on board the British Fleet in the West Indies. That the contract, on Mr. Smeathman's plan to settle them in Africa, has not been fulfilled in their favour, but a Mr. Irwin has contrived to monopolize the benefit to himself.—That they fear a right plan has not been formed to settle them in Africa with any prospect of happiness to themselves, or any hope of future advantage to Great Britain.— They cannot conceive, say they, that Government would establish a free colony for them, whilst it supports its forts and factories to wrong and ensnare, and to carry others of their colour and country into slavery and bondage—They are afraid that their doom would be to drink of the bitter water, and observe that it will be their

---

2. Ottobah Cugoano, *op. cit.*, see *Introduction* to the reprint by Dawsons, 1969, in the *Colonial History Series*.

prudence and safety to take warning from the cautious in Scripture: 'Doth a fountain send forth at the same place sweet water and bitter?'—That they fear the design of some in sending them away, is only to get rid of them at all events, come of them afterwards what will.—In that perilous situation they see themselves surrounded with difficulties and danger; and what gives them the most dreadful presage of their fate is, that the white men set over them have shewn them no humanity or good will, but have conspired to use them unjustly before they quitted the English coast.—And that they had better swim to shore, if they can, to preserve their lives and liberties in Britain, than to hazard themselves at Sea with such enemies to their welfare, and the peril of settling at Sierra Leone under their government.

It was not long before counter-charges were being made against Equiano and others. Comment in the *Public Advertiser* of April 11th 1787 takes a very different line from that of the issue of April 6th: though it should be noted that it is not strictly editorial, but an insertion into an editorial column of the letter of a correspondent, X:

> The Public will naturally suspend their disbelief as to the improbable tales propagated concerning the Blacks, especially as the cloven foot of the author of these reports is perfectly manifest. That one of the persons employed in conducting those poor people is discharged, is certainly true, his own misconduct having given too good reason for his dismission. The Blacks have never refused to proceed on the voyage, but the ships have been delayed at Plymouth by an accidental damage which one of them received in a gale of wind. To sum up all, should the expedition prove unsuccessful, it can only be owing to the over-care of the committee, who, to avoid the most distant idea of compulsion, did not even subject the Blacks to *any* government, except such as they might choose for themselves. And among such ill-informed people, this delicacy may have total consequences.
>
> X

A fuller defence appearing in the *Public Advertiser* of April 14th 1787 accused Equiano of "advancing falsehoods as deeply black as his jetty face", and made a number of puns about "black reports" and the "dark transactions of a Black", which hardly suggests freedom from race-prejudice, though allowance should be made for the abusive strain of much 18th century journalism. The full text is as follows:

> The expedition of the Blacks to Sierra Leone is not the least retarded by the dismission of V——— the Black who was appointed to superintend the Blacks.
>
> The assertions made by that man that the Blacks were to be treated as badly as West-India negroes, and that he was discharged

to make room for the appointment of a man who would exercise tyranny to those unfortunate men, show him to be capable of advancing falsehoods as deeply black as his jetty face. The true reason for his being discharged, was gross misbehaviour, which had rendered him not only disagreeable to the officers and crew, but had likewise drawn on him the dislike of those over whom he had been appointed.

The person since appointed is the purser, a man of good character and unimpeached humanity, under whose care, for control it cannot be called, the Blacks, so far from entertaining any apprehensions, are perfectly happy.

The cloven foot, as observed by a judicious correspondent X in Wednesday's paper, is perfectly manifest in the tales propagated on account of the above discharge. No man endowed with common sense can credit for a moment that the committee (all men of acknowledged humanity and honour) would give any countenance to the least ill-treatment of the objects of their compassion, whom they have endeavoured to snatch from misery and place in comfortable situations.

The proceedings of the committee do them the greatest honour, and as Christians they have provided for the poor Blacks every necessary of life, and will on their arrival at Sierra Leone place them in such a situation as to enable them to live happily. Another provision they have also made for those men, and one which ought not to be forgotten; they have provided for them schoolmasters to instruct them in reading and writing, and have sent out books to have them instructed in the Christian religion.—Are such the measures which would have been pursued if the intention had been to enslave them? Would inculcating the principles of the Christian religion cause the so instructed tamely to submit to unchristian oppression? Or does it not seem far more probable that such measures were adopted for the purpose of inspiring the intended settlers with such elevated ideas of the blessings of liberty, as to induce them to resist any endeavour which may hereafter be made to encroach on their freedom? Let us hear no more of these *black* reports which have been so industriously propagated; for if they are continued, it is rather more than probable that most of the *dark* transactions of a *Black* will be brought to *light*.

In fact, the expedition turned out to be little short of disastrous, though this is no proof of ill-will on the part of the Committee. Because of the delays in sailing, the ships reached Sierra Leone just before the rains, which were usually heavy that year. The tents provided for the settlers were inadequate, planting was impossible, and sickness continued to kill off the disheartened settlers so that within three months a third of them were dead. Blame for the failure of the 1787 expedition was placed on the inadequate diet and the degenerate lives led by the settlers, but the reasons were clearly more complex. However, Equiano's doubts about the preparations for the expedition appear to have been justified by this disastrous start to the Sierra Leone settlement. The fears, which he appears to have encouraged amongst the settlers, that they were being returned to slavery, were not justified; but it may be that the strain of the delays at Plymouth, the sickness aboard ship, the growing uncertainty about prospects in Sierra Leone and the adequacy of the expedition's equipment, the paternalism of the white leaders of the expedition and the negligence or dishonesty of the Agent, Irwin, all this may well have overburdened Equiano and led him into wilder accusations than the facts would support.

At the time there was a considerable body of opinion against Equiano, for in addition to his enemies, both Captain Thompson and Granville Sharp spoke against him. Granville Sharp's comment, however, was probably based on hearsay and there is good reason to think that he soon revised his opinion of Equiano. Sharp wrote to his brother in June 1787 that "all the jealousies and animosities between the Whites and the Blacks had subsided, and that they had been very orderly since Mr. Vasa and two or three other discontented persons had been left on shore at Plymouth".[3] * * * Equiano clearly thought highly of Sharp in his comments in the *Narrative* (see II.248) [176], and Sharp, in a letter to his niece Jemima written many years later in 1811, refers to Equiano as "a sober honest man".[4] Sharp's unsympathetic view of Equiano in 1787 derives, most probably, from letters sent from the expedition at Tenerife, such as one, presumably from "Fraser the Parson" published in the *Public Advertiser* on July 2nd 1787, and both the *London Chronicle* and the *Morning Chronicle and London Advertiser* the next day:

> I have the pleasure to inform you that we are all well, and that the poor blacks are in a much more healthy state than when we left England. Vasa's discharge, and the dismission of Green and Rose, are attended with the happiest effects. Instead of the general misunderstanding under which we groaned through their means, we now enjoy all the sweets of peace, lenity, and almost uninterrupted harmony. The odious distinction of colours is no longer remembered and all seems to conspire to promote the general good. The people are now regular in their attendance upon divine service on Sundays, and on public prayers through the week. Now they do not, as formerly, absent themselves purposely on such occasions, for no other reason whatever than that I am *white*. We have upwards of twenty Blacks who receive instruction

---

3. Prince Hoare, *Memoirs of Granville Sharp*, London, 1820, p. 313.
4. Amongst the Granville Sharp papers at Hardwicke Court, Gloucestershire, Sharp to his niece Jemima, February 22nd 1811. The letter continues: "I went to see him when he lay upon his death bed, and had lost his voice so that he could only whisper."

every day from the schoolmaster, and I am happy to acquaint you that some of them promise to make excellent scholars. I am this day to appoint another school on board of the Vernon under the direction of Mr. Smith. In short, Sir, our affairs upon the whole are so changed for the better, that I flatter myself with the pleasing hope that we may still do well, and enjoy the blessing of Providence in the intended settlement.

Editorial opinion in the *Public Advertiser* the following day, July 3rd, was that this and other letters confirmed

... what we asserted of Vasa the Black, some months since, and have proved what we expected, that the expedition would be carried on with more harmony by his absence.

But in a letter reported on July 14th 1787, again in the *Advertiser*, Equiano defended himself against these criticisms:

An extract of a letter from on board one of the ships with the Blacks, bound to Africa, having appeared on the 2nd and 3rd inst., in the public papers, wherein injurious reflexions, prejudicial to the character of Vasa, the Black Commissary, were contained, he thinks it necessary to vindicate his character from these misrepresentations, by informing the public, that the principal crime which caused his dismission, was on information he laid before the Navy Board, accusing the Agent of unfaithfulness in his office, in not providing such necessaries as were contracted for the people, and were absolutely necessary for their existence, which necessaries could not be obtained from the Agents. The same representation was made by Mr. Vasa to Mr. Hoare, which induced the latter, who had before appeared to be Vasa's friend, to go to the Secretary of the Treasury, and procure his dismission. The above Gentleman impowered the Agent to take many passengers in, contrary to the orders given to the Commissary.

While all this was going on, the matter had been taken up by the Navy Board, as a result of this letter written by Capt. Thompson to the Board:

Nautilus, Plymouth Sound, March 21st 1787

Gentlmen,

I am sorry to be under the necessity of complaining to you of the conduct of Mr Gustavus Vasa, which has been, since he held the situation of Commissary, turbulent and discontented, taking every means to actuate the minds of the Blacks to discord: and I am convinced that unless some means are taken to quell his spirit of sedition, it will be fatal to the peace of the settlement and dangerous to those intrusted with the guiding it.

I am equally chagrined to say that I do not find Mr. Irwin the least calculated to conduct this business: as I have never observed

any wish of his to facilitate the sailing of the Ships, or any steps
taken by him which might indicate that he had the welfare of the
people the least at heart.

The general conduct of the Blacks, since the Transports have
been under my orders, has been troublesome and discontented; I
have taken such methods as I could to keep them in order, but as
these have yet failed, I fear, as I am not authorized to take any
rigorous steps, unless You interfere, the people who are intrusted
with the care of them, will be inadequate to accomplish the
designs of the Government.

As Mr. Irwin the director, has declared to me his intention of
leaving the Ships, and going immediately to London, I beg to
know your instructions how I am to act, and have the honour to
be, Gentlemen, etc. etc. etc.

Tho. B. Thompson[5]

The Navy Board, however, had reasons for thinking more highly of
Equiano than did Captain Thompson, and forwarded Thompson's letter with this covering note to the Treasury:

Navy Office, 23 March 1787

Gent.

Inclosed We send you a Copy of a letter We have received from
Capt Thompson of His Majesty's Sloop Nautilus relative to disputes between the Agent and Commissary on board the Ships
with the Blacks, and desire you will please to acquaint the Right
Honble the Lords Commiss. of the Treasury that in all the Transactions the Commissary has had with this Board he has acted with
great propriety and has been very regular in his information but
having from the beginning expressed his Suspicions of Mr. Irwin's
intention in supplying Tea and Sugar and other Necessaries
allowed for the use of the Women and Children on their Passage
and having complained from time to time of his conduct in this
particular We are not surprised at the disagreement that has taken
place between them. We submit therefore whether in order to
avoid the temptation of going on shore that must naturally arise
while they lay in the neighbourhood of a great town it may not
be proper to order them to Torbay and there wait for a favourable
Wind and in the mean time We submit to their Lordships what
power it may be necessary to entrust with Capt Thompson in
order to prevent the Blacks from getting ashore and to quiet that
Spirit of Turbulence and dissatisfaction which appears among
them

We are
Gent:
Your very humble servants

5. Public Record Office, London: T.i/643, 681, for this and the letter which follows.

So the Navy Board seemed more inclined to blame the troubles on the delays, and the temptations offered by the port to the restless and discontented settlers on whose behalf Equiano appears to have been working diligently. Irwin seems to have been a bad leader, if we are to trust Captain Thompson's opinion, and the Navy Board did so. In circumstances such as these, anyone who put the case for his people persistently and forcefully, as Equiano did, would be likely to win the reputation of a troublemaker. And not only did Equiano continue to speak with respect of Sharp, Clarkson and other leaders of the abolitionist movement;[6] the testimonials given him by such men as Thomas Clarkson, and Dr Peckard, Dean of Peterborough and Fellow of Magdalen College, Cambridge, indicate the respect in which Equiano continued to be held by the leaders of the movement.

Some Sources, Borrowings and Quotations

One of the most striking passages in Equiano's *Narrative* is his account of how he tried to talk to the book:

> I had often seen my master and Dick employed in reading; and I had a great curiosity to talk to the books as I thought they did, and so learn how all things had a beginning. For that purpose I have often taken up a book, and have talked to it, and then put my ears to it, when alone, in hopes it would answer me; and I have been very much concerned when I found it remained silent. (I. 106–7) [48]

But this episode, though it may have been true enough, did not originate with Equiano. In a book published some years before, probably in the 1770's, another African living in Britain named Gronniosaw, described a similar experience:[7]

> (My master) used to read prayers in public to the ship's crew every Sabbath day, and when I first saw him read, I was never so surprised in my life, as when I saw the book talk to my master, for I thought it odd, as I observed him to look upon it and move his lips.—I wished it would do so to me. As soon as my master had done reading, I followed him to the place where he put the book, being mightily delighted with it, and when nobody saw me, I opened it, and put my ear down close upon it in great hopes it would say something to me; but I was very sorry and greatly disappointed when I found it would not speak, this thought imme-

---

6. A letter from Equiano thanking the Committee for the Abolition of the Slave Trade for their good work on behalf of the black poor was published in the *Public Advertiser* on February 14th 1789. [See p. 205 of this NCE. *Editor.*]
7. James Albert Ukawsaw Gronniosaw, A *Narrative of the most remarkable particulars in the Life of James Albert Ukawsaw Gronniosaw*, Bath, 1770?, pp. 16–17.

diately presented itself to me, that everybody and everything despised me because I was black.

The last sentences of these two passages are so particularly alike that Equiano might have had Gronniosaw's book before him when he was writing. On the other hand it seems more plausible that he was remembering the passage, or else had a note copied from Gronniosaw's book: it would be unlikely that Equiano should have deliberately plagiarized a work which would be read by the very same audience as that to which his own book was directed. It is a common experience that words remembered or noted down can sometimes be mistaken for our own when, as often happens, we forget their source.[8] Indeed, the experience described here must have been quite common, since to most Africans at that time the idea of communicating in words other than orally would be unimaginable, and the movement of the lips of an indifferent silent reader would certainly be interpreted in these circumstances as "talking to the books".[9]

Equiano also used Constantine Phipps' A *Journal of a Voyage towards the North Pole* (London, 1774), as the following parallels show:

Phipps p. 31 ". . . had not the mildness of the weather, the smooth water, bright sunshine, and constant daylight, given a cheerfulness and novelty to the whole of this striking and romantick scene."

Equiano II. 107 [132] ". . . we had generally sunshine, and constant daylight; which gave cheerfulness and novelty to the whole of this striking, grand, and uncommon scene."

Phipps p. 42 ". . . the ice was one compact impenetrable body."

Equiano II. 106–7 [132] ". . . we were stopt by one compact impenetrable body of ice."

Phipps pp. 57–8 ". . . At six in the morning the officers returned from the island; in their way back they had fired at, and wounded a sea-horse, which dived immediately, and brought with it a number of others. They all joined in an attack upon the boat, wrested an oar from one of the men, and were with difficulty prevented from staving or oversetting her; but a boat from the *Carcass* joining ours, they dispersed."

Equiano II. 108 [132] ". . . Some of our people once, in the boat, fired at and wounded a sea-horse, which dived immediately; and, in a little time after, brought up with it a number of others. They all joined in an attack upon the boat, and were with difficulty prevented from staving or oversetting her; but a boat from the Carcass having come to assist ours, and joined it, they dispersed."

8. An instance has been pointed out to me in this introduction.
9. Cugoano tells a rather similar story in his *Thoughts and Sentiments*—see p. 80: "The Inca opened it eagerly, and turning over the leaves, lifted it to his ear . . ."

Presumably Equiano would use Phipps' *Journal* to check his own facts,[1] and would have had either the *Journal* or notes taken from it in front of him as he wrote this section of the *Narrative*. The latter again seems more likely as there are one or two minor discrepancies in the figures given in the two accounts.

Equiano refers several times in footnotes to Anthony Benezet's *Some Historical Account of Guinea* (1771) and there are occasional slight echoes of Benezet in Equiano's opening chapter:[2]

> Benezet: That part of Africa from which the Negroes are sold to be carried into slavery, commonly known by the name of Guinea, extends along the coast three or four thousand miles. (p. 5, 1788 edition)
>
> Equiano: That part of Africa, known by the name of Guinea, to which the trade for slaves is carried on, extends along the coast above 3400 miles . . . (I.4) [20]

Equiano's "3,400 miles" looks rather like a misinterpretation of a hand-written note copied from Benezet, i.e. 3–4000 miles.

In later editions of Benezet, for example that of 1788, Equiano would have found arguments similar to those he uses in his final chapter[3] on the economic soundness of ending the slave trade, and developing commerce with Africa. For instance, Appendix X to the 1788 edition of Benezet is a list of "Queries proposed in the Universal Dictionary of Trade and Commerce, by Malachy Postlethwait, who was a Member of the African Committee". These queries include:

> I. Whether so extensive and populous a country as Africa is, will not admit of a far more extensive and profitable trade to Great Britain, than it yet ever has done? . . .
>
> III. Whether . . . there is not a probability that this people might, in time, by proper management of the Europeans, become as wise, as industrious, as ingenious, and as humane, as the people of any other country has done? . . .
>
> V. Whether it would not be more to the interest of all the European nations concerned in the trade to Africa, rather to endeavour to cultivate a friendly, humane, and civilized commerce with these people, into the very centre of their extended country, than to content themselves only with skimming a trifling portion of trade upon the sea coast of Africa?

---

1. He describes in his *Narrative* (II. 104)[131] how he kept his own journal of this expedition.
2. Benezet, *op. cit.* pp. 122–3.
3. See below pp. 330–32 for Equiano's letter in the *Report on the Slave Trade* which argues in very similar terms.

It is worth quoting at some length an example of the kind of argument which Postlethwait[4] and others, including Equiano, were countering. The following is taken from an anti-abolitionist tract published in 1772:

> . . . all our pretended reformers of the age, who, under a cloak of furious zeal in the cause of religion and liberty, do all they can to throw down those essential pillars, commerce, trade, and navigation, upon which alone must depend their own enjoyment of any freedom, civil or religious . . . "That trade", says Voltaire, "which has enriched the English, contributed to make them free", as the enlargement of our commerce so vastly increased the value of our lands, as well as our general riches, it is no less certain and self-evident, that any sensible decrease of it would sink the values of rents and lands, in a similar proportion. Our cities and manufacturing towns, which now consume such immense quantities of the products of our lands, being then depopulated, our farms will thereby be deserted, and, perhaps, even the entire rents might in time be insufficient to support the numberless poor, then destitute of employment.[5]

It is important to bear in mind that the arguments against the slave trade on moral and religious grounds, such as those principally proposed by Granville Sharp, were not enough. It was necessary to prove to the public that virtue could go hand in hand with economic advantage. Equiano would have come across similar arguments in other works that he had read. He had, for example, been reading the controversy between James Tobin and James Ramsay—he refers to Tobin's reply to Ramsay (I. 219) [81] and writes admiringly of Ramsay in a footnote (II. 248) [176]. And in, for example, one of Ramsay's pamphlets published in 1788, he would have read:

> This country (i.e. Africa) abounds in natural wealth well adapted for a mutual profitable exchange, instead of the present quantity bartered for slaves . . . On the abolition of the Slave Trade, we may reasonably look forward to a commerce, that may indefinitely be extended with Africa, till every manufacturing hand in Britain be employed in supplying her market.[6]

Equiano appears to have done a considerable amount of reading during his life, particularly of his bible and the large number of theological and abolitionist works mentioned regularly throughout the *Nar-*

4. Malachy Postlethwait's arguments can be found in detail in his book, *Britain's Commercial Interest Explained and Improved*, London, 1757, in particular Vol. II, pp. 215–220. Since Postlethwait was a member of the abolitionist Committee Equiano may well have known him, and would almost certainly be acquainted with his work.
5. *Reflections . . . on what is commonly called The Negroe-Cause*, by a Planter, London, 1772.
6. James Ramsay, *An Address on the Proposed Bill for the Abolition of the Slave Trade*, London, 1788.

rative. Equiano quotes directly from Clarkson (I. 40–41) [30], and the words which follow the quotation, though not placed in inverted commas, are nevertheless almost word for word Clarkson's own. This evidence of persistent reading, and the use of books, or notes taken from books, in the preparation of the *Narrative* helps to account for Equiano's fluency and articulacy in English.

The quotations from poetry also indicate Equiano's method of working, in that he manages to get his quotations wrong from Milton, Pope and Thomas Day, and clearly did not have the text in front of him. The four quotations from Milton all come from *Paradise Lost* Books I and II and while Equiano gets the short quotations right, the longer quotation (I. 226) [83–84] has several errors in it. The quotation from Pope's *Iliad* (I. 145) [60] is way off the mark, and clearly quoted from memory, though a single quotation does not prove a knowledge of the work, as the four Milton quotations indicate a knowledge of the first two books of *Paradise Lost*, and the mistakes a quotation from memory. The quotation from Cibber (II. 210) [164] is also slightly wrong, but this was something of a proverbial utterance and again is no evidence of knowledge of the work. But the oddest case is that of Equiano's extensive quotation from Thomas Day's *The Dying Negro* (I. 188) [72]. The first line of the quotation appears only in the Second and Third editions of the poem, as its final line, but Equiano gets it wrong, using the word "slaves" where Day uses "souls". Lines 10–11 of Equiano's quotation occur only in the First and Second editions of Day's poem, so that at this point it looks as if Equiano is quoting from the Second edition. But then lines 14–15 in Equiano's quotation occur only in the Third edition of Day. To add to the chaos, Equiano's use of the Third edition seems confirmed by the occurrence of the words "as coarse as fair" in line 17 of his quotation—the Third edition has this, but the Second and Third have "to coarser fare". But how, in this case, do we account for those two lines which only occur in the First and Second editions? And finally, what about the half-dozen occasions when Equiano puts in words of his own? The only explanation seems to be a memorial reconstruction of a text from memories of all three editions of the poem; or a manuscript note of Equiano's own, which he modified as other editions of the poem came into his hands; both of which would indicate a remarkable degree of enthusiasm for abolitionist verse.

Equiano and the abolition of slavery

Equiano settled in England in the late 1770's, and within a few years there is evidence of his involvement in the abolitionist movement.[7] In

---

7. In April 1779 Equiano was given a book by "that truly pious and benevolent man Mr Granville Sharp" according to a note in his own handwriting—see above p. 307—and was presumably already on friendly terms with him.

this respect he is something of a contrast to the one other African in
late 18th century England who achieved a reputation for his writings,
Ignatius Sancho, butler to the Montagu family and friend of Sterne
and Garrick. Sancho reached Britain at the age of two, had no memories of Africa, and was almost wholly assimilated into middle-class
British society. His letters, published in 1782, two years after his death,
contain only occasional comments, mainly of a jocular or sentimental
kind, on race and slavery.[8] He had been brought up in Britain at a time
when there was no centre of protest, such as was to develop later under
the leadership of Granville Sharp, Thomas Clarkson and others, during
the 1770's and after, when British legislation began to move in favour
of the slaves. In 1729, the year of Sancho's birth, the Attorney-General,
Yorke, and the Solicitor-General, Talbot, had given their decision that
any slave in Britain remained a slave whether or not he had been baptized. Twenty years later the judgment was reinforced when Yorke, or
Lord Hardwicke as he had then become, declared that an escaped slave
in Britain could be legally recovered by his owner. But by the 1760's,
strong currents of opinion were flowing that in a Christian country,
proud of its traditions of personal freedom, such decisions were legally
questionable. So, when in the winter of 1762–3 Equiano was re-sold
and returned to slavery in America, he spoke out against his master:

> I was so struck with the unexpectedness of this proceeding, that
> for some time I did not make a reply, only I made an offer to go
> for my books and chest of clothes, but he swore I should not move
> out of his sight; and if I did, he would cut my throat, at the same
> time taking his hanger. I began, however, to collect myself; and
> plucking up courage, I told him I was free, and he could not by
> law serve me so. (I. 174–5) [68–69]

Later he repeated his plea to the captain of the ship returning him to
America:

> I told him my master could not sell me to him, nor to any one
> else. "Why", said he, "did not your master buy you?" I confessed
> he did. "But I have served him", said I, "many years, and he has
> taken all my wages and prize-money, for I only got one sixpence
> during the war; besides this I have been baptized, and by the laws
> of the land no man has a right to sell me." And I added that I had
> heard a lawyer and others at different times tell my master so.
> They both then said that those people that told me so, were not
> my friends; but I replied, "It was very extraordinary that other
> people did not know the law as well as they." Upon this, Captain
> Doran said I talked too much English . . . (I. 176–7) [69]

8. *The Letters of Ignatius Sancho*, Dawsons, 1968; see *Introduction*, pp. i–iv, for a more detailed
  discussion of Sancho and Equiano.

Two years after this incident the abolitionists won the first of a series of legal victories. In 1765, Granville Sharp took up the case of a run-away slave, Jonathan Strong, who had been recaptured and was being reclaimed by his owner. Sharp gained Strong's release, though on a legal technicality, but this success encouraged him to go further. In 1771 he took up the case of Thomas Lewis, and a year later that of James Somersett. The latter was to be a turning point in the history of abolition. Justice Mansfield gave his decision that once a slave had set foot in Britain his master had no right to return him to American or West Indian slavery. It is not the case, as is sometimes claimed, that Mansfield's decision gave freedom to the slaves in Britain. The decision was couched in ambiguous terms and was debated in the courts for more than a decade.[9] But it did give a far greater degree of security than they had enjoyed before, and encouraged the abolitionists to even greater efforts.

Equiano was associated with Granville Sharp and other abolitionists some years before the expedition to Sierra Leone. There is an undated letter amongst the Sharp Papers at Hardwicke Court from General Oglethorpe to Sharp: ". . . Gustavus Vasa was with me this morning. It may give rise to things of such extent as makes me wish to have time to consult you at your leisure." Sharp, Oglethorpe and Equiano were associated over the *Zong* case, and the letter probably refers to this. The *Zong* incident was a particularly brutal episode in the slave trade, in which over 130 slaves were thrown overboard for the sake of insurance money. It took place in 1783, and on March 19th of that year Sharp recorded: "Gustavus Vassa, a negro, called on me, with an account of 130 negroes being thrown alive into the sea."[1] Later he wrote to the Admiralty demanding that action be taken, "having been earnestly solicited and called upon by a poor negro for my assistance to avenge the blood of his slaughtered countrymen."[2] Besides being active in Britain, Equiano appears to have wished to return to Africa to give help there. He describes (II. 218–223) [167–68] how he applied unsuccessfully to be ordained by the Bishop of London in order to go out as a missionary. In a list of names of volunteers to go exploring in Africa on behalf of the African Association Equiano's name appears along with that of his friend Ottobah Cugoano.[3] And after his failure to return to Africa as a member of the Sierra Leone expedition, the thought of return seems to have stayed with him, according to a letter

---

9. For a discussion of the status of slaves after the Mansfield Decision see E. Fiddes, "Lord Mansfield and the Somersett Case", in the *Law Quarterly Review*, Vol. 50 (1934), pp. 499–511.
1. Prince Hoare, *Memoirs of Granville Sharp*, London, 1820, p. 236.
2. *ibid.*, p. 242.
3. In the Banks Papers from the Sutro Collection, of which there are photostats at the British Museum. The list is on p. 11 of the papers dealing with the African Association.

he wrote to a group of abolitionists in Birmingham. Equiano travelled round Britain speaking against the slave trade and selling copies of his book. After a particularly successful visit to Birmingham in 1789, he wrote thanking his hosts:

> These acts of kindness and hospitality have filled me with a long-ing desire to see these worthy friends on my own estate in Africa, where the richest produce of it should be devoted to their enter-tainment. There they should partake of the luxuriant pineapples, and the well flavoured virgin palm-wine, and to heighten the bliss I would burn a certain tree, that would afford us light as clear and brilliant as the virtue of my guests.[4]

The letters published in later editions of the *Narrative* show Equiano to have remained on good terms with supporters of abolition, in spite of disagreements over the organization of the 1787 expedition to Sierra Leone, Shortly after this affair, Equiano was co-signatory, along with Cugoano and ten others, of a letter to Granville Sharp, written on December 15th 1787 and entitled "The Address of Thanks of the Sons of Africa to the Honourable Granville Sharp Esq."[5] and there is also his letter of thanks to the Committee for the Abolition of the Slave Trade published in the *Public Advertiser* of February 14th, 1789.[6] In the same year, a letter of Equiano's addressed to Lord Hawkesbury was published in the evidence of the Committee investigating the slave-trade:[7]

> A System of Commerce once being established in Africa, the Demand for Manufactories will most rapidly augment, as the native Inhabitants will insensibly adopt our Fashions, Manners, Customs, etc. etc.
> In proportion to the Civilization, so will be the Consumption of British Manufactures.
> The Wear and Tear of a Continent, nearly twice as large as Europe, and rich in Vegetable and Mineral Productions, is much easier conceived than calculated. A Case in Point. It cost the Abo-rigines of Britain little or nothing in clothing, etc. The Difference between our Forefathers and us in point of Consumption, is lit-erally infinite. The Reason is most obvious. It will be equally immense in Africa. The same Cause, *viz.* Civilisation, will ever produce the same Effect. There are no Book or outstanding Debts, if I may be allowed the Expression. The World Credit is not to be found in the African Dictionary; it is trading upon safe Ground.

4. Quoted in J. A. Langford, A *Century of Birmingham Life* (1868), I. 440–I.
5. Quoted in Prince Hoare, *op. cit.*, pp. 374–5.
6. See p. 205 of this NCE [Editor].
7. *Report of the Lords of the Committee of the Privy Council . . . concerning the present State of the Trade to Africa, and particularly the Trade in Slaves* (1789), Part I, No. 14. The letter is dated March 13th 1788. The argument here is in words almost identical to those used in the *Narrative* (II. 249–54)[177–78].

A commercial intercourse with Africa opens an inexhaustible Source of Wealth to the manufacturing Interest of Great Britain; and to all which the Slave Trade is a physical Obstruction.

If I am not misinformed, the manufacturing Interest is equal, if not superior to the landed Interest as to Value, for Reasons which will soon appear. The Abolition of diabolical Slavery will give a most rapid and permanent Extension to Manufacturers, which is totally and diametrically opposite to what some interested People assert.

The Manufactories of this Country must and will in the Nature and Reason of Things have a full and constant Employ by supplying the African Markets. The Population, Bowels, and Surface of Africa abound in valuable and useful Returns; the hidden Treasuries of Countries will be brought to Light and into Circulation.

Industry, Enterprise and Mining will have their full Scope, proportionately as they civilize. In a word it lays open an endless Field of Commerce to the British Manufacturer and Merchant Adventurer.

The manufacturing Interest and the general Interest of the Enterprise are synonymous; the Abolition of Slavery would be in reality a universal Good, and for which partial Ill must be supported.

Torture, Murder, and every other imaginable Barbarity are practised by the West India Planters upon the Slaves with Impunity. I hope The Slave Trade will be abolished. I pray it may be an Event at hand. The great Body of Manufactories, uniting in the Cause, will considerably facilitate and expedite it; and as I have already stated, it is most substantially their Interest and Advantage, and as such The Nation at large. In a short Space of Time One Sentiment alone will prevail, from Motives of Interest as well as Justice and Humanity.

Europe contains One hundred and Twenty Millions of Inhabitants; Query, How many Millions doth Africa contain? Supposing the Africans, collectively and individually, to expend Five Pounds a Head in Raiment and Furniture yearly, when civilized etc.—an Immensity beyond the Reach of Imagination: This I conceive to be a Theory founded upon Facts; and therefore an infallible One. If the Blacks were permitted to remain in their own Country they would double themselves every Fifteen Years: In Proportion to such Increase would be the Demand for Manufactures. Cotton and Indigo grow spontaneously in some Parts of Africa: A Consideration this of no small Consequence to the manufacturing Towns of Great Britain.

The Chamber of Manufactories of Great Britain, held in London, will be strenuous in the Cause. It opens a most immense, glorious, and happy Prospect.

The Cloathing, etc. of a Continent Ten thousand Miles in Circumference, and immensely rich in Productions of every Denomination, would make an interesting Return indeed for our
Manufactories, a free Trade being established.

> I have, my Lord, the Honour to subscribe myself
> Your Lordship's very humble and devoted Servant,
> GUSTAVUS VASSA, the late Commissary
> for the African Settlement.

53 Baldwin's Gardens,
Holborn.

Equiano's manuscript letter of 1792 quoted earlier also refers to his
continuing activity against the slave trade:

> I Trust that my going about has been of much use in the Cause
> of the accu(r)sed Slave Trade—a Gentleman of the Committee
> the Rev. Dr. Baker has said that I am more use to the Cause than
> half the People in Country—I wish to God I could be so.

In view of the very large number of copies of the *Narrative* which must
have been sold—the subscription lists are extensive and the above letter speaks of the sale of 1900 copies of the Dublin 4th edition alone—
one can take quite seriously the statement of Thomas Digges in one
of the letters in the Appendix, that Equiano was "a principal instrument in bringing about the motion for a repeal of the Slave-act".

The Narrative *as literature*

Equiano made no claim to be a literary artist, only a man telling the
story of his life; and so it would be unreasonable to insist on a serious
comparison between his book and the works of the major writers of
fiction and biography at this time. All the same, the situation of Equiano has a touch of both Robinson Crusoe and Gulliver: from one point
of view, his is a story of economic and moral survival on the barren
rock of slavery, a study in initiative and adaptability not entirely unlike
Robinson Crusoe's; and from another, it is a tale, like Gulliver's, of new
perspectives gained by physical alienation, in this case of the black man
in a white world. An important difference, of course, is that Crusoe,
Gulliver, and their adventures, emerge from their creators' imagina-
tions and have the distinctive marks of conscious creative artistry about
them, whereas Equiano is apparently doing no more than trying to tell
the direct truth about his own experience. At the same time, he has
many of the qualities of the more interesting 18th century literary
heroes, particularly those of Defoe, revealing himself in the narrative
in a wholly convincing way and never resorting to affectation or self-
display merely in an effort to sentimentalize and to conceal his true
nature. At times he reveals himself at a total loss, ignorant, confused

and helpless: at others he acknowledges himself to be self-seeking and is ready to satirize his own weaknesses, as in the comic account of the dying passenger from whom he and Captain Farmer are hoping to extract a small fortune. (II. 7–11) [103–05] Within a few pages he confesses to taking a lighted candle into a powder-magazine (II. 98) [129–30] and to setting fire to Dr Irving's store room which "was stuffed with all manner of combustibles", (II. 104–5) [131] incidents which present his negligence in a distinctly ludicrous light. Comic self-revelation occurs again and again in the narrative, in such incidents as those of the grampuses (I. 101–2) [47] or the ride on horseback (I. 165–6) [66]. This is not to say that these episodes are presented simply comically, but that the comic potentialities are at no time avoided in the effort to present a more heroic or pathetic figure. Even more interesting are the ambivalent feelings which emerge from time to time about those who help him, particularly in Chapters 9 and 10, where there is a considerable tension between his affection for Captain Farmer, and the nagging irritation of his subordinate place in life: what becomes apparent is Equiano's need to release himself not only from his enemies, but from his friends. This whole section is a remarkable revelation of the psychology of paternalism and subordination, as regret for Farmer's death mingles inextricably with the pleasure Equiano feels (and is prepared to reveal as having its boastful and complacent side) about the opportunity which Farmer's death has given him to display his own skills as a navigator and leader of men:

> The whole care of the vessel rested, therefore, upon me, and I was obliged to direct her by my former experience, not being able to work a traverse. The captain was now very sorry he had not taught me navigation, and protested, if ever he should get well again, he would not fail to do so; but in about seventeen days his illness increased so much, that he was obliged to keep his bed, continuing sensible, however, till the last, constantly having the owner's interest at heart; for this just and benevolent man ever appeared much concerned about the welfare of what he was intrusted with. When this dear friend found the symptoms of death approaching, he called me by my name; and, when I came to him, he asked (with almost his last breath,) if he had ever done me any harm? "God forbid I should think so", I replied, "I should then be the most ungrateful of wretches to the best of benefactors." While I was thus expressing my affection and sorrow by his bedside, he expired without saying another word; and the day following we committed his body to the deep. Every man on board loved this man, and regretted his death; but I was exceedingly affected at it, and I found that I did not know, till he was gone, the strength of my regard for him. Indeed I had every reason in the world to be attached to him; for, besides that he was in general mild, affable,

generous, faithful, benevolent, and just, he was to me a friend and
father; and had it pleased Providence, that he had died but five
months before, I verily believe I should not have obtained my
freedom when I did; and it is not improbable that I might not
have been able to get it at any rate afterwards.

The captain being dead, the mate came on the deck, and made
such observations as he was able, but to no purpose. In the course
of a few days more, the few bullocks that remained were found
dead; but the turkies I had, though on the deck, and exposed to
so much wet and bad weather, did well, and I afterwards gained
near three hundred per cent. on the sale of them; so that in the
event it proved a happy circumstance for me that I had not bought
the bullocks I intended, for they must have perished with the rest;
and I could not help looking on this, otherwise trifling circumstance, as a particular providence of God, and was thankful
accordingly. The care of the vessel took up all my time, and
engaged my attention entirely. As we were now out of the variable
winds, I thought I should not be much puzzled to hit upon the
islands. I was persuaded I steered right for Antigua, which I wished
to reach, as the nearest to us; and in the course of nine or ten
days we made this island, to our great joy; and the next day after,
we came safe to Montserrat.

Many were surprised when they heard of my conducting the
sloop into the port, and I now obtained a new appellation, and
was called Captain. This elated me not a little, and it was quite
flattering to my vanity to be thus styled by as high a title as any
free man in this place possessed. When the death of the captain
became known, he was much regretted by all who knew him; for
he was a man universally respected. At the same time the sable
captain lost no fame; for the success I had met with, increased
the affection of my friends in no small measure. (II. 32–5) [110–
11]

There are a number of reversal situations like this in the narrative.
For instance, the former slave who has been saved by the paternalistic
attentions of others, dreams that his master's ship "was wrecked amidst
the surfs and rocks, and that I was the means of saving every one on
board". (II. 38) [112] The dream comes true. As in the previous chapter, Equiano again takes over from the ship's captain, and remarks with
some satisfaction on the superior conduct of the "three black men and
a Dutch creole sailor" to that of the white men. (II. 46–7) [114] Significantly, when the Captain orders the hatches to be nailed down on
the slaves in the hold, Equiano the former slave takes over from him
and the hatches are not nailed down. (II. 44) [113] Of course, this is
not to say that the racial attitudes taken up by Equiano are simple
ones, for the white men of his experience from a very mixed company,

and for this reason his responses to the world into which he has been thrown at the age of eleven are bound to be complex, as the episode of the death of Captain Farmer shows. But the emancipation of the slave Equiano is brought about by more than the mere payment of forty pounds sterling: he also has to act out roles of dominance through which he can shed his past.

It would probably be unwise to make much of the rhetorical passages in the *Narrative* in view of the doubts that have been expressed about whether these might not have been added by another hand; though there is really no good reason why Equiano, an avid reader of 18th century religious tracts as well as the Bible and, bearing in mind the frequent quotations, at least the first two books of *Paradise Lost*, should not have written with some degree of expansive eloquence. But these passages are in a way less interesting than the plainer ones. One reason for thinking them to be additions by another author might be their occurrence alongside episodes described in a very much plainer language, and nowhere is this more marked than in Chapter 2, which begins in the plain style and ends with a fine rhetorical flourish. But if we look closely at this chapter it becomes clear that these two manners of writing are being used deliberately and appropriately, and that the plain style is perhaps the subtler of the two. This style occurs in its most naive form when Equiano is describing his initial fear and perplexity at the ways of the white men:

> One white man in particular I saw, when we were permitted to be on deck, flogged so unmercifully with a large rope near the foremast, that he died in consequence of it; and they tossed him over the side as they would have done a brute. This made me fear these people the more; and I expected nothing less than to be treated in the same manner. I could not help expressing my fears and apprehensions to some of my countrymen; I asked them if these people had no country, but lived in this hollow place (the ship): they told me they did not, but came from a distant one. "Then," said I, "how comes it in all our country we never heard of them?" They told me because they lived so very far off. I then asked where were their women? had they any like themselves? I was told they had: "and why", said I, "do we not see them?" they answered, because they were left behind. I asked how the vessel could go? they told me they could not tell; but that there were cloths put upon the masts by the help of the ropes I saw, and then the vessel went on; and the white men had some spell or magic they put in the water when they liked in order to stop the vessel. I was exceedingly amazed at this account, and really thought they were spirits. I therefore wished much to be from amongst them, for I expected they would sacrifice me; but my

wishes were vain; for we were so quartered that it was impossible
for any of us to make our escape. (I. 75–7) [40]

What is distinctive here is Equiano's skill in creating a dramatic
language, not merely to describe in literal terms, but to recreate the
very sense of the speakers' past simplicity and incomprehension and
to distinguish this from an articulate and informed "present". Thus
objects are described in naive terms—the ship is "this hollow place",
the sails "cloth put upon the masts" and the anchor becomes "some
spell or magic they put upon the water, when they liked, to stop the
vessel". Equiano does not merely write about his perplexity, his language becomes, dramatically, that of the perplexed boy that he once
was. This is true of the whole dialogue, in the naive assumption behind
"how comes it in all our country we never heard of them?", the implied
ignorance of the more "knowledgeable" people who are replying to the
boy's questions, and the very simplicity of the sentences in which question and response are formed, itself suggesting an innocent, untutored
view of life.

Many of the best effects of the *Narrative*, in fact, are gained by this
kind of dramatic or ironic simplicity—the episode of the dying man
on board ship already referred to (II. 7–11) [103–05], the account of
Equiano's petty trading and the theft of the bags of fruit (I. 236–40)
[172–74], or the following episode, another reversal situation, where
the Indians are now the perplexed innocents and Equiano is in the
position of authority and wisdom. Notice in particular how a complex
sentence structure and a literary vocabulary are suddenly and dramatically discarded for particular effect:

> The Indian governor goes once in a certain time all about the
> province or district, and has a number of men with him as atten-
> dants and assistants. He settles all the differences among the peo-
> ple, like the judge here, and is treated with very great respect. He
> took care to give us timely notice before he came to our habita-
> tion, by sending his stick as a token, for rum, sugar, and gunpow-
> der, which we did not refuse sending; and at the same time we
> made the utmost preparation to receive his honor and his train.
> When he came with his tribe, and all our neighbouring chieftains,
> we expected to find him a grave reverend judge, solid and saga-
> cious; but instead of that, before he and his gang came in sight,
> we heard them very clamorous; and they even had plundered some
> of our good neighbouring Indians, having intoxicated themselves
> with our liquor. When they arrived we did not know what to make
> of our new guests, and would gladly have dispensed with the hon-
> our of their company. However, having no alternative, we feasted
> them plentifully all the day till the evening; when the governor,
> getting quite drunk, grew very unruly, and struck one of our most
> friendly chiefs who was our nearest neighbour, and also took his

gold-laced hat from him. At this a great commotion took place; and the Doctor interfered to make peace, as we could all understand one another, but to no purpose; and at last they became so outrageous that the Doctor, fearing he might get into trouble, left the house, and made the best of his way to the nearest wood, leaving me to do as well as I could among them. I was so enraged with the governor, that I could have wished to have seen him tied fast to a tree and flogged for his behaviour; but I had not people enough to cope with his party. I therefore thought of a stratagem to appease the riot. Recollecting a passage I had read in the life of Columbus, when he was amongst the Indians in Mexico or Peru, where on some occasion, he frightened them by telling them of certain events in the Heavens, I had recourse to the same expedient; and it succeeded beyond my most sanguine expectations. When I had formed my determination, I went in the midst of them and, taking hold of the Governor, I pointed up to the heavens. I menaced him and the rest: I told them God lived there, and that he was angry with them, and they must not quarrel so; that they were all brothers, and if they did not leave off, and go away quietly, I would take the book (pointing to the Bible) read, and *tell* God to make them dead. This was something like magic. The clamour immediately ceased, and I gave them some rum and a few other things; after which they went away peaceably; and the Governor afterwards gave our neighbor, who was called Captain Plasmyah, his hat again. When the Doctor returned, he was exceedingly glad at my success in thus getting rid of our troublesome guests. (II. 184–7) [157–58]

It is perhaps worth noting that up to this point the Indians had been built up as at least moderately noble savages, with many of the virtues of Equiano's "Eboes" of the opening chapters, to be compared advantageously with the Europeans. But it is at this moment that the drunken Indian governor appears to disrupt the happy proceedings, the situation being saved by a combination of the trickery of the original white adventurer Columbus, the doctrines of Europeans Christianity, and the wit of a former negro slave, who adds characteristically a note on Doctor Irving's reliance on him to settle the situation. Equiano's simplicities are not so simple after all. But besides being comical or ironic they can at times be distinctly moving, as in this final example, a paragraph describing an incident taken, admittedly, from Gronniosaw, but nevertheless substantially in Equiano's own words, where he tries to speak to the books:

> I had often seen my master and Dick employed in reading; and I had a great curiosity to talk to the books as I thought they did, and so to learn how all things had a beginning. For that purpose I have often taken up a book, and have talked to it, and then put

my ears to it, when alone, in hopes it would answer me; and I have been very much concerned when I found it remained silent.

*   *   *

CHARLES T. DAVIS

From The Slave Narrative: First Major Art Form in an Emerging Black Tradition†

*   *   *

Though they cared little for matters of tradition, the activists of the 1830s gave new life to an old form. Charles Nichols reports that the genre of the slave narrative began in 1703 with *Adam Negro's Tryall*, written by John Saffin, a well-known colonial author, who was moved to respond to Samuel Sewall's antislavery tract *The Selling of Joseph*.[1] Saffin was white, but other writers who cultivated the genre in the eighteenth century were black, Briton Hammon, John Marrant, and Gustavus Vassa. There were not many accounts of this kind published during the century, and in general they possess no claim to artistic distinction. This is not true of *The Interesting Narrative of the Life of Olaudah Equiano, or Gustavus Vassa, the African*, published in London in 1789. * * * Though Equiano's story is far superior to many of the accounts appearing in his own century and later, it is separated in fundamental ways from the Afro-American tradition and from the nineteenth-century narratives.

Equiano considered himself to be English, not American, or indeed what would be thought of in the mid-eighteenth century as a colonial. His phrase of self-identification during his years of wandering was "almost an Englishman."[2] Crucial to understanding *The Interesting Narrative* is the recognition that Equiano had two homes rather than one: first, the charming valley of Essaka in Eboe, loosely connected with the Kingdom of Benin, and, second, "old England," deeply yearned for while he was forced to labor in the West Indies. The fact is that Equiano spent all of his years as a slave (except for journeys elsewhere with his master) in the West Indies, and these years account for a relatively modest portion of the narrative as a whole. Indeed, more

---

† From *Black is the Color of the Cosmos: Essays on Afro-American Literature and Culture, 1942–1981*, ed. Henry Louis Gates, Jr. (New York: Garland Publishing, Inc., 1982), pp. 85–86. © 1982. Reproduced by permission of Taylor & Francis/Garland Publishing, http://www.taylorandfrancis.com.

1. Charles H. Nichols, *Many Thousands Gone: The Ex-Slaves' Account of Their Bondage and Freedom* (Bloomington and London: Indiana University Press, 1974), pp. ix–x.
2. Paul Edwards, ed., *Equiano's Travels, His Autobiography* (London and Ibadan: Heinemann Educational Books, Ltd., 1969), p. 43.

attention is given to Equiano's precarious existence as a free black. Many of the adventures are trials of body and spirit at sea in which unpredictable elements, sea battles, and sea explorations are prominent. Incompetent and unscrupulous sea captains represent rather more of a danger than do evil and sadistic slave masters. It would seem that *The Interesting Narrative*, looked at strictly, is neither an Afro-American work nor slave narrative, though a part of the whole consists of memories of enforced servitude in the West Indies. And that part may account for the American edition in 1837.

Equiano's narrative was very different from the American slave auto-biographies and biographies of the nineteenth century in style and manner of telling, as well as in matter. Edwards has commented in the "Preface" to an abridgment of *The Interesting Narrative* that the hero resembles Gulliver as he desperately sought to adjust himself to the enlarged perspective in Brobdingnag and Robinson Crusoe in his intense preoccupation with economic and moral survival. We do not need to accept that slavery is Equiano's desert island[3] in order to sense the strong eighteenth-century character of the tale. Not only were the realities of black slavery more urgent and brutal for the nineteenth-century author, but the literary traditions that touched these stories demanded a radically altered technique. *The Interesting Narrative* is a respected forerunner of the slave accounts that began to appear in the 1830s; it is also a remote one, which did not impose upon its successors precedents that might be followed.

* * *

HOUSTON A. BAKER, JR.

From Figurations for a New American Literary History†

* * *

The locus classicus of Afro-American literary discourse is the slave narrative. Appearing in England and America during the eighteenth and nineteenth centuries, the thousands of narratives produced by Africans in England and by fugitive slaves and freed black men and women in America constitute the first, literate manifestations of a tragic disruption in African cultural homogeneity. When the author of *The Life of Olaudah Equiano, or Gustavus Vassa, the African. Written*

3. Ibid., p. xvi.
† From *Blues, Ideology, and Afro-American Literature: A Vernacular Theory* (Chicago: University of Chicago Press, 1984), pp. 31–39. Reprinted by permission of the University of Chicago Press. Bracketed page numbers refer to this Norton Critical Edition.

by Himself (1789) arrived at the African coast in the hands of his kid-nappers, he had left behind the communal, familial way of life of his native village of Essaka in the province of Benin.[1] The family member whom he has a final opportunity to embrace is a sister kidnapped in the same slave-trading raid. His sibling serves as sign and source of familial, female love. And the nature of the final meeting is emblematic of the separations that a "commercial deportation" effected in the lives of Africans: "When these people [Africans carrying Vassa and his sister to the coast] knew we were brother and sister, they indulged us to be together; and the man, to whom I supposed we belonged, lay with us, he in the middle, while she and I held one another by the hands across his breast all night; and thus for a while we forgot our misfortunes, in the joy of being together" (p. 24) [35–36]. The phrase, "The man, to whom I supposed we belonged," signals a loss of self-possession. The man's position "in the middle" signals a corollary loss of familial (and, by implication, conjugal) relations. The narrator introduces a senti-mental apostrophe to represent his emotional response to loss:

> Yes, thou dear partner of all my childish sport! thou sharer of my joys and sorrows! happy should I have ever esteemed myself to encounter every misery for you and to procure your freedom by the sacrifice of my own. Though you were early forced from my arms, your image has been always riveted in my heart, from which neither time nor fortune have been able to remove it.(p. 24) [36]

But the full import of loss is felt less in sentiment than in terror. Having arrived at the coast, Equiano encounters the full, objective, reality of his commercially deportable status:

> The first object which saluted my eyes when I arrived on the coast, was the sea, and a *slave* ship, which was then riding at anchor, and waiting for its *cargo*. These filled me with astonishment, which was soon converted into terror, when I was carried on board. I was immediately handled, and tossed up to see if I were sound, by some of the crew; and I was now persuaded that I had gotten into a world of bad spirits, and that they were going to kill me . . . When I looked round the ship too, and saw a large furnace of copper *boiling*, and a multitude of *black people* of every description *chained* together, every one of their countenances expressing dejection and sorrow, I no longer doubted of my fate; and, quite overpowered with horror and anguish, I fell motionless on the deck and fainted. (P. 27, my emphasis) [38–39]

The quotation captures, in graphic detail, the peremptory consignment of the African—body and soul—to a chained and boiling economic

1. In *Great Slave Narratives*, ed. Arna Bontemps (Boston: Beacon Press, 1969), p. 79.

hell. He will be forced to extract relief and release through whatever instruments present themselves.

At one interpretive level, the remainder of *The Life of Olaudah Equiano* is the story of a Christian convert who finds solace from bondage in the ministerings of a kind Providence. The Christian-missionary and civilizing effects of the slave trade that were so much vaunted by Europeans find an exemplary instance in the narrator's portrait of himself after a short sojourn in England: "I could now speak English tolerably well, and I perfectly understood everything that was said. . . . I no longer looked upon . . . [Englishmen] as spirits, but as men superior to us [Africans]; and therefore I had the stronger desire to resemble them, to imbibe their spirit, and imitate their manners" (p. 48) [56]. Through the kindly instructions of "the Miss Guerins," Englishwomen who are friends of his master, the young Vassa learns to read and write. He is also baptized and received into St. Margaret's church, Westminster, in February 1759 (p. 49) [57]. As a civilized, Christian subject, he is able to survive with equanimity the vagaries of servitude, the whims of fortune, and the cruelties of fate. After his manumission, he searches earnestly for the true, guiding light of salvation and achieves (in chapter 10) confirmation of his personal salvation in a vision of the crucified Christ:

> On the morning of the 6th October. . . . [1774], all that day, I thought that I should either see or hear something supernatural. I had a secret impulse on my mind of something that was to take place . . . In the evening of the same day . . . the Lord was pleased to break in upon my soul with his bright beams of heavenly light; and in an instant, as it were, removing the veil, and letting light into a dark place, I saw clearly with the eye of faith, the crucified Saviour bleeding on the cross on Mount Calvary; the scriptures became an unsealed book. . . . Now every leading providential circumstance that happened to me, from the day I was taken from my parents to that hour, was then in my view, as if it had but just then occurred. I was sensible of the invisible hand of God, which guided and protected me, when in truth I knew it not. (Pp. 149–50) [143–44]

The foregoing passage from *The Life* represents what might be termed the African's providential awakening and ascent from the motionlessness that accompanied a coerced entrance into the mercantile inferno of slavery. To the extent that the narrative reinforces a providential interpretation, the work seems coextensive with an "old" literary history that claims Africans as spiritual cargo delivered (under "special circumstances") unto God Himself.

If, however, one returns for a moment to the conditions of disruption that begin the narrator's passage into slavery and considers the truly "commercial" aspects of his deportation, a perspective quite different from that of the old history emerges. Further, by summoning an ideological analysis grounded in the genuine economics (as opposed to the European-derived "ethics") of slavery, one perceives quite a different *awakening* on the part of the African.

To bring together perspectives of Jameson and White in a discussion of *The Life of Olaudah Equiano* is scarcely to designate "the African" of the narrative's title an exclusively religious product of a trans-Atlantic trade's providential mission. For Vassa's status as transportable property is finally ameliorated as much by his canny mercantilism as by his pious toiling in the vineyards of Anglicanism. *The Life of Olaudah Equiano* can be ideologically considered as a work whose protagonist masters the rudiments of economics that condition his very life. It can also be interpreted as a narrative whose author creates a text which inscribes these economics as a sign of its "social grounding."

The Life, therefore is less a passive "mirroring" of providential ascent than a summoning "into being [by a narrative of] that situation to which it is also, at one and the same time, a reaction."[2] If there is a new, or different, historical subtext distinguishing Vassa's narrative from traditional, historical, and literary historical discourse, that subtext is, at least in part, a symbolic "invention" of the narrative itself. This subtext becomes discernible only under an analysis that explores a determinate relationship between *The Life* and the economics of slavery.

"Now the Ethiopian," writes Vassa, "was willing to be saved by Jesus Christ, the sinner's only surety, and also to rely on none other person or thing for salvation" (p. 150) [144]. The religious "voice" and conversion narrative form implied by this statement stand in marked contrast to the voice and formal implications characterizing *The Life's* representations of West Indian bondage. In the "West India climate," according to Vassa, the most savage barbarities of the trade manifest themselves, resulting in the catalog of horrors that appears in chapter 5. The savage tides of the Caribbean are to the calm harbors of England as the gross deceptions and brutalizations of Montserrat are to the kind attentions of the Guerins and others in London. It would surely seem, therefore, that if "the Ethiopian" were anywhere "willing to be saved by Jesus Christ . . . and to rely *on none other person or thing*" (my emphasis), a "West India climate" would be the place for such reliance. Yet when the narrator enters the West Indies in chapter five, the voice dominating the narrative is hardly one of pious long-suffering.

After a year's labor for Mr. Robert King, his new owner, Vassa writes, "I became very useful to my master, and saved him, as he used to acknowledge, above a hundred pounds a year" (p. 73) [76–77]. Thus

2. Fredric Jameson, "The Symbolic Inference; or, Kenneth Burke and Ideological Analysis," *Critical Inquiry* 4 (1978): 504.

begins a process of self-conscious, mercantile, self-evaluation—a meditation on the economics of African, or New World, black selfhood—
that continues for the next two chapters of *The Life.* "I have sometimes
heard it asserted," Vassa continues, "that a negro cannot earn his master the first cost; but nothing can be further from the truth. . . . I have
known many slaves whose masters would not take a thousand pounds
current for them. . . . My master was several times offered, by different
gentlemen, one hundred guineas for me, but he always told them he
would not sell me, to my great joy" (p. 73) [77]. These assertions of
chapter 5 seem far more appropriate for a trader's secular diary than a
devout acolyte's conversion journal.

Having gained the post of shipboard assistant, or "mate," to Captain
Thomas Farmer, an Englishman who sails a Bermuda sloop for his new
master, Vassa immediately thinks in secular terms that he "might in
time stand some chance by being on board to get a little money, or
possibly make my escape if I should be used ill" (p. 83) [85]. This
conflation of getting "a little money" and freedom conditions the narrative experiences leading from the slave's first trading venture (chapter 6) to his receipt of a certificate of manumission in chapter 7.
Describing his initial attempts at mercantilism, the narrator writes in
ledger-like detail:

> After I had been sailing for some time with this captain [Mr.
> Farmer], at length I endeavored to try my luck, and commence
> merchant. I had but a very small capital to begin with; for one
> single half bit, which is equal to three pence in England, made
> up my whole stock. However, I trusted to the Lord to be with me;
> and at one of our trips to St. Eustatius, a Dutch island, I bought
> a glass tumbler with my half bit, and when I came to Monserrat,
> I sold it for a bit, or sixpence. Luckily we made several successive
> trips to St. Eustatius (which was a general mart for the West
> Indies, about twenty leagues from Montserrat), and in our next,
> finding my tumbler so profitable, with this one bit I bought two
> tumblers more; and when I came back, I sold them for two bits
> equal to a shilling sterling. When we went again, I bought with
> these two bits four more of these glasses, which I sold for four bits
> on our return to Montserrat. And in our next voyage to St. Eusta-
> tius, I bought two glasses with one bit, and with the other three
> I bought a jug of Geneva, nearly about three pints in measure.
> When we came to Montserrat, I sold the gin for eight bits, and
> the tumblers for two, so that my capital now amounted in all to
> a dollar, well husbanded and acquired in a space of a month or
> six weeks, when I blessed the Lord that I was so rich. (P. 84) [86].

Manifold ironies mark the foregoing account of the slave's transactions. Rather than describing a spiritual multiplication of "talents"
in providential terms, shipboard transactions are transcribed as a

chronicle of mercantile adventure. The pure product of trade (i.e., transportable "property" or chattel) becomes a trader, turning from spiritual meditations to canny speculations on the increase of a well acquired and husbanded store! The swift completeness of this transformation is apparent when, amidst the lawless savagery visited upon blacks in the West Indies, Vassa calmly resolves to earn his freedom "by honest and honorable [read: mercantile] means" (p. 87) [88]. In order to achieve this end he redoubles his commercial efforts.

Eventually *The Life*, in its middle portion, almost entirely brackets the fact that a mercantile self's trans-Caribbean profit-making is a function of an egregious trade in slaves plied between the West Indies and the southeastern coast of the United States. We find, for example, the following statement by the narrator: "About the latter end of the year 1764, my master bought a larger sloop, called the *Prudence*, about seventy or eighty tons, of which my captain had the command. I went with him in this vessel, and we took a load of new slaves for Georgia and Charleston . . . I got ready all the little venture I could; and, when the vessel was ready, we sailed, to my great joy. When we got to our destined places . . . I expected I should have an opportunity of selling my little property to advantage" (p. 91) [92]. One explanation for the bracketing of slavery that marks this passage is that the narrator, having been reduced to property by a commercial deportation, decides during his West Indian captivity that neither sentiment nor spiritual sympathies can earn his liberation. He realizes, in effect, that only the acquisition of property will enable him to alter his designated status *as property*. He, thus, formulates a plan of freedom constrained by the mercantile boundaries of a Caribbean situation.

With the blessings of a master who credits him with "half a puncheon of rum and half a hogshead of sugar," Vassa sets out to make "money enough . . . to *purchase my freedom* . . . for forty pounds sterling money, which was only the same price he [Mr. King] gave for me" (pp. 93–94, my emphasis) [94]. By chapter 7 the slave's commercial venture is complete. Having entered the "West India trade," he has obtained "about forty-seven pounds." He offers the entire sum to Mr. King, who "said he would not be worse than his promise; and taking the money, told me to go to the Secretary at the Register Office, and get my manumission drawn up" (pp. 101–102) [105]. In the act of exchange between lord and bondsman, there appears a clear instance of the West Indian slaveholder's willingness to substitute one form of capital for another. Mr. King's initial reluctance to honor his promise is overcome by a realization that his investment in black bodies can be transformed easily enough into other forms of enterprise.

The most monumental linguistic occurrence in the process that commences with Vassa's shift of voice in chapter 5 is the transcription of his certificate of manumission in chapter 7. The certificate is, in effect, an economic sign which competes with and radically qualifies the ethical piousness of its enfolding text. The inscribed document is a token of mastery, signifying its recipient's successful negotiation of a deplorable system of exchange. The narrator of *The Life* (as distinguished from the author) is aware of both positive and negative implications of his certificate, and he self-consciously prevents his audience from bracketing his achievement of manumission as merely an act of virtuous perseverance in the face of adversity. "As the form of my manumission has something peculiar in it, and expresses the absolute power and dominion one man claims over his fellow, I shall beg leave to present it before my readers at full length" (p. 103) [106].

The document—which gives, grants and releases to "the said Gustavus Vassa, all right, title, dominion, sovereignty, and property" that his "lord and master" Mr. King holds over him—signals the ironic transformation of property by property into humanity. Chattel has transformed itself into freeman through the exchange of forty pounds sterling. The slave equates his elation on receiving freedom to the joys of conquering heroes, or to the contentment of mothers who have regained a "long lost infant," or to the gladness of the lover who once again embraces the mistress "ravished from his arms" or the "weary hungry mariner at the sight of the desired friendly port" (p. 103) [105].

Two frames of mind are implied by the transcription of the manumission certificate and the response of the freeman. First, the narrator recognizes that the journey's end (i.e., the mariner's achievement of port) signaled by manumission provides enabling conditions for the kind of happy relations that seemed irrevocably lost when he departed his sister (i.e., familial relations like those implied by "mother-infant" and conjugal ones suggested by "lover-mistress"). At the same time, he is unequivocally aware that the terribleness of the economics he has "navigated" separated him from such relationships in the first instance. There seems no ambivalence, or split opinion, however, on the part of the *author* of *The Life of Olaudah Equiano*.

The structure of the text of the narrative seems to reflect the author's conviction that it is absolutely necessary for the slave to negotiate the economics of slavery if he would be free. The mercantile endeavors of the autobiographical self in *The Life* occupy the very center of the narrative. (Chapters 5, 6, and 7 mark an economic middle passage in a twelve-chapter account.)

The work's middle section represents an active, inversive, ironically mercantile ascent by the propertied self from the hell of "commercial deportation." It offers a graphic "re-invention" of the social grounding of the Afro-American symbolic act par excellence. It vividly delineates the true character of Afro-America's historical origins in a slave economics and implicitly acknowledges that such economics *must be mastered* before liberation can be achieved.

Vassa's hardships do not end with the purchase of freedom. Subsequent episodes make it clear that life for a free black in eighteenth-century England was neither simple nor easy. Nonetheless, the dramatic impact of the text following chapter 7 is qualitatively less than that of preceding chapters. This reduction in dramatic effect is at least in part a function of the predictability of the narrator's course once he has undergone economic awakening in the West Indies. The possibility of amorous heterosexual relationships, for example, is introduced immediately after manumission with the narrator's tongue-in-cheek comment on the community's response (especially that of black women) to his liberation:"The fair as well as the black people immediately styled me by a new appellation, to me the most desirable in the world, which was freeman . . . Some of the sable females, who formerly stood aloof, now began to relax and appear less coy . . ." (p. 104) [106]. Vassa knows that it is scarcely "coyness" that has distanced him from "sable females" during his servitude. The impediment to union has always been the commercial "man in the middle" first encountered on his departure from his sister.

The economics of slavery not only reduced the African man to laboring chattel, but also reduced African women to sexual objects. After his description of separation from his sister, Vassa concludes the apostrophe cited earlier with the fear that she may have fallen victim to "the lash and lust of a brutal and unrelenting overseer" (p. 24) [36]. The probability of such a fate for a young African girl is implicitly heightened in The Life by the narrator's own later account of the behavior of his shipmates on a trading sloop:

> It was almost a constant practice with our clerks, and other whites, to commit violent depredations on the chastity of the female slaves; and these I was, though with reluctance, obliged to submit to at all times, being unable to help them. When we have had some of these slaves on board my master's vessels, to carry them to other islands, I have known our mates to commit these acts most shamefully, to the disgrace, not of Christians only, but of men. I have even known them to gratify their brutal passion with females not ten years old. (Pp. 73–74) [77].

Not "coyness," then, but a disruptive economics that sanctions rape and precludes African male intervention causes sable females to stand aloof. Yet the successful negotiation of such economics is, paradoxically, the only course that provides conditions for a reunification of woman and sable man.

It is, ultimately, Vassa's adept mercantilism that produces the conflation of a "theory" of trade, an abolitionist appeal, and a report of African conjugal union that conclude The Life of Olaudah Equiano. After attesting that "the manufactures of this country [England] must and will, in the nature and reason of things, have a full and constant employ, by supplying the African markets" (p. 190) [177], the narrator depicts the commercial utopia that will result when the slave trade is abolished and free commerce is established between Africa and Britain. The abolitionist intent of his utopian commercial theory is obvious. If British manufacturers become fully convinced of the profitability of ending the slave trade, then it must of necessity come to an end for lack of economic and political support. The African who successfully negotiates his way through the dread exchanges of bondage to the type of expressive posture characterizing The Life's conclusion is surely a man who has repossessed himself and, thus, achieved the ability to reunite a severed African humanity.

The conflation of economics and conjugal union is strikingly captured by the last sentence of the penultimate paragraph of Vassa's work. The narrator says: "I remained in London till I heard the debate in the House of Commons on the slave trade, April the 2nd and 3rd. I then went to Soham in Cambridgeshire, and was married on the 7th of April to Miss Cullen, daughter of James and Ann Cullen, late of Ely" (p. 192) [188]. A signal image, indeed, is constituted by the free, public African man, aware of and adept at the economics of his era, participating creatively in the liberation of his people and joined, with self-possessed calmness, in marriage. It is an image unique to a discourse that originates in "commercial deportation" and recounts with shrewd adeptness the myriad incumbencies of the economics of slavery."

The ideological analysis of discursive structure that yields the foregoing interpretation of The Life of Olaudah Equiano is invaluable for practical criticism. It discovers the social grounding—the basic subtext, as it were—that necessarily informs any genuinely Afro-American narrative text. What I want explicitly to claim here is that all Afro-American creativity is conditioned by (and constitutes a component of) a historical discourse which privileges certain economic terms. The creative individual (the black subject) must, therefore, whether he self-consciously wills it or not, come to terms with "commercial deportation" and the "economics of slavery." The subject's very inclusion in an Afro-American traditional discourse is, in fact, contingent on an encounter with such privileged economic signs of Afro-American discourse. The "already-said," so to speak, contains unavoidable preconditions for the practice of Afro-American narrative.

ANGELO COSTANZO

From The Spiritual Autobiography and Slave Narrative
of Olaudah Equiano†

* * *

One critic has stated about Equiano that by "defining himself as a bicultural man, he found the means to imagine his relationship to the world in terms that did not require his becoming either totally co-opted by or totally alienated from the Western socio-cultural order."[1] Equiano immersed himself in eighteenth-century Western literary culture and resorted to many of its literary traditions when he wrote his narrative. One tradition Equiano used was that of the young individual picaresque hero or anti-hero, a popular subject in the eighteenth century. This hero or rogue journeys from place to place in search of experience that contributes to his growing awareness of the world and to his sense of maturity. The picaresque tradition can be traced from the Spaniards of the sixteenth century, to the Elizabethan prose writers, and to the eighteenth-century novelists that included Swift, Defoe, Smollett, and Fielding.

Equiano's use of the picaresque tradition helped to fix the role of the picaro type of character in slave narrative writings. His accomplishment widely permeated later slave literature. Henry Louis Gates, Jr., has pointed out the affinities that exist between the picaresque and the slave narrative writings: "There is in the narration of both a profusion of objects and detail. Both the picaro and the slave, as outsiders, comment on if not parody collective social institutions. Moreover, both, in their odysseys, move horizontally through space and vertically through society."[2] Gates credits much of the success of the slave narrative in large measure to the popular appeals of the picaresque narrative convention.

Equiano's figure of the picaro is in the portrayal of himself as a young and innocent African who, after being kidnapped and sold into slavery, journeys all over the world, thereby gaining knowledge and education that make possible the great work of his life: the writing of his autobiography. At times, he satirizes his own weaknesses when he presents

† From *Surprizing Narrative: Olaudah Equiano and the Beginnings of Black Autobiography* (Westport, CT: Greenwood Press, 1987), pp. 46–49. Copyright © 1987 by Angelo Costanzo. Reproduced with permission of Greenwood Publishing Group, Inc., Westport, CT. Bracketed page numbers refer to this Norton Critical Edition.

1. William L. Andrews, "The First Fifty Years of the Slave Narrative, 1760–1810," in *The Art of Slave Narrative*, ed. John Sekora and Darwin T. Turner (Macomb: Western Illinois University, 1982), p. 22.

2. Henry Louis Gates, Jr., "Binary Oppositions in Chapter One of *Narrative of the Life of Frederick Douglass, an American Slave, Written by Himself*," in *Afro-American Literature: The Reconstruction of Instruction*, ed. Dexter Fisher and Robert B. Stepto (New York: Modern Language Association of America, 1978), p. 214.

himself as a naive and ignorant youth. We can observe his use of ironic humor in the account of the dying silversmith from whom Equiano and Captain Farmer hope to inherit a fortune, but instead they are duped by him (2: 7–11) [103–04]. Another time Equiano admits his stupidity in taking a lighted candle and holding it in a barrel of gunpowder (2: 98) [129–30] On a voyage to the North Pole, while writing in his journal one night, a spark from his candle sets the storeroom on fire, and Equiano is nearly burned to death (2: 104–5) [131] During his first trip to England, he thinks the grampuses are responsible for stopping the ship when the wind dies down (1: 101) [47] He also describes his gullibility in the episode relating his fear that the whites are preparing to eat him and his friend Dick Baker (1: 99–100) [46–47] One morning upon awakening, he sees his first snow and thinks "somebody in the night had thrown salt all over the deck" (1: 104) [48] In Virginia, he is under the impression that a watch and a picture hanging in a room are spying on him as he fans a sleeping gentleman (1: 92–93) [44] Equiano thinks people carry on conversations with books when he sees crew members reading, and he movingly describes his foolish attempts to learn from books by talking to them (1: 106–7) [48] Once while riding a runaway horse, he nearly is killed and expresses his determination not to be "so foolhardy again in a hurry" (1: 166) [66]. A humorous and ironic situation takes place when Equiano attends a religious love feast expecting a banquet of food but instead is "astonished to see the place filled with people, and no signs of eating and drinking" (2: 130) [139]. In his attempts to free a slave, Equiano tries to serve a writ of habeas corpus on a gentleman from whose house he is barred. Equiano comically relates how he fools the people in the gentleman's house: "My being known to them occasioned me to use the following deception: I whitened my face, that they might not know me, and this had its desired effect" (2: 121) [136]

In writing about the picaro in the slave narrative, Raymond Hedrin states that the early narrative figures were picaresque because their lives were picaresque. In the later narratives, however, the survival techniques of the picaro became important to the slave, but he had to depict himself as being righteous in the cause of freedom. As a result, the slave narrators attempted to "purify the picaro."[3] While it is true that many of the picaresque happenings in Equiano's story are told simply for their humor, the incidents demonstrate Equiano's use of the picaro behavior for survival purposes. In addition, Equiano portrays himself as a justified picaro fighting for the abolition of slavery. Contrary to what Hedrin says, we need not wait for the later narratives to reveal the higher type of character, for Equiano created the "purified picaro" and probably influenced the use of this character in the later narratives.

3. Raymond Hedrin, "The American Slave Narrative: The Justification of the Picaro," *American Literature* 53 (1982): 630–45.

This claim can be reinforced by the careful observation that what is notable about Equiano's adaptation of the picaresque figure is that he makes his hero an instrument of social purpose in the antislavery crusade of the eighteenth century. Up to that time, picaresque heroes were depicted primarily for their entertainment value or for the religious propaganda that showed the wayward person finally seeing the light by converting and freeing himself from sin and subsequently dedicating his life to God. Equiano delights readers with the account of his naive, youthful self journeying through new lands and over strange seas, all the while having perilous but thrilling experiences. Later he undergoes a religious conversion and devotes his life to serving the Lord, but Equiano adds to this the depiction of himself as the now mature young man dedicating his life to social and humanitarian principles in the fight against slavery.

The influence of eighteenth-century primitivism on the slave narratives was strong. Several of the autobiographers, such as Gronniosaw, Cugoano, Equiano, and Smith, recalled their memories of idyllic days that ceased when European influence spread over Africa. These writers knew of the powerful sentimental attraction that such ideas as primitivism and the noble savage had on the eighteenth-century Western world, and thus the narrators described their memories of Africa according to the prevailing primitivist notions popularized by the numerous travel books written by autobiographers and historians. These included books by the Quaker antislavery writer Anthony Benezet, whose works on Africa and the slave trade were widely read in the 1770s and 1780s. Equiano and Cugoano mentioned Benezet in their narratives and borrowed information from him.

The eighteenth century saw a great deal of primitivist travel literature—fictional and nonfictional—written as personal narrative. The outstanding examples in the nonfictional realm are such works as Captain Cook's *Voyages* and John Green's *New General Collection of Voyages and Travels, the World Display'd*. Of more significance are the fictional writings of Defoe, to which Equiano's narrative is closely allied. In Equiano's work, there is close attention to specific circumstantial detail and to the sense of verisimilitude that we see in *Robinson Crusoe*, and Equiano also shares with Defoe the delineation of the protagonist's sense of discovery of strange and awesome objects and of people in hitherto unknown lands. The fictional and nonfictional travel literature stresses the physical journey or voyage over strange areas of the globe as being also a journey of awakening consciousness to life on this earth. Implicit in some of the narratives is the concern also for spiritual awareness and development that a physical journey of education allows the traveler to undergo.

*   *   *

CATHERINE OBIANJU ACHOLONU

The Home of Olaudah Equiano—A Linguistic and Anthropological Search†

*   *   *

I

If we take some words that appear in Equiano's story (Paul Edwards's edition), we will see some crystals of anthobiographical evidence that the alphabet he used in transcribing sounds of Igbo words would not have been used by him if he had the option of writing his story today. Equiano wrote his story at a time when West African languages had not yet been put into writing. Therefore he was struggling to put into writing, using English orthography, Igbo words and sounds. Thus we have him transcribing his name as Equiano using a -q- which does not exist in Igbo orthography today. Its equivalent is- kw-. Even more striking is his use of the English - e- alphabet to transcribe the Igbo sound [i]. Thus we have *Eboe* rather than *Ibo* (notice the reproduction of the English diphthong [ou] or [əu] in *Eboe*), *Embrenche* rather than *Igbur-ichi* and so on.

I have prepared a table that reflects Equiano's dilemma and his possible choice of alphabets in the description of sounds, some of which had no equivalent in the English language as orthography. The fact that some English alphabets such as - a- are used to describe more than one or two different sounds, e.g. *hand*, *table*, constituted another problem to the bi-lingual author. The following table reflects some Igbo sounds, equivalent alphabet-names in English orthography and their possible English spellings in usage, i.e. when put in units of words.

	1	2	3	4	5	6	7	8	9	10	11	12	13
Igbo sound	[a]	[e]	[i]	[ai]	[u]	[o]	[ọ]	[ụ]	[kw]	[gb]	[ny]	[nw]	y
Equivalent English Alphabet name	—	a	e	i	—	—	—	—	(q)	—	—	—	—
Equivalent English Spelling	a	e	i	ai, y	u	oe	-v-	-o-	qu	b	y	w	y

---

† Catherine Obianju Acholonu, "The Home of Olaudah Equiano—A Linguistic and Anthropological Search," *The Journal of Commonwealth Literature* 22.1 (1987): 5–16. Reprinted with the kind permission of Bowker-Saur, a division of Reed Business Information Ltd. Bracketed page numbers refer to this Norton Critical Edition.

Equiano laboured hard to transcribe Igbo words into English; it was a
very arduous task indeed, considering the age at which he must have
ceased to interact in the indigenous language and the age at which he
wrote his autobiography. If we go through the list of Igbo words in his
book we find a number of inconsistencies in his transcription. Sometimes he simply chose to use the alphabet-name, especially if this conforms with the sound he wanted to represent. At other times he tried
to conform to the norm by incorporating changes which take place
when an alphabet is no longer standing on its own but has been joined
with other alphabets to make a word. Equiano's most striking use of
alphabet-names is to be found in such words as

Eboe, Essaka, Embrenche, oye—Eboe

The name of the English alphabet -e- is used to describe the almost
identical Igbo sound [i]. The phonetic symbol for these two sounds is
[i:]. Examples are the first -e- in *Eboe* and *Essaka*, and the three -e-
alphabets in *Embrenche*. Today Equiano would have written *Ibo* or
Igbo, *Isseke* and *Igburichi*. Equiano also sometimes used the name of
the English alphabet -a- to describe the almost identical Igbo sound
[e] or [ ]. Thus we have Ess*a*ka rather than Isseke, even though in
some of the later words, he endeavoured to keep close to the English
usage. The reason for this is not far-fetched. He must have realized
that if he had written *Isseke* the actual name of his town would have
been lost forever, for the normal English man would have pronounced
the word *Isseke* as (aisi:k) (-e- at the end of an English word is always
silent) therefore he opted for -a-. We also notice a similar dilemma in
the rendering of the word *Eboe*. Since most English words that end
with an -o- are pronounced [oe] or [ou] and since the closest similarity
to this sound at the end of words can be seen in such words as foe,
woe, toe, Equiano had more problems with such words as *Ah-ffoe, Ah-
ffoe-way-cah*, and his own names Equiano and Olaudah, etc. When I
first came across the word *Ah-ffoe*, I was convinced it is made up of
two words that mean the same thing, only a dialectic difference. These
are 'Ahọ' and 'Afọ'. Ahọ is from the Orsu dialect while 'afọ' is more
widespread among people of the Isu district, around Onitsha and the
Ika Igbo the word '*arọ*' is used. The word *Ah-ffoe* tells an entire story
in itself; a lot of meaning and direction can be drawn from this single
word. 'Aho' is a word that one encounters in a very small proportion
of Igboland—namely the Orsu district, which spans the area between
Ozubulu (West) and Orlu (exclusive) on the East, and between
Mgbida (South) and the Ideato Local Government Area on the North
(both exclusive). Within this distance of about forty to fifty square
kilometres the only town whose name sounds closest to *Essaka* is *Isseke*,
a town in Ihiala local government area in Anambra State. This town
was formerly in Orlu division before the creation of states in Nigeria.
　　Equiano's use of the -f- (Affoe) rather than the -r- (Arọ) spoken in

Onitsha, Mid-West Igbo and Awka areas, is a pointer to the fact that he was neither from any of these areas, nor did he journey through them in his captivity. Equiano was most likely taken through the Igbo hinterland, through the Isu district (Orlu, Owerri, Okigwe), and down to the Delta region before he was finally shipped off. We cannot rely on his sense of direction, judging from his age and state of mind during the journey.

Embrenche is a combination of the words *Igbu ichi* and *Mgburichi*. *Igbu ichi* is the act of scarification of the face, while *mgburichi* is the term used for the generality of men who bear the scarification. The singular form is *nwichi*. Equiano at his later age must have found it difficult to grasp the difference between the first two words, which he merged into one word "Embrenche", i.e. *Igburichi* (from the prefix of one and the suffix of the other). The -n- sound, I strongly suspect, is Equiano's way of rendering the nasal sound in *ichi* or *ich(n)i* in Isseke or Orsu dialect. Also he could have confused the word *ichi*—scarification, with *ich(n)i*—to crown, which is still in line with nobility. This word is also nasalized in Isseke or Orsu dialect, but in Isu dialect the word, though nasalized *ish(n)i*, goes with a voiceless -sh- rather than a voiced -ch- sound.

Equiano's first name Olaudah could be a rendering of *Ola-ude*: a ring with a sonorous sound; or *Ola-uda*: ring with a loud sound; or *Ole-ude*: where is the breath, or energy or life? The first two suggestions are more likely to fit into Equiano's explanation that his name "which in our language signifies vicissitude, or fortunate; also, one favoured and having a loud voice and well spoken". *Ola*—ring, is a symbol of good fortune in Igbo world view.

II

Before I get down to the description of my journey to Isseke and its results, I shall first put across my views and personal attempts at unravelling some of the pieces of information supplied by Equiano which have constituted stumbling blocks to scholars.

Equiano writes about the Kingdom of Abyssinia, a "kingdom divided into many *provinces* and districts in one of the most remote and fertile of which, called Eboe, I was born . . . in a charming fruitful vale named Essaka."[1] The kingdom is Abyssinia, the province or district is Eboe, while Essaka is described as a "vale". Then the author goes on to indicate his impression of the distance between this province (Eboe) and the capital of Benin and to indicate that "our subjection to the king of Benin was little more than nominal, for every transaction of the

1. *Equiano's Travels*, ed. Paul Edwards, London: Heinemann, 1980, p. 1 [20]. First published 1967 as an abridged edition of *The Interesting Narrative of the Life of Olaudah Equiano, or Gustavus Vassa the African, Written by Himself* (1789).

government . . . was conducted by the chiefs or elders of the place."[2] Equiano's point here is that although it was generally understood that the empire of Benin had subjected all the other 'provinces' in the region of Abyssinia, the Igbo country could only be said to be nominally (i.e. in name or word, not in fact) subjected to the king of Benin. This point is illustrated by Equiano's description of the Igbo system of government which being run by chiefs and elders does not indicate subjection to any king. Hitherto scholars have tended to interpret the foregoing lines as evidence of Essaka's subjection to the king of Benin and have thus placed Essaka towards the western side of the Niger.

Many things in Equiano's narration point to the fact that Equiano could not have been a western or Ika Igbo.

The Western Igbo are not known to have been conversant with facial scarification, or *ichi*.[3] Also I do not know the mid-western Igbos to venerate the python (Eke) as we do in Isu and Orsu districts of the Igbo hinterland. In fact, as far as I am informed the python is killed and eaten among the mid-western Igbo. Equiano tells of the way the python was venerated and courted among his people. "I was desired by some wise men to touch these that I might be interested in the good omens. . . ."[4] Even among these people who venerate the python, most notable of which is Njaba and environs, it was difficult to find a people who not only respected the animal but also courted its friendship, to the extent that children were asked to touch them for the good omen they brought. These were some of the initial questions which my visit to Isseke helped me to answer. Isseke is one such place where the python was courted as a welcome visitor and good omen.

Oye Eboe, which has been interpreted severally as *Onye Ibo*, *Onye Aboh*, etc., was not very difficult to unravel. At first I suspected that the word which was used to describe "stout mahogany-coloured men from the South-west of us: we call them Oye-Eboe, which term signifies red men living at a distance," was Equiano's transcription of the Igbo word *Oyibo* (see No. 13 in table above). *Oyibo* is a word that signifies a very lightly coloured person, among our people, i.e. not a European (for the word existed among us before the Europeans appeared). Also this term was used in describing albinos. However, Equiano describes these as "red men" who moved from one village to the other trading on fire-arms, gun-powder, beads, etc., and exchanging these for slaves, men who instigated wars[5] and took away slaves in their long sacks.[6]

I thought that these people must be the Aros, there is no other group of people who are associated with the slave racket, as much as the Aros

2. ibid., p. 1 [20].
3. Paul Edwards, *Equiano's Travels*, 2 vols., London: Dawsons, 1969, p. xix [308–09].
4. *Equiano's Travels*, op. cit. p. 14 [29].
5. ibid., p. 9 [24].
6. ibid., p. 7 [24].

of the Long Juju of Arochukwu. I had heard that in the olden days the
Aros were generally very lightly coloured, almost red. I cross-checked
this with Eze Silver Ibenye Ugbala, Ezeugo III of Okporo in Orlu Local
Government Area. Says Ezeugo, "Yes, the Aros were the people to
whom slaves were sold throughout Igboland. They had a very powerful
syndicate for organized slave trade. They were also very huge and fair
in colour. People used to refer to them as *oyibo*, especially children,
because of their colour."[7]

I also asked this very knowledgeable traditional ruler of Okporo community if he knew of any anchor shaped coin or currency that was used
in the olden days in Igboland. He said there was, and that it was called
Ego Ikpechi, otherwise called *umumu*. He showed me one he had in his
collection and told me it was used in parts of Igboland including Orsu
area (his area) which included Isseke.

From the Eze's house I drove to Isseke. I got to the house of Eze
Anthony Osakwe, the Ezeoha I of Isseke. The Eze received me very
well. And after the traditional kola had been eaten I told him why I
had come. He said he would conduct a research with his people. He
took the book, *Equiano's Travels*, from me and asked me to repeat my
visit after a number of days. When I went back to the Eze after some
days his first word was—"Eureka! We have traced the man. He was
indeed a native of Isseke, from one of the two ruling families of our
town." I expressed my happiness and then the Eze went on:

> When I read what he wrote about *Igbu ichi* and that his father
> was from one of the ruling families of 'Essaka', I knew that *if* he
> was from our town, he could only have hailed either from my
> kindred, Ubaha, which is the first ruling family of Isseke, or from
> Dimori kindred, the second of the two ruling families here. You
> know in Igboland it is not common or easy to capture children
> from royal families, such a thing never goes unnoticed. I asked
> the old men in my kindred if, as far as they could remember, there
> had in the olden days, been any boy sold into slavery at a tender
> age from our kindred. I mentioned the names Equiano, Ikwuano,
> Ikwuno, Ekweanu etc. but they said there was no such name and
> that as far as their family histories went there was no member of
> the kindred sold into slavery. Then I went to the Dimori kindred.
> I spoke with the ofo title holder of the family. Igwe Agbaka about
> 95 years old. Igwe told me in confidence that there was a little
> boy who was sold at a very tender age: and that nothing had been
> heard of him since then. When I mentioned the boy's surname
> and asked Igwe whether there was any such name in his kindred,
> he said there was, till this day, a family going by the name of
> *Ekwealuo* and that in fact the boy who had been sold was from
> the Ekwealuo family.

7. Interview with Eze Silver I. Ugbala, Ezeugo III of Okporo.

I said I must see this family at once and that I must see Igwe. Eze Osakwe further told me that when he went to see one of the extended families of the Ekwealuo household he saw a small boy of about fifteen who resembled the man in the portrait on the cover of the book *Equiano's Travels*. I could not believe my ears. I said I wanted to get there immediately. So the Eze's second wife Eunice Ogechi Osakwe was asked to take me and my crew (Miss Chika Olumba, my sister, who helped in taking records, a student of Theatre Arts, and a photographer) to the Dimori kindred. When we got there we met Igwe in his obi with some of his kinsmen and we talked to them about some of the customs of his people, especially the ones mentioned in *Equiano's Travels*. In all we made a total of three visits to Isseke during which we spoke to people and took photographs.

We were opportuned to meet the entire elders of the Dimori kindred in a large family meeting on one of our visits. Many of them still bore the *ichi* marks on their faces. We asked several questions about the customs of the village and of Isseke as a whole. I also visited one of the Ekwealuo extended families and took photographs of the young head of the family, his wife, baby boy and little brother. I was told that the old men in the family had all died off, leaving only the young ones who would not be in a position to say much about the family pedigree. There is a tragic story behind this unfortunate state of affairs which discretion does not allow me to expose to the public. However, I saw the members of the Ekwealuo family and took photographs. I made personal portraits of the two members of the family who so closely resembled Olaudah Equiano—they were Bright Nwabueze Ekwealuo, aged fifteen, and the little boy in the arms of Mrs Paulina Ekwealuo, wife of Innocent Orusaemeka Ekwealuo. I was told that Bright Nwabueze was a carbon copy of their grandfather and that many of the members of the extended family, most of whom were off to other towns, had features like those of Bright. I noted the small, protruding and bright eyes, the rigid clearly marked lips, the long nose, the long neck; but what struck me most was the receding hairline and the forehead, the small scalp and the resemblance between the shape of the boy's scalp and forehead and those of Equiano. I could imagine his looks in the next thirty-five years. At that stage I had no doubt that I was standing on the ground that Olaudah Equiano had trodden two hundred years ago as a young boy full of prospects before the slave raiders struck, or so he had thought.

Olaudah Equiano was not simply captured, he was sold, according to his kinsmen (which is a very shameful thing for a noble family to admit). Igwe could not tell me why the boy was sold but I believe I can guess why. People sold their children in those days when they were highly in debt and could not find no way out. But I believe Olaudah was singled out for sale because of his effeminate nature; his strong tie to his mother could have raised doubts in his father's mind or in any of his uncles who was in dire need of money. Hence he was sold off with his sister (who was soon forgotten, being a girl). Olaudah was destined to get the *ichi* marks—in Isseke custom boys received the *ichi* marks at the age of fourteen or fifteen. A man of large means, an *ogaranya*, was expected to bestow the *ichi* marks on all his sons. It was a very expensive venture, and was the first step in a series of ceremonies that would lead to the *nze* or *ichie* position in the land. Ichie Ekwealuo must have been at a loss for what to do with this boy who even accompanied his mother into seclusion during her menstrual cycle. No man would have risked spending so heavily to bestow the *ichi* marks of manhood on a boy who was obviously more of a woman than a man. Olaudah, quite unknown to him, must have been the cause of much misunderstanding between his parents. His mother may have wanted him spared the scarification, and his father, to avoid the risk of the shame and chagrin that Olaudah might bring him by constituting a sort of Dauda, or by not surviving the ordeal (many were known to have died on the scarification stool), must have opted for the much 'simpler' task of getting rid of the boy. The kidnapping of Olaudah and his sister must have been arranged. Otherwise why were they not at the *ilo* or *ama* where children were more safely guarded by adults and where Equiano himself had often played the role of the spy?

III

My interviews with the people of Isseke and with the members of the Dimori kindred yielded the following results which I have translated into English.

Mr Ambrose Osakwe (aged about 65) of Ubaha, Isseke confirmed Equiano's story about a sentry who climbed trees and waited to raise alarm if he sighted slave raiders. He said, "According to what our father told us, boys were sent up trees with the horn, *odu*; while hefty men stood guarding children who always played together in the village playground. As soon as an unknown person was sighted, the *odu* was blown and the enemy was apprehended."

I asked about the people who carried long bags and exchanged white men's goods for slaves. He said they were Aro people who took away slaves to be sold to Azumili. He said, "The Aros and their neighbours from Abam, Abiriba, Item etc. always sought for and incited wars among our people and our neighbours because this was an easy way of obtaining heads and slaves. They made wars throughout Igboland, and they were the main agents of the white slave raiders. They were also hired by any party seeking revenge of war against another party." On war he said "Our people fought with bows and arrows (*uta*), as well as pointed sticks with metal tips (*ube*) or (*otundu*) and shields."

Igwe Agbaka (aged 95) told me, "Our people were very warlike, the Dimori kindred was known as war Lords". I asked him whether their women also went to war and he said, "Our women played their own part in a war situation. Our fathers told us stories of women who were known to have captured and killed soldiers during wars. Nwibe Ezike was a woman among many who captured and killed enemy soldiers." This was confirmed by Nze Egwuatu Onwuezike and others in the gathering.

I asked about the people who counted the years whom Olaudah had referred to as *Ah-ffoe-way-cah*.[8] All those present confirmed that the men who counted the years had performed all religious rites among the people of Isseke and the entire Igbo nation were people from Nri, who were called *Nwanhi* (*nwanchi* or *nwanshi* in other Igbo dialects). They were midgets or dwarfs. At this I burst out with my suspicion— "don't our people refer to dwarfs as Nwika (or Nwaika)?" The answer was a general "yes!" A small person was scornfully referred to as *Nwaika* (ugly monkey). I had no doubt in my mind that Olaudah had in mind the term "Afo-nwa-ika"—a word which must have been used by children to describe the funny looking midgets that went from compound to compound rattling out history and legends like local tape recorders. Olaudah must have confused these with the local medicine men and priests, and with the *Nze Nzus*, the highest title holders in the land. When they died they were buried by fellow Nze Nzus, no ordinary person (non initiate) was allowed to come near the corpses of priests and *Nze Nzus* and they were buried in the dead of night. Those who buried them always came back from a different route. (Igwe Agbaka.) How do you compute the year? "We know that a year has ended when we hear the rattling noise made by an unknown phenomenon that passes through our land once a year and only in the evening (as soon as the sun sets).[9] The noise is so deafening and yet you can never see the thing. We do not know what it is. When it happens all Isseke men, women and children throw out their old utensils and roar in jubilation: 'Aho gbara aka la o!' 'Year, please, go home empty handed!'." "Igwe, is this the way that people of other towns count the year?" I asked. "Not necessarily. Every town has its own symbol for recognizing the end of the year. This is how we, the people of Isseke, recognize the end of the year among us. Our neighbours, as far as we know, have other signs from nature for recognizing the end of the year." (Igwe Agbaka, Egwuatu Onwuezike.) Achebe's *Arrow of God* shows one example of how some Igbo people compute the year.

"Equiano wrote that there were *two* offerings or ceremonies that

8. *Equiano's Travels*, p. 13 [28].
9. Compare with Equiano's description of the end of the year, p. 11 [27]. Equiano is obviously describing the same phenomenon.

were made at harvest, 'before the fruits are taken out of the ground'.[1]
What do you say to this?"

> Yes, as soon as the phenomenon which we have just described has
> taken place we begin to prepare for Ahiajoku (New Yam Festival).
> Before the fruits are taken out of the ground we make two cere-
> monial offerings called *Isa Ire*) (washing of the tongue) and *Ite
> Nsi* (rubbing of medicine), preparatory to the actual *Ire Iji* when
> the yam seedlings are taken out of the ground and eaten with
> thanksgiving to the gods. (Igwe Agbaka.)

As to the smoking of pipes, which Equiano described as the "favorite
luxury" of the people of Essaka,[2] and that these were made from earth
and were fashioned by the women, several people confirmed that smoking of pipes was a favorite sport among the people of Isseke, perhaps
more than any other people around the same vicinity. In Isseke men
especially old men smoked long earthenware pipes (which were made
by the women), women and girls smoked shorter pipes.

About Olaudah, the author's first name, the Eze's wife Eunice, along
with others present, confirmed that there were names such as Ola-ude
(loud ring, sonorous ring) in Isseke. Igwe and Egwuatu affirmed that
the Dimori kindred was known as spokesmen of Isseke, and many of
their children had names that reflected this fact; Olaudah or Olaude
is one such name. They also told me that the Dimori family, being a
family of judges (king markers), took the *ichi* very seriously. I could see
that this was so for even today many of them still bear the *ichi* marks.
This cannot be said of other Igbo communities I have been to (I could
not remember when I last saw a man bearing the *ichi* marks, before I
met these people). I could begin to imagine why the *ichi* (or Embrenche) occupied such a pride of place in Equiano's anthropological data.

Equiano's claim that "we were almost a nation of dancers, musicians
and poets" was confirmed during the third visit to Isseke when I had
the opportunity of meeting the elders of the Dimori kindred. These
men told me, "our people are known by our neighbours as music makers, singers and dancers. Every joyful occasion in Isseke is an occasion
for the display of several dances by men, women and children . . ."[3]

Equiano's claim that his people produced corn, tobacco, and cotton
was only partly confirmed by these men.[4] They said that their people
produced cotton in abundance and exported to the neighbours. But
they did not produce tobacco though they smoked it a lot. (Equiano
must have nurtured the wrong notion that because his people made
much use of tobacco they produced it themselves.)

1. ibid., p. 11 [27].
2. ibid., p. 10 [26].
3. See Equiano's explanation about dances, pp. 3–4 [21–22].
4. p. 7 [24].

Equiano claims, "our principal luxury is in perfumes; one sort of these is an odeferous wood of delicious fragrance, the other a kind of earth, a small portion of which is thrown into the fire diffuses a more powerful odour. We beat this wood into powder and mix it with palm oil with which both men and women perfume themselves."[5] Igwe and Egwuatu told me that their people frequently burned a kind of fruit which looked like a piece of wood (six inches or more in length) for its delicious odour. They called it *Ughịghịhị*. It was thrown into the fire and the smoke diffused a powerful but delicious perfume in the compound. The *Uhie*, cam wood, which to a child might appear like red earth, was mixed with palm oil and rubbed on the skin. These men told me that as far as they knew it was the *uhie*, cam wood, and not the *Ughịghịhị*, that was mixed with palm oil and applied to the skin.

Equiano's claim that the women in his town wore golden ornaments must have been an exaggeration. Igbo women of mettle in the olden days, including Isseke women, wore the *aka* (choral beads) and *esuru* (heavy ivory beads) on their arms and legs.

Although Isseke people produced cotton, they did not weave cotton, rather they wove raffia into bags, mats and bed covers. They also wove baskets. These were coloured with the blue colour derived from leaves such as the *alulu*, or the *edo* derived from earth; there were other colours derived from earth, wood and leaves. Uri or *uli* which was derived from berries was not used for dyeing cloth, but rather for making marks on the skin. I was made to understand that the *uri* or *uli* was the commonest colour, the source of which was known to every child, unlike the other colours with more exotic origin. Equiano was therefore mistaken in assuming that the colours used in dyeing material was derived from berries.

The wood ash which provided salt, is nothing but *Ngụ*, a type of salty substance derived from burnt palm sponge. It is still used today in Igboland for cooking breadfruit and hard foods. It is also used for making soap.

CONCLUSION

I have pictures in my possession taken of Equiano's kinsmen to indicate the resemblance which is still discernible between Olaudah Equiano and some members of the Ekwealuo's family in Isseke. I also have included pictures reflecting the *ichi* facial marks on men who are still alive today in Isseke, as well as a photograph of the *Obi* of the custodian of custom in the Dimori family—the Igwe Agbaka; this photograph reveals beautiful wall paintings which reflect the beauty and artistry of the people and their local culture.

5. p. 5 [23].

Over the years in which the little boy Olaude Ekwealuo travelled from country to country and from continent to continent, changing his name to Gustavus Vassa and seldom speaking or hearing his language, so much could have happened to account for the discrepancy between Ekwealuo and Equiano. It is possible to assume that his original name was Ekweanuo which he retained but which since had shifted from -n- to -l- among his people. *Ekwealuo* and *Ekweanuo* both mean the same thing (if they agree we shall fight) i.e. Ekwekorita-aluo (a name that portrays a warlike people). It is equally possible that a change from -l- to -n- was made (consciously or unconsciously) by Equiano himself. It is possible that the Igbo people he met after he left home (who include those in the West Indies and London) used -*nuo* (to fight) rather than -*luo* (to fight), and thus helped corrupt Equiano's Igbo.

In any case Equiano had plenty of linguistic difficulties which must have accounted for the discrepancies in spelling. These not withstanding, the closeness between Isseke's customs and those described by Equiano, the existence of a family by the name of Ekwealuo in one of Isseke's ruling kindreds, the little boy from this family who had been sold, the resemblance between Equiano in the portrait and Bright Ekwealuo, all accumulate as evidence that Olaudah Equiano was none other than Olaude Ekwealuo from Isseke in Anambra State of Nigeria, an Igbo from the Eastern hinterland.

HENRY LOUIS GATES, JR.

From The Trope of the Talking Book†

*   *   *

* * * In 1789, * * * Olaudah Equiano published his slave narrative, *The Interesting Narrative of the Life of Olaudah Equiano.*[1] Equiano's *Narrative* was so richly structured that it became the prototype of the nineteenth-century slave narrative, best exemplified in the works of Frederick Douglass, William Wells Brown, and Harriet Jacobs. It was Equiano whose text served to create a model that other ex-slaves would imitate. From his subtitle, "Written by Himself" and a signed engraving of the black author holding an open text (the Bible) in his lap, to

---

† From *The Signifying Monkey: A Theory of Afro-American Literary Criticism,* pp. 152–58. Copyright © 1988 by Henry Louis Gates, Jr. Used by permission of Oxford University Press and of Henry Louis Gates, Jr. Bracketed page numbers refer to this Norton Critical Edition.

1. Olaudah Equiano, *The Interesting Narrative of the Life of Olaudah Equiano, or Gustavus Vassa, the African. Written by Himself,* 2 vols. (London: the author, 1789). I shall be using Paul Edwards's 1969 edition of Equiano's first edition, published at London by Dawsons and hereafter referred to as Equiano.

more subtle rhetorical strategies such as the overlapping of the slave's arduous journey to freedom and his simultaneous journey from orality to literacy, Equiano's strategies of self-presentation and rhetorical representation heavily informed, if not determined, the shape of black narrative before 1865.

*   *   *

Equiano told a good story, and he even gives a believable account of cultural life among the Igbo peoples of what is now Nigeria. The movement of his plot, then, is from African freedom, through European enslavement, to Anglican freedom. Both his remarkable command of narrative devices and his detailed accounts of his stirring adventures no doubt combined to create a readership broader than that enjoyed by any black writer before 1789. When we recall that his adventures include service in the Seven Years War with General Wolfe in Canada and Admiral Boscawen in the Mediterranean, voyages to the Arctic with the 1772–73 Phipps expedition, six months among the Miskito Indians in Central America, and "a grand tour of the Mediterranean as personal servant to an English gentleman," it is clear that this ex-slave was one of the most well-traveled people in the world when he decided to write a story of his life.[2]

Like his friend Cugoano, Equiano was extraordinarily well read, and, like Cugoano, he borrowed freely from other texts, including Constantine Phipps's A *Journal of a Voyage Towards the North Pole* (London, 1774), Anthony Benezet's *Some Historical Account of Guinea* (London, 1771), and Thomas Clarkson's An *Essay on the Slavery and Commerce of the Human Species* (London, 1785). He also paraphrased frequently, especially would-be "direct" quotations from Milton, Pope, and Thomas Day.[3] Nevertheless, Equiano was an impressively self-conscious writer and developed two rhetorical strategies that would come to be utilized extensively in the nineteenth-century slave narratives: the trope of chiasmus, and the use of two distinct voices to distinguish, through rhetorical strategies, the simple wonder with which the young Equiano approached the New World of his captors and a more eloquently articulated voice that he employs to describe the author's narrative present. The interplay of these two voices is only as striking as Equiano's overarching plot-reversal pattern, within which all sorts of embedded reversal tales occur. Both strategies combine to make Equiano's text a representation of becoming, of a development of a self that not only has a past and a present but which speaks distinct languages at its several stages which culminate in the narrative present. Rarely would a slave narrator match Equiano's mastery of self-representation.[4]

2. Edwards [Equiano], p. v [302].
3. Ibid., pp. xlv–liii [323–27].
4. See ibid., pp. lxvii–lxix [335–36].

Equiano refers to his literacy training a number of times. Richard Baker, an American boy on board the ship that first took Equiano to England, was, Equiano tells us, his "constant companion and instructor," and "interpreter." At Guernsey, his playmate Mary's mother "behaved to me with great kindness and attention; and taught me every thing in the same manner as she did her own child, and indeed in every way treated me as such."[5] Within a year, he continues,

> I could now speak English tolerably well, and I perfectly under-stood everything that was said. I not only felt myself quite easy with these new countrymen, but relished their society and man-ners. I no longer looked upon them as spirits, but as men superior to us; and I therefore had the stronger desire to resemble them; to imbibe their spirit, and imitate their manners; I therefore embraced every occasion of improvement; and every new thing that I observed I treasured up in my memory. I had long wished to be able to read and write; and for this purpose I took every opportunity to gain instruction, but had made as yet very little progress. However, when I went to London with my master, I had soon an opportunity of improving myself, which I gladly embraced. Shortly after my arrival, he sent me to wait upon the Miss Guerins, who had treated me with such kindness when I was there before; and they sent me to school.[6]

Equiano also used the sea as an extension school, as he did on the "Aetna fireship":

> I now became the captain's steward, in such situation I was very happy: for I was extremely well treated by all on board; and I had leisure to improve myself in reading and writing. The latter I had learned a little of before I left the Namur, as there was a school on board.[7]

Equiano, in short, leaves a trail of evidence to prove that he was fully capable of writing his own life's story. Despite these clues, however, at least the reviewer for The Monthly Review wondered aloud about the assistance of "some English writer" in the production of his text.[8]

Equiano uses the trope of the Talking Book in his third chapter, in which he describes his voyages from Barbados to Virginia and on to England. It is on this voyage that he begins to learn English. Equiano uses the trope as a climax of several examples sprinkled throughout the early pages of this chapter of sublime moments of cross-cultural encounters experienced by the wide-eyed boy. His encounters with a watch and a portrait are among the first items on his list:

5. Equiano, Vol. I, pp. 98, 109 [46, 49].
6. Ibid., pp. 132–33 [56].
7. Ibid., pp. 151–52 [62].
8. Monthly Review (June 1789): 551. [See p. 295 in this NCE. Editor.]

> The first object that engaged my attention was a watch which hung on the chimney, and was going. I was quite surprised at the noise it made, and was afraid it would tell the gentleman any thing I might do amiss: and when I immediately after observed a picture hanging in the room, which appeared constantly to look at me, I was still more affrighted, having never seen such things as these before. At one time I thought it was something relative to magic; and not seeing it move I thought it might be some way the whites had to keep their great men when they died, and offer them libations as we used to do our friendly spirits.[9]

When he sees snow for the first time, he thinks it is salt. He concludes just before introducing as a separate paragraph the Talking Book scene, "I was astonished at the wisdom of the white people in all things I saw."[1]

Equiano returns to Gronniosaw's use of the trope for its details and refers to gold only implicitly, in his reference to the "watch which hung on the chimney." The trope is presented in a self-contained paragraph, which does not refer directly either to the paragraph that precedes it or to the one that follows. Nevertheless, the trope culminates the implicit list of wonderments that the young African experiences at the marvels of the West. As Equiano narrates:

> I had often seen my master and Dick employed in reading; and I had a great curiosity to talk to the books, as I thought they did; and so to learn how all things had a beginning: for that purpose I have often taken up a book, and have talked to it, and then put my ears to it, when alone, in hopes it would answer me; and I have been very much concerned when I found it remained silent.[2]

A watch, a portrait, a book that speaks: these are the elements of wonder that the young African encounters on his road to Western culture. These are the very signs through which Equiano represents the difference in subjectivity that separates his, now lost, African world from the New World of "white folks" that has been thrust upon him.

Significantly, Equiano endows each of these objects with his master's subjectivity. The portrait seems to be watching him as he moves through the room. The watch, he fears, can see, hear, and speak, and appears to be quite capable of and willing to report his actions to his sleeping master once he awakes. The watch is his master's surrogate overseer, standing in for the master as an authority figure, even while he sleeps. The painting is also a surrogate figure of the master's authority, following his movements silently as he walks about the room. The book that speaks to "my master and Dick" is a double sign of subjec-

9. Equiano, Vol. I, pp. 92–93 [44].
1. Ibid., pp. 104, 106 [48].
2. Ibid., pp. 106–7 [48].

tivity, since Equiano represents its function as one that occurs in dialogue between a human being and its speaking pages. What can we make of these elements that comprise Equiano's list of the salient signs of difference?

While dramatizing rather effectively the sensitive child's naiveté and curiosity, and his ability to interpret the culture of the Europeans from a distinctly African point of reference, Equiano is contrasting his earlier self with the self that narrates his text. This, certainly, is essential to his apparent desire to represent in his autobiography a dynamic self that once was "like that" but is now "like this." His ability to show his readers his own naiveté, rather than merely to tell us about it or to claim it, and to make this earlier self the focus of his readers' sympathy and amusement, are extraordinarily effective rhetorical strategies that serve to heighten our identification with the openly honest subject whose perceptions these were and who has remembered them for us to share. But Equiano is up to much more. Under the guise of the representation of his naive self, he is naming or reading Western culture closely, underlining relationships between subjects and objects that are implicit in commodity cultures. Watches do speak to their masters, in a language that has no other counterpart in this culture, and their language frequently proves to be the determining factor in the master's daily existence. The narrative past and the narrative present through which the narrator's consciousness shifts so freely and tellingly are symbolized by the voice that the young Equiano attributes to the watch. Portraits, moreover, do stare one in the face as one moves about within a room. They are also used as tokens of the immortality of their subjects, commanding of their viewers symbolic "libations," which the young Equiano "thought it might." Portraits are would-be tropes against the subject's mortality, just as Equiano imagined them to be. Books, finally, do speak to Europeans, and not to the Africans of the eighteenth century. The book recognizes "my master and Dick," acknowledging both their voices and their faces by engaging in a dialogue with them; neither the young African's voice nor his face can be recognizable to the text, because his countenance and discourse stand in Western texts as signs of absence, of the null and void. The young Equiano has read these texts closely, and rather tellingly, while the older Equiano represents this reading at a double-voiced level, allowing his readers to engage this series of encounters on both a manifest and a latent level of meaning.

But what can we make of the shift of tenses (from "had" to "have," for example) in Equiano's passage on the Talking Book? One key to reading this shift of tenses within the description itself is Equiano's endowment of these objects of Western culture with the master's subjectivity. Equiano, the slave, enjoys a status identical to that of the watch, the portrait, and the book. He is the master's object, to be used and enjoyed, purchased, sold, or discarded, just like a watch, a portrait, or a book. By law, the slave has no more and no less rights than do the other objects that the master collects and endows with his subjectivity. Of course the book does not speak to him. Only subjects can endow an object with subjectivity; objects, such as a slave, possess no inherent subjectivity of their own. Objects can only reflect the subjectivity of the subject, like a mirror does. When Equiano, the object, attempts to speak to the book, there follows only the deafening silence that obtains between two lifeless objects. Only a subject can speak. Two mirrors can only reflect each other, in an endless pattern of voided repetition. But they cannot speak to each other, at least not in the language of the master. When the master's book looks to see whose face is behind the voice that Equiano speaks, it can only see an absence, the invisibility that dwells in an unattended looking-glass.

Through the act of writing alone, Equiano announces and preserves his newly found status as a subject. It is he who is the master of his text, a text that speaks volumes of experience and subjectivity. If once he too was an object, like a watch, a portrait, or a book, now he has endowed himself with his master's culture's ultimate sign of subjectivity, the presence of a voice which is the signal feature of a face. The shift in verb tenses creates irony, because we, his readers, know full well by this moment within the narrative that Equiano the narrator no longer speaks to texts that cannot see his face or that, therefore, refuse to address him. Equiano the author is a speaking subject, "just like" his master. But he is not "just like" his master and never can be in a culture in which the blackness of his face signifies an absence. Nevertheless, Equiano's use of shifting tenses serves to represent the very movement that he is experiencing (in a Middle Passage, as was Gronniosaw) as he transforms himself from African to Anglo-African, from slave to potential freedman, from an absence to a presence, and indeed from an object to a subject.

If the master's voice endows his objects with reflections of his subjectivity, then the representation, in writing, of the master's voice (and this process of endowment or reflection of subjectivity) serves to enable the object to remake himself into a subject. Equiano's shift in tenses enables his readers to observe him experiencing the silent text, within a narrative present that has been inscribed within a passage from his past; but it also serves, implicitly, to represent the difference between the narrator and this character of his (past) self, a difference marked through verb tense as the difference between object and subject. The process by which the master endows his commodities with the reflection of subjectivity, as figured in the African's readings of the watch, the portrait, and the book, is duplicated by Equiano's narrator's account of his own movement from slave-object to author-subject. The shift of tenses is Equiano's grammatical analogue of this process of becoming—of becoming a human being who reads differently from the child, of becoming a subject by passing a test (the mastery of writing) that no object can pass, and of becoming an author who represents, under the guise of a series of naive readings, an object's "true" nature by demonstrating that he can now read these objects in both ways, as he once did in the Middle Passage but also as he does today. The narrator's character of himself, of course, reads on a latent level of meaning; the first test of subjectivity is to demonstrate the ability to read on a manifest level. By revising the trope of the Talking Book, and by shifting from present to past and back to present, Equiano the author is able to read these objects simultaneously on both levels and to demonstrate his true mastery of the text of Western letters and the text of his verbal representation of his past and present selves.

What does this complex mode of representation suggest about Equiano's revisionary relationship to his friend and companion Cugoano? Cugoano had left Equiano very little room in which to maneuver, both by implicitly naming the "original" of the Anglo-African tradition's central trope and then by representing it as a fiction of a fiction, as a story about a story. Cugoano's bracketed narrative of Atahualpa calls attention to itself by removing it from the linear flow of the rest of his narrative, in a manner not found in the usages of either Gronniosaw or Marrant. By 1787, then, the trope could not be utilized without a remarkable degree of self-consciousness. So Cugoano engages in two maximal signs of self-consciousness: he uses the trope as an allegory of storytelling, allowing the characters even to speak in direct discourse, and simultaneously names its source, which is Gronniosaw and Marrant in one line of descent and an Inca historian in another line of descent. Equiano could not, as Gronniosaw and Marrant had done, simply make the trope a part of a linear narrative. So he subordinates it to a list of latent readings of the "true" nature of Western culture and simultaneously allows it to function as an allegory of his own act of fashioning an Anglo-African self out of words. Equiano's usage amounts to a fiction about the making of a fiction. His is a Signifyin(g) tale that Signifies upon the Western order of things, of which his willed black present self is the ironic double. If Cugoano names the trope, Equiano names his relation to Western culture through the trope. But he also, through his brilliant revision, names his relation to his three antecedent authors as that of the chain of narrators, a link, as it were, between links.

* * *

GERALDINE MURPHY

Olaudah Equiano, Accidental Tourist†

As most readers will recognize, my title refers to Anne Tyler's recent novel, *The Accidental Tourist*. Macon Leary, the protagonist, writes travel guides for business types who loathe traveling. The logo for his series is a stuffed living room chair sprouting wings: "While armchair travelers dream of going places, travelling armchairs dream of staying put." Like his readers, the leery Macon resists travel to territories unknown, psychological or geographical; living in a cocoon of familiar and familial habits to ward off the contingencies of postmodern life, he is an accidental tourist who stubbornly takes the *heimlich* with him wherever he goes. The author of an eighteenth-century slave narrative, *The Interesting Narrative of the Life of Olaudah Equiano, or Gustavus Vassa, the African*, is an accidental tourist of another sort. Kidnapped from his home in Benin (now Nigeria) at the age of eleven, he is transported from owner to owner in a bewildering series of transfers from the interior of the continent to a slave ship bound for the new world. Unlike Macon, of course, the young Equiano doesn't have the luxury or resources to take his home with him.

"Travel," bell hooks observes, "is not a word that can easily be evoked to talk about the Middle Passage, the Trail of Tears, the landing of Chinese immigrants, the forced relocation of Japanese-Americans, or the plight of the homeless."[1] On the contrary, travel connotes a voluntary, temporary change of environment. The autonomy, leisure, self-cultivation, and intellectual curiosity associated with this activity bespeak the privileges of class, gender, and—as hooks's examples pointedly suggest—race. Although actual travelers have been a fairly heterogeneous lot, the symbolic traveler is constituted as white, male, and European, as subject rather than object, observer rather than spectacle. It takes no great leap of imagination to see how European travel writing from the Renaissance to the modern era has figured in the production of a "non-west" available for colonization and empire building. In this binary scheme, westerners are travelers, and nonwesterners are travelees—static spectacle or hapless pawns.[2]

---

† Geraldine Murphy, "Olaudah Equiano, Accidental Tourist," *Eighteenth-Century Studies* 27 (1994): 551–68. © 1994 American Society for Eighteenth-Century Studies. Reprinted by permission of the Johns Hopkins University Press. Bracketed page numbers refer to this Norton Critical Edition.

1. bell hooks, *Black Looks: Race and Representation* (Boston: South End Press, 1992), 173.

2. In *Orientalism*, Edward W. Said speaks of the *"positional* superiority" of the westerner: "The scientist, the scholar, the missionary, the trader, or the soldier was in, or thought about, the Orient because he *could be there*, or could think about it, with very little resistance on the Orient's part." (New York: Vintage, 1979), 7.

Nevertheless, Equiano, the travel*ee* ripped from his family and culture and westernized perforce, becomes a travel*er* himself when he grows up, observing Europe and other continents just as Europeans had observed Africa. After surviving the middle passage, Equiano (whose Igbo name means "one favored, and having a loud voice"),[3] is purchased by a British naval officer and accompanies him through several campaigns of the Seven Years War with France. Captain Pascal renames the unwilling boy Gustavus Vassa—ironically, after the sixteenth-century Swedish king who liberated his country from Denmark. Though fond of Equiano, Pascal is enraged by his assumption, apparently encouraged by the common sailors, that he is free and entitled to the prize money he has won in boxing matches; as a result, Pascal sells him to a Quaker merchant in the West Indies. Equiano becomes the first mate on his new master's sloop and manages to buy his freedom in Franklinesque fashion by painstakingly accumulating capital through his trading ventures among the islands and the southern coast of the United States. In his early twenties he returns to England, but still of a "roving disposition," he ships out on voyages to Asia Minor, southern Europe, and the West Indies and on the Phipps expedition to the North Pole. Although he had been baptized as a boy by Captain Pascal, Equiano becomes preoccupied with his spiritual condition after escaping death on the polar trip, and he undergoes a conversion experience. Other notable adventures he records in the *Narrative* include a stint as a plantation overseer on the Muskito coast and a role in the ill-fated recolonization effort in Sierra Leone. Throughout the course of the *Narrative*, Equiano often longs for death and bemoans his removal from Africa, but his spiritual and material development reveals a pattern of acculturation and self-authorization as a British subject. That which was *unheimlich* to the African child became conventional to the Anglicized adult.

What interests me in this "interesting narrative" is the intersection of the slave narrative and the travelogue. Equiano's Narrative initiates the tradition of African-American slave narrative and serves as a palimpsest for Frederick Douglass's well-known autobiography.[4] What had become a highly conventionalized genre by the mid-nineteenth century, however, was a much more fluid enterprise for Equiano. His *Narrative* incorporates elements of spiritual autobiography, the newly emerging secular success story, and the political discourse of the humanitarian/abolitionist movement, not to mention travel writing. Many critics have noted that slave narratives are "transcultural" or "hybrid" productions, written within and against the terms of the dom-

3. Olaudah Equiano, *The Interesting Narrative of the Life of Olaudah Equiano, or Gustavus Vassa, the African* in *The Classic Slave Narratives*, ed. Henry Louis Gates, Jr. (New York: NAL Penguin, 1987), 20 [27]. Subsequent references are cited parenthetically in the text.
4. Gates, "Introduction," *Classic Slave Narratives*, xiii-xiv.

inant culture, and Equiano's is no exception.[5] The discourse of travel embedded in his text seems one of its most incongruous features, because it implicates Equiano in the imperial gaze as well as western modes of knowing. Yet at the same time, his race complicates what feminist film theorists have called "the look" and calls into question the stability of European identity. (Through the ethnographic gaze of the Other, Equiano negotiates a position that I will call "dissident colonialism.")

The colonizing gaze of the imperial *imaginaire* is in some respects congruent with the male gaze described by Laura Mulvey, and it is worth examining such theoretical paradigms of power relations before turning to the historical moment of Equiano's *Narrative* and its relationship to eighteenth-century travel literature. In her now-classic article, "Visual Pleasure and Narrative Cinema," Mulvey argues that the patriarchal unconscious activates a series of gendered oppositions in classical Hollywood cinema: male/female, active/passive, sadistic/masochistic, narrative/spectacle. "The determining male gaze," she asserts, "projects its fantasy onto the female figure, which is styled accordingly. In their traditional exhibitionistic role women are simultaneously looked at and displayed, with their appearance coded for strong visual and erotic impact so that they can be said to connote *to-be-looked-at-ness*."[6] The woman as icon, however, to continue with Mulvey's argument, represents the threat of castration and provokes two responses on the part of the male—voyeuristic investigation of the female (a sadistic enterprise associated with film noir) or "fetishistic scopophilia" (a camp celebration à la Sternberg and Dietrich), which, by over-exalting the female object of desire, renders her harmless. In the corresponding hermeneutic of imperial desire, the colonial Other, in this case Africa, is spectacle to Europe's controlling gaze.[7] Moreover, if we think of stereotypes of the ignoble and noble savage as the European responses to the "threat" of the other, then these two contrasting images could be construed, respectively, as sadistic and fetishistic. The figure of the ignoble savage, which I am associating with investigative

5. "Transcultural" is Mary Louise Pratt's term in *Imperial Eyes: Travel Writing and Transculturation* (London and New York: Routledge, 1992); Homi K. Bhabha uses "hybrid" in "Signs Taken for Wonders: Questions of Ambivalence and Authority under a Tree Outside Delhi, May 1817," *"Race," Writing, and Difference*, ed. Henry Louis Gates, Jr. (Chicago: Univ. of Chicago Press, 1986), 163–84. Americanists, perhaps following DuBois's example, tend to stress the bicultural character of African-American writing. For a useful exception, see Susan M. Marren, "Between Slavery and Freedom: The Transgressive Self in Olaudah Equiano's Autobiography," *PMLA* 108 (1993): 94–105. Marren describes the "transgressive self" in terms of "a fluid positioning, a mode of articulation of newly imagined, radically nonbinary subjectivities," 95.

6. Laura Mulvey, "Visual Pleasure and Narrative Cinema," *Narrative Apparatus, Ideology: A Film Theory Reader*, ed. Philip Rosen (New York: Columbia Univ. Press, 1986), 198–209, quoted 203. This 1975 essay is widely anthologized.

7. In addition to the travel narratives, there are those nonwestern peoples who were brought back to Europe for display, from Columbus's cargo of Native Americans to Saartjie, the "Hottentot Venus."

voyeurism, was an ideological prop to the slave trade. This particular response, according to Mulvey, lends itself to narrative. "Sadism," she says, "demands a story, depends upon making something happen, forcing a change in another person, a battle of will and strength, victory/defeat, all occurring in linear time with a beginning and an end."[8] The concept of the noble savage, on the other hand, corresponds to fetishistic scopophilia, which is static and pictorial rather than linear and developmental. Whereas the ignoble savage initiates the story of Europe's civilizing mission, the noble savage, living in a timeless, Arcadian simplicity, demands nothing more than nostalgic appreciation on the part of the European beholder.

As suggestive as Mulvey's argument is for understanding the dynamics of the European gaze, it does not provide any clues as to what is at stake when the African looks. Film theorists such as Linda Williams and Mary Ann Doane, who have studied the woman's look, note that the "good girl" is often literally or figuratively blind and that the woman who exercises the active gaze reserved for male desire is usually punished for her assertiveness. Race, as well as gender, however, needs to be factored into this relay of looks because for African-American males, at least, the gaze has been similarly fraught with danger.[9] "Reckless eyeballing," for example, which means looking appropriatively at a white woman, was grounds for lynching. As a child, Frederick Douglass was astonished that his new mistress, who had never owned slaves before and was uncorrupted by the institution of slavery, "did not deem it impudent or unmannerly for a slave to look her in the face."[1] For Equiano, as a sailor who had witnessed the rape of African women by white men on board and was powerless to intervene, there could be no simple conflation of sexual and imperial conquest.

Several critics have commented on the two voices of Equiano's *Narrative*, that of the naive African child and the Westernized adult; I would like to suggest that these voices are accompanied by two opposing gazes. The African boy's gaze—at the slave ship, sailing instruments, the Europeans, books, grampuses, snow, and the streets and houses of Falmouth—is often indulged by whites because it is the diametrical opposite of the voyeuristic, appropriative gaze. Indeed, it can prompt voyeurism in the European. When on his first voyage to England Equiano wakes to another first, a snowfall, he runs below to fetch the mate and show him the extraordinary quantity of salt on the

8. Mulvey, 205.
9. See, for example, Linda Williams, "When the Woman Looks," in *Re-Vision: Essays in Feminist Film Criticism*, ed. Mary Ann Doane, Patricia Mellencamp, and Linda Williams (Los Angeles: Univ. Publications of America, 1984), 83–99. Deborah E. McDowell briefly addresses the issue of race and the gaze in "Negotiating between Tenses: Witnessing Slavery after Freedom—*Dessa Rose*," *Slavery and the Literary Imagination*, ed. Deborah E. McDowell and Arnold Rampersad (Baltimore: Johns Hopkins Univ. Press, 1989), 153–54.
1. *Narrative of the Life of Frederick Douglass* in Gates, *Classic Slave Narratives*, 48.

ship's deck. "He, knowing what it was," Equiano recalls, "desired me to bring some of it down to him; accordingly I took up a handful of it, which I found very cold indeed; and when I brought it to him he desired me to taste it. I did so, and was surprised above measure" (43) [48]. According to Jean-Paul Sartre, "to see is to *deflower*. If we examine the comparisons ordinarily used to express the relation between the knower and the known," he continues, "we see that many of them are represented as being a kind of *violation by sight*."[2] The African child's look, however—either of terror or wonder—collapses the distance and the hierarchical, gendered relationship between knower and known. He is ravished by the spectacle, rather than vice versa. The center of power shifts, then, from the beholder to the object beheld—the technological achievements of the west, for example—and of course to the European witness whose gaze encompasses both.

Equiano's adult gaze, as I mentioned above, cannot be equated with the appropriative, colonizing gaze, the "violation by sight" that Sartre describes, because he is marginalized by race, nation, and class, if not by gender. On the contrary, he "sees" violations, literally as in the case of African women, but other instances of injustice as well. In describing Turkey, for example, he notes "how the Greeks are, in some measure, kept under by the Turks, as the Negroes are in the West Indies by white people" (124) [127]. After praising the beauty of Genoa's architecture, he concludes by saying "all of the grandeur was, in my eyes, disgraced by the galley-slaves, whose condition, both there and in other parts of Italy is truly piteous and wretched" (125) [128]. In his account of the Phipps expedition to the North Pole, Equiano expresses pride in their advancing farther than any other explorers; nevertheless, his introductory sentence encompasses both secular ambition and Christian humility: "I was roused by the sound of fame to seek new adventures and find toward the North Pole what our Creator never intended we should, a passage to India" (128) [131]. Equiano invokes Columbus only to mock his own ambitions. He further spoofs them by revealing that in trying to keep a journal of the expedition, he almost blew up the ship when he lit candles in a tiny chemical storeroom.

On the other hand, Equiano's adult gaze is not, cannot be, entirely dissociated from the colonizing project. Recalling the six- or seven-month journey from his homeland to the coast, he describes the lands through which he travels not from the perspective of a captive child but with an evaluating, entrepreneurial eye, in a manner reminiscent of John Smith's descriptions of American plantations:

> It would be tedious and uninteresting to relate all the incidents which befell me during this journey. . . . I shall therefore only

2. Quoted in Tania Modleski, *The Women Who Knew Too Much: Hitchcock and Feminist Theory* (New York: Routledge, 1989), 63.

observe, that in all the places where I was, the soil was exceedingly rich; the pomkins, aedas, plantains, yams, &c. &c. were in great abundance, and of incredible size. There were also large quantities of different gums, though not used for any purpose; and everywhere a great deal of tobacco. The cotton even grew quite wild; and there was plenty of red wood. I saw no mechanics whatever in all the way. . . . The chief employment in all these countries was agriculture, and both the males and females, as with us, were brought up to it, and trained in the arts of war. (32) [38]

In Equiano's *Narrative*, Africa is not the dark continent, but it is the undeveloped continent waiting to be cultivated by Europe. The colonizing eye of such passages is consistent with several of the roles Equiano plays once he has acquired his freedom: overseer of his friend Dr. Irving's short-lived plantation on the Muskito coast; mentor to a young Muskito Indian prince on the voyage to Jamaica from England; and commissary for the Sierra Leone colony. His assumptions of these duties may represent to some modern readers assimilation or capitulation,[3] but they also subversively expose the positionality of European–and African–identity. This is obvious to the Muskito prince, who asks, "How comes it that all the *white men* on board, who can read and write, observe the sun and know all things, yet swear, lie, and get drunk, only *excepting yourself?*" (154 [154], italics added). On the plantation, Equiano once adapted Columbus's ruse of taking credit for an eclipse to strike fear in unruly Indians: "it succeeded beyond my most sanguine expectations," he notes (157) [157]. Clearly, defining Equiano's gaze is no easy matter.

The concept of the male/colonizing gaze is valuable because it insistently foregrounds the power relations of point of view, yet at the same time its binary oppositions can occlude the historical dimensions of looking. In order to understand the uses of travel in Equiano's *Narrative*, we must situate it in the appropriate historical contexts, namely the imperial moment of the late eighteenth century (especially the relationship between England and Africa) and the genre of travel writing with which that process is so closely allied. Unfortunately, history does not conform to the neat schemata that I have presented. My analogy between the ignoble/noble savage and Mulvey's psychoanalytical categories of voyeurism/scopophilia, for example, implies that primitivism marked an *end*, that imperial desire had given way to nostalgia; however preferable that might have been, we know that it was

3. One commentator, for example, in an essay generally sympathetic to Equiano, refers to instances of "mental colonization." See Chinosole, "Tryin' to Get Over: Narrative Posture in Equiano's Autobiography," in *The Art of the Slave Narrative: Original Essays in Criticism and Theory*, ed. John Sekora and Darwin T. Turner (Macomb: Western Illinois Univ. Press, 1982), 45–54.

not the case. While primitivism lent aid and comfort to the abolitionist cause, it was not so much incompatible with European colonization efforts but rather served them in a different way than did the concept of the ignoble savage or (as "he" is often called) the Wild Man.[4]

The lengthy description of the "manners and customs" of his native Benin with which Equiano opens the *Narrative* has to be considered in the context of travel writing on Guinea, both overtly racist and more enlightened accounts. Much of the early literature on West Africa was written by travelers engaged in the slave trade, who represented African culture as so dehumanized that New World slavery was actually a providential blessing. According to William Bosman, John Barbot, and William Snelgrave, among others, the African was indolent, idolatrous, deceitful, and depraved; moreover, these writers manifested what one historian calls a "Kinseyan interest" in African sexuality: both men and women were lascivious, but in Barbot's view the latter were "hotter than the men" and readily prostituted themselves to Europeans, "so great is their inclination to white men." Pro-slavery discourse offered accounts of cannibalism and often provided lurid scenes of torture and execution that matched the barbarity of Orientalism without its accompanying luxury. The crude racism and sexism of these travelogues not only underwrote the authors' own interests but provided ideological justification for any qualms that might arise in the metropole. Toward the end of the eighteenth century, when the slave trade was increasingly under attack, pro-slavery forces revived stereotypes of the ignoble savage provided by the earlier travelogues in order to refute the arguments of the abolitionist movement.[5]

Abolitionists and humanitarians were themselves obliged to engage the travel literature on Africa in making a case *against* the slave trade. They did so by reading racist accounts against the grain and by relying on more enlightened, "scientific" travelogues, the fruits of what Mary Louise Pratt calls "anti-conquest." In his preface to *Some Historical Account of Guinea* (1771), for example, the Quaker abolitionist Anthony Benezet announced his intentions to set straight a record that had been distorted by pro-slavery interests. He cited James Barbot

4. On the other hand, Hayden White, in his consideration of the fetishistic status of the noble savage in eighteenth-century thought, argues that it had nothing to do with the inhabitants of distant continents and archipelagos. The true referent of the concept was to be found in the upper ranks of European society: "the idea of the Noble Savage is used," he says, "not to dignify the native, but rather to undermine the idea of nobility itself." It served an insurgent bourgeoisie in its own struggle for hegemony, a bourgeoisie that was largely indifferent to the interests of natives abroad or the working class at home. "The Noble Savage Theme as Fetish" in *Tropics of Discourse: Essays in Cultural Criticism* (Baltimore: John Hopkins Univ. Press, 1978), 191, 194.

5. J. Robert Constantine, "The Ignoble Savage: An Eighteenth-Century Literary Stereotype," *Phylon* 27 (1966): 171–79; John Barbot quoted, 174. See also Wylie Sypher, *Guinea's Captive Kings: British Anti-Slavery Literature of the XVIIIth Century* (1942; New York: Farrar, Straus and Giroux, 1969), 32, 38.

(John's brother) on the severe punishments in Benin for adultery—not, however, to illustrate the Other's barbarity but rather to contrast African respect for the family (which such penalties implied) with British indifference (which was apparent from the slaveholders' casual separation of slave families).[6] In drawing a more sympathetic portrait of the African, Benezet drew extensively on Thomas Astley's *A New General Collection of Voyages and Travels* (1746). Astley's volume included some sensationalistic material but concentrated more on topography and the sorts of manners and customs that Europeans would find unexceptional. Turning the African wilderness into a cultivated garden, and dwelling on the "innocent simplicity" the natives maintained, even among Europeans,[7] Benezet substituted a positive stereotype for a negative one. His rhetorical maneuver was by no means idiosyncratic, for by the 1770s, thanks to the influence of the abolitionist movement, Africans were increasingly perceived according to the same conventions of primitivist idealism as American Indians and Polynesians. "Here," said Philip Curtin, speaking of Benezet's abolitionist account of Guinea, "the literary figure of the noble savage, so often painted in fiction, reappeared as 'fact.' "[8]

The dramatic transformation of the African from a dehumanized beast into a noble savage (and the African landscape from a wilderness to a garden) had, of course, more to do with European imperatives than African realities. The momentum of British imperialism stalled in the late eighteenth century for a number of reasons. For one, the North American colonies had achieved their independence. For another, in Africa and elsewhere, tropical diseases impeded the next step after coastal trading posts were established—namely the exploration of the interior—until the Victorians realized the benefits of quinine. Perhaps most importantly, the oppression and enslavement of Africans could not be squared with either Enlightenment philosophies of natural rights and humanitarianism or the precepts of evangelical Protestantism. In no small measure, abolitionist movements in France and England helped undermine imperial confidence. The response to these developments was complex; on the one hand, England strengthened its hold on the sugar islands and turned to Latin America as a fresh field for colonization. On the other, it began to imagine a new relationship with West Africa, one in which the slave trade was abandoned in favor of commerce. From the turn of the century, then, until the invention of a Dark Continent legitimated a new phase of impe-

6. Anthony Benezet, *Some Historical Account of Guinea: Its Situation, Produce, and the General Disposition of Its Inhabitants, with an Inquiry into the Rise and Progress of the Slave Trade, Its Nature, and Lamentable Effect*, 4th ed. (repr., London, 1788), 31–32.

7. Ibid., 2.

8. Philip D. Curtin, *The Image of Africa: British Ideas and Action, 1780–1850*, vol. 1 (Madison: Univ. of Wisconsin Press, 1964), 49, 54.

rialism, Africa was portrayed in a relatively benign light, as befitted a potential trading partner.[9]

Along with prominent British abolitionists, Equiano saw "legitimate" trade as a pragmatic and enlightened alternative to the slave trade and, with an eye to the Parliamentary debates of the late 1780s, concluded his narrative with arguments to that effect:

> The manufacturers of this country must and will, in the nature and reason of things, have a full and constant employ by supplying the African markets.
>
> Population, the bowels, and surface of Africa, abound in valuable and useful returns; the hidden treasures of centuries will be brought to light and into circulation. Industry, enterprise, and mining, will have their full scope, proportionably as they civilize. In a word, it lays open an endless field of commerce to the British manufactures and merchant adventurer. The manufacturing interest and the general interests are synonymous. The abolition of slavery would be in reality an universal good. (First ed. II, 253) [177]

With postcolonial hindsight, we wince at such sentiments. Rarely do commentators on Equiano's *Narrative* address them. It is important to remember, however, that Equiano did not have classic underdevelopment in mind for his homeland; his vision of "an universal good" included Africa as well. "Dissident colonialism," my term for Equiano's political stance,[1] may be oxymoronic for us, but in the context of the immediate struggle, it is hard to argue with his judgment—based on bitter experience—that purchasing British commodities was preferable to being one.

This newly imagined commercial relationship with Africa provides the rationale for Equiano's report, quoted above, on soil conditions, cotton, tobacco, and gum trees; here he implies that many of the cash crops grown in the West Indies and southern United States for European markets could be cultivated in the Niger valley. (It is worth remembering that Equiano was kidnapped from the same African interior that the trade-oriented African Association, which funded Mungo Park's exploration, was so eager to penetrate thirty years later.) The idea of trade also influences Equiano's description of Igbo society. Neither demonic nor Edenic, it is remarkably similar to the village life that English poets idealized:

---

9. Ibid., xii, 5–6; Keith A. Sandiford, *Measuring the Moment: Strategies of Protest in Eighteenth-Century Afro-English Writing* (London: Associated Univ. Press, 1988), 43–72; Patrick Bratlinger, "Victorians and Africans: The Genealogy of the Myth of the Dark Continent," "*Race*," *Writing, and Difference*, 189, 192; Pratt, *Imperial Eyes*, 70–74.

1. Dissident colonialism, I should add, is only one aspect of his political identity. Peter Linebaugh describes the influential part Equiano played in the London working-class movement of the late eighteenth century. See *The London Hanged: Crime and Civil Society in the Eighteenth Century* (London: Allen Lane, 1991), 415–16.

Agriculture is our chief employment; and every one, even to children and women, is engaged in it. Thus we are habituated to labour from our earliest years. Every one contributes something to the common stock: and as we are unacquainted with idleness, we have no beggars. The benefits of such a mode of living are obvious.—The West India planters prefer the slaves of Benin or Eboe, to those of any part of Guinea, for their hardiness, intelligence, integrity and zeal. (17) [24–25]

There is no intended irony in the last sentence, at least as I read it. Industry and intelligence are affirmed as universal virtues, and a work ethic—not enslavement—is the "obvious" consequence of a life of self-discipline and cooperation in an agricultural community. Eighteenth-century social philosophers posited four developmental stages of civilization, moving from an economy of hunting-gathering, to pastoralism, to farming, and finally to commerce;[2] by emphasizing the importance of agriculture, Equiano implicitly refutes theories of tropical degeneration and native indolence and puts Africa, chronologically, on the threshold of Western development.

As his remarks on agriculture suggest, Equiano's account of Igbo culture exists in dialogue with pro-slavery and antislavery travel literature. He is most eager to counteract the stereotypes of African women as sexually promiscuous. They were, according to him, "modest to a degree of bashfulness; nor do I remember to have ever heard of an instance of incontinence amongst them before marriage" (17 [25]; he turns the tables on the slave traders' accounts completely when he recalls his first unfavorable impressions of the forwardness of white women: "I thought them not so modest and shamefaced as the African women," 43 [48]). Equiano repeats (and footnotes) Benezet's observation on the severity of the punishment for adultery, which in turn highlights the value of female chastity. When it comes to sex and violence in Igbo culture, he treads much more delicately around the former. In describing marriage customs, for example, he westernizes polygamy by associating it with male adultery. "The men . . . do not preserve the same constancy to their wives, which they expect from them; for they indulge in a plurality, though seldom in more than two" (13) [21]. Such a practice would scarcely seem foreign to Europeans, though its wisdom would more likely be evident to male readers.

Equiano's sketch of Igbo manners and customs manifests his debt to the primitivism and cultural relativism that antislavery polemicists drew upon. "We are almost a nation of dancers, musicians, and poets"

2. On these four stages, see Ronald L. Meek, *Social Science and the Ignoble Savage* (Cambridge: Cambridge Univ. Press, 1975), 5–36. Peter Hulme and Ludmilla Jordanova note in their Introduction to *The Enlightenment and Its Shadows* (London: Routledge, 1990) that the eighteenth century produced "a different kind of map . . . in which all the stages of mankind's 'development' could be visible at a glance: the history of the world could be superimposed upon its geography" (9).

(14) [21], he says—echoing countless descriptions of the eloquence, dignity, and creativity of traditional societies.[3] Moreover, he cannily equates Igbo culture with primitivist Others closer to England: the Africans, for instance, dance like the Greeks; their clothing resembles a Highland plaid, and their pipes are like those found in Turkey (14–15) [22]. He concludes with a tentative theory that black Africans are descended from the Jews of the Old Testament "before they reached the Land of Promise . . . while they were yet in that pastoral state described in Genesis" (22) [29]. A Calvinist, Equiano would be inclined to read his culture in typological terms, spiritually awaiting the good news of the Gospels and materially achieving fulfillment in commercial partnership with the west. Equiano parts company with the primitivists in some respects, however; where Benezet (whose account he relied on extensively) focused on the good nature of the natives, Equiano unblinkingly notes their "warlike disposition" and mentions scarification and the display of severed limbs as war trophies—both of which practices invoke the ideology of savagery. According to Angelo Costanzo, "Equiano was trying to paint a picture of the African as a noble savage of heroic dignity, while Benezet perhaps was describing the African from the viewpoint of Quaker virtue."[4] It is also true, however, that Equiano has less invested in the tropes of noble savagery than enlightened Europeans; he refuses to adopt wholesale stereotypes of alterity, even positive ones. To Equiano, who served in the Seven Years War with Captain Pascal, the warrior ethos provided yet another parallel to European culture.

The portrait of manners and customs with which Equiano opens his *Narrative* is a highly conventionalized and stable feature of European travel writing whose purpose, most critics agree, is to rehearse Otherness. Michel de Certeau asserts that the travel account is organized according to an "*a priori* of difference," its three-part scheme consisting of an ahistorical ethnographic description of the savage "body" flanked by the narratives of departure and return.[5] Pratt describes manners and customs discourse in similar terms. It serves, she says, "to fix the Other in a timeless present where all 'his' actions and reactions are repetitions of 'his' normal habits"; its panoramic gaze is oddly impersonal and derives its authority "from a seat of power that should

---

3. Paul Goetsch compares this statement by Equiano to the following couplet in a contemporaneous antislavery tract: "Musicians, Poets, too, by nature taught, / A song spontaneous bursting from a thought"; he argues that Equiano was deliberately revising the "ignoble savage" image of Africans. "Linguistic Colonialism and Primitivism: The Discovery of Native Languages and Oral Traditions in Eighteenth-Century Travel Books and Novels," *Anglia* 106 (1988): 348.

4. Angelo Costanzo, *Surprising Narrative: Olaudah Equiano and the Beginnings of Black Autobiography* (New York: Greenwood Press, 1987), 55–56.

5. Michel de Certeau, "Montaigne's 'Of Cannibals': The Savage 'I,'" *Heterologies: Discourse on the Other*, trans. Brian Massumi (Minneapolis: Univ. of Minnesota Press, 1986), 69.

probably be identified with the state."[6] Equiano's detailed account of Igbo culture owes as much to the conventions of manners and customs as it does to his childhood memories, yet it is ambiguously suspended between memoir and ethnography. As an indigenous ethnographer, he upsets the classic three-part form and blurs the boundaries between self and Other. The speaking "I" is not effaced, for he employs the first person almost consistently throughout his sketch: "My father was one of those elders or chiefs of whom I have spoken, and was stiled Embrenche; a term, as I remember, importing the highest distinction, and signifying in our language a mark of grandeur" (12) [20]. "Our vegetables are mostly plaintains, eadas, yams, beans, and Indian corn" and so on (15) [22]. Only in describing religious beliefs does the converted Equiano shift into the third person: "the natives believe that there is one Creator of all things. . . . They believe he governs events, especially our deaths or captivity . . . some believe in the transmigration of souls" (19) [26]. Formally as well as thematically, then, Equiano's portrait of manners and customs affirms similarity as much as Otherness.

Equiano's travels, of course, are not confined to retrospective portraits of Igbo society. As a slave and a free man, he spent much of his adult life at sea, and his *Narrative* includes accounts of shipwreck and providential deliverance, successful trading ventures, and many more miscellaneous travel notes. Among the latter are manners and customs portraits of the various cultures he encounters. There are the Muskito Indians, for instance, who build houses communally, like the Africans:

> I do not recollect any of them to have had more than two wives. These always accompanied their husbands when they came to our dwelling, and then they generally carried whatever was brought to us, and always squatted down behind their husbands. Whenever we gave them any thing to eat, the men and their wives ate separate. I never saw the least sign of incontinence among them. The women are ornamented with beads, and fond of painting themselves; the men also paint, even to excess, both their faces and shirts: their favorite colour is red. The women generally cultivate the ground, and the men are all fishermen and canoe makers. Upon the whole, I never met any nation that were so simple in their manners as these people. (155–56) [156]

There are also the Turks, among whom he lived for five months on one trip. Briefly describing their architecture, their fruits, their hospitality to blacks, and the veiled women he occasionally glimpsed, he concludes with "one remarkable circumstance," the large, heavy tails

6. Pratt, "Scratches on the Face of the Country; or What Mr. Barrow Saw in the Land of the Bushmen," *"Race," Writing, and Difference,* 139, 145.

of their sheep. "The fat of them is very white and rich, and is excellent in puddings, for which it is much used. Our ship being at length richly loaded with silk and other articles, we sailed for England" (125) [127].

Equiano shifts into a more "scientific" mode in recounting his expedition to the North Pole (on which he almost blew up the ship, as noted above), incorporating what appear to be pages of his journal:

> On the 20th of June we began to use Dr. Irving's apparatus for making salt water fresh. I used to attend the distillery; I frequently purified from twenty-six to forty gallons a day. . . . On the 28th of June, being in lat. 78° we made Greenland, where I was surprised to see the sun did not set. . . .
>
> On the 30th, the Captain of a Greenland ship came on board, and told us of three ships that were lost in the ice; however, we still held on our course till July the 11th, when we were stopped by one compact impenetrable body of ice. We ran along it from east to west above ten degrees; and on the 27th we got as far north as 80°, 37'; and in 19 or 20 degrees east longitude from London. (129–30) [132]

Equiano describes an earthquake in the West Indies, an eruption of Mount Vesuvius ("we were so near that the ashes from it used to be thick on our deck" [126] (128), and a marriage at the foot of the gallows in New York City (170) (169). In subsequent editions of the *Narrative*, the penultimate paragraph mentions "a great variety of scenes" in the British Isles which unfortunately cannot be included, "as this would swell the volume too much"; the irrepressible traveler, however, cannot forgo a footnote:

> Viz. Some curious adventures beneath the earth, in a river in Manchester,—and a most astonishing one under the Peak of Derbyshire—and in September 1792, I went 90 fathoms down St. Anthony's Colliery, at Newcastle, under the river Tyne, some hundreds of yards on Durham side. (177) [187]

Travel discourse in Equiano's *Narrative* is an informal medley of natural wonders, remarkable sights, proto-ethnographic description and scientific information. Indeed, anything "interesting" is fair game.[7]

Mary Louise Pratt has coined the term "anti-conquest" to describe the bourgeois repudiation of an earlier, frankly imperialist rhetoric.

7. This is precisely the kind of discourse that the nineteenth-century slave narrative cannot accommodate. Douglass's *Narrative*, for example, is preoccupied with authenticity ("Written by Himself") rather than interest, and it is organized around the thematics of escape rather than travel. His journey from south to north, slavery to freedom, constitutes the central aporia of the text. Although he would like to reveal the details of his escape, doing so, he explains, would compromise his abettors and enlighten his enemies, the slaveholders. Douglass's well-known apostrophe to sailboats upon the Chesapeake Bay (the "most thrilling" passage in the narrative, according to William Lloyd Garrison) is a threnody of the stasis that defines his condition: "You are loosed from your moorings, and are free; I am fast in my chains, and am a slave!" (*Classic Slave Narratives*, 315, 293).

Both types of anti-conquest narratives—natural history on the one hand and sentimental egalitarianism on the other—maintain their "innocence" as they simultaneously elaborate European hegemony; in eighteenth-century travel writing, "science and sentiment code the imperial frontier in the two eternally clashing and complementary languages of bourgeois subjectivity."[8] Pratt situates the slave narrative within the sentimental camp, but Equiano's *Narrative* clearly includes both currents. The most striking example of his empiricist inclinations, to my mind, occurs fairly early in the text, while Equiano is still enslaved in the West Indies. Having described his lot as a slave on the island of Montserrat, Equiano seems determined to undermine the affective force of his own experience at a time when he felt the yoke of slavery most acutely. He forbears the litany of punishments and instruments of torture the slaves are subject to because "it cannot any longer afford novelty to recite them," and abruptly interpolates a visit to a sulfur spring:

> In the variety of departments in which I was employed by my master, I had an opportunity of seeing many curious scenes in different islands; but, above all, I was struck with a celebrated curiosity called Brimstone-Hill, which is a high and steep mountain, some few miles from the town of Plymouth, in Montserrat. I had often heard of some wonders that were to be seen on this hill, and I went once with some white and black people to visit it. When we arrived at the top, I saw under different cliffs great flakes of brimstone, occasioned by the steams of various little ponds, which were then boiling naturally in the earth. Some of these ponds were as white as milk, some quite blue, and many others of different colours. I had taken some potatoes with me, and I put them into different ponds, and in a few minutes they were well boiled. I tasted some of them, but they were very sulphurous; and the silver shoe-buckles, and all the other things we had among us of that metal, were in a little time, turned as black as lead. (82) [84–85]

What is the point of including this little excursion to Brimstone Hill? Aside from pointing out a local curiosity to visitors in the sugar islands, its value lies in the way it constitutes Equiano as the bourgeois subject. For a European naturalist, the discourse of scientific empiricism may provide, in Pratt's terms, a "way of taking possession without subjugation or violence."[9] For Equiano, too, a displaced, enslaved African still in his teens, it is a way of taking possession—not so much of the world, but of himself. Here, the universalist language of science doesn't serve to *mask* a bourgeois subjecthood already taken for granted but

8. Pratt, *Imperial Eyes*, 39.
9. Ibid., 57.

to *establish* one; the gaze equalizes black and white travelers.

Equiano's journey from "accidental tourist" to "dissident colonialist" is a remarkable achievement. His decision to continue his travels, to gaze at the west as Europeans had gazed at Africa, may have engaged him in the imperialist project despite himself, but it also opened up European identity to question in ways the west hadn't bargained for; in a very real sense, today's *Gastarbeiter* are the descendants of Equiano. His responding—and redefining—gaze was in itself testimony to the cultural parity that he so poignantly and mistakenly anticipated through the commercial development of West Africa.

ADAM POTKAY

From Olaudah Equiano and the Art of Spiritual Autobiography†

To read Equiano as he asks to be read, we must first reexamine his well-known "Talking-Book" episode, which, strictly speaking, is about a book that refuses to talk. Here, the older and quite literate Equiano recalls his first encounter with books, and his innocence of what they signified:

> I had often seen my master and Dick employed in reading; and I had a great curiosity to talk to the books, as I thought they did; and so to learn how all things had a beginning. For that purpose I have often taken up a book, and talked to it, and then put my ears to it, when alone, in hopes it would answer me; and I have been very much concerned when I found it remaining silent.[1]

What does this anecdote signify? What is its point? Surely, at the most basic level it is a tableau of considerable pathos and charm, soliciting a smile and engaging our sympathy on behalf of the young outsider. It is, too, Equiano's reflection on the daunting but ultimately not prohibitive chasm that separates the orality of his childhood from the literate culture to which he crossed over. And, as Henry Louis Gates has demonstrated, it affords an instance of the central topos of eighteenth-century African-English writing.[2]

† Adam Potkay, "Olaudah Equiano and the Art of Spiritual Autobiography,"*Eighteenth-Century Studies* 27 (1994): 677–90. © 1994 American Society for Eighteenth-Century Studies. Reprinted by permission of the Johns Hopkins University Press. Bracketed page numbers refer to this Norton Critical Edition.

1. *The Interesting Narrative of the Life of Olaudah Equiano, or Gustavus Vassa, the African* (1789; rev. ed. 1814), reprinted in *The Classic Slave Narratives*, ed. Henry Louis Gates, Jr. (New York: Mentor, 1987), 43–44 [48] hereafter abbreviated SN.
2. Gates, "The Trope of the Talking Book," ch. 4 of *The Signifying Monkey: A Theory of African-American Literary Criticism* (New York: Oxford Univ. Press, 1988), 127–69; hereafter abbreviated SM.

Gates traces this topos of the talking book back to the slave narrative of Ukawsaw Gronniosaw (1770); as Gronniosaw writes, recollecting a scene from his youth: "I was very sorry, and greatly disappointed, when I found that [the book] would not speak. This thought immediately presented itself to me, that every body and every thing despised me because I was black." Gates comments on this passage: "This desire for recognition of his self in the text of Western letters motivates Gronniosaw's creation of a text [his autobiography]. . . . The next refuses to speak to Gronniosaw, so some forty-five years later Gronniosaw writes a text that speaks his face into existence among the authors and texts of the Western tradition" (SM, 136–38). In other words, Gronniosaw's failure to "hear" the book—like that of Equiano after him—figures his alienation from Western literary culture, an alienation relieved by adding his own distinctive books to that culture.

Gates is drawn to the "talking book" topos because it establishes an African-English literary tradition: repeated and revised by successive black authors—Gronniosaw, Marrant, Cugoano, Equiano, and finally John Jea—it becomes an illustration of black texts talking to one another across time. I would argue, however, that the creation of a peculiarly black canon is only half the work performed by the particular talking book anecdote recounted by Equiano. Although Equiano may here be talking back to Gronniosaw, he is, in the very act of doing so, participating in a theological quest for origins. Equiano talks to books, quite specifically, "to learn how all things had a beginning." His curiosity about ultimate causes follows hard upon a series of questions about agency: upon first landing in England and seeing snow, the twelve-year-old Equiano asks his ship-mate "who made it; he told me a great man in the heavens, called God." The narrative voice continues:

> After this I went to church; and having never been at such a place before, I was again amazed at seeing and hearing the service. I asked all I could about it; and they gave me to understand it was "worshipping God, who made us and all things." I was still at a loss, and soon got into an endless field of inquiries, as well as I was able to speak and ask about things. (SN, 43) [48]

It is in light of Equiano's ultimately theological curiosity that his "great curiosity to talk to books" must be read: indeed, the book that Equiano as yet unwittingly desires to read is not just any book, nor just a synecdoche for Gates's "Western letters," but specifically the Bible, a book that claims to explain the genesis of all things.

Theological curiosity is precisely what links Equiano back to Gronniosaw.

*   *   *

In the early black autobiographies, the concern with origins always prefigures a devotion to the book that bespeaks origins. Indeed, the topos of the talking book last appears in the early nineteenth-century autobiography of John Jea, an ex-slave who recalls an ecstatic moment in his illiterate youth when an angelic vision taught him to "read" these words and these words only: "In the beginning was the Word, and the Word was with God, and the Word was God" (quoted in *SM*, 161). Thus, from Gronniosaw to Equiano to Jea, the true moral of the talking book is that an inquisitive spirit represents a perfection of the faculties and leads toward the literacy that enables one to find answers in the Bible.

The tug toward the solution is always, in these autobiographies, away from Africa (or at least, as we shall see, a literal understanding of Africa): surely and not unreasonably a delicate issue today. The fear that the black self will be assimilated into a larger white corpus is no less real than the eleven-year-old Equiano's persistent fear of being "eaten by those white men with horrible looks, red faces, and long hair" (*SN*, 33 [39]; cf. 40–41 [42]). The happy outcome of Equiano's literary life, however, is that he is not devoured by the white men—neither literally nor, I would argue, figuratively. He is not "digested," in the sense of being passively converted into something he might not have wished to become. Any transformation he undergoes is one he wills, guides, shapes, and controls. Of course, the neatest way to shape a life is in writing it down, fashioning it into the particular artifact one chooses—art being typically more full of willful choices than any life could be.

My argument is that Equiano reads and renders his own life—and perhaps, by extension, the life of his race—as mirroring the movement of Biblical history from the Old Testament to the New. That is, he reads the pattern of his life as reduplicating the pattern of salvation history found in the Christian Bible.[3] I will, in what follows, refer to this manner of reading by its traditional name of "tropology." Tropology is one aspect of the "fourfold interpretation" of Biblical texts, a hermeneutic famously elaborated in Dante's "Letter to Can Grand":

> And for the better illustration of this method of exposition, we
> may apply it to the following verses: "When Israel went out of
> Egypt, the house of Jacob from a people of strange language;
> Judah was his sanctuary, and Israel his dominion" [Psalms 114:1–
> 2]. For if we consider the letter alone, the thing signified to us is
> the going out of the children of Israel in the time of Moses; if we
> consider the allegory [typology], our redemption through Christ
> is signified; if the moral sense [tropology], the conversion of the

3. My argument is anticipated by remarks in Angelo Costanzo, *Surprizing Narrative: Olaudah Equiano and the Beginnings of Black Autobiography* (Westport, Conn.: Greenwood, 1987), 63–64.

soul from the sorrow and misery of sin to a state of grace is signified; if the anagogical, the passing of the sanctified soul from
the bondage of the corruption of this world to the liberty of everlasting glory is signified.[4]

To summarize the first three levels of Dante's fourfold exposition: the
literal level relates to a presumably historical event in the Hebrew Bible;
the typological level relates that event to an aspect of Christ's life; and
the tropological level, the level that interests us, relates the historical
event to an occurrence in our own spiritual lives.

In early modern Britain, writing one's life as a figural gloss on key
Biblical passages was no more than all good Puritans were apt to do.
Still, Equiano does so, as we shall see, with a number of distinctive
twists. First, unlike other Puritan spiritual autobiographies, Equiano's
"progress" is not *just* the tropological freeing of the soul from the symbolic Egypt of carnality; rather, his journey proceeds on a literal as well
as an allegorical level. According to Equiano's telling of his life, he
literally retraces the course of the Bible from patriarchal mores (mores
that are, quite directly, a patriarchal inheritance, traceable back to the
sons of Abraham and Keturah [SN, 22] (30)) to captivity in a strange
land; and from deliverance to repatriation in a Beulah land of the spirit.
In short, Equiano literally reenacts the basic narrative pattern of the
books of Genesis and Exodus, as well as learning, by his conversion or
Christian rebirth, to read Israelite history along with his own experience as an allegory of spiritual deliverance.

The second distinctive twist that Equiano applies to the genre of
spiritual autobiography is a startling mode of ethical irony: the irony
of at once affirming and renouncing a natural desire for violent revenge
upon one's captors. It is an irony that skirts what we might call the
"Egyptian quandary," or the question of how to condone the vengeance of Moses when writing in light of the Christian injunction to
turn other other cheek. Equiano delineates this quandary with subtle
power, and indeed, as I will suggest, bequeaths his method to later
African-English writing.

Both of Equiano's characteristic twists on the genre of autobiography will come into focus if we retrace the steps of his literal—and
figural—journey. The "progress" of his life consists of three main
stages. The first stage comprises his boyhood within his native "Eboe"
(or Igbo) culture, in the part of West Africa that is now Nigeria. To
the mature Equiano, Eboe society resembles nothing so much as the
society of the patriarchs. Indeed, recalling the time when his shipmate
Daniel Queen first taught him to read the Pentateuch, Equiano records
as his first response, "I was wonderfully surprised to see the laws and

---

4. *Dantis Alagherii Epistolae*, trans. and ed. Paget Toynbee, 2nd ed. (Oxford: Oxford Univ.
Press, 1966), 199.

rules of my own country written almost exactly here" (*SN*, 64) [68]. His entire presentation of Eboe society is designed to flesh out this parallel. As he writes at the virtual outset of his book, "I cannot forebear suggesting what has long struck me very forcibly, namely, the strong analogy, which . . . appears to prevail in the manners and customs of my countrymen and those of the Jews, before they reached the Land of Promise, and particularly the Patriarchs, while they were yet in that pastoral state which is described in Genesis" (*SN*, 22) [29]. He carefully explains the basis of the Eboe/Hebrew analogy:

> Like the Israelites in their primitive state, our government was conducted by our chiefs and judges, our wisemen, and elders; and the head of a family, with us, enjoyed a similar authority over his household with that which is ascribed to Abraham and the other Patriarchs. The law of retaliation prevailed almost universally with us as with them: and even their religion appeared to have shed upon us a ray of its glory. . . . For we had our circumcision (a rite, I believe, peculiar to that people): we also had our sacrifices and burnt offerings, our washings and purifications, on the same occasions as they had. (*SN*, 23) [30]

Of all the points of comparison between Hebrew and Eboe culture, the two upon which Equiano most insists throughout his narrative are a belief in the potency of names and a respect for the law of retaliation. The mature Equiano professes always to have been aware of the significance of naming and remarks that "like [the patriarchal Jews], our children were named for some event, some circumstance, or some fancied foreboding at the time of their birth. I was named Olaudah, which, in our language, signifies 'vicissitude or fortunate,' also, 'one favoured, and having a loud voice and well spoken' " (*SN*, 20) [27]. Equiano's narrative, evincing at once his eloquence and his ultimately fortunate fall, intends to confirm the foresight of his original naming.

The second shared element of Eboe and Hebrew culture stressed by Equiano is the law of retaliation. Equiano maintains that among his people legal proceedings "were generally short; and in most cases the law of retaliation prevailed" (*SN*, 13) [21]. This legal principle—or ethical imperative—is designed to limit violence to a more or less exact reciprocity; as the Mosaic Book of the Covenant codifies it, an "eye for eye, tooth for tooth, hand for hand, foot for foot, / Burning for burning, wound for wound, stripe for stripe" (Exodus 21: 24–25). Although this code is given to Moses on Mount Sinai, Equiano supposes that the general law of retaliation prevailed among the Israelites in the pre-Mosaic patriarchal era. And surely, before Moses receives the law there is already in the early chapters of Exodus the overarching pattern of retaliation between Pharaoh's ordering the death of all male Hebrew infants and Yahweh's tenth plague on Egypt, the extermination of the first born.

Although the pastoral state of Eboe/Hebrew culture thus represents the first stage of Equiano's life, its second stage is enslavement—an event that corresponds, of course, to the captivity of Israel in Egypt, the bondage of the house of Jacob among strangers. Equiano is kidnapped at the age of eleven, and sojourns among diverse African tribes on his way to the coast, where he is ultimately loaded upon a slave ship bound for Barbados. From the West Indies he is shipped to a Virginia plantation, where he works as a household servant. Here, as Equiano writes, "I thought that these [white] people were all made up of wonders. In this place I was called JACOB" (SN, 39) [44]. Now, empirically this act of naming may or may not be true; but literarily it is surely appropriate. For Jacob, as "Israel," is the eponymous patriarch who descends into Egypt—the land of wonders that turns into the land of bondage.

But like the patriarchs, Equiano does not live by one name alone. As a young slave he receives a succession of new appellations, each of which resounds with a significance not lost on the Equiano who narrates. Thus in America Equiano becomes "Jacob"; and, later, aboard a ship bound for England—the land in which Equiano finally settles, and gains renown as an abolitionist—he is renamed "Gustavus Vassa":

> While I was on board of this ship [to England] my captain and master named me GUSTAVUS VASSA. I at that time began to understand him a little, and refused to be called so, and told him, as well as I could, that I would be called JACOB; but he said I should not, and still called me Gustavus. And when I refused to answer to my new name, which at first I did, it gained me many a cuff; so at length I submitted, and by it I have been known ever since. (SN, 40) [45][5]

The ironies here are manifold. The young Equiano, like Jacob at the river Jabbok, figuratively "wrestles with a man" (Genesis 32:24)—here, that man is his captain and master. (Later in his *Narrative*, Equiano will recall another time in his life when "It pleased God to enable me to wrestle with him [God] as Jacob did" [SN, 142] (143).) Unlike the Biblical Jacob, however, Equiano does not prevail against his antago-

---

5. In her novel *Oroonoko*, Aphra Behn explains the ostensible purpose, and hints at the ironic significance, of the English habit of renaming black slaves: "the Christians never buy any Slaves but they give 'em some Name of their own, their native ones being likely very barbarous and hard to pronounce; so that Mr. Trefry gave *Oroonoko* that of *Caesar*; which Name will live in that Country as long as that (scarce more) glorious one of the great Roman: for 'tis most evident he wanted no part of the personal Courage of that Caesar, and acted things as memorable, had they been done in some Part of the World replenished with People and Historians, that might have given him his due" (New York: Norton, 1973), 40.

nist; nonetheless, along with the victorious Jacob, the vanquished Equiano undergoes a pivotal name change.

The name that Equiano reluctantly accepts in lieu of Jacob is "Gustavus Vassa," a name with wholly secular and political connotations. Vassa, a sixteenth-century Swedish patriot who freed his country from Danish tyranny, became in 1738 the hero of Henry Brooke's well-known play, *Gustavus Vasa, the Deliverer of His Country*—a play all the better known for being suppressed by Robert Walpole as an alleged attack against his ministry, and in turn defended by Opposition writers such as Samuel Johnson.[6] Eighteenth-century Britons viewed Gustavus as a hero who stands firm against tyranny and corruption; who puts the political good of his people above all else. This secular and political mantle is, as Equiano presents it, literally forced upon him—a local act of compulsion that prefigures the broader inevitability of accepting some form of humanist discourse as an African spokesperson in later eighteenth-century England. The mature Equiano presents his earlier self as instinctively preferring to be read into a sacred Hebrew script; it is with some dramatic irony that the young Equiano demands to be called Jacob, accepting the name Gustavus only under duress. And it is presumably to this primal constraint that we are to attribute the mature Equiano's fluency in the idiom of civic humanism: a fluency he demonstrates when, in his early sketch of Eboe manners, he presents his native people not only as the descendants of Abraham, but also as the true heirs of Cincinnatus—small farmers and militia-warriors, utterly unacquainted with the "luxury" of modern Europe.[7]

Thus Equiano reluctantly accepts the persona of Gustavus and the destiny of a liberator. Perhaps the mature Equiano, a fervent evangelical, intends the irony of his renaming to point to the Christian moral that only those who have been humbled will be exalted; only those who have submitted will be set free and given the power to free others. Indeed, something of this bit of Christian wisdom hovers behind the drama of what is doubtlessly the most powerful section of Equiano's *Narrative*: his fifth chapter, in which he recounts his slavery in the West Indies from 1763 to 1766. (Chronologically, this enslavement occurs

6. On the contemporary context and the continued fame of Brooke's play throughout the century, see Helen Margaret Scurr, *Henry Brooke*, Ph.D. diss. (typeset), University of Minnesota, 1922, 62–68. The persistence of Gustavus Vassa's reputation as a heroic patriot is attested by Wordsworth's claim, in the *Prelude*, to have considered making him the subject of an epic poem (1850, 1:212–13).

7. For example, Equiano writes: "As our manners are simple, our luxuries are few" (*SN*, 14) [22]; "Agriculture is our chief employment; and every one, even to children and women, is engaged in it" (17) [24]; "All are taught the use of . . . weapons; even our women are warriors, and march boldly out to fight with the men. Our whole district is a kind of militia" (18) [26]. Equiano's frame of reference here is the classical republican paradigm that J. G. A. Pocock sees reborn in the modern world with Machiavelli's *Discorsi*, and that the later eighteenth-century English reader would associate most closely with a certain strain of Scottish Enlightenment thought and, of course, with the ideology of the American Revolution. See Pocock's *The Machiavellian Moment: Florentine Political Thought and the Atlantic Republican Tradition* (Princeton: Princeton Univ. Press, 1975).

after Equiano, who had expected his manumission after dutiful service
in the Seven Years War, is inexplicably sold by his master, Captain
Pascal, to a slave trader en route to Montserrat.) Equiano introduces
his experience in Montserrat with recollections of his then inchoate
faith: having "miraculously" survived a fall from his ship's upper-deck,
he "thought [he] could very plainly trace the hand of God; without
whose permission a sparrow cannot fall" (SN, 60) [64]; and upon first
learning of his destined enslavement back in the West Indies, he "considered that trials and disappointments are sometimes for our good;
and . . . thought God might perhaps have permitted this, in order to
teach . . . wisdom and resignation" (67) [70–71]. En route to the
Indies, then, Equiano suspects—in a way he did not yet do when
dubbed "Gustavus"—that submission is the sign of future exaltation.

As in any good spiritual autobiography, however, the young Equiano
vacillates between his dawning confidence in providential design, and
a despair that invites sudden death. Equiano describes his first sight
of Montserrat in these terms:

> On the 13th of February 1763, from the mast-head, we described
> our destined island, Montserrat, and soon after I beheld those
>
>> Regions of sorrow, doleful shades, where peace
>> And rest can rarely dwell. Hope never comes
>> That comes to all, but torture without end
>> Still urges.
>
> At the sight of this land of bondage, a fresh horror ran through
> all my frame, and chilled me to the heart. My former slavery now
> rose in dreadful review to my mind, and displayed nothing but
> misery, stripes, and chains; and in the first paroxysm of my grief,
> I called upon God's thunder, and his avenging power, to direct
> the stroke of death to me, rather than permit me to become a
> slave, and to be sold from lord to lord. (SN, 68) [73]

Of course, the region of sorrows where hope never comes is none other
than Milton's Hell (Paradise Lost 1.65–68); the mature Equiano, from
his very knowledge of Milton's work, ironically implies that while Montserrat looks like hell, a place of torture and despair, it cannot be hell,
a place where hope never comes. His earlier self may not yet have
known Milton or Milton's faith, but—according to Equiano's later representation—he did then have some intimation of a divine telos, both
in history and in his own life.

Still, the second stage of Equiano's life is continuously marked by
his struggles with despair: both the despair of the literal slave in Montserrat, and later, when he becomes a freeman, the despair of the unas-
sured Christian in the evangelical community of England, who frets
about being a slave to sin and death. It is despair of ever knowing

whether or not he might count himself among the elect that drives Equiano to the brink of suicide: "One day I was standing on the very edge of the stern of the ship, thinking to drown myself, but this scripture was instantaneously impressed on my mind—'That no murderer hath eternal life abiding in him.' (1 John 3:15)" (*SN*, 141) [142]. Through the intervention of this apt Biblical passage Equiano triumphs over his doubt and receives some surety of his ultimate conversion or "new birth" in Christ. It is with the assurance of his salvation that he arrives at the third and final stage of his tropological progress.

This third stage of Equiano's life is freedom from captivity, a literal freedom that also allegorizes spiritual deliverance from innate depravity. Equiano's freedom from bondage comes when he has amassed the sum of forty pounds sterling (*SN*, 100–1) [104]; freedom from his figurative bondage, more arduously won, arrives with the assurance of his salvation, a revelation that attends his reading of Acts 4:12: "Neither is there salvation in any other: for there is none other name under heaven given among men whereby we must be saved, but only Jesus Christ" (*SN*, 142–45) [143–45]. That Jesus Christ's is the only *name* that can save neatly caps Equiano's earlier concern with the weight of nomenclature, signifying that the chain of nominal substitutions that constitutes his earlier career might now come to a close. The centrality of this verse from Acts is commemorated in the original cover illustration of Equiano's *Narrative*: it displays Equiano in elegant European dress, holding a Bible open to a page on which Acts 4:12 is printed in boldface.[8] The illustration announces quite clearly that the Equiano who pens his own history does so from the perspective of a Christian, and, more specifically, of an evangelical—the verse he brandishes was a particular favorite of George Whitefield's.[9] Or, to phrase it as Equiano probably would, his portrait shows that he writes from the perspective of the New Covenant. And from this vantage, he surveys his Eboe or Old Testament self, in an act of writing he calls his life.

In its finest moments, however, Equiano's writing ignites through the friction of his new and old perspectives. Thus throughout the fifth chapter's account of slavery in Montserrat, the youthful Equiano's

---

8. Gates reproduces this portrait of Equiano on the cover of *The Classic Slave Narratives*.

9. Equiano presents his serious interest in Christianity as originating in a glimpse of George Whitefield's preaching (*SN*, 97) [102]; in doing so, he keeps step with the earlier black autobiographies of Gronniosaw (22–34) and John Marrant (*A Narrative of the Lord's wonderful Dealings with John Marrant, A Black* [London, 1785], 10–13), as well as with Phillis Wheatley's elegy, "On the Death of the Reverend George Whitefield" (1770). An excerpt from Whitefield's sermon "The Folly and Danger of Being Not Righteous Enough" serves to typify the reading of Pauline theology that Equiano inherits: "I say, salvation is the free gift of God. It is God's free grace I preach unto you; not of works, lest any one should boast. . . . your own works are but as filthy rags, for you are justified before God without any respect to your works past, present, or to come. . . . Acknowledge yourselves as nothing at all, and when you have done all, say you are 'unprofitable servants.' There is no salvation but by Jesus Christ; there is no other name given under heaven amongst men whereby we may be saved, but that of the Lord Jesus" (*Sermons* [London: William Tegg, n.d.], 128–29).

anticipations of Christian resignation grate against his coeval desire for violent revenge. The wish to retaliate first flashes upon him in the following episode:

> A poor Creole negro I know well, who . . . at last resided in Montserrat . . . used to tell me melancholy tales of himself. Generally, after he had done working for his master, he used to employ his few leisure moments to go a fishing. When he had caught any fish, his master would frequently take them from him without paying him; and at other times some other white people would serve him in the same manner. One day he said to me very movingly, 'Sometimes when a white man take away my fish I go to my maser, and he get me my right; and when my maser, by strength, take away my fishes, what me must do? . . . I must look up to God Mighty in the top for right.' This artless tale moved me much, and I could not help feeling the just cause Moses had in redressing his brother against the Egyptian. (SN, 79–80) [82]

Equiano here alludes to Moses's first adult action: his slaying the Egyptian whom he saw "smiting an Hebrew, one of his bretheren" (Exodus 2:11–12). But even while the narrating Equiano casts himself, at this point in his far-from-artless tale, as a future liberator—as a type of Moses or Gustavus—he simultaneously knows that he cannot be Moses, because the Christian dispensation has no room for the violent retaliation imagined by his younger self.

Thus, although Equiano in mature indignation may applaud those "negro-men" who "still retain so much of human nature about them as to wish to put an end to their misery, and to retaliate on their tyrants!" (SN, 75) [78], he complicates both his appeal to nature and his sympathy for the *lex talionis* by later remarking, "the reader may easily discern, if a believer, that I was [then] still in nature's darkness" (SN, 136) [138]. The older Equiano professes having passed to the other side of the "nature" that urges him to murder both others and himself. As John Marrant declares in his sermon to the First African Lodge of Freemasons, Christians are obliged "to love and bless those who hate them and injure them, to endeavour to have peace with all men, to abstain from revenge, and to render them good for evil."[1] According to the reborn Marrant—and to the new mind of the Equiano who writes—the Eboe or Hebrew law of retaliation thus becomes an ungodly, indeed a Satanic code. Nonetheless, Equiano's text tends (as all tropology does) to preserve even as it cancels the old law. His *Narrative* presents a palimpsest of old mind and new, with neither wholly sacrificed to the other. For in recounting his "natural" Eboe or

---

1. Marrant, *A Sermon Preached on the 24th day of June, 1789 . . . at the Request of . . . the Grand Master Prince Hall and the Rest of the Bretheren of the African Lodge of Free and Accepted Masons* (Boston, 1789), 4. Marrant paraphrases Matthew 5:38–39.

Hebrew thirst for retaliation, the older Equiano at once distances and affirms that thirst: he both renounces and reannounces it.

This double-voiced mode is nowhere more apparent than at the end of Equiano's account of Montserrat, in his vehement apostrophe to those who traffic in slaves:

> Why do you use those instruments of torture? Are they fit to be applied by one rational being to another? And are ye not struck with shame and mortification, to see the partakers of your nature reduced so low? But, above all, are there no dangers attending this mode of treatment? Are you not in hourly dread of an insurrection? Nor would it be surprising: for when
>
>> No peace is given
>> To us enslav'd, but custody severe;
>> And stripes and arbitrary punishment
>> Inflicted—What peace can we return?
>> But to our power, hostility and hate,
>> Untam'd reluctance, and revenge, tho' slow,
>> Yet ever plotting how the conqueror least
>> May reap his conquest, and may least rejoice
>> In doing what we most in suff'ring feel? MILTON (SN, 81) [83–84]

Equiano coyly fails to complete his identification of this quotation. As he would expect his reader to know, these lines do not simply belong to Milton but quite specifically to Milton's Satan. And in quoting without identifying Satan, Equiano manages at once to endorse and to reject the rule of revenge. His artistry here, carefully duplicitous, allows him to voice a desire for vengeance, indeed to express it with passionate conviction, all the while casting it in the evidently untenable voice of Milton's ruined archangel, a persona that has not quite yet acquired, in Equiano's pages, its Romantic cachet.

*   *   *

[The story of Equiano's life] begins as Eboe-Hebrew pastoral, falls into Egyptian bondage and the desire for revenge, and ends up a divine comedy, closing on a Pisgah-sight of the spiritual Canaan. His final home, in the *Interesting Narrative*, is thus Christianity and its exegetical methods: methods that allow him to read his life as a progress, without closing off the paths that circle back to where he began.

ROBERT J. ALLISON

Equiano's *Narrative* as an Abolitionist Tool†

* * *

Equiano was uniquely qualified to write an antislavery book, and he began to do so in the spring of 1788. He knew the whole system of slavery, from the kidnapping of slaves in Africa, to the brutal middle passage across the Atlantic, to the plantations of the West Indies and the American mainland, to the intercolonial slave trade. He had experienced every part of the slave system. But he had also lived as a free man for twenty years. His life was more than a testament against slavery: it was a record of one man's survival of both a brutal institution and a savage age.

In presenting the case against slavery, Equiano presented himself as a human being. He kept his book focused on his own life and made himself a sympathetic character, one with whom his readers could identify. Thus he could make his readers see that if slavery was wrong for him, it would also be wrong for them. He was not "a saint, a hero, [or] a tyrant," he wrote. He knew that he was not perfect, and he understood that no other person was. His book was intended to move different readers in different ways, but to bring all to the same conclusion: that Equiano was a decent person, that he did not deserve to be enslaved, and that therefore no African deserved to be enslaved. That this seems obvious now shows how successful Equiano and other abolitionists were; that we have not completely overcome the legacy of slavery and racism should bring home to us the enormous obstacles in Equiano's way.

Equiano's *Narrative* came at a critical moment in the British antislavery movement. Opposition to slavery in England had already come from different segments of British society. Granville Sharp, Thomas Clarkson, and their intellectual or religious allies were moved by moral revulsion against the brutality of the institution. Ottabah Cugoano, Equiano, and other black refugees had directly experienced it. Working people feared that their own status as free men and women was in jeopardy if the wider British public accepted slavery, and some industrialists in the emerging cities of Manchester and Birmingham had to compete for capital with the slave traders of Liverpool. Each group—religious reformers, intellectuals, blacks, working people, capitalists—pursued its own agenda, often working against one another. But in

† From the Introduction to *The Interesting Narrative of the Life of Olaudah Equiano*, Robert J. Allison, ed. (Boston and New York: Bedford Books of St. Martin's Press, 1995), pp. 14–17. Copyright © 1995 by Bedford/St. Martin's Press, Inc. Reprinted with permission of Bedford/St. Martin's Press, Inc.

1788 this diverse coalition banded together to form one of the greatest mass movements in British history. Activists collected tens of thousands of signatures on petitions urging Parliament to end the slave trade. Equiano presented his own petition to Queen Charlotte, wife of George III, on March 21, 1788.

Equiano's *Narrative* became one crucial link between these segments of the British public. He knew the great English abolitionists Sharp, Clarkson, and Ramsay, but he also knew sailors and dockworkers, black refugees from the West Indies and America, and leaders of London's emerging radical working class. He was recognized by virtually every segment of the antislavery and reform movements, and he could speak of his own experiences in a way to move men and women at every level of society. Among the subscribers to the first edition of his book were members of the English royal family and political radicals who in a few short years would be charged with treason, pacifists and admirals, Anglican bishops and dissenting ministers, Africans living in London, and women and men committed to reform.[1]

After Equiano sold nearly two thousand copies of the *Narrative* on a trip to Ireland in 1791, a white abolitionist said that Equiano was "more use to the Cause than half the People in the country." Always wary of his own vanity, Equiano responded, "I wish to God, I could be so."[2] In the *Narrative*, Equiano presented two strong arguments against slavery. Though the moral arguments is on virtually every page, Equiano knew that Englishmen would not stop doing something that earned them money just because it was sinful. So he also made an economic case for ending the slave trade. He appealed to an English audience whose own economic world was changing. The *Narrative* sold especially well in the rising industrial centers of Manchester and Birmingham. England's industrial transformation was well under way by the 1780s, and Equiano argued that freedom for slaves in the West Indies and an end to the African slave trade would actually speed up the transition to an industrial economy. Africa, he argued, could be a lucrative market for European goods. If England would stop making Africans their slaves and instead would sell them textiles and tools, English manufacturers could enjoy tremendous profits far beyond what English slave traders and sugar planters enjoyed. Equiano thus appealed to both the British soul and the British purse.

Equiano understood the economic change taking place in England. He offered a way out for planters fearful of an insurrection but not certain that the former slaves could be incorporated into society. White people feared that the former slaves would retaliate and shared

1. See James Walvin, "British Popular Sentiment for Abolition, 1787–1832," in *Anti-Slavery, Religion, and Reform*, ed. Bolt and Drescher, 149–53.
2. Gustavus Vassa to Rev. G. Walker, February 27, 1792, ". . . written by himself: A Manuscript Letter of Olaudah Equiano," Paul Edwards, ed., *Notes and Queries* (June 1968).

James Tobin's suspicion that the freed people would not work. Equiano himself was hardworking and diligent, and he told the slaveholders that by "treating your slaves as men, every cause of fear would be banished. They would be faithful, honest, intelligent, and vigorous," and all would enjoy "peace, prosperity, and happiness."[3] England and America could survive, but only by treating their slaves as men and women, only by living up to the Christian precepts and ideological positions staked out by Europeans and Americans.

It would not be enough, he knew, for masters to be nicer to their slaves. Nor would it be enough to abolish the slave trade. The problem was that slavery gave some men too much power, and men with power would abuse those without power. He had learned this lesson both as a slave and as a free man. Five of the *Narrative*'s twelve chapters chronicle his life after slavery, and some of the most brutal evidence against slavery is from the stories of men like John Annis and Joseph Clipson, who escaped from slavery only to be forced back into it. Though free, these men could at any time be tricked or overpowered by whites.

Equiano's *Narrative* was such a successful tool that slavery's defenders tried to challenge his authority: they claimed he was not an African at all but had been born in the West Indies. If he had been born in the West Indies, he could not have experienced the middle passage. Two anonymous notes were planted in the London papers in 1792, while Equiano was in Scotland selling the fourth edition of his *Narrative*, charging that Equiano was actually from the island of St. Croix.[4] This was an easy charge to refute: Equiano still had friends in England who remembered his arrival there as a slave thirty years earlier.

These critics saw what a powerful weapon Equiano's *Narrative* was. It appealed to people at many different levels of British society, particularly men and women of the working class who might have regarded abolition as an upper-class hobby. Equiano was distinctly ordinary; he made clear that what had happened to him could happen to anyone. Ordinary readers could identify with him, as they might not identify with the nameless bodies in Clarkson's drawing of a slave ship or with the nearly naked slave kneeling in Josiah Wedgwood's medallion entitled "Am I Not a Man and a Brother." * * * Though the drawing and the medallion became popular antislavery symbols, Equiano was a real person. He spoke directly to many different men and women in his audience, confessing his own sins and urging them to face their own.

* * *

3. Equiano, *Narrative*, 100 (See also Edwards, in two volumes, *Editor*).
4. The squibs are reprinted in Shyllon, *Black People in Britain*, 265 n.

Olaudah Equiano:
A Chronology

1740–1800	Approximately 3,130,000 Africans enslaved and transported to the New World.
1745	According to *Narrative*, Equiano born in Essaka, present-day Nigeria. (According to Vincent Carretta, Equiano may have been born elsewhere, possibly South Carolina, and in a different year).
1748	Montesquieu publishes *Spirit of the Laws* (English transl. 1751).
1754	Slave ship *Ogden*, having sailed from Liverpool to the Bight of Biafra, arrives in Barbados May 9. On May 21, sloop *Nancy* leaves Barbados with slaves for Virginia. Equiano may have arrived in Virginia on *Nancy*, two years earlier than *Narrative* suggests. John Woolman prints tract *Some Considerations on the Keeping of Negroes*. Pascal arrives from Newfoundland at Falmouth, on *Industrious Bee*, December 14.
1755	Names of Gustavus Vassa and Richard Baker appear on Pascal's muster list (August) of the *Roebuck*. Rousseau publishes *A Discourse upon the Origin and Foundation of the Inequality among Mankind* (English transl. 1761).
1756	"Gust. Vasa" on muster book of *Roebuck* as captain's servant.
1756–57	Trial for cowardice of Admiral John Byng.
1756–63	Seven Years' War.
1757	"Gusta Worcester" serves on *Savage*, January 12–21. Probably meets the Guerins in London, February or March. Byng executed on March 14, 1757.
1757–59	November 10, "Gustavus Vavasa" joins Pascal and serves for him on *Jason*, *Royal George*, and *Namur*, returning to London, 1759.
1759	February 9, "Gustavus Vassa a Black born in Carolina 12 years old," baptized at St. Margaret's Church, Westminster. "Gustavus Vasser" serves on *Etna* for Pascal. English

Narrative of the Lord's Wonderful Dealings with John Marrant, A Black published. James Tobin's *Cursory Remarks upon the Reverend Mr. Ramsay's Essay* printed, to which Equiano responds in public letter in 1788.

1786   Appointed commissary to Sierra Leone by Committee for the Relief of the Black Poor. Thomas Clarkson publishes *An Essay on the Slavery and Commerce of the Human Species, Particularly the African*. Sir Philip Gibbes writes *Instructions for the Treatment of Negroes*.

1787   Society for the Abolition of the Slave Trade formed in London. Equiano dismissed from Sierra Leone expedition for political reasons. Quobna Ottobah Cugoano publishes *Thoughts and Sentiments on the Evil and Wicked Traffic of . . . Slavery*.

1788   Samuel Jackson Pratt's poem *Humanity; or, the Rights of Nature* appears, to which Equiano responds in print. John Matthews publishes *A Voyage to the River Sierra-Leone*. French abolitionist *Société des Amis des Noirs* formed. March 21, Equiano petitions Queen Charlotte to end slave trade. Abolitionists petition parliament.

1789   February 14, writes Letter to the Committee for the Abolition of the Slave Trade for *The Public Advertiser*. March 24, publishes *Interesting Narrative*, which goes through nine English editions by 1794. May 13, William Wilberforce, "Speech in the House of Commons." Parliament votes to regulate slave trade. July 14, storming of the Bastille; French Revolution begins.

1790   Dutch edition of *Narrative, Merkwaardige Levensgevallen Van Olaudah Equiano Or Gustavus Vassa, Den Afrikaan/Door Hem Zelven Beschreven*, published at Rotterdam.

1791   Lectures in Ireland.

1792   April 7, marries Miss Susan Cullen of Ely, Cambridgeshire. German translation, *Olaudah Equiano's oder Gustav Wasa's, des Afrikaners merkwürdige Lebensgeschichte von ihm selbst geschrieben/Gustav Wasa / George Friedrich Benecke aus dem Englischen übersetzt*, published at Göttingen.

1793   October 16, birth of daughter Ann Maria.

1795   April 11, birth of daughter Joanna.

1796   Susan Cullen Vassa dies; buried on February 21.

1797   March 31, Equiano dies in London. Daughter Ann Maria Vassa dies, July 21.

1807   Britain and United States agree to abolish the slave trade.

1833   Britain emancipates slaves in West Indies.

Selected Bibliography

• Indicates works included or excerpted in this Norton Critical Edition.

EDITIONS

• Allison, Robert J., ed. *The Interesting Narrative of the Life of Olaudah Equiano*. Boston and New York: Bedford Books of St. Martin's Press, 1995 (follows first American printing of 1791, with introduction, illustrations, and chronology).

Bontemps, Arna, ed. *Great Slave Narratives*. Boston: Beacon Press, 1969, (includes Equiano).

Carretta, Vincent, ed. *The Interesting Narrative and Other Writings by Olaudah Equiano*. New York: Penguin, 1995 (reprints ninth edition, with introduction and 700 notes).

• Edwards, Paul, ed. *The Life of Olaudah Equiano or Gustavus Vassa, the African*. 2 vols. London: Dawsons of Pall Mall, 1969. The Colonial History Series (reprints first edition, with indispensable 70-page introduction and with annotations).

Gates, Henry Louis, Jr., ed. *The Classic Slave Narratives*. New York: Penguin Mentor, 1987 (includes Equiano, based on 1814 Leeds and London imprint, with introduction).

Potkay, Adam, and Sandra Burr, eds. *Black Atlantic Writers of the 18th Century*. New York: St. Martin's Press, 1995 (includes selections from Equiano in the 1814 Leeds, London, and Darlington imprint, with introduction, overview of all known editions, and 190 notes).

CRITICAL WORKS

• Acholonu, Catherine Obianju. "The Home of Olaudah Equiano—A Linguistic and Anthropological Search." *The Journal of Commonwealth Literature* 22.1 (1987): 5–16.

———. *The Igbo Roots of Olaudah Equiano: An Anthropological Research*. Owerri, Nigeria: Afa Publications, 1989.

Andrews, William L. *To Tell a Free Story: The First Century of Afro-American Autobiography, 1760–1865*. Urbana: University of Illinois Press, 1986.

• Baker, Houston A., Jr. "Figurations for a New American Literary History." In *Blues, Ideology, and Afro-American Literature: A Vernacular Theory*. Chicago: University of Chicago Press, 1984.

Bitterli, Urs. *Die "Wilden" und die "Zivilisierten": Die europäisch-überseeische Begegnung*. München: C. H. Beck, 1976.

Brawley, Benjamin. *Early Negro American Writers: Selections with Biographical and Critical Introductions*. New York: Dover, repr. 1970.

Bultman, Charles Keene. "Economies of Violence: Race, Property, and the Rewriting of History in Post-Revolutionary America (Thomas Jefferson, Olaudah Equiano, Stephen Burroughs, Charles Brockden Brown)." Ph.D. diss., University of California, Berkeley, 1998.

Caldwell, Tanya. " 'Talking too Much English': Languages of Economy and Politics in Equiano's *The Interesting Narrative*." *Early American Literature* 34.3 (1999): 263–82.

Carretta, Vincent. "Olaudah Equiano or Gustavus Vassa? New Light on an Eighteenth-Century Question of Identity." *Slavery and Abolition* 20.3 (December 1999): 96–105.

———. "Three West Indian Writers of the 1780s Revisited and Revised." *Research in African Literatures* (Winter 1998): 73–86.

Christadler, Martin. "Selbstkonstitution und Lebensgeschichte in der Autobiographie der Aufklärung: Benjamin Franklin und Olaudah Equiano." In *Skepsis oder das Spiel mit dem Zweifel. Festschrift für Ralph-Rainer Wuthenow zum 65. Geburtstag*, ed. Carola Hilmes et al. Würzburg: Königshausen & Neumann, 1994. 191–212.

• Costanzo, Angelo. *Surprizing Narrative: Olaudah Equiano and the Beginnings of Black Autobiography*. Westport, CT: Greenwood Press, 1987.

401

402 SELECTED BIBLIOGRAPHY

Curtin, Philip D., ed. *Africa Remembered: Narratives by West Africans from the Era of the Slave Trade*. Madison: University of Wisconsin Press, 1968.

———. *The Image of Africa: British Ideas and Actions, 1780–1850*. Madison: University of Wisconsin Press, 1964.

Curtius, Ernst Robert. "The Book as Symbol." In *European Literature and the Latin Middle Ages* (1949). Transl. Willard Trask. Bollingen Series 36. New York: Pantheon Books, 1953. 302–47.

• Dabydeen, David, ed. *The Black Presence in English Literature*. Manchester, Engl.: Manchester University Press, 1985.

Davis, Charles T., and Henry Louis Gates, Jr., eds. *The Slave's Narrative*. New York: Oxford University Press, 1985.

• ———. "The Slave Narrative: First Major Art Form in an Emerging Black Tradition." In *Black is the Color of the Cosmos: Essays on Afro-American Literature and Culture, 1942–1981*, ed. Henry Louis Gates, Jr. New York: Garland Publishing, Inc., 1982. 83–119.

Doherty, Thomas. "Olaudah Equiano's Journeys: The Geography of a Slave Narrative." *Partisan Review* 64.4 (Fall 1997): 572–81.

Donnan, Elizabeth. *Documents Illustrative of the History of the Slave Trade to America*. 4 vols. Washington, D.C.: Carnegie Institute, 1930–35.

• Dykes, Eva Beatrice. *The Negro in English Romantic Thought*. Washington, D.C.: Associated Publishers, 1942.

Earley, Samantha Manchester. "Challenging 'African American': Construction of Slave Self as Counterposition to the Hegemony (Olaudah Equiano, Frederick Douglass, Harriet Jacobs, Frances E. W. Harper, Pauline Hopkins, Toni Morrison)." Ph.D. diss., Kent State University, 1998.

Edwards, Paul, and James Walvin, eds. *Black Personalities in the Era of the Slave Trade*. Baton Rouge: University of Louisiana Press, 1983.

Fichtelberg, Joseph. "Word Between Worlds: The Economy of Equiano's Narrative." *American Literary History* 5.3 (Fall 1993): 459–80.

Fryer, Peter. *Staying Power: The History of Black People in Britain*. London: Pluto Press, 1984.

• Gates, Henry Louis, Jr. "The Trope of the Talking Book." In *The Signifying Monkey: A Theory of Afro-American Literary Criticism*. New York: Oxford University Press, 1988.

Hinds, Elizabeth Jane Wall. "The Spirit of Trade: Olaudah Equiano's Conversion, Legalism, and the Merchant's Life." *African American Review* 32.4 (Winter 1998): 635–47.

• Huggins, Nathan I. *Black Odyssey: The Afro-American Ordeal in Slavery*. New York: Pantheon, 1977.

Ito, Akiyo. "Olaudah Equiano and the New York Artisans: The First American Edition of *The Interesting Narrative of Olaudah Equiano, or Gustavus Vassa, The African*." *Early American Literature* 32.1 (1997): 82–101.

Jordan, Winthrop D. *White over Black: American Attitudes toward the Negro, 1550–1812*. Baltimore: Penguin Books, 1969.

Loggins, Vernon. *The Negro Author: His Development in America*. New York: Columbia University Press, 1931.

Marren, Susan M. "Between Slavery and Freedom: The Transgressive Self in Olaudah Equiano's Autobiography." *Publications of the Modern Language Association* 108 (1993): 94–105.

Mays, Benjamin E. *The Negro's God as Reflected in His Literature*. 1938; repr. New York: Antheneum, 1973.

Mtubani, Victor C. D. "The Black Voice in Eighteenth-Century Britain: African Writers against Slavery and the Slave Trade." *Phylon* 45 (1984): 85–97.

• Murphy, Geraldine. "Olaudah Equiano, Accidental Tourist." *Eighteenth-Century Studies* 27 (1994): 551–68.

• Nichols, Charles H. *Many Thousand Gone: The Ex-Slaves' Account of Their Bondage and Freedom*. Leiden, E. J. Brill, 1963.

Ogude, S. E. "Olandah Equiano and the Tradition of Defoe." *African Literature Today* 14 (1984): 77–91.

Orban, Katalin. "Dominant and Submerged Discourses in the Life of Olaudah Equiano." *African American Review* 27 (1993): 655–64.

Piccinato, Stefania. "Olaudah Equiano Gustavus Vassa: Un Uomo del '700 fra due culture." In *Il senso del nonsenso*, ed. Lynn Salkin Sbiroli. Roma: Edizioni Scientifiche Italiane, 1994. 237–245.

• Potkay, Adam. "Olaudah Equiano and the Art of Spiritual Autobiography." *Eighteenth-Century Studies* 27 (1994): 677–90.

Rust, Marion. "The Subaltern as Imperialist: Speaking of Olaudah Equiano." In *Passing and the Fictions of Identity*, ed. Elaine K. Ginsberg. Durham, NC: Duke University Press, 1996. 21–36.

Samuels, Wilfred D. "Disguised Voice in *The Interesting Narrative of Olaudah Equiano, or Gustavus Vassa, the African*." *Black American Literature Forum* 19 (1985): 64–69.

Sandiford, Keith A. *Measuring the Moment: Strategies of Protest in Eighteenth-Century Afro-English Writing*. London: Associated University Press, 1988.

Sekora, John, and Darwin T. Turner, eds. *The Art of the Slave Narrative: Original Essays in Criticism and Theory*. Macomb: Western Illinois University Press, 1982.

Shyllon, Folarin. *Black People in Britain: 1555–1833*. London: Oxford University Press, 1977.

Starkey, Marion L. *Striving to Make It My Home: The Story of Americans from Africa*. New York: Norton, 1964.

• Sypher, Wylie. *Guinea's Captive Kings: British Anti-Slavery Literature of the XVIIIth Century*. Chapel Hill: University of North Carolina Press, 1942.

Walvin, James, ed. *Slavery and British Society, 1776–1846*. Baton Rouge: Louisiana State University Press, 1982.

———. *An African's Life: The Life and Times of Olaudah Equiano, 1745–1797*. Washington, D.C.: Cassell, 1998.

Woodard, Helena. *African-British Writing in the Eighteenth Century: The Politics of Race and Reason*. Westport, CT: Greenwood Press, 1999.

Zafar, Rafia. *We Wear the Mask: African Americans Write American Literature, 1760–1870*. New York: Columbia University Press, 1997.